GREAT CHARITY
AGGER GAP
HEUGH SYKE
WHISTLING
GREAT HOPE
SMIDDY
BRIDGE
GLORY
NOGGIN MOOR
OLD WIFE
MARY
MARTHA
NOTION
NOTION
BRIDGE
JOSS
FOSS
BUCKER
FLUE
SLEETY SLAPE
GT DEEP
LEVEL
MINE ROAD
SORROW NEAR
ALF
WINTERINGS
WEST
END
NICK
TOWN
FOOT
MODESTY
MAIN
STREET
YEW TREE HOUSE
LOW
BANDS
THE BRIG
TURN
DOLLY BRIDGE
BACK
LANE
IDDLE SORROW
JOM HIGH ROAD

ADAM BRUNSKILL

By the Same Author

KING COTTON
THE CROWTHERS OF BANKDAM
DOVER HARBOUR

THOMAS ARMSTRONG

ADAM BRUNSKILL

COLLINS
ST JAMES'S PLACE, LONDON
1952

For
W. A. R. COLLINS
1939-1952
Years of Happy Association

PRINTED IN GREAT BRITAIN
COLLINS CLEAR-TYPE PRESS: LONDON AND GLASGOW

PROLOGUE

I

THE ROAD ran upwards for two or three hundred yards before disappearing behind a tongue of ground, part of the foothills of the great range which, in the distance, blue-hazed, raised its peaks six or seven thousand feet into the evening light. It was Autumn, and the keen nip in the air foreshadowed that before long the countryside would be enveloped in an icy grip.

In the immediate neighbourhood of the village, from the gaunt stone-built Wesleyan Chapel at its outskirts to the turn of the road, the prospect was decidedly less beautiful. Hereabouts the land was scarred by the crumbling headgear of disused mine shafts: the many lead- and silver-extraction plants had been erected without regard to the observer's eye, and a vast area within the orbit of the poisonous fumes from the chimneys of the smelt mills had been converted into a wilderness whose sickly herbage could bring painful death to cow, sheep or hen straying into it.

Nevertheless, there was undoubtedly much happiness in that grim place. From somewhere beyond the bend, becoming gradually stronger, came the sounds of men on the march. Above the tramp of feet could be heard the hum of voices, a snatch of song, and the whistling of the inevitable whistler. Down they came, a company of several hundred spread over half a mile of narrow road, miners, smelters, ore washers and other surface men, leaving behind them the ladanum bushes of the high lands and the modernly-equipped mines and smelt mills which, with the advance of the industry, now crept farther and farther away from the village.

These trudging feet, each kicking up its cloud of dust, were eager indeed. Not only was the day's work done, but this, great day, was the day of the monthly 'Pay.' For the younger ones it meant an evening's jollification without stint; for the others, whose feet moved less springily, it meant the means to care for those near and dear. Perhaps the thoughts of those who walked more stiffly at the tail-end of the company slipped now and then to another place, so conjuring up many a fragrant memory.

But soon the smiles of recollection vanished, to be replaced by a sadness of expression as further memories came: of constant poverty, of days when a man and his family existed on blue milk and ' gulls,' when hope went and only desperation stayed.

Yes, it was good to draw an adequate Pay.

Two young men walked together, one of whom was speaking of a mutual friend and his recent promotion.

"Aye, Adam's doing well for himself," he said, brown eyes for once solemn. "It's no small thing to be made assistant agent in a big concern like this."

"It isn't that," Simon Sunter agreed. "B-B-But Adam's had the makings of a first-rate lead-miner ever since the three of us started together when we were twelve years old. And if you——"

"He has an' all," Daniel Dolphin interposed. "And I'll be right glad to see him for the first time alongside Mr. Phillips at the Pay."

"Aye, and if you'd spend a bit more of your spare time in studying," Simon Sunter insisted, "y-y-you might be next on the list when there was another vacancy for an assistant."

"We'll let that pass," Daniel grinned. "Anyroad, don't forget to touch your forelock to Adam when we go in."

Despite a lack of humour sometimes the despair of his wife, Simon Sunter did not swallow this, and began to speak about the problem arising from the smelting of refractory ore. As opposed to his two friends, both of whom were miners, he was a smelter, and worked at one of the smaller smelting mills on the sett. But, like Adam Brunskill, he had risen out of the common rut, and nine months before had been appointed Head Smelter at that mill.

By the time he had finished they were in the village, nearing the offices of the mining company, where they joined the crush filing through the doors.

"After we've drawn," Daniel remarked, licking his tongue in a fantastically wide circle about his mouth, "we'll sample that new place. Real beer, my lad, though," a chuckle escaped him, "the old stagers say it hasn't the body of Appleby ale."

"What about Adam?" Simon Sunter inquired. "He'll noan be able to come with us."

Daniel thought differently. At bait time he had heard that Jim Brunskill had taken a turn for the better, in which case Adam need not hurry home to his father's bedside.

The Pay Room was lengthy. At the far end, to the accompaniment of chinkling coin, the officials of the Company busied themselves behind a barrier of tables. Mr. Phillips, the General Manager, was there, and with him the head agent, the cashier and two clerks. In addition there were four assistant agents, amongst them Adam Brunskill, whose special duty it was to explain, when necessary, any variation in the mode of assessing the monthly earnings.

As he drew nearer, Daniel's face became excessively controlled. High authority might be present, but this surely was the time when a little fun was excusable. The General Manager, however, nipped all that in the bud.

Meantime, while his friends walked along to the new room provided for the Company's workmen, Adam Brunskill continued with his task. He was a clean-shaven young man with deep-set, keen eyes, mouth firm but humorous, in age between twenty-five and thirty. About six feet in height, he was well-proportioned, the litheness of his movements suggesting perfect muscular co-ordination, and, if not handsome, he had a ruggedness of feature not without its attraction.

Each in his own way the three friends, Simon Sunter, Daniel Dolphin and Adam Brunskill, were known amongst their companions—Simon for his devotion, first, to his wife Jane and their small daughter and, second, to his chosen occupation; Daniel for a nature which landed him in every manner of peccadillo; Adam for the many outstanding feats which, even in a community where strong men were obviously many, marked him out as one on his own. In this connection the classic story about Adam Brunskill was that of a watchman alongside the main road to the South-East who, box and all, was transported to the cemetery three-quarters of a mile away. There the burden was set down, opposite a decaying tombstone, so gently as not to disturb the still slumbering occupant. That story of single-handed strength, together with another epic, soon to be made, was likely to remain a topic not so much of amusement as of wonder to the miners of the Company for many a year to come.

Joiners and others had finished work in the big room only the day before, but two huge fires warmed the tobacco-filled air, in which as yet the smell of drying paint was strong. More and more men crowded in as the Pay in the offices proceeded, and the servers at the bar were hard pressed to keep pace with demands.

Simon Sunter and Daniel Dolphin, each carrying a pint tankard of foaming Old and Mild, were just sitting down in a corner when their attention was attracted by a youngish man. He was a veritable giant, not a pound under sixteen stones; his powerful frame bulged out of his clothes, and he seemed not to carry an ounce of surplus fat. Grinning broadly, he held up a tumbler of neat whisky in a ham-like hand.

"Adam be long yet?" he bawled.

"Any minute I reckon, Humphrey lad," Daniel shouted back.

The big Cornishman nodded, a further few pleasantries were exchanged, and then each turned back again to particular cronies.

"Mmm . . ." Simon murmured. "Looks as if he's out for a g-go with Adam."

Daniel wiped his moustache with a knuckle. "Aye, Humphrey's never got over the last do he had with him."

"Well, Adam wasn't meaning to, I know," Simon said seriously, "but he d-d-did make him look a right fool."

"He were too quick for him," Daniel observed with authority. "As well an' all, for if Humphrey had got one of them fancy Cornish locks on him even Adam wouldn't have got away without breaking a limb."

"Anyroad, there won't be owt to-night, n-not with Adam's father being as h-he is," Simon remarked.

"Not unless Humphrey gets awkward and forces summat," Daniel said. "As he's apt to do if he sups much more o' that stuff."

Which was precisely how it happened about twenty minutes later. What passed in the early stages was hidden by the general hubbub, but shortly afterwards, when the noise ceased as if by signal, the onlookers saw the Cornishman discard linen undercap and rosin-stiffened felt hat.

"Now then, lad," Adam Brunskill laughed, his eyes wary. "Another time, Humphrey, but not now."

"No time like the present, Adam," the other chuckled thickly, half-crouching, outstretched hands manœuvring for a hold. "No, now'll do for me—no, you don't," he roared.

In the space cleared by common consent Adam Brunskill tried to slip past, but his opponent, perhaps anticipating the move, dived for him, a projectile of steely sinew and muscle. The result was not all the pursuer desired. Swiftly side-stepping, Adam's arms flailed scissors-wise, the flat of his right hand crashing behind his adversary while swinging scythe-like left forearm swept massive legs from off their feet. Before anyone could quite realise what was what, the Cornishman had been half-somersaulted, his boots pressing upon the still soft daub-plaster on the high ceiling. In this attitude, swearing vividly, he struck downwards, but Adam, transferring with a quick shift the weight to one hand, grasped a hairy wrist with the other.

"By God!" somebody breathed.

Slowly Adam walked down the long room. "I reckon you'd better come along with me, Humphrey," he laughed. "And you'd better keep your feet marching or I won't answer for the consequences if a mountain like you comes down with a wallop."

Fascinated, the company watched, their glances now and then returning to the line of footprints left on the ceiling, tension not being relaxed until, near the far fireplace, the blaspheming miner was allowed to fall; he was caught about the middle and placed lightly on the floor.

"All right, Humphrey?" Adam asked.

The swaying figure, dizzy after this ordeal, was still cursing freely but neither viciously nor with real ill-temper. It was characteristic of the Cornishman that, a struggle ended, he immediately became a very decent-dispositioned fellow indeed.

"Yes, I'm all right, Adam," he said wryly. "But if ever I can get you properly on the mat . . ."

Adam grinned. "I'll see you don't, lad."

Interest elsewhere was now concentrated on the footmarks overhead. It was agreed that, for the sake of keeping permanent record of a mighty feat, neither the Company's management nor men would wish the plasterers to repair the damage, and it was further suggested that Humphrey should be weighed before witnesses on the lead scales at one of the smelt mills.

Amidst the ensuing laughter a young woman, breathing deeply, appeared in the doorway, her anxious glance searching the room. Of those most concerned Daniel Dolphin saw her first.

"There's Jane!" he ejaculated, but her husband reached her before him. "Has summat happened to our Bessie, love?" Simon Sunter asked.

Adam Brunskill arrived there at almost the same time, and, after assuring Simon that all was well with their little daughter, Jane Sunter spoke to him. "You'd better get back sharp, Adam," she told him. "Your father were all right when I went home to see to Bessie's bath, but he took queer afterwards an' my mother sent for t'doctor. Well . . ."

Adam looked steadily at her. He saw a tall and thin young woman whose air was of wholesomeness and shining cleanliness. Her eyes, redeeming a plain face, were large and luminous and just now their soft, grey depths were misting.

"It's all up, is it, Jane?" he said.

After a moment she nodded. "The doctor's coming again later, Adam," she said. "But . . . but he says there isn't anything we can do."

Adam hastened through the gathering dark to his dying father.

Inside the Spanish miners' common room on the corner, the wine server busied himself with tall jars, while from the pot hanging over the fire on the earthen floor appetising odours wafted outdoors as a reminder to a group of satisfied customers who, in broad-brimmed hats and snuff-coloured cloaks, were enjoying a smoke and final gossip before departing homewards.

Responding with equal gravity to the dignified salutations given him by these somewhat threadbare loiterers, Adam Brunskill turned off the main thoroughfare to enter a narrow lane which, at the speed he then was running, quickly brought him to the place in which the English community dwelt. Here, margining a rectangular piece of land whose grass no amount of loving care had persuaded into the verdure of a village green, were the cottages of those who had been compelled to seek a livelihood abroad.

At first glance the array of little houses seemed to be a perfect representation of many a tiny hamlet in the Yorkshire Dales. But a closer examination showed that there were significant differences now and then. The pitch of a roof, the style of a doorlatch, the squat massiveness of a chimney, these details bespoke connections elsewhere: with the Lead Hills of Scotland, Derbyshire, and the Mendips farther south.

Adam Brunskill, long legs swiftly covering the sorry turf, neared a row of four cottages faithfully characteristic of the western dales of Yorkshire. He headed towards a door at which, the soft light from the oil-lamp behind making a halo of her hair, Jane Sunter's mother was waiting.

"I'm glad you're here, Adam," she said. "I thought our Jane mightn't find you so quick, an' . . . an' . . ."

She was deeply moved. As she fumbled with the corner of her apron Adam put his arm around her plump shoulders and, as a faint slurring of feet came from above, eased her into the most comfortable chair of an austerely furnished kitchen.

"What about a nice cup of tea, Mrs. Caygill?" he persuaded her. "The kettle's on, I see."

"That's t'Minister upstairs," she said inconsequentially.

Adam nodded while deftly spooning tea from a wooden caddy into the teapot he had scalded. Tea-making is usually something of a social office, but he went about the business with an engineer's economy of effort, as perhaps only could be expected from a man who throughout his remembered life had lived in a house which had never seen a woman's touch.

"There we are," he murmured, carrying a small round-topped table upon which he had placed a milk jug and sugar basin. "You can pour for yourself, can't you?" he rallied her.

Such as it was, her remaining composure slipped a little more. "I know it's wrong, Adam, but in a way it isn't just because your father's going that I'm behaving this road, and it isn't even because I can remember both him and your mother when I were a tiny tot in Yorrel and they were a little lad an' lass who lived down t'Dale at Winterings. It isn't even because at times I've heard him rambling about things I can myself remember just as clearly as if I'd seen 'em yesterday . . . you know, the sound of the waterfalls, the juniper bushes and rowan trees, the shadows moving across the fells, and t'feel of springy turf beneath your feet. It isn't because his time has come, like your mother's did, an' as I expect mine will, in a foreign land far away from Skewdale. No, it isn't that."

Adam coaxed her into trying the tea. She sipped a little and then, as the stirring above became more pronounced, she looked at him solemnly.

"It's . . . it's because he's so cheerful, lad," she said.

"He's always been a good plucked 'un, Mrs. Caygill," Adam nodded.

She nodded, too. "But this time it isn't just pluck, Adam," she said. "It's because he's glad to go, glad to go to your mother. You know, lad," she continued, her eyes reminiscent, "I've always said an' I always shall say that never could there have been a man and woman who loved each other more than Jim Brunskill and Mary Nattrass. I can recall when they first came here, just after they were wed, him a fine upstanding young fellow and her a gentle little lass bubbling over with happiness. Then, in due course, you made your appearance, lad, and . . ." involuntarily, a soft understanding laugh escaped her, "and never in this world was there a bairn like Jim and Mary's Adam, never. But . . ." her face fell, "less than two years after they'd run off together, your mother died, and since then your father's been a changed man. He did his duty at the mine, he gave you all the care and attention a lone man can give a little baby, but in a way only the husk of him were left."

Adam Brunskill's deep-set eyes were sad. "He never talked much to me about my mother, never seemed able to," he said. "But I've always known it was that way with them."

Mrs. Caygill, whose tears had come in a flood, glanced quickly towards the stair-foot. As a step sounded on the top tread, she muttered a choked: "It was that," and then, a plump comely body greatly differing from her daughter Jane, hastily made what amends she could towards improving her appearance.

For the spiritual comfort and physical well-being of their English servants the London and Andajoz Lead and Silver Mining Company had brought out from England a parson and a doctor. Mr. Shields, the minister, was a good man and well liked.

"How is he, Mr. Shields?" Adam asked.

The clergyman slowly shook his head. "I don't think it can be very long, Adam," he said. "He's perceptibly weakening."

Jim Brunskill's son turned towards the stairway. "I'll get up to him . . . and thanks, Mr. Shields. I owe a lot to you, an' to Mrs. Caygill, for all you've done."

The tribute apparently passed over the minister, who was faintly frowning. But, though he restrained Adam with a movement of the hand, he did not speak immediately about the cause of his perplexity. At last, fingering his chin irritably, he admitted that he was troubled.

"Rightly or wrongly, Adam," he said, "I've got it into my head that your father's something on his mind," he said.

"Something on his mind!" Adam ejaculated.

Seemingly, in these final moments, Mr. Shields had come to a decided conclusion. "Yes, I think he has," he said.

Lips firm, Adam climbed the dark staircase towards the candleglow above.

The resemblance between son and father was unmistakable. Both had the same steady, deep-set eyes and the height of Norsemen ancestry, the younger one almost touching the low ceiling, the other resting diagonally in the bed, a habit acquired in too fast growing youth.

"Now then, old lad," Adam said as he pulled up a chair. "How goes it, eh?"

Jim Brunskill smiled from his pillow. "An' what about you, lad?" he asked. "About t'Pay, I mean. That's my one regret, not seeing you among the top-notchers."

Adam was filling a pipe, pressing the tobacco into the bowl. His father could be extremely testy if the room were treated with the deference due to an invalid's quarters, and he knew the smoke would not harm.

"There'll be another Pay, won't there?" he grunted.

An air of sternness spread over Jim Brunskill's thin face. "If there's one thing I thought I'd drummed into you, Adam," he began, "it's that a chap has to face up to whatever trouble he's in and stick it out to t'bitter end."

Adam chuckled. "You drummed it in all right," he confessed. "An' many was the hiding I got from bigger lads because of it."

"Let's have no more of it, then," the other snapped. "I'm going, and I know an' you know that I haven't long."

At first it seemed as if this outburst had tired him, but to his son it seemed also that, as his father stared at the candle, his thoughts were elsewhere. Then, as if pulling himself together, Jim Brunskill began to speak on practical matters. He told Adam that the London office of the Company had charge of his will, adding with patent pride that his savings, over six hundred pounds, were in the same keeping.

"So with what you've put by yourself, you'll be very nicely off for a young fellow. An' you're going to go much farther, lad," he continued, showing signs of excitement. "Maybe even farther than taking on as head agent when Jim Calvert retires. Aye, Mr. Phillips hinted the other day that the Company had their eye on you for a management job at one of their mines up in the North."

"Steady," said Adam.

Fortunately there was intervention, Mrs. Caygill entering with a steaming cup, from which the sick man managed to take a few sips of broth. By the time his pillows had been shaken and they were alone again, he had become quieter, and in that mood began to reminisce about his family, whose names were recorded in Greets Church even before the days of Queen Elizabeth. Indeed he could remember one learned visitor to Skewdale on a fishing holiday, a real scholar, declaring that the Brunskills had been in the Dale long before that, perhaps for nearly a thousand years.

"Skewdale's in our blood and bone, lad, an' that's why I ought to have taken you to see it. For that matter I ought to have gone back myself, though ..." his voice sank, "... that's for another reason. Summat I've fretted myself about ever since me and your mother ran off together ..."

His head slipped back, his eyes closed, and his pallor deepened. But Adam had hardly stretched for spoon and brandy bottle when, disjointedly, he started to relate how he and Mary Nattrass, nothing else possible for either of them, had climbed the fells into an adjoining dale, and how, sometimes walking and sometimes favoured with a lift by farmer or carrier, they had at last reached the railway more than thirty miles away, where both first saw a train, and both gave themselves to the perplexing and embarrassing business of sending a telegram. Then, he with a label in his buttonhole for identification, they travelled to London where, at King's Cross, as was the custom when miners used only to a lonely countryside were engaged, a representative from the Company's London office met them. This gentleman, nonplussed by the arrival of an unmarried couple, had nevertheless reacted gallantly, and before nightfall Jim and Mary were installed in separate lodgings. Thereafter, in their kindness, the officials of the Company and their wives took the pair in hand; berths were booked in the next but one steamer to Seville, and Jim Brunskill was granted an advance against his first Pay. Pending their wedding, highly intimidated to begin with but gradually growing more confident, they explored the greatest city in the world hand in hand. Next came their marriage, attended by the staff of the London office, the five days' sea journey to Spain in idyllic weather, and, to round up, a thrilling trip by rumbling cart and mule.

Jim Brunskill's eyes were open again and, if sunken eyes can glow, his were glowing.

"By, but me an' your mother were happy, lad, and it were only occasionally, like when she had the one letter from home, that I thought of what my own folk were saying about me. But it weren't true, no, by God it weren't."

Adam leaned forward, sure now that Mr. Shields had been right. "An' what did you think folk were saying?" he asked.

His father's lips quivered. "That we'd bolted like we did because ... because I were frightened of what her brothers 'ud do to me," he said, adding with the irritation of ill-health: "An' if I weren't as weak as a kitten I wouldn't be acting this womanish road."

"Never mind about that," Adam urged. "You ... they reckoned *you* were frightened?"

The dying man tried to nod. "Aye, lad. But it weren't so, and I haven't been acting a lie all along when I've tried to teach you always to square up to whatever difficulty were before you. Right enough, George and William Nattrass were ugly customers, but it was your mother, and not fear of them, that deterred me from doing what I wanted to do."

With a simplicity investing his story with utter reality, Jim Brunskill told of that day long ago when, safely away from Skewdale, he had suggested to Mary Nattrass the deferment of their journey to London, she to find a lodging until his return, he to go back to Winterings and there have it out with George and William Nattrass. So vividly did the figures of his parents stand out that Adam could almost see the distress on the pictured face of his sweet and gentle mother, almost sense her horror at the idea of her Jim matching himself against her brutal brothers.

"It's a rum thing, lad," Jim Brunskill smiled, " but when you love somebody, I reckon they must appear differently to you, an' I don't think your mother ever saw me as I really was: a chap who could stand up to anybody in Skewdale. All she saw was me broken an' bleeding on the ground, with my face kicked in by George's and William's clog-irons."

"The towelling wouldn't have been all one way," Adam commented.

His father snorted faintly. "It wouldn't, lad, but that was how your mother saw it, an' as I came to the conclusion she'd be half-dead with fright if I went . . . well, I gave up the thought."

"You couldn't have done owt else," Adam retorted.

"It's pestered me though," sighed the older man. "Th'idea of it—me, a Brunskill, to run from a Nattrass."

"There's never been much love lost between Brunskills and Nattrasses, has there?" Adam murmured.

"No," his father replied. "When I was a little 'un I've heard my grandfather say as how his grandfather telled him that the trouble started when a Brunskill and a Nattrass had a difference just after a battle called Agincourt. Anyroad, I'd have tackled William and George, for all that none of our lot were left to see fair play. As you know, lad, all my four brothers had gone away to try their luck, two of 'em to th' United States, one to Australia and one to Canada."

Adam took time to mend the fire in the hope that his father, now extremely exhausted, would doze off. But the sick man, sunken face brightly illuminated by the leaping flames, started to talk again.

"It was when your mother died, lad," he said, "that I nearly went back to Winterings, not so much because George and William Nattrass had written calling me a coward, but because I was so out of my head about your mother that all I wanted to do was to smash both of 'em because of th'awful and untrue things they'd said about us. But I didn't, partly because you were nobbut a baby, and partly . . ." The silence lasted so long that Adam cautiously leaned across the bed.

"Partly," his father at last began haltingly, "no, *mainly* because I couldn't leave the place where she was laid to rest."

"No . . ." Adam said, sympathy and understanding in his deep voice as he grasped the mottled and scarred hand which lay on the coverlet. "An' don't think any more about it, Father," he continued. "You've worked here among men for nearly thirty years, an' I'll vouch that not one of 'em doesn't hold your courage to be as high as anybody's."

A tear winked in Jim Brunskill's eye. "I hope so, lad," he said wearily. "But it's hurt me, because I'd always been proud in my own strength and I couldn't forget that George and William Nattrass were saying what they liked, with nobody left to speak up for me. Most of them who would had gone away, to work in the Durham coal mines and the cotton and wool mills of Lancashire and Yorkshire, or to adventure in lands afar. The truth was that as the years went by lead-mining got so bad in Skewdale that them who hadn't a cow to eke out with were nigh to starvation."

This time the exertion was too much for him, and he slipped into an uneasy sleep, his breathing ragged. But shortly he was so still that Adam once again approached more closely. Soon, however, his eyes opened, and by then Adam had made up his mind.

"Father," he began, "I've been thinking while you've been having a nap, and I've decided to go to Skewdale when spring comes round."

That remark, of design made so casual, had all the effect of a powerful stimulant. "You have, lad?" his father cried out.

"Yes," Adam nodded. "Moreover, if any of that Nattrass lot say owt to which I take exception I shall deal with 'em in a fitting way."

Jim Brunskill tried to raise himself. "Aye, but you'll keep a grip on yourself, won't you?" he begged. "You must, lad, for if you once let yourself go it'll be murder all right."

"I'll take care not to get myself hanged," Adam promised, smiling.

"By . . ." Jim Brunskill breathed expansively and, for a brief space, gathered vigour as he planned the trip to Winterings, where Adam's Aunt Eliza would give him a rare welcome.

"She's wed to a chap called Pedley, Ambrose Pedley, who when I last heard fro' her three year ago were still struggling to make a living in t' mines there. A mealy-mouthed 'un he is, an' . . . an' . . ."

His voice had weakened perceptibly. "I think you're overdoing it," Adam warned him. "What about having a bit of a snooze?"

Jim Brunskill made an effort to smile. "That's noan bad advice, lad," he admitted, tired eyes closing. "And at after we can have another yarn, can't we? You know, lad, you've made me very happy."

One by one the minutes ticked by. At intervals either Jane Sunter or her mother left their families, gathered in the kitchen below, to creep up the stairs. At nine o'clock the doctor came, shook his head with surety, and then departed on his round.

At eleven o'clock Adam Brunskill's vigil ended. Bending, he caught his father's last words.

"Adam, lad, you mustn't grieve for me. You see . . ." His glance wavered uncertainly while searching for a faded, over-posed daguerreotype, of an exceptionally solemn young man and grave young woman, taken in London on the day of their marriage. "You see, lad," he whispered, "I'm going on a journey all right, but at th'other end I shall be met by somebody who's always meant more to me than everybody in the world. And . . ." Adam bent still lower, "you'll not take that amiss, lad," the fading voice continued, "if ever it's your blessed fortune to love and be loved by the one lass that matters."

"I've not taken it amiss, old lad," Adam told him tenderly.

There is always a degree of mystery for whomever may be present when a soul passes into eternity. Adam Brunskill experienced something of that mystery when, for a fleeting instant, he saw a radiance on his father's face and heard a choked word which was, in so far as he could judge, his mother's name.

* * * *

Notwithstanding icy rain squalls driving fiercely from the Sierra Morena, the Wesleyan Chapel was full.

All were there, Spanish miners from the South who made much more of their grief than the grave men of the Asturias in the North; men in tight, embroidered velvet jackets and knee-breeches, with a manta over all for protection; men in good leather boots and men inadequately shod in sandals made of esparto.

And men from the lead mines of Durham, Northumberland, the Isle of Man, and Alston Moor in Cumberland; from Cornwall, Derbyshire, Wenlockhead in Dumfriesshire, and the once famous Lead Hills of Lanarkshire; from the Western Dales of Yorkshire: Skewdale, Swaledale, Arkengarthdale, Wensleydale, Wharfedale and Nidderdale.

Afterwards, with a chosen company largely invited from those with Skewdale connections, there was a funeral tea at the dead man's house. So was the ageing Jim Brunskill laid to rest, alongside the remains of the young wife of his youth.

2

The whisper of spring was more pronounced, and in the foothills a rapid thaw had begun. A bright sun shone upon the front of the mining company's Counting House, from which Adam Brunskill, early that Saturday afternoon, was emerging after making arrangements to draw from the London office such additional monies as he might need when in England.

On the threshold he paused to watch the antics of a young bull destined for the ring, but soon was walking along the street. In this wise, responding to many a salute, the friendly wave, a smile, or the graceful doffing of a sombrero, he proceeded homeward, where Jane Sunter had just completed the task she had set herself.

"There," she greeted him. "All that you're getting rid of is tidied up, an' everything you want to keep is in that sea-chest."

From the chest, bought by his mother and father on arrival in Seville, Adam picked out a highly-scrolled Testimonial which proclaimed the meritorious attendance of 'Mary Nattrass' at 'Winterings Wesleyan Sunday School.' The daguerreotype which had hung in his father's room was also there, and he and Jane examined the stiffly-posed pair.

"She's a sweet face, hasn't she?" Jane murmured.

"It'd have been sweeter if the photographer had taken 'em about two minutes sooner," Adam smiled.

The sea-chest was locked, Jane, at Adam's request, taking charge of the key. She and Simon were also attending to the sale of the furniture.

"An' thank you for what you've given us, Adam," she said. "An' don't forget, when you come back we expect you to live with us."

"You're a grand lass, Jane," Adam said.

"Don't be so daft," Jane Sunter retorted.

"Simon thinks you're a grand lass, too," Adam teased her.

Young Mrs. Sunter flushed. "You great dunderhead."

They were crossing towards her own home before she perceived an opportunity for retaliation. Adam, besides carrying a big carpet bag containing his clothing, had with him the mining instruments of his profession: a dial with its compass needle, the whole in a varnished box strapped to which were two short-legged tripods, a portfolio for squared dialling paper, and books both for mathematical calculation and for pleasure.

"I suppose you'll be trying to get a job so that the trip won't cost so much?" she jeered.

"Well," he agreed, just aggravating, "I wouldn't mind surveying down in them long Skewdale levels if the chance offered."

"For nowt . . . no pay?" Jane inquired, with offensive disbelief.

Companionably they differed as far as her home, where Simon Sunter, who had hurried from work on this special day, was already washed and changed. Daniel Dolphin arrived soon afterwards, to be greeted as rapturously by the bright-eyed little daughter of the house as Adam had been a few minutes before. From Adam's knee Bessie imperatively ordered the latest arrival to perform her favourite trick, shrieking with joy when he, as bidden, generously licked the tip of his nose with his long tongue.

For Adam's convenience, Jane had arranged a meal in the middle of the afternoon, and chairs had been pulled to the table when another visitor came, Mr. Calvert, the Head Agent. His purpose in calling, he told Adam, was to ask him to convey greetings to a couple of old friends in Skewdale, Mr. Titus Alderson and Mr. Henry Hird. Adam learnt that both these gentlemen were concerned in lead mining, Mr. Hird as agent for the mineral owner, Sir Charles Grafton, and Mr. Alderson as Chief Agent for the West Side Lead Mining Company at Winterings, an undertaking struggling bitterly to survive.

"Do you wonder?" Daniel Dolphin observed. "Here we've plenty of good lead ore and a bonus in the shape of up to a hundred ounces of silver out of every ton dressed. Why, in Yorkshire the proportion of silver never exceeds five ounces, and so isn't worth th'expense of extraction."

"It's our lead that counts most, Daniel," Simon Sunter said. "There they're just about worked out."

"Aye, I think that's it," Mr. Calvert agreed. "I know Titus Alderson has had a terrible time. Anyway, Adam, give him my best respects."

This Adam promised to do but, to his surprise, the Head Agent now appeared somewhat indifferent about the message to Mr. Henry Hird. Meantime an argument on topography had broken out between Jane and her husband, with Simon, despite interesting interruptions, doggedly reciting the villages and hamlets beginning from the head of Skewdale. First there was Yorrel, he said, and next came tiny Snorr; Winterings followed, then Half, renowned for geese.

Mr. Calvert was regarding the young people with plain astonishment.

"Bless my soul!" he ejaculated. "I've only just realised that none of you have ever seen Skewdale. You were all born here, the lot of you."

"Some of th'older ones talk a fairish amount about it," Adam said slyly. "It's not surprising we've picked a bit up."

Laughing, Mr. Calvert was taking the point when Daniel Dolphin remarked that Greets, the main village of the upper Dale, came next below Half.

"That's where Henry Hird lives, Adam," he said. "He's my uncle, by the way, though we've never kept in touch with him like we have with my Aunt Ellen."

Other people present had greetings to send, too. Carefully Adam enumerated them—at Yorrel there was Jane's Aunt Rosie, Miss Caygill; at Snorr, Simon wanted him to call on his Aunt Minnie, Mrs. Skidmore, who lived at Badger Hall, one of the best farms in the district.

"Yes, Anthony Skidmore's father had a good bargain or two at the mines," Mr. Calvert nodded. "An' he were wise enough to get out and put his brass into land. Aye," he calculated, "that were thirty-four year ago, in eighteen forty-five."

Then at Winterings, Adam continued, there was Mr. Titus Alderson, whom he would certainly see for Mr. Calvert; and also at Winterings was Daniel's Aunt Ellen, who lived at Malaga.

"An' she's rolling," Daniel grinned. "So don't forget to impress on her that in Spain she's got a nephew who's t'finest, steadiest——"

"Leave it to me, Daniel," Adam promised. "Now next comes Half, where I haven't a commission, and after that we arrive at Greets."

"Aye, Greets," echoed the Head Agent. "Yes, it used to be rare an' prosperous when t'mines were in full swing, but now it's just ground down in poverty."

"All the same, I suppose I shall be there sometime or other," Adam said. "So I'll pop in an' give your good wishes to Mr. Hird."

Mr. Calvert was preparing to leave. "Aye, if it happens to be convenient," he said. "But don't put yourself to any trouble about it, lad."

Time was passing and all too soon after the meal Adam had to go. Daniel grasped the traveller's carpet bag, Simon the surveying instruments, and Adam shouldered Bessie. All together, with Jane, they walked to the Mining Company's premises close to the offices, into the big shed where vehicles were loaded with pigs of lead and bars of silver. The drivers had finished their meal, and the atmosphere was redolent with strong cheese, mealy beans dressed with rancid oil, salt cod, boiled rice, haricots, pimento and, permeating all else, dung. For private refreshment wine in leather bottles was being stowed, and the silver guards were inspecting their weapons.

"You'll write, lad?" Simon asked.

"An' tell us everything," Jane said in her husband's support.

"I wish I were going with you, lad," Daniel grumbled. "Anyway, you'll be back a month after Christmas, so we can have it at second best."

There was a sudden bustling about, the crack of a whip, and the jingling of harness as the mule teams began to move. Quickly Adam shook hands with Simon and Daniel, stooped to receive an enthusiastic kiss from Bessie, and bent a little to kiss Jane Sunter's cheek. Then he jumped alongside the driver, and, with a sharp jolt, the wagon started protestingly to move.

Like his father six months before, Adam Brunskill was setting out on a long journey, but his was to the wild countryside of their ancestry.

CHAPTER ONE

I

FOR THOSE North Country exiles employed in Spain the cheapest way home was from Seville to Newcastle-on-Tyne, in one of the grimy ships laden with a certain type of ore which, partially treated beforehand, was sent to Northumberland to be reduced. The return journey was made in a similar ship, when she carried coal for the smelt mills and refining plants.

Adam Brunskill decided, however, to make the trip as varied as possible, and booked a passage in a Thames-bound ship. He spent a week in London, sightseeing by day, the evenings fully occupied at music-halls and suchlike in the company of various young men he met when paying a duty visit to the Leadenhall Street offices of the London and Andajoz Lead and Silver Mining Company.

The round of interest and pleasure ended, Adam very early one morning caught an express at St. Pancras. From a corner seat he stared eagerly as the English countryside flashed by, delighting in the rush of speed and enjoying the sights in busy stations at each brief halt. The long run to Yorkshire passed quickly, to Sheffield, overhung by a pall of industrial smoke, and then on to Normanton, reached dead on time, where a thirty minutes' stop was scheduled, so that passengers could take advantage of the piping hot meal waiting in the refreshment rooms.

It was good and appetising food, especially taken with a tankard of sparkling beer which Adam, along with most fellow travellers, preferred to the bottles of Burgundy and Hock, price-tickets suspended around necks, standing on each snowy-white tablecloth—Scotch broth, sole, two choices of entrée, prime roast beef or tasty leg of mutton, three different sweets, and cheese and biscuits to wind up.

Replete, Adam lighted his pipe and climbed aboard again as the warning bell sounded. The guard blew his whistle, the train began to move, leaving Normanton and its revolving pit-head wheels, with Leeds next, another giant with a multitude of factory chimneys. Then through the textile districts with here and there, sometimes in a pleasant green setting and sometimes cheek-by-jowl with hideous back-to-back dwellings, a glimpse of the mullioned windows of an exquisite Elizabethan manor house. The next stop was at Skipton, on the threshold of the north-western border of that other Yorkshire so breathtakingly beautiful, and there Adam changed. From far up the platform, idly waiting, he watched the express driver wipe off with cotton-waste a splash of oil marring a cherished engine and, a few moments afterwards, as gleamingly varnished coaches began to slide past, he saw comfortable swivelled armchairs and flashes of coloured plush which, as the speed increased, formed one continuous glow of Midland Railway red.

Picking up his luggage, he walked back and entered a compartment of the slow train which, on its way northwards, stopped at stations growing more and more widely spaced as progressively more lonely and mountainous country was reached.

The air, on this the roof of England, was much colder. Adam, leaning out to stare at a mountain mass of limestone, now saw a short cutting ahead, with a tunnel beyond into which the engine was disappearing with a sustained whistle. Again the tunnel was lengthy, and lengthy also was the lofty viaduct at the farther end, from which, a hundred feet or more above the beck cascading beneath, Adam's entranced eyes perceived still another scene of Alpine beauty, foaming streams tumbling down colourful hillsides, a stone-built farmhouse perched crazily, a grey hump-backed bridge spanning a ravine, an occasional cottage, blue smoke curling from squat chimney.

"Aye," he murmured, glancing now at the railway telegraph lines above, the wires of which were twisted into one thick strand the more easily seen by grouse on the wing, "it's all they made it out to be . . . and I reckon here's where I get out."

At this point, when the regular sounds of the coach wheels were becoming slower, the track ran high up the flank of a fell, the ground to one side falling steeply to a winding road, while on the other it rose sharply, the view of the summit spoilt by the snow barrier, a screen of stout woodwork designed to keep drifts from blocking the line.

"Yes, it's Wham," Adam nodded.

A little later he alighted, and inwardly chuckled while warding off plain but somehow not impertinent questions as to the why and wherefore of his presence there. Then, bidding good-bye to the stationmaster, he started to walk as directed.

There were many matters of interest to occupy Adam Brunskill's attention as he trod the rough road. Apparently hereabouts the railway was involved in construction of magnitude. Within sight were hundreds of Irish navvies, and Adam was wondering how they were housed when, beyond a two-wheeled farm cart creaking through a field-gate, he noticed a temporary village. Laid out in avenues were wooden huts, with pipe chimneys sticking through tarred felt roofs. Reflecting that this incursion might have caused upheaval locally, he voiced his thoughts on catching the cart driver's eye.

"Aye," said that individual, spitting.

It was not until the lichen-stained, stone-slated roof of the Packman's Rest came into sight that the farmer became more communicative. Adam then learnt that not until the intruders departed would a woman be able to walk unmolested, or a man step abroad without a ferocious cudgel hidden away under coat or tucked down trouser leg.

"Fair terrorised everybody, they have," the farmer continued.

" Managed to give 'em anything back?" Adam asked.

A red gleam of battle glinted in the other's eye. "It's noan so easy in a spot like this, when we all live miles apart. Still . . ."

Adam grinned. "A few sore heads amongst 'em, eh?"

Exchanging jokes on this, they went along, Adam walking alongside a plump mare with the thick coat of winter still on her, her feet, unshod, making little noise. The cart was piled with manure from a cow-byre, and, with prudence, he had taken station to windward. By now the Packman's Rest was close by, and Adam was reminded of stories he had heard. Not so very long ago the Packman's Rest had been a prosperous house, when the pack-horse trains, each pack-horse with its silver-tinkling bell, used the inn freely.

". . . and think on you tell your bosses." He was recalled to earth by the farmer. "Or some of your chaps'll get worse hurt."

The misconception was cleared up as soon as Adam realised that his instruments were responsible for the assumption that he was one of the special surveyors the railway company sent up from time to time.

The same mistake was made in the Packman's Rest. Almost immediately, however, the landlord found another explanation.

"Going to one of t'lead mines, I suppose," he said, nodding as if satisfied. "Another of these mining experts they keep calling in."

He took a great deal of convincing to the contrary.

"Nay . . ." he tried a new tack, "seeing them tripods it were nobbut natural for me to think so."

"Right enough," Adam agreed.

"You should know if anybody should," the landlord remarked handsomely. "'Course it's none of my business . . . but . . ."

This verbal sparring continued some little while longer, final honours in the match being even, each of the adversaries finishing with a high regard for the other. The landlord, indeed, was so pleased with the duel that his hitherto poker-like expression slipped into a smile when Adam plumped for tea with the family in preference to the back parlour by himself.

"Reet, mister," he said, lifting the flap of the bar counter. "Now we'll find t'missus, an' at after you've washed it'll be about time to shove your knees under the kitchen table. An' that," he switched with foreboding, "will be th'end of peace for to-day." He nodded towards the railway. "Them Irish hooligans."

"Aye, I've heard already they cause some bother," Adam remarked.

The landlord stopped in his stride and, in a spate of words, forcefully expressed his opinion. Like most innkeepers in the upper dales, his livelihood derived from farming, but though the Packman's Rest was now making money at a rate as never before, he yearned for life to resume its old serenity.

"Bother!" he repeated with disgust.

Even his clogged feet proclaimed his disbelief in the adequacy of the word as he led the way through a stone-flagged passage.

The noise in the overcrowded tap-room was deafening, meantime the landlord and three assistants strove to keep pace with the hoarsely-strident demands of the ever-thirsty navvies who had flocked in. The Irishmen, in the mud-spattered clothing of everyday use, took up every available inch of space, and although it was still early the atmosphere was already foul, its scent compounded of rank tobacco, ale and spirits, damp corduroy, and sweat-encrusted bodies.

Just as Adam, hemmed in beneath a hanging lamp, decided upon seeking a quieter spot to scrutinise the map he had bought in London, the door opened and in came a tall and powerful young man of about his own age, whose advent was greeted with mixed feelings by those in authority.

"Well now, Reuben lad," the landlord shouted. "An' what are you doing over here? Been sending away a broken part by train?"

The newcomer clove a way through the throng and tossed off the brandy waiting for him, sliding the glass back before replying.

"Trouble with a hydraulic pumping engine," he growled. "An' I've been getting off t'slide-valve for re-planing."

"Come over the top by trap, Reuben?" an assistant barman inquired.

The stranger was eyeing the scowling faces nearby. Beer had been spilt as a result of his tempestuous entrance and there was much abuse in consequence. It was significant, however, that none of the blasphemous navvies seemed inclined to take the first steps towards hostilities, and from this Adam concluded that the man's fighting abilities must be recognised. These talents, he mused, lips curving at another recollection, must be of an unusual order to quell born fighters.

"Aye," Adam heard the lead-miner say, for such he now deduced him to be. "And I'm off back just as soon as I've downed another glass. That is," he amended as he stared about, "that is unless one o' these pigs from t'bogs is thinking of detaining me."

"Reuben!" the landlord cried.

The warning, and the sound of a tumbler splintering the mirror at the back of the bar, was lost in an angered murmur. Meanwhile Adam was smiling as he recalled a friendly adversary's idea of a perfect evening. Nothing would have suited Humphrey the Cornishman better than to have been in the tap-room—with unerring eye he would have selected his target.

"Nay, I'se nobbut looking at 'em," the miner gibed.

Snarling mouths disclosing blackened stumps bawled obscenities, brutalised faces thrust savagely forward, but, as if perfectly assured, his glance ranged contemptuously, halting only when he discerned a broad smile. Then, convinced he was confronted by challenge, his dark eyes narrowed and swiftly he shouldered forward.

"Now Reuben," the landlord shouted, "I'm noan having any fighting . . ."

Adam found himself facing, at close quarters, a man somewhat taller than himself and rather more massive, a powerful and virile figure whose good looks were not seriously impaired by a nose broadened as the result of some fight. He had raven-black hair which, below his cap, curled freely about his ears before descending to sideboards.

"You seem tickled about summat, mister," he began, a deadly intent about him. "It wouldn't be, would it," he leaned nearer, "because o' me?"

Adam laughed. "Not exactly," he said. "You see——"

The miner's lips thinned, his right hand closed, his elbow went back. "Not exactly," he repeated. "You'd better explain yourself or you'll find the front of your face has been knocked to t'bloody back."

Deep-set eyes alert, Adam Brunskill remarked evenly that he preferred to explain when not under threat. This said, he spoke briefly about Humphrey the Cornishman's liking for a bout when a suitable opponent presented.

"An' you'd just about fit the bill for him," he ended.

The other's lips curled as he prepared to turn away. "It's plain, anyroad, that you're noan anxious to fit t'bill in the same connection," he said. "But you can remember this," he added, jabbing a finger, "that if you and me ever light on one another again you'll do well to keep your face straight."

"It seems so indeed," Adam agreed.

On the public side of the bar there was certainly disappointment at this tame ending, but excitement rose again when Adam spilled half a tankard of beer from a neighbour's hand.

"Look phwhat you've done, ye Protestant bastard," the labourer howled. "But . . ."

It had happened very simply. The lead-miner had thrust several men sharply aside when returning and the movement had passed along.

"A pity," Adam murmured, smiling cheerfully into a pair of piggy, inflamed eyes. "But it's one of them accidents that can be remedied, eh? So you just sup up what drops are left, mister."

Relieving the navvy of his tankard he squeezed through to the counter, where the raven-haired young man started to nod ironically.

"Well . . . well . . . well," he marvelled. "First it were Humphrey t' Cornishman as saved your bacon, an' now you're nearly breaking your neck to pacify a potato eater. Tell me this, is there owt you wouldn't do to dodge a scrap?"

Adam Brunskill was becoming weary of this persistence, but he realised that three half-glasses of brandy, taken on an empty stomach, might not have been without their effect.

"Not much," he admitted. "I'm not one to go seeking quarrels."

The lead-miner sneered. "I guessed as much."

Then he went out and, shortly afterwards, the yellow-gleaming lights of a trap passed the misted windows of the tap-room.

A little later Adam stood at the door, beneath the small porch. It was raining heavily, but the cool air was good to breathe after the fug indoors. For almost a quarter of an hour he remained there when, avoiding the tap-room, he made his way to the rear of the house where, in the kitchen, he found a peaceful little party assembled, farmers of the neighbourhood, with a couple of gamekeepers and three shepherds. Here the talk was simple and yet profound, and good ale was savoured, not gulped down.

"An' here's where I ought to have been long ago," he thought.

While charging his pipe he listened to gossip about the young man who had tried to force a fight, learning that the miner was so feared by the bruisers that there was not a fair between Brough and Bedale where the barkers would throw out a money challenge unless sure he was not there.

"An' look at the belting he gave last Michaelmas to that ginger-whiskered Irish hooligan who thought so much of himself," a red-faced man remarked. "Why, t'chap's never been fit to work on the railway since."

The landlord, taking a spell from the bar, glimpsed Adam on the settle. "I'm sorry he picked on you, mister," he said. "But he's always in a black mood if things go wrong at t'mines."

Adam Brunskill's ideas about the lead-miner began to change. It seemed as if his job, though in lead-mining, might be one of greater authority. He inquired about this.

"Yes, it is," he was told. "Reuben's the head agent for the East Side

Lead Mining Company in Skewdale. 'Course it isn't the big job it was thirty years ago, but still . . ."

"Skewdale!" Adam exclaimed. "So he lives in Skewdale, does he?"

The landlord clapped his knee. "Aye, an' you could have driven over with him!" he ejaculated. "Not that I'm wanting to lose a night's custom, but it would have saved you a rare tew."

"If Reuben had been willing," Adam smiled.

The innkeeper guffawed. "He didn't altogether warm to you, did he? But hereabouts the miles are long an' folk help one another. Anyroad you'll manage all right . . . up High Straits an' along Jom High Road is the best way when you're on foot. It's a grand walk," he went on, eyes reminiscent, "and when I weren't so rewmatticky I oft did it . . ."

Adam was anxious to be away as early as possible in the morning.

"Afore dawn if you like, mister," his host promised. "Aye, it's going to be a shortish night for some of us an' all."

The lambing season would soon be beginning and he and his nearest neighbour would be starting out first thing to ride to the tops, to round up and drive down to pastures nearer home the ewes who had wintered on the high moors.

In due course, warm, well-fed, and happy with anticipation, Adam went to bed.

2

The heavy rain had ceased and now, while flossy white clouds sailed beneath a soft-blue vault, the sun steadily foretold a fine day.

High Straits was an unusual thoroughfare, a green lane confined between stone walls without a trace of mortar, its surface short turf through which here and there an outcrop of limestone appeared.

It was time for a breather. Adam put down his luggage and faced about, to gaze at the larger panorama now unfolding. The Packman's Rest was lost from view but, beyond the point where he had left his companions of the first two miles, where High Straits began, he could see that the landlord and the farmer neighbour, mounted on stocky dales ponies, were already on the lower slopes of the farther moor. No longer, however, could he glimpse three excited but very competent working dogs whom he had seen as rapidly moving dots travelling in great sweeps. But the result of their efforts was there, a sinuous and long-extended whitish-grey line of ewes which, like some biblical tribe, moved from the bleak heights of the moors to the sweet lushness of the promised land below.

"Well," he murmured, "if I keep stopping so oft I shan't get to Skewdale to-night."

Taking up bag and instruments, he resumed a journey in which everything was of interest to him—the sparkling sheen given to bent and long grasses by millions of drops of water, the rushing becks and plunging waterfalls coloured brown with peat, and the heavy-horned sheep who, seldom staying long in one place as a horse, ran from patch to patch to nibble the most tender shoots.

In due course, the prospect ever becoming more majestic, he rounded the second of two snake-like curves, to enter a sunless defile where foothold was precarious on the icy surface of long-lying snow.

"Yes, an' at that they say it were a mild winter here," Adam mused.

The awkward stretch negotiated, he continued forward with the special zest discovered when a good grip is obtained after bad. About half a mile along, where the ground began to flatten, there was an indication that High Straits entered another thoroughfare. From this point the moors rolled northward without interruption to Skewdale.

Near the summit of High Straits, where the light airs of the lower country had increased into a steady breeze, Adam heard the sound of wheels trundling over the sharp, gritstone surface of Jom High Road. Turning round, he saw a white-bearded old man pushing a knife-machine on whose side was painted the name 'Peg Stephen,' in bright gilt; below this was added in home-done lettering progressively more cramped: 'Knife, scissors and razor grinder, tinker, pots, horn-worker, dowser, educator and conjuror.'

The old gentleman came to a standstill with apparent relief, relinquished the handles, and mopped his brow with a ragged sleeve.

"Well, I never!" he ejaculated. "It's not oft I drop on anybody who's come up High Straits."

Adam smiled. "For that matter I shouldn't suppose you're frequently here yourself."

"Twice a year, young man, i' Spring and in Autumn," the knife-grinder replied solemnly. "Aye, an' without a single miss, for sixty-two years now, ever sin' I were a nipper."

Within a minute or so he had learnt Adam's destination, whereupon he insisted that the carpet bag and other gear should be placed on the knife-machine, Adam in his turn insisting that the pushing of the machine should be his job alone.

"Well . . ." Peg Stephen finally conceded, "it's noan my idea of a fair division of t'labour, but . . ."

That walk, over the 'top' to Skewdale, was an exhilarating one for Adam Brunskill. There was enchantment in this wild moorland coloured in russets and greens, from the thousands of sheep to the startled flap of moor game, and the purling beck which disappeared into a limestone bed never again, so far as the eye could see, to reappear. And then, where the land began to dip, there was a few minutes' lively gossip with the Hawes tailor and draper who, trap laden with cardboard boxes and rolls of material, was returning from his quarterly round.

A mile along, on the lower slopes of Silver Seat, they sat down, Peg Stephen generous with onions and prime Wensleydale cheese, Adam likewise sharing the bacon sandwiches provided by the landlady of the Packman's Rest. From that elevation two other mountains crowning the fells to the south of upper Skewdale were in sight, the juniper-clad sides of Virgin Hill to the east and, to the left, reaching up more than two thousand feet, the clear-cut line of Lovely Lady.

"A grand view," Peg Stephen remarked, rummaging in the tool-box for a quart bottle of beer. "It'd take some beating."

To one who had known the much-sullied lead-mining areas of Spain, the miracle was that this countryside, mined for centuries, was so unspoiled. True, there were indications of large mining operations, and within a narrow sector Adam perceived signs of pits and shafts and levels, each with its dead heap: a mound of debris, often smoothly carpeted with grass, formed by the spar and stone brought from underground.

"It would that," he murmured.

A deep gully passed close to their feet. The bottom, quite dry, was lined with turf upon which boulders were strewn, as if in a river bed, but the ravine started abruptly in the hillside and its banks lacked the rowans and birches fringing running watercourses elsewhere.

"That's it," Adam muttered.

Old Peg Stephen had seen the young man's interest, and promptly proceeded to demonstrate his claim to be an 'educator.' His knowledge, however, could not have included an ability to recognise his companion's instruments.

"Aye, yon's a hush, lad," he orated, handing back Adam's tobacco box, "an' that were the earliest way known o' winning bouse—which is lead ore. In fact, till t'landowners stopped it, they've alway hushed whenever somebody were lucky enough to find a vein near the surface."

In full swing, Peg Stephen went on to explain that hushing consisted of releasing a big volume of water which, surging downhill, scoured away the top-soil and exposed the mineral vein. At a subsequent period, he went on, the ore was mined by broad but shallow pits, these in turn being succeeded by deeper pits or shafts, until finally, in modern days, the ore was reached by levels, long tunnels driven horizontally into a hill side.

"Ye-es," he ended, "methods have improved since th'Old Man first used flint and such-like tools to get the lead out at after a hush."

He broke off to laugh heartily, apologising for the use of expressions which must be beyond his companion's comprehension. This led to his explaining the Old Man as a term applied both to miners of another age and the underground workings excavated by them.

"Might be nobbut fifty year ago, or it might be in Johnny Gaunt's day, or as far back as Red Rufus, but it's always called the Old Man when they come across old workings," he went on.

Surreptitiously Adam had taken a look at his map. Three peaks showed themselves to the north and he had, he thought, identified them as the main landmarks on the other side of Skewdale: Great Barg, Spout Fell, and Usha Beacon.

This pleasant interlude came to an end and the journey was resumed. Peg Stephen's mind was still on mining and, as they followed the ten-feet tall timber posts which guided horsemen in heavy snow, he went on to reveal his knowledge. And when Jom High Road ran high alongside the edge of a gill, he showed Adam a mining enterprise which in its heyday must have filled this silent place with the sounds of many men and much machinery at work.

"It finished about thirty-five years ago," said Peg Stephen.

This was Adam's first sight of a Yorkshire lead mine and, though derelict, he paid it close professional attention. The entrances of two levels looked very much like miniature railway tunnels, and from each a tramway ran to the grinding mill and washing floors lower down the gill, where the bouse was cleaned in preparation for its processing at the smelt mill farther down the beck.

"It's noan worked out either," Peg Stephen said, his tone peculiar.

Too interested to notice that a further question was expected of him, Adam continued to stare below, at nettle-overgrown waterwheels which had once driven the now rusty rolls of the grinding mill and, seen through the skeleton roofwork of the smelting mill, at massive ore hearths.

"Aye, they say there's plenty of bings o' bouse still to be got," the knife-grinder persisted.

Adam's glance was following the course of the smelt mill's flue: a solidly-built stone passageway which climbed steadily up the fellside for three-quarters of a mile, until it reached the shelf of a scar some five or six hundred feet higher. The flue terminated in a square, stone erection which, its sides without taper, suggested a medieval watch tower rather than a chimney.

"Why don't they get it out?" Adam asked, still preoccupied.

"Because," Peg Stephen told him a trifle tartly, "three men were killed there on successive days. And at after . . . well, t'other chaps could often hear 'em walking about, an' then their warning taps started."

Adam nodded sympathetically. While not particularly influenced by tales of bargests and other hobgoblins, he knew the futility of endeavouring to persuade men to the contrary.

"Aye, they all cleared out after one Pay," the old man said on taking up the journey. "Never another bat struck since."

Soon Jom High Road began to curve away from the hill and, half an hour later, the moor-gate came into sight, a peregrine falcon swooping over it. Beyond the gateway the moor was changing to rough pasturage, coarse and benty, studded with juniper. Skewdale, the valley itself, was not very distant.

The first outpost of human habitation was not more than a mile below the moor-gate, and when the farm came into view, Peg Stephen stretched across the knife-machine to release the clapper of a bell.

"They'll know who's here now," he chuckled. "And even if they haven't over much for me they'll noan forget to come out to hear all t'gossip. I oft think I'm better than a newspaper for 'em."

The loud tinkling bell indeed gave advance notice and immediately on arrival he was handed a pig knife, a pair of wool shears, and a rivetless saw blade and handle.

While treadling he enjoyed himself elaborately detailing the sensational increase of business which had necessitated an assistant, whom they could see for themselves.

"Aye, they're a grand lot, is Skewdale folk," he said when they left, smiling at Adam. "Rough customers if they think you're a bad 'un, but if they size you up as being all right—well, there's nowt they won't do for you."

Meantime, keeping his tongue wagging, there was more evidence of mining ventures, fairly recent shafts, fenced off or walled over for safety, and old shafts which, being 'run,' showed only as a saucer-like depression in the ground.

It was a one-sided conversation and at last he remarked, with rueful understanding: "Jawed your head off, haven't I? Anyroad, there isn't much now you don't know about lead-mining, is there?"

Hiding a smile, Adam pondered. "Excepting one thing," he suggested. "You haven't mentioned so far where the ore is found."

This apparently simple question momentarily nonplussed the old gentleman.

"Well, now," he began, tugging his beard, "th'ore is in veins . . . and veins stand up on end instead of being flat under the ground, if you see what I mean."

"Aye . . ." Adam said, full of inquiry.

With some thankfulness Peg Stephen noticed that he could abandon a most unprofitable line without loss of prestige. Grasping Adam's elbow, man and knife-machine accompanying him to the outer edge of the road, he pointed to the narrow dale which, a long way below them, steadily unfolded with every step round the bluff.

"An' there's Skewdale, lad," he proclaimed, his air that of a successful showman. "Champion, isn't it?"

The valley, steep-sided in the main, rose in three great terraces opposite. This immense land mass, upon which slowly-moving cloud shadows continuously varied the prevailing tones of green, purple and brown, climbed to a far-extending summit which stood out as a boldly-drawn line against a background of pale blue sky and gold-tinted cloud. The purity of this high line was not blemished by building or tree; indeed the whole of the clean-swept landscape was unwooded save for trees marking finely the downward courses of becks, and belts of Scots pine, larch and spruce serving as windbreaks for dwellings or shelter for beasts. Everywhere were glimpses of palpitating threads of running water, water tumbling down gills and falls on its breakneck journey to the River Skew, a winding ribbon racing tumultuously over rock and pebble.

In his role of guide, Peg Stephen's arm was again outstretched, towards the light grey fumes drifting from two towers some way above that first terrace.

"There's two smelt mills that *are* doing summat, though I shouldn't imagine it's much," he said. "That one to the left belongs to the West Side Company and th'other to the East Side Company."

Adam gave them but a quick glance, his attention captured by miles and miles of walling, walling of indeterminate shade which framed and made a small-patterned patchwork of the little green meadows and, immediately up the hill slopes above the meadows ran in great but irregular sweeps to contain both the rough grazings belonging to individual farms and the big common pastures, many of which were seven or eight hundred acres in extent. And, on the higher side of the common pastures, the walls again marked and guarded the division between common pasture and moor.

Peg Stephen was still holding forth: "'Course all that used to belong to the Skewdale Lead Mining Company."

It was at once all so familiar to Adam that he could do nothing but marvel. That, through the eyes of others . . .

"But when they came to grief two companies were formed," the old man continued. "And Winterings Gill—that's it climbing straight up bang in front of us—were decided upon as being t'natural boundary between the two mining setts, as it undoubtedly were."

Flanked by sharply rising ground, frequently changing direction in bold curves or sly twists, it was impossible to see very far either up or down Skewdale. Yorrel was completely hidden from sight by a lofty spur to the left, but Adam was sure he had recognised Snorr—there was the three-arched bridge, the central span alone used by the river, an overlarge giant straddling a pigmy, and nearby, to confirm, an ancient highway which sped with but slight deviation across the mining grounds.

That surely was Legatt's Way, upon which Roman soldiers had marched and a Roman Emperor's pigs of lead had been conveyed.

Peg Stephen clicked his tongue. "But neither's been successful."

Gravely Adam nodded, an act mainly of courtesy. Again he looked down at Snorr, and from there, his glance following the winding course of main road and swift-rushing river, never very far apart, he came at last to a huddle of grey-roofed and grey-stoned little houses clustered at the foot of Winterings Gill. And, as he stared at Winterings, the village in which generations of his ancestors had lived, the village beloved by his mother and father, from which they had run away, never to return, a lump came into his throat.

Peg Stephen's soliloquy went on: "No, Titus isn't having it easy. And it comes harder when an older chap makes mistakes."

Adam emerged from his reverie. "Titus!" He tried to pick up the thread.

"Aye, Titus Alderson, the Head Agent for the West Side Company," Peg Stephen went on. "He lives at Town Foot, Yew Tree House it's called, at the bottom of this road just over Dolly Bridge. It's the first house I pull up at, an' I'll bet that as soon as his niece hears this bell o' mine she'll be getting summat on the table for me . . . an' sharp-like," he added with a mysterious chuckle.

Adam was at once struck by the fact of Mr. Alderson's name coming up just as he, bearer of James Calvert's greetings to him, was on the point of entering Winterings. And so, out of special interest, he referred to a previous remark made by Peg Stephen.

"Aye," the old gentleman was grave. "He made an error in the direction of a cross-drift or summat, and it nigh finished him. A matter o' underground surveying, like."

Rather inexplicably there was then silence, but the reason, much to Adam's amusement, duly came to light when the 'educator' made his effort.

"Course there's veins *and* veins," he declared, "and it's only when they're wick wi' mineral that they're worth owt. An' as to t'veins, well, they're nobbut sort o' cracks, if you follow me."

Adam avoided a hopeful glance. "Not quite yet," he said.

There was a 'tch!' either of irritation or embarrassment and a vigorous hawking prior to spitting. But the bleating of many sheep had become close, and Peg Stephen again shirked the issue, by mounting the high grass verge.

"Looks like as if this lot'll be later wi' their lambing than usual," he shouted, knowledgeable once more.

Adam joined him at a wall where, arms resting on loosely-fitting coping stones, they were able to watch what was going on.

"Now then," Peg Stephen called out.

"How do," came the reply.

As prelude to a lively conversation this seemed hardly propitious, but after leisurely exchanges to do with the weather, hay prospects and certain newsy items, the fun started, the controversy being as to the barter-price for the conversion of beef bones into spoons.

Smiling as doughty blows were delivered, Adam's main interest nevertheless was in the work. Penned in a corner by a couple of sheep dogs were perhaps a hundred and fifty ewes, a tight-packed oscillating mass of dirty grey giving full voice. Foul hair and unsavoury adherences on the bags were being cleaned away so that when lambs were dropped they would enjoy a sweet suck. Each animal desperately resisted the pull on her horns until a deft swing finally brought her upright between a man's legs, in which position, sitting, she miraculously became perfectly resigned. When released she tore off, a mad progress halted in a stride as a few succulent grasses caught her eye.

It was good to witness this intimate pastoral scene, but it seemed probable that badinage would continue yet awhile, for there had also been a preliminary reference to the unique difficulties arising between a couple at Reeth in Swaledale after a courtship of twenty-six years.

So Adam said good-bye; he and the old gentleman shook hands, arranging to have a drink together the next evening.

"At the Plug, Lucy Peacock's that is," Peg Stephen confirmed.

Adam eyed the remaining stage of Jom High Road, whose downward slope was exceedingly precipitous. Tactfully he suggested the machine be entrusted to him.

"Aye, by God," the knife-grinder grunted. "T'last time I went down I shot so fast over Dolly Bridge that I damned nearly finished up across Town Foot i' Richard Blenkiron's Smithy."

"Right," Adam said, pulling out the stone with which he had wedged a wheel. "An' where shall I leave this for you?"

"Outside Titus Alderson's gate, by the big yews," Peg Stephen responded. "An' nip in, will you, an' say I'll noan be long."

The bell of the knife-machine sending forth its ringing tone, Adam started down the winding road. Every step changed the appearance of the fell at the other side of Skewdale, and soon the smelt mills lying back on the first great terrace of land began to disappear from view. From that point progress became extremely rapid, and shortly afterwards he reached Dolly Bridge, a grey stone erection spanning the Skew in one slim curve. Sitting upon the mossy parapet he looked upstream, on the left of which the sole dwellings near were a couple of cottages alongside a rough track joining Jom High Road just above the bridge. To the immediate right was a house he guessed to be Mr. Alderson's, beyond which a big woodyard extended up-river as far as stone dam-stakes over which water leapt. Past the woodyard, their lines varied and irregular, were the backs of other houses.

"Well, I'm here at last," Adam muttered. "Winterings, eh?"

He stayed there quite a while, his glance roving, noticing, as he had done before, that almost every other field had a massive stone barn in it. And for a little longer, leaning over the parapet, he peered into a shadowy pool, searching for the brown trout whose protective colouring made them so difficult to discern.

Adam smiled. "Come on, lad," he admonished himself.

There was not much farther to go, just thirty or so yards between Dolly Bridge and the highway, on gaining which he saw that two tall yews flanked the gate of the house on the corner.

The brown-grained door of Yew Tree House was open, but Adam for some moments stared about him, first gazing along cobbled Main Street into the village and then, in the opposite direction, down the road which wound through the dale to Half and Greets. Facing Mr. Alderson's house, across the street, a lane opened out between lofty walls; the Roe Inn, an establishment with many cracked windows, occupied the left-hand side of the entry, while at the other there was a blacksmith's shop, house adjoining, with a sign: 'Richard Blenkiron—Farrier and Smith.'

Having briefly surveyed Town Foot, Adam gathered together his possessions and, unlatching a green-painted gate, went up the stone-flagged path.

Knocking on the door, he was promptly bidden to enter.

As seen from the front door of Yew Tree House, an oil-cloth covered passage reached to the full depth of the house; to the right was the doorway into the kitchen, where Adam glimpsed a brightly-glowing peat fire, tiny blue flames dancing on the top.

A remark made while he was wiping his boots brought his feet to a standstill. The voice came from a remote part of the house, but the distance hid neither its sweetness nor the quiver of mirth.

"You needn't think you've surprised me," was called out gaily.

Adam coughed, but this merely evoked a peal of laughter. There were further observations, not very clear owing to the combined clatter made by clogs and the iron handle of a bucket.

"I should have thought . . ." the young woman jeered between resounding bumps, "that even a complete stranger like you would have known . . . that Skewdale folk aren't caught all that easy."

Adam chuckled. "I never made out they were."

Another heavy thud coincided with this retort, but he must have been partially heard, for afterwards there was a silence which, if short, was notable enough to cause creases of amusement to appear around his eyes.

"You ought to join the strolling players," the reply came at last. "Anyway, your tea's ready an' you can't say it isn't."

"H'mm . . ." Adam responded, his deep voice dubious.

The lady laughed. "An' you'd better be sitting down to it when I come back," she cried out, her footsteps receding. "I shan't be long."

Smiling, Adam put down his luggage on the worn but clean red-striped matting. Then, appreciatively, he glanced about, from the corner cupboard, with its display of china, to the grandfather clock whose regular tick fell pleasantly on the ear. The fire burned soundlessly, its light reflected at many a point in copper, brass and well-polished furniture. Against the hearth, on a brightly-coloured cloth rug, a red-cane rocking chair stood cosily, and nearby, on the wall, a rack held a good dozen clay pipes.

"We'll see who has the surprise . . . eh, Fatty?" Adam grinned as he stooped to fondle the portly black cat which, jumping down from the side of the hob, had begun to weave around his legs. "But it's some game they have between 'em," he nodded, recalling the mystery Peg Stephen had made about Mr. Alderson's niece hurrying with tea. "Yes, that's it, and the bell heralded me."

The distant squeals made by shovelling had ceased and now footsteps pattered in the back kitchen. A door closed and then followed the sounds of splashing water.

"Well, she invited me," Adam smiled.

As he pulled a Windsor chair to the table his face assumed that expression of gravity normally upon it. Only once, fleetingly, did his seriousness relax when, seating himself with his back presented squarely to the fireplace, he felt the well-furnished body which, in a lithe spring, alighted upon his knee.

With the family cat padding steadily on his lap, Adam awaited events.

CHAPTER TWO

I

THE WOOD YARD at Winterings, left on Sir Charles Grafton's hands when the Skewdale Lead Mining Company collapsed, did business with all comers, whether farmer, local carpenter or group of groovers who, a bargain negotiated with Sir Charles's mineral agent, clubbed together to adventure in some mining project.

Yew Tree House stood at the Dolly Bridge end of the yard. It was a comfortable-looking house and, although not large, had three entrances: the front door; a way out through the back kitchen to outbuildings and stable; and a third door on Jom High Road into Mr. Titus Alderson's office. Inside, the house lived up to its outward appearance; its rooms were snug and reflected great credit upon the young woman who tended them.

There was scant space between the four-poster and the wall, but Titus Alderson's niece had no difficulty in squeezing out. Her movements were supple and, although an all-enveloping apron made guessing hazardous, the manner in which she walked to the open window gave the impression that her figure was graceful. After shaking the duster she comprehensively inspected the bedroom.

"Yes, that'll do nicely," she remarked. "And the next thing is, how long will Uncle be before he comes down from the mine?"

She turned again to the window, her glance following the upward course of Sorrow Near from the Smithy opposite. The sunken road was bounded by a wall high enough to hide a pedestrian, but her uncle, on Ben, would have been visible throughout the entire length.

Her face clouded. "No," she murmured. "Oh, I do wish he'd take it easier until he gets better, but he won't give himself a chance."

Even that ridiculous garb, crowned by a grandmotherly mobcap, could not conceal the truth that Cherry Dinsdale was a very pretty girl. There was a vividness about her, too, as if she enjoyed every moment of living. And as for the rest, her teens were a few months behind, she had a laughter-curved mouth, and she was neither short nor tall.

Just then her attention was attracted by a plump, golden-haired young woman who had been hurrying towards Smithy House until she noticed the window, when she paused at the gate.

For quite three seconds Cherry Dinsdale stared down blankly, until vague recognition began to dawn. "Now who is it?" she puzzled, very audibly. "Her face is somehow familiar, but . . ."

The blacksmith's daughter giggled, meantime the absurd soliloquy overhead went on. In due course Cherry, scowling ferociously, pinned the stranger down as some person encountered in a millinery establishment. The final stage came when, triumphantly, she identified the unknown as the milliner.

"You are awful, Cherry," Fronick Blenkiron tittered. "An' I'm right sorry, really I am."

A spirited discussion ensued about a bonnet which should have been worn at Chapel the previous Sunday. An undertaking followed that at the latest it would be brought across by Saturday teatime. After which the conversation took an easier turn.

"No, I'm not going out to-night, but Dinah's calling," Cherry said. "It isn't time yet for them to start cheese-making."

Richard Blenkiron kept cows, too. His only daughter grimaced.

"No, thank heavens," she agreed, "we've still a good month."

Some few details of current gossip passed between the two girls and then Fronick Blenkiron tripped across Main Street, waving to her father in the Smithy doorway before entering her home.

A smile still lingering, Cherry collected her dusters, cloths and bottle of furniture cream, and glanced once again up Sorrow Near. As she turned away she heard, rather thinly, the jingle of a bell.

"Peg Stephen!" she gasped.

Skirts and apron streaming behind her, she flew out of the bedroom, shot down the narrow staircase, and scampered along the passage. In the kitchen she laid the table, whisking crockery from a cupboard, cutlery from a drawer, food from the larder.

"There!" she said. "Well, he hasn't caught me napping."

Next she filled the kettle, suspending it above the fire. Another household task still remained and, though unconnected with the old scissors-grinder, she decided to do it before he arrived.

Changing into clogs from the shoes she usually wore indoors, she went into the back kitchen. While there she heard the knock on the front door and, as it was unknown for Winterings folk to do other than pop their heads inside and shout, Peg Stephen's latest departure merely made her laugh.

Nevertheless the old man was most certainly improving in his methods, for he almost tricked her once.

"I don't know who he's pretending to be," she smiled in the stick-place, "but he's better than when he tried to imitate Dr. Seaton."

The buildings at the rear occupied the greater part of the space between the end wall of the Saw Mill and the tail race of the big waterwheel. There were Ben's stable and several stone-built sheds. In the coal-house Cherry filled half a bucket for lighting the fire next morning, on top of this stuffing kindling from the stick-place next door, the second bucket being piled with hard black peats from the peat house.

Loaded, she returned to the house and washed her hands. When hanging up the towel, a movement in a looking-glass caught her eye. Unmindful of workaday cap and apron, she rushed into the kitchen.

"Oh!" she gasped, pulling up sharply. She said "Oh!" again, this time the tone a little outraged, adding to this an imperative but slightly disgusted: "Sambo!" when, passing behind broad shoulders, she saw that spoilt creature comfortably settled.

A young man rose, carefully placed the cat in the vacated chair, and then turned to her. "I think he's taken to me," he explained. "Of course . . ." he said with nice respect, "this is a very friendly household. I knew that the instant after I'd rapped my knuckles on the door."

Hastily Cherry glanced out to see if the familiar knife-machine were in the usual position. This brief spell enabled her to fight off a wild impulse to laugh for which, to her extreme annoyance, the unexpectedness of his opening remark was responsible.

"I thought it was Peg Stephen," she answered with dignity.

"No," the tall young man said with regret. "Nobbut his assistant."

"His assistant!" Cherry ejaculated.

"His assistant," nodded the visitor.

They stared at each other, this young man and this young woman. As for Adam Brunskill, he was very content to do so, for she made, he decided, the bonniest of pictures with her sweet mouth, her cheeks delightfully flushed, and wavy tendrils generously escaping from a too slack mobcap. Meantime Cherry inconsequently thought that she liked a bronzed and roughly-hewn face, until she became sharply aware of a quizzing pair of grey eyes whose impact, she confusedly felt, was bringing a deeper blush to her cheeks.

"Then you'll know how long he'll be," she said, striving to sound very aloof.

A moment afterwards she bit her lip. While the young man replied he patently started to examine the table. His glance passed longingly from a piece of cold brisket to the crock of rich yellow butter, from a wedge of Skewdale cheese to the spice cake and golden-brown treacle tart.

"Yes," he sighed, the painstaking scrutiny ended, "he mentioned you'd have summat ready for him."

Cherry Dinsdale gave up the struggle. "An' you'd like your tea, too, would you?" she inquired, dimpling.

His reply came without hesitation. "I'd like nowt better."

His deep voice conveyed so surely his sincerity that Cherry immediately ensured he did not see her face again until its latest fiery flood subsided, taking her time with the brown earthenware teapot until, herself again, she picked up a cloth pad to grasp the kettle. It was then, as the young man was rolling Sambo, that she saw the luggage. Her eyes widened when she recognised an expensive mining dial and tripods, and then they darkened with anger.

Slowly she put the pad aside. "And how long have you been Peg Stephen's assistant?" she asked, containing herself.

Adam confessed to the trivial period of the association, his smile vanishing at the change in her.

"You're a mining engineer, aren't you?" Cherry continued.

"I haven't quite reached them sort of heights," Adam responded.

Impatiently she brushed aside the palpable evasion. "Are you connected with lead-mining or not?" she demanded.

"Yes," Adam retorted.

Wondering how he had offended, he saw her in this other mood, pale but holding herself proudly.

"Well, perhaps soon you'll get promotion," she said, her mouth scornful. "An' then you'll be able to do like the big pots: hire a trap instead o' walking over the tops from Wham Station as I expect you have. You've come from London, haven't you?"

"Aye," Adam nodded.

Anger when a loved one is ill-treated is often fiercer than when oneself is involved. That is how it was with Cherry Dinsdale. She knew that often nowadays, in desperation, lead-mining companies called in experts, but never had she imagined the West Side Company's directors doing so before consulting her uncle. Mr. Rutter might have agreed, Mr. Plews *would* have, but to realise that the Chairman, Mr. Wade, was capable of such a low-down trick. . . . To this further ignominy her uncle would return to-night—Uncle Titus who had put his savings into the Company to assist it through its greatest trial, Uncle Titus who had voluntarily forgone half his salary of a hundred pounds a year.

"And I suppose you want to see my uncle?" she said, dangerously quiet.

"I do," Adam agreed, not helping her.

His seeming indifference fired her, for there were also certain long-recognised courtesies between mining agent and mining engineer.

"Then why didn't you write to him beforehand?" she flamed.

Mildly Adam replied: "Because I didn't think it were necessary."

On this, colour flooded her cheeks. "It was the first thing you should have done," she said with withering contempt. "And anybody would who had a ha'porth of decency."

"Mmm," Adam Brunskill murmured.

But she was not goaded this time. Instead she told him with a very proper dignity that she did not wish him to stay.

He gave Sambo a friendly poke before picking up his possessions. It seemed unlikely he would speak to her again, but he did.

"Don't tell Peg Stephen I've owt to do with lead-mining," he begged.

The promise slipped out before Cherry could check it, and afterwards she was furious with herself.

"Thanks," he smiled, actually smiled.

Her temper, because of that smile, rose to a new height, but he was gone and so she could not vent it. Nevertheless the opportunity soon occurred, for in the passage he turned and, his expression preternaturally grave, looked round the jamb of the door.

"There's just another thing," he began.

"Well . . ." she said.

He was all innocence. "Only that your cap's not all that plumb," he replied before unhurriedly departing.

Cherry Dinsdale could do no more than gasp. "Of . . . of all the impertinence!" she told herself tempestuously as she sought the most accurate part of the kitchen mirror. Then she surveyed herself, her mouth opening in dismay when she saw the mobcap hopelessly askew, weighted down to one side by her hair. At the other side she resembled a drummer boy whose jaunty cap covered only half his head.

"Of all the sights," she murmured, horrified.

Fascinated, she continued to eye herself. But it was not long before her mouth began to curve, her dimple to assume larger proportions, and soon after that she was laughing helplessly.

"How ever he kept his face straight, I don't know," she gurgled.

This was the sole tribute the young man received, and her brightness faded when she saw him talking to Mr. Blenkiron near the Smithy door.

On leaving Yew Tree House, Adam crossed Town Foot to obtain more precise directions, when he learnt his aunt had died two years before.

"And you're her nephew, eh?" the blacksmith said.

Mr. Blenkiron was big built. He wore a leather apron, and his shirt sleeves, rolled above the elbow, revealed a pair of powerfully muscled arms. From young manhood he had enjoyed feats of strength and even now in this, his middle age, had the reputation of being one of the two strongest men in the Dale, Reuben Nattrass, the East Side Company's head agent, not claiming to be more than his equal.

Thoughtfully he combed his fingers through a gingery beard. "Then

I reckon you're a Brunskill," he remarked. "An' if so you'll have come some way. All the Brunskills went to th'ends of the earth."

"I'm Jim Brunskill's son," Adam answered. "If you remember him."

"Yes," the blacksmith pondered, "I believe I do, though I were nobbut a lad when he left."

When, a little later, Adam mentioned he would be remaining in Skewdale until the end of the year, he was warmly invited to Smithy House.

"Next door, lad," Richard Blenkiron said. "Just when you've a mind, we don't stand on ceremony here."

"Right, Mr. Blenkiron, I will," Adam accepted gratefully. "And now I think I'd better be off to Back Lane."

He recrossed Town Foot to enter Jom High Road, on to which, a short distance up, a wing of Yew Tree House abutted. There was a door, and two windows through which he glimpsed underground plans and a large-scale map. Heaped in the windows were geological specimens of fascinating colour and exquisite formation, trifles miners can never bear to throw away.

"That'll be Mr. Alderson's office," Adam decided.

He was quickly over Dolly Bridge, and then turned to the right. Back Lane was little more than a cart track, and the solitary pair of cottages he had noticed earlier were just above the dam stakes conserving water for the Saw Mill waterwheel. The house in which his aunt had lived, the nearest, was in a sorry state, mortar crumbling and paint flaking.

"Yes," he reflected, noticing the paltry stack of criss-crossed timber in the vast wood-yard across the swift-flowing river, "it certainly seems as if a blight has fallen over everything here."

Nevertheless he was not oppressed as he savoured the reek of peat drifting from the chimneys of the village, and watched long shadows darkening great areas of pasture and moor, for soon the sun would be down. In some queer way he felt that this was home.

Ambrose Pedley's cottage was two-storied, but at the back the land rose so sheerly that it would have been easy to vault on to the stone slates of a roof pitched low to offer the least resistance to winds which could tear along the Dale as though confined in a tunnel.

A short, sallow-complexioned man, of between fifty and sixty, opened the door in response to the knock.

"I'm Adam Brunskill," Adam announced himself. "You'll have opened the letter I sent, I expect."

A pair of dark, almost burning eyes, set in hollow cheeks, fixed their gaze on him. "I did," Ambrose Pedley said. "But there were no point i' writing you, seeing as you were coming."

Adam followed him into a dingy kitchen. "I've heard about Aunt

Eliza," he said, when settled in a lumpy-bottomed, straight-backed chair. "I'm sorry."

Ambrose Pedley shook a head profusely clothed with a tangle of whiskers and beard. "You should rejoice an' not mourn," he said. "She's at peace, and where all things are pure. Aye, pure . . ." A lingering sigh escaped him.

While endeavouring to find subjects less gloomy, Adam studied a man whose clothes were pitiably poor, though a brush would have worked wonders on greeny-black, thigh-length coat and cloth breeches, on heavy-ribbed stockings and dirty clogs.

"Yes, I should know how it is in mining," Ambrose Pedley continued heavily. "I'm a groover for th'East Side Company, and my share of the last partnership I were in 'mounted to just two pounds for the month."

"Bare existence," Adam commented. "But why haven't you chucked it long ago and gone elsewhere where you could earn a fair livelihood?"

Ambrose Pedley leaned forward to grasp Adam's knee, his dark eyes intently on him.

"Don't you understand, lad, that there's more important things than material 'uns?" he beseeched. "Every Sunday . . ." he brought the other arm into play, using upthrust finger as signpost sweeping the heavens, "every Sunday, near or far, storm or sunshine, I carry the Word over mountain an' dale. Isn't work like that, serving the Lord among them I know, better nor going off as you say? A thousand times, aye."

In part, only inherited instinct of the obligations of kinship deterred Adam from seeking other quarters. But, as he looked about, he realised that lodging-money would help his cousins.

Ambrose Pedley's soft lips were smiling. "But don't think you're noan welcome, lad, despite cruel difficulties. What there is we'll share right willingly, down to the last dry crust, as t'Lord would have us do."

By now Adam suspected that this kind of long-windedness might go on interminably if given licence. And so, starting off by saying he had always intended to pay his aunt for board, he made forthright inquiry as to the proper weekly sum. Pinned down by a will stronger than his own, the older man was brought to mention half a sovereign. To this Adam demurred.

"Well, Agnes will have to do your washing, I suppose," Ambrose Pedley said, "so we'll say another sixpence for that. But . . ." his beard quivered, "I think instead of you rushing things like you are——"

Adam cut in: "We'll make it twelve and six to begin with. I reckon that's a sight too little, so we'll see how it pans out."

Ambrose Pedley asserted himself. "It's too much an' that means it's charity," he declared. "Never yet have I accepted a pennypiece that——"

Adopting the example set him a little while before, Adam's arm shot out. He pointed to the calf-bound Bible resting on a low shelf.

"Charity . . . nowt of the kind," he denied. "Anyroad, doesn't it say in there that those who have shall help them who haven't? And . . . and isn't there also mention of folk who are too stiff-necked with pride?"

Ambrose Pedley gaped. "You've getten the sense of it," he admitted. "Though the exact phrasing——"

"Twelve an' six, then," Adam interposed.

A heavily-bearded head was nodded before it sank on to its owner's breast. "Out of the mouths of babes and sucklings," Ambrose Pedley whispered, his eyes closed.

Ignoring this manifestation, Adam stood up and delved into his pocket.

"I'll pay it every week in advance," he said, and then, at the sight of the forlorn figure, tried to enliven the proceedings. "Save trouble," he chuckled, "if I'm ever minded to run off in the middle of the night."

Ambrose Pedley straightened in a spasmodic jerk. "What do you mean by that?" he asked, his voice high-pitched.

It was Adam's turn to gape. "Nowt," he replied.

For some seconds Ambrose Pedley's dark eyes were probing, until, satisfied by the younger man's astonishment, he relaxed.

"It were nobbut that in my frailness I were mortified because you'd used Holy Writ to point out th'error I were in," he mumbled from the depths of unkempt whiskers. "*Me*, who's reckoned as good a student of Divinity as there is in t'district . . . aye, and nearly as moving a preacher as my brother James is. And . . ." he groaned, "that's sinful pride again."

The chink of coins, as Adam poked in the gold and silver compartments of his purse, did not disturb him. This was how they were respectively engaged when the door-sneck clicked.

As Ambrose Pedley's partnership was not resuming work in Martha Level until the following week, he spent his time in memorising the address shortly to be delivered in the Chapel at Keld in Swaledale.

This made it difficult for his younger daughter, Agnes, to leave home without genuine excuse. Nevertheless she slipped away in the late afternoon of the day Bull Waggott checked mine timber in the Wood Yard. It was very wicked of her, she knew, but she always consoled herself that there was nothing harmful in trying to obtain a glimpse of him; with perfect truth she could say they had never exchanged a single word.

This did not mean that Bull Waggott, Reuben Nattrass's crony and right-hand man at the East Side Company's mines, was not interested in women. In point of fact, Waggott, whose nickname of 'Bull' was extremely apt both as to appearance and disposition, had never really noticed her. She looked very young, far less than her eighteen years.

"No . . ." she said to herself, quite woebegone, "he's not in there and," she panicked as she thought of her father, "I'd better hurry back."

The main gate of the Wood Yard, in Main Street, was about a hundred yards from the point Jom High Road entered the village, and so, first making sure nobody was watching her, she glanced again through the gap between a pile of tramroad sleepers and a heaped mass of elm slabs. Disappointed, she started off homeward and, half walking and half running, soon reached the green-painted gate of Yew Tree House, where she was hailed by a young man who, canvas mail-bag slung over a shoulder, was striding up the main road from Greets.

"You're in a big hurry, lass," Wingy Blenkiron called, waving his one arm. "Summat wrong?"

"No . . . no," she gasped, startled out of her preoccupation.

"Right," Fronick Blenkiron's brother laughed.

Shaking his head as if slightly amused, Wingy crossed Town Foot towards Smithy House. Since losing his right arm through a premature explosion when driving the Sun Cross-cut in Notion Level he had been postman of Winterings, and was returning from Greets after taking down the collection.

Agnes Pedley's flying feet soon took her over Dolly Bridge and into Back Lane, her exertions bringing a touch of colour to alabaster-like cheeks. The shepherd who lived next door was outside, cutting off Y-pieces of thorn for weasel traps, and he let her know at once that a young man was with her father.

"It'll be my cousin Adam," she blurted out.

"In that case, love," Mark Iveson said, "you'd better go in."

A moment later she was standing before the door of her home, hand outstretched to the thumb-sneck, thumb briefly arrested, as always, before she pressed it down. As the door swung open she saw her father in his chair and a tall young man who was tucking in the flap of a purse.

At her entry, Ambrose Pedley, bowed in self-humiliation, aroused himself to twist round.

"Where have you been, girl?" he asked, his voice plaintive. "Anyroad, this is your cousin Adam, and he's staying wi' us for a bit. Have you got everything ready as you should?"

Her big cousin smiled down at her. "So this is Agnes," he said. "Well, there isn't much of her but what there is looks very nice to me."

Actually, at first sight, Adam thought her to be no more than a child of thirteen or fourteen, hence his teasing compliment. Now he perceived his cousin's hair was up and that she was on the verge of womanhood. But she deceived greatly.

Still marvelling, and vaguely perturbed, he looked at her again. In build she was small and fragile and this, together with flaxen hair and, before she coloured painfully when addressed, the two daubs of red in her smooth, white cheeks, brought to mind a doll. Even her eyes were china-blue but, instead of being vacant, he began to feel sure they reflected a haunting fear.

Apparently her mother had instilled into her what was due to a guest. Adam, as Ambrose Pedley embarked on an account of how he spent himself in the Lord's service, saw her peer at a stone shelf in the larder, and caught her glance when, directly afterwards, it went to the money he had placed on the table.

She waited for her father's effusion to end.

"Would . . . would Cousin Adam," she then faltered, "like summat to eat now . . . or would he sooner wait till I've been to the shop?"

Adam patted his stomach. "I'm just stuffed, lass," he boasted. "No, not a single bite."

"But later on, Cousin Adam?" she asked, brightening.

Unaware that Ambrose Pedley's eyes were darting, Adam chaffed her.

"Well . . ." he closed one eye, "I'm a rare 'un for a pot o' tea——"

"And a slice of fruit cake, Cousin Adam?" she said.

"With a piece of cheese, eh?" Adam insinuated.

"Yes, Cousin Adam," she nodded.

"It's ordered, Agnes," Adam said grandly. That, at last, made her smile.

She then busied herself, taking out of the oven a pillowcase which had been airing there, blankets from a clothes-horse, and bedclothing off the line across the fireplace. Bearing a big bundle, the top of which she held down with her chin, she went upstairs, subsequently making two more journeys, one to fill an ewer and the other to fetch the primroses she had arranged in a pot jam-jar.

"Your bedroom's ready, Cousin Adam," she said when finally done. "An' . . . an' when you want to take your things up I'll show you where. And . . ." after a halting start she was gaining more confidence, "an' if you find you need another blanket——"

"I'll show your cousin where he's sleeping," her father interrupted harshly. His dark eyes were still on her when he spoke to Adam, whose mouth had hardened when he saw her shrink. "This road after me, lad," he said, moist lips a-tremble.

Adam, pulling out his silver watch when alone, decided he had plenty of time before dusk. But, as he stood at the window his thoughts were grim, not upon the deepening colours which invested the high fells and swift-flowing river below with a new charm.

"Aye, he's a queer 'un is yon," he summed up Ambrose Pedley.

He glanced about him, from the iron bedstead to the wallpaper hanging down in a drooping arc from the damp wall; from the battered chest to the clean but threadbare towel.

"She's done what she could anyway," he mused, bending to smell the fragrance of the primroses in their commonplace receptacle. "She's a nice lass, too, an' ought to have a chance."

Poor as it was the bedroom did not unduly dismay him, for his home surroundings in Spain had always been grey. But, by contrast, it recalled the brightness in the kitchen of Yew Tree House. Nodding, he determined to take a stroll, during which he intended to call for a drink and something to eat. This resolve he acted upon forthwith.

2

With the exception of a small area around Calvert's Wynd, Main Street was lined thinly with buildings of a single depth only. The backs of those on the north side looked up the meadows and pastures flanking Winterings Gill, while their counterparts opposite reached down towards the Skew.

When the river was low dwellers in Back Lane, by using the Hippy Stones below the dam stakes, could enter Main Street near the Wesleyan Day School, so saving the round by way of Dolly Bridge. And, as in all mountainous districts, a spate of water subsides with fine weather just as quickly as it comes with rain or thaw, the Hippy Stones were less than awash. Adam, noticing this, slithered down the steep bank to the river and picked his way gingerly across the green and slippery slabs of rock. On the farther side he scrambled up the pebbles, crossed the race supplying the Saw Mill waterwheel, and then entered Dirty Bottom, a dark quadrangle lined by tumbledown cottages. From there he went along Calvert's Wynd, an irregular passageway.

"Well, it's a short cut," he grunted. "But it could be sweeter."

For a minute or two he stood at the entrance to Calvert's Wynd, in Main Street, between a cobbler's shop and the gate-post of the Wood Yard. The school was across the road, with house next door.

"No," he muttered, rejecting the tempting idea of a walk towards Town Foot and Yew Tree house. "I'll go to the left instead, and get some grub somewhere."

Eyeing everything and eyed curiously, he sauntered up grey Main Street, passing an empty public house and a long, open cart shed with considerable range of stabling facing which, set well back, was a commodious residence. A grocer's shop and a crockery shop came after that, each of which, to judge from window displays, departed from rightful spheres, the former offering a mackintosh for seven-and-sixpence, the latter parading moleskin at two and seven pence a yard.

Beyond there, another disused public house alone intervening, Main Street bent sharply and narrowed momentarily, the pavement reduced to a mere shelf eighteen inches wide. From here the street ran in a straight line to Winterings Gill, the road beyond being hidden by the high-waisted hump of a bridge. Within view, in addition to cottages and houses, was the Romanesque-styled Wesleyan Chapel, with burial ground and tree-planted garth, and the Reading Room and Literary Institute. There were three more shops which, with others in similar plight, made seven in all either shuttered or dimly revealing the aftermath of removal through small-paned, cobweb-festooned windows. One small general store had survived at the West End, and this, from the higgledy-piggledy of widely varied stock in its bow front, competed in many lines for what trade there might be with the two establishments still doing business towards Town Foot.

"Three shops open an' more than twice as many closed," Adam mused. "An' as for pubs, they've been knocked even harder."

He noted further examples. An inn used as a private house, another declined to an off-licence, and a third boarded up.

At the approach to Winterings Brig there were two more, but while that on the low side, the Bridge Inn, seemed advanced in decay, the other, the Plug and Feathers opposite, looked exceedingly prosperous.

"Aye," Adam murmured, as he leaned over the bridge, "everything proves that lead-mining here long ago ended its day."

It was pleasant on the peak of Winterings Brig, watching the lively beck leaping to join the Skew no more than a stone's throw away. On the higher side the stream came into sight over a jutting lip of limestone, and from there, between hazels and silver birches, tumbled down three falls, the third so deep that, at the foot, just above the graceful bridge, its force had scooped out a dangerous sump.

Adam stretched over, to gaze down at the turmoil of waters more than twenty feet below.

"I shouldn't like to be chucked into there," he decided, noting the strange eddies. "Yes, I can well believe all I've been told about that."

Winterings Brig was the traditional place of punishment for those who gravely offended the community. Adam remembered the story of the Lord of the Manor's Steward who, when an unmarried Winterings woman gave birth to her fourth child by him, had the desirability of naming the wedding day impressed upon him at this place. That gentleman was fortunate, escaping with a severe fright and the loss of an eye when dashed against a boulder, but the young lead-miner who, notwithstanding many warnings, continued to whistle while working underground had not got off so lightly. Hurled over the bridge, the whirlpool had closed over him finally, and he was not seen again until the flood subsided, when his battered body floated out of a pot-hole down at Half, a proper end, it was held, for one whose defiance of the mining code had involved the death of a partner by a fall of rock and the maiming of another, crushed against the side by a bouse wagon.

"You'd better not tumble over there," someone called cheerily.

Adam looked round. Two young men were passing, both unbuttoning jackets in anticipation of a game of hand-ball.

"I'll look out," Adam laughed.

The one-armed young fellow grinned. "I should, lad."

Idly, Adam watched the game as the opponents, shirt sleeves rolled up and clogs pattering madly on the paved yard, smashed the ball, with powerfully swinging, flattened palm, against the end wall of the Bridge Inn, from the roughly-dressed stones of which it occasionally came off at an unexpected angle, to be retrieved only by a wild dash and hand outstretched to the utmost.

Still eyeing the players Adam walked down the village side of the hump. "Aye, he's out o' balance because of having only one arm," he thought, "but he's more than a match for the long-haired 'un. . . . Well . . ."

He looked at the Plug and Feathers with its gleaming windows and fresh brown paint, at the well-brushed cobblestones before the doorway, and a mounting-block as clean as if scrubbed every day.

Across the road a good-humoured wrangle had broken out. "I tell you it did, Bart," Wingy Blenkiron shouted. "An' I say it didn't," Bart Hugill countered. "Nay, dammit, Wingy . . ."

Half smiling, Adam Brunskill paused with his foot on the yellow-ochred door-step of the Plug and Feathers. When the debatable point was cleared up, he went inside.

The tap-room was very cosy and, although the evening was not cold, a blazing apple log sent out a pleasing aroma and added a touch of welcome.

Towards the inglenook a youngish man limped with a pewter tankard, a piebald bitch in whose veins every conceivable hunting strain appeared to have been mixed following faithfully at his heels.

When settled Matt Tiplady resumed the argument, Floss sitting between his legs. As was usual when he had had a drink or two, her master's bone of contention was the law which denied a man the right to take game when and where he wished.

A neighbour winked. "But that's poaching, Matt," he deplored.

"Aye, an' that's what the magistrates down at Corvy 'ud say," Matt Tiplady grunted. "But the fact is that t'lawyers, for their own good reasons, don't choose to go back far enough. If they did——"

"Your brother-in-law wouldn't have the job o' trying to nobble anybody for a few brace o' grouse, eh?" a red-faced man chuckled, glancing up from his knitting. "Anyroad, Matt, have you telled Will he's in the wrong?"

Matt Tiplady grinned. "It has been mentioned betwixt us."

There was a roar of laughter, brought about as much by his manner as by his words.

Adam now began to be interested in a group gathered about an old gentleman who, kneeling, was illustrating his remarks by drawing diagrams on the flag-stones. His attention became keener on discovering that the sharp exchanges concerned Titus Alderson.

"Now here's Doomsday High Shaft . . . an' there, a bit beyond, is Jamie's Mint, where th'ore is supposed to be," the old fellow explained, busy with the chalk. "So after Titus's New Drift meets the bottom of Doomsday——"

"If it does," a young man broke in.

Painfully, on stiff knees, the aged miner turned round. "An' what d'you mean by that, Arthur?" he demanded.

"I'm nobbut thinking of his Short Cut," the other jeered. "If it'd been driven half a fathom lower it'd have gone right under an' beyond Old Joss Level, an' that tells how cockeyed the junction were. As unminerlike a piece of work as I've ever heard on."

The veteran fired. "Titus Alderson knew more about lead-mining by he was eighteen than you'll know in your natural, my lad," he thundered. "Oh, aye, he made that slip, I'll admit, but as for him making another mistake, when it's nobbut a matter of accurate dialling——"

"He's doddering," his young opponent shouted. "An' that's why his New Drift'll noan hit the bottom of Doomsday."

"Of course it will, you damned fool."

The bellicose young man made rather an unusual study, so Adam thought. He was tall, weedy, and weak-faced. His stance attempted to offset these disadvantages: jaw out-thrust, clenched fists dangling and elbows a shade out, his attitude was that of a prize-fighter. Notwithstanding, he suddenly was surprisingly conciliatory on the prospects of Mr. Alderson's New Drift, though he certainly was not pandering to an old man.

"Oh, maybe he'll do better this time, but we shall see," he conceded, adding: "You bloody dafthead."

An incisive voice brought a period even to the old man's bellow, and Adam saw that the mistress of the Plug and Feathers had taken her place behind the bar.

"Arthur," Mrs. Peacock said, "take yourself out of here."

"Now, Lucy . . ." the young man began, sickly jovial.

Lucy Peacock's lips tightened. "Mrs. Peacock to you, if you please. An' remember, I'm not having foul language here . . . an' I'm not having folk called behind their backs either."

The weedy young man laughed. "A bit sweet on Titus, eh?" he sniggered. "I have heard it rumoured, you know."

"You get yourself off to Greets an' no more lip," the widow told him, her fine eyes hot. "Of all the impertinent windbags."

"It's all right, Mrs. Peacock," someone called out. "Arthur'll be stopping at Half to see Annamaria Rutter, an' you know who wears the britches of them two. Just write a note like the Schoolmaster does, an' she'll give him a rare salting."

That caused a real hullabaloo, laughter vieing with the cries of those who endeavoured to implement the document to be sent to the dominating Miss Rutter. It spoke volumes for Mrs. Peacock's reputation that none of these suggestions even verged on the vulgar, the opportunity above all not being lacking when the butt of this merriment turned on the company.

"When I'm wi' a woman there's no question as to who's getten the britches on," he snapped. "And if anybody wants to step outside——"

"Get stepped outside yourself, as I telled you." Mrs. Peacock pointed.

The victim glared about him. "Right, I will," he growled, before swaggering off. "And to hell with all of you."

In the milder hubbub which ensued, while those present tried to mollify an ancient miner bent on vengeance, Adam edged to the bar. Mrs. Peacock, seated on a stool, had taken up her needlework. She was a well-preserved woman of about sixty, with not a strand of grey in her dark hair.

"Do you think I could have a sandwich or two?" he inquired.

Lucy Peacock eyed him over. "Aye, if you like, but you'll be the first Brunskill I ever knew who didn't prefer summat with a knife and fork."

"And how do you know I'm a Brunskill?" Adam smiled.

Mrs. Peacock, however, continued unsmiling: "News travels fast about here, and I can put two and two together. Ham an' eggs do you?"

Shortly afterwards Adam was sitting with a big plate before him, in a kitchen appointed to cater for the parties of sportsmen who, in August, would occupy every bedroom in the inn.

There were two buxom girls and, once their giggling ceased, they were not at all averse to chattering. So, when disputatious voices arose in the bar, Adam learnt something about the tangled skein of Skewdale mining finance.

"Eee, the mistress won't half be cross if he goes on," one of the maids remarked. "It's Droughty Tom, chuntering about that pump again."

"And who's Droughty Tom, and what's his trouble?" Adam asked.

"He's a limeburner," the other girl began. "And . . . well, it's to do with a donkey pump at Old Wife Shaft set up two years ago."

Neither knew the finer details but, as they supplemented one another, Adam gleaned that the controversy revolved around the ownership of the pump. The state of affairs was quite unique: the East Side Company disclaiming ownership of a piece of machinery essential to them.

The clash was less heated when Adam left the kitchen. But Droughty

Tom, a bulbous-nosed old man in lime-dusted clothing, had not quite done.

"What happened were plain enough," he said grimly. "I were i' Newcastle on business with a bag of sovereigns along of me, and I lighted on Reuben. Well, we called in a pub, and there, and I reckon it were done deliberately, he got me on to whisky instead of ale, and the next thing was that I were handing out brass in an office. But," his knotty old fist crashed down, "I nobbut loaned Reuben that brass, an' owt different is a lie."

The two elderly men he was addressing were still powerfully-built. Both were broad-shouldered and tall, and although the senior was more gross than his better-dressed companion, they were obviously related. It was perhaps a little extraordinary that, when Droughty Tom was making a most damaging charge, they were far more interested in Adam.

"Anyway," Droughty Tom growled, "I'se asking once again what the Board says. You're both directors of the East Side Company, aren't you?"

The dressier of his opponents countered persuasively: "Look here, Tom, the bill for the pump were in your name, so how could the brass be a loan?"

"That was how I were tricked," the lime-burner stormed.

The other clicked his tongue. "Now, Tom, no slander, please," he said, before suggesting, unofficially, that a settlement might be reached either on the basis of a modest rental or outright purchase at a figure which, he intimated, must take into full account wear and tear.

"I'll neither rent it to you nor accept a penny less nor the amount I paid," Droughty Tom roared.

The third party took a hand. He was more aggressive than his smoother-spoken co-director. "If you don't like the situation, why don't you fetch the pump out?" he asked with scarcely veiled triumph.

There was a brief silence. When the lime-burner resumed, his tone was quieter though his manner was not a jot more accommodating.

"Th'East Side Company 'ud be looking silly if I did," he commented. "Jenny Incline 'ud flood, an' *that's* one of the best mineral grounds you've getten. But all t'same, William, you have me fast, haven't you?"

A flabby jowl wobbled with laughter. "You're saying it, Tom, not me."

"Aye," Droughty Tom reflected. "You know I shouldn't get a quarter back at after I paid for taking the pump out of Old Wife Shaft and paid again—to a carrier like yourself, William—for carting it off to be selled."

The better-dressed director smiled. "You've hit t'position off to a T, Tom," he said, slyly complimentary.

The discussion died after that. Droughty Tom began slaking a lime-dried gullet, and the two directors approached Adam.

"Well, I never thought a Brunskill 'ud ever show his face here again, George," the heavier one wheezed.

"So you're Jim Brunskill's lad, are you?" the other inquired.

"Aye, and who are you?" Adam asked.

The slightly bigger individual laughed shortly. "I'm William Nattrass an' he's my brother George, and fro' that it'll noan surprise you to hear that your mother were sister to both on us."

"My uncles, in fact," Adam said.

Faintly smiling, George Nattrass looked about him before speaking. "So it seems, but I'd better tell you it's not a connection to be presumed on."

A few sycophants tittered. George Nattrass, in addition to his large general shop and wholesale warehouse down at Greets, was the chief cheese factor in the Dale. He had other irons in the fire, too.

Adam's jaw firmed. "That suits me as well."

"Your father never came back to see me an' my brother," George Nattrass went on, derisive, "but maybe you'll not know what I mean."

"I know all right," Adam retorted. "But I can pledge you that if he had returned, and if a fight had come of it, he'd have manfully taken any hammering you two could have given him . . . if you could have given him one, that is."

"If we could, you say," William Nattrass roared. "Why, we'd have bloody well smashed him up till——"

The voice of the mistress of the house rang out peremptorily. Before Mrs. Peacock could get into her stride, however, George Nattrass checked her with an upraised hand.

"It's all right, Lucy," he assured her. "William nobbut got a bit over-excited and there'll be nowt more said that's unsuitable. It's just been that me an' him were a little too inquisitive as to what the effect would be o' mixing good blood with tainted."

Adam's mouth curved imperceptibly. "You've misjudged my father," he murmured with deep regret. "Is it likely that a chap of a grand strain like his 'ud ever contemplate wedding a lass of rotten stock?"

The tables turned, inflamed by the general amusement, George Nattrass was venomous.

"I didn't mean as how . . ." he shouted.

Blotchy-faced with anger, he endeavoured to cope with the witticisms he suffered, William Nattrass lending blustering support. Meantime their nephew was able undeterred to pay for his meal before leaving a gathering not unappreciative of the stand made on behalf of one no longer able to answer for himself.

The little bow-fronted shop, over which a signboard read 'Hannah

Batty,' seemed a likely place for Adam to replenish his tobacco-box, and so, to the accompaniment of a jingling door-bell, he went in.

Here needs of every description were supplied—groceries, chocolates, rolls of flannel, bacon from the side hanging beneath the low-beamed ceiling, yeast contained in a canvas bag, and paraffin from a big drum.

When the door at the back opened Adam first glimpsed the silvery-white cloud of hair of an elderly woman who bore herself as if only the other day she had mastered the trick of carrying a heavy book on her head for correct deportment.

"What have you in the bacca line?" Adam asked.

"Them there," she replied, nodding at a row of gilt-lettered canisters. "You'd better look inside 'em, as you won't be used to t'sorts here."

Adam eyed her. "A good idea," he agreed.

After fingering and sniffing, he chose Dinwiddie Cut Flake, the transaction so expeditiously completed as virtually to confirm that this was indeed the shop's owner. Mrs. Batty lifted the scales clear of the counter, and filled a well-polished pan with tobacco. The purchase was wrapped in a twist of paper, change counted without hesitation, though by a method of numeration unknown to the customer who, in no time at all, would have started the shop bell tinkling again had he not received an invitation which would have been surprising had it not been for his suspicions.

"Now what about us having a wee crack in t'kitchen?" Mrs. Batty suggested.

"So you're another who knows who I am," Adam grinned.

She cackled. "Aye, and I knew your mother an' father long afore they ever thought of bringing you into t'world."

Adam entered an overcrowded room in which a small girl was rising from a stool. A solemn-faced child of about eight years old, she held up for inspection her knitting.

Mrs. Batty scrutinised the work. "That's grand, Mary Jane, but stop when you get to t'heel. Turning a heel properly is noan a simple matter."

"I know it isn't," Mary Jane said. "Well, I'll have to go . . . and thank you, Hannah."

"You're welcome, love," Mrs. Batty smiled. "And where are you off to now? It's getting near your bed-time, isn't it?"

"Home," the little girl replied, "to make supper for Ward an' my father. But I'm calling at the Plug first to see if my father's ready."

At his hostess's signal, Adam had lowered himself cautiously into a small rocking-chair, where his head was close to a shelf on which many varieties of medicinal herbs were arrayed. Behind him was the long swinging pendulum of a Dutch clock whose face covered one of the many unnaturally coloured bunches of roses on the papered wall.

More than once Adam had caught the inquiring eyes of the child. He smiled again, this time eliciting a response.

"Who are you?" Mary Jane asked, emboldened.

"I'm Adam Brunskill," he told her. "And I've come to stay up in Back Lane. Now what about you, lass?"

"I'm Mary Jane Tiplady," she piped. "I live up Lane End at Snorr, and I've kept house for my father since my mother went to heaven."

"Have you, love?" Adam nodded. "Well, now we know one another, don't we? So when next we meet we won't have to pass with our noses stuck in the air, will we?"

Mary Jane gurgled, the joyousness of childhood replacing the over-seriousness in her little face.

When the last echoes of the shop-bell were dwindling behind the small visitor, Mrs. Batty shook her head.

"You'd hardly credit, lad, how that little lass tries to keep the promise she made her mother to look after her father." A very unwrinkled face clouded. "Poor Matt," she sighed, "just gone to bits he has since his missus died. He lost the toes o' one foot through crossing a waterwheel when he were drunk, and now he spends his time poaching."

"I think I've seen him already," said Adam.

"Been to t'Plug, have you?" Hannah Batty returned as, stretching to the mantelpiece, she grasped a blackened clay pipe. Between puffs, at ease in a wing chair, she complained that Edmund Kearton, Mary Jane's grandfather, had dealt with Matt Tiplady's backsliding in quite the wrong way.

This reminded her of a sash which could drop like a guillotine when she was sitting out to clean the window, and she asked Adam to call with a message at the joiner's.

"On this side of the street it is," she went on, "but well past Nick Turn, that's what we call t'bend in Main Street."

Soon she was plying Adam with questions about dalesfolk in Spain, but in due course referred to his father and mother.

"Never was there a sweeter girl nor Mary Nattrass," she said, her gaze distant. "Jim Brunskill were a grand fellow, too, and he did right to take your mother off, for nobody here could addle a decent Pay. Besides . . ." she was almost speaking to herself, "it were the only road to escape the predicament he were in."

Adam's throat felt dry. "Because of my mother's brothers, because he were frightened of them?"

"Not he," Hannah Batty replied, sharp. "Your father would have tackled a mountain if needs be, let alone William an' George Nattrass."

"What was the mess he'd got into, then?" Adam persisted.

A pair of wise eyes looked with kindliness at him. "Nowt that need trouble you, Adam," he was told. "All I'll say is that your father was as straightforward as they're made."

Then Mrs. Batty, who had known Winterings when its twelve hundred inhabitants were prosperous, talked of their present calamitous condition.

"Yes, there's noan aboon three hundred now," she grieved. "An' some of 'em, them with an interest in lead-mining companies, oft can't sleep o' nights. You see, mining shares aren't what they term 'fully-paid,' so there's always a liability if owt goes seriously wrong. Anyway, no more of this dowly stuff, lad."

She enlivened matters by relating a few of the pranks in which Jim Brunskill had played a leading part, and then, eyes softening reminiscently, talked of Adam's mother, whom she had first dandled on her lap a couple of years before becoming a grandmother herself.

"Hold on, Methuselah," Adam grinned.

With fishing visitors Mrs. Batty had often had the present experience. "As to that, maybe," she said staidly. "But I'd nobbut entered my teens when young Mr. Billy fro' Greets Hall jumped from his horse on to t'mounting-block outside the Plug and read out about poor Admiral Nelson's death. Yes, I'se eighty-eight next."

"You're a marvel," Adam said in all sincerity. "For that matter," he added, "as likely a lass as I've come across."

Mrs. Batty positively bridled. "You great big barmpot," she declared.

"I'll tell you what," Adam continued in a whisper, inspecting the door into the shop, his conduct so mysterious that the old lady's beam changed into wide-eyed astonishment, "what about you and me having an outing some day? That is, if you can manage to give the go-by to your present chap. Say I hire summat from that livery stable in Main Street."

Hannah Batty's face was a picture. Then she went off into a convulsion of laughter, traces of which were still evident when she saw her visitor off.

"You must come an' see me again, lad," she said weakly. "This has done me more good than a week o' supping camomile tea."

"I will," Adam promised. "I've enjoyed myself an' all."

Her shrewd old eyes were on him, and she looked at him more searchingly than she had done before. "You know, lad," she said, "I've rather got t'idea as you're a bit of a deep 'un."

"Nay," Adam protested. "Just because I——"

"All t'same, I think so," Hannah Batty interposed firmly. "But never mind," she cuffed him lightly, "I'll be expecting you."

"Right," Adam smiled.

As he walked past the Literary Institute towards Nick Turn, he puzzled about the unknown episode in his father's life, nearly reaching the Wesleyan Day School before remembering Mrs. Batty's commission. Fortunately Mr. Kearton's workshop was close-by, plainly recognisable by wood shavings and the smell of turpentine and boiled oil.

Edmund Kearton, a sparsely-built, lantern-jawed individual, comported himself soberly. Without looking up he spoke when Adam's shadow fell upon the coffin frilling he was examining.

"What do you want?" he inquired.

Hearing an unfamiliar voice, he eyed the newcomer from top to bottom. Winterings folk declared that this was merely his way of measuring a future customer for grave clothes.

"It's her sash weight," he said irritably. "But my first duty is to attend to the befitting laying-away o' them who's passed over."

Two coffins were being made, and a third was completed, a pathetic little varnished box with cheap black handles and plate.

"You'll be Jim Brunskill's lad?" the undertaker grunted.

"Yes," Adam replied.

"Thought so," Mr. Kearton snapped. "Well, I've other things to do more important nor gossiping, young man."

Dismissed abruptly, Adam strolled past the School and, at the Master's house beyond, was diagonally crossing the road towards the Town Foot end of the Wood Yard when a young lady whom Daniel Dolphin would certainly have described as ' a right dasher ' hurried past him. He glimpsed an attractive face and, as she turned into a gateway between two tall yews, trim ankles beneath fluttering skirts.

"Somebody's in front of me," he mused. "But all the same . . ."

A couple were leaving Smithy House, a plump young lady hanging on to the arm of the long-haired young man who had played hand-ball. The door had hardly closed behind them when it was re-opened by a tight-expressioned woman who shouted: "Fronick, was that Dinah Skidmore who went in opposite? If it were, your father promised Mr. Skidmore he'd see if we'd any honey left."

"I've looked, an' we haven't, Mother," the young woman cried back.

Mrs. Blenkiron sounded more relieved than otherwise. "Oh, in that case, lass," she said, and entered the house again.

The long-haired young man nodded to Adam, and the fair-haired girl smiled. Meantime, even while responding, Adam cogitated.

"Skidmore," he said to himself, "that's the name of Simon's Aunt Minnie. I wonder if that lass is related. Well, I'll find out afore long . . . and here goes."

For the second time he approached the open door of Yew Tree House.

3

As Mrs. Skidmore of Badger Hall had decided not to go to market, Cherry Dinsdale and her great friend Dinah Skidmore were planning how, unhampered, they could have the most fun at Corvy the next day.

"We'll get the butter and eggs sold first," Dinah said with glee. "And . . . was that a——"

"We'll have our elevenses at that nice new place in Friargate," Cherry clapped. "Where—— Yes, you're right, Dinah, it was a knock, I've heard it now."

She ran from the kitchen into the passage, which was why Adam Brunskill, within a very short space, saw another extremely neat pair of ankles.

"Oh!" she gasped. "Well . . . well, what do you want, please?"

"I'd like to see Mr. Alderson, if it's convenient," Adam replied, overwhelmingly courteous.

"Mr. Alderson," Cherry said distantly, "is at a meeting of the Chapel trustees."

"Well, then," the tall young man declared, unabashed, "I'll have to look in again."

"Perhaps I can save you the trouble," Titus Alderson's niece retorted, "if you'll let me know your business."

Adam's whole attitude was of censure. "I can't possibly," he said. "It's a private matter."

"Is it?" Miss Dinsdale commented, each word iced.

Grinning inwardly, he heard the tap-tap of a small foot on the threshold. He noticed, too, soft hair and the slightly bustled dress in an inexpensive but fetching blue-and-white spotted print.

"It is," he confirmed. "But I can tell you one thing," he resumed, "that it's nothing to do with . . ." His attention was caught by the gleaming brass door-knocker. "I ought to have used this, oughtn't I, instead of banging on the paint?"

Pent-up, the young lady made a serious mistake. "Nothing to do with what?"

An air of surprise came into his face. "Lead-mining," he explained. "It was you, wasn't it," he went on, beginning to frown, "who thought I'd called to see your uncle about the mines?"

Adam Brunskill, at that point, was very near to having his face slapped, but Cherry Dinsdale was a very fair-minded girl.

"I'm . . . I'm sorry about that," she confessed. "I made a right fool of myself."

"Don't we all now and then?" Adam observed largely.

Cherry's hand itched again, but there was interruption from two sources, a powerful young man flinging open the gate a few seconds after Dinah Skidmore appeared from the kitchen.

"I promised Mother I wouldn't be long," Cherry's friend said as she edged down the path. "You're sure you can't walk part way with me?"

"No, I can't, lass," Cherry told her. "You see I want to leave everything ready for Uncle Titus while we're off."

"All right, love," Dinah smiled nervously. "An' I'll be here with the trap about eight. We'll . . ." She heard the steps behind her, looked quickly over her shoulder. "Look who's here," she hissed.

Adam, who in the big, black-haired young man recognised a short-lived acquaintance of the evening before, saw the girls' glances briefly meet.

"I've got to see your uncle, Cherry lass, as soon as he gets back from t'Chapel," the latest comer started off, staring at Adam.

"What's the West Side Company done wrong this time, pray?" Cherry Dinsdale inquired.

"Now, now." The East Side Company's head-agent was vastly amused. "You know I've always done what I could for your uncle."

"Then you can see him in the morning, when he isn't tired out."

"Nay, I'd rather keep you company, love, till he gets back," the miner winked.

Cherry was coldly decided. "I'm walking Dinah home, so you won't be able to," she said.

The dark-eyed young man scowled, but for the moment switched to Adam.

"Well . . . well . . . well!" he marvelled. "The chap who were at the Packman's Rest. And what are you doing i' Winterings?"

"Visiting relations," Adam said equably. "And trying to make friends."

The other laughed. "You'll make no enemies, I'll be bound."

"Nowt like turning the other cheek," Adam agreed.

The two young ladies were listening to these extraordinary exchanges with considerable surprise, but their turn soon came. Dismissing Adam with a final: "You should know," the mine agent transferred his attack to Cherry.

"I just heard you say you were stopping in," he said brusquely.

"Can't she change her mind?" Dinah Skidmore demanded.

"You shut your clap, and get back to Snorr," he swung round, mouth ugly.

Cherry Dinsdale's cheeks were pale. Then, with a deadliness of purpose which, by contrast, made her previous dealing with Adam innocuous, she asked him to leave. His face became redder than the westering light which silhouetted the unbroken edge of Great Barg.

Dinah Skidmore looked both frightened and concerned for her friend. "It's getting chilly, love, so go in and put a coat on," she urged.

Cherry turned indoors. "Yes, I will," she smiled, her lips tremulous.

"All right, my girl," the enraged young man shouted thickly after her, jabbing a finger. "Well, we'll see. By God, we will."

This threat made, he spun angrily on his clog heel but, perceiving the stranger, paused momentarily.

"By the look of you," he jeered, "you didn't come to any harm at the hands of them *rough* railway navvies at Wham."

"Not a scratch," Adam revealed himself gratified to report. "But remember, he who fights and runs away——"

The other's stare was ludicrous. "Well . . . well, I'se damned!" he ejaculated, spitting expertly. "Fancy any chap owning to . . ."

With an oath at himself for so wasting his time, he clattered away, and, outside the holly hedge, proceeded up Main Street.

"Now I happen to know his name's Reuben," Adam murmured. "But what goes along with it?"

"Nattrass," Dinah Skidmore gulped.

In stages, Adam learnt that Reuben Nattrass was the son of William Nattrass, the carrier, whose stables and residence, Ash Grove, faced each other across Main Street, at the near side of Nick Turn.

"So he's my cousin," he observed.

"Your cousin!" His companion gaped.

There are extremely modest young ladies who, either by looks, or carriage, or clothes, put quite wrong ideas into the minds of males. Dinah Skidmore was of these. In point of fact she was absurdly shy with young men, and became practically tongue-tied when the stranger started to ask the most inquisitive questions—he even proposed walking home with her, to see her mother.

That was the state of affairs as Cherry came out, when, with Adam at the rear, they filed down the pathway. Arm-in-arm, the two girls walked towards the West End, neither vouchsafing a word to an intruder who, most terribly provoking, seemed to be quietly enjoying himself.

Just beyond Hannah Batty's shop, Cherry Dinsdale endeavoured to solve the mystery, discreetly nodding her head one way while sepulchrally inquiring out of the corner of her mouth nearest her friend. This manœuvre nearly ended in disaster, for Adam leaned slightly forward to glance round the bonnets framing two very pretty faces. One young lady was flushed rosily and the other so empurpled as to arouse fear that a seizure might be in the offing.

"Nowt wrong, is there?" he asked, with sympathy.

"No," Cherry replied fiercely. Nearing Winterings Brig, however, she could stand it no longer. "Where are you supposed to be going?" she demanded.

Adam was contemplating the sign of the Plug and Feathers, a wedge or plug suspended vertically with its point between the flat sides of two half-round iron rods: the old method of splitting rock before gunpowder was used.

"It's all arranged with Miss Skidmore," he answered, turning politely.

Dinah Skidmore may have been sent over the abyss on hearing herself described so formally, or possibly her friend's grotesque expression and gruff whisper had been too much for her. Whatever it was, she went off into an uncontrollable fit of giggles.

"Really, Dinah, you *will* have to see Dr. Seaton," Cherry fretted. "You're having too many of these awful attacks."

On Adam's side of the highway, across Winterings Gill from the Plug and Feathers, there was a curtainless but charming little farmhouse. Though he eyed it with a very real pleasure, the grey, creeper-clad building provided him with a reason for keeping his head that way. Miss Dinsdale's attempt to save the situation had brought a revealing grin to his face.

Beyond the hump of Winterings Brig the rough highroad wound its lonely way up the Dale, the land to the right climbing steadily towards Water Ling Moor, from which side came the plaintive cry of a curlew sailing above a belt of trees, umbrella-headed Scots pines whose soft, dusty green was overtopped from behind by the darker green, arrow-shaped tips of towering, straight-limbed spruce.

To the left of the road, across a narrow line of meadows, the Skew splashed along, its nearer side heightened by a flood bank dangerously pockmarked with rabbit holes. At the other side the ground rose towards Lovely Lady, distant and high.

The girls and Adam, stepping out briskly, soon reached the Royal Alfred at Snorr, three-quarters of a mile away. There, rounding the corner of an establishment partly house-of-call but chiefly farm, they left the main road to go along a lane between hedgerows beginning to bud. A squat chimney came into sight a little farther on, Snorr Bridge being beyond the solitary cottage.

The bridge indeed appeared too large for its purpose, but Adam, glancing upstream, appreciated that without the spans flanking the central arch a big flood might be irresistible.

"Aye," he thought, glimpsing fragments of older foundations, "there's been another bridge afore this, and I'll bet it was washed away."

At the far side of the bridge the party took the fork to the right, the lane now running alongside the river. In it were two more cottages, adjoining, and beyond these Badger Hall.

The grey, weathered home of the Skidmores was simply but graciously built, the porch recessed between two projecting wings, each of which looked out through a polygonal shaped bow window divided by mullions. Like many old dales houses, it was much more moderately-sized than its imposing name suggested.

They went into an old courtyard, along the back of the house as far as an arched doorway, inside which was a flagged lobby. The kitchen was off this and, when the little procession entered, Mrs. Skidmore, a capable-looking woman, was reinforcing with buckskin the more wearing portions of a pair of breeches. The wife of one of the best and most respected farmers of the district, her own particular pride consisted of knowing that she was regarded as being the finest cheesemaker in Skewdale from Greets upwards.

"Here's a young man wants to see you, Mother," Dinah told her.

"My name's Adam Brunskill, Mrs. Skidmore," Adam started off at once, "and I've brought you greetings from your nephew Simon i' Spain."

"Simon . . . Simon *Sunter*," Minnie Skidmore said excitedly.

Adam nodded. Then, all eyes on him, including those of the master of the house, who had appeared at the kitchen door, he gave them news of Simon, of Simon's wife Jane and little Bessie, and indeed of anyone originating from Skewdale.

"That's fair interesting, lad," Anthony Skidmore remarked warmly. He was a good-looking man with fine-boned face, his iron-grey beard carefully tended. Continuing, he said he supposed Adam had similar messages to deliver in the neighbourhood.

"Well," Adam said, "there's Jane's aunt up at Yorrel, Miss Caygill."

"Rosie Caygill, t'dressmaker," Mrs. Skidmore murmured. "But," she shook her head, "you mustn't go there yet awhile, lad. They've had the worst epidemic of scarlet fever they've ever had."

"Aye," her husband supplemented, "I reckon Edmund Kearton's been almost as throng as when the typhoid swept folk off ten year ago."

Later, with genuine hospitality, he supported his wife when she insisted the young man should spend the next Sunday evening with them.

"And in the meantime, lad, I expect you'll be finding your way about," he went on. "Well, there's one thing," the indulgent way in which he eyed his daughter and her friend revealed his fondness for them, "you'll have had a couple o' real talkative guides to-night."

"Never . . . *never* has a chap had two such guides," Adam said with utter conviction.

Mr. Skidmore chuckled. "When them two chatterboxes——" There was a muffled noise, the scutter of feet and a thump, the sounds made when more than one person decide to go through a doorway at the same time. "Now what's up?" he asked. "And what have t'lasses made off for?"

"Nay, they'll nobbut be up to some of their silly games," Mrs. Skidmore said comfortably.

For a little while longer the three of them talked, until Adam said good-bye to Mrs. Skidmore. Outside, he made the acquaintance of Nell, the Badger Hall sheepdog. She was black, spotted white on legs and breast, with soft eyes and well-pointed nose and, in her owner's matter of fact terms, was: "the finest working bitch i' Skewdale, bar none, and known by everybody as such."

"A marvel with both sheep and beasts," Mr. Skidmore declared as

Adam fondled the prodigy. "Tackles a bull without flinching, an' lets bairns half-pull her ears off without saying a word."

Adam was stroking the silky, longish hair. "You're worth your weight in gold, lass," he told her.

"Noan so far off," Anthony Skidmore said seriously, before going about his affairs. "Her pups fetch two go'den sovereigns apiece, choose how, an' that's real brass."

Drawn by the volume of bleating to the more remote side of the garth, Adam climbed a battlemented wall and saw a hundred or more ewes and their young. Close by, a ewe methodically cleaned a couple of lambs born a few minutes before; elsewhere, day-old youngsters were rapidly becoming less shaky on their tall legs, and, dotted about, each resembling a small heap of white material, were slumbering babies. The air was filled with family cries, the thin note of the children and the deeper, imperative call of anxious mothers. Just before Adam turned away, another set of twins, veterans of over a week, detached themselves from a frisky game of follow-my-leader to tear towards their parent. Diving under her from each quarter, knees down and sterns high, they sought until they found, when slowly-wagging tails began to rotate ecstatically. Meantime their provider bent to sniff first one and then the other, to assure herself that no alien creature was drawing of her bounty.

There was much else to interest Adam—the neat, shorthorn roans in the sweet-smelling cow-house, the haysweeps and coup carts in the shed, the three-week old calf which ceased to bellow on receiving a supper of half-fresh and half-skim milk.

"Taking everything in, lad?" Anthony Skidmore smiled. "Well, if time hangs on your hands I can always find you a byre to muck out."

"Oh, I'll be along," Adam laughed.

"Hasn't Cherry come out yet?" Mr. Skidmore asked. "Now when I go in again I'll send her off to you double sharp. Yon two lasses are going to market to-morn and they'll have to be up early."

It was infinitely peaceful there, as dusk began to fall. The birds were singing their final songs, though, in the orchard, two blackbirds and a third were still involved, a little wearily perhaps, in the pavan of courtship they had probably begun at dawn.

When a young lady who considers she has reached woman's full estate is hurried outdoors, she experiences a feeling of wholly justified indignity, the reaction from which is certain to be vented on the first suitable person. In Cherry Dinsdale's case this proved to be Adam who, standing against a wall, was making friends with the farm cat. Perversely she chose to express surprise.

"Whatever are you still doing here?" she inquired.

"Waiting for you," he retorted with annoying frankness.

That, from a stranger, was enough to make any young woman haughty. "I don't remember asking you to," she said.

"I don't remember you asking me not to . . . or owt else," he countered.

Hastily she decided the conversation was becoming too personal and so told him her Uncle Titus would be delighted to hear about friends in Spain. Unfortunately this surmise caused not the least variation in the impassivity of the young man's face.

Much less sure of her ground, she nevertheless tried to carry it off. "That was why you wanted to see him, wasn't it?" she said.

As Adam left the wall to walk beside her he threw over his shoulder a few words of solemn warning: "Hear that, puss," he said, deep voice bloodcurdling. "That's what you've to guard against if you want to save some of them nine lives."

Miss Dinsdale turned on him like a flash. "I weren't being——" she started off, adding with greater fury: "Yes, I was being curious, you . . . you nasty thing."

"Shame, shame." Adam sounded stricken.

With this inauspicious beginning it was not surprising they continued in silence down the lane, past the two cottages, and then round the curve leading to Snorr Bridge. On the sloping approach, however, Adam made a most intriguing remark.

"Aye," he muttered, "it's that business earlier that's responsible for the misunderstanding. I'd have been better biting my tongue off."

Cherry allowed him to maunder, but only for a while. "Don't think you'll catch me," she said at last.

He was quite shocked. "By, but you're suspicious. Nay, it were nobbut that I'd never seen Spanish young ladies look like you did."

"We don't wear combs in our hair and . . . and such-like," Cherry reminded him.

"No . . ." the young man drawled, "and they don't wear mobcaps either."

She darted a glance. "Mobcaps . . ." she said.

Ruminating, he eyed the darkening waters of the Skew. "'Course things 'ul be different here and if I'd had any gumption I'd have guessed you were wearing it at the latest fashionable angle."

Thoughts chaotic, Cherry Dinsdale took a deep breath. Unhappily, for her undoing, she began vividly to recall the image she had seen in the kitchen mirror. At that, her mouth curled, her shoulders began to shake, until her state, despite an averted head, could no longer be hidden.

"I . . . I did look a cut, didn't I?" she laughed.

The young man considered. "No," he pronounced, "that's noan exactly the idea I've been carrying about since then."

Miss Cherry Dinsdale blushed violently, her heart hammered most disturbingly and, for once, she was unable to find a word.

Gradually the ice was broken and, before arriving at the main road, they were on good enough terms for her to tell him that Dinah's brother and his wife Susan lived in the solitary cottage. Will Skidmore, she explained, was gamekeeper to the gentleman who leased the sporting rights of the moors. Thereafter she talked more freely, though once, between the Royal Alfred and the village, she became a little reserved when he said he had brought kind thoughts for Mr. Henry Hird of Greets and his widowed sister, Mrs. Ellen Alderson.

"Mr. Hird's at home, but Mrs. Roberty Will's away," she said. "She won't be back at Malaga for a bit."

"Mrs. Roberty Will?" Adam queried.

"She married Uncle Titus's brother, Robert William." Cherry was no more communicative.

All too soon for Adam was Winterings Brig reached and Nick Turn in Main Street left behind. Just beyond Calvert's Wynd they were hailed by an old gentleman rushing from the cobbler's shop on the corner.

Peg Stephen opened with a surprising inquiry: "You know what one of them round sponge cakes looks like?"

Receiving an amazed affirmative, he then asked for such a cake to be considered when a layer of raspberry jam was in it. Would not the jam represent a seam of coal, he urged.

By now, Adam suspected what was afoot. "Certainly," he said.

Next, the knife-grinder desired him to imagine the same cake without jam and, in mime, went through the movements of breaking it into two pieces. Finally his calloused hands closed again as if once more to make whole the two halves.

"Now then, lad," he looked up, "where they joined there'd be a sort of crack right across, wouldn't there?"

"There would," Adam agreed.

Peg Stephen spat with pleasure. "That crack," he resumed, very much the instructor, "is just t'same as a vein. In other words, veins of lead stand more or less upright, an' are noan found laid flat like coal is. 'Course it doesn't follow that there's bound to be lead in a vein . . . though that's outside t'agenda, isn't it?"

Cherry Dinsdale's expression was soft when, jauntily, the old fellow eventually retraced his steps to Blind Kit's snug workshop. But, impishly, she made a remark which, to her joy, caused her companion some embarrassment.

"That's why you asked me not to let on to him you'd to do with mining: to spare his feelings. He'd been airing his knowledge, hadn't he?"

He smiled down in response, a smile which she thought transfigured his stern face. "Just a bit," he replied.

All journeys end and, in due course, Cherry was explaining from the inner side of a green-painted gate why she preferred him to visit her uncle the next day.

"Aye, he'd nobbut want to stop up yarning," Adam nodded.

Just visible in the deepening dusk, wearing the dark suit suitable for a Chapel trustees' meeting, Richard Blenkiron was talking to a thin, shambling youth who held his head stiffly sideways. The lad was holding a bunch of wild flowers.

"That's Mazy Bill. He'll be off up to your cousin Agnes," Cherry said.

"Agnes isn't walking out, is she?" Adam ejaculated.

Cherry shook her head. "No, but you see poor Bill isn't quite sharp and so even Ambrose Pedley 'lows him to go there. He thinks there's nobody in the world like Agnes . . . unless it's his mare Polly—he's a trammer up at Uncle Titus's mines."

Mr. Blenkiron spotted the couple. "You're evidently finding your bearings, lad," he roared.

"I must go," Cherry said hurriedly.

"Right," Adam said over the iron gate. "Good night, Cherry."

For a space they stared at one another. "Good night . . . Adam," she whispered before speeding away.

Very content, Adam crossed for a chat with the blacksmith and then, with Mazy Bill Rutter, only son of Mr. Martin Rutter, Auctioneer, Farmer, Livestock Dealer and a director of the West Side Lead Mining Company, he went up Jom High Road, over Dolly Bridge and along Back Lane.

Though Adam, talking of flowers and other simple delights, tried to get a word out of Mazy Bill, he had not succeeded. Indeed he had given it up as a bad job when suddenly the youth began to speak of his own accord.

"What're you going to Agnes's for?" he demanded, tiny bubbles of froth appearing at his mouth. "If . . ." his jaws started to quiver, "if . . . if you hurt Agnes . . ."

"Now, lad," Adam checked him. "I'm going there because I'm Agnes's cousin, and——"

"If you hurt her . . ." Mazy Bill hissed.

Stopping abruptly, Adam spun the youth round and, firmly grasping the bony shoulders, held him so that they were face to face.

"Listen, Bill," he urged, "I like my cousin Agnes and I'm not going to harm her, and nobody else is either. D'you understand?"

The wildness in Mazy Bill's eyes was diminishing. His lean body was ashake, a tear trickled down his cheek.

"Aye . . ." he cried. "But . . . but I thought you might be doing."

"Nowt of the kind, Bill," Adam retorted, giving an encouraging clap. "Now come on, lad."

Fortunately Agnes was on the look-out for her cousin's return and so, while she thanked Mr. Rutter's crazed son for the primroses, Adam chatted with Mark Iveson. Both men, however, soon found themselves glancing at the young people, and each shook his head. No witness could fail to be moved either by the half-witted lad as, face contorted, he struggled to express delight, or by the frail slip of a girl who possessed the gift of dealing so gently and yet so firmly with him, until at last, dispatched homewards to Half, he shuffled off, eerily smiling.

"Has he always been that road?" Adam asked. "An' how's he manage at the mine?"

"Does champion," Mark Iveson said. "Unless . . ." he added, becoming grim, "he imagines anybody's going to lay a finger on that Polly of his, an' then there's like to be trouble."

"He used to sit next to me at t'Wesleyan Day School," Agnes joined in. "It wasn't till he had that awful accident . . ."

The shepherd took up the sombre story, of a boy who was fond of exploring the Old Man and how he, crawling through an ancient drift, had become jammed.

"I'll go in, I think," Agnes Pedley shuddered.

The shepherd waited until the door closed. "An' that's it. He couldn't move forward or backward."

"Aye, fear makes your body swell," Adam nodded.

"They found him on the Monday, weak but sensible enough until somebody mentioned they daresn't blast for fear of injuring him," Mark Iveson continued. "As ill luck would have it, he misconceived what they were saying, an' thought they meant to use black powder. That did it, and he lost his reason in a snap of a finger."

It was a busy part of the year for him and not long afterwards his wife popped her head out to say supper was ready. Adam bade them both good night and went indoors himself, into a kitchen meagrely illuminated by a tallow-dip which, placed near the big bible, partially silhouetted Ambrose Pedley's face and made black pools of the hollows in his cheeks. His eyes were closed as he lay with his head against the chair-back, but his lips were moving as he repeated the ill-spelt lines he had laboriously composed in the penny exercise book resting on his knees.

Agnes pointed to a chair, and to the provender on the marble-patterned oil-cloth covering the table. "My father's had his, Cousin Adam," she said, her voice low.

Adam rubbed his hands as he sat down. "You've got everything I wanted, Agnes lass. Cheese, fruitcake . . . an' there's the teapot with its cosy on."

Her pale cheeks flushed with pleasure. "Yes, Cousin Adam."

"Food for t'Gods," Adam declared. He was taking a cautious sip of very hot tea—meantime from behind there were alarming references to a congregation shovelled ' to feed the scorching flames of hell '—when a thought occurred to him. He leaned over the table.

"Agnes, I know I've another cousin, but where is she?"

Whatever colour there was in her cheeks vanished as her glance went affrightedly towards her father.

"Margaret . . ." she trembled, "she went away two years ago an'——"

A fearsome cry of rage shrilled through the air as the master of the house sprang up. The room was filled with strange shadows as the smoky candle-flame, buffeted by eddies raised by the swiftness of his move and the fluttering exercise book's falling from his lap, dipped into gloom or flared into a pennant of tawny light.

"Haven't I telled you that's a name as never must be mentioned in this house?" Ambrose Pedley shrieked. "Haven't I telled you what I'd do to you——"

Adam placed himself in front of his cousin. "Hold on," he said sternly. "Agnes is noan to blame for anything. It was me who——"

"She knows that *whatever* t'circumstances she hasn't to soil her lips with her—wi' that name," the older man raved. "Don't you, girl, don't you? And you'll never do it again, swear by th' Eternal Truth as you won't, either here or elesewhere."

Adam thought his cousin not far from fainting, and he pressed her into a chair. "Take it easy, lass, and try a sip of tea," he said.

"Swear you will never," her father passionately demanded.

Her head drooped. "No . . . no, I never will again, Father," she said.

Ambrose Pedley collapsed, too, his head sunk on his breast in the attitude Adam was beginning to know. He spoke painfully. "You don't understand, Adam," he muttered, near to tears. "I once had another daughter, but she left here wi'out a word. She were evil, and——"

"You've no need to take it out of the one daughter you've got left," Adam told him.

Ambrose Pedley's sigh came from the depths. "I went too far, lad, I know," he mumbled. "But t'Lord will scourge me as I deserve."

With little appetite Adam ate a piece of cake and swallowed a morsel of cheese. And, while he sat at the table, he tried to bring his cousin nearer to normality by suggesting jaunts they might have together. But it was not of great avail.

When she stumbled upstairs the idea of a freshening walk to Jom High Road made an instant appeal to him, and on his return he paused on the bluff above the river. Winterings was going to bed, too, and the candles which greyly illuminated many windows were being snuffed one by one.

"Aye, an' me an' all," he murmured.

Indoors again, he picked up a candlestick and, calling good night to Ambrose Pedley, who was still sunk in despair, mounted the steps to his bedroom. Stripping to the waist, he washed himself before undressing and pulling a nightshirt over his head.

Then he padded to the open window. In the fields beyond Main Street a light bobbed as search was made for a ewe needing help in her labour, and nearby an owl hooted, the call returned more faintly by a mate. The air was cold and pure and, still staring at the clear-cut mass of the high fells, visible against a blue-black vault housing a host of glittering stars, he took three or four deep breaths.

At last, shivering slightly, he slipped into bed, the thin straw mattress crackling beneath him. But no sooner had he blown out the candle than he was asleep.

CHAPTER THREE

I

ADAM BRUNSKILL soon settled down in Winterings, and within a short while he learned a great deal about the district, sometimes roaming on foot and at others mounted on a Skewdale pony loaned by a friendly farmer. Recreation in plenty he found—with the young ladies he tried his hand at quoits and his feet at step-dancing; with the young men he played hand-ball or went swimming in deep, ice-cold pot-holes in the river; and, under the tuition of two brothers-in-law, respectively a gamekeeper and a poacher, he picked up useful fieldcraft.

As Mr. Blenkiron had told him, dalesfolk did not stand on ceremony, a change to which he had to accustom himself, this not altogether surprising in a young man brought up in a community unconsciously influenced by the grave courtesy of the Spaniards amongst whom they lived.

But it was all very homely.

* * * *

Beneath Ambrose Pedley's roof, breakfast invariably consisted of 'gulls'—oatmeal with a little milk—and barley bread, the other meals being of the same calibre. This, Adam decided, was adequate neither for himself nor for a cousin he considered seriously underfed, and so he set about remedying these deficiencies. So far as breakfast was concerned the result was a side of bacon bought from Francis Harker of Low Bands Farm, between the highway and the river, just across Winterings Brig.

On the morning Ambrose Pedley's new partnership started in Martha Level, Adam mopped up the remaining traces of sweet-tasting fat and then, slipping into a side pocket the small package his cousin handed him, left the breakfast table.

"Champion, Agnes love," he smiled. "Well, I'm off now, so tell your father I'll be waiting for him by the Smithy."

Already this big cousin had brought brightness into Agnes Pedley's face. "I've made you beef sandwiches, Adam," she said, eager for his approval. "And I've put in some thin slices off them pickled onions Old Hannah gave me."

Gravely Adam remarked that the pair were becoming real cronies. "I suppose you're putting your heads together . . . to get me to take you both for another day's outing in a trap."

He was pleased with the indignant reaction. "We're not," she said. "Though maybe," her blue eyes shone, "someday we can go again like you said."

"We'll see about it, lass," Adam promised.

Laughing, he put on his cap and went out, to walk briskly along Back Lane, which now he had discovered was really part of Middle Sorrow, this in its turn being part of an ancient thoroughfare passing from Yorrel to Greets in three great loops, each differently named.

A raking stride soon brought him to Yew Tree House where, after announcing himself from the threshold, he was bidden to enter.

"Morning, Cherry," he said, on going into the kitchen.

Miss Dinsdale was arrayed suitably for serious business. "Good morning, Adam," she replied, smiling but slightly preoccupied. With one hand she was beating eggs and with the other endeavouring to measure out flour. "And what are you doing here? I thought you were meeting Uncle Titus?"

"Not till this afternoon," Adam said. "So I thought it'd be a good idea if I'd another look at that strata."

"Well, off you go then," she said. "Can't you see I'm throng?"

"Baking Day," Adam murmured. "An' that's another thing I've never properly known. You see me and my father . . ." he went on, embarking upon a doleful story of two men who made out for themselves. "Of course neighbours were kind . . ."

Cherry's eyes were dancing. "Are you ever going to the office?" she asked.

With that he left the kitchen, walked along the passage to enter, at the far end, the room facing on to Jom High Road.

Mr. Alderson's office was equipped much the same as any mining agent's. There was a desk, and a laboratory balance, in a glass case, stood on top of a safe; elsewhere were plumb lines, measuring chains, a dial and other tackle.

Adam's interest, however, was in a neatly coloured plan on the wall which, from millstone grit found on the surface of the hills, gave each successive stratum down to the fifth limestone. Intervening were some twenty-five to thirty beds, composed of plates, cherts, limestones and grits.

"Mmm . . ." he muttered, "I think I've got that lot in my head."

Next he eyed a plan which showed in section a vein which, not quite upright, haded or leaned perhaps fifteen degrees. The same beds were there, each in a different shade of watercolour, but, volcanic action being responsible, those to one side of the fissure were not in alignment with the corresponding colours of the other.

"Yes, an' where the throw's been trivial, one or two fathoms, aye two to four yards, that's where the most ore has been found," Adam thought, next scrutinising a neighbouring plan revealing a whole set of beds thrown up forty fathoms. "An' hardly anywhere it's large."

Cherry had come into the office, her idea being that Adam might find it useful to look at specimens of rock the old Skewdale Company had used in their night-school.

"Here's a piece of plate, that shaley stuff," she pointed. "And there are the cherts, sparkling like flints. These are the limestones: underset limestone, grey and Red Beds limestone, that pinkish lump . . ."

The little museum was housed in the glass-fronted top half of a battered mahogany bookcase, and from its sundry contents some of the remote history of Skewdale could be gleaned. There were Roman coins, the tine of a deer's horn, an axe-head of stone, and a wooden spade; an iron tinder box and steel, a pocket-dial hinged to close, a bucker used for hammering and breaking up ore before crushing mills were thought of, and a piece of level rail, of elm, not iron.

"That's the Ten Fathoms Grit," Cherry continued to expound. "And this dark grey, grainy piece is Main Lime . . ."

Adam gave her the closest attention. "My words," he remarked with great respect, "but you've a real gift for explaining. You know, Cherry, you ought to have been a teacher."

Her glance flicked suspiciously to him. "I am a teacher sometimes," she flashed, "an' it would do you no harm to come to Sunday School either."

The sound of clogged feet in Jom High Road was heard above the whine of the Saw Mill as Ambrose Pedley passed the window. And so Adam went through the passage to the front door, where he lingered a little longer.

"What time on Sunday?" he asked.

More and more was Cherry coming to know this somewhat peculiar young man. "One o'clock," she said, dimpling. "But be off with you an' less of your silliness."

To her increased amusement he seemed quite disgruntled as he crossed Main Street towards the gap between the Smithy and the Roe Inn where Sorrow Near began its course down the dale to Greets.

The lofty walls bounding Sorrow Near were not reduced in height for more than a quarter mile of stiff climbing from the Smithy, and it was only then, on looking back, that the village could be seen. At this point the old thoroughfare curved sharply to the right to run roughly parallel with the line of the valley, but Mine Road branched off, following

Winterings Gill upwards until, at Notion Bridge, it reached the lowermost properties respectively of the two mining companies. The East Side Company's Bucker Level with its dressing floors and small smelting mill came first, and then, across the beck a little higher up, the big smelt mills of the West Side Company.

Ambrose Pedley had not been very communicative that morning, but now he remarked that Bucker Level was twenty-four fathoms below Martha Level.

"The entrance looks just about the standard size," Adam commented.

"Aye, the tails are nearly all t'same. Four feet wide an' six foot high above the tram rails, wi' an arched top."

A noise, steadily becoming louder, came from the interior of the working, a rumbling bass with squeaky overtones, and, very shortly, a horse emerged from the stone-built tail. Behind it were six wagons laden with bouse, on the foremost of which a candle was stuck. The train of ore continued along the tramroad towards the bouse-teams, semi-circular stone bays assigned to every ore-getting partnership.

Water, about two inches deep, was running from Bucker Level.

"Ever get it much deeper than that?" Adam asked.

The older man snorted. "We do an' all, but it's better coming out that road than creeping about inside doing mischief. You know, don't you, that a level's as much for draining as it is for drawing bouse to bank?"

As he then retired within himself again, Adam was left to his own devices. There was much to occupy him, however. Across Winterings Beck were the two fine-looking smelting mills of the West Side Company, the North and South Mills separated by a stream which, after tumbling seventy or eighty feet over a waterfall farther back in the hill, seemed as large as the main beck it entered a few yards below Notion Bridge.

Still remaining on the Noggin Moor side of Winterings Gill and continuing upwards for another twenty minutes, Adam and his companion arrived at Martha Level, just behind a huddle of grey buildings, consisting of another smelt mill and a grinding mill, together with dressing floors protected from the weather by corrugated iron shades supported upon timber pillars. The office of the East Side Lead Mining Company was there also.

Adam was aroused by a dreary observation. "Well, I reckon I'd better change my clothes," Ambrose Pedley said. "Another bargain starting and I expect t'result 'ul be as it always is."

"But riches," Adam said, "profit not in the day of wrath, the Book says."

"Aye," Agnes's father responded, a trifle short.

The suspicion of a grim smile about his mouth, Adam watched him trudge off towards the Shop, a small building used by the groovers to put on garments which, so long as they hung together, were good enough for work.

The partnership joined by Ambrose Pedley was a large one, of eight men, and, until the partners had drawn tools, candles, gunpowder and fuses from the store, Adam wandered about. In one of the semi-circular bouse teams, partnership bouse was being shovelled from the plank floor. It was thrown on to a big, rectangular grate and played upon by powerful jets of water which swept away dirt and clay, lumps of useless rock being picked out. Then, loaded into small durk wagons, the bouse was pushed along to the crushing mill where it was broken down to the size of a walnut. Inside the crushing mill the din was enormous, with the roar and clatter of the massive iron rolls, and the never-ending hiss of high-pressure water.

The partnership members were walking towards Martha Level tail and Adam hastened back. Picks, shovels, borers, sledges and powder canisters had been placed in a wagon, on the front of which, base embedded in a small piece of very adhesive clay, a candle had been stuck.

"Ready, lads?" the head of the partnership shouted.

The wagon was trundled into the level, and, in file, the partners followed, each carefully shielding from draught a lighted candle. They were an oddly dressed crew, some in deerstalker caps and others in hard felt hats, but all showing glimpses of white flesh through rents in their rags.

As the last glimmer faded away up Martha Level, Adam was roughly accosted by a beefy young man.

"This is th'East Side's private property," Bull Waggott growled. "So tak' your bloody self off."

A quick surge of anger stayed Adam's feet, but, during that almost imperceptible, halt he remembered the welcome given him by so many Winterings folk. The hostility of the Nattrasses and their friends was irritating to be sure, but . . .

"But it'll die down if I keep a hold on myself," he mused. "And if it doesn't, well . . ." his thoughts narrowed upon Cherry Dinsdale and Reuben Nattrass's evident interest in her, "well, I'll pick on the ring-leader. Aye," he promised himself, his eyes gleaming, "I'll tackle the mighty man himself."

The day was too lovely and the lonely moorland surroundings too beautiful to dwell overlong on such ideas, nevertheless Adam, climbing at a steady pace, was guilty of this fault until he came to a smelting mill close-by the tumbledown bridge which carried Legatt's Way over Winterings Gill.

There he paused, entranced by the road-making skill of Roman military engineers, but, on re-starting uphill, had not gone far when, below, he noticed on the opposite of the beck another fine piece of engineering.

"By . . ." he smiled, "but you couldn't teach these chaps much about using water for power."

The axis of Glory waterwheel was at right-angles to the line of the beck, so that as the wheel rotated it moved to-and-fro a series of long timbers. These " rods," supported at regular intervals by tower-like frames of massive woodwork, extended for a quarter of a mile up the slope, when their horizontal motion was transferred into a vertical one to work a spear-rod in a shaft, this being connected to a pump in the sump.

From this point, until reaching a tributary of Winterings Beck, he kept strictly to the trod. An extensive bog, innocent looking indeed, stretched to the right, but when the trip was planned Will Skidmore had warned him of the danger.

After slithering down the steep side of the syke to jump across the fast-moving little stream, he pulled himself up the opposite bank by grasping clumps of benty grasses. After that progress became quicker, and shortly he was passing two unused levels with Dagger Gap not more than three or four hundred yards farther up Winterings Gill, about the same distance from the monumental dead heap of Great Charity Shaft, his place of meeting with the younger of Dinah Skidmore's brothers.

For three hours, with the exception of an interval spent eating the midday bait, Adam and his companion had circled a part of Noggin Moor, passing along the southern side of a vast moss, from which the East Side Mining Company annually dug out smelting peats.

"And talking about Titus Alderson's misfortune with his Short Cut," Will Skidmore said, reminded by a well-fenced shaft close by Legatt's Way, "take that spot yonder. An air-way through to the day was needed quick, and so at the same time as they began a rise from the level underneath they started to sink from the surface to meet it."

"A tricky job to make 'em coincide exactly," Adam commented.

"They didn't even meet," the gamekeeper said. "No, them coming up completely missed them going down."

Adam shook his head. "A sad business for a mining man when he slips that much in his calculations. How was the agent treated at after?"

The incident had taken place before Will Skidmore was born, but he had been told the outcome.

"The chap hanged himself," he remarked as they crossed on to a stretch of blackened moor burnt off by the keepers to provide tender green shoots for the game birds in their charge. "But sssh, lad."

Gun held ready, he waited, a square-jawed young man of medium height with kindly, far-seeing blue-grey eyes finely netted with weather creases. Some distance away, a pin-point in the sky, a bird soared, but, though fleetingly it came nearer, he did not risk a premature shot.

Eventually, however, the chance came; a sharp report reverberated over the moor and a limp, feathered little mass fell like a stone.

"Good shot, lad," Adam complimented him.

"A bit off t'usual beat, that'un," Will Skidmore grunted as he retrieved the sparrowhawk, which would be added to a macabre collection hung out as warning to other marauders. "Aye, he's nobbut vermin, but God made 'em, and they're entitled to a painless death."

Striding through vegetation and scrub higher than the keeper's shining leather leggings, they passed Charity Shaft's big dead heap, with Dagger Gap quite near. There Winterings Beck had as close neighbour another stream not a whit less than itself.

"That's Foul Syke, Adam," Will Skidmore said. "It runs in a huge loop and encloses a fairish part of Water Ling Moor."

"Does it?" Adam said, a thought surprised. "Nay, I were wondering why it's allowed to waste when a twenty-yard trench 'ud send it down Winterings Gill."

Will Skidmore, chuckling, began to explain Foul Syke's course. He pictured, too, Titus Alderson's face if ever Adam's project were carried out.

Adam was staring, but then memory jogged him. "Foul Syke isn't that beck, is it, that joins Winterings Gill just below Notion Bridge? Comes out between the North and South Smelt Mills?"

"That's it," the gamekeeper laughed. "Aye," he indicated the narrow rib of land dividing Winterings Beck from Foul Syke, "if you cut through that the West Side lot 'ud be in a sad plight for their waterwheels and ore-dressing."

At Dagger Gap they were to separate, Will Skidmore continuing towards Spout Fell, Adam to return to Notion Bridge by following the downward course of Winterings Gill on the Water Ling Moor side. But, before parting, both paused to gaze down into Skewdale and to look at the heights beyond.

From that commanding position, the mining grounds of the two companies were spread out before them, that of the East Side Company extending to the left across Noggin Moor, the West Side Company's reaching over Water Ling Moor from Winterings Gill to Yorrelgrain with its glint of rushing water and margining trees.

"Round about seven thousand acres apiece," Will Skidmore said.

"A fairish mining sett when it were all one," Adam observed.

The gamekeeper weighed his words. "Maybe it'll be under one management again. That is if your cousin Reuben can arrange it."

"So you think the land lies that road?"

"Well, that's my idea," Will Skidmore admitted. "And I'm damned sure that if old Titus Alderson comes another cropper Reuben Nattrass 'ul do it and all."

"You mean he'll take over the agent's job of the West Side Company as well?" Adam suggested.

"That's how it appears to me," Will Skidmore replied.

For perhaps five minutes longer they discussed this and other matters and then Adam jumped Winterings Gill, its sides very low here. Glancing now and then at the plan loaned him by Cherry's uncle, he began to descend.

Adam was soon well down Water Ling Moor, approaching Mirk Gutter, the upper of two tributaries swelling Winterings Beck from that side. Doomsday High Shaft was beyond and, because of the speculation whether Titus Alderson's New Drift would successfully effect a connection with the bottom of the shaft, he briefly halted. There was nothing to see, of course, merely a circular, stone-lined shaft whose masonry was in a parlous condition.

The landscape was becoming more familiar. After climbing the farther side of Worm Gutter, the second watercourse, he sighted Glory Shaft again, its mighty spear-rod steadily moving up and down. Then came the tumbledown bridge on the Roman road, and next the trod alongside Winterings Gill down to Mary Level and Mary Dressing Floors, which faced across the beck the East Side Company's Martha Level and Dressing Floors.

Adam would have preferred to inspect the Floors, but the afternoon was advancing and so he pushed on, following the tramway along which the bing ore, bouse after preparation at the dressing floors, was taken down to the Bingstead at Notion Bridge, to await smelting in the mills.

Soon the North and South Mills came into view downstream, with another set of rails, from Notion Level nearby, joining the double lines in the middle of which he was walking. The switchpoints of the junction were opposite the joiner's shop, and from there he passed many buildings —the mine wood store, the blacksmith's shop, changing shop, stables, engine-man's house, oil store and coal-house—until he reached the impressively-sized North Smelt Mill, with its ore hearths, slag hearths and furnaces.

At the extreme end of the smelt mill, Big William, a seventy-five horse-power, overshot waterwheel, regularly maintained its five revolutions to the minute, high above it a launder pouring water to fill over-brimmingly each bucket disposed across the wheel's five-foot beam.

About then, from the direction of the West Side Company's office, he heard voices in altercation. Despite the noise of falling water and the hiss of compressors supplying air to the blast furnaces, the argument carried fairly clearly.

"I know the price o' lead is going up," Titus Alderson was retorting.

"But isn't it as much to the Company's advantage as to the Lessor's to get out as much as we can?"

The office was across the stone bridge connecting the North and South Mills, squeezed between the bank of Foul Syke and the towering end wall of the South Mill. Two men had come through the doorway, Titus Alderson and a gentleman Adam had not seen before. The pair walked gradually towards the bridge.

Adam began to saunter out of earshot, but heard the unknown's contribution: "Eighty-one bings o' crop ore raised last quarter," he complained. "And production steadily falling off in t'North Sun Vein . . . as it's bound to do if you don't improve your pumping arrangements at Maybe Shaft."

Adam strolled to the back of the North Mill and then up Foul Syke Gill, the flue of the mill, as it climbed the steep slope to the side, ever growing higher above his head and the launder supplying water to Big William ever coming nearer. The launder, a wooden channel supported on strong wooden trestles, lessened in height as it proceeded up the gill, finally being replaced by a little canal, which in turn was reduced in height until an intake was reached at the level of Foul Syke. Joss Foss, the waterfall Adam had seen from the other side of Notion Bridge that morning, was a short distance beyond, misty spray rising at its foot.

"Well, I should think they'll have finished the row by now," he thought, turning back.

Nevertheless, as he emerged on to the wharf-like road in front of the North Mill, the differences had not been resolved. Fortunately, however, the pair had meandered to the bingstead, outside which a horse was hitched.

"What you're doing, Titus," the big-nosed rider pronounced, "is spending too much brass i' driving that new drift. How can you have many ore-getters when you've got so many chaps on Dead Work there?"

Titus Alderson laughed mirthlessly. "How can we open out new ground if we don't have dead work?" he asked. "A year ago it were all th'other way round, when you were telling me I'd broken the lease because I hadn't the stipulated number of men at dead work."

"What I said," stormed the other, "were that you were taking out any easy ore without regard to developing the mine in new places."

Adam, slipping across to the other side of Foul Syke, was seen through the office window by Bart Hugill, who came to the door, where he threw back his head to rid himself of the hair which had fallen down his forehead.

"Bart," Adam began, "how much is a bing? In Spain we reckoned up bouse and bing ore differently, and summat I heard made me wonder."

"Eight hundredweight," Bart Hugill answered.

Adam was thinking how trivial was the output of the West Side Company in comparison with the figures to which he was accustomed when his attention was diverted by the horseman who, having left Titus Alderson, rode past with lowering brow. Watched by both young men, the rider crossed Notion Bridge but then, instead of continuing down Mine Road, turned up Winterings Gill.

"Henry Hird from Greets is yon. Sir Charles Grafton's mineral agent," Bart Hugill sniffed. "Seemingly he's going up to th'East Side Company's office at Martha Level. Well, they're noan doing so champion for all their shouting, but I'll bet he doesn't rate there like he has here this afternoon."

"That's Mr. Hird, is it?" Adam cogitated.

It rankled with him that an ill-mannered scolding had been delivered in the presence of many of Mr. Alderson's subordinates. James Calvert's greetings to Henry Hird could wait.

"If you see Fronick," Bart Hugill was saying, "tell her I'll be a bit late. You see, I'm taking my brother for a little walk first . . . he settles down better when he's tired."

Adam was hardly thinking of Bart Hugill's demented elder brother, Rive Rags. As he stood there he could perceive Titus Alderson, who was staring towards a boulder over which Winterings Beck rippled, upon the tired face the same sadness he had noticed before when the older man had been off-guard.

"I'll let her know, Bart," Adam promised as Mr. Alderson turned.

The mine agent saw him, smilingly waving his hand in salute.

The Great Deep Level, the driving of which had brought the old Skewdale Mining Company to bankruptcy and subsequently carved a considerable slice from the Grafton family's small fortune, was situated farther down Winterings Gill, on the same side as the North and South Smelt Mills. As Titus Alderson had arranged to show Adam something of this white elephant, they were to walk there together, and so Ben was sent off home by himself.

Before the snuff-brown galloway departed, however, Titus Alderson reminded Bart Hugill about " the usual bit o' miner's yarn," and Adam watched the clerk tuck a piece of scarlet thread through a girth-buckle.

"That's to satisfy that niece of mine, Adam, the fond lass that she is," the mine agent laughed. "You can scarcely credit it, lad, but a couple o' months ago Cherry got into a real stew when he arrived without me. She set off up Sorrow Near . . ."

When Ben was homeward bound at the businesslike pace he set himself, Titus Alderson bustled about to attend to several matters, Adam not for the first time thinking his appearance slightly nautical—the white, pointed beard favoured the fancy, as did a sprightliness of gait, though leaden grey cheeks, blue-tinged lips and eyes strained with anxiety did much to rebut the idea.

"Come on with me, lad," he beckoned to Adam. "I want a word wi' Jonas Cottingham in the top smelt-house and then we can be off."

The smelting-place was long and very lofty, its roof supported by great oak ribs. There were four vast hearths, each with canopy up which a shower of brilliant sparks flew occasionally. At one, men were piling coal, timber and ore to the glowing peats, and at another preparations were being made for casting pigs of lead.

It seemed a day for discord. When Adam went inside, the chief smelter, Jonas Cottingham, was giving a vicious dressing-down to his chief assistant, a pallid, middle-aged man whose fell disease was plainly revealed.

Titus Alderson did not say anything until Harry Blaydes went back to his work.

"Has Harry been spitting badly again, Jonas?" he asked. "Because if he has you should have sent him home. You know Mr. Wade fixed him up in t'Lodge of Half House so as he needn't tew when he ought to be resting."

The corners of Jonas Cottingham's thin-lipped mouth drooped lower. "Maybe so, but this is a smelt mill, noan one o' them new-fangled sanatoriums."

"Aye, and it's about smelting I'm here," Mr. Alderson said briskly. "Or roasting rather. There's about forty bings o' good slime to come down from the circular buddle at Mary Dressing Floors . . ."

The chief smelter was immediately pugnacious. "I thought all hands had to be kept on th'ore hearths. If you want brass quick——"

"The sharpest way is to start the roasters," Titus Alderson said. "You should make eighteen pigs a shift . . ."

Adam wandered away. A silver stream of lead had been run off one hearth into a tank, and its surface was being skimmed to remove impurities. Moulds stood in readiness on the stone-flagged floor, small iron troughs a few inches in width and depth and less than two feet long, from each of which, nevertheless, a pig weighing approximately a hundredweight would later be turned out.

Ladling into the moulds had begun, the molten metal betraying not the least sign of its immense heat, when, for still another time that day, high words were spoken.

"I'm the smelter, aren't I, an' shouldn't t'smelter know which is best?" Jonas Cottingham was demanding.

"And I'm the chief agent, the chap who's ultimately responsible," Titus Alderson replied. "So I want no more objections from you, Jonas."

Later, when they started off together, the sole reference Mr. Alderson made to this incident was that: "Jonas were always crotchety."

That was an estimate Adam darkly suspected fell far short of the mark.

After crossing the mill bridge over Foul Syke, and then passing the office, the South Mill and the Weigh Place, Mr. Alderson and Adam kept to Sleety Slape, a steep and tortuous track close to Winterings Beck. Within the last ten days the increase in the animal population of Skewdale had been enormous, and, as they proceeded downwards, more and more lambs came into sight, with more still expected, for, as Titus Alderson told Adam, Anthony Skidmore and other progressive-minded farmers had, the previous November, divided their flocks into three, allowing the tups to them at intervals. In this wise lambing was spread over a longer period than usual.

"Two year ago we'd a cruel hard winter," he went on. "One big storm covered the ground with snow for week after week, and of course the herbage afterwards were foul and unfit to eat. And when the time came for th'ewes to drop their lambs they were so weak and impoverished that they either died or hadn't any flush of milk, and as for the lambs, all too frequently they were born dead or died soon after."

"Loss of stock must have been terrible," Adam said.

Titus Alderson's expression became graver. "Francis Harker lost nearly a hundred and twenty ewes out of two hundred, and from the remaining ewes nobbut thirty lambs lived. The worst part was that the previous hay-crop had been very thin, and there wasn't enough to see the beasts through the winter let alone spare some for t'sheep."

"So what's been tried is sort of spreading the risk, eh?"

"Aye," Mr. Alderson nodded. " 'Course there's disadvantages, because a later lambing naturally reduces the prices bid at the lamb auctions at the end of the summer."

By now they were almost at the bottom of Water Ling Moor, not far from the wall barring it from Winterings Common Pasture. And, as Sleety Slape curved again in sympathy with the tree-lined gill, a cluster of grey, weathered buildings came into view, and the Great Deep Level.

As they stood at the tail, the old mining agent told Adam the reasons for driving the level: to reach the Master Abbey Vein and open up maiden ground, and to drain waterlogged workings above.

"A goodish flow coming out," Adam pointed. "But is it enough?"

Titus Alderson shook his head. "No, it failed in every respect, and when it became known I think that were Winterings' saddest day. Chaps had been hanging on desperately, and almost two score had to leave their families right away, some just wi' steerage brass and others to tramp in search of work. Aye, it were a sorry end to what had been started fourteen years afore with such high expectations. You see, lad, the Master Abbey Vein, specially in the bottom limestones, had been fruitful enough elsewhere, and as much as thirty thousand pounds' worth of ore had been taken out on it every year."

While he spoke, they had sauntered as far as a waterwheel which, in its thronged heyday, had needed a thousand gallons of water every minute to keep its buckets efficiently moving.

"It must have been a big undertaking," Adam remarked.

"Wasn't it just," Titus Alderson said. "Why, from the tail here the level runs straight for eight hundred fathoms to Great Faith Shaft, and that's nearly a mile. Moreover, after that, it winds to Great Hope Shaft afore striking easterly to Great Charity."

Adam halted at a solitary window in a long wall. Within, dimly seen, was machinery which once had been expensive and gleaming.

"All that belongs to Sir Charles Grafton," Titus Alderson explained. "After the Skewdale Company collapsed he raised the brass somehow, an' restarted driving by more modern methods. It were quicker, to be sure, but the groovers never took properly to dynamite."

At Great Charity Shaft, the Great Deep Level was within the East Side Company's sett, and idly Adam wondered which company possessed the working rights in it.

Titus Alderson smiled broadly. "Nay, lad, neither me nor Reuben Nattrass is ever likely to conjure up some way o' utilising the Great Deep. But the lease allows either of us to do so if we wished."

Adam could not help thinking that such an arrangement might prove awkward, and he said as much.

The older man glanced sharply at him. "Meaning they'd differ just to be contrary. You've been hearing a tale or two, eh?"

For the next two or three minutes, as they resumed in single file down Sleety Slape, he ranted about the growing proclivity of Skewdale folk to make something out of nothing.

"Oh, aye," he went on, "I've had hints as your cousin Reuben were tricky and needed watching, but I treat such nonsense with the contempt it deserves. He's over-keen, I'll allow, but he'll fine down i' time, and whatever else there's one thing that makes me warm to him—it's that, like me, he believes there's still plenty o' lead in these hills."

Modesty, the creeper-clad little farmhouse at the foot of Sleety Slape, across the gill from the Plug and Feathers, was not far away. Soon the two men reached the main road where, over Winterings Brig, they parted, Titus Alderson heading across the cobblestones ostensibly to "look in on Lucy an' maybe have a glass o' beer," the latter part of this promise Adam taking leave to doubt. Cherry's uncle too often sucked a cold and empty pipe.

2

Adam was almost level with Mrs. Batty's bow window when the shop bell tinkled, and he saw his cousin Agnes coming out. She was closely followed by an ample-bosomed, elderly lady, soberly but expensively clad, whose upper lip had a suspicion of dark down, above a mouth compressed with anger.

Agnes Pedley was stealing a glance at this figure of wrath, but when she perceived Adam the awe which had made her face even more youthful than usual was changed into quick alarm.

"You're earlier than I'd thought," she gasped, hastening to him. "Your tea won't be ready for you, but I'll run on——"

"Hey!" Adam grabbed her arm. "Haven't I rammed it into you yet that it isn't a matter of life and death if t'fatted calf isn't steaming on my plate as soon as I put my foot indoors?"

"Yes," she nodded, still flurried. "But——"

"But nothing, lass," Adam insisted. "You're walking on with me."

He continued to hold her as they went along. Main Street clattered with clogs, and the oddly-sized couple evoked many a smile, for the people of Winterings had become vastly tickled, and perhaps touched, by the association of the cousins.

"You're rarely interested in summat, lass," Adam smiled.

Head twisted round, she was raptly staring at the lady who, after leaving Hannah Batty's shop, was now disappearing over the hump of the Brig.

"Off to visit Mrs. Skidmore at Badger Hall, I expect," she half-whispered in her excitement. "Oooh, Cousin Adam, there's been a right upset betwixt Old Hannah an' her niece . . . that's her: Mrs. Roberty Will of Malaga."

"So *she's* Daniel's aunt," Adam grinned.

Full of her thrilling story, Agnes paid little attention to this, and so Adam heard how Old Hannah had vocally lambasted her niece about a cottage whose tenants had been given notice to quit, on Mrs. Alderson's behalf, by her man of affairs, Mr. Lodge Trotter, the Postmaster of Greets.

Daniel, so Adam was thinking, had not erred when estimating his aunt as of considerable substance, even if the dual capacities of Mr. Lodge Trotter were rather unusual. On his mentioning the latter point, Agnes took another of her long breaths. Mr. Trotter, Adam then learnt, was a gentleman of many more parts: he was the Rate Collector, representative of a clothing firm, and his quasi-legal practice was so extensive that Mr. Miles Buckle, the Corvy solicitor, swelled with rage on hearing his name.

"And besides all them jobs," Agnes ended, very pleased with herself, "he's the Secretary of the West Side Company an' all."

At Cuthbert Daykin's, one of the two shops almost opposite the gates of Ash Grove, Mr. William Nattrass's residence, Adam called to collect two galvanised iron pails.

"I'm leaving these at Blind Kit's, lass," he explained on rejoining his cousin. "He's letting us have two hundred eggs as soon as he can, and then you can preserve 'em as you said you'd like."

Agnes's eyes began to film when she protested she had never meant him to buy the eggs, and besides—a teardrop crept down her smooth cheek—he would have gone back to Spain long before the contents of one bucket had been seriously diminished.

"Less o' that, or folk might think I'm ill-treating you," Adam jollied her. "Anyway, what about the grand times we'll have together afore then?"

In a gesture almost animal-like in its affection, she pressed the side of her bonnet against her cousin's hard-muscled arm. This little action was seen by a ruddy-faced man swinging out of the Wood Yard gateway. The sawyer, Nathan Wharton, winked at Adam and made a facetious remark to the girl about her 'young man.' Agnes was a favourite of his: as she was with many of the older men; her slight figure, flaxen hair and blue eyes made great appeal.

"Here's Blind Kit's, lass," Adam laughed as Nathan Wharton passed by. "Shan't be a minute."

The errand at the cobbler's took no longer than that, but when he came out Agnes had gone. Still perturbed about tea, she was flying down Calvert's Wynd towards Dirty Bottom and, at that pace, would soon be jumping across the Hippy Stones.

Smiling a little ruefully, Adam continued to Town Foot, where he glanced at Yew Tree House. He saw nothing of Cherry Dinsdale nor, as he turned in the other direction to look at Smithy House, could he glimpse Fronick Blenkiron's golden-haired head in her workroom. At the Smithy, leaning over the half-door, he again drew blank, but fortunately, close at hand, he heard hammering. Richard Blenkiron's cow-byre was not more than twenty yards up Sorrow Near, just before the sharp bend.

While three cows munched hay contentedly, Fronick's father was repairing his property. Adam joined him in the cloyingly-sweet atmosphere of the byre, putting away his pipe before entering.

"Joinering this time, Mr. Blenkiron," he remarked.

The blacksmith's gingery beard quivered, his deep-chested voice rumbled into laughter. "Jack on all trades, me," he said. "Village blacksmith, smith to t'West Side Company, cow keeper, bee keeper, an' what not. And yet all told it doesn't add up anywhere near to my grandfather's one job."

"What was that?" asked Adam.

Richard Blenkiron jerked his head towards Water Ling Moor. "Head smith to t'mines there, lad, with four first-class smiths under him. Aye, most chaps who met him didn't feel any shame i' doffing their hats to a man in his position. Ah, well . ."

Adam helped to lift a big door on to its crooks and, what with this and topics mutually interesting, he nearly forgot Bart Hugill's message to Fronick. This, however, caused the blacksmith to fall into a reverie so deep that he failed to hear the sound of clogged feet approaching.

"You know, lad," he murmured, "it's a sorry state of affairs hereabouts for young women an' their chaps."

Mrs. Blenkiron came round the corner, a thin woman with a small and not very generous-looking mouth. She told her husband that Dr. Seaton was waiting for him at the Smithy.

"His horse has lost a shoe an' he's to get up to Yorrel sharp."

"I'll attend to it, Grace," Richard Blenkiron promised.

Adam accompanied them to Main Street, where he was promptly buttonholed by the doctor, a middle-aged gentleman who appeared to know all there was to be known about him. Dr. Seaton was far too diminutive for a horse as large as the one which, apparently sunk in slumber, stood near him, and, as further incongruity, he was attired in an ancient suit of sporting tweed and a very formal hard black hat.

The conversation did not last long, for Dr. Seaton's keen eyes discerned a patient endeavouring to slip by. "You!" he yelled. "You! . . . Bottle finished . . . why didn't you call surgery? . . . Corvy Market Day . . . saw you driving through Greets . . . don't deny it . . ."

Leaving Adam, he advanced upon his shrinking victim.

While crossing to Jom High Road Adam began to reflect about the blacksmith, of whose three sons two had emigrated to Canada. It was small wonder that such a man should view with anxiety the courtship of his only daughter with a young man whose livelihood depended upon the West Side Company.

"Bart ought to get off and find himself a decent job," he decided.

His glance roved over the river, passing from the small heap of sale-coal piled in the Wood Yard to the thin blue pennant of smoke drifting from the kitchen chimney of Yew Tree House.

"That's what I'd do anyroad," he told himself.

His steps grew more springy as his thoughts dwelt upon personal matters to do with himself and the girl he knew he loved. Half wonderingly he gazed at the steep-sided hills, from buttercup-tinted meadows in the 'bottoms' to a travelling shaft of light which brightened a small larch plantation high up Snorr Out-Pasture before climbing to transform the gloomy recesses weathered in the face of grey and sheer Snorr Scar above.

"But it grows on you, does all this," he murmured, his eye following the long, unbroken sweeps of the 'tops.' "It does that."

After tea, first arranging for his cousin to meet him later, he went outdoors again. As he walked along Back Lane he determined how there and then he might best fill in a spare interval.

3

Malaga, a handsome, square house with pediment supported by pillars flanking the front entrance, was a short distance down the main road from Town Foot. After crunching along a semi-circular, gravel drive, Adam rapped the knocker, and shortly afterwards was smilingly asked in by a maid. He had barely stepped on to the mat, however, when his further movements were arrested by a sharp voice. The mistress of the house summarily dismissed the servant girl and then bore down on the caller.

"You'll be that Brunskill I've heard about," she began, from as far back as the innermost of a line of Raphael's sacred pictures. "I'm telled you know my nephew Daniel Dolphin."

"Yes, he's a friend o' mine," Adam said. "And as I was coming to Winterings he asked me to pay you a visit."

"What for?" Mrs. Roberty Will asked.

Adam looked at her more closely. Her dark and still fine eyes were a-smoulder, and it struck him that a woman of much self-importance might be very enraged if she suspected that the castigation she had received could become common gossip. She would take it for granted, he was sure, that Agnes had told him of the scene in Hannah Batty's shop.

"Well . . ." he replied, "to start off I've to give you his love."

"He could have sent it in a letter, couldn't he?" Mrs. Roberty Will retorted. "An' more often if he'd wanted."

Adam smiled. "You don't know Daniel, Mrs. Alderson. He's a grand chap, but settling down to write is summat that—well, it's summat he'll generally put off to the next day."

There was no easing, no meeting half-way. Mrs. Alderson, acidulously mentioning the scanty number of times Daniel had written to her, then made it clear she did not care to discuss her kin with strangers, adding that it was not one of her habits to stand at the door, either.

Adam's lips tightened. "Right then, Mrs. Alderson," he said when the tirade ended. "All that remains is for me to pass on t'rest of his message. He said he's coming to see you one fine day."

"That's the lot?"

"The lot," Adam confirmed. "And now I'll take myself off."

"Well, I'll noan detain you," said Mrs. Roberty Will, beginning to close the door. "And thank you for your trouble, young man."

"It's nowt," Adam grunted.

He reached a conclusion when in the main road again.

"Evidently Daniel hasn't done the homage to her money bags that she expects."

A few young people were gathered outside Smithy House and, when he saw them, the disagreeableness of the last minutes was forgotten as he hastened forward.

The little group had decided to escort Dinah Skidmore to Badger Hall, Fronick Blenkiron going also to meet Bart Hugill. The clerk lived at Slackrigg, a tiny hamlet about three-quarters of a mile up the fellside behind Anthony Skidmore's house.

Dinah was beginning to lose her shyness with Adam, and, in Main Street, she told him that, starting in the morning, Ned Mason would be working up Snorr Beck.

"And my father said, Adam, that if you wanted to have a shot at walling for a few days, now was your chance."

Wingy Blenkiron cheerfully remarked that the fossils in the stones slit hands to ribbons, but Cherry reproved him, quoting Adam with some wickedness: "You have to take the rough with the smooth when you're learning," she said, a reference to his tumbling into a particularly noisome muck-heap at Badger Hall.

"Now then." Adam tried to make himself heard above the laughter.

It was an enjoyable stroll. At the farther side of the Brig, between the highway and the purling Skew, a streamer of misty vapours rested on the low meadows, but over it a line of blackthorns flaunted ivory-white blossom. Nature had begun her life-flooding wiles, and the evening air spoke her promise.

Near the Royal Alfred, before turning into Blenk Bottom Lane, Cherry pointed out Bloody Sigh to Adam. The ancient earthworks were towards Yorrel, on a flattish piece of ground, the tip of a spearthrust which Water Ling Moor sent almost to the main road.

"But I've heard Mr. Skidmore say," she continued, "that they'd have been able to win both meadow and pasture from it if they'd wanted."

"Well," Adam said, "everywhere here were moor or forest at one time, so I don't see why not."

Dinah shivered. "But fancy milking there late in Autumn, or turning out in the night for a sick cow. No, I wouldn't go there for a pension after dark."

Adam was staring at Bloody Sigh, an irregular, moat-like trench and massive cairn overshadowed by a belt of oak trees.

"I wouldn't, either, nor in daytime for that matter," Agnes chirped, which revealed she had never been to Bloody Sigh, and caused Wingy Blenkiron to suggest repairing the omission forthwith. "No, I won't, Wingy," she screamed, to become immediately more upset upon using the nickname which had arisen out of his maiming. "I'm ever so sorry, Clarkson," she gulped. "I shouldn't have."

"No, you oughtn't, Agnes," Fronick Blenkiron said severely.

A discussion upon by-names kept them going as far as Will Skidmore's cottage. The gamekeeper was out, but Susan, his wife, was in her neat kitchen and they stayed there until the children, Alice the oldest and Walter Heseltine the youngest, drank their bed-time milk. Nine-year-old Bob Skidmore had not so far bethought himself to come home, so his mother informed her visitors.

Afterwards, on Snorr Bridge, Wingy Blenkiron chuckled. "Aye, he's a right young rip is your nephew Bob, Dinah," he grinned. "Him and his cousin Ward . . . when they get together . . ."

"Hidings don't stop 'em either," Cherry smiled. "You'd bother, hadn't you, Agnes, because of them the other night?"

The trick played by Bob Skidmore and his cousin, Ward Tiplady, the poacher's son, was an old one, the root of the mischief a big sod which the boys, stepping on to Ambrose Pedley's roof from the high ground behind, had used to seal the kitchen chimney. The Pedleys, father and daughter, had been at a mid-week service.

"Yes, and Adam were at the door talking to Mark Iveson," Agnes gloated. "An' he thought the place were afire when the smoke started to pour past him."

"Have you seen 'em since, Adam?" Dinah inquired.

"We've had a chat across the river," Adam replied. "They were right polite an' all."

There was a burst of laughter. The tactics of the pair were well enough known and, apart by victims, relatives, or the stricter-minded, their misdemeanours were generally appreciated.

When Adam had learnt from Mr. Skidmore exactly where Ned Mason would be employed the next day, he climbed the battlemented wall of the garth and walked towards the house, but as soon as he saw that Cherry and Dinah were still in lively conversation outside the arched back door, he selected a grassy seat, and pulled a small Bible from his pocket.

When Cherry joined him he was busily searching for suitable broadsides with which to confound Ambrose Pedley.

"You know, I . . . I think it's awful you have to use t'Bible for such a purpose," she said, troubled. "I suppose it's because I can't forget that Agnes's father is a lay-preacher and—well, if he were as he ought to be it wouldn't be necessary."

Adam scrambled up. As they sauntered together his eyes were focused in the distance, following the course of Sorrow Near from Mine Road down dale to Milton Hall and Juniper Wood. The previous Sunday he had met Cherry and Dinah out of Sunday School and, on Titus Alderson's recommendation, they had walked that way for him to see laminated strata of rock almost two hundred feet high. The scrub-filled quarry was very remote and, lay-preacher notwithstanding, he felt certain that

Ambrose Pedley would have believed the worst of any young couple frequenting the place.

"What are you thinking about, Adam?" Cherry looked up.

"Oh, nowt very much, lass," he smiled, bringing himself to the present. "Only about where we went last Sunday."

Cherry fought valiantly to ward off a gurgle, but failed. Milton Hall was a favourite courting place, and near the ruined, old shooting-lodge they had inadvertently surprised Arthur Nattrass and his young lady, Annamaria Rutter. For a self-sufficient young woman, Annamaria had looked incredibly silly when discovered.

"As if we should spy on them," she said, laughing. "But really, both me an' Dinah thought your cousin Arthur was going to hit you when he began to unbutton his coat."

Arthur Nattrass, son of George Nattrass of Greets, was the weedy young man whom Adam, on his first evening at Winterings, had heard throwing out challenges at the Plug and Feathers, after scorning Titus Alderson's mining abilities.

"But Annamaria soon settled his hash," Adam chuckled.

Titillated by this recollection, they continued their way, so unhurried as not to catch up to the others until close upon Snorr Bridge, where Fronick seated herself comfortably on the lichen-stained parapet to await Bart.

For a change it was decided to return home along Middle Sorrow. The hill was abrupt and deeply rutted by cart traffic between Snorr Bridge and the lonely farm at its summit, but once at the top there was a slight but steady descent on short, firm turf to Back Lane.

They paused, as hill folk do, for a breather and the view.

"It's lovely, isn't it, Adam?" Cherry's voice was soft.

The blood-red sun was sinking, and the Skew a thin line quivering with reflected fire. Their glances ranged upwards, from the greenness of new growth in the bottom of the winding dale to tops which, though the heather would not bloom for many months, nevertheless hinted of purple. Behind the line of the tops, as though snow-covered mountains remotely away, clouds, pink-shaded to one side and dove-grey to the other, raised their peaks into the pale blue sky.

"Yes," Adam murmured, recalling a sad scene in William Nattrass's yard, when the Corvy-bound carrier bore three young men and their possessions on the first lap of a very long journey. "Yes," he repeated, "I can understand chaps who're emigrating feeling down in t'dumps."

The animation and joyousness in Cherry Dinsdale's pretty face faded. "Yes, I know how heartbroken I was when we'd to go, Adam," she said.

Adam stared. "Why, I thought you'd lived here all your life."

She shook her head. "No, I left when I was thirteen, and I didn't come back again for four years . . ." She broke off to point to the solitary farmhouse.

"That's Silence, Adam, where Dinah's eldest brother Ralph lives. He's wed to Isa Nattrass that was, Reuben Nattrass's sister."

"I've seen her but we haven't spoken," Adam said. "They've two little girls, haven't they, that go to school on a white horse?"

Cherry laughed. "Yes, that's Nancy and Harriet all right, on Gem."

Silence was a small farmhouse, cow byre built on at one end with hay-baulk over it. Hemmed in too closely by a crescent of scrub-birch, it was rather a forbidding place.

"It's supposed to be haunted," she went on, "and one day a year, on the anniversary of the death of a former tenant, Isa always takes the children down to her father's at Ash Grove for the night."

"And nobody's laid the ghost?" Adam inquired.

"No," Cherry said soberly, "though Ralph's used special prayers and recited passages from the Bible backwardsway."

There was a shriek ahead, where Agnes had just beaten Wingy Blenkiron in a sprint. The postman, as Adam noticed, treated the girl as though she were a child and, a handball event in prospect, was using her for training purposes, to free muscles he believed bound by his plodding eighteen miles' daily round.

Both Cherry and Adam were smiling, but the next thing they spoke about was in a sadder vein, her father's fatal accident in a durk drift near Mary Level Forehead.

"Anyroad," Cherry swallowed, "at after the funeral my brothers decided mining here were no good, an' so we all went off."

It was a picture of mixed pathos and humour she then drew, describing their life; the new and pathetic loyalty which claimed for the moors outside a grimy Lancashire town a charm comparable with the fells at home, and the reunions with other migrants from Skewdale, all as homesick as themselves.

"Then one night when we came back from the mill," Cherry's dimple began to reassert itself, "there was a letter from Uncle Titus to say his housekeeper was getting wed. Well . . ." she started to laugh, "I were never so humiliated in my life, Adam, because my brothers almost began to pack my bag there an' then. You see they knew that in America they could get a job mining straight off."

"Aye," Adam said. "But why hadn't you all gone to America beforehand? You'd have the brass for the fares."

As one under the spell of beauty, Cherry's soft eyes looked towards the wild, rocky region around gold-tipped Virgin Hill.

"Because they were that fond o' me," she murmured, a great affection for them in her. "They knew that all I dreamed about were of coming back to Winterings some day."

From then onwards Adam was slightly preoccupied, until foolishly she imagined that earlier he might have thought she did not agree with him about Ambrose Pedley. So she tried to explain the pride of Winterings folk in the preachers for which the village had long been renowned.

"Even now, Adam, there's never less than a dozen set out every Sunday morning, up dale and down dale and over the tops to both sides, tramping miles and miles in all conditions to chapels and to spots so lonely that the services have to be held in a house. And you can't but respect and look up to such men, for they're grand 'uns, Adam."

Despite being oppressed by the problem with which, quite innocently, she had confronted him, Adam smiled down at her.

"I'm sure they're the salt of the earth, lass. Only," he slapped the volume in his pocket, "I've a particularly peculiar customer to deal with."

"As Agnes shows in her face," Cherry said, nodding towards the couple in front, who were making plenty of noise. "What she wants is more of that, more fun and acting silly. And even apart from how Ambrose Pedley keeps her under his thumb, there's lots who don't agree with him in other matters. I know Mr. Blenkiron and several more preachers don't hold with the way both he and his brother James conduct services. They say it's making the chapel into a bear-garden."

These were grave issues and it was full time for foolishness. Adam, pointing to a boulder ahead, proposed a race, suggesting with gross insult that a start of half the distance might make the contest not so one-sided.

Cherry's red lips curled. "I can beat you with a sight less than that," she proclaimed.

Marks more mutually acceptable were chosen, and then they were off, a tall young man tearing along Middle Sorrow in headlong pursuit of an animated young woman who, determined upon victory, showed decidedly more white cotton-stockinged limbs than elders not as rigid as Ambrose Pedley would have approved.

Where the track narrowed, a slight collision brought them momentarily into each other's arms. Both were rather silent for a while.

Pewitt Pillar, on Middle Sorrow, was level with Winterings Brig, and here the other couple waited, near Droughty Tom's cottage and stone limekilns. From this point onwards walkers were in sight of Main Street and Back Lane, and so for Agnes Pedley, frightened of her father, there was no more romping. Henceforth she kept in close company with her cousin, when the chief topic was the entertainment and dance in the Literary Institute towards the end of the month.

Dancing would naturally be anathema to Ambrose Pedley, but Adam was stirred when Agnes blurted out that she would not be permitted to attend the concert either.

"Nay, lass," expostulated Wingy Blenkiron. "Whatever harm is there i' listening to a bit of singing and a comic or two?"

"None," Cherry blazed. "But it's easy for us to talk, Wingy. She's the one who has to deal with him."

"Not for this once, lass," Adam promised. "Yes, I'll have a go at him . . . for th'entertainment part that is."

To their astonishment Agnes seemed in a dilemma.

"You'd like to go, Agnes, wouldn't you?" Wingy exclaimed.

"Oh, I *would*," she replied. "No . . . maybe after all . . . I don't much really want . . . you see . . . well . . ." Stammering ended, her voice trailed off and she was not far from tears.

From behind, Cherry made signs wholly unfathomable to Adam, for whose meaning he had to wait until they were alone, when Agnes, across the road at Smithy House, was gossiping with Wingy and Mrs. Blenkiron. After reaching Jom High Road, the party had loitered on Dolly Bridge, watching a dipper which winged under the bridge half a dozen times before sweeping to its nest in a crevice beneath the arch. Between there and Town Foot, Cherry and Adam managed to detach themselves from their companions.

Cherry kept her voice low. "It's clothes she's bothered about, Adam. But I'll have a talk with Dinah and somehow or other we'll see she's turned out nicely if you can persuade her father to let her go."

"So that's it, is it?" Adam grunted. "Well, it's right champion of you," he continued, his tone warm, "but I'm wondering if I can't kill two birds with one stone."

He explained that, realising more and more the conditions in which Agnes lived, he had been puzzling what he could do. Supposing he gave his cousin money for an outfit? That would solve the other difficulty, too.

"Aye, it's stingy, but I were bent on not benefiting that father of hers," he admitted.

"I don't call it stingy, Adam, not with a mean creature like him," Cherry differed. "And as for clothes . . ." her eyes glowed, "there's nothing she'd like better, *nothing*. The poor lass has never had owt worth wearing."

"That's that, then," Adam smiled. "And can I tell her you'll give her any advice she needs?"

Cherry wrinkled her nose. "You can—but *don't*. Leave her to do just as she wants. It's better, Adam."

Gently he began to stroke the shapely but work-roughened hand clasping the top of the gate.

"You're a wise . . . and a bonny lass, Cherry," he said quietly.

"Adam, you mustn't say things like that, please," she protested, her blush visible in the fading light.

For a brief span they stood quite still, her hand now covered by his. Then she glanced over her shoulder.

"Adam," she whispered, "I must go in. Uncle Titus'll wonder what on earth I'm doing."

"Tell him you an' me have been coming to grips on a little matter," Adam said. "And speaking of grips," he added, casting out sentiment in favour of a poker-faced solemnity she now estimated more accurately, "we've been at 'em already, come to think of it."

"Now!" Cherry said.

"Aye," he chaffed her, "we shall have to do a bit more racing, me and you. A right exciting finish it were."

A foot stamped on the flagged path. "Adam!" she threatened.

Then, swiftly, her defences fell as confusedly she remembered how tightly he had held her. Never had he seen her so shy, and it moved him immeasurably.

"Cherry, lass," he said.

But she had turned away and, skirts fluttering, was scampering towards the door, from which he faintly heard her breathless: "Good night, Adam."

A great gladness in him, Adam crossed Main Street. As he glanced at the darkening rim of the hills he thought that never before had they seemed so much a part of him, and he of them, as in this somehow precious hour.

With girls of Agnes Pedley's temperament direct measures pay, and on Dolly Bridge Adam told her his plans without preamble.

"So make a list of everything you want," he wound up. "The whole lot—shoes, stockings, blouse, underlinen . . ."

Her eyes were wide with fright. "Under . . ." she gasped, and, half-whispering, covered her face with her hand. "Oh, Cousin Adam, how . . . how could you . . . you speak o' such private things to me?"

Adam had a pronounced feeling that he might have had a nasty situation to tackle if Mazy Bill had seen them just then.

"Now listen here," he began firmly. "My part ends when you've told me the total, and I neither want to see the list or anything else. But one last thing: you haven't to buy the cheapest you can find."

Her mouth was still open and she looked so dumbfounded that, as novel restorative, he said she reminded him so much of a fish on a marble slab that it would perhaps be better if she provided herself with shining scales instead of clothing.

Agnes's lips quivered. "Oh, Cousin Adam."

"But I'm noan escorting a cod to Chapel next Sunday night," Adam remarked, adding lugubriously: "A right idiot I'd look, wouldn't I?"

She smiled wanly."I . . . I could cry," she announced.

By good fortune, he made exactly the right reply. "You'd do better, lass, to start thinking about what you'd like to buy."

As, eventually, she did, to such purpose that along Back Lane she was in another turmoil, whether to risk the epidemic at Yorrel to see Rosie Caygill about a dress or to visit Greets to examine the stock in George Nattrass's emporium. In the same febrile state of excitement she entered her home, where the outcome was a supper-making of error upon error, with knives and forks lacking, and the teapot pouring nothing stronger than scalding water.

Adam laughed. "You don't know whether you're on your head or your heels, do you, lass?" he asked.

She was so long in answering that he became aware of the silence. Turning, he saw two painful spots of colour in her white cheeks. Her eyes had their old haunting fear, and she was holding, still unopened, the tea-caddy.

"What's amiss now, Agnes?" he inquired.

She hesitated, gulped, and then tried to tell him.

"Cousin Adam," she whispered, "you mustn't buy me them . . . underthings, and you mustn't tell my father you were thinking o' doing. He'd . . . kill me if he knew owt like that had ever been mentioned betwixt us."

Adam smiled at her. "Eh, lass, your father's going to know only what you want to tell him. All I shall do is to hand you a few sovereigns and what you do with 'em is your own concern. So don't worry yourself any more."

She sniffed again, however, and, as another crisis appeared close at hand, Adam left the table. He was squeezing her slim shoulders when the door latch clicked and, at the sharp sound, she sprang away as if possessed.

From the threshold Ambrose Pedley stared at them, sallow complexioned face framed ovally by the tangle of hair and beard, the yellow candlelight reflected in his dark eyes.

"What's going on here?" he demanded.

"You . . . you made me jump, Father," Agnes mumbled.

He closed the door and walked towards the fireplace before putting the next pregnant question. "Why should you jump because your father's come home?" he asked with uncanny restraint.

"Because the unexpected noise startled her like it startled me," Adam intervened irritably. "And that's noan the only shock I've had to-day. Yes," he snorted, "I've had a right 'un, bearing in mind what *you'd* telled me."

"Me!" ejaculated Ambrose Pedley.

Whatever else, Adam had certainly gained their entire attention. Agnes gaped and her father shuffled his weight from one foot to the other.

"Well, an' what——" the older man began.

The lodger was in an awkward mood. "How much longer, Agnes?" he asked with scant patience. "Skipping about in a flurry doesn't help, you know." He jerked his head her way but spoke to her father. "She forgot to put the tea in the pot."

"Carelessness," Ambrose Pedley said bleakly. "How many times, girl——"

"You can chide her later," Adam was brusque. "I've summat important just now and it's this . . . why did you say t'Chapel here were gaining membership when the real truth is that you're losing ground to the Congregationalists?"

"You what?" Ambrose Pedley shouted. "And who telled you that? The Congregational minister at Yorrel, him that sends forth a stinking savour worse nor an apothecary's ointment tainted wi' dead flies?"

"No, he didn't," Adam insisted. "But let's stick to the point."

At half-past ten, original suspicions completely forgotten, Ambrose Pedley was still pouring venom on to Mr. Waddington, the Congregational minister at Yorrel, and in all, until close upon midnight, Adam suffered the chastening experience of hearing one so-called Christian maliciously condemning a Christian of another body. After that, Ambrose Pedley lay back exhausted. But, strangely enough, his humour then became more mellow, and Adam not only obtained permission for Agnes to attend the entertainment in the Literary Institute, but successfully broached the question of his gift to her.

CHAPTER FOUR

I

THE REPAIRS to Anthony Skidmore's pasture wall almost complete, Ned Mason decided to do a small job at home the following morning before starting out. His time of meeting Adam was therefore advanced from half-past seven to nine o'clock.

Next day the rain had diminished and a patch of brightness in the grey sky foretold the end of the drizzle. At least that was Titus Alderson's cheery belief. He was setting out for the bank at Corvy, to draw money for the following Pay, when Adam passed Yew Tree House.

In Main Street, taking joy in getting as wet as possible, children bound for school scuffed their clogs through muddy pools, and Nancy and Harriet Skidmore, just arrived from Silence, were slithering down from Gem's broad back before tethering the aged white horse amongst the veterans who already had brought in more than a dozen youngsters from outlying farms.

Adam called at the shop on the corner of Calvert's Wynd. Blind Kit's workplace was a favourite spot for assembly, but at this hour his cronies were otherwise occupied.

"Sole and heel, lad?" Blind Kit asked, his fingers delicately feeling around the welts of the boots. "Aye, they'll do another."

He was a man in the late forties, with a face scarred by particles driven below the skin, sad relics of the accident in which he had lost his sight.

Both had work to do and when the schoolmaster, Mr. Kidd, began to ring the bell, the cobbler stuffed his mouth with nails, and Adam grasped the door latch.

Over the narrow-waisted hump of Winterings Brig a funeral was approaching from Yorrel, the coffin, heaped with bunches of primroses, borne in a two-wheeled coup cart, the shafts and body of which, scrubbed scrupulously until every vestige of farm usage had been removed, were embellished with crape material, as was the over-bellied, wind-swollen mare.

Francis Harker, of Low Bands Farm, soberly clad, was waiting to join the tail of the *cortège*, and he and Adam stood side by side until it passed, Adam with his cap off and the farmer holding a curly-brimmed hat. It was not too pleasant in the wet, but their ordeal was as nothing compared with that of the main body of mourners who, after crawling from Yorrel, had still the journey to Greets Church before them.

"Looks as if there might be mutiny in t'ranks, Adam," Mr. Harker whispered. "But he's allus the same, is Edmund Kearton."

A sufferer ventured a hushed expostulation. "It's all reet, Edmund," he said, "but we'll get our deaths o' cold . . ."

"He's looking for more undertaking business," a cynic grunted.

Mr. Kearton's lantern-jawed face betrayed only a greater resolve. "Now *not* so fast," he snapped. "This is noan a bun-fight, an' the only seemly road to pay respect . . ."

Mr. Harker, with a doleful reference to " congestion of the lungs," added himself to the procession.

The worst fears were not justified for, when Adam reached the Royal Alfred, the rain had stopped and, by the time he came to Will Skidmore's cottage in Blenk Bottom Lane, conditions were so rapidly improving that Susan Skidmore was putting up a clothes-line.

Will's wife was a plump, easy-dispositioned young woman who did not take greatly after her sparsely-built father, Edmund Kearton. She did not allow Adam to go by without an allusion to what, for four days, had been a standing joke in one small circle.

"I think I'd better inform you, Susan," Adam retorted, acquiring an air of dignity, "that last night Ned said I were in the way o' becoming a right outstanding waller."

Susan Skidmore, in no wise impressed, merely giggled.

There seemed little doubt that the weather had really 'faired' up, and a few bullfinches and a couple of yellow wagtails were celebrating the change farther down the lane.

Ned Mason occupied one of the pair of cottages up the riverside lane across the Skew, his neighbours the Waggotts, whose son, Bull, was often a source of annoyance.

"Looks like clearing up nicely, lad," he greeted Adam, falling in with him.

"Aye, when we're about at the end of getting soaked every day," Adam grinned.

"You haven't seen Skewdale rain yet," the mason scoffed.

At the point where the lane curved sharply behind Badger Hall to wind up the fell-side, they were joined by Matt Tiplady and his sundry-ancestored bitch, Floss. The poacher lived at Lane End, a short distance upstream from the Skidmores' old house. He was carrying over his shoulder a pick and shovel.

"Beck-bottoming, lad ?" Ned Mason inquired.

Matt Tiplady grimaced. "Aye, I'm trying near Old Flout Level."

The little party climbed the steep track to Slackrigg, a hamlet formerly serving the groovers of a mining ground above. Over half its twenty or so dwellings were derelict, and of the remainder only four had tenants.

Above Slackrigg Matt Tiplady left them to follow the right-hand feeder of Snorr Beck, while Adam and his companion continued up the watercourse to the east, which soon brought them to Anthony Skidmore's top pasture.

Adam took off his coat and set to work with zest. It was good to watch the two faces of the wall grow, to stuff the middle with rubble, to develop the power of selecting from a heap the exact stone for a destined purpose, to put a 'through' now and then, a stone which, stretching from back to front, provided a stable foundation upon which to erect anew. And, when an occasional straightening was permissible, there was always the view to enchant.

Ned Mason missed little passing-by far-away below, neither horseman nor vehicle, and more than once he doubled Adam with his drollness. When the old Quaker roadman, Luke Close, on the main road near Bloody Sigh, abandoned his shovel to smoke on a wall in the Council's time, he commented suitably; later, glimpsing Mrs. Emma Ann Metcalfe and bachelor Cuthbert Daykin, her neighbour and fellow shopkeeper, talking together from their respective doors, his observations were sufficiently ribald, if his voice had carried, to have caused both parties to seek the advice of either Mr. Lodge Trotter at Greets or, more professionally, Mr. Miles Buckle at Corvy. That is, if either of them had dared allow Emma Ann's husband, Cyprian Metcalfe, the engineer to the East Side Company, to learn how they had been trifling.

By midday, when they ate their meal, the walling had practically been completed.

"Aye, I'll soon be on my way down," Ned Mason said.

"And I'll be going to see how Matt's getting on," Adam decided.

Often they were lost in contemplation of the scene, the fell opposite which appeared as if three different qualities of rug, unevenly scalloped, had been laid on it—the uppermost, the moor, curving down to the frontier to which man had forced it back, its islands of pale green becoming daily more prominent; the middlemost, pasture land and common pasture, where wintertime tints of brown were steadily being subjugated by the increasing growth of long grasses; and the meadows themselves, a strip of thickening fresh green carpet covering the bottom and lower slopes to each side.

Adam was eyeing a wall three or four miles long which sprawled across the exposed heights to the north.

"Yes, but leaving aside objections like that, Ned," he said, "wouldn't a wall like that be stronger with mortar?"

"Maybe." The waller laughed. "But in a real gale where would t'gaps be to ease the pressure?"

"The lot 'ud tumble down, you mean," said Adam.

"The whole bloody length," the mason agreed with relish. "But wi' dry-walling, nobbut part goes."

At two o'clock the job was finished, and Adam surreptitiously compared his own contribution with that of a skilled man's. Ned Mason, however, a wiry, brown-complexioned individual, gave Adam's small section an attention far from cursory. "Noan so bad, lad," he remarked in due course. "Aye, I've seen worse attempts."

Adam Brunskill had already mastered many of the technicalities of a profession vastly more intricate than that of a country craftsman, but nevertheless it was infinitely satisfying to contemplate the result of his labour, and to receive a tribute, guarded perhaps, from a direct descendant of a Breton brought to Corvy in England to help build a great castle for a Norman overlord.

From a mile or two away, the abandoned mining ground was indistinguishable from Snorr Moor surrounding it, but on the sett itself the story was different, the scree and debris of mining abundant.

Beyond a dam with rotting wooden sluice Adam came to a level from which water gushed to a depth of nearly three feet. The stone-built tail was sound, but what mainly attracted his attention was the luckstone securely fixed on to the keystone. He had seen these emblems before, in places where it was considered they would be of good fortune to the groovers. The luckstones were circular pieces of limestone with a hole in the centre; miniature specimens were extremely rare and highly prized for wear as an ornament.

To cross the dressing floors he jumped several masonry-lined channels, and then picked a path through a dump of old plant: tubs of all sizes and rust-eaten cog-wheels, tramway rails, wagon frames and such-like.

The smelt mill came next, its water-wheel still coupled to the antiquated leather-and-metal bellows which had provided blast in the era before double-acting cylinders and wrought-iron receivers for compressed air. Below the smelt mill were the usual dead heaps, and it was only by pure chance that Adam noticed an unfamiliar gleam.

"Why!" he ejaculated, stopping.

Then he hastened towards the hillock, scattering a party of dishevelled, dirty-looking tups, one of which trailed a long length of bramble caught in its unkempt wool.

A brief examination satisfying him, he went to work more systematically, providing himself with an iron bar to dig deeper into slags buried in a mass of hardened slimes. Eventually, to make a rough test, he broke one of the slags and scraped the rough edge across the top of a light-coloured freestone rock. It left a grey smear, proving the presence of lead.

"That's it," he muttered. "By the old-time smelting methods they couldn't extract to the extent we can now, and lots of valuable metal was thrown away."

The next steps were soon completed. Watched expressionlessly by the tups from the lofty summit of an adjacent dead heap, he slipped a few slags into his pocket and, quartering a small quantity of the slimes, made a fairly representative sample for assay purposes.

He stumbled upon Matt Tiplady suddenly, beyond a small waterfall. The poacher had recently taken up a portion of the beck's bed, for the water below was muddy, but when Adam saw him, he was bending down immersed almost to his thighs, shaking below the surface a stone-filled tub. Without looking up he spoke to Adam, and it appeared that Floss, who was sitting sedately on the bank, had given warning ten minutes before.

"Well, making anything out, lad?" Adam inquired.

Matt Tiplady was very impressive. "If I keep on this road, an' put in plenty of overtime, there's every prospect I shall have won a bing of ore by Christmas."

"And by then, Mary Jane and Ward 'ul just about have starved to death," Adam said, chuckling as he threw down the specimens. "Why not try with these instead, Matt? I got 'em up yonder, and I reckon they'll pay for re-smelting. Taking the slimes and both kinds of slags, black and grey, I shouldn't be surprised if they averaged around five per cent o' pig lead."

Matt Tiplady left the water to scrutinise the slags, but did not seem very sanguine.

Adam laughed as he pocketed them. "That's all right, Matt," he said, when heartily thanked. "Now let's lend you a hand to see if together we can't increase t'production of beck tailings."

They went turn and turn about in shovelling out of the bed when the stream was diverted to the other side, in breaking up large pieces on a flat stone with the bucker, in jigging in the water. The result was always the same: the upper layer of rock in the tub extended deeper than it should, the middle band, which ought to have been progressively richer, was not, and the bottom of the tub, into which the heaviest constituent, lead ore, should have sunk, revealed never more than an inch or so of debatable bouse.

"I've had enough," Matt Tiplady exclaimed in disgust two hours later. "Aye," he winked, "and I'se making off for a spot where there will be a bit o' profit. Between Lovely Lady an' Legatt's Way, Adam lad. Some night you must come wi' me afore you go back. It can be fair exciting, you know."

Adam grinned. "I'll keep you to that."

"Right," Matt Tiplady nodded. "And let's hope Will Skidmore and Luther Thwaites—he's the Lord's keeper, the bandy-legged bastard—are out on t'scent."

The tools were left to be collected on the return from nefarious business, and then the poacher, Floss close at his heels, limped up the moor.

Slackrigg and its melancholy atmosphere were behind when, from the edge of a scar, in a pasture steeply below, Adam sighted Cherry and Dinah, each carrying a young lamb. Both girls were in the big aprons Skewdale young ladies wore always save for strictly social occasions.

Climbing down the rock face, Adam headed in their direction, his route taking him across half a dozen walls, over which he was now adept at passing without disturbing a few stones in the process.

"Oh, Adam," Cherry said in distress when he caught up to them, "their mother's just died. The poor thing had got right away from any help, but we happened to hear her groaning."

"Lucky you did," Adam replied, looking at an orphan who had made a feeble cry. "At anyroad it'll give them a chance of living."

Dinah remarked that, at home, there was a ewe who had lost her twins the previous day. "We'll have to persuade her to mother these. And we're trying rum this time, whatever my father says."

Through pastures and meadows they hurried to Badger Hall, where Adam was sent for a bottle of Demerara Dew and the two cracked teacups kept on a shelf behind the back door. On his return Dinah and Cherry started to dress the lambs' curly coats with rum while he, with a quarter cupful, was dismissed to the garth, there to secure the ewe and rub her nose with the spirit.

"Right!" Adam nodded. "But . . ." he eyed two suspiciously straight faces, "I'm having Nell wi' me. I'd enough when you inveigled me into putting a hobbling strap on to one o' these woolly mountaineers as wanted to wander."

Both girls glanced up with a surprise too plainly depicted to be real, but his stony-eyed stare was too much for them. His biting comment did not improve matters. "A merry heart doeth good like a medicine," he said.

Their unrestrained laughter in his ears, he left for the front of the old house, from which, fortunately, he saw Mr. Skidmore at once, up the riverside towards Lane End, resting on a crook and contemplating his lands. Adam whistled, held up the cup, a sign which the master of Badger Hall understood. Quickly Nell arrived, tongue hanging out of the side of her mouth.

"Come on, lass," Adam said. "You and me have a job to do."

So far he knew few of the cries, whistles and discreet hand-signals which at once dispatch a good working-dog on a variety of errands, from rounding up miles away to crawling inch by inch on the belly. In the present instance Nell virtually took control. She immediately penned the ewe in an angle of the battlemented walls, holding her victim petrified while Adam daubed its nose freely enough to cause a complete kinship of scent between prospective foster-mother and the twins to be adopted. And, on the return, she marshalled the bereft creature without fretting it unduly.

Anthony Skidmore was passing, his destination the meadow behind the cottages of the Masons and Waggotts, to which his daughter and her friend had gone.

"So's th'ewe you're bringing doesn't see the lambs being popped down, lad," he continued. "She'd be extra suspicious otherwise."

Adam was thinking of the dead ewe, and he inquired what would be done with the carcass. Sadly Mr. Skidmore replied that soon someone would be along to beg it.

"They'll hand me back the fleece, Adam, but t'meat will be cut up, and the best joints 'ul sell like hot cakes at three-ha'pence a pound. Aye," he went on, fingering his iron-grey beard, "and many's the carcass black wi' flies that has been disposed of similarly. Yes, this top part o' Skewdale's gone through it, lad."

The orphans had been placed at the far side of a field full of contented families and, as always with ewes who have lost their lambs, their potential mother was uneasily alert, ever moving. It was not long before she heard the weak cries. The youngsters tottered towards her; when they tried to suck she pushed them away or warned them off with a toss of her head, her manner less severe than it would have been had she not been deeply perplexed. When they were still, however, she smelt them thoroughly.

"Aye, they'll be having their suppers afore bedtime," Anthony Skidmore said. "But in the meantime," his smile widened, "just keep your eye on that ewe by t'byre."

A conscientious mother was becoming wearied of shooing off a boisterous lamb which repeatedly pestered her own offspring, a lamb of much inferior physique at least ten days younger. Twice more she took short runs at the playful molester and then, patience exhausted, marched off, a determined, thin-legged woman in a very long and outsize woolly coat.

"Watch," Mr. Skidmore guffawed. "She's found th'other's mother."

Bony impact of head against head was distinctly heard as the ewe with a grievance butted. That ended the lesson for the careless one, who beat a retreat, her frolicsome son gambolling along with her.

"By, that's clever!" Adam marvelled. "Teaching her to bring up her child properly, eh?"

Four abreast, they began to saunter homewards, facing the pale sun, amidst crying lambs and deep-bleating sheep whose apprehensive glances never strayed from Nell, quietly at heel. In this fashion the first gate was reached when Dinah, fingers shooting to her mouth, recalled the activities in the dairy: the big buttermaking.

"Cherry, my mother!" she squealed.

"And we promised we wouldn't be long," Cherry gasped.

When the girls scampered off, Adam was free to talk about local agriculture, as increasingly he was doing. Lead-mining, once the overriding factor in the Dale's economic life, was now of negligible importance. Farming had taken its place, and farming, in Skewdale, meant the modest profits from the sale of cheese, milk, wool and stock. These various gains in turn depended upon the yield of hay every year.

"You see, Adam, we're hill farmers here, and to us good sweet grass means everything," Anthony Skidmore was saying. "It's th'only crop we have and we always hope and pray it'll be a big 'un. That's why we win every blade we can at haymaking, an' that's why the fog, which is the grass that grows after haymaking, is worth so much to us for fattening cattle and sheep. Aye, hay's our life-blood. We spread our muck to secure it, and we dress the land wi' lime to improve it."

Adam, clearing up problems easy and acute as he came to them, continued to meditate about the simple round. Throughout the winter the vast majority of cows were dry, but when, in March or April, they calved and gave milk, buttermaking started and went on until shortly after Old May Day, when the beasts left the byres for the open air. The cheese-making season then opened, to rage unabated until November, when the cows were brought indoors once more.

"If buttermaking earns nowt much—excepting," he grinned, "the wherewithal for the ladies to buy a few extra geegaws more than the egg money 'ul let them, why doesn't cheesemaking start straight after calving?"

Anthony Skidmore chuckled. "Ask t'missus that, lad?"

As Adam did in the big kitchen of Badger Hall, where a handsome tea was laid, and a bright-blazing wood fire lighted up a recess large enough to allow passage to a coach and pair.

Mrs. Skidmore had a bone to pick with Adam. She charged him with detaining the girls when they should have been in the dairy.

"It isn't what t'lasses have said, but I can read between the lines, Adam, and . . ."

Simultaneously Cherry and Dinah began to squabble noisily about a fruit cake. With justifiable scepticism Adam concluded they were more concerned in hiding their delight than in deciding whether the heat of the oven or an over-abundance of fruit were responsible for the cake's slightly depressed dome. Nevertheless, he apologised before putting his poser.

"Aye . . . it's this, Mrs. Skidmore," he continued. "Just why don't you start with your cheesemaking as soon as your cows calve?"

Mrs. Skidmore stared. "Why, lad, th'only cheese worth eating is a grass cheese. If you made 'em when the beasts were still indoors . . . well, they'd taste of nowt." Quite forgetting her complaint, not very serious, she chattered away on a subject she knew, oblivious of anything else.

"Isn't he clever in dodging things?" Cherry remarked, falsely admiring.

"Low cunning, love," Dinah amended. "Of all the——"

"Of all the baggages," Adam mumbled to Mrs. Skidmore's patent astonishment.

The master of Badger Hall dryly interposed to inquire about tea, and to point out that the 'young 'uns' were 'up to their tricks as usual.'

After tea Adam milked with Mr. Skidmore, and fed a couple of sturdy calves whose diet, at six weeks old, was skim milk with a dash of oatmeal and wheat flour shaken on it. There were other jobs to do: skinning a dead lamb, filling in the grave in which rested ewes and lambs, the casualties of the season's lambing, and turning the handle of the grindstone while the prongs of a pair of hay forks were sharpened. Finally, filled with well-being, the walk homewards with Cherry in the gathering dusk.

"You're becoming a right farmer, Adam," she teased him. "Enjoying it?"

"I am that," he said, loving her vividness. "Yes, it's a grand life, lass . . . for a man, that is. Of course it's different for a woman."

"Why should it be?" Cherry demanded.

With overwhelming compassion Adam dwelt upon the sorry lot of the hill farmer's wife . . . the few but hectic weeks of buttermaking, the many months' grind of cheesemaking, haymaking and the provision of food and drink for a host of helpers, in winter the eternal drying of clothes soaked on the fells, the . . .

"Don't be silly, Adam," Cherry broke in indignantly. "Of course a farmer's wife is kept at it, but there's all sorts o' compensations, and I'm not meaning the Fairs, though they all go to them, cheesemaking or no. She's helping her husband to build up summat real, isn't she? And besides . . ." there was a moving earnestness in her, "I'm thinking of them two lambs, Adam. They'll live now, and . . . well, it's wonderful to be able to help like that . . . to watch things grow, and . . ."

They were near the village and, happier than ever, Adam stared at Modesty, but revealed nothing of his thoughts as he eyed the little farm. He had not been long enough in the Dale, he knew, to decide what the remainder of his life's work should be.

"Bart's soon left Fronick," Cherry exclaimed when the milliner's young man appeared over the hump of the Brig. "Because of working out the Pay I expect. He'll be wanting to make an early start to-morrow."

Reminded by thumps against his thigh at every step, Adam pulled up the oncomer to inquire about a mining analyst. This information he obtained, but not until he had satisfied the suddenly eager clerk that the find, if of value at all, was trivial.

"Nay," he told Cherry, when they were alone again, "it's more a question that I'm curious about the slags than owt else."

Along Main Street, aware that gossip was linking their names, they walked quickly, their conversation largely to do with Agnes.

"She came to ask my opinion of some patterns," Cherry smiled. "And I know she's often at Smithy House to see Fronick."

"And she's legged it twice to Greets," Adam laughed. "Yes, she's coming more out of her shell."

They did not linger at the gate of Yew Tree House. This allowed Adam time before supper to write a letter for enclosure in a parcel on whose contents he desired a professional report.

2

Stylish clothes effect a transformation in anyone hitherto shabbily dressed, but in Agnes Pedley's case they did more. From a childish-looking little creature she became at once a young woman, a tiny, doll-like young woman it was true, but one whose figure, equally staggering discovery, was nicely ripening.

On the evening of the entertainment, before leaving the cottage in Back Lane, Ambrose Pedley repeated his warning from the threshold.

"Yes, that's understood," said Adam. "I'll bring her home then."

"Wi' tinkling ornaments about their feet," Agnes's father remarked obscurely.

Soon after that the stairs creaked and, in striking contrast to the dingy kitchen, Agnes entered.

"*Well*, lass," Adam greeted her, dumbfounded. "It is Agnes, isn't it? Now then, turn round and let's have a proper look at you."

Skirts fluttering, she pirouetted for him, her manner shyly arch. Then she took off the new dark blue mantle, to display a light blue dress and a thin necklace of jet, her sole ornament. A dark blue bonnet, trimmed with ribbon matched to the dress, framed her alabaster-like cheeks, allowing a glimpse of flaxen hair, the whole blue-eyed effect perfection.

"How do you like me, Cousin Adam?" she asked.

"You're a real knock-out, lass," Adam laughed. "From now on I reckon I shall have to keep a sharp watch on you and the lads."

She crowed with pleasure, and half-bemazed with sheer joy buttoned up her mantle before going out with him. Cold easterly winds crept round the shoulder of Usha Beacon but, more important, it was fine.

"It'd never do for a peacock such as you to get bedraggled." Adam smiled.

"Oooh, I am pleased you're pleased," she said excitedly, "because I were so anxious about everything. I couldn't make up my mind about shoes—I've getten new ones, Cousin Adam."

She insisted upon stopping to show him her soft, black calf shoes, but the footwear amply discussed, became quite mute, a flood of painful colour investing her cheeks. On Dolly Bridge her hand tightened upon her cousin's arm, until the gloved fingers began to nip.

"Cousin Adam," she started off, her voice quivering. "I . . . I . . ."

"Now what is it, lass?" Adam encouraged her.

After several false beginnings, the answer arrived with a rush: "Cousin Adam, I bought everything new, as you telled me. New under . . . underthings an' all."

"Very sensible, too," Adam remarked. "But," he closed an eye, "that's one thing I haven't heard, remember."

She forgot her embarrassment. "You haven't heard . . ." Then she guessed what he meant. "Oh, you are funny," she giggled.

At Town Foot the younger Blenkirons had been leaving their home when Cherry came out of her uncle's, and as Arthur Nattrass and his young lady, Annamaria Rutter, walking up from Half, were crossing the bottom of Jom High Road, Agnes had a foretaste of the surprise her appearance would cause. The young men were frankly complimentary, and the young ladies enthused over her, though Miss Rutter rather spoilt things by inquiring, with genuine interest, where the money had been found.

As the party passed Ash Grove, Reuben Nattrass joined in.

"Well, Cherry love, I'se looking forward to hearing you sing tonight," he shouted, "but I'm a sight more looking forward to swinging you off your feet at after."

Arthur Nattrass invariably followed his redoubtable cousin's lead. "Aye," he boasted, "we'll make t'lasses wonder where they are."

The East Side's agent was jabbing a finger towards Adam, his dark-eyed glance hard. They had seldom met, but latterly, in their small encounters, his antagonism had been more sharp-set.

"So you're still here," he mocked.

"In person, mister," Adam nodded. "And likely to remain a fairish while."

Reuben Nattrass laughed. "I shouldn't have thought that there big company i' Spain could have spared your valuable services so long."

"Yes," Arthur Nattrass lowered his tone for comic relief, "he's a real important figure in lead-mining out there."

"Which is more than you are here, lad," Wingy Blenkiron grinned.

Fronick tugged her brother's arm. "Clarkson!" she reproved him.

This affront, in the presence of young women, particularly incensed Arthur Nattrass.

"I'm noan one, Blenkiron, who'd let out at a chap who can't defend himself properly," he said in measured accents. "But I can tell you this: you'd be flattened on t'ground by now if——"

"Don't talk so daft, Arthur," Annamaria Rutter broke in. "You're just aping that big gorilla cousin of yours, and I'm sick and tired of——"

"Gorilla, eh! Annamaria, my love," Reuben Nattrass chuckled. "All the same, my girl," he continued, his mood changing, "if you don't guard——"

Miss Rutter snorted. "Gorilla, that's it," she declaimed. "Wi' nowt above the eyes save the one idea that beef and brawn is superior to owt else."

To the ill-concealed pleasure of all, she relentlessly attacked him until they reached the fringe of the crowd near the Literary Institute.

With Cherry and his cousin on either side, Adam stepped off the kerb for quicker going when their path was barred by a man who, if wealth of hair and tangled beard were any criterion, had renounced the barber's scissors to the same extent as Ambrose Pedley.

James Pedley held up his hand. "Agnes," he demanded, "for what purpose are you here?"

Superficially he was the counterpart of his younger brother, with the same sallow complexion and hollowness of cheek. But the essential differences were marked. Whereas Agnes's father's lips were full and moist, his eyes dark and gloomy, and his character basically insignificant, James Pedley was dominant, his lips thin lines, his eyes extraordinarily pale.

"To enjoy herself at th'entertainment I hope, Mr. Pedley," Adam said. "But she won't be dancing, there'll be none of that . . ." some demon put the words into his mouth, "of that tinkling bells round the ankles business."

There was another resemblance: under stress of feeling James Pedley's voice, too, rose higher.

"You . . ." he spluttered. "You . . . you'd stand afore me an' garble the Word, holy words that——"

Lightly Adam patted his shoulder. "I'm not standing long, Mr. Pedley, because I'm off inside . . . for a pleasant evening that'll noan earn a black mark in the Maker's book either for me or them I'm wi'. Good night."

Leaving behind an orator adept at swaying a gathering, Adam grasped the girls' arms and urged them into the throng.

Already most of the chairs in the back room of the Literary Institute were taken up, with Mrs. Roberty Will and her friend Mrs. Skidmore amongst the elect in the centre of the front row. Adam, Dinah joining them in the side aisle, piloted his charges to convenient seats, Cherry and her friend, as artistes due to appear, selecting the two end ones. A few minutes later Mrs. Richard Blenkiron's brother, Mr. Martin Rutter, opened the proceedings with a few repetitive references to the Sunday School harmonium, to whose reconditioning the proceeds were being devoted.

The Winterings Glee Party occupied the platform first, but subsequently the items were individual: Adam's cousin Isa, Mrs. Ralph Skidmore, a tall and angular young woman, obliged with *Evening bringeth my heart back to thee*, and dismal-faced Sam Kirkbride, engineer to the West Side Company, brought the house down with *Don't be after ten.* Mrs. Emma Ann Metcalfe, a crushed-looking little person, sang *Little Gipsy* with unbelievable vivacity, and Cuthbert Daykin, a gentleman of uneasy aplomb and no chin, made the rafters ring with *A Warrior Bold.*

"I'll bet," Will Skidmore grinned, screening the side of his mouth, "I'll bet Cuthbert's noan so much of a warrior bold if Cyprian Metcalfe ever cops him sweethearting with Emma Ann."

"For shame, Will." Susan Skidmore laughed.

"Well, the two shops are convenient for 'em," Annamaria Rutter said loudly.

Amongst other talent, Cherry Dinsdale and Dinah Skidmore received a great ovation for the duet *Far Away*, and the room resounded for the schoolmaster, Mr. Kidd, a volley of handclapping masking an undercurrent of tittering when, from the old square piano, long coat-tails dangling, he bowed in acknowledgment. As usual the march in *Judas Maccabeus* had been his choice, and as always his fingers sped ever faster, the later stages a mad race with more split notes than true.

The real stars, however, were Mark Iveson, wonderful in imitating birds and beasts, and Mark Tiplady, a superb baritone. There was not the slightest sound while the shepherd recaptured the dawn awakening of moor life, and long before the voice of Mr. Kearton's poacher son-in-law had died away in *Good-night, Beloved* many in his audience were fumbling for handkerchiefs.

"A grand do." Adam nodded enthusiastically at the end.

After an aside to Cherry, he began to search for his cousin amidst the general confusion; the musicians were pushing through with their stands; chalk, dusted on the floor, was being slid on; and eager helpers whisked away the chairs. Agnes was not in sight, nor, when he edged into the Reading Room, could he see her there.

The fact was that Agnes, aglow with her triumph, felt capable of coping with anything. When, in the lobby, she found herself close to Bull Waggott, she was quite confident, though her legs trembled. She even risked a glance under her long lashes—he was still staring at her, deliberately staring.

"So this is where you are, Agnes lass," her cousin called.

She tossed her head, becoming for a few seconds a very consequential little miss indeed. Aware of being observed, she protested prettily about leaving so soon.

"Can't I stop for just *one* dance?" she wheedled.

"Do you think it's wise, lass?" Adam asked her.

She laughed lightly. "You can't always be wise, Cousin Adam."

Adam considered. "No, maybe not, lass. But if you remember we agreed it was advisable to make changes gradually."

All at once her eyes brimmed. "All right, I'll . . . I'll go if I have to." Cruelly disappointed, she hardly spoke while walking to Town Foot, but Adam coaxed her into better spirits before they reached Back Lane.

Ambrose Pedley peered at his daughter, and then, rising, picked up the candlestick, With the light held above his head he goggled at her, fascinated, speechless.

"A right knockout, isn't she?" Adam chuckled.

"Oh, I have enjoyed myself, Father," Agnes cried. "And ever so many nice things were said to me. Mrs. Harker o' Low Bands telled me as how——"

Abruptly, gripping her shoulders, Ambrose Pedley held her at arm's length, his dark eyes demanding.

"You've getten some idolatrous perfume on you, girl. It assails my nostrils wi' it's wicked scent an'——"

"It's nobbut lavender water wi' summat else, Father," Agnes shivered. "Lots of young women have it . . . it's refreshing like."

Adam laughed heartily, the gist of his succeeding observations that though he had every respect for the man who kept to the narrow path there were also certain disadvantages.

"A chap like that knows nowt about the world," he scoffed. "Lavender water, eh! Why, Mr. Gladstone never steps out without reeking of it, and t'ladies of the royal family dollop it on all ends."

Ambrose Pedley's head jerked forward. "How do you know?"

"Advertisements," Adam replied unblushingly. "Huh . . . lavender water, eh! You know . . ." he was very serious, "I can't but think that such as you, as yearns to save folk, would forward the matter better if you went about more. Say you investigated for yourself whether or not there was harm in . . . well, a decently conducted public house, young people dancing, a hand o'——"

Agnes's father started. "I'll never lend my presence to——"

"No, it'd take courage, the highest courage," Adam interposed.

"I've got courage," Ambrose Pedley retorted.

"Yes, but could you stand your name ringing through the Dale as the one who, heedless of pain to himself, had probed deeply before pronouncing?" Adam demanded. "No, it'd be too hard, a sort of—what's the word? . . . martyrdom, isn't it?"

"That's it, martyrdom," Ambrose Pedley muttered.

Adam held up a warning finger. "And what happens to martyrs, eh? Oh aye, I know that folk gather in good numbers to listen to your brother James, but dare you face a storming multitude maybe four or fivefold bigger? That's t'sort of courage you'd need." This said, he then referred to a more commonplace matter: James Pedley's interference outside the Literary Institute.

His mood somewhat pensive, Ambrose Pedley announced he would speak to his brother. "As if I'd 'low my daughter to set forth on owt unseemly," he complained. "Me, who when all the chapels' preaching plans is arranged is almost as much in demand as he is."

"Aye, I'm telled you don't quite draw the crowds as he does," Adam murmured before calling attention to Agnes. "A bonny young lady, isn't she?"

From then, it seemed as if fear were invading Ambrose Pedley's burning eyes. But when, perhaps relieved by his acceptance of the change in her, she put her arms about his neck, his grasp tightened around the budding figure.

"I . . . I were in error i' reproving her," he stammered.

Suddenly Agnes Pedley became daring. Releasing herself, she scolded him for crumpling a beautiful dress, to hang up which she must go upstairs immediately. Gaily, too, she ordered her cousin to return to the Literary Institute.

"Yes, off you go, Cousin Adam," she said imperiously as she slipped towards the stairfoot. "And thank you for taking me an' bringing me back. . . . It's been right lovely, Cousin Adam, and I'll leave something on the stone shelf for you for when you get back an' . . ."

"Take a breath, lass." Adam smiled.

Finally, her blue eyes loving, she told him how much she hoped he would enjoy himself the remainder of the evening.

"Thanks, lass," Adam replied, his glance very kind.

Even after the pattering sounds of her feet had died away, her father stared towards the darker corner where she had stood. Then, a little uncertainly, he found his chair.

"Well, I think I'll be off," Adam announced.

"Aye, do," Ambrose Pedley muttered. "Because I want to be alone, to devote serious thought to what you've said, lad. An' soon also I shall sink down to express thanks in another matter, for your presence here to-night. You see when my nostrils were offended wi' that smell . . . well," he moaned, "I were wicked enough to wonder if she were bedecked like them who set snares for the gross appetites o' sinful men . . . them who perfume their beds with myrrh, aloes, and cinnamon, them who anoint themselves an' use t'powders of the merchants."

Pity in him, Adam eyed the woebegone figure, the tortured face.

"Do all the praying you feel the need of," he said into the stillness. "But just remember this, that you've got as good and sweet a daughter as any man could wish for."

More time had been spent at Back Lane than he had reckoned on, and the short cut by Calvert's Wynd was tempting. When outside, he slithered down the bank to the river and, springing from slab to slab of the Hippy Stones in the gloom, crossed the low but swift-moving waters of the Skew.

Mrs. Hannah Batty, wearing an old cloth cape, elastic-sided boots and high black bonnet, was standing at her door, on her arm the waterproof, draw-string bag she always carried on errands of compassion. Handicapped by slack, black cotton gloves, she was making heavy weather of the search through a dozen or more dog-eared cards, each with a loop of twine, for use on certain occasions. The inscriptions varied; amongst them were: CLOSED INDEFINATELY, LYING IN BED, and BACK IN ONE HOUR, HELP YOURSELF. On each was a small drawing, a sheep's head, a coffin, and so on, word pictures far easier for an unlettered old woman to recognise than the phrases written out for her.

"Here it is, t'rascal," she muttered, picking out a baby's head, with wording: OPEN TO-MORROW AFTERNOON.

"Well, now!" The deep voice startled her. "When exactly does that mean you're open? Supposing I'd nobbut seen it in t'morning?"

Mrs. Batty smiled broadly at Adam. "Less o' your cleverness, young man. If it'd meant th'afternoon *after* to-morrow I should have put the Siamese twins up. That 'ud mean I suspected the labour were going to be prolonged."

"Oh," said Adam.

"Hey!" she cried, the change unexpected. "You gallop off to th' Institute and tell Harry Blaydes I've had word from Half that his wife's pains have come on sudden."

"Harry Blaydes . . . right. That's . . ."

"Th'assistant smelter to Jonas Cottingham," Mrs. Batty explained. "You know, him with the bad chest. Whist mad he is."

The clue sending him post-haste to the card-room, Adam quickly rooted out his quarry, who promptly abandoned leg-pulling table companions.

One end of the entrance lobby of the Literary Institute was in use as an unofficial smoke-room. Adam, while hanging up his overcoat, saw Reuben Nattrass striding towards the outer door. The mine-agent jerked his head sideways to summon two henchmen along with him, but whereas Bull Waggott responded the other wavered.

"Come on, lads," Reuben Nattrass grunted. "A few brandies at t'Plug 'ul put us in better fettle for the women when we come back."

"Eh, I don't know, Reuben," Arthur Nattrass mumbled.

His cousin stopped. "Suit yourself, but if you intend to wed Annamaria Rutter I reckon it's about time you started teaching her summat . . . to keep her mouth shut an' ask no questions for one thing."

Arthur Nattrass's face was scarlet. "Who the hell says it's owt to do with Annamaria?"

"Me," Reuben Nattrass jeered. "An' for why—because she frightens the daylight out on you."

"Don't talk bloody silly," Arthur Nattrass blustered. "And bloody well lead on."

The dancers were raising plenty of dust to the tune of the *Dolly Varden Polka*, played by a band of four: Hugh Bearpark, the West Side Company's carpenter, bassoon; Nathan Wharton, the Wood Yard sawyer and Nick Pratt, the archer, whose every knuckle was mal-shaped, crushed in carrying out his occupation, fiddlers; and Mr. Kidd, piano. Many young ladies were dancing together, another indication of the blight which had taken so many young men away from Skewdale.

When the music ended and the majority of the gentlemen were mopping their brows and the ladies wafting small handkerchiefs, Cherry, in a pretty lace jacket, came to Adam.

"What did Agnes's father think of her?" she asked.

Adam grinned. "She made the same kind of impression that I imagine Dinah does on chaps."

"How do you mean?" Dinah's friend inquired coldly.

"Nowt," Adam replied in haste. "But at afterwards . . ." He eyed her suspiciously. "And if behind that frozen front you've put on you aren't giggling, then I'll eat my hat. Now come on, out with it."

Cherry almost choked. "I know," she confessed. "When me an' Dinah's at Corvy, gentlemen raise their hats to her, and talk about staring——"

"Their whole attention 'ul noan be on Dinah, I'll bet," Adam remarked.

" 'Course if you're going to talk that silly way," Cherry said.

"All right, then," Adam smiled.

Bustling about began as Mr. Kidd's sausage-like fingers pounded the preliminary notes for the *Lord of Lorne Lancers*, forerunner of further waltzes, galops, barn dances, polkas and quadrilles, none of which Adam missed.

At the interval young ladies hastened off to repair damages sustained at the hands of over-vigorous partners, and on their return were provided with cups of tea and plates of buns, fetched for them by the young men, from the refreshment counter set up in the Library.

Just before the resumption Reuben Nattrass appeared, curly black-hair dishevelled. He reeled towards a small group.

"Now, Cherry love," he said, "what about showing 'em what you an' me can do?"

"I'm sorry but I'm booked up," she told him.

"All th'extras and all?" he growled. "Now look here——"

"Aye, I've been lucky enough to get the promise of any extras there might be," Adam interrupted. "A case, isn't it," he continued affably, "of the early bird catching the worm?"

Reuben Nattrass rocked round and with lowering brow listened while Adam, with a courtliness which would have done credit to a Spaniard, apologised in flowery terms to Cherry for so likening her. Then he stabbed a finger into the speaker's shoulder.

"I'm beginning to think I shall have to do summat about you," he hiccoughed, blinking owlishly. "But that can wait. Aye, I ought to have been back sooner, Cherry lass, but I'se no grudge against you. I've never valued owt that fell into my lap."

He turned again, saw Adam and, still swaying, doubled his arm back, "No," he muttered, before lurching off, "not in the presence of ladies."

Meantime, nearby, there was a disturbance of a more serious nature.

"You'll never do this again to me, Arthur," Annamaria Rutter stormed. "Oh no, you'll never again make me into a wallflower while you're out half th'evening in a public. And just because——"

"Ssssh." Dinah Skidmore tried to quieten her.

Arthur Nattrass was not drunk and, as usual, endeavoured to carry off a difficult situation as befitted his own conception of himself. Leaning negligently against the wall, he toyed with the watchchain visible beneath a cutaway coat, swinging the charm which dangled from it.

"Just because you think it's grand to bask in your cousin Reuben's supposed glory," Miss Rutter went on, dogged as ever. "How much longer——"

"Don't go on any more," Fronick Blenkiron begged, her face red with embarrassment. "Everybody's listening."

"That's an unusual luckstone," Adam remarked. "Have you seen this, Cherry, on Arthur's chain?"

"Yes, it's right unique," Cherry nodded. "And so dainty."

The luckstone was a pretty little thing, about the size of a sixpence and as thick as a wedding ring. Its colour was pale grey, with a single, fine, purple vein.

"Never have it off me 'cept when I'm abed," Arthur Nattrass informed them. "As to how it's kept watch and ward over me," he leered at Adam, "and I'm noan speaking about t'dangers met with underground——"

Adam coughed significantly. Annamaria was glancing their way.

"Nearly made another mullock, didn't I, Adam lad?" Arthur Nattrass chortled.

The band struck up the opening bars of the *No Name Galop* and Adam, dispatched by Cherry's approving smile, lost not a moment in claiming Miss Rutter.

If anything the second part of the evening was jollier than the first, right to the final waltz, the *Beautiful Danube*, which Adam had with Cherry, his arm, lightly round her waist, not being withdrawn until, under Mr. Kidd's tearaway hands, *God Save the Queen* terminated the proceedings. After that was the usual scramble for coats and scarves hung one above another along an inadequate number of hooks, and then, inch by inch, dancers and whist-players shuffled towards the door. In this tight press Mr. Kearton was a close neighbour of Cherry and Adam.

"Your uncle hasn't been to-night, lass." The joiner frowned as though personally offended. "An' isn't he fishing this season at all? First time he hasn't been wi' me to teach Mr. Wade and t'vicar of Greets what trout fishing really is."

Outside, a small party of friends gradually congregated. They talked together a while before Wingy Blenkiron departed for Snorr with Dinah, when the remainder began to walk towards the bracket lamp at Nick Turn, the sole street light in the village.

Adam, Cherry's evening slippers tucked into his pocket, held her arm. She was very quiet, and he inquired if she were tired.

She shook her head. "No, it's nobbut that I'm bothered about Uncle Titus. They're finding the New Drift very hard to drive, which makes it cost more, and he's fretting a lot, though he does his best to hide it."

"He's getting on," Adam said very tentatively. "Couldn't he retire?"

She did not speak again until they were beyond the yellowing rays of the oil-lamp. "He wouldn't even if he could, Adam, not till the West Side Company is better placed. He feels it's his responsibility."

Neither of them said much after that and, as Annamaria Rutter and Arthur Nattrass were even more silent, it was left for Fronick Blenkiron to fill the gap. She did it nobly, chattering all the way about her orders for Whitsun bonnets.

At Town Foot farewells were not delayed. Cherry went in home, Fronick and Bart crossed to say good-bye in the inky blackness a few yards up Sorrow Near, Annamaria and Arthur continued down the highway, and Adam turned up towards Dolly Bridge, from the middle of which he heard that his cousin Arthur's young lady had by no means lost her tongue.

On entering his lodgings, Adam lighted a candle, threw off his overcoat, and unloosed the laces of his boots. Next he foraged in the pantry, bringing out a glass of milk, the top of which was covered by a plate with a broad wedge of seed cake on it. No sooner had he seated himself than footsteps creaked the stairs, and appreciably later Ambrose Pedley stumbled into the kitchen in his night-shirt, feeling for the furniture as if needing support.

"You're right bad!" Adam exclaimed in concern. "Now get into your chair while I nip up for my whisky flask."

"Whisky!" Agnes's father repeated, horrified. But he did not rant on about a suggestion which, to him, must have been monstrous. "No, I want no fiery spirit that . . ." his soft lips trembled, "that fires a man's brain."

"What about tea, then?" Adam persisted. "I'll get some kindling blazing, and enough water for a pot 'ul boil in two tic-tacs."

There was a weary refusal. "I'm ill, lad, but my ailment's spiritual an' noan material," came the shaky response. "But leave me be, leave me be, I tell you."

Adam ate and drank, occasionally glancing at the man whose stricken eyes never left the fire-back, whose lips ever moved soundlessly. The snack finished, he quietly placed glass and plate on the stone slab and, Ambrose Pedley in the same unvarying position, tip-toed upstairs.

In the bedroom he indulged in thoughts more important than those concerning an unbalanced individual. "No . . ." he concluded, perhaps a quarter of an hour later, "I've th'inclination, but as yet I don't know enough to weigh up properly the pros and cons of settling in Skewdale. And that, anyhow, depends on whether somebody else will ever think of me as I do of her. Then there's her uncle to consider—she's noan one who'd leave him in the lurch, specially at a time when he needs plenty of care and sympathy."

In less than five minutes he had decided there could be no harm in keeping money quickly available. With as little noise as possible he opened a swollen drawer in the old chest, lifting out writing paper, pen, and a bottle of ink. The candlelight emphasising the strong lines of his face, he wrote to the Leadenhall Street office of the London and Andajoz Lead and Silver Mining Company requesting them to transfer a substantial portion of his funds to a Corvy bank.

3

The last days of the month were cheerless, with showers of sleet driving from the north-east, and it was particularly desolate on the evening when the men of the village carried the Maypole on their shoulders to Francis Harker's pasture at Low Bands, the strongest supporting the butt-end of the lengthy larch.

May Day was better, but conditions up the fellside, a skin of thaw on frozen ground, made going treacherous in the race for the Maidens'

Garland, an event taking place in the morning. Both start and finish were on the hump of Winterings Brig, the course along Sorrow Near to Juniper Wood, thence up icy Heugh Syke Gill to the trod high above Half, which the runners followed, along the cliff-like edge of the first great terrace of land overlooking the Dale, to reach Mine Road and Notion Bridge.

The competitors were seen off by a large crowd, the traditional signal for the start being given by Dinah Skidmore who, the previous evening, had drawn the longest apple twig. Scarlet with embarrassment, she was hoisted by a couple of muscular young men on to the square, stone post at the end of the bridge parapet, and from that elevated position dropped a handkerchief. A cheer went up, the clatter of clogged feet resounded in Main Street, and the race for the Garland had begun.

At Milton Hall Adam was running third, but in the slippery ascent of Heugh Syke Gill he lost ground to the agile dalesmen. On the trod he gained once more, attaining his former place at the bridge connecting North and South Smelt Mills.

From there the route led up Foul Syke Gill, easy enough as far as the intake supplying the buckets of Big William, but thereafter extremely tricky. The track, mounting alongside the deepening gill, rose abruptly towards the summit of thundering Joss Foss, its surface an outcrop of shale sloping towards the ravine. Near the top a minor accident occurred which might have had fatal consequences.

In his own fall Adam pinned the legs of the heavily-breathing man in front, arresting him when head and shoulders, hanging over the void, pointed to the spray and jagged rocks sixty or seventy feet below.

" No . . . damage, Len," he winced, feeling a scraped elbow. "Lucky I came a cropper, too."

Len Rukin, a groover hailing from Wensleydale, who with his friend Hugh Bearpark lived during the week in one of the changing shops of the West Side Company, pulled himself up. He was a dark-complexioned young man, with a marked blue jowl.

"Aye, or otherwise," he nodded into the depths, "there'd have been a right grand funeral our way, Adam lad."

The remaining yards of the ascent they took cautiously together, but after that, up the switchback sheep-trod which wound amongst the birches and rowans fringing Foul Syke Gill, it was each man for himself. Over this kind of country Adam once again improved and, on reaching Legatt's Way, along which the course continued as far as the towering shoulder of Kettle Dub, he was not far behind the leader.

From Kettle Dub homewards, down moor and pasture towards Modesty, the contest became a nightmare. Apart from an occasional levelling out, the slope was that of a high-pitched roof, with the further hazards of gullies, scars and old hushes. Hesitation was often more disastrous than calculated recklessness, with the result that every man, selecting his own line, tore downhill without imposing much check.

There were many misfortunes: Bart Hugill somersaulted, finishing below the icy slush of a pool; Wingy Blenkiron skidded on the flat of his back the full length of the rough approach road to Dubbing Quarry; Bull Waggott went over a small waterfall, to emerge with blood streaming down his cheek; and Hugh Bearpark crashed amidst a band of hushing debris.

It was exhilarating, Adam found, this wild competitive progress, and of it all nothing was more exhilarating than the spectacle of a raven-haired giant who, on one amazing leap, dramatically brought himself far ahead of any rival.

"By God!" he panted after a tumble, watching Reuben Nattrass from his knees. "I believe he's going straight for yon deep gorge."

The ravine towards which the mine-agent raced was guarded on the moor side by a wall. He took it unflinchingly, to fly in an arc with a drop beneath him the height of a three-storied house. On the farther side he landed with not more than a few inches of secure foothold behind him, and then, crouching low, shot down the steep slope beyond, his clog-irons acting as runners on the frozen surface.

"Champion!" Adam ejaculated, in warm praise of a magnificent feat. "He could have bashed himself to bits if he'd faltered."

The runners were spread over the black-and-white mottled fellside, and although those behind had no prospect of winning, none abated his efforts, a hell-for-leather company still. Adam, like them, put his best foot forward, to speed down towards the crowd on the Snorr side of Winterings Brig.

The entrants for the Maidens' Garland wore their oldest breeches or trousers and, despite the cold morning, were in shirts and braces. When the last of the tatterdemalions had disappeared round Nick Turn, Cherry and Dinah, taking Agnes with them, entered the cheery kitchen of the Plug and Feathers, where many ladies were gathering to pass the interval before the runners' return. Meantime Mrs. Peacock hospitably provided sweet biscuits and steaming cups of coffee for all comers.

Cherry had hardly got indoors when Mrs. Roberty Will beckoned to her. She went across to the older woman, to be promptly greeted with a sharp question. "You're oft with that lass of Ambrose Pedley's," the mistress of Malaga began. "How is it you're taking up with her all of a sudden?"

In time, Cherry remembered that her uncle had to be careful with his sister-in-law, who had a large interest in the West Side Company. "I don't know as I have, Mrs. Alderson," she answered civilly. "But she's going about more now, you know."

A gold locket heaved on an ample bosom. "Is that th'only reason?" Mrs. Roberty Will inquired.

Desperately Cherry hoped she was not blushing when she replied lightly: "Whatever other reason could there be, Mrs. Alderson?"

As Mrs. Roberty Will did not deign to reply, Cherry was able to return to her friends, all of whom, save Agnes, were savouring the hot coffee. The explanation of the omission soon followed, when Lucy Peacock arrived with a ruby-filled glass.

Agnes eyed the wine as if it were the Devil's brew. "I . . . I couldn't, Mrs. Peacock," she stammered. "I . . ."

"It's medicinal," her hostess snapped. "Now sup it up an' no more nonsense."

Cajoled by those about her, Dr. Seaton's name being freely invoked in support of the drink's tonic effects, her scruples were at last overcome. The centre of interest, she continued to be discussed.

"But she *is* looking a lot better, isn't she?" Cherry urged.

"And I should hope so," nodded Dinah, sternly eyeing the culprit. "Fancy excitement making you poorly for days an' days."

The sequel to Agnes Pedley's heady triumph on the evening of the entertainment had been grievous, and for some days afterwards she had been pitifully lethargic. She was far less wan now, and the greyish-purple shadows beneath her eyes had almost faded.

This social occasion lasted about half an hour longer, when everyone crossed the Brig to walk a little up the main road, to a point beyond Modesty allowing an uninterrupted view of the high line of Water Ling Moor. Interest tautened when Puke Hastwell, head man at the Wood Yard, announced the impending appearance at Kettle Dub of the first of the runners.

In the ensuing silence Agnes Pedley's not very robust voice was heard clearly. "I hope Cousin Adam wins 'cause he won't have t'chance next year. But if——" a belch checked possible revelations.

Annamaria's horse-laugh rang out, and, despite her cousin Fronick's anguished nudge, she persisted in stating the obvious: "It's that port wine, it's gone to her head."

Cries were now rising. Four fast-striding competitors for the Garland were silhouetted against the pale grey sky, and when Reuben Nattrass made the fifth his adoring sister let it be known. She exhorted him the whole way down and kissed him with abandon when he trotted in an easy winner.

"Eh, Reuben lad," she shouted, her angular face wreathed in smiles, "you've done it again. But talk about having my heart in my mouth . . ."

Dinah Skidmore looked thoroughly disgusted. "I think Isa's awful. Reuben might be her husband by the way she carries on."

"Ralph doesn't seem to care, does he?" Cherry remarked.

"Because he's just a cold fish," Dinah retorted.

When the last runner arrived, the crowd streamed back to form up in a close semi-circle before the Plug and Feathers. There, standing on the cobbles in front of the mounting block, Reuben Nattrass's head was crowned with the victor's garland by a very small girl, the youngest scholar in the Day School, who received a kiss for her pains.

Three cheers terminated the ceremony and the gathering was thinking of dispersing when, in the narrow gap between Modesty and a clump of spruce and Scots pines behind the farmhouse, a couple of small figures were perceived plodding down the fellside. Ten minutes later, between lines of spectators clapping every step, two fair-haired boys, each about nine years old, panted on to the Brig, to end up dramatically sprawling on the parapet.

"Champion, lads," Mr. Kearton shouted to them, watch in the palm of his hand. "Allowing for the state underfoot I reckon you've improved nicely on last year."

"It were real bad i' places, Grandfather," Ward Tiplady, the snub-nosed one, said. "Weren't it, Bob?"

The other, Bob Skidmore, square-jawed like his father, straightened up manfully. "Never seen owt like it in my experience," he summed up.

That not only raised a roar of laughter but gave Arthur Nattrass a suitable opening. Annamaria's tall young man had had a nasty toss on Water Ling Moor, tripping over a stone protruding from the arched top of the South Smelt Mill's flue. His right leg had stiffened and he supported himself with an arm around Miss Rutter's shoulders.

"With all th'experience you two lads have got," he guffawed, "I should have thought you'd win as you liked."

Bob Skidmore eyed his cousin and was eyed in return. In consequence, suddenly acquiring a leg as rigid as a ramrod, Ward Tiplady besought Bob's aid, leaning heavily on him.

"It's noan that I'se the sort to make excuses, Bob lad," he announced jauntily. "But I've getten a real crack . . ."

"An' though I says it as shouldn't," Bob Skidmore swaggered, "I'm noan the sort to give in so long as I can stand on——"

There was another howl of amusement during which, despite the handicap of a genuinely damaged limb, Arthur Nattrass hobbled vainly in pursuit. He was not angry, however, and took the business quite philosophically.

"I were a rip myself at their age," he grinned. "An' they're not any worse for it, are they?"

"I don't like impertinence all the same," their grandfather snapped. "An' when I see them youngsters next . . ."

Greatly pleased by this entertaining wind-up, the crowd, in mass, began to move along Main Street. Amongst the closely-packed company was Mrs. Ralph Skidmore, heading for Ash Grove with her brother, upon whose shoulders perched his nieces Nancy and Harriet, a position enabling them to examine in detail the garland of yellow, glossy-petalled celandine.

"Oooh, Uncle Reuben, an' when you did that there big jump," Harriet Skidmore crowed, "I shut my eyes ever so tight, Uncle Reuben."

Her sister Nancy's eyes were not closed. She was favouring Adam with a languishing smile. "Adam . . ." she twisted farther round, "did you see Uncle Reuben do that ever so big jump?"

"I did, love," Adam said. "I were in a grand position to watch, and it were the biggest jump I've ever seen."

Mrs. Ralph Skidmore turned angrily. "Stop your chattering, Nancy, an' look to your front."

Her brother paused and, burdened with the little girls flanking his yellow garland, slewed towards Adam.

"Well . . . well, so we're going in for buttering-up, are we?" he sneered. "You've seen which way the wind's blowing, have you?"

Adam considered. "I think I have, Cousin Reuben."

"Noan so much of your *Cousin* Reuben," Reuben Nattrass growled. "Anyroad, how did you get on in t'race, or couldn't you manage the full course."

From out of the press, ruddy-faced Nathan Wharton, the sawyer, took a caustic hand. "He finished sixth, and there were some fair good foot-racers behind him at that, Reuben. Aye, he did very well."

"You reckon so, Wharton?" the mine-agent grunted. "Well, if you do you can bet your life he does an' all."

Smiling faintly, Adam eyed him. "Yes, noan so bad, taking into account as it were mostly country strange to me, Cousin Reuben."

Pressure from the rear thrusting them along, nothing more passed. Few of those present gave another thought to the matter, but Cherry Dinsdale, an exception, looked more troubled than the occasion would seem to warrant.

* * * *

After dinner Agnes Pedley, in her full array of finery, left with Adam for the May-day sports. Her father remained indoors, turning the leaves of the Bible, stubbornly bent on discovering items more unanswerable than: 'A false balance is an abomination to the Lord,' his best to date. The previous evening, hinting upon the wisdom of ascertaining whether or not some specific activities were damning sin, Ambrose Pedley had been routed by his brother James's overpowering quotations.

On the way down to the village Agnes chattered more than Adam had heard her before, but he discovered that this was merely to cloak nervousness about a request she wished to make. The cause duly emerged when she stopped on Dolly Bridge.

"Before we meet anybody there's summat I want to ask you, Cousin Adam," she faltered. "It's . . . it's summat I want to do a . . . a lot, Cousin Adam."

Adam became judicial. "State your case, lass," he advised her.

In a welter of emotion, she was too much in earnest to smile. Her blue eyes were beseeching, and her alabaster-like cheeks, framed in the blue bonnet, were flushed with anxious colour.

"I . . . I want to . . . to call you like . . . as Cherry Dinsdale and the other lasses does," she gasped. "Can I, Cousin Adam?"

"Call me like . . .?" Initially it was beyond Adam's comprehension, but then he laughed. "Oh, I see, you're another who doesn't care for the word cousin, eh? Aye, of course you can . . . Adam it is."

She gulped. "Eh, I am pleased, Cousin—Adam, I mean."

She still had something to say, but before saying it seemed to shed the air of a young lady with which her clothes invested her, to become, so Adam thought, a very young girl again.

"Adam," she began near the door of Titus Alderson's office, "there's summat else an' all."

"Aye, lass," he said, waiting.

Simply, she told him. "I'm right fond o' you, Adam . . . *ever* so."

Next, the oration high-flown, he remarked that now all these important matters had been concluded, they could all the more look forward to a thoroughly lively afternoon.

Agnes glanced at him, tittered, and swung herself on his arm.

Swelled by many from distant fellside farms and tiny hamlets, the pasture at Low Bands was crowded already when Adam and his cousin entered. Immediately inside they were intercepted by Mr. Martin Rutter's unfortunate son who, a few nights before, when bringing a bunch of soldiers' buttons to Back Lane, had excitedly told Agnes of an idea which would give his loved mare Polly great pleasure. Briefly, it was that, on Sundays, after feeding and watering her at the mine, he would ride her to Winterings Common Pasture for a change of scene. It was now discussed again.

"Yes, and I'll tell you what, I'll meet you an' Polly at t'pasture," Agnes said, smiling. "Maybe Adam'll come with me sometime."

"I will that," Adam nodded. "And between us we'll think up some tit-bit for Polly that even Bill's never taken to her."

Dribbling at the corners, Mazy Bill's mouth opened still wider in his delight, which made it all the more difficult for him to explain another idea. This concerned the staunch friendship between Polly and Ben.

While the young pair examined seriously this proposition, Adam's attention lingered on a party of three whose conversation had little to do with May-day afternoon. In strict truth, Mr. Wade, of Half House, was doing scant talking, this devolving upon Mr. Rutter, who appeared not at all loath, and Mrs. Alderson, the latter often emphasising her points by tapping the ferrule of her black silk umbrella upon the rough grass. Suspecting that these deliberations concerned the West Side Company, Adam wondered, when Titus Alderson approached, a sea-captain ashore, if the small party would be augmented.

"Hey, Titus!" Mrs. Roberty Will shouted, favouring Adam's length with a glance more reminiscent of Mr. Kearton, the undertaker, "we want you over here."

Farther along the pasture, Mr. Kidd rang the school-bell to announce the first of the children's races.

"Ha!" the aldermanic proportioned chairman of the West Side Company exclaimed, palpably relieved. "Must be off now or I'll never dare drive past my own lodge again. Promised Blaydes' eldest, Mrs. Alderson, that I'd watch her run to-day. Never do to break my promise, would it?"

Mrs. Robert William Alderson smiled bleakly. "I suppose not, Mr. Wade. But perhaps at after the race we might resume our chat. Of course I'm not a director, and I recognise I've no right to put my fillings in, but nevertheless it shouldn't be forgotten that I'm deeply involved."

"Quite," said Mr Wade.

"To be proper frank, Mr. Wade," Mrs. Roberty Will continued, "I think sometimes that it's lost sight of that I am t'largest shareholder in the Company. Yes, I do really."

"No, I won't have that, Mrs. Alderson," Mr. Wade replied, absolute conviction in his fruity voice. "None of us is ever . . . er . . . forgets it. And there's the bell again." Raising his hat hastily, and mumbling about 'Blaydes'' girl, he departed with considerable alacrity.

Two shamed spots coloured Titus Alderson's grey cheeks; his sister-in-law's tone had been very sharp.

"Who'd be a mining-agent i' Skewdale, Adam lad?" he inquired with a laugh, passing it off. "An' now then, Bill, what is it you're up to with this well-turned-out young lady?"

As his cousin seemed perfectly happy with her escorts, a white-bearded old man and a shambling youth whose stiff-necked head wobbled with joy, Adam wandered off to search for Cherry. She was with Dinah, helping to place the younger children on their marks for the handicap race.

In the last two events of the series, the inseparables, Bob and Ward, cantered home in the three-legged race; and Ward's sister, Mary Jane, briefly relinquishing the cares of housekeeping at Lane End, emerged third from the final barrel in the obstacle race for the 'under nines.'

A hectically beaten drum heralded the next diversion.

"Let's run across," Cherry proposed. "Fronick said that Wingy and her father had been doing something ever so secret lately."

Adam propelling the young ladies, the three of them speedily arrived at the site of the weight-lifting displays, where much gear was in evidence: spring-extenders, big sledge-hammers for driving stakes, and wooden clubs and weights of all sizes. The largest exhibits, however, were two pairs of black-painted spheres, joined by a round iron bar about a yard long, one of which rested at Puke Hastwell's feet.

"Nay, I'll noan be able to raise it off t'ground, never name swing it above my head," the Wood Yard foreman protested. "Why, the two ends are as big as cannon-balls."

"It's belief as 'ul do it," the blacksmith comforted him.

Mr. Hastwell, a bow-legged man with a wart on the tip of his nose, bitterly eyed a sea of grinning faces.

"Belief, nowt," he differed. "Getting me out here i' front of everybody."

Richard Blenkiron clicked his tongue despairingly. "If you do *exactly* as I say, Puke, you'll perform t'feat. I'll guarantee that. But the thought o' failure mustn't enter your head . . . you must regard picking up that appliance as if it were made of summat noan so much heavier than . . . well, say cardboard."

"You'll guarantee it?" the Wood Yard man demanded.

A ham-like fist cracked into a broad palm. "So long as you've confidence in yourself, Puke, an' *provided* you put everything you've getten into th'effort."

Puke Hastwell's wart twitched as he snorted: "I'll do that all right, if for nowt else but to make you swallow your words."

A buzz of anticipation began. Mr. Hastwell was precisely instructed how he must grasp the bar, and, when he stooped, was made to stand up again to dig heel-holes for a more secure stance. Lastly the blacksmith, impressively addressing the throng, requested absolute silence.

"I can't see properly," Cherry squeaked. "You can't either, Dinah."

Miss Skidmore had hastily withdrawn from a more favourable position on discovering herself in very close contact with a young man whom she had sent about his business the previous autumn.

"Neither of you can, eh?" Adam murmured. "Right!" He bent and, scooping his arms, lifted two young ladies each of whom only just succeeded in biting off a betraying squeal before reaching an elevation not much less commanding than that in which Reuben Nattrass had held his nieces Nancy and Harriet. "There, that do you better?" he remarked with satisfaction.

Neither of the scarlet-cheeked young women could think of any response then.

The crowd, very much on tip-toe, was watching developments.

"Now when I say 'go,' Puke," Richard Blenkiron said. "Are you ready, lad? Then . . . GO."

The roar of laughter must have carried well towards Yorrel. Puke Hastwell, in one mighty heave, certainly fulfilled his obligations, for the contraption, with its light spheres of thin copper, flew above his head. On the other hand, the iron connecting bar was reasonably weighty, and its momentum could not at once be arrested. In one unbroken movement, arms stretched high above his head, the Wood Yard's foreman fell on the flat of his back, dropping with noisy suction into the quagmire.

"A dummy," he snarled, scrambling up, "an' I might have known you Blenkiron lot were up to your tricks. And what about my clothes? My best trousers mucked fro'——"

Gently Adam lowered Cherry and Dinah who, when he left them subsequently, were still speechless. In the hubbub, unobserved by a crowd laughingly intent on Puke Hastwell, he made certain arrangements. The two sets of spheres were as alike as two peas and, smiling to himself, he thought that with care it would not be impossible to confuse their owners. Then he waited until the ripe moment, when he caught the younger Blenkiron's eye—for this once he intended to do his utmost to deceive a friend.

"Wingy," he winked expansively, "I've a mind to have a shot myself."

The postman winked back and nodded appreciatively, previous to beating a tattoo until all eyes were his way. In the midst of a public announcement, he attempted to allay any suspicions.

"Mark you, it's with the proper 'un, Adam lad," he challenged. "I'll noan be a party to any further deception."

"What do you think?" Adam inquired, up in arms.

Richard Blenkiron was quite austere, too. "Naturally," he remarked. "We've had our fun wi' Puke, but now for a genuine artiste."

While Wingy Blenkiron re-attacked the drum with one-armed frenzy, and the crowd was marshalled into its former ring, Adam devoted himself to ensuring there was no untoward investigation.

"Roll up, ladies an' gentlemen," Wingy roared. "Don't miss this opportunity of witnessing Mighty Brunskilli, the strongest man i' Spain. Aye, he's been amongst us, but only to-day has he graciously revealed . . ."

When his son's sensational exhortation ended, Richard Blenkiron, as master of ceremonies, addressed a few serious and extremely audible words to the central figure, who had divested himself down to his shirt-sleeves, Bart Hugill, as steward, taking charge of coat and overcoat.

Adam, loosening cuff-links, confided that, as opposed to lifting the spheres with a jerk, he proposed to do so slowly, a much greater test of strength and skill.

"Ah!" the blacksmith commented, deeply knowing, "the Spanish school o' levitation."

"Basque," Adam said.

"Eh . . . er . . . aye, Bask," Mr. Blenkiron floundered. "Course," he resumed, recovering gallantly, "course that's very different to th'English method. I take it, lad, you're aware of the grave risk involved?"

Relieved on this, he begged those present to bear witness that the young man had been warned, a wise provision indeed.

"Aye," he went on, plucking a gingery beard, "I've nobbut seen it attempted once afore by . . . er . . . by t'Bask way, but . . ." he shook his head, "the poor chap dropped dead a minute afterwards. Fatally ruptured, aye."

"An' where did you see that?" Matt Tiplady sang out.

"At the Great Exhibition, more years ago than I care to mention," the blacksmith retorted. "An' them who's inclined to scoff, Annamaria, 'ud better go elsewhere."

He harangued the company a little longer and then, when Wingy had sounded another volley, he gave Adam the sign, when slowly the two spheres left the ground.

There were many amused sceptics in the throng, but even the worst amongst them conceded one thing: that the young man offered a most realistic impression of the performance of a Strong Man, right down to his last step which, incidentally, was near a set of counterfeit objects. From that position, as grand finale, Wingy inspired to accompany him with a roll increasingly louder and faster, Adam lowered the spheres at full stretch, until they touched the ground, the gradual rate of descent never varying.

"Mag-nificent, lad," Richard Blenkiron boomed, shaking hands. "It'll be remembered as long as there's a Skewdale," Wingy added. "Champion, Adam," clapped Bart Hugill.

There was a good-humoured cheer. "Oh, you've all acted your parts real well, Richard," Hannah Batty cackled. "But don't think you've had us on, because you haven't."

As the crowd dispersed, Mr. Blenkiron's daughter and niece admitted to being tricked. "You know," said Fronick, wide-eyed, "how you can easily persuade yourself."

Annamaria's reason was more tangible. "It were your muscles, Adam," she declared. "They were sticking out like whipcord."

"He did that wi' gripping the connecting bar," Bart Hugill laughed.

Two other young ladies were less forthcoming with Adam. "Yes, I'm in the way o' being a fairish weight lifter," he remarked complacently to them. "You'd say that, wouldn't you?"

Cherry's attitude was ominous. "What me an' Dinah are going to say to you is something very different, Adam Brunskill," she began.

"You're not in the wilds o' Spain now," Dinah pointed out.

"And here you don't pick up young women without so much as asking their leave," Miss Dinsdale continued.

"Ingratitude!" Adam sighed, his glance sad as it rested on a scene of small activity nearby. Wingy was putting the clubs in order and Bart was inspecting a home-made chest-expander whose merit was that it would squirt a stream of black fluid into an unfortunate gymnast's face. At that moment Mr. Blenkiron bent to pick up a pair of spheres. Expecting modest resistance only, the reaction was enough to bring him down on one knee, in which position he glanced with perplexity from one set of spheres to the other.

"I could have dropped," observed Miss Skidmore.

"You could?" Adam exclaimed in concern. "Well now, I thought I were holding you firmly enough."

Blushing again, the two girls were girding themselves for relentless war, when Mr. Blenkiron's bellow aroused everyone.

"Whatever's the matter with my father?" Fronick gasped.

The blacksmith's deep laugh resounded, he slapped his thigh with force enough to stagger a two-year-old bull. "Adam, lad," he roared, "for almost a minute you've had me wondering whether at after all you'd been juggling with the real 'un."

"Juggling with that!" Bart Hugill yelped. "Not likely. Why if we hadn't stopped at Edmund Kearton's for a couple o' battens it'd have bumped a hole through t'bottom of the cart afore we got here."

"He's strong enough," Cherry murmured.

With determination she and Dinah set about reducing the object of their joint attention to a more humble frame of mind.

It was one of those strange attractions of extreme opposites, for, just as Agnes Pedley was drawn irresistibly by the sheer masculinity of Bull Waggott, so was he, who had known most of the drabs of the upper Dale, attracted in equal degree by her fresh daintiness. If he had reservations at all, these concerned his friends, who would laugh themselves silly at the notion of his pursuing in decent courtship a lass who stood not much higher than his heart.

"Anyroad," he grunted, eyeing her again, "to hell wi' other folk's opinions. She's small, right enough, but she's a real likely lass and noan one of t'flat-chested sort."

His thoughts in part pure and in part tinged with desire, he once more stared the length of Mr. Harker's crowded cart-shed, where refreshments were being served by the ladies' May-day committee.

"Aye," he remarked to himself, "at the first opportunity I'll have another go at talking her into th'idea of a walk."

Agnes Pedley was gossiping over a cup of tea with a lady much too youthfully clad, whose bright yellow hair, so the unkind vowed, owed its shade to an aromatic plant which grew in the garden she passionately cherished at Yorrel.

"A right pleasant chap, is your cousin, Agnes," Miss Caygill was saying. "But," she tittered, "a young lady can't be all that open as to how fond she is of a young man, even if they are cousins."

Agnes Pedley's chin went up. "I don't care who knows."

The dressmaker, to whom Adam had given Jane Sunter's love, might have followed up with sage advice, but she glimpsed an acquaintance. Left by herself, Agnes replaced her cup on the trestle table and, a little affectedly, sauntered from the shed. Outdoors, a powerful hand grasped her elbow and she was drawn into a narrow gap between the end wall and an old cart.

"We could go to Bloody Sigh instead," Bull Waggott urged. "Then neither your father nor anybody else 'ud see us. An' I'd have you away fro' there afore the edge of dark."

"No . . . I couldn't really," she stammered.

His bull-like face became more determined. "There's no harm in it, lass, an'," he reddened, "you'd come to no harm either. I promise that."

"No . . . no," Agnes breathed.

Her heart thumping deliriously, she backed away from him, to find and re-join her cousin.

There were still many attractions: the scholars dancing round the Maypole; the Winterings Plate, won by Wingy Blenkiron, with Adam as steed; the pole-leaping event in which Reuben Nattrass surpassed all others; the tandem race for unmarried ladies, won by Cherry and Dinah on a disqualification for obstruction; the wrestling competition final in which Bull Waggott, encouraged almost at his ear by Reuben Nattrass, pinned Cyprian Metcalfe squarely on his back. And, again, more dancing round the Maypole.

In the prevailing conditions dancing was not comfortable, and so Dinah Skidmore's friends accepted her invitation to Badger Hall with great enthusiasm.

"An' what about having a toffee-join?" she cried.

Adam had learnt what that meant. "I'll buy the sugar," he shouted.

"Right, and I'll fetch some treacle," Wingy Blenkiron declared. "Agnes lass, you'll go back wi' me for it, eh?"

Agnes started guiltily. Bull Waggott was near and, as some reward, she was glancing at him beneath her lashes and smiling slightly. This was a little womanly attention she was beginning to think men of all ages rather appreciated. When she had done it to Ned Mason, an old friend, he had raised his dark eyebrows drolly, grinned and whistled.

"Yes, I'd like, Wingy—I mean Clarkson," she said, confused.

In due course the party was made up of young folk and old, for, when

Mr. and Mrs. Skidmore gleaned what was afoot, they insisted upon the inclusion of any of their own friends who were about.

Few residences in the upper Dale could have dealt as effectively as Badger Hall with the incursion of a host of people. The brass pan was brought out for a laughing, argumentative toffee-making by the girls in the kitchen, with the young men bent on a share in stirring the bubbling-brown contents; there was dancing in the shelter of the court-yard in the shadowy light furnished by a couple of old horn lanterns; and, the ancient house providing many secluded niches, magnificent games of hide-and-seek.

Then a big supper and, after the younger women, despite Mrs. Skidmore's protests, had washed up, ballad-singing and glees, poetry reciting and the telling of old tales. And, at last, when everyone was drowsy, the final few minutes of quiet talk before the homeward trek.

"Farming for you to-morrow again, Adam?" Cherry asked, stifling a yawn. "Still lots to do?"

Adam counted off on his fingers: cutting tails, marking lambs, driving ewes and lambs to the moors, washing fat sheep, shearing . . . "Have I missed owt?" he asked his neighbour.

Anthony Skidmore, a few extraordinary spasms ravaging his features, said nothing.

Cherry gently reminded him that he had been asked a question, Dinah bestirred herself to point out it was only civil to reply, and Richard Blenkiron consulted Titus Alderson about restorative steps.

Mr. Skidmore found voice, to berate the culprits. "How many times must I tell you lasses not to make t'toffee so sticky? If you'd nobbut——"

His teeth clamped again and his efforts, as he struggled to free himself, crowned the evening. Only one thing more was needed and this the master of Badger Hall asked for as soon as he could speak.

"My own special, lad," he said.

So Matt Tiplady sang *Jesus, lover of my soul.*

With rich and lovely notes dwelling in their ears the party broke up, to walk homeward as they wished, the young people uproariously, in lines linked arm-in-arm across the width of the highway to Winterings Brig, feet in soldierly step ringing out on the frozen ground. The occasional cries of ewes and lambs and nightbirds carried very clearly and, gleaming in the starlight, the snow-dusted fell-tops looked down.

CHAPTER FIVE

I

WHEN THE lambs were three or four weeks old they and their mothers were driven back to the moors. Early one fine but windy morning, Adam and Mark Iveson, watched reproachfully from the end of a chain by the shepherd's bitch, awaited Anthony Skidmore and his son Ralph, both of whom had grazing rights on Noggin Moor.

"Aye," Mark was saying when, from along Middle Sorrow, sounds of the approaching flock were heard, "true enough it'd be gainer if this lot could just nip up behind Badger Hall on to Snorr Moor, but these ewes come fro' Noggin Moor and to Noggin Moor they've to return. You see, lad, sheep regard their heaf as their own home, an' you've summat on to stop 'em trying to get back if they're shifted."

The oncoming flock was in sight, a tight-packed confusion of deep-baaing mothers and plaintively bleating youngsters, the long shaggy fleeces of the ewes dirty grey, the black-faced Scotch lambs with curly coats ivory white. Each was marked with its sign of ownership, a daub of red rudd on the near quarter of Badger Hall stock, those from Silence with a streak of blue on the shoulder.

When the noisy company arrived Anthony Skidmore called out a cheery 'good morning,' and brandished his stick at Agnes Pedley and Mrs. Iveson, who were standing at their doors. Ralph Skidmore, however, a lean-faced man with a forehead permanently creased, was more reserved.

"You'd better take charge now, Adam lad," Mr. Skidmore smiled.

Not very quickly, but quite nicely, the ewes and lambs were steered to Town Foot, where a party of them decided upon a tour of Main Street, while others favoured the highway winding down the dale.

Mr. Skidmore's stick moved a few inches. "Nell lass," he said, a couple of words between friends.

"Hey! Thoo!" Ralph Skidmore snapped. "Go on, lad."

Whether or not the short-coated, Silence sheep-dog had a name, he responded eagerly enough to his master, in a boisterous sort of way. He flew in aggressive pursuit, so forcing the sightseers into wild retreat, and in the end he had to run as far as William Nattrass' stables before he was able to cut them off. On the other hand, Nell merely jumped a wall, not to be seen again until she appeared on the top of it somewhat farther down the Greets road, when her unsuspicious quarry, slowed to an amble, were gently but firmly turned back.

"That's a grand bitch o' yours, Anthony," Mark Iveson said.

As the grey-and-white flood began to press into Sorrow Near, Adam made much use of his new ash plant, rapping it against the ground to discourage loiterers or slapping his leg once or twice, by-play seen, as was intended, by Cherry, who had brought out a stool for window-washing. The din was overpowering, but her comment, he thought, sounded uncommonly like: "Good morning, Farmer Brunskill," this increasing his grin so much that when, at the window of the millinery department of Smithy House, he glimpsed Fronick Blenkiron, she half rose in astonishment.

Up the sunken track of Sorrow Near, between lofty walls, there was little for either man or dog to do, and so Mr. Skidmore returned to a matter he had not been able to take up a few minutes before.

"Yes, she's a right champion is Nell," he declared fondly. "As a matter o' fact, Francis Harker is always at me to mate her again wi' that dog over at Raydaleside. He's after a pup, like."

"If you do, can I have another?" Adam asked on the spur of the moment. "To buy, I mean, and I'd prefer a bitch."

They all stared at him, but probably Mark Iveson's conclusion was theirs, too. "You couldn't take owt back to Spain with you, lad, that'd better remind you o' being here," he said.

"No, he couldn't," Nell's master smiled. "And a bitch is best, Adam. They're just that bit extra sensitive and, well . . ." his eyes were reminiscent as he pictured many a loved animal, "well, th'only thing they care about is the master, him only, till the day the light dies out on their eyes."

"I've booked one then, have I?" Adam inquired.

Fine-boned face serious, Anthony Skidmore replied that if Nell littered in time, Adam could have one of her offspring, as a present.

"I say present, lad," he laughed, "because afore you sail the sea again I'll have had that much work out on you as to make you the cheapest servant-man that ever stood up in a hiring-fair."

"Right," Adam grinned. "It's a bargain."

Solemn again, Mr. Skidmore extended his arm a little widely, Adam doing likewise, so that, when palms swung together, they slapped in a noisy handshake.

"An' that's the bargain sealed," the farmer said.

About a mile farther along Sorrow Near, where the little hamlet of Half was within view below, men and stock bore left across land once part of a royal chase, pursuing a winding track through juniper bushes to Milton Hall.

Mark Iveson jerked his head towards the ruins of the old shooting-lodge. "This is t'courting quarter, Adam," he joked. "I expect Ralph and your cousin Isa did plenty o' canoodling in these parts."

"Ralph and Isa did their courting by correspondence, Mark lad," Mr. Skidmore said dryly. " 'Course, I believe they had a few words together after Sunday chapel."

The shepherd chuckled, but the reference reminded him that James Pedley was planned to preach at Winterings, on Sunday evening fortnight. "You'll be making special arrangements, won't you, Ralph?" he said. "Getting in brandy and such-like for them who swoons."

Ralph Skidmore remained unperturbed. "You'd look well, wouldn't you, if I brought that insinuation up at the Chapel?"

A good man, Mark Iveson realised he was behaving in a most ill-natured way. "Aye, I should," he admitted, shamefaced.

This slight clash had its effect as far as an old level where a small independent partnership of men was endeavouring to scrape up a few bings of bouse from places worked over twice or thrice already. But, higher up Heugh Syke Gill, tongues were completely loosened when Ralph Skidmore stumbled on a dead grouse. The finding of the inquest was that of death by accident.

"No need to worry about that," the shepherd said. "But there was a touch of disease amongst 'em earlier on."

"Aye," confirmed Anthony Skidmore. "I know our Will was bothered, but he says they're looking well now an' laying champion."

Nell and Hey! Thoo! were busier, with Ralph Skidmore's piercing whistles more frequent and his father's quieter signals more often necessary. To each side Noggin Moor opened out widely, its spring-green tufts of new bracken restful to the eye, the long grasses elsewhere bending in waves to the vagaries of the wind, as the whisper of an oncoming breeze smears its dulling strokes on the mirror surface of an idle sea.

"I see th'East Side directors are having their annual ride over the sett wi' Sir Charles," Mark Iveson exclaimed as the cavalcade of ewes and lambs moved up towards Sweet Tarn, from which, as Adam noticed, a pressure pipe-line ran down to the engine-house of Old Wife Shaft, in whose sump, thirty fathoms below ground, was a donkey pump the cost of which Droughty Tom stubbornly claimed.

The horsemen to whom the shepherd had pointed were riding in single file along a winding track. There were seven of them: Sir Charles Grafton, Henry Hird and Reuben Nattrass; and a full board of directors: William Nattrass, George Nattrass, Mr. Miles Buckle, who also was secretary of the Company, and Mr. William Storey, of Corvy, the Chairman.

While Anthony Skidmore and Mark Iveson exchanged yarns about

Mr. Storey, who apparently was a strange mixture, a prudent banker on the one part and a wildly enthusiastic lead-mining adventurer on the other, Adam scanned the moor to the west of the tower terminating the flue of Martha Smelt Mill. It did not appear greatly affected by the fumes. No doubt modern condensers and long flues prevented the emission of dangerous 'flight.'

"No," Mr. Skidmore told him, his eyes still streaming with amusement, "mining companies don't have to pay for damage to stock like they once did. Of course there's odd spots, old 'uns, where a sheep can still get poisoned, but every year rain and thaw reduces the risk."

Steadily the flock continued upwards. Sweet Tarn, with waves made respectably sized by the strong wind, was left behind and then, higher along Heugh Syke Gill, came Sun Hade Pump Shaft, with waterwheel and pump on the surface. Beyond there, from the crest of a spur, the Noggin Moor shepherd whistled in greeting, and a quarter of an hour later met the oncoming party.

Various consultations were held on the gusty height, the Skidmores mainly discussing pasturage, Mark Iveson arguing with his colleague about certain proposals the shepherds of the Dale intended to submit to the conservators in the autumn.

Adam, who had an appointment with Mr. Alderson at Notion Bridge, did not stay until these deliberations were completed. Bidding farewell to his companions, he set out for Dagger Gap.

Descending Water Ling Moor, Adam crossed Mirk Gutter and Worm Gutter before drawing level with Glory Shaft, whose quarter-mile length of massive rods inexplicably were stationary. Seeking the reason, he paused, at once perceiving Richard Blenkiron and several men in the ravine clustered around the fifty-feet diameter waterwheel, to whose rim they were bolting a large tub. Others were loading the tub with stones, work in which the blacksmith soon shared, elbowing aside two assistants to pick up himself the biggish rock whose weight they had been testing jointly.

"Trying to give the waterwheel more power," Adam reflected. "Looks as if the pump hasn't been able to cope wi' what it had to do."

In due course Richard Blenkiron raised his hand to a man standing by at the sluice farther up the beck, and then slowly the wheel began to turn. When the line of rods once more was moving backwards and forwards at its proper rate, and water, lightening the problems of groovers forty-five fathoms below, spilled out in regular spasms from a pipe at the eye of Glory Shaft, Adam resumed his journey along the brink of Winterings Gill. The going was easy down to Mary Dressing Floors, and in another ten minutes from then he was crossing Mill Bridge. As he had surmised since watching the makeshift adjustment to Glory water-wheel, Cherry's uncle was not at the little office.

"He's at Mary Forehead," Bart Hugill told him glumly. "It's flooding to the tune of three hundred gallons a minute till they get the pump off again."

"You don't sound so lively, lad," Adam ventured. "Anyhow, it is."

"Lively!" the clerk scoffed. "What, with Glory pump in a losing battle to keep Mary Forehead Ground free o' water, the New Drift to reach th'ore at Jamie's Mint—we *hope*—swallowing every penny, and t'North Sun Vein Ground, our best for mineral, dependent on how long the old pump at Maybe Shaft can hold out. Lively, eh!"

"Noan so good," Adam agreed. "But in most cases levels act as natural drains. Why is it you have to do so much pumping?"

"Never enough brass for a clear-cut scheme, so there's been God's amount o' burrowing, like a worm twisting up an' down. You see, for years now, what has been scratted out has never done much more than cover the Pay. A bright prospect, eh?"

"Why don't you try for a job elsewhere?" Adam asked bluntly.

Bart Hugill brushed off his forehead a strand of hair before answering. Indeed, he accepted Adam's tobacco tin and charged his pipe before beginning properly. It was a story old in parts, with parts new. There was a reluctance to leave Skewdale, the responsibility he felt towards a stricken brother, and doubts whether his experience in a specialised industry would be sufficient when competing with smart city clerks.

"Me and Fronick have talked it over and over, Adam," he went on. "And . . . well, we've come to the conclusion that we'd prefer to make do on little, so long as we can stay here."

For a while neither spoke, each wrapped in his own thoughts, until the clerk, unburdening himself of the rest, confided his and Fronick's plan. There was a cottage near Barfoot, with three nice fields, which could be rented cheaply, and as soon as they could scrape together the money to buy a couple of milk cows, they were taking the plunge.

"Like most chaps about here I've done a bit o' farming now an' then, Adam," he continued earnestly. "And what I lack one road I can make up wi' hard work in another, so I tell myself."

"I'm sure, Bart," Adam nodded.

A rueful smile played about the other's lips. "But when we shall be able to do it, lad. . . . Three shillings is the top price Fronick gets for a bonnet an' so she can't make more than a few coppers out of the most expensive of 'em. And as for myself, I never can put aside more than eighteen-pence a week, do what I will. Still . . ."

As if opening his heart had greatly improved his spirits, he started to explain how, in former days of lead-mining prosperity, shrewd young women reserved their smiles for the best catches of all, young groovers with a lucky reputation in mining bargains.

"Oh, aye," he laughed, "farmers were small beer then, but to-day it's different. Yes, if my ambition comes off, Fronick'll be in t'latest fashion. But as to the sort of bargain she'll be getting . . . you know I tell her her head can't be screwed on right."

Adam smiled. "Maybe her other parts have been assembled better. Perhaps her heart's in the right place."

"Aye, I think so," the clerk chuckled. "Yes . . ." he sobered a little, "yes, I'm sure on it, dead sure, Adam."

For almost an hour longer Adam remained there, but as Mr. Alderson did not appear he left a message and started down Sleety Slape towards the village.

* * * *

About noon of the second day when three neighbours joined forces to wash fat sheep, Wingy Blenkiron, on his round to Slackrigg, delivered Adam a letter from a Newcastle analyst.

The figures stated exceeded Adam's estimate, varying from twenty per cent of lead in the slags to a shade under five in the slimes, of which there was a preponderance at Flout Level. All in all, approximating to seven per cent, a feasible proposition was certainly present.

"Well thanks, Wingy," he said. "Aye, I'm here all right."

"That's why I didn't bother to walk up to Back Lane," the postman grinned.

After crossing to his coat, hanging on an alder branch, to put the letter away, Adam took over from Mr. Harker once more, his turn to hand the sheep to the washers, Anthony and Ralph Skidmore. The work was being carried out in a moderately deep pool, about a hundred yards down Snorr Beck from Slackrigg. Each awaiting batch of sheep was penned into an enclosure of hurdles which, near the flowing water, narrowed into an alleyway along which each struggling victim had to be dragged before being seized by those who stood waist-deep in the chill mountain stream. Many more sheep nibbled away in a more remote corner of the big pasture.

"Nobbut one good thing about sheep," Anthony Skidmore grunted when, teeth chattering, water dripping from him, and hands slippery with grease, he left the pool, "an' that's the brass you get paid for 'em."

"Aye," Francis Harker said, gasping as he joined Adam in the water, "and that's greasy and all. Every sovereign the market man pulls out seems as if it's been rubbed wi' mutton fat aforehand."

There were compensations, however: the beck, frothing tunefully over shallow limestone steps, sunshine glinting on dappled water, the yellow-flowered celandine margining the stream, the faint almond scent from masses of lily-white bird-cherry blossom, the strutting of a pied wagtail using its long tail as balancer, the song of the robins, chaffinches and blackbirds, even the mirth of those not involved when a particularly obstinate creature buck-jumped in the pool, its desperately clinging attendants faithfully following the frantic curveting.

By the early evening, when young Bob and Ward came puffing uphill, no more than a handful of sheep remained to undergo an ordeal which, for them, really began when, strong hands grasping their horns, they were thoroughly ducked before being permitted to struggle out on to the opposite bank, where they vigorously shook themselves, sending up a shower of spray.

"You've nearly finished, Grandfather!" Bob exclaimed.

"These jobs have to be got on wi', lad." Mr. Skidmore remarked with severity. "We hung about long enough, but as you two didn't show up we'd to make the best on it."

Ward's snub nose wrinkled. "Go on with you, Mr. Skidmore."

It so happened that the rotation of duties had left Adam's final task of the day the one least onerous, merely to usher, with an embarrassing plenitude of sheepdog assistance, the last few sheep from pasture into pen. This done, he lazily watched a party of black-headed gulls, returning from the daily foraging expedition to lower and less harsh country, sail up the Dale as far as Bloody Sigh where, full white span fleetingly revealed when banking, they swung right, to wing leisurely over Water Ling Moor towards their nesting-places below Little Barg.

"It's right interesting up at Deer Pot just after t'baby gulls have come out of their shells," Bob remarked, following Adam's glance.

Ward joined in hard at the heels of his cousin. "Aye, it is that. Would you like to go up there wi' me and Bob sometime, Adam?"

Adam promptly accepted the boys' eager invitation. While they were there he also seized the opportunity to dispose of another matter, sending a message to Ward's father asking him, if possible, to call at the Plug and Feathers early the same night.

Matt Tiplady was very definitely taken aback by the assayer's report, but on realising the means were there to make a modest profit, he began excitedly to plan. He decided to visit Henry Hird the next morning, and thought he might be able to arrange for a take-note at a royalty of one in twelve. As to carrying the slags and slimes from Flout Level to Notion Bridge, he felt convinced that Anthony Skidmore would lend him a horse and cart. Money would be needed to buy the coal for smelting, but to cover this he had a partner in mind, a man to whom he owed a good turn, who would just about be able to get together the small sum needed.

"You see, Adam," he explained, keeping his voice low, "the West Side Company is in no condition to allow much credit, an' it'll be as much as they can manage if they supply t'wood and peat. Anyroad, I'll pop along in a few minutes to catch Titus Alderson . . . he'll noan let owt pop out fro' under his hat until I've secured the take-note, an' I might as well get fixed up with him. You'll come wi' me, of course, lad."

Though conducted quietly for secrecy's sake, a battle-royal then ensued when Adam flatly refused any part of the profit. It ended in a compromise: Adam was to be repaid the analyst's fee of two guineas out of the first sale of lead; a set of pie dishes were to be bought for Mary Jane; and Agnes Pedley, with suitable safeguards to conceal the origin from her father, was to be provided weekly with a prime rabbit, hare or other game.

"Well, I'm not over suited," the poacher grumbled. "An' what's this about Mary Jane wanting pie dishes?"

"It slipped out one day when she was showing me her ducklings an' their foster mother, that favourite hen of hers, down by the river," Adam replied. "She's a canny little lass."

"Yes," Matt Tiplady said, "never a better, lad . . . only . . ." He blinked and, to hide his face, bent to stroke Floss who, as always in these circumstances, was sitting quietly between his legs.

Neither of them as yet had had a drink, so Adam went to the bar where he ordered a tankard of Old and Mild for himself and a pint of porter for Matt.

"Aye," Mrs. Peacock nodded, her fine eyes angry. She was crewelling a daffodil upon a chair-back cover and, before she attended to him, in silence, this work was carefully put aside. Adam was not without his suspicions as to the reason for her temper, and these were confirmed when he carried the drinks back.

"Thanks, lad," Matt said, still dim-eyed. "Would you believe it, Adam, but there's somebody else on about that New Drift of Titus Alderson's, them chaps yonder. Why it is so oft jawed about I can't fathom, but it is. An' I've been telled, an' this is t'biggest licker of all, that there's been some sizeable betting as it'll never hit the sump o' Doomsday High Shaft."

A fantastic theory flashed into Adam's mind. "Why should it miss?" he asked abruptly, conscious of being irrational.

"Why should it?" Matt Tiplady scoffed. "'Course it won't, lad. It's t'simplest matter for a skilled mining-agent to lay off the direction correctly, an' you can be sure Titus took special pains this time. No, it's just a handful of malicious folk who'd be only too suited if by any wild fluke summat went wrong."

Adam glanced at the trio in the inglenook: Bull Waggott and his Company's engineer, Cyprian Metcalfe, a shortish, deep-chested man almost square in build, so wide were his shoulders; the third was Jonas Cottingham, against whose feet four bottles of brandy were standing, presumably obtained from Mrs. Peacock to tide him over until his wholesaler's next delivery to the Groovers Welcome, of which he was the landlord. The three were still discussing Titus Alderson's problems, but Adam, deliberately eavesdropping, was utterly convinced that none of them guarded any sinister knowledge. It was, he concluded ruefully, arrant foolishness in himself to have conjured up such a preposterous notion.

"All the same, Adam," Matt Tiplady ruminated, "it's noan nice to think o' chaps taking such a delight in running somebody else down."

On that same issue, Mrs. Peacock was just about to become active. She patted into position her dark hair, a preliminary to deeds.

"There's some," she announced, stony gaze on the inglenook, "there's some as say Christian conduct and keeping a public-house is like trying to mix oil an' water. Maybe so, but . . ." Ruthlessly she advised Cyprian Metcalfe to hasten home to the shop so that he could enjoy a longer evening in knocking Emma Ann about. As for Jonas Cottingham, she suggested that, while walking down to Half, he should reflect upon the merits of loyalty to a senior.

"If Emma Ann's been opening her mouth," Cyprian Metcalfe blustered.

"She never breathes owt," Lucy Peacock retorted swiftly. "But folk aren't blind, not they. Besides, I happen to know as Cuthbert Daykin once found her bleeding on t'kitchen floor when he'd called to borrow a sup o' milk. An' you'd nobbut just gone out, you squat, hulking brute."

Aching to intervene, Jonas Cottingham began to speak before the angered East Side Company's engineer could reply. "Loyalty!" he snapped, mouth corners drooping. "What about Titus Alderson's loyalty to them under him? Yes, as sure as I'se here——"

"Summat tells me you'll noan be here much longer, Jonas," Matt Tiplady said.

The smelter glared at the interrupter before resuming: "If Titus Alderson goes on as he is, it'll noan be long afore every man-jack in t'West Side Company is out o' work. Where's the loyalty in——"

A throat was cleared effectively, and Droughty Tom rumbled into speech. "Titus doesn't dodge his obligations, choose how, Jonas, which is more than you can say about t'directors of them two chaps you're hobnobbing wi'."

"That bl——" Bull Waggott checked himself. "That pump," he jeered.

"Alderson ought to retire," Jonas Cottingham proclaimed.

Lucy Peacock, a woman of affairs, became most businesslike, reminding the smelter that he had not paid for the spirits. He was further nonplussed when she stated, gruffly but civilly, that recently she had been considering distinctions in the matter of credit.

Jonas Cottingham forgot Titus Alderson. "I've always chalked up wi' you," he shouted, enraged. "And I'se always paid an' all. Why should you single me out all of a sudden?"

Mrs. Peacock turned her head slightly sideways while she fingered a coil of hair. "You've just telled me . . . 'cause seemingly you're going to be out o' work any day. So . . ." She waited impassively until a sigh of pure joy faded away. "So I want eighteen an' eightpence, four quarts at four and eight, and I want it *now*."

Matt Tiplady gave Adam a hearty dig in the ribs. "Come on, let's be off, lad," he guffawed.

Pushing through a grinning company to reach the front door, the last words they heard on a vexing subject were those of Lucy Peacock. In the same level tone she was offering Jonas Cottingham the choice, either to surrender the brandy forthwith or to have her send one of the girls along Main Street to fetch Albert Gibson, the constable.

Declining Len Rukin's and Hugh Bearpark's challenge, shouted from the stone-flagged hand-ball court against the end wall of the Bridge Inn, to a handicapped foursome at the next change but one, and pausing only to inspect a card on Hannah Batty's door which, in large letters, inquired ANYBODY GOING SLACKRIGG WAY, with a drawing in the corner of derelict cottages and a baby's dummy, the two men walked towards Town Foot.

Titus Alderson opened the front door of Yew Tree House and seemed pleased to see his visitors, but Adam thought he looked far too fine-drawn, the result probably of anxiety that day in Mary Level Forehead. After Matt Tiplady had explained his errand, the old mining-agent, who preferred to discuss business in a business setting, led the way down the passage to his office. Adam, however, went into the kitchen, where Cherry put down her book: Mrs. Oliphant's *The Primrose Path*.

"Sit down, Adam," she said, smiling.

Reaching for her sewing-basket, she slipped a well-scrubbed potato into a sock before starting to darn, meantime Adam, from the opposite side of the hearth, leisurely eyed a room which had always captivated him. As usual the kitchen was neat and bright, and even Sambo was on the hob, though not asleep this once, his yellow eyes, round as saucers, directed unwaveringly towards the door, beyond which he had glimpsed Floss silently padding behind her master.

In that restful retreat, Adam should have been at peace with the world, but he was not. When at last he pinned down the cause of this unease, he discovered to his irritation that the same ridiculous idea was responsible. His wry smile must have appeared strange to the young woman who, now and then, glanced at him wonderingly.

In these circumstances the conversation was naturally desultory.

"Aye, it was very pleasant up Snorr Beck," Adam remarked.

"You'll know all about washing sheep now," she teased him.

Gradually he relapsed into silence, the concentration of his expression ever more acute. In point of fact he was puzzling as to what conceivably could prevent a drift, if exactly headed, from attaining its desired destination. Even the hardest rock was not impassable and if there were fear of cutting into dangerous water who would know better of its potential presence than the mine-agent in whose sett the work was proceeding.

Cherry leaned forward, her tone very gentle. "Adam, there's another box of matches on the shelf by you. You've struck nine of 'em in a row, and four you threw straight into the fire. And——"

"Have I?" said Adam, aghast.

She dimpled. "And you'll do better if you fill your pipe. You knocked it out a while ago . . . that'd be about number three match."

The culprit was still staring. "I'm sorry, lass. I must have got absent-minded because o' summat I can't make out."

It was not her intention to pry, but rather to shelve the matter on the lightest of notes. "I know," she said gaily, "it's a very grave problem indeed, an' I know what it's to do with . . . farming."

His reply was laconic. "No, mining."

"*Mining!*" Cherry exclaimed, bolt-upright in her surprise. "You're noan thinking of trying your hand here at mining now, are you?"

Again he surprised her, though she was unable to be sure whether or not he were serious.

"Not so far, lass, but you never know," he laughed.

Cherry decided to be no more serious than he was. "You've had a vision of a vein somewhere that's shining wi' ore."

Adam grinned. "It wouldn't be my first vision either. I remember one boiling hot *festa* day when me and Simon got stretched out in a field. I was just nodding off when suddenly a woman, clutching t'lace mantilla on her head and hoisting her skirts up, came tearing along chased by a couple o' chaps with knives. Well, I thought her face were Daniel's . . ." He broke off, shoulders shaking. "It was, too, as I found out that night, wig an' all."

Cherry rocked with laughter. "But all the same that wasn't a vision," she demurred.

Adam's smile died away, his expression growing solemn. "No, maybe not, but I've seen one all right, one I'll never forget." He sighed profoundly.

"Go on," Cherry begged.

He made an effort. "It took place in a room, an empty room, but somewhere away I could hear a voice, a sweet, welcoming voice. There was a door at the far end and suddenly a young lady appeared, as bonny——"

Cherry rose with extreme dignity. "Uncle and Matt'll soon be finished, so I'll lay supper—currant teacake an' cheese. You can stay if you want, but——"

"Yes, lass?" he encouraged her, blandness itself.

"Only if you behave yourself," she retorted.

"*Con muchisimo gusto, senorita*," he replied with humility.

The latter part of that evening was another evening Adam added to his many delightful memories of Winterings. His talk with Cherry as she busied herself, the soothing tick of the grandfather clock, the blue-flamed peat fire offsetting the night's chill, the company of friends.

Until he strolled homewards he never gave another thought to the New Drift.

2

One morning it seemed as if, for the second time that year, the animal population of the Dale had been vastly augmented, but this was merely due to the appearance of cattle which, inside so long, had been put outdoors for the summer and autumn. Everywhere, in fields and along grassy roadsides, the neat shorthorns were browsing.

The vacating of the byres provided an opportunity for refurbishing, and this was the next stage in Adam's farming education. The morning but one after the beasts had been turned out he thoroughly cleaned the smaller cow-house at Badger Hall, and might have completed lime-washing on the following day had not Francis Harker asked him to milk two of the Low Bands cows which were grazed on the Common Pasture—a serious crack had become visible in the structure of Yorrel Congregational Chapel, of which Mr. Harker was a prominent member, and an emergency meeting was to be held at once.

In the early evening Adam went along to Low Bands to collect a back-can, a vessel hollowed out at one side to rest snugly against the back. Slipping into the leather straps as if into a schoolboy's satchel, he then picked up a milking-stool and one of the pails freshening on the binks: stone shelving outside the farmhouse door. Thus, lightly burdened, he walked across to the mainroad, where he joined in the traffic passing to and from the Common Pasture: men with back-cans, women with buckets and, where a considerable number of beasts were concerned, donkeys with milk receptacles to either side.

Fortunately he had milked the two cows before and so did not suffer a temperamental feminine display. The job completed, he shouldered the back-can once more and started down the steep slope, pausing occasionally to chat with milkers, amongst them Fronick Blenkiron and Mrs. Emma Metcalfe, who was terrified she might not be at home when her husband returned from the mines.

Lower down Adam halted, to watch Blind Kit. This was the first opportunity he had had of seeing the blind man pick out his own cow, but the feat was done, a placid red roan receiving a kindly slap after her owner had weaved unerringly amidst nine or ten beasts.

"Unbelievable!" the observer muttered. "You can hardly credit it."

The cobbler was in the lower part of the Pasture and, when Adam neared him, he had already drawn the first milk to waste on the ground, the succeeding flow squirting into the pail with a hollow, pinging sound which grew deeper as the contents became greater.

"Now then, Adam lad," Blind Kit called out.

"How did you know it was me?" Adam asked.

The explanation was too trivial even to make the cobbler smile. "Because of the whip of the hard grasses, t'round ones, against the front of your boots," he said. "It'd have cracked differently if you'd been wearing clogs like everybody else."

"And now I'll tell *you* summat, Kit," said Adam, still astounded. "That after what I've just seen you'll be my man for darker places if ever I want anybody to show me some out-of-the-way spot underground. Anyhow, I'm told there's few know the Old Man like you do."

He set down the milking-stool and, back-can standing off his shoulders like a soldier's knapsack, seated himself for a talk.

"Aye," Blind Kit deliberated, not braggingly, "I suppose that me and Reuben Nattrass knows us way about the mines here more than anybody, th'old groovers included. 'Course I learnt it afore I lost my eyes," he went on. "I started nosing round as a youngster, like Reuben did at after me, an' as that poor lad o' Martin Rutter's did at after both of us. Yes, if ever you require a cheap guide, Adam, one as'll noan cost you a candle, I'm him."

In the end they walked down to the village together, their conversation having then reached, by devious routes, that of the preparation of addresses, the most important part of which the cobbler firmly believed he did best of all when milking.

"Why it is, I don't know, but when I'm pulling at t'beasts dugs I feel right at peace, an' my thinking is at its clearest." Involuntarily he chuckled, before describing the outraged attitude of a rather patronising lady, a visitor, whom he had once told the same thing. "An' you know, lad, I still can't credit I were being indecent."

Adam laughed. "A narrow-minded 'un," he said.

Blind Kit's head turned, his blue-pitted face and the sightless eyes towards the young man. "You'll be listening to th'high priest of 'em all on Sunday night, lad," he observed, a touch of grimness in him.

Sunday evening chapel duly came and, as James Pedley's diatribe proceeded, it seemed a positive certainty that, before concluding, he would attain those terrifying heights associated with his name. Nevertheless, the final part fell flat. But few, in addition to the lay preacher himself, bore any grudge against Adam, whose fault undoubtedly it was.

Latterly, there had been rising discord between the Pedley brothers, and although not planned to preach anywhere on the evening James Pedley was to speak in Winterings Chapel, Ambrose Pedley preferred to attend Greets Chapel in a private capacity rather than witness crowds of worshippers streaming towards the West End to sit under his brother.

Because of this dog-in-the-manger attitude Adam and his cousin were alone for tea after returning rather late from the Common Pasture, where they had met Mazy Bill and Polly. However, by five minutes past six, Agnes was quite ready to leave home again, and a quarter of an hour later they were nearly at Nick Turn, in the midst of a throng of chapel-goers.

At Ash Grove, probably calling for his boon companion, Bull Waggott was opening the gate. To Adam's surprise, he passed a pleasant word.

The narrowing of Main Street, with people closer together, made comment difficult. When it was more possible, Agnes's fiery flush was subsiding.

"Well, that's the first civil word I've had from yon chap," Adam remarked. "Maybe," he smiled, "he's more careful on the Sabbath."

Agnes had an alternative theory: that the presence of a lady might have been responsible. And, to Adam's secret amusement, she spoke of the groover as if he were in his callow youth, not a man close upon thirty.

"He'll change before long, they all do," she declared with great wisdom. "Take your cousin Arthur, fr'instance, who's always imitating Reuben Nattrass. But he'll grow out of it and Annamaria knows he will, just as any young woman 'ud know, 'cause young women are always a sight older than young men, an' it's nowt to do with their ages."

"I don't think Annamaria's just patiently leaving it until Arthur abandons his roistering ways," Adam said. "As far as I can judge she keeps giving him a real hard shove in the right direction."

Agnes spoke as if imparting an important secret. "An' that's where she makes a mistake, Adam. She'd do better if she were more gentle, more . . . more womanly-like. Arthur 'ud respond quicker that road and . . . and come under her influence all the sooner."

Adam Brunskill had always been able to control his features, but at this juncture he began to have his fears. Fortunately the crush near the chapel was greater, and so, in the nearby presence of another young woman, he found a suitable outlet. This was why Cherry Dinsdale and, because they were with her, Titus Alderson and Mrs. Robert William Alderson, received a demonstrative salute which, as far as the older people were concerned, caused the mine-agent to gape and his sister-in-law's black silk-clad bosom to heave with annoyance. As for Miss Dinsdale, she probably appreciated the situation more exactly, for she whispered to the young man who had so dashingly raised his hat, when, squeezed together, they filed small step by small step into the chapel.

"You can tell me at after, Adam," she said sepulchrally.

Adam, his expression that of polite inquiry, gazed down at the pretty and roguish face. "I beg your pardon?" he said.

With considerable artistry, while simultaneously smiling with syrupy sweetness at a dear friend, Dinah Skidmore, she trod on his foot.

Mazy Bill was close-by, head as usual stiffly to one side, fixed grin of delight on Agnes, with whom he and his mare had enjoyed a wonderful afternoon. The trammer's family was there, too, and it was to his father, the auctioneer, that Adam confided the reason for a sudden cry of anguish.

"You haven't been in at that bull-fighting, bull-fighting——" Mr. Rutter broke off to frown at a friend of his daughter. For all his experience on the selling rostrum he could not compete with such frantic nose-blowing.

"You were saying, Mr. Rutter?" Adam asked with interest when Cherry's paroxysm diminished. "No, I haven't actually taken part . . ."

Aching with restrained laughter, fearful of the calamity which might befall her if she met his glance, Cherry Dinsdale stared fixedly to her front as, along with others, she moved slowly forward, past a table upon which, in a large vase, fragrant wall-flowers added a note of rich colour to relieve an otherwise austere interior.

When his time came to address a packed congregation, James Pedley began quietly enough, describing his life since he had started, when ten years old, as a wash-lad on the dressing-floors of the Skewdale Mining Company; his years as a groover at Keld Head in Wensleydale; the step upwards to leadership of a partnership of six for the B.G. Mining Company at Greets, and penultimately his post as an assistant agent at Yorrel Mines, one he retained until that company went into its third and, as it proved, final bankruptcy.

"And now, brothers an' sisters, look at me now," he implored his hearers. "Nobbut a humble groover again, glad to draw whatever God's pleased to grant me when th'East Side's Pay comes round."

Adam, shifting a little askew, did not respond to the invitation. While in this attitude, as he tried discreetly to glimpse Cherry, Hannah Batty noticed him. The old lady's demeanour was solemn, which made all the more extraordinary her girlish gesture. Slyly she closed one eye, a trick which, seventy or so years before, must have had an uncommon effect upon the young men who went to war with Sir John Moore in the Peninsula.

James Pedley's theme was 'humility,' and he was beginning to warm to it. Gifted with an appreciable imagination, and glorying in censure by name, it was not surprising he gripped the majority.

"But what about th'other sort, them that doesn't know what humbleness means?" he asked. "Well, brethren, I'll tell you about them, and what's going to happen to 'em here in Skewdale."

For a few still moments his pale eyes roved, and then, almost conversationally, he detailed a new and gargantuan smelt mill bridging the Dale above Yorrel. More than one gasp was heard as he repeated the fantastic specifications—a building as large as Spout Fell, ore hearths greater than Virgin Hill, and tanks not one of which was less than Little Barg.

"Filled wi' molten lead . . . and noan of 'em smaller than Little Barg," he said slowly, tone still low. "Now, brothers and sisters, what do you reckon 'ud happen to t'sinful among you if them tanks burst, an' all that there scalding lead started flowing down the Dale? What do you reckon, eh?"

Possessed of the true spellbinder's art, he allowed the precise interval needed before his voice rose frighteningly.

"Well, the tanks has burst, and a wall o' molten lead is rushing down on Yorrel," he screamed. "It's divided now, into five or six streams, each bent on executing the Lord's judgment. One of 'em has just wiped out what that popish lot at Greets Church call their chapel-of-ease, and another's swallowed t'Rose an' Crown; that one that's been hanging back, you can see it, can't you, has whipped round to Rose Cottage, to frizzle Rosie Caygill alive for her vanity, and look yonder, there's t'Congregational Chapel gone in a puff o' smoke . . ."

Before leaving Yorrel, he had one piece of condign punishment to relate which plainly filled him with malignant satisfaction. At Yorrel the Manse of the Congregational minister was the last house the destroying flood would reach, and vividly he portrayed Mr. Waddington's contemptible actions when, from outside his back door, the minister first saw the fearful danger.

"He's off, off as fast as his legs 'ul carry him, running to save his skin without a thought for the misguided 'uns who are his flock, without even going indoors to warn his nearest an' dearest. Down t'road he's racing, wi' his black hat on, but it's after him, burning trees an' consuming the beasts in the fields . . ."

Agnes Pedley, gloved hands clasping and unclasping, blue eyes transfixed with terror, stared at her uncle.

"It's nobbut his yarn, lass," Adam comforted her.

James Pedley's paean of joy shrilled to the rafters. "It's at his heels now . . . he's round th'old Corn Mill and over Yorrel Bridge, but it's there, creeping up, creeping up . . . it's touched him, he's faltered, he's fast. His feet's burnt off . . ."

Adam was concerned. "I'd better take you out, Agnes," he said.

The unfortunate Mr. Waddington disposed of, the preacher brought the terrifying wave surging down the Dale. With every artifice he strove to impress those before him with their imminent peril, and, in attempting to achieve stark reality, was not without success. The pitch-pine pews squeaked, the gallery creaked, and the oil lamp and its lengthy suspension chain began to swing slightly; from one part of the chapel came a choked cry, and elsewhere sounded a muted thump as though a limp figure had slipped sideways in a faint.

"No . . . no, Adam," Agnes whimpered.

Her uncle quickly dealt with Snorr, his picture of Lane End being particularly horrific, Ward and Mary Jane both suffering the same gruesome fate as the evil man who was their father.

Hearing his cousin's moan, Adam patted her hand. "Well, if you won't go out, you won't, lass. But don't take a ha-porth more notice of him," he rapped, angered, "for he's nowt better than a mountebank."

James Pedley's head turned, his pale eyes venomous as he endeavoured to outgaze the young man whose words had carried clearly enough in one of those telling silences he found so profitable. He was vastly too experienced not to know the interruption was fatal, nor to appreciate that, occurring as it did at the point to which throughout he had been dramatically leading, the threshold of Winterings, when a Winterings congregation was before him, he had been robbed on the very eve of triumph.

"An' there's . . . there's someone else who's high on t'list to be seared to the bone," he screeched, extending a quivering arm. "That young chap yonder, him that's a stranger amongst us because his own blood here won't acknowledge him, him that's deluded my own brother into harbouring him . . . him . . ." his voice sank pregnantly, "him that's made a mock o' me, me who's the servant of the Lord."

But the spell was broken. Necks were craned, a buzz resounded, and those who had shivered lest their names should be mentioned were revived.

James Pedley's thin-lipped mouth closed tightly but then opened again. In a few withering words he concluded his address and, less than ten minutes afterwards, the double doors were unlatched by Puke Hastwell.

There was to be no subsequent counting of heads for James Pedley that evening—every person present, including those who had faltered earlier under the power of his suggestion, left the Chapel on two feet.

Few of the chapel-goers grouped in Main Street seemed inclined to leave. To begin with, Adam was the centre of interest, until Matt Tiplady's grimly-expressed determination to punch James Pedley's nose "for scaring my little lass" created a diversion. The poacher, in clean linen collar and neatly knotted black tie, looked very different from the everyday figure he presented in corduroys and coat of many hidden and voluminous pockets. But his weather-beaten cheeks were a dull red and, while Susan Skidmore and Bart Hugill were urging him to be reasonable, Mary Jane clung desperately to his hand.

"Mr. Blenkiron'll stop him," Cherry exclaimed with relief as the blacksmith elbowed through the thickening throng. "Even if he does it reluctantly, as I suspect he will."

"Do you wonder, love?" Dinah said, lowering her voice. "Just look at them two woebegone little things, wi' tear-streaks all down their faces."

Reuben Nattrass, who was riding his nieces high, overheard the remark nevertheless. "Aye," he said, "these two sweethearts o' mine have been rare bothered, but they're getting over it now, aren't you, loves?"

Apparently this was so. "But we know what to do next time, 'cause Uncle Reuben's telled us," Harriet vouchsafed with importance. "When James Pedley stops an' stares at folk we shall say, ever so loud——"

Nancy obviously felt she should be playing a bigger part. "We shall say," she squeaked hurriedly, "well, well, well, I *never*."

Whatever were the likes, dislikes and other differences between them, the children provided a common meeting ground for their elders, who laughed uproariously.

"My words, Reuben lad," Isa Skidmore shook a finger, "if you teach these bairns o' mine summat as you shouldn't . . ."

Her brother, although he exchanged a few words more with the older young ladies, made no real attempt to stay with them, and Adam, who had noticed the episode from across the street, vaguely wondered why. The East Side's agent was unquestionably attracted by Cherry and it seemed out of keeping with his nature not to take active steps about anything he desired.

"Unless . . ." Adam mused, glancing upwards to watch the swallows which, at dazzling speed, winged around the chapel, from tree-planted garth to burial ground, "unless he realises he hasn't an earthly with her by ordinary means. And if so——" His sudden chuckle might have startled Agnes, but she, almost recovered now, was chatting to Fronick and Annamaria. "A few more o' these fancies of mine," he told himself ruefully, "an' soon I'll be put away somewhere."

Wingy Blenkiron gravitated near. "Adam lad," he began in mock solemnity, "you'd better look out fro' now on. You must never forget jungle-whiskers has got you down in his black book."

"I'll watch my p's and q's," Adam smiled.

The postman broke into a broad grin. "Aye, or he'll stir up a holy crusade against you, lad."

The red orb of the sun was sinking towards the Brig when James Pedley, face taut with suppressed feeling, left without incident for Yorrel. Then, everything to do with his extravagant address thoroughly discussed, the crowd started to disperse, some homeward-bound and others for a stroll before supper.

For their late Sunday evening jaunt, one small party crossed Francis Harker's meadow in Blenk Bottom to reach the flood-bank and the grassy slope beyond, where some decided to sit, while others explored the Skew up-stream.

In the shade of an overhanging shelf of rock, Adam discerned a trout, facing the flow. Apart from barely detectable movements of the fins it was as stationary as if riding at the end of a gossamer line secured to an invisible anchor. It chanced that Will Skidmore was close-by and, on Matt Tiplady's mischievous instigation, Adam discoursed authoritatively upon a method of catching fish which would have been heresy to any self-respecting sportsman, gamekeeper or water-bailiff.

"Could you, Adam?" Agnes's eyes widened. "How?"

Nonchalantly Adam went into details, from the initial stage of rolling shirt sleeve to the shoulder until the crucial second when, laid flat on the bank, adroitly tickling finger-tips worked sufficiently forward on a lulled creature's underbelly to reach the point when a secure grip could be obtained on an infinitely slippery body.

"Mmmm . . ." Will Skidmore ruminated. "You're picking up a trick or two, though that's noan one I recall teaching you, Adam lad."

"Oh, he's got other instructors besides you, Will," Cherry laughed.

The gamekeeper's eyes crinkled, but his warning was as blunt as his jaw. "Seemingly, lass," he agreed. "But, friend nevertheless, he'd do well to understand that if ever I nab him on t'moors doing owt as he shouldn't it'll be the same for him as for any of th'instructors you've mentioned—an appearance afore the magistrates at Corvy."

"Nay, Will," Dinah protested.

Matt Tiplady, who had really intended to inquire aloofly why his brother-in-law should glance so significantly at him, post-haste demanded what there might be on the moors which legitimately could be prohibited from any man. On this, an amused but alarmed company decided it was full time to return, and on the way back co-operated wholeheartedly to bring about a change of subject.

Mark Iveson and his wife, both in Sunday best, were strolling down the highway from Snorr, the shepherd leisurely swinging a walking-stick silver-chased on the curved handle. A short distance behind this pair Bull Waggott stepped out briskly and, as Skidmores and Tipladys bade farewell to their friends, he joined in with those returning to the village.

Cherry whispered to Adam. "You don't often see him out enjoying the beauties of nature."

The groover, in high good humour, evidently, had just passed a remark which made Mark Iveson chuckle, and, on the joke being repeated for the benefit of rosy-cheeked Mrs. Iveson and Agnes, they laughed, too.

Bart Hugill shared in the fun also and, commenting appropriately, received a friendly clap on the back which sent him reeling.

"He seems very pleased with himself," said Adam, grinning.

Until a big, raven-haired young man bawled from the cobbled space in front of the Plug and Feathers, Cherry was entertained by the groover's painstaking attempts to be agreeable to all, including Fronick Blenkiron who, puce-coloured with embarrassment, shrank almost visibly whenever he looked her way.

"Hey, Bull!" Reuben Nattrass grunted as they came up to him, "have you gone deaf or summat? Anyroad . . ." he proceeded to give instructions about certain work to be done at the mine first thing the next morning, finishing up with: "I'll be up there as soon as I can." Business matters completed, he referred to a personal grievance. "An' where the hell have you been? I didn't say t'Royal Alfred."

Bull Waggott did not appear particularly troubled, his grin exposing several gaps where teeth had been knocked out in fights. "You didn't?" he replied. "Ah, well, these mistakes do occur, lad."

Irritated by an unprofitable evening, Reuben Nattrass was in the mood to be unpleasant. It was perhaps natural he should select Adam as his victim, inquiring of him how much longer yet the farmers would reap profit from his many talents.

"Nay," he continued, "I'se nobbut wondering when us poor miners can hope to draw upon your skill i' problems like you've just heard me mention."

Regretfully Adam explained the situation. "I'm fully booked till after haymaking," he said. "But then, who knows?"

"Well, don't forget th'East Side Company's got the first call on your valuable services," sneered the mining agent who, turning to Cherry, guffawed: "You hear that, lass, me offering to burden t'Company with this chap, so never again say as I'm unmindful of your Uncle Titus's true interests."

Just as in a very brief space the whole of his life is supposed to be reviewed by a drowning man, so Adam Brunskill, in a flash of revelation, perceived his future path, one which might enable him to determine much that in the present was the wildest surmise. When he spoke the slur in his tone and the form of address were both designed to provoke an antagonism which would advance his purpose.

"I doubt, Cousin Reuben," he drawled, "I doubt very much if you'd like me to see some of t'mining methods I imagine you'll go in for. You must remember I've had the advantage o' being trained in one of the world's finest and biggest lead-mines, where only the most modern——"

"I don't care a damn where you've been trained," Reuben Nattrass growled. "An' afore you start criticising us lot here, you'd better have a go yourself."

Adam took the little gathering into his confidence. "I reckon that's almost a challenge, isn't it? But he'd look silly, wouldn't he, if I accepted it and one o' these days showed him a thing or two?"

Reuben Nattrass flared. Adam, he declared savagely, was at liberty whenever he wished to join any of the East Side Company's ore-getting partnerships who would have him. "I'd like nowt better," he snapped. "It's men's work i' these Skewdale levels, an' I'll wager a fair trifle you'd noan be long in finding an excuse for getting out."

"You're tempting me, Cousin Reuben," Adam said, smiling broadly.

The dark eyes were dangerous. "Tempting you, you say?" the mine-agent shouted. "I nobbut wish you'd bloody well try your——"

"Here, no more o' that language," Mark Iveson intervened.

Mildly, Adam smoothed things over. "Aye, I think we'd better let it drop," he went on. "Though," he shook his head, "I'm inclined to reckon that I'll have to manage a Pay or two for th'East Side lot, or I'll never be able to hold my head up again."

No one took him very seriously, not even Cherry Dinsdale, who prided herself that she was beginning to understand him much better. All the same, she was perplexed on another count. Never before in her hearing had he been the least boastful or superior, and yet undoubtedly that had been his attitude towards his cousin.

A little worried, she reflected on these things as she accompanied her friends along Main Street.

3

Shearing also was a neighbourly business, with Low Bands taking the first turn, this not a very long affair owing to a disastrous loss of stock from which Mr. Harker would take another year or two to recover. The shearers then shifted to Badger Hall, amongst them Adam in a tattered shirt and borrowed pair of white shearing drawers. From morning until night, apart from intervals for refreshment—foodstuffs brought from the house, liquid sustenance drawn on the spot out of a forty-gallon barrel of beer—the Skidmores' garth was noisy, on those warm days, with the clicking of shears, the clamour of sheep, and the occasional laughter of men.

In his preliminary attempts with the shears, Adam was ignominiously directed to operate only in the regions around filthy tails, but by the final evening at Anthony Skidmore's, while wool was being trodden down into a canvas sheet held up at each corner by a rope, two experts examined a sheep upon which he had exercised his skill unaided.

"Aye, cropped nice an' close," Mr. Harker rumbled. "An' I can't sight any blood where he's jabbed the points in."

"Yes, I contend it'll live, Francis," Mr. Skidmore observed.

"'Course he can't do his thirty moorland sheep a day yet," Low Bands remarked, slightly disparagingly. "An' you've to do that afore you can call yourself a real clipper."

"Still . . ." said Badger Hall.

"Aye." Francis Harker winked.

At this, the tribute ended. The sheet, a vast bag containing between two and three hundredweights of oily wool, was skewered-up and then rolled on to a sled: a low conveyance dragged about as much on the grits and grassy surfaces of rough roads and fields as on snow and ice in winter. With Adam walking alongside the horse, the wool was carried to the small wool barn, where room was limited owing to the presence of the previous year's shearing. That year prices had been exceedingly low and Mr. Skidmore, one of the few with the resources to do so, had resisted the blandishments of the Bradford wool merchant who, each season, drove round to the farms in a finely varnished dog-cart. Until values improved, the master of Badger Hall was quite prepared to retain his stock.

Adam was not asked to take any part in the festivities at Silence, for such, despite the hard toil, shearing had always been: a time of fun and pleasure. His cousin Isa's attitude was the root of the matter, of course, and of this Adam had further proof that night when, reaching the top of the steep hill on Middle Sorrow above Snorr Bridge, he passed Ralph Skidmore's farm. The two little girls were grooming Gem, the old white horse as still as a statue while one or other of his small mistresses darted under his belly or mounted a pair of rickety steps.

Harriet's smile was less in evidence than her sister's, which was decidedly coquettish.

"Now then, young ladies," Adam laughed. "Giving Gem a polish up?"

"You don't polish hosses," Harriet informed him primly.

Nancy was dancing about, flourishing a well-worn hearth brush. "He's nobbut being silly," she shrieked. "Adam's nobbut being silly."

"Don't be silly yourself," her sister reproved her.

If little Harriet, in her childish antagonism, was taking her cue from her Uncle Reuben, she was certainly influenced also by her mother, who just then clattered round the side of the house, a well-filled milk-pail in each hand. Mrs. Ralph's response to a polite greeting was very boorish.

"Aye, well, seeing as you're so throng I'll noan stop for a chat, Cousin Isa," Adam remarked with consideration.

Her angular face reddened. "Who's asked you to, pray?"

And so Adam left Silence behind, striding along the springy turf of Middle Sorrow until he came to a sow kiln made of sods, used by the Skidmores for burning lime subsequently spread over their meadows.

Here he heard himself hailed and, glancing up the land on the higher side of the track, saw Bob and Ward sprinting through the heather.

The boys' errand was brief: to inquire about climbing to Deer Pot on the following day. It appeared they knew he would not be amongst the shearers at Silence and, with the least encouragement, Bob Skidmore would have vented an opinion about his Uncle Ralph.

"It'll suit me grand," Adam said, glance fixed on Ward's side-pocket, which moved about in an extraordinary fashion until a narrow, fawn-coloured head emerged, when a deadly little creature surveyed the world with bright eyes. "An' what are you lads doing with that ferret and who does it belong to?"

"It's me an' Ward's, Adam," Bob grinned.

"And does your father know about it?" Adam asked.

Ward spluttered. "If my Uncle Will did, he wouldn't half give Bob a tanning."

Smothering the thought of Will Skidmore's face if he realised how much his son might be advancing towards becoming a poacher of the moors he guarded so zealously, Adam shook his head, patently disturbed by their depravity.

"Yes, I think he would," he agreed. "Aye, I reckon it's my duty to . . . to impound it . . ." Before he could say any more, the two youngsters darted away, whooping with joyous defiance.

After a hard day's work it was pleasant to stroll along Middle Sorrow, breasting a cool evening breeze. In the dale the meadow grass was growing taller and more lush, and everywhere milkers could be seen, in the Common Pasture, at the sides of lanes, in small garths and other enclosures. A couple of donkeys, milk cans slung on either side, were daintily picking the easiest path down Sleety Slape; cattle, with dogs in attendance, were sauntering from the second of their two most important engagements of the day; the blue smoke of peat drifted up the valley, its tang merged with the lovely scent of blossom which, in shades from deep pink to pale and then white, copiously clothed the hawthorns; and a cuckoo on urgent affairs winged purposefully, to land upon one of the top spurs of a towering spruce whose new growth against the darker green of old made an effect enchantingly variegated.

"Yes," Adam murmured, eyeing the warm brown trunk of a Scots pine and the pinpoints of yellow flowers sprinkled upon its dusty green head, "yes, I wish my father had seen all this again. He'd have revelled in it and maybe he'd never have gone back to Spain . . . perhaps he'd have settled here, as I'm half contemplating doing. Aye . . ."

At Pewitt Pillar he decided that, when haymaking was over, he would tell Cherry Dinsdale he loved her. He would not know then with absolute certainty whether his future life could best be spent hill-farming in a remote Yorkshire dale, nor could he have rid himself by then of that bug of foolish fancy whereby Reuben Nattrass was cast as the unscrupulous party scheming Titus Alderson's undoing. But did those things matter?

"The truth is that she's th'only lass there is for me, and if she feels the same about me . . . well, the sooner we enter into our happiness the better. My father had nobbut two years, but I'm greedy, and . . ."

At this stage Adam was jarred out of his daydream by a rusty-voiced inquiry. He and the old man who was smoking a pipe outside his cottage had frequently exercised their wits upon one another. This time the younger was to triumph.

"Well, lad, they say that i' spring young chaps' thoughts turns to love," Droughty Tom remarked. "An' I feel bound to add thoo's looking very intent."

Adam pulled himself together. "I were evaluating some very important matters, Mr. Woodward," he said with an air.

A broad thumb, in which the underpart of the nail was lined with white, was placed against the side of a bulbous nose, which was then blown powerfully.

"You were, were you?" the lime-burner said at the completion of these exertions. "In that case I were wrong, lad. You see I were trying to make out which of three very bonny lasses it were. There's that little cousin o' thine, her as oft hugs your arm when you're walking out together, an' next we have Titus Alderson's niece and Anthony Skidmore's daughter."

As he earnestly pointed out that there was a true and fine faith which saw no sin in a man taking to himself more than one woman, Adam might have been a hierophant sent out by the Latter-Day Saints.

"Does Salt Lake City mean anything to you?" he persuasively inquired of the stupefied lime-burner.

"*Salt Lake* . . ." Droughty Tom was gasping when he noticed a betraying gleam. Then, his spit implicit of self-disgust, he conceded the round. "That makes it four-three, wi' you leading," he growled. "But you'd never have nabbed me if you hadn't heard that there were a rumour last year as a young Mormon missionary might be coming up t'Dale from Corvy."

Adam shook his head. "If there's owt worse than a bad loser——"

Obeying an alarming-sounding but quite good-natured order to remove himself, Adam was soon at Back Lane, where neither Agnes awaited his coming nor was tea laid. In the last fortnight, this was not the first occasion such a thing had happened. Far from being annoyed by this neglect, Adam considered it a sign that his cousin was acquiring a semblance of character. It was more girlish, anyhow, and less the action of the crushed little creature she had been.

* * * *

During the cheese-making season, Anthony Skidmore often declared that the dairy at Badger Hall resembled the battle headquarters of a great army. Beyond question only the highest standards were permitted, and his wife's commands were meant to be obeyed.

When Adam arrived at the farm, his meeting place with Bob and Ward, it was still too soon for moments of expert decision in the dairy, and so the possessor of ' the finest pair of cheese-hands in Skewdale ' was able to attend to her cheese factor. This gentleman, Adam's Uncle George, would in two or possibly three collections before November take the bulk of the Badger Hall output. No prices were fixed, these being dependent on that current at the time of sale—by way of contra account George Nattrass supplied the household and farm with such groceries, draperies, corn and meal as were required, with cash adjustment at the end of the year.

Adam spoke from the dairy door. "Good morning, Mrs. Skidmore. Good morning, Uncle George, you're up early from Greets, aren't you?"

Mrs. Skidmore spared a fleeting smile from amidst her business preoccupations, but George Nattrass made no response whatsoever.

Dinah and Mary Jane Tiplady were attired similarly to the commanding officer, in freshly laundered, close-fitting white mobcaps and big aprons. Their sleeves were rolled above the elbow.

"No more gallivanting to Corvy market, Dinah," Adam remarked. "Anyway," he added, deep with understanding, "it might save a lot of chaps' lives, mightn't it? You know, them who cranes their necks too much."

Dinah, scarlet under the shock, glanced hastily at her mother, who luckily was engrossed in a pet subject, the iniquity of mixing good cheeses with indifferent ones, and as she provided George Nattrass with a grade so reputed that often, on the strength of allowing a customer a proportion, he was able to gain up to a farthing a pound on others less renowned, he listened carefully.

"You wait, Adam Brunskill," Dinah said under her breath.

"Tch, tch," clicked Adam, turning his attention to Mary Jane. "So you're adding to your accomplishments, are you, love?"

A conscientious little girl, Mary Jane passed on her father's message before dealing with personal ambitions. This was that more than twenty loads of slags and slimes had been carted to Notion Bridge, the results of the first smelting confirming the Newcastle chemist's analysis.

Mrs. Skidmore had reached her climax, which was that all Skewdale cheeses should be of a certain quality or not sold as such. She did not wish to mention names . . .

"You've no need, Minnie," George Nattrass shrugged. "It's Grace Blenkiron you're meaning, isn't it? Well, she will make her skim-milk cheeses, though I've telled her she loses by it."

"All t'same, George," Mrs. Skidmore persisted. "Mind you, it's you who's brought her name up."

Adam was glancing around the stone-flagged dairy, from brine vat to cheese press. Everything was in readiness, a pile of wooden moulds, scrubbed scrupulously, and rolls of white cotton bandaging, the outer covering for each cheese. There were two big cheese kettles, one of brass and the other of copper, bowls a yard across and deep, both gleaming to perfection.

"Adam!" He heard Dinah's whisper and, following her smiling look, his own eyes filled with amusement when he watched Mary Jane, with an utterly professional air, test the temperature of the milk. The child dipped her elbow into the liquid, a most sensitive part for such assessment, and then, nodding wisely, washed her arm carefully.

"Well, you're starting cheese-making in the right hands, I should say," Adam said to her. "And you've plenty of time afore you."

Little Mary Jane was very grave. "You can't begin too young, Adam," she explained. "An' then when you're a young woman you've got everything at your finger-tips, haven't you?"

Hastily Adam fought back a grin. "Yes, I suppose so, love. Anyhow one thing seems clear, an' it's that you're going to be a farmer's wife."

Mary Jane had no doubt on that, though the date was more dubious. "You see I promised mother I'd look after my father for always," she confided. "So maybe I'll have to wait until he's gone to heaven."

"And we don't want that to happen," Dinah said.

"Makes it a bit awkward, love," Adam observed.

Mary Jane frowned thoughtfully. "Perhaps when I got wed I could take my father with me. I've seen lots of old grandfathers sitting in t'corner of a kitchen, right comfortable an' all."

She was so much in earnest that the appearance of her brother and cousin afforded real relief. Lively Matt Tiplady, calmly delegated by his small daughter into the role of the old man who, presumably, kept an eye on the younger children, was enough, as Dinah managed to convey to Adam, "to make a cat laugh." Fortunately Mary Jane, hearing Ward's and Bob's noisy entrance, forgot to probe further.

"You don't come in here with your mucky clogs on," she screamed. "A speck o' dirt can do all t'harm in the world when there's owt like cheese-making or butter-making going on."

"Quite right, love," Minnie Skidmore said with approval.

"Aye, you start as you mean to go on, lass," the cheese-factor advised the termagant. "An' then maybe some day you'll make as good cheeses as is made in this very dairy."

Mrs. Skidmore bridled, and everyone else, for their various reasons, looked very pleased, even the boys, who seemed inclined to be proud of the small virago. Shortly afterwards Adam and his young companions left for the strenuous climb to Deer Pot, on Water Ling Moor.

Entering Sorrow Far opposite the Royal Alfred, the route was along this portion of the old byway as far as the intersection with Legatt's Way, a very short distance only from the burial mound at Bloody Sigh, and thence up the Roman road to a point where it crossed the two-mile long flue of the North Smelt Mill. From there, following the unwavering course of the flue, the ascent was so precipitous as to demand real effort, correspondingly arousing an even greater admiration for the flue builders whose heavy task, in rocky ground and with often tricky foothold, had been to hew a trench eight feet deep and six feet wide, before flooring, lining and capping the long-extending cut with a barrel-arch, all in rough-dressed but workmanlike-shaped stones.

"We're nearly there now, Adam," Ward said, breathing heavily. "It's on the flat piece just above the next rise."

At that altitude it was surprising to encounter a lake of perhaps four or five acres in extent, but the spring responsible evidently preferred to thrust upwards rather than seek egress lower down. From that lofty plateau the great fells and hills to the south of Skewdale, Lovely Lady, Silver Seat and Virgin Hill, so impressive from the 'bottoms,' were now humbled; beyond them and around, many more mountain ranges were visible, land masses of which the nearer were blue-shaded and those remote soft-hued, barely discernible.

"I see Deer Pot serves t'mines as well as the gulls," Adam remarked, pointing to the turn-wheel valve of a fourteen inches diameter pressure-pipe which dipped into the distance, eventually to reach a small, stone building nearly a mile off. "Goes to the eye of Maybe Shaft, doesn't it?"

"Aye," Bob Skidmore nodded. "To t'hydraulic engine there, which drives the pump in the shaft sump."

"So long as the old crock can keep going." Ward shook his head. "It's at the far end—the pump I mean."

Adam grinned. "You lads believe in being well informed."

The boys took him more seriously. "It's best to have your e'en open," Ward vouchsafed, while his cousin added sagely: "In this world," thus making their joint meaning more clear.

Every step forward through the rushes fringing Deer Pot caused greater resentment amongst its native inhabitants. And, when the little party reached a sandy strand thickly encrusted with yellowish-white droppings, the commotion assumed alarming proportions. The air, darkened by a multitude of furious gulls, was filled with a cacophony of angry cries against a background of whirring wing beats as, in hundreds, anxious parents dived upon the intruders. But, despite the tumult, it was interesting to approach one mother who, for all her fear, never budged from the untidy nest in which she was sitting; and, more fascinating, to handle downy chicks just out of the shell and others old enough to peck sharply at a stranger's hand.

"Why are they frightened on us when they're that young?" Bob puzzled.

The situation was hardly suitable for a discussion on such lines—already Adam had received a stinging crack from the tip of a strong wing, and Ward's cap had been flung backwards a good ten yards, struck from his head by the clawing feet of a fast-flying bird. So a retreat was made, up the remaining portion of the flue until, at its conclusion, they attained the square, stone tower, of height that of a Norman village church, out of whose top light grey smoke drifted from the ore hearths and furnaces of the North Mill.

Pausing briefly, a start westward was then made, leaving the more barren regions for the moorland below where, scrambling along the gullies traversing it, they set clucking many a startled water hen and flushed into talkative flight dozens of game birds. Next, Bob in the lead, keeping carefully to a not very well defined trod, the party crossed a bog brilliant with the violet flowers of butterwort, this bringing them out not far away from a cliff-like edge where a merlin had been reported a few days before. Nothing was seen of it, but the three were favoured with a more majestic sight: that of one of the great lords of the air, a buzzard of immense wing span sailing along the face of the scar.

"Wouldn't it be champion if we could do that?" Bob said, envying.

"We could go round t'Dales of an afternoon," Ward gloated.

While slithering down the scree to Foul Syke, and as far beyond as the high ridge of ground over the beck, the boys lent themselves to the extravagant fancies this opening encouraged. But when Yorreldale, an offshoot of the main dale, stretched out below, they resumed their duties, pointing out everything of interest. There was a small village nearby, quite deserted.

"Aye . . ." Ward mourned, "aye, there used to be nine public-houses i' Yorreldale, doing a good trade an' all. And now there's nobbut one, down at Yorrel, and it's doing nowt."

For once Bob did not supplement his cousin but, stalwart and weather-wise, shaded his eyes while inspecting the sky towards a sun rapidly being obscured. Then ensued a colloquy which left Adam thinking his feelings should be those of the mountaineer in a most dangerous part of the snowy Alps, whose guides discern a catastrophic change in conditions.

"Up bank, Ward," said Bob quietly.

"Aye, lad," agreed Ward. "Yes, there."

"We'll have ten minutes, think you?" Bob inquired.

"We'll be going afore it," his cousin pointed out.

"Aye, there's that," Bob nodded. "But twelve at th'outside."

This weighty discussion related to the imminent appearance of a heavy rain squall, and the need of seeking shelter. Forthwith Adam was piloted carefully towards the rim of a basin-shaped depression in the ground, the remains of a shaft which had ' run,' his blood meantime being chilled by an account of what his fate would be if, assuming that the bottom consisted only of a sprinkling of grass-covered earth resting on old timbers, he jumped into it.

Cover was shortly found in the lee of the wall separating Water Ling Moor from Yorrel Side. Crouching there, it was inspiring to watch the ragged wall of rain whose misty advanced spear partially blotted out Slackrigg, but allowed a glimpse of a lane which in its higher part suddenly glistened with water while the lower portion remained dry.

"Oh, that oft happens," Ward observed, very worldly-wise. "Why, me an' Bob once saw the main road wet at one side and dry at th'other, right from Town Foot to Malaga."

"And the joining were as straight as if t'Schoolmaster had laid his round ruler down," Bob interposed.

"But a bigger 'un than he uses to whack us wi'," Ward chuckled.

Still staring into the Dale, Adam smiled and nodded. The rain was sending warning splashes ahead, for regularly, in pasture after pasture, cows which had been peacefully grazing began to comport themselves with an abandon not generally conceded to their lumbering kind. They bucked wildly, before racing off to take refuge behind a copse or other windbreak, at the side of a barn or beneath the riot of colourful flowers on a tall bank.

The boys were reconnoitring, over the wall top. "It's here now, Adam," they shouted together.

While the big drops slashed overhead an instructive conversation took place. Adam not only heard plans for Whitsuntide but also, more indifferently, that the previous goose season had been quite satisfactory, so that those youngsters who otherwise might not have had new clothes would be fortunate, on the money received from the dealers for the sale of goslings. The Coopers, however, fathers, mothers, and broods of children, would as usual on Whit Sunday crowd to Chapel in their rags. It seemed that although as a result hard-pressed folk would make them gifts of serviceable second-hand clothing the charity arose not from pity but from Winterings' desire to hide from outsiders that the village sheltered such good-for-nothings.

Amused by the lads' disgust, Adam inquired further about the Coopers, who he knew lived at Dirty Bottom. "They're groovers for th'East Side Company, aren't they?"

The by-names given to the three brothers precisely expressed local opinion. "Aye," grunted young Bob. "They're called: ' Nowt Much,' ' Nowt,' and ' Less Nor Nowt,' and it suits 'em. Why, their ash heap is as big as the house itself, because they'll noan bother to shift it into the river."

"All they think about is beer," Ward scoffed.

"And begatting children," Bob said with contempt.

"Aye, that an' all, Bob lad," Ward snorted.

The storm was passing and soon four or five diffused shafts of sunlight caressed the purpling fellside above Yorrel and, as the last wisps of grey rain cloud trailed over Great Barg, the bare outline of that height was revealed.

"Well now, lads," said Adam, glancing at his watch before standing up and flexing knees and arms, "it's me who's in charge from here onwards, and you two who's doing the chasing after."

And chase him they did, across a moor in which myriads of tiny raindrops shone brilliantly, diamond-like; to Dubbing Quarry where crystals in the massive limestone winked out a greeting; thence, diagonally, to reach the sheer upper end of Winterings Common Pasture and, later, a small, walled-in fir plantation half a mile above Modesty. So to the Brig and, at last, the back door of the Plug and Feathers, where the mistress of the house and two rosy-cheeked maids gazed at the callers.

"Can we come in, Mrs. Peacock?" Adam smiled.

Lucy Peacock did not smile. "What do you think the boot-scraper's for?" she demanded.

The broad hint acted upon most vigorously, Adam tried again. "So what could you do for three hungry chaps?" he ventured.

"I've nowt in," Mrs. Peacock replied, "but such as there is . . ." she sounded extremely grudging, "you can have. Tea or coffee?"

'Such as there is' started off with a couple of boiled eggs each, followed by platefuls of tongue and ham, the accompanying bread lavishly spread with butter; there were also, to fill up any niches, stewed fruit, scones, custard tart, currant pasty, three varieties of sweetcake and an assortment of buns.

When Adam had his last word of that afternoon with the cousins they were prostrate on the parapet of Winterings Brig, as they had been after the race for the Maidens' Garland. The beck was very low and had they tumbled into the lazy whirlpool below, at the foot of the three fern-margined terraces of the falls, the consequences might not have been dire, though from such a height it would have been serious if they had alighted on heaped household rubbish which awaited the next real spate.

Beyond Nick Turn, Adam met Cherry as she was leaving Cuthbert Daykin's shop, which gave him the opportunity to discuss a project he had previously consulted her upon. In Winterings he had received much kindly hospitality, and this in his circumstances he could never repay. But, some time before, he had had the notion that a wagonette trip and picnic at Whitsuntide might enable him to express gratitude in some small degree. Further details of this he now talked over with Cherry, along Main Street and at the gate of Yew Tree House. The survey was comprehensive; food hampers, ginger pop, cigars, bottled beer, spice, and surprise packets for everybody.

"My words, I'm fortunate," Adam continued, his stance that of one prepared to devote the remainder of the day to this theme, "to have you. To bring my troubles to, I mean."

Very ostentatiously Cherry shifted her shopping basket from one hand to the other, opened the gate, and placed herself at the opposite side.

"And what about the wagonettes?" she asked.

A slow smile curved his lips when he told her he had engaged two at his uncle's. In point of fact the negotiations for these had aroused scant enthusiasm at the livery stables, where William Nattrass would certainly not have come to terms at all had not his financial position been such that any profitable hire must be accepted.

"Adam," said Cherry, the fun gone out of her, "why did you bother with your Uncle William? There's a place in Greets who'd have been only too glad."

"Well . . ." Adam cogitated, "you know how all my Nattrass relations treat me, don't you? So why shouldn't I get a bit of amusement out o' them?" As he smiled down so easily at her she thought, miserably, that he had not the least conception of the danger into which he might be running. "Aye, I find 'em amusing, lass," he laughed.

"But . . . but, Adam," she said, "it'll nobbut cause bother in the end."

"Let it," he retorted.

For the rest of the evening, and as she lay in bed, Cherry Dinsdale peered into nothing but a future in which, step by step, Adam was bringing himself nearer and nearer to bloody conflict with a man many of whose utterly-broken opponents she could recall.

"If I could only make him see what a terrible brute Reuben Nattrass is once he starts," she whispered to herself.

But, within her, she was aware that Adam would not be stayed in his lightsome treatment of the Nattrasses. And, as she slipped at last into sleep, tears of impotence and anxiety filled her sweet eyes.

4

Wherever he went Adam was offered cheese-cakes and, as a refusal was considered either as a reflection upon the quality of the cakes or a deplorable idiosyncrasy in himself, he ate them until he was satiated. Whit Sunday also, at two o'clock chapel, was much as he had expected, apart from the greater poignancy caused by direct contact with people who strove so hard to conceal poverty. There were new garments here and there, but, on the whole, mothers and fathers made do, the ladies brightening old attire with fresh ribbons, the men in coats and trousers sponged a few days before and pressed beneath the mattress since. The girls came off better, their cheap frocks, either worn the first time or so beautifully washed and ironed as to seem so, making a splash of colour amidst the sombre broadcloth, as did their pretty bonnets; the boys, they shone, faces, laced boots and home-done, stiffly-starched collars.

At evening chapel, old James Guy of Greets, who with his lifelong friend, John Dougill, also of Greets, shared the distinction of being the most eminent retired mining-agents in the entire Yorkshire lead-mining districts, delivered a really wonderful address; and after chapel, as so often in fine weather, the congregation did not disperse, but enjoyed themselves singing hymns on Winterings Brig until nearly dark.

Monday was fine and, towards Silver Seat, the slight sultriness of the bottoms was replaced by a light breeze. For the horses the climb up Jom High Road might have been more arduous but, at each stiff ascent, it became a regular feature for the young people to jump from the vehicles. As Wingy Blenkiron declared, he had walked five miles and ridden a tenth of that. "It's worth it, but thank God we can put us seats on to a comfortable cushion on t'way back, except down the steepest bit," he summed up.

"Clarkson!" his sister gasped. "Of all the vulgar things to say."

The postman mopped his brow and, beneath the cover of the handkerchief, winked at several boon friends. "Never mind what *I* say, lass," he advised her. "What you want to do is to take care o' Bart. You ought to have heard what *he* said when we'd to give t'wagonette a shove just below the moor gate."

Unluckily for Bart Hugill, he remembered far more clearly his future father-in-law's extremely ripe sally.

"An' what are you spluttering about?" Fronick demanded.

Her young man was rash. "Summat a sight worse that your father said," he replied, unable to check a subsequent howl of glee.

"As if my father . . ." Fronick began, and then turned her back on him, but not before she added: "You common thing."

Their little difference was adjusted long before a fine array of victuals was spread at the site chosen for the picnic. This was on the lower approaches to Silver Seat and, at the conclusion of the meal, the majority decided not to stir from where they were. Others more active, however, toiled to Sybil's Well, in the middle of the oval-shaped, perfectly flat summit of the towering hill, where the girls and young men gossiped leisurely while cooling off.

In due course fresh diversions were sought. Wingy Blenkiron launched suitable boulders down the steep slope, and Bart Hugill, on all fours, stalked a party of ewes and lambs who peeped curiously over the nearby edge at the strangers; Dinah and Fronick dropped stones into the pagan well and discussed clothes, while Adam and Cherry wandered across to the far side until they were able to enjoy a wonderful view of upper Skewdale.

"It wasn't as high as this, an' there weren't any leaves on the trees," Adam soliloquised as he shook out a handkerchief for her to sit on, "but all the same this is very much like the first glimpse I had of the Dale."

"Are you glad you came, Adam?" Cherry asked.

He stared below, seeing the silvery, winding river, grey villages and hamlets, the fine green lines of pack-horse tracks, and moors which day by day grew nearer to assuming their richest hue. Then, searchingly, he turned towards her.

"Aye, I'm glad I came, lass," he said.

Each happy in the other's presence, they started quietly to talk, the minutes speeding faster than they knew, until the sound of footsteps disturbed them. Bob Skidmore and Ward Tiplady and his sister, obviously rehearsed, lined up to make a set speech. "We're a deputation," Mary Jane began breathlessly, "as comes . . . as comes——"

"With the humble respects of t'company awaiting," Bob prompted her.

Adam chuckled and Cherry, though blushing perceptibly, laughed as the gist of the message became more plain, which was that the guests had no desire to behave ungraciously, but if their host and the young lady with him did not immediately march downhill they must reconcile themselves to walking home.

"Champion, Mary Jane," Adam grinned as he pulled out his watch. "But they're in a hurry, aren't—— Whew!"

"What time is it, Adam?" Cherry asked, to which, without a word, he twisted the dial towards her, to reveal the fatal figures on it. "Adam!" she screeched, "it *can't* be."

"It is, lass," he smiled.

Then he pulled her up and, still holding her hand—an attention which caused Ward to wink at Bob, and Mary Jane to scowl at both lads—they crossed the table top of Silver Seat and, encouraged by faint hoots from below, began to descend.

CHAPTER SIX

I

BY THE beginning of June, Adam's spare cash was low and so, as he had been advised by Messrs. Richardson and Storey, the Corvy banking house, that he was credited there with funds received from the London and Andajoz Lead and Silver Mining Company, he decided to visit them on the next market day. This meant riding with the weekly carrier, leaving William Nattrass's yard at five o'clock in the morning. Two evenings before, however, he was asked to fetch a couple of beasts from a breeder in Wensleydale.

"It's a fairish stretch, lad, an' you'll noan drive 'em in here much afore ten or eleven o'clock to-morrow night, but t'evenings are light," Anthony Skidmore said. "And we'll have some supper waiting for you."

It would be a pleasing errand over fresh country, with Nell, but it caused a slight problem—how could Adam, on the day but one following, after perhaps only four hours in bed, be sure of waking early enough to wash, dress, cook his own breakfast, and catch the carrier's cart.

Ward and his cousin promised to arrange *that*, with the loan of what, poker-faced, they termed their 'alarum clock.' The deliberations took place outside the pig-place, which they were cleaning out while its tenant, an enormous sow, skipped about the Badger Hall orchard like a lightweight, and the offer was made when Bob's grandfather had gone off to examine a cow which, 'off its cud,' was covered with an old eiderdown whose ends she chewed, despite her reluctance to eat more sustaining fodder, with every semblance of relish.

"We'll take it to Back Lane for you to-morrow," said Ward.

Susan Skidmore was houseproud, and some part of the example she set must have filtered down to her dare-devil son. "An' we'll put summat down, newspaper like, so as your cousin Agnes 'ul noan have to do any siding-up," Bob added.

"Aye, and just chuck it out of t'window when you've wakened, Ward continued helpfully. "It'll noan harm it."

Adam eyed them. "What kind of an alarm-clock is this?" he asked.

When he was told he laughed so uproariously that Will Skidmore, who often worked as a part-time hind for his father, paused to discover what it was about. When Adam informed him the lads were arranging to do a good turn, he smiled as one who hopes for the best but fears the worst.

The 'alarum clock' performed most efficaciously. On the second morning after these undertakings, as the eastern sky brightened, Adam woke with a sudden start in a mighty din. The previous night, after a scorching fourteen hours on foot, he had tumbled into bed too dog-tired to notice a dark shadow in the window-bottom.

"Just a minute, old cock-a-lorum," he begged, rapidly swinging his legs out, to hasten across the floor before the rooster, whose magnificent red comb still quivered from the last effort, threw himself into another ear-splitting cry. "Aye, just a minute, for pity's sake."

The cock turned a beady and malignant eye, but was sufficiently interested to remain silent until the lower sash was raised. Probably of a less venomous nature than his mien suggested, he suffered himself to be thrust into space, to be followed by a screwed-up bundle of the paper Bob had prudently spread upon the temporary perching-place.

"Seems used to it an' all," Adam grinned when the bird completed the flight with less squawking than might have been expected. "And now what?" he wondered, when Mark Iveson's cock strutted out importantly.

The two gentlemen circled each other warily, but fortunately hostilities were not pursued beyond that point.

Refreshed by the sweetness of the early morning air, Adam was wide-awake enough to appreciate everything he saw as the wagon bumped along between hedgerows colourful with pink and white wild roses.

At Half, where Heugh Syke, a meagre stream during dry weather, joined the Skew after tumbling down Noggin Moor, the discords of many geese echoed in the foot of the narrow gill. The hamlet was very small, with one of its more outstanding buildings the Old Cow Inn, bought for a song by Mr. Martin Rutter and still used, despite his wife's entreaties, as a residence for himself and his family. Then there was the Groovers Welcome, whose host was Jonas Cottingham; and next, shaded by a noble Dutch elm, the lodge of Half House, from which the drive to Mr. Wade's mansion extended about three hundred yards.

From there, leaving the Skew, the main road climbed easily as far as the place where Sorrow Near crossed it, the old byway dipping down towards the river, a roundabout course to Greets Church. The dusty highway, to attain the same destination, rose more steeply, heather to either side, to reach a lofty brow before finally descending to the largest village in the upper dale, whose first habited abode on that side, the

B.G. Inn, named after the old B.G. Mining Company on Hart Moor, had in its day coined money from the patronage of that once famous undertaking's groovers. After that came Greets Hall, Sir Charles Grafton's seat, within tall, castellated walls, and, facing this, on the opposite side of the road, the grey-towered church; the Vicarage, formerly the Old Hall, was farther along, a Jacobean house with many voided windows, walled up when window-tax was onerous.

Beyond the Vicarage the village green opened out, bounded at intervals by a chapel, the Society of Friends' Meeting House, and a few dwellings. The highway divided the spacious, grassy oval, passing in the middle an ancient elm, beautiful in its full dress of foliage, whose trunk was not less than two yards in diameter.

A bird's-eye view of Greets would have shown the village's lay-out, apart from stray erections, as not being dissimilar to two unequally-sized eggs laid end to end, the Green being the larger. The Market Place, weathered Saxon Cross in the centre, was more compact, hemmed in by houses and shops, cheek by jowl.

Amongst the shops to the right of the road's egress to Corvy, Adam saw his uncle George's, its three windows devoted to drapery, ironmongery and groceries, with an enclosure for loading adjoining. In addition to the usual sign there was also one less conspicuous: 'Agent for Nobel's Explosives Company.'

"So he supplies the mines an' all, does he," Adam thought.

On the other side of the Market Place, an apprentice lad was sweeping the pavement in front of a curved, small-paned window, within which Adam perceived a treadle-lathe and several pendulums. This, he guessed, was the workshop of a tradesman whose frequent calls at Yew Tree House were, he was sure, hated by Cherry.

"Is that Thomas Plews' place?" he inquired. "Him as makes grandfather clocks and is a director of the West Side Company."

The driver looked back. The horse was already close to the bridge spanning Greets Beck, and the angle of view was narrowing. "Aye, that's Screw Tom's," he grunted. "Full of t'brotherhood o' man on the Sabbath, a real shark on other days."

Adam next nodded to the left, at a three-storied mill, powered by a water-wheel, of whose ownership he was not in doubt. A few women were leaving it, and others, carrying various woollen goods, were walking towards it.

"Yes, that's Mr. Wade's," he was informed. "Makes carpet yarns mainly, but he spins a bit of another sort that folk who wants to earn a trifle by knitting at home can go for. They do such things as mittens, long stockings and seamen's caps an' jerseys. He pays about a shilling for a jersey."

"It doesn't seem much," Adam remarked.

The carter said dourly that beggars could not be choosers. "All t'same, I don't think Mr. Wade could pay more if he wanted. He's a real decent sort."

Below Greets, with every mile farther from mountainous country, the landscape became more wooded, and prospects increasingly restricted, though once, through a clearing, Adam glimpsed otter hounds exercising by the river. The day promised to be hot, and by and by, following the example of two calves behind him, each of which, head alone protruding, was tied in a sack, Adam's eyes closed and he, too, slipped into sleep.

When he awoke Corvy stood on its eminence a short way ahead, a little market town whose roofs, less austere than those in the upper dale, were as often of red tiles as of stone slates. Dwarfing all else was the massive grey Keep of the Norman castle, the tower of the Nunnery and, sharply outlined against the azure sky, a graceful arch, perfect fragment of a great Cistercian monastery.

After leaving the Bank, no longer under the necessity of restraining a smile, Adam stood in the doorway, enjoying the spectacle of the crowded Bull Ring . . . ladies gossiping, gentry driving in, farmers—mainly from the arable regions to the east—talking in groups on matters perhaps a little different from those which would be discussed by hill-farmers from the west.

"Aye," he murmured, his thoughts going back to the recent interview, "Mr. Storey's pretty much as Mr. Skidmore said."

It was the policy of the partners of Messrs. Richardson and Storey to meet each new customer personally. Adam had found William Storey a very precise gentleman, insistent upon the due observance of proper banking procedure. On the other hand the banker, through the Leadenhall Street introduction, knew Adam was closely connected with mining in Spain and, shedding the role of quiet-spoken banker for that of Chairman of the East Side Lead Mining Company, blossomed into a rakish optimist ardent about long-term prospects in Skewdale.

"Yes, lead-mining is a real romance to him," Adam mused.

The Bull Ring was lined by Elizabethan and Georgian buildings, with others characteristically Scottish in style. Some were private dwellings, while the ground floors of many houses had been converted for commercial purposes; in height they ranged from two to four stories with a dormer above that, giving a widely-irregular skyline which, with chimneys of every pattern and roofs whose pitch was low to extremely steep, made a captivating sight. On the cobbles, outside the kerb, the scene was no less pleasing—rows of stalls, canvas shades overhead protecting butter and cream, poultry, game and flowers from the hot sun, thronged by folk from the outlying countryside who, men and women alike, were making the most of their weekly treat.

Adam laughed. "Yes, you can see why lasses like Cherry and Dinah miss their trips here. A real change for 'em, all the hustle an' bustle."

Speak of the devil and you are supposed to see him. After walking along the crowded pavement between shops at one side and stallkeepers crying their wares at the other, Adam arrived at the corner of Mercenary Lane, where he had a clear view of the opposite side of the Bull Ring. To his astonishment he saw Prue, the Skidmores' piebald mare, mincing into the arched stable entrance of the William and Mary. Two young ladies, in zephyr gingham dresses, were sitting in the trap behind her, and though their faces were concealed by big straw sunbonnets of a colour somewhat lighter than the smaller model Prue's ears pricked through, Adam was equally certain who they were.

"Cherry and Dinah!" he ejaculated.

Within a minute or so he would have joined them had not a high-spirited horse at his shoulder shied at a piece of fluttering paper. Adam grabbed the lively fellow, patted the glossy coat and discussed the affair with him, gradually soothing him down until he was calm enough to be led past the danger zone.

Delayed by this, Adam did not reach the William and Mary until Prue had been removed from the shafts and the girls were on the eve of departing on their business, with a basket of eggs and a second basket, much larger, in which, beneath a snow-white cloth, pounds of yellow butter wrapped in grease-proof paper rested, each with the farm's sign, the Badger, embossed on it.

He looked them up and down. "I thought that once cheese-making started there'd be no more o' this gallivanting for months an' months."

"It's butter as my mother promised a special customer," Dinah laughed, when they had recovered from their astonishment. "For just this time," Cherry pointed out, seeing no relaxation of a condemnatory expression. "Dinah *had* to come."

Becoming a trifle easier, Adam picked up the baskets and, proceeding sideways in the crush, carried them safely to their destined places, this completing the official mission. Then he accompanied the young ladies shopping and, at the dinner-hour, escorted them to the Saracen for the one o'clock Ordinary. Afterwards, more shopping, and sight-seeing visits for his benefit to the Castle and the gracious old priory church of St. Peter-on-the-Wall, with a call for water-ices sandwiched in between. Next, to round off the day, tea at the new tea-shop in Friargate, and then back to the stables of the William and Mary.

As the man of the party Adam took the reins during a drive which was on the whole uneventful, except for the repeated necessity of stirring Prue when, from trot to amble, she declined to a crawl, and the incident some distance short of Greets when William Nattrass overtook them.

Hearing the jingle of harness they all glanced back, to see a dog-cart rapidly approaching, the horse stretching out as if, rather than with a wheeled vehicle to draw, it was being hard-ridden in a point-to-point. As the thoroughfare was narrow Adam pulled Prue against the hedge, but the oncoming driver was not too much in his cups as to risk at speed a passage which, at the offside, fell sheerly to the boulder-strewn Skew, the drop so considerable that the tops of pines growing by the water's edge were not much more than a few feet above the road level.

"Do you want all t'bloody room?" William Nattrass shouted thickly, flabby jowl quivering as, fighting his wayward animal, he brought it to its haunches. "I said," he struck his beast again, "did you want——"

"I heard what you said," Adam broke in.

A pair of whisky-inflamed eyes were turned towards him. "So it's Jim Brunskill's god-damned——"

Adam again intervened. "Aye, it's Jim Brunskill's lad. But if you've owt else to say about that or anything else you'd better keep your mouth clean or I'll clean it for you . . . t'river's nice and handy."

"Don't take any notice, Adam," Cherry whispered. "It's because he's market fresh."

Snarling obscenities, William Nattrass succeeded in forcing his big body upright when, swaying dangerously on a lofty perch, he raised his whip.

"I reckon thoo needs summat to remember me by," he wheezed. "And nowt'll be better than to lay that face o' thine open."

The lash swished viciously but failed to find its target, the sound its owner's undoing, for he was lucky not to be thrown from the dog-cart. Bolting ahead, hoofs and wheels raised a cloud of dust those behind had to suffer for the next few minutes.

Dinah was furious. "I'd tell my father if I knew where it'd end, but you never can be sure with wild beasts like t'Nattrasses," she said.

The memory of this unpleasantness soon passed and, on a lovely evening, there were more interesting things to discuss. The three of them, with Agnes, had been invited to Rosie Caygill's for tea towards the end of the month, on the day of the Loyal-Dale Independent Friendly Society's annual walk from Greets. This, together with the ensuing argument as to how best they might journey to Bainbridge Sports in Wensleydale, kept them going until, passing Mr. Wade's mill and crossing the bridge, they entered Greets Market Place, where, in the vicinity of the Grafton Arms, traps, gigs and horses were clustered by the score.

"Huh!" Dinah derided, pointing towards the inn's Early English arched doorway. "That's where my father is just now."

"At least he doesn't roll home like some, you've said so yourself, love," Cherry laughed.

"What is it this time?" Adam smiled.

"The Lord's yearly audit-dinner," Dinah answered. "With Mr. Buckle fro' Corvy at the head of the table lifting his elbow as much as any of them."

"He's the Steward of the Manor, Adam," Cherry chimed in. "He presides for the Lord."

Hitherto Adam had thought that Sir Charles Grafton was the Lord of the Manor, but now, before reaching the stocks on the village green, he learned something of the intricacies of ownership in Skewdale where, for example, a man might own land but not the herbage which grew on it. In the matter of mineral ownership the position was no less peculiar, Sir Charles enjoying the rights of these but not necessarily the ground above, this in the main belonging to a largely unknown Kentish gentleman, Mr. Philip Alexander Moyle Digges—the girls had his name pat—Lord of the Manor of Greets.

"Well, it sounds a rare mix-up," Adam commented. "If the lawyers have brought about a position like that no wonder Matt Tiplady declares they're not all that secure on laws to do wi' game."

On the right, the belfry of the stables of Greets Hall peeped out between the trees, and on the left, against the high wall of the churchyard, two or three games of hand-ball were in progress.

Then came the B.G. Inn and, beyond it, a hill up which Prue really had to exert herself. From the top the remainder was easy, a long ride down moor and pasture to the river and meadows at Half, where Harry Blaydes and his wife waved from the lodge of Half House, Jonas Cottingham and two of his customers watched from the bar-room of the Groovers Welcome, and Annamaria Rutter, glimpsing the trap from one of the new farm buildings her father had erected behind the Old Cow Inn, rushed out for ten minutes' gossip.

Then, the bright sun so low as to be blinding, the jog-trot along the road to Yew Tree House, where Miss Dinah Skidmore set down her passengers and did not take much persuading to alight for a cup of tea herself.

* * * *

Between then and Midsummer Day Adam continued to work at Badger Hall, with odd days off for sports elsewhere and other festive occasions. He also went away with Mr. Skidmore on a buying round of the Northern livestock fairs and, at a later date, with the master of Badger Hall and Nell, drove back a flock of Scotch wethers from the south of Carlisle . . . a wonderful walk in good company, a journey throughout the whole long distance of which he barely saw a main road, his feet always on the soft turf of ancient highways and pack-horse tracks, the six nights spent in the houses of friendly farmers and shepherds. The weather delightful, it was an experience not to be forgotten.

2

Although the Loyal-Dale Independent Society's Walk to Yorrel was regarded as a general holiday, Agnes Pedley excused herself from accompanying her cousin, but, far from seeming disappointed, she was quite gay. Whether or not she suddenly became aware of this, her blue eyes grew more solemn. "Oh, I'd have liked to have gone with you, Adam," she said. "But I've a right lot to do what wi' one thing and another. And you'll tell Rosie Caygill as how sorry I am, and you'll thank her for me, won't you?"

Adam promised faithfully to execute these commissions and then, on a bright morning freshened by the rain of the night, strolled down to Yew Tree House. As he and Cherry walked through thronged Main Street, where the Winterings contingent of Independents was assembling to join the main body from Greets and Half, he explained Agnes's default.

"Oh, she'd be upset all right," Cherry said. "I expect she was trying to put a good face on it because of you."

Farther up the highway, outside the Royal Alfred, there was another crowd of families from Snorr and Slackrigg and the high farms on the fringe of Water Ling and Snorr Moors. Five or six of the men were in the distinctive rig-out of the Independents, white trousers and big blue rosette on the coat lapel.

Some twenty minutes later the procession came into sight, filling the road four abreast, legs moving with that unmistakable springiness which is the hall-mark handed down by many generations who have been used to striding through ling and long grasses. Their leader, a very notable exception to this, however, stepped out at the head by himself, an elderly man with a puffy, big face who, arms swinging extensively, was taking a longer stride than his height conveniently allowed. Fascinated by this individual, from whose *pince-nez*, the plum-shaped lenses of which were inordinately large, a loop of inch-wide black ribbon dangled, Adam bent to Cherry.

"I say, lass," he said, grinning, "who's the rum cut in front?"

Her vivid, always expressive, face sobered. "Lodge Trotter," she replied. "He's t'secretary of Uncle Titus's company."

Adam reflected; then he remembered. "And a lot besides, isn't he, including being . . ." he was overcome again by the black ribbon, "a sort of lawyer, eh?"

"He pushes himself to the fore in everything," Dinah snapped.

In the wake of the parade, on foot, horseback, or riding, were a host of folk whose passage would soon soil with dust the purplish-red of campion which richly coloured banks and hedgerows. When the worst of the crush was over, Adam and the two girls started off.

As always, the old procedure was followed on the Society's arrival at Yorrel: a brief service was held before the members sat down to dinner in a big tent. Others, less fortunate, either ate the food they had brought or struggled in and then out of the Rose and Crown, next door to the garth in which the annual Love Feasts were celebrated. Despite these inconveniences everyone was enjoying the outing and later in the afternoon, as the last spirited line of *Blow ye the trumpet, blow* died away, there was real regret. Singing hymns and listening to good preachers had always been to the taste of Skewdale folk.

It was still too early for tea and so Cherry and Dinah showed Adam over the village, the most remarkable feature of which was the Wesleyan Chapel, whose foundations had been hewn out, and every stone quarried and dressed, by Yorrel groovers in the first fervency of the new religious discoveries more than a hundred years before.

When returning across the bridge carrying the main road over Yorrelgrain, Titus Alderson's sister-in-law and Mrs. Skidmore were encountered. Mrs. Roberty Will hardly acknowledged Adam's and Cherry's greeting and was not too forthcoming with Dinah either.

Later, Dinah was the most angered of the three. "Well, seemingly I'm in disgrace because I mate wi' you, Cherry, and Adam here isn't worth speaking to because she's seen him with you a few times."

"Nay, I think I got off on the wrong leg with her right from the beginning," Adam said.

Dinah brushed aside his suggestion. "It's 'cause Cherry stands up to her about her uncle. She thinks herself so important because of all her brass that she can't abide opposition fro' anybody."

Hitherto, with him, Cherry had always been quite non-committal about the mistress of Malaga, but now the strength of her resentment was a revelation to Adam.

"I think," she said a little tersely, "that when my Uncle Titus gets the New Drift through to Doomsday, and the groovers start opening up Jamie's Mint—I think I shall throw summat over her to mark th'occasion . . . . maybe a bucket of water. I'd like to, anyway."

Even Dinah was momentarily stayed with surprise. "You do, love," she laughed, the initial shock over.

Rose Cottage was only a few yards up the rough road into Yorreldale, between the lane and Yorrelgrain, its front door and garden facing the beck and, at the other side of the stream, the thorn tree beneath which John Wesley had once preached.

On rounding the end of the cottage they saw the dressmaker, whose hair, recently washed for this special day, was an unbelievable shade of gold. Suitable excuses were made for Agnes's absence.

"Now lad, I'm very proud o' my flowers," Miss Caygill said, professionally eyeing Cherry's and Dinah's spotted prints, "so while t'lasses take off their bonnets you look round. The garden," she coughed meaningly, "goes right down to the bottom of the gill, so you've plenty to see."

The social decencies thus provided for on both sides, she ushered the girls indoors, leaving her male guest to wander amidst columbine and brilliantly-hued gaillardia; there were flags and geums, heavily-scented stocks and mauve cushions of thrift. Over walls were more cushions: of purple aubrietia, white arabis and yellow alyssum.

Before descending to the stream shining and rippling at the foot of the slope, Adam glanced back. "A work of art," he muttered.

Yorrelgrain, which formerly had turned many waterwheels and supplied the dressing-floors of Yorrel Mines, was a watercourse only slightly smaller than Winterings Beck. Its flow at present was scanty.

"Aye, an' that'll be another of Titus Alderson's anxieties," he nodded. "Yes, I'm not surprised that to-day and for the last few days he's been on the moors prospecting for springs to divert."

Muffled by the high bank behind him, he faintly heard Cherry's sweet voice calling him in to tea. With alacrity he began to climb the steep ascent.

After tea Adam lazed in a sweep-back chair, seeing little beyond a gleaming mahogany tray, shining china, a well-polished rocker with spotless antimacassar, and flowering plants in pots on the window-ledge. The ladies were chatting, Rosie Caygill amused in particular about Jane Sunter, of whom he had told her all he could.

"Imagine it!" she was exclaiming. "*Me* with a niece who's got a little lass three years old! Of course I've never seen Jane, but I haven't a doubt that if she were here folks 'ud take us for sisters."

Someone had to say something and, as Adam failed and the cat diverted Dinah by jumping on her knee, it was left to Cherry.

"It sometimes happens in big families, Rosie," she said.

The dressmaker's mouth screwed into a preliminary button. "Oh, that were it, lass. There were years an' years betwixt me and my next brother. Of course I shouldn't like to be vulgar, but . . . well, long afore I arrived on t'scene people thought as how my father an' mother were beyond . . ." She coughed, her cheeks definitely aflame. "I . . . I needn't say any more, need I?" Hastily and unanimously she was assured that further explanation was not necessary.

These references to Simon Sunter and his family naturally touched upon Adam's work in Spain, and from that it was only a step to the mines of Skewdale. It was then that Rosie Caygill, who owned twenty shares in the East Side Company, forgot her pretensions.

"I suppose I could be in a worse plight," she continued. "If they'd been West Side 'uns—with all due respect to your Uncle Titus, Cherry lass."

"It's all right, Rosie," Cherry said sadly.

That released the dressmaker's pent-up flood of woe. The shares, she explained to Adam, were of a nominal value of twenty pounds, of which six pounds was paid up, leaving a liability of fourteen pounds each. And, she added, lips quivering, fourteen times twenty was two hundred and eighty.

"I must have been out of my head all them years ago when I 'lowed Puke Hastwell to talk me into buying 'em," she cried, betraying more than she knew.

"Sometimes the worst never happens," Adam remarked.

"Takes a man, doesn't it, to comfort us poor women," said Miss Caygill, rallying, and forthwith became so cheerful that, on their leaving, she put on a bonnet to walk with them as far as the old Corn Mill, an intention nearly frustrated when, amongst her beloved flowers, she glimpsed one of her greatest enemies. "Drat them slugs," she stormed.

With Yorrel Mines completely closed, the village had suffered even more grievously than Winterings, and this, on reaching the main road, she was so busily demonstrating that a man of profuse beard and hair was almost on them before she saw him. Confronted unexpectedly, she blurted out a remark she doubtlessly regretted later.

"Here's James Pedley," she gulped. "But if he dares again to mention owt about my hair . . ."

The pale eyes of the hot-gospeller were for one person only, Adam. "So it's you," he opened, without compromise. "Him as slanders the Lord's servant in the house o' God, him as sets brother against brother. But you'll be punished for your infamy, you idolatrous, loose-tongued helot."

In a tone by contrast quite conversational, Adam observed that as there were still many people about it was an exceptional opportunity for a ranter to rant. But, for himself, he proposed to be absent.

"Aye, you'll creep away," James Pedley shouted.

Adam's thumb jerked up the road, Yorrel-wards, and his eyes, as Cherry likened them, seemed twin blades of piercing grey.

"Get off," he said. "Or folks *will* have summat to discuss."

And this James Pedley did, leaving Miss Caygill to express her indignation volubly as far as Yorrel Bridge, where she turned back.

The evening was balmy, the sights and smells delightful—the aroma of Sweet Cicely in the pastures, the prettiness of pink and white clover in the meadows, the hum of bees flitting from flower to flower, and the harebells which patterned with blue the cairn and mounds of Bloody Sigh.

Adam was staring up the fellside, watching a herd of small, very shaggy cattle with ponderous brows and heavy horns. The neat shorthorns were almost universal in the dale up to Greets or even Half, but above there, in the wilder regions between Winterings and Yorrel, a proportion of hardy Scotch cattle were kept. It would be interesting, he thought, to know precisely how the two breeds compared in performance. Well, if at the end of the summer he reached the conclusion he now felt he would, that would be a matter he could examine.

"Hallo, love," he smiled as Mary Jane skipped up from behind. "It's been a grand day, hasn't it?"

"It were too hot this morning," Mary Jane announced. "My words, I had a tew with the baking. And to cap all th'oven wouldn't draw."

"Why did you bake this morning of all times, lass?" Dinah inquired.

"Because we'd run out," the small housekeeper replied. "I've never in my life seen two chaps wi' appetites like my father and our Ward."

"Couldn't you have managed for another day, Mary Jane?" Cherry said.

"You wait," scoffed Matt Tiplady's little daughter, "till you've a man an' a growing lad of your own to provide for, and then you'll see, Cherry."

Giggling had always been Dinah Skidmore's greatest weakness and, at this point, she began one of her most devastating bouts.

Near Winterings Brig, while glancing at the creeper-covered farmhouse at the foot of Sleety Slape, Cherry made a remark about which her escort had great difficulty in concealing his pleasure. Simply, it was that in childhood her dream had been of living there.

"Aye?" Adam observed, politely interested. "Yes, it looks a very nice spot. I suppose I needn't inquire why it's vacant?"

Between the Plug and Feathers and Nick Turn he learnt all Cherry knew about Modesty, which was that would-be tenants had not the means to stock it, and investors avoided it in the absence of tenants to bring a return on capital outlay.

Adam was humming and his comment seemed just casual. "So it could either be rented or bought?" he murmured.

Cherry had slowed her step to read a notice on the board against the policeman's cottage. This informed tenants, lessors and lessees of minerals and other persons interested, that, on four consecutive days at the beginning of July, Philip Alexander Moyle Digges, Esquire, or his representative, would 'Perambulate the Boundaries of the Manor of Greets.' It was signed by Miles Buckle, Steward of the Manor.

"Why don't you go?" said Cherry. "I believe that some o' the things they do are right quaint."

"It's a good idea, lass," Adam said.

He smiled at her, and she smiled up at him. Both were pleased with themselves, although for vastly different motives; Cherry because she had thought of something he would enjoy, he because of the discovery that she loved a house he favoured. Her pleasure lasted for long after she had gone in home, and his was certainly strong enough as he crossed Dolly Bridge. By then he was attempting to estimate the price which would be asked for Modesty, with its meadows, pastures and moor rights.

"I'll do a bit o' cautious sounding," he decided as he turned into Back Lane. "Mr. Skidmore's the best chap, and——"

Fleetingly he caught a quick movement across the river, a thin figure which slid from the semi-gloom beyond the waterwheel into the concealing darkness of the Saw Mill's passage-way. It was over in a flash and such vague impression as he had was of a head held stiffly to one side.

"It were like Mazy Bill," he reflected. "But what would he be doing in the Wood Yard?"

The crazed are guilty of the craziest actions and, as he had been told frequently, even by Agnes, Mr. Rutter's son was capable of the queerest, so he did not trouble himself further. At the cottage, Ambrose Pedley was on his way out, with the intention, he informed his lodger, of climbing up to the moors where, the broad heavens above him, God might be pleased to clarify his thoughts.

"I met your brother in Yorrel, an' we'd words again," Adam said.

Ambrose Pedley sighed heavily. "I'm noan ready to tackle him yet, lad. When students of t'Scriptures such as me and James fling us-selves into the clash o' battle, we've to have all the weapons by us."

Their succeeding conversation was of a domestic nature, merely that Agnes would be home shortly, her father having given her permission to go along to Hannah Batty's for an hour. Ambrose Pedley's parting words were that Adam must not make a meal for himself—women, he declared, were men's handmaidens.

When the door-sneck clicked, Adam was grasping the carving-knife to cut another slice from the leg of lamb delivered by the travelling butcher who drove down Jom High Road every week. He glanced up, to see his pretty little cousin flushed of cheek and smiling happily.

"Well, you seem to have enjoyed yourself with Old Hannah," he teased her. "Anyway, I'm glad, because I've had a grand day myself, every minute of it."

"Oh, I am suited, Adam," she said. "Now tell me everything."

Singing gaily, Agnes washed up when he had finished, and the sole cloud to cross her face that evening was when, after he had suggested they should stroll as far as Pewitt Pillar, he made inquiries as to what she had been doing that day. In reply she was hardly frank, the catalogue of her activities not very interesting.

At the conclusion Adam spoke with supreme disgust. "And to think that I reckoned you looked right lively."

"But I have had a nice time, Adam," she persisted. "A won—special nice time."

Making great play about it, Adam would not hear another word. Assuming gruffness, which usually pleased her, he told her that, if she wished to change into clogs before walking along rough-surfaced Middle Sorrow, she must hurry or he would leave her.

"All right," she said, but lingered to repeat what she had already said. "I have had a nice time, Adam."

"A nice time," her cousin twitted her.

As if raising a small issue to one of consequence, she took an impulsive step towards him, her voice acquiring a shrillness not wholly agreeable. "Yes, I have," she declared. "A real grand 'un."

Astounded, Adam stared down into resentful eyes. "Easy, lass," he said. "It were nobbut that I didn't think the list sounded all that entertaining—washing a bedroom floor, black-leading the fireplace, an' so on."

Defiance still uppermost, she faced him. "I enjoyed it, anyroad."

"All right, lass," Adam nodded. "Now if we're going out . . ."

She went obediently enough, leaving him tugging the lobe of his ear in bewilderment. As for Agnes, she whispered to herself as she kicked off her shoes: "I'm right fond on Adam, but . . ." her lips went mutinous, "but I'm noan having him or anybody else nosing into my affairs, I'm noan that." She stretched out a leg and, hooking a clog with her toes, dragged it towards her. "No, him and Cherry and th'others always treat me as if I were a child . . . but if they only knew."

She smiled strangely, her eyes darkening secretively.

3

Even in bygone days when they were kings, and farmers little esteemed, the lead-miners of the western dales had been expert with the scythe, and, able to afford it, regarded haymaking as a period of holiday and pleasant change. This outlook altered gradually with the decline of the major industry, until the time came when the groovers eagerly anticipated haymaking, for the additional money it would earn them and the plenitude of food they and their wives and daughters, who also went along to assist, could eat in the fields.

Amongst the groovers engaged at Badger Hall was John Raisbeck, a Quaker from Half, known as Freestone John from the ownership of a small quarry up the fellside above his home. He was a man of about fifty, who more than twenty years before had realised he could obtain a livelihood in Skewdale only if he found other modest sources of income. He now had two cows, and filled in any spare time at the mines. Reasonable-minded, he took only single-handed bargains so that, whenever he received an urgent order for flag-stones, he could leave at once his place underground without imposing an unfair handicap on partners.

On the third afternoon at Badger Hall since the first whetting of the blades had been heard that haymaking, Freestone John chanced to mention to Anthony Skidmore his belief about a promising lead in a cross-cut at Martha Level Forehead.

Owing to the vagaries of the weather in the mountainous backbone of England, where the most important task was to secure the hay immediately it became dry, the building of haystacks was unknown, the many stone barns serving in their place. In these, where cow-house and store were on one level, the hay was kept on the ground; in others, two-storied, the hay was packed into the top compartment, a convenient method allowing feed to be dropped easily into the cattle racks below.

One of the most strenuous jobs, when barns were two-storied, was that of forking the hay to the upper storey, the baulk, from the horse-drawn sleds which brought it in. It was back-aching work and even Adam was not sorry when Matt Tiplady arrived to relieve him.

"Right, lad," he said. "I think I'll cool off by doing a bit o' spreading in that meadow they've just started cutting."

"Yes," the poacher replied, without the semblance of a smile, "and you'll be in congenial company an' all."

Mopping blinding sweat off his forehead, Adam sauntered away. Everywhere haymaking was in progress and, as every blade of grass counted, men in shirt-sleeves and women in faded prints and aprons were busy on the steepest and most awkward meadow slopes, where it was a gymnastic feat to swing a scythe. There were fields in which the hay was being raked into wind-rows, in others it stood piled in small cocks and big pikes. Broadly speaking methods were alike, but as between farmer and farmer there might be variation. It was Anthony Skidmore's pet insistence, for instance, that when the mowers had passed the new-cut grass should be shaken out by hand.

"Adam lad," he had said with immense gravity the previous evening, "a rake shifts whole lumps at a time. No, the hands is th'only tool as is needed."

The weather was perfect, blue sky, a bright sun and light easterly airs welcome to all, including the horses who pulled the sleds, carts and sweeps; horses whose everyday life was that of the farm, and Skewdale ponies, surprisingly tractable, caught and led down from the moors and commons upon which, foraging for themselves, they ran wild for nearly eleven months of the year.

"Grand," Adam thought, breathing in a mixed scent of freshly-cut grass, drying grass and sweet hay. "Mind you, it's noan so oft like this, as Mr. Harker telled me. Sometimes the weather's so bad that they don't start haymaking until . . . well, I've heard as far on as late into August."

It was extremely difficult then, he knew, the hay left out the evening before so wet with dew the next morning that re-spreading was necessary, the success of this depending upon a hot sun, for the days were shortening. Often, too, there was the bugbear of alternate rain and sun, the repeated drying and re-drying rotting the crop, leaving it fit for nothing better than bedding, and so grimly intensifying the eternal problem of adequate fodder for the cattle in winter, with a margin for sheep in the event of prolonged snow.

"Yes, that's th'unpleasant side of it," Adam told himself. "But I'll figure it all up soon . . . an' in the meantime I might as well make the most of days like this. Everybody else is doing, choose how," he smiled, as a snatch of song came to him.

He waved to Walter Heseltine Skidmore, perched on the summit of a sled-load of hay drawn by Prue, by whose side Alice Skidmore was walking. They waved in response, as also did Mrs. Hugill with her idiot son, Rive Rags, who could use a rake if supervised.

There were more women and youngsters than men, for, just as Agnes would spend the whole of haytime with her father in the Rutters' meadows at Half, the Skidmores had many volunteers, too. Altogether it made a jolly party, but though quips might be shouted and pranks sometimes played, there was no flagging. Paramount was the feeling that advantage should be taken of every second.

"Yes, they all buckle to," Adam soliloquised. "And they're instilling it into the children as well."

He leaned on a stone gate-post to allow himself a rare treat, a spectacle seldom seen in this hilly country, where but few meadows were as even and level as that in Blenk Bottom. Seven mowers advanced in line, scythes swinging in unison, each cutting the same sized arc from the tall grasses before them.

"Like soldiers drilling," thought Adam. "And five of 'em are groovers at that. Well, I'll improve my own performance before long."

He entered the meadow, as he crossed it replying in kind to the back-chat of those who followed the mowers to open out and scatter the green-brown swathes, this delaying his arrival at the far side where Cherry, quite near a wall beyond which Mr. Skidmore and another man were repairing a scythe, was the last of the line.

Her slim brown arms were busy enough, but beneath her sunbonnet she looked very cool.

"It'd be awful if you got sunstroke, Adam, an' you do right to take it easy," she remarked, her voice quivering with sham concern. "Why don't you rest yourself in a shady spot under that clump of elders?"

"I think, lass," said Adam, his brow knit as he studied the suggestion, "it might be better for me if I'd a swim in t'river afore I settle down. Last night we'd a good splash in that big pot-hole towards Lane End . . . icy it was . . . then a refreshing drink afterwards—can you imagine summat really cold slipping down your parched throat——"

"You're going to make me hot afore you've done," Cherry protested. "And you're doing it deliberately, too."

Adam was pained. "Nay, lass."

Cherry would probably have attempted to restore her position, but Mr. Skidmore beckoned and then pointed to the young man with her, who a few moments later was talking to the master of Badger Hall and a groover he liked at first sight.

For Adam the matter was settled by just six words, those with which Freestone John informed him that the proposition concerned the East Side Company, when his acceptance was so crisp as to have raised many a suspicion in men more prone to seek motives than the pair at the other side of the wall.

"Well, I bethought mesen you once mentioned you wouldn't mind a bit o' practical experience here in the mines, Adam?" Anthony Skidmore remarked, pleased to have done a favour. "And as neither of you wants to be tied hard an' fast it suits you both."

"It does me," Freestone John exclaimed, stretching over to shake Adam's hand. "And as to when we'll start, friend . . ."

That depended on how long haymaking lasted. But the Bargains would not be put up for bidding until the final Saturday of the month and if the weather were not unreasonable it was thought they might make a beginning together in the early days of the next month.

"But don't keep him at it too long, John," Anthony Skidmore chuckled. "There's t'price of a pup he's to work out with me."

A certain amount of cajolery resulted, but then Freestone John brought practical details to the fore—tools for Adam would be furnished by the Company and, under the Truck Act, charged only at bare cost against the two men's joint Pay, as were fuses, powder and candles. Then there was clothing—Adam, with autumnal farming slush in mind, had already been measured by Blind Kit for a pair of clogs, but ancient reach-me-downs would be required.

"Well, let's hope you've a real good adventure," Anthony Skidmore encouraged them before reverting to an alert, time-saving hill-farmer. "Now, Adam lad, Cherry shot off like a flash a minute or so since, so I suppose that means another sup o' tea for us lot down at this end. You'd better go along to the house to give her a lift with t'basket."

Adam would have reached Badger Hall sooner had he not been intercepted in the next field but one by Bob and his cousin who, in absolute charge of a big dales' pony and hay-sweep, were labouring manfully.

"Hey, Adam," Ward cried.

Three perspiring creatures ceased action, the two boys and the sweat lathered horse. Cautiously Bob glanced around and then, between them, he and Ward told Adam about an outcropping vein they intended to hush. Already a channel to direct the flow of water had been dug, their next task the building of a turf-bank dam.

"You'll noan let on, Adam?" said Ward.

"Cut your throat first," his cousin added.

Adam duly spat and completed the full oath, when he was allowed to depart. He paused only once before entering the old courtyard at the rear of Badger Hall, to pay a call upon Nell, who was shut away safely in the calf-house, where she had cried mournfully all day. So long as the mowers swung their scythes she would remain in custody, lest in her enthusiasm for the rabbits which bolted from the grass she were mutilated by a razor-sharp blade.

It was the sole time throughout the year that she misbehaved herself and, as slight consolation, Adam presented her with a few broken pieces of warm-damp oatcake he delved out from the depth of a trousers pocket.

Of all the ladies in the roomy kitchen of Badger Hall only Hannah Batty had nothing to do with haytime preparations. She was there on an errand of mercy, begging old clothes on behalf of a poor family.

"You can have a dress of Alice's, Hannah," said Susan Skidmore, glancing up from the ham she was slicing.

Cherry was squeezing into one end of a butter basket a gallon, enamel jug of scalding tea, Dinah was dividing jam pasties into broad strips, Mary Jane Tiplady, standing on a footstool, cut bread as if her life depended on it, and Mrs. Skidmore, an incredible twist to her mouth, dazedly watched Mrs. Blenkiron lavishly buttering.

"Right, Susan love, it'll be welcome," said Mrs. Batty. " Now you, Minnie? No, it's noan so long sin' I cleared you out, is it?" This question had to be repeated.

If ever a woman looked as though she would have liked to proclaim that, at Smithy House, a magnifying glass was required to see the butter on the bread, it was the mistress of Badger Hall. Good manners conquered, however.

"No, I've nowt just now, Hannah," she replied wanly.

Old Hannah next turned her attention to her niece, Mrs. Roberty Will, of whom it was said in Winterings that this was the one season when she shed the influence of her money-bags. In a big apron as were the others, she was not sparing herself.

"Yes, I think I've rummaged out everything at Malaga, Ellen," the old lady reflected. "But there is summat else . . . when next you're in Corvy, I want you to call at t'chemist's there . . . now let's see . . . tubing an' a nipple for a feeding bottle . . ."

Mrs. Roberty Will whispered humorously: "So far so good," before confiding in Susan, her friend Minnie Skidmore now being lost to everything save Grace Blenkiron's abandoned sweeps with the butter-knife: "Do you know, lass, I'm sure t'last time the chap behind the counter were puzzling what on earth ailed me—I could see it in his eyes."

Hannah Batty, her smooth forehead wrinkled, strove to capture a missing item. "There were lots others, I'se certain," she murmured. "Castor oil, aye . . . then there were suppositories——"

"I'm not, Aunt Hannah," screeched Mrs. Roberty Will.

The laugh then was as nothing to that succeeding it, when Old Hannah, after remarking mildly: "I don't know what's up wi' you daft lot," remembered another requisite. "Fancy forgetting that!" she exclaimed, smiling at herself. "Aye," she went on, sobering, "an enema, Ellen. Now there's a special sort o' bone-piece as you can insert easier nor . . ."

That was why, when Adam entered the kitchen, he found several ladies convulsed, Mrs. Roberty Will declaiming: "I never, *never* will," and Old Hannah's face gathering the lines of determination she wore whenever the question was that of the alleviation of sickness.

Too deeply hurt to join fully in the fun, Cherry's smile had little heart. It vanished when she saw him.

"Well, this sounds a lively party," Adam remarked to her. "I've come to carry the basket, lass, when you're ready."

"I'm not ready," said Cherry coldly. "An' you needn't wait until I am, thank you."

Adam stared. "You can't manage it by yourself, lass."

"Will's helping me," she answered. As if to make the hint plainer, she added: "I went out to ask him."

Adam gazed steadily at her. Her cheeks were completely drained, but her eyes met his unflinchingly. What was amiss he could not conceive, but for the moment nothing could be done.

If the Skidmores' kitchen just before had resounded, it was eerily silent when he left. Shocked faces were on Cherry and, with one notable exception, she was treated to the scrutiny of one suddenly bereft of her senses.

"Well, Cherry, I'm fair glad to hear that," Mrs. Roberty Will remarked with approval. "You should have sent that young chap about his business long since."

Dinah Skidmore, who had perceived her friend's distress, tried to shelter her. "Why?" she demanded. "What's he done wrong?"

"What's he *still* doing wrong?" snapped Mrs. Roberty Will. "That's more like it."

"Well, what is he?" persisted Dinah.

Mrs. Alderson's bosom swelled as she took a deep breath. "Summat that if I'd done my duty, knowing *you* went about with him an' all, I should have talked over wi' your mother two or three weeks ago," she retorted. "You know, Dinah, no young woman can afford to have her name soiled."

Mrs. Skidmore forgot about Grace Blenkiron in her anxiety about her daughter. "What is it, Ellen?" she asked.

"His association with his cousin Agnes," Mrs. Roberty Will rapped. "Disgraceful!"

Hannah Batty's shrewd eyes never left her. "In what way, Ellen? Now if you're on th'eve of making a serious insinuation, be careful."

"I've no need to be careful, Aunt Hannah," Mrs. Roberty Will retorted. "Because more nor me have seen how they behave . . . like *lovers.* She hangs on to him, and looks up at him coyly, and . . . an' I've heard tell as how she rubs her cheek against his sleeve. And if that happens outdoors, what happens elsewhere?"

"*Nothing!*" Cherry flamed. "An' it's nobbut your nasty mind as makes summat out of these things. She's very fond of him, that's all, though I daresay me an' Dinah know why better nor anybody else——"

"If you don't apologise to me, miss," thundered her opponent.

"There's nowt wrong wi' Adam," Dinah declared.

Her mother was worried. "It's all right saying that, Dinah, but if folk are talking——"

Old Hannah broke in sarcastically. "An' there's no smoke without fire, is there, Minnie?"

"I'm not blaming Agnes," said Mrs. Roberty Will, recovering her temper. "She's nobbut an inexperienced girl, younger than most of her age, but he's a grown man. In other ways I've nowt against him, of course."

"Are you sure, Ellen, you've nowt against him?" Hannah Batty insisted.

"Of course I'm sure," her niece blustered. "Why I'd never set eyes on t'chap afore I came back from away."

"Aye," sighed Old Hannah.

The fierce conflagration had died but the embers still remained, so the diversion made by Mary Jane, when she peered round Dinah, was not unwelcome.

"About th'eggs, Mrs. Skidmore, I've——"

"Lord's mercy!" gasped Minnie Skidmore. "I'd forgotten about 'em."

Mary Jane, unmoved, piped on: "I took 'em off for you when t'sand ran out, Mrs. Skidmore. Shall I shell 'em or are they to stop as they are?"

There was no further talk about Adam and his cousin, not then.

All that Cherry Dinsdale desired was to go home as soon as she could, but before she left Badger Hall, a little earlier than the others, very blunt words were said to her.

"I don't for a moment believe there's ever been owt as shouldn't betwixt Adam and Agnes," Dinah asserted in the seclusion of the open shed. "But you could have telled me you'd heard whispers. I am your friend, aren't I?"

Cherry shook her head. "I haven't heard a whisper."

"Then why," Dinah demanded, "were you so nasty with him when he came into the kitchen? It were only afterwards she began about it?"

Cherry's lip trembled. "Oh, Dinah love, it were summat else. He's going partner with Freestone John for th'East Side Company, and it hurt me 'cause my uncle could have arranged it for him if he'd known he wanted to try his hand at grooving here."

"I am sorry, love," said Dinah, very upset. "I mean because . . . well, I thought you were keeping summat from me an' wouldn't own to it."

Mutual regrets are not without their compensations and, when the two girls parted, they were probably more devoted friends than ever. Just before Cherry hurried off, however, Dinah had a most awkward afterthought.

"I've thought of that, too," Cherry nodded unhappily. "Yes, I shall have to tell him why I were so uppity-up, because if that silly story about him an' Agnes ever gets to his ears he'd think it were because of it . . . an' that 'ud be awful."

The last hay-laden sled was moving slowly across a meadow, and all the hay which could not be brought to the barns that night had been heaped into tall pikes which would for a while resist the weather if it broke.

Cherry Dinsdale, prey to her thoughts, ran down the lane, alongside the river, past the cottages of the Masons and Waggotts, and so on to Snorr Bridge, where a further trial awaited her.

"Now then," said Reuben Nattrass, "just the lass I want to meet. What do you say if we sit on t'parapet for a while?"

"No, I've to get back home," said Cherry, halted perforce.

"Or do you mean you don't want to talk to me, is that it?" the big mine-agent inquired.

"That's summat I've not even considered," she informed him.

He looked down at her good-naturedly. Then, grinning a little, he remarked that, if she preferred to receive his proposal standing there was no objection. He grinned even more at her start on hearing this, but, more earnestly, began to explain the proposal, which turned out to be an invitation to accompany him to Greets First Fair.

"We'd drive down in the dog-cart, lass, behind t'finest piece of horseflesh you've ever seen, that new 'un my father's got," he urged. "And at after we'd have a slap-up spread at either t'Grafton Arms or the Royal Oak, whichever you'd prefer——"

"No, thank you," said Cherry.

"And for why, lass?" he inquired.

"Because it doesn't suit me," Cherry said haughtily. "And kindly stand out of my way an' let me go."

"Well, well, well," he taunted her. "No, lass, that's noan good enough, so I reckon I'll keep you here till I get a better explanation."

Foolishly Cherry tried to slip past him. "Let me go," she cried, desperate when he caught her tightly to him. "If you don't leave-hold," she threatened, to be answered by a mocking, but more excited: "An' what if I don't let you go, lass."

Salvation came from the end of the bridge where, above the parapet, a slender tip began to rise inch by inch, until eventually, held erectly by Edmund Kearton, a nine-foot fishing-rod appeared.

The joiner edged through the narrow stile at the top of the steps leading down to the bank and, on the roadway, absentmindedly tried a cast which landed within three inches of Reuben Nattrass's ear.

"Be careful what you're doing or you'll be having somebody's bloody eye out," the victim bawled.

Mr. Kearton looked across. "You saw my arm go back, why didn't you open your mouth?" he snapped.

"Why should I have done?" growled the mine-agent.

Testily the joiner observed that it had never been his practice to bandy words on a public highway, and he had no intention of beginning. That said, he dismantled his rod.

"Coming my way, lass?" he asked abruptly. "I know Reuben's going th'other, because I saw him from the river."

Watched angrily by Reuben Nattrass, Cherry was escorted towards the Royal Alfred and home.

"Did he bother you much, lass?" she was asked.

Cherry shook her head. "No . . . an' thanks, Mr. Kearton. You heard, didn't you?"

He was too complacent to answer that. "Your Uncle Titus couldn't have flicked as close to his face as that," he boasted. "And as for such as Mr. Wade an' the Reverend Penrose at Greets . . . huh!"

Deeply grateful to him, Cherry paid full attention to a series of amazing stories, an account which did not terminate until they reached the house and joinery premises in Main Street. Edmund Kearton was a true fisherman.

4

The tumbledown building opposite Yew Tree House, on the Half side, had been erected for the convenience of pack-horse trains using Jom High Road and the two Sorrows. There, beasts had fed while packmen lightened their own rough provender with draughts of herb beer, pasties, fruit and cakes bought at the tables of Winterings ladies who had an eye to turning an honest penny. Since this traffic ceased the Bait House had been used by the local mining companies for 'Putting up the Takes,' a form of auctioning the work to be done during the next month, the lowest bidder obtaining the bargain.

On the day before the East Side Company's groovers assembled for this purpose, Adam heard from Freestone John and so was with him on the following afternoon when Reuben Nattrass started the proceedings before a crowd of men.

"Now then," the mine-agent shouted. "Drawing eighty fathoms o' tramway from t'Black Drift an' laying it down again in Blind Trial Crosscut. What are your offers, lads?"

Timbering, walling, arching, sludging-out and every description of mining enterprise was dealt with during the next hour. Bargains were entered into with ore-getters at a price per bing, this depending on prospects. Contracts for Dead Work were arranged at a figure per fathom driven, whether horizontally in level or drift, or vertically in upwards rise or downwards sump, both these being shafts below the surface between gallery and gallery. In some cases, when extensions were taking place in fruitful ground, Dead Work was agreed upon a combined basis, a price per fathom together with a rate on every bing of ore won.

It was a lively social occasion, but, though tobacco smoke eddied towards holes in the roof, arguments were often spirited, chiefly in two cases of driving: a drift at Sun Hade ultimately clinched at the general head price of forty-eight shillings per bing plus thirty shillings a fathom, and the Horse Level at Jenny Incline, in excessively tough rock, at one hundred and ten shillings each fathom advanced.

As for Freestone John, he put forward the precise return he required, thirty-six shillings a bing, for heading in the cross-cut at the Common Rully Gate off Percival's Rise, and this was noted without question. Actually, after nodding acceptance, the sole remark made by Reuben Nattrass hinted at the Quaker's partner.

"Well, John," he grinned, "I expect that when t'Pay comes you'll need a helping hand to carry all your sovereigns back to Half."

"I doubt it, friend," Freestone John said gravely. "But if this young fellow an' me wins a nice parcel o' bouse it'll be a change that's noan unwelcome."

A slack-tongued cock sparrow of a groover, who might have suffered physical damage had he been younger or his reputation other than it was, then took a hand. "It'll noan be unwelcome to the Company either, John lad," he sniggered. "Just now it's t'West Side lot that's going through the mill, but it's noan so long since Reuben there were fluttering about like a hen wi' its head off."

Though there were no serious consequences this remark initiated a certain amount of commotion, during which Adam and his partner squeezed outdoors, where an unexpected order for flagstones was discussed.

"Not a bit on it, John," Adam laughed on hearing the details. "Any-time 'ul do for me, whether it's a week or ten days afore we can start together. Just let me have a word when you've finished 'em, that's all."

On this understanding they separated, the Quaker going down the highroad and Adam across the way to Yew Tree House, where Cherry was cutting the lawn.

"I've come post-haste, lass," Adam announced from the gate.

Cherry smiled. "What for?" she asked.

"What for?" he repeated. "Why, to use them shears . . . to save you kneeling on dampish ground. At your age you should be thinking of warding off t'rewmatticks, not deliberately seeking 'em."

An observer, listening to the couple, a tall young man and a pretty girl who, on relinquishing the garden shears, sat on the grass with her feet tucked out of sight beneath wide-spreading skirts, would have been sure that here was a pair in complete harmony.

That was not so, for a shadow had clouded their relationship since Cherry had apologised for her behaviour at Badger Hall. Adam had understood the reason for her hurt, but it had not been possible for him to say why he had chosen the East Side Company instead of asking her uncle. She, unhappily, had sensed the half-truths in his tale.

* * * *

The second day of the 'Riding and Perambulation of the Boundaries of the Ancient Copyhold Manor of Greets' was fine, and as haymaking was largely over a regular stream of people entered Sorrow Near, amongst them Adam. Will Skidmore was with him, together with two fine labradors belonging to Mr. Hesketh, the Liverpool cotton-broker who rented the shooting rights. It had been rumoured that there would be a considerable rally and, on reaching a high, level stretch of Sorrow Near, once used by the Romans for chariot-racing, that became quite evident. Crowds were also ascending Heugh Syke Gill from Half, and beneath the striking scars of Usha Beacon many more were marching easily down the slope of Legatt's Way towards the last stage of the first day's walk. The rendezvous was near the end shaft of a long line whose old dead-heaps, on a bearing slightly south of west to north of east, the prevalent direction of Skewdale veins, marked the course of the lode far below.

The Lord of the Manor's party was headed by Mr. Miles Buckle, a gentleman of appearance more befitting an eighteenth century squire than a lawyer; there were also representatives from the adjoining Lordships, land agents, mine agents, mineral agents, gamekeepers, tenants; and of horsemen more than thirty, amongst them Mr. Henry Hird of Greets.

As the gathering was very jovial, Adam saw little harm in disposing of a matter he had neglected too long, and so he went up to Sir Charles Grafton's agent, James Calvert's message to a friend in mind.

The big-nosed man brusquely interrupted his introduction of himself. "I know you've come from Spain, and I know who you are," he grunted. "You're cousin to that little lass of Ambrose Pedley's, aren't you?"

Adam eyed him curiously. "Yes, I'm Agnes's cousin."

The mineral agent leaned down from the saddle to make a remark he believed significant. "She used to be a nice little lass, I'm telled," he said. "It's to be hoped them new clothes she's getten from somewhere hasn't changed her."

Curtly Adam discharged his mission before attending to personal matters. In the latter, his tone was such as to convulse Henry Hird's full face with fury.

"My cousin's clothes are her affair, Mr. Hird," he said. "As for the other . . . well, she's still as nice a lass as could be, and you'll do well while I'm about to let owt else like that stick in your throat."

"Why——" Henry Hird gasped. "You . . . you byebigiten . . ."

The exchanges ended there, as words quilled in the remote past boomed out. For Adam it had been a nasty incident, but he did not mean to allow it to spoil his day. "Yes," he mused, "I suppose folk will guess who bought the clothes, but it doesn't speak much for 'em if they don't realise that whatever difference there may be in her . . . well, it's nobbut the airs and graces of a young girl who never before has had anything to preen in."

Documents to do with the previous day's 'perambulation' had been discharged by signing. Luther Thwaites, gamekeeper to the Lord of the Manor and Standard Bearer, started ahead of Mr. Buckle and other mounted gentlemen on the second day of the ceremonial walk.

The route cut south of Spout Fell, to a stone stoup marked: 'T.A. 1696,' when direction was changed towards an old wash-fold, thence to Dagger Gap; next, in the term of ancient deeds, 'As Heaven Water Deals,' which meant following the thinning flow of Winterings Beck steeply upwards to its source below a sugar-loaf currack. Then westerly, across a vast region of moorland from which not a glimpse of Skewdale could be seen, past a needle-shaped outcrop of limestone and the waterfowl flighting in alarm from a tarn. Finally, northward of Great Barg, to a spot where there were traces of the foundations of two buildings of purpose unknown, where the boundary ran between them.

Here lunch was taken and, washed down with draughts of beer, Adam ate the bacon sandwiches Agnes had made for him and listened to the tales of dalesmen who revelled in a day on the high fells as much as he himself was doing.

"All very well, this yarning," Richard Blenkiron complained, stirring himself. "But what about my haymaking?"

Francis Harker's wink embraced a circle comfortably squatting. "Good gracious, lad, haven't you done it yet?" he said, much surprised.

"An' you know damned well why," the blacksmith roared. "Because all through haytime chaps like you, who doesn't know how to handle their tackle, keeps breaking it, an' bringing it to me to repair."

A few minutes later, when the Steward gave the signal, bandy-legged Luther Thwaites swung the flag-pole over his shoulder and, horsemen and pedestrians strung out astern, the cavalcade resumed the journey across fine, sweet grasses towards Yorrelgrain, the watershed boundary of the Manor. At the stream, progress was denied by an army of eight keepers who, with shotguns, supported a land-agent standing to their front.

A scene of two hundred years previous was enacted. An ivory and silver-embellished flintlock pistol was produced and there were sundry references : 'ever faithful to my good Lord'; 'that water shall be fouled with thy life-blood'; 'I bare my breast.' Then a shot reverberated, Mr. Buckle spoke to his Maker, and the estate-agent, sobered by shock, covered his eyes in horror.

On the resumption, after much joking and laughter, Trembling Hags came into view a little below, where the West Side Company's men were cutting peats, stacking the blocks so that sun and air would dry them thoroughly before the end of the summer. This sight, of one phase of his concern's activities, reminded Titus Alderson of an invitation he had extended but not yet honoured: to show Adam through the workings. Reining in Ben, he waited.

"Th'only trouble, lad, is that there's nowt very lively for you to see," he said afterwards. "Unless . . ." his glance was a little sharper, "it's that Short Cut o' mine as you'll have heard about."

Adam did his best, devoutly thankful that Mr. Phillips, manager of the London and Andajoz Lead and Silver Mining Company, was not within hearing.

"No, I don't suppose an odd mistake 'ud stick out so much in a big undertaking," Mr. Alderson commented, lightening. "An' dialling even in great mines can go wrong, can it?" For a few seconds he slipped into a brown study, until with very honest dignity he turned to Adam. "No, lad, the stark truth is that I made a right blunder, an' nowt alters the fact."

The Perambulators were passing an old level whose keystone was elaborately carved with a lion's head. A short distance away Adam noticed a shaft over the eye of which a handwinder had newly been set up, a wooden roller with a handle. Alongside this a boy of nine or ten, in tatters, steadily rotated the wheel of a crude air-pump.

That day's Boundary Walk ended at Yorrel Bridge, but as Adam was more attracted to returning by the moors, he decided against going farther down Yorreldale. But, before starting easterly, he walked to the shaft, there being told that the lad was piping air to his father and brothers below, an arduous and responsible job.

"Aye, but if they can keep going down there, I'm noan being licked up here," the youngster declared stoutly.

A crackle in Adam's pocket reminded him of the packet of butterdrops bought from Old Hannah. "Well, you seem to be managing all right," he pronounced. "But the point is, could you manage some butterdrops?"

Even when Adam was quite distant, striding along a trod towards Foul Syke, he could hear an excited boy who, forgetful that his kin were many fathoms below ground and a considerable way from the shaft's sump, was shouting down the news.

At a few minutes before five o'clock Adam reached the shooters' luncheon hut below Deer Pot, where the trod forked. He swung right, down a rock-strewn hush to Foul Syke Gill, which soon brought him to the summit of Joss Foss.

There, level with the beck as it curved over the jutting lip of the fall, he sat down and pulled out paper and indelible pencil, preliminaries to writing a letter to be addressed jointly to Simon Sunter and his wife, their daughter Bessie and her adopted uncle, Daniel Dolphin.

As he locked up the mine-office, Bart Hugill glimpsed Adam and so, hoping to save himself a trip to Yew Tree House, walked up Foul Syke Gill and then began to climb the awkward, outward-sloping track mounting alongside Joss Foss. Half-way up the steep ascent he halted, facing about for the view while resting. The smelters and groovers had left long before and so his eye was caught immediately by an unmistakable figure below. But Mazy Bill, instead of crossing Notion Bridge, continued erratically and surprisingly over Mill Bridge and into Sleety Slape.

"I wonder where he thinks he's off to, poor chap," he muttered, on starting upwards again. "I reckon he's getting worse lately."

Adam saw the clerk just afterwards. "Aye, 'course I'll leave the papers for Mr. Alderson," he said on hearing Bart's request. "Saves you a bit, does it, going down to Snorr on the trods?"

"Except in snow an' ice, when we avoid it like poison," Bart Hugill said, laughing. "Oh, aye, me an' several more, Bull Waggott and Ned Mason amongst 'em—Ned when he's working up here, that is—always makes for home this road."

That evening he was taking Fronick to Annamaria's and so did not linger unduly, though he paused sufficiently for a decider of three games of handball to be touched upon.

"Wish I could watch you an' Wingy to-night," he grunted, torn between two desires. "Anyhow, you've come on enough to give him a run for his money, lad."

Adam did not remain much longer either. Leisurely he descended the steep track and sauntered along the bottom of the ravine to the South Mill. At the Great Deep Level, lower still, he wandered from Sleety Slape, crossing to the waterwheel, a respectably-sized erection thirty-six feet in diameter and four feet on the face, of the usual overshot type.

"Noan past working," he thought, "for all it's been neglected."

Nor had the tail-race seriously deteriorated, a well constructed stone-lined little canal used for carrying away water which for almost half a revolution had served its purpose in the buckets of the waterwheel. The race emptied into Winterings Beck, at a point where the side of the gill opposite was cliff-like. Here was another manifestation of the incalculable forces of nature, for the slabs in the bed of the stream dipped sharply to one side, so that the beck, as if a giant had tilted the landscape, slid against the foot of the smooth, sheer precipice rising beyond.

Adam was in the mood for exploring and, when the chimneys of the Plug and Feathers came into sight, he opened a gate on the right of Sleety Slape. Entering a meadow, he kept along the wall as far as a narrow gap, through which he squeezed to enter a cobbled yard enclosed by several buildings: a peat house, stick place, cow byre, and hay barn. Next he glanced at Modesty itself, from the stone binks for the milk cans and pails to the staircase window, round-headed, slender and very lofty.

"Aye, it's a nice spot," he murmured.

Experimenting, he found a window the lower sash of which he could raise about a foot. Working head and shoulders inside, and then padding forward on his palms, he brought his legs after him.

It was a pleasant house, with kitchen and dairy at the rear and a living-room at each side of the front door. From that aspect, through small-paned windows, there was a view along Main Street as far as the fir trees in the Wesleyan Chapel garth, and, seen over the lichen-stained roof of the Bridge Inn, juniper-clad slopes rose to colourful moors on which a flock of sheep was grazing, with farther behind, sharply-etched and magnificent, the remote height of Silver Seat.

"Mmm," Adam said to himself. "And the house is noan so damp as most are here."

Mounting the stone staircase, his hand sliding along the Spanish mahogany rail, he went from bedroom to bedroom, each of which conformed in shape with the principal rooms below. When coming down again he paused on the half-landing, to look out through a window which, beginning a few inches above his toes, extended to the upper ceiling.

"I don't know which is best," he pondered, "t'front or the back."

It was lovely on that side, too; neat outbuildings, water bubbling from a spring, water gleaming in the tree-overhung depths of Winterings Gill, walled fields with solid, little grey barns; the screen of Scots pines and spruce through which the evening sun filtered, a fir-plantation higher up, beasts peacefully browsing on the Common Pasture, the land always rising towards Kettle Dub and Water Ling Moor.

"It's a compact farm an' all," he thought, incuriously watching the hump of a back whose owner, concealed by hazels, crawled cautiously across a depression between Winterings Beck and Sleety Slape. "Some of the youngsters having a game of some kind," he smiled, his mind really elsewhere. "Maybe a Red Indian stalking the whites."

One of the peculiarities and disadvantages in Skewdale, he knew, was that in so many farms there was much wasteful walking or riding. In Blenk Bottom, two of Mr. Skidmore's meadows were separated by one of Mr. Harker's, and the tenant of Low Bands was even more seriously incommoded, for he hardly had one meadow adjoining another, and his pastures, too, were equally widely dispersed. On the other hand the whole of Modesty was contained in the corner made by Sleety Slape and the main road to Snorr.

"Yes, if it were anywhere else, it'd be what the agents call a desirable property," Adam soliloquised. "Even though it is small."

Some time later, before finally leaving the curtilage, he probed the outside woodwork with a knife. "Sound as a bell," he pronounced.

As it seemed advisable that people should not link him with an interest in Modesty, he returned past peat-house and garth to the meadow above, so lost in thought that he failed to hear a subdued murmur near the gateway. But, as he knocked back the rusty catch, a feminine shriek aroused him to the present. To his utter astonishment, on stepping round a clump of thorn, he collided with his cousin. Receding down Sleety Slape was a beefy-looking young man whose thick neck and heavy shoulders could just as aptly have earned him the nickname he had as that of his appearance in front.

The apprehension in Agnes Pedley's china-blue eyes sped swiftly as soon as she saw who it was, long before he had got over his surprise. Indeed she took the initiative, chiding him for alarming her. Later, recognising his own tactlessness, Adam wondered if he had been responsible for the change in her. Young girls could be very thin-skinned.

"I'll blow a whistle next time I'm abroad, lass," he said. "Anyhow, how did you come to be with that chap?"

Agnes's lily-white cheeks flushed. "How do you mean, with him?" she asked. "An' is there owt wrong with Cecil, for that matter?"

"Cecil!" Adam ejaculated.

"That's his proper name, an' . . . an' I'm like Fronick, I prefer to use proper names when I'm speaking about folk," Agnes said. "Nicknames such as Wingy and . . . well, such as Bull, say, are nowt but daft."

"I see," Adam nodded. "But you still haven't told me how it was you were here with . . . wi' Cecil. Mind you, lass, it's noan of my business——"

"Then why ask," she said.

Adam was laconic. "Curiosity."

"An' that killed the cat." Her response was no less quick. "Like as you're always teasing Cherry Dinsdale."

At this pat answer, Adam scrutinised her. "Well, it's no use hanging about here," he said. "Come on, lass."

"You seem to forget I'm grown up now, Adam," she reminded him as they approached the Brig. "An' young women don't take to being questioned like you've questioned me."

"They don't," Adam observed.

Privately he was thinking that silly little creatures might have good manners instilled into them if they could be put across the knees and slapped well. Some evidence of these reflections may have shown on his stern face, for his cousin began rapidly to explain.

"I were just out for a walk an' I lighted on Cecil, and he stopped just to pass the time o' day an' that's all there were about it." Drawing another deep breath, she continued the story of a fortuitous meeting, an account so very childishly circumstantial that her cousin took himself to task. "Adam," her hand slid under his arm. "I've . . . I've . . ."

"Steady on, lass," Adam comforted her.

"But . . ." she gulped, "I know I've been right naughty i' talking back at you, but . . . but I'll noan do it again."

Adam made much to do with his threat. "If you do, young lady," he promised at the end, "I'll give you what I've been contemplating already, a real spanking."

A little girl once more, she giggled, tightening her grip to swing gaily alongside him, an affectionate little trick which, beyond Nick Turn, caused Mrs. Emma Ann Metcalfe—who often seemed to inspect the stock in her window at the same time as her neighbour appeared on the pavement to examine his display—to speak out of the corner of her mouth to Cuthbert Daykin. And, still farther along, it brought a tightening of Edmund Kearton's stringy face as, his stare hard, he watched them from his work-bench.

At Agnes's light-hearted insistence, she and Adam turned into Calvert's Wynd and, after hurrying through Dirty Bottom, crossed the Hippy Stones, with much laughter on the passage.

Ambrose Pedley had arrived home from the mine ten minutes before, and, from being a happy little girl, Agnes Pedley became a frightened little girl.

"Well," he greeted her, sallow face colouring, his burning eyes on her, "well, it took you a while to come over t'river, didn't it? Since when have you had to be handed fro' stone to stone?"

"Since we decided at the other side that I'd be a grand gentleman an' she'd be a fine lady," Adam grunted, as he went off to wash himself in the end-place. "Play, it's called."

With uncertain fingers, Agnes was taking off her bonnet. "I'll be right sharp wi' tea, Father," she said. "I thought you were all staying behind to put up timbering for the new rise."

Ambrose Pedley licked moist lips. "I stopped back all right," he admitted. "But," his voice was soft, "it were to talk a grave matter over with your Uncle James if you'd like to know."

"I'll be right sharp, Father," she repeated in a flurry.

"Anyroad, where have you been, girl?" he demanded.

Holding the smoke-grimed kettle, Agnes swallowed. "For a walk, Father. An' then I met Cousin Adam."

"That were *very* fortunate, weren't it?" Ambrose Pedley smiled.

As perplexed as Adam might have been had he heard, Agnes stared at him briefly before hastening with her task.

5

When Titus Alderson rode out of the Wood Yard to rejoin Adam, who was talking to Blind Kit through the cobbler's open door, he could not conceal his annoyance about Puke Hastwell. The Wood Yard foreman, unblushingly so Mr. Alderson declared, had vowed that he had neither sycamore sleepers for horse-tramways nor larch planks for wagon sides. For once, Adam thought as, tea-filled whisky bottle bumping in his pocket, he walked abreast of Ben, Cherry's uncle was really roused.

"But I know what it is," the old mine-agent bawled, to make himself heard above the piercing whine of the Saw Mill. "It's because we're behind wi' our account . . . and because Hastwell's got shares in th'other company."

That morning the horn had sounded for a trail-hunt, and hounds and followers were racing up the rough pasture above Malaga. In days of prosperity as many as forty or fifty sporting Winterings groovers had kept a hound apiece, but though the number was now trivial the hunt had succeeded in remaining in existence, and a day out with it highly relished. The spectacle made Adam wonder whether his companion had chosen this morning deliberately, so that nobody would be in the workings. In suspecting that, he did an injustice to Mr. Alderson and, as he found later, a much greater injustice to the West Side Company's groovers who, fully aware of the company's parlous state, put in their shifts to a man.

Mr. Alderson's fiery mood did not persist indefinitely, and he was his old bright self when they came to the East Side Company's smelt mill and dressing floors at Bucker Level, silent in the absence of men enjoying themselves. And, on Notion Bridge, when bidding Adam provide himself with candles, he had all the zest of a man eagerly anticipating showing another of the same occupation round the realms he controlled.

"Say three-quarters of an hour, lad," he called out, as Ben's hoofs clattered stable-wards on reaching the paved, wharf-like road in front of the North Mill. "Meet me at Mary Level, eh?"

Nodding understanding, Adam crossed Mill Bridge, heading towards a door on which a brass plate, filmed with verdigris, announced the 'Registered Office of the West Side Lead Mining Company, Ltd.'

"Morning, Adam." Bart Hugill, thrusting a pen behind his ear, slipped from a tall stool. "Now I'd better let you have agent's candles, not groover's, so as you'll see better." The difference, he explained as he rummaged in the candle-box, was appreciable; those for the groovers, at sixpence a dozen, were good enough for their purpose, but inadequate for accurate dialling, the measurement of Dead Work, and other essential matters.

"Here's a candle-holder an' all," he added, producing a socket with pointed sidepiece to insert into crevices.

As Mary Level was some distance up the gill Adam did not prolong his stay, but started off at once . . . passing Big William, the red-glowing smelt hearths of the North Mill, and the range of buildings beyond; following the air-pipes which, carried on high posts, supplied air to those advanced workings in Notion Level lacking sufficient ventilation.

Near the great Peat House, with its long ladders for stacking the four thousand loads of peats it would hold, Adam paused to look about him. Everywhere was activity and, although there was nothing remarkable in men strenuously engaged, the scene was set against a background of moorland wild and bare. With the exception of Sam Kirkbride's house not another habitation, or even barn, could be seen, either at this side of Skewdale or the other, whose upper limits only were visible.

"It's like a world apart," he reflected, his glance roving from game birds flying low to black-faced sheep chewing expressionlessly, from men shovelling and hammering to others wheeling barrows and pig-moulds. Horse-teams were busy on the double tram-road, hauling Notion Level bouse uphill to Mary Dressing Floors and rattling downhill with bing ore for storage in the Bingstead, to await the smelters.

"So Mary Level ore is dressed on the spot, but the Notion Level stuff is taken up there," he said to himself. "And then it's all brought back to Notion Bridge. Well, it's trailing it about, but a sight better than they manage at th'other side. It can't be economic for th'East Side Company to use three small mills an' three different dressing floors."

Hearing an increasing rumble of wheels, he diverted towards Notion Level, the swing door at the tail of which was closed. Of Skewdale levels this was one of the few so provided—but without the door groovers half a mile or more inside would have been chilled by the draught and their smoky candle flames bent horizontally whenever the wind blew from the S.S.E.

Adam was fortunate. A grey head appeared, with a mane so profuse as to bring the Pedley brothers immediately to mind. The arch-shaped door was shoved back until caught by a spring-hasp when, this necessary operation completed, Polly advanced farther into view, grey of plump body and long tail. She drew five large, bouse-laden wagons whose iron sides, outward sloping, made a broad-based V.

"Well, Bill lad," he shouted, as the trammer, stooped in the queer attitude imposed by a head permanently to one side, thriftily blew out the train's single candle, "now I've seen Polly do it for myself. Yes, she's a real clever 'un."

Mazy Bill straightened like a jack-knife opening, to stare unwinkingly. This rigid stance changed suddenly, when his face puckered as though he were crying, but without tears. "Come on, Polly love," he mumbled. Then he, his beloved mare, and the creaking wagons started towards the bouse-teams.

"Aye," Adam murmured, resuming the trip up Winterings Gill, "the poor lad must be having one of his queer spells."

He stepped out again, walking in the middle of the two sets of rails laid on the narrow shelf of ground between beck and a steeply-rising, gorse-overgrown bank. In due course, beyond another of the ravine's sharp bends, he sighted the vast dead heap made from worthless rock wagoned out of Mary Level.

Nearer the slime pits and buddles of Mary Dressing Floors, which occupied a broader stretch overlooking water tumbling down miniature falls, the bubbling song of the stream as it rippled over smooth sandstone pebbles and lapped against moss-covered boulders died away, lost in the clatter of dolly tubs and jigging machines, drowned by the splash from waterwheel buckets, the hiss from pipes and hose. When the roar of the crushers in the grinding mill, in its turn, fell away behind him, Adam bore to the left, along a tramroad up an offshoot of the gill, until he reached a low, stone building divided for its different uses: horse house, blacksmith's shop, and a 'Dry' or changing place outside which an abstract from the Metalliferous Mines Regulations Act was posted.

Titus Alderson had finished his business and, their paths coinciding, they strolled towards Mary Level.

"A piece o' clay 'ul do better for you than that candle-holder," the old agent said, tossing a greyish, sticky ball, but he was more approving about the decrepit hard hat Adam had been given by Blind Kit.

Within the tail of the level matches were struck. As soon as both candles were burning they entered the mine, stepping in single file upon wooden sleepers at times above but as often below ankle-deep pools, the slit of daylight behind gradually fading away. The wavering flames revealed sides damp and glistening, a level walled and arched in parts, cut through solid rock occasionally, and supported elsewhere by timbering of great strength. Here and there the passageway widened into a chamber, with turn-rail and space enough for a horse to face about; at intervals refuge niches were hewn into the side.

The three main grounds were visited, two of which were winning mineral, the third an attempt to attain an area where profitable ore was supposed to be.

At Mary Level Forehead, ten fathoms beyond the sump in which a pump, worked by the immense spear-rod in Glory Shaft, clank-clanged monotonously, Adam saw an onrush of water through the rock face. As he knew already, the boundary common to the two mining companies ran almost equidistant between this forehead and the forehead of the East Side Company's Martha Level. The two levels were designedly driven at the same depth and would have been connected had not the old Skewdale Company failed. To Adam it seemed feasible that the water might quite easily have seeped from the neighbouring company's side, in which case the remedy was obvious.

"No, lad," Titus Alderson shook his head, "it's been tested for just that, wi' oil, an' nobbut the merest trace came through. These underground streams i' limestone are oft mysteries."

In cross-cuts off the main horse level, and in drifts off the cross-cuts, Adam heard poll picks at work, the thud of sledge hammers meeting the heads of borers, and here and there, twinkling yellow, were the lights of candles—candles, as many at times as eight of them close together, a smoky-bright zone in which the same number of partners toiled in sweet air; elsewhere, the atmosphere foul, a pair of dimly-burning candles lit the labours of three or four slightly lethargic, heavily-breathing men. In most cases the bases of the candles were embedded in a small piece of clay which, pressed against rock or timber, held securely to form a convenient wall bracket. But some of the groovers, usually the older ones, preferred a lantern—as less susceptible to draughts, though the cylindrical canister and the shield, especially when of horn, cut off or absorbed a great deal of light.

"Well now, lad," Titus Alderson said when, still in Mary Level, Noddy John's Rise gaped blackly at their feet, "take care here, t'ladders aren't all they should be."

Disdaining a holder, his candle was stuck by the inevitable clay-ball to the brim of his hat, so leaving both hands free when he put his foot over the edge. At the bottom, stepping off the last rung on to the sole of Notion Level, they went along the tramway, turning sharp left at Great Hope Shaft and sharp right at Maybe Shaft where, its performance causing so much concern, was the old and overburdened pump which drained the North Sun Vein.

Sam Kirkbride was there, oilcan in hand, his face more gloomy than usual, if that were possible, as the ailments of the pump were reviewed.

"It's a new 'un that's wanted," said Mr. Alderson. "But . . . well, you know how things are, Sam."

The engineer nodded. "Aye, Titus, I do," he said simply. "Maybe if we nurse her she'll last out longer than we think."

In the North Sun Vein the partnerships were cruelly hampered by inroads of water along the cross-cuts and in the sumps Adam descended, and hardly a man was not soaked through. Up the rises it was better and, leaving the ladders, he entered quite dry drifts in which durk-wagons, on extremely narrow gauge lines, were pushed to the rises for their contents to be emptied down the hoppers, box-like conduits whose mouths, in the level below, discharged into tall horse wagons placed there in readiness.

Titus Alderson did not accompany his guest throughout this series of exhausting trips, but he was present when the young man from Spain saw his first, Yorkshire master-vein. Beyond a stationary train with a Skewdale pony in gears at the front, the animal's head in gloom but glossy brown rump illuminated by the candle on the leading vehicle, a partnership was hewing and shovelling the precious mineral.

"There you are, Adam," he pointed. "Now if we'd plenty like that."

Recalling Peg Stephen's effort to describe a vein by means of a sponge-cake, Adam smiled slightly as he surveyed the scene. The fissure, hading a shade from the vertical, was about two feet wide with sides of grits and limestone respectively; this space was filled with gangue and spar, through the middle of which, a broad grey ribbon with a sheen, ran the ore of lead.

An elderly man, black-bearded, raised his hand. "I'se firing a shot, Titus," he called across. "Now out of t'way, lads, an' shift that horse."

An immediate withdrawal was made by all to a safe distance, where the explosion of the blasting charge was awaited. When it came there was a thunderous report, a violent rush of wind with blackish smoke and fumes in its wake, the report continuing to echo and re-echo through the levels and drifts of the mine. Afterwards the havoc was inspected, the great slabs of rock which had been riven out.

"Well, lad," Titus Alderson said to Adam at the end of a bout of coughing, "we've a lot to see yet, so we'll . . . aye, we'll get back to that renowned Short Cut o' mine."

On the return, a few fathoms short of Noddy John's Rise, he stopped to indicate a hand level of recent construction driven out from the horse level.

"This is where it begins, Adam," he said. "It's noan very long either, which makes what happened at the fore end all the more incredible. Yes . . ." he spoke almost to himself, "incredible is th'only word for it, for I still can't make out how I went wrong."

The inner end of the Short Cut was in truth a terrible witness to a mining man's lack of skill, and Adam was hard put to hide his dismay. It was evident that Arthur Nattrass's assertion was justified, for if the new working had been driven a trifle lower it would have missed Old Joss Level altogether. As it was the connection had been effected with a curving slant which must have taken a month or two to effect and cost money the West Side Company could ill-afford.

"What about the plan you'd use showing Old Joss Level, Mr. Alderson?" he inquired. "It'd be an old one, wouldn't it? Had it been checked?"

Titus Alderson's colourless lips quivered. "Yes, lad, an' there were nowt wrong there. And since then I've re-calculated from t'figures in my dialling book time without number. My dial were all right, too."

"Is there any ironstone?" was Adam's next question. "That'd pull the compass needle out o' truth."

"Not about here," the old man replied, as he started off again. "And afore the survey I took the precaution o' having the tram-rails uprooted out of the level for a fairish distance."

Old Joss Level, which ran in parts through even older workings of the Old Man, was being repaired in the most dangerous stretches. At one point Hugh Bearpark, the rosy-cheeked carpenter from Swaledale, was setting up round timber in side-legs and caps to support a dubious eleven fathoms of roof. Farther along still, beyond slush a foot deep on the sole, Nick Pratt, on contract, was walling and arching the ancient level through a soft area, his shapeless fingers as useful with massive stones as they were delicate in inserting small, packing pieces.

Near the forehead Mr. Alderson's aghast: "Good gracious, lad!" meant it was half-past two, and so, forthwith, they entered a cavern-like chamber to eat their bait, swilling down the food with cold tea. During the meal Titus Alderson outlined how it was proposed to reach the ore at Jamie's Mint.

"Straight on fro' here, lad, through the New Drift to Doomsday, and then right on to Captain Tregoning's Stoping, where all the water is," he explained. "If Doomsday hadn't been in th'awful condition it is, an' if we'd had the brass for real up-to-date tackle, I should have gone for it another way, but it'd have been a sight more costly even than what we're doing, which is bad enough."

"How do you know for sure the ore's there?" Adam asked.

"Because my great-grandfather handed the story down," the old mine-agent replied. "Until they were flooded out for good he earned any amount every Pay there."

As proof, this was not entirely convincing, but years later, so Adam gleaned, a party of Cornishmen, the finest miners and engineers in the world, had thought well enough of the prospects to make an attempt, but, just as initial expenses had been recouped, a continuous torrent forced them out. There was reason now to believe, however, that water-pressure was much less.

"Aye, I shall be glad when we're through," Mr. Alderson said, winding up with every confidence. "Then we can make a start wi' putting the Company on its feet."

He accepted a quid of tobacco from Adam and, happy in purely professional topics, sat talking of such matters as the slope of levels, which, in Skewdale, was usually a quarter-inch to a yard.

"Anyway, lad, I'm sticking to my guns and never mind your one in one hundred and thirty," he chuckled at the termination of a vigorously-conducted argument. "I still contend that wi' one in one hundred and forty-four the tractive force required to pull a loaded train down the slope is just the same as is exerted when the same wagons, empty, are hauled back up the slope."

"We'll have to settle it by putting the question to them as does both," Adam said. "Th'hosses."

"Aye, lad." The mine-agent's guffaw was unseemly in the serious atmosphere of the mine. "Well, now . . ."

So then to the forehead of Old Joss Level and along the New Drift, the noise increasing with every stride nearer to the partnership of Dead Men driving forward through Black Flints and Chert.

"It's still very stiff, Mr. Alderson," said their leader, Len Rukin, wiping off a dirty streak which had trickled to his blue jowl. "I don't know as how many drill points we're blunting in a week, but Richard Blenkiron says he's doing nowt else but sharpen an' temper 'em for us."

"Yes, it's been as hard as owt ever encountered in t'Great Deep Level," his senior remarked before turning to Adam. "We'd expected to hit Doomsday by June, but at this rate I fear it'll be August."

As only two men could work at the confined forehead the discussion was protracted.

The eventual outcome for Adam and Mr. Alderson of this day underground was a meal of ham and eggs, cooked by Mrs. Peacock's own hands, eaten in the kitchen of the Plug and Feathers, where they had called for a drink after walking Ben down Sleety Slape. On their arrival the proprietress heard of the lengthy exploit, whereupon she promptly raised the flap of the bar-counter and, smiling more than Adam had ever seen her, led the way to the back premises, from which, to anticipate any objection on the spot, she then slipped away to arrange for Ben to be taken home and word left with Cherry.

The finer points of lead-mining were still being debated unflaggingly when, just before half-past nine, Lucy Peacock turned them out. At the gate of Yew Tree House Mr. Alderson broke off the theme, but this was only to issue an invitation.

"Nay, you scraped your clogs at th'Plug, lad," he said. "An' you'll noan muck owt seriously either—sit in t'leather chair when we go in."

Indoors, watched by Cherry partly with amusement and partly with a lump in her throat, Titus Alderson went on expounding, eyes lively and white, pointed beard seeming to jut rather than droop. However, after a cup of tea, during the two minutes' interval between the preparatory whirr of the grandfather clock and its subsequent striking, the bowl of her uncle's pipe sank on to his chest; he fell asleep, as quickly as that.

Cautiously closing the kitchen door, Cherry saw Adam off, the breeze wafting her soft hair. "He's enjoyed it so much because he could talk his head off to somebody as understands what he's talking about, Adam," she whispered. "And without—well, there being owt sort o' nasty in the background. I nobbut wish . . ."

The tinge of regret in her voice reminded Adam of that one thing which loomed as barrier to perfect accord. Thereupon he brought it up, as much as he dared. "Cherry, lass," he began, "if I'd wanted an ordinary spell o' grooving here it'd have been for your uncle. I'm nobbut starting for the East Side lot because I'd like to size my cousin up."

"Why?" she asked.

To advance farther would be to reveal overmuch. "Maybe because I can't quite make the chap out," he hedged. "Anyroad, you'll have noticed how he treats me, so for one thing I'm minded to see how far he will go."

Her red lips parted. "Oh, Adam, you must be careful," she implored. "Reuben Nattrass is dreadful when he gets savage."

Adam teased her. "I could be a nasty customer myself, lass."

"But you've haven't any idea, Adam," she persisted. "He's *terrible*."

Adam's tone changed, to become comforting. "Don't worry, lass, I shan't come to much harm. Besides, an' you can take this for gospel, I've always done my best to avoid fighting."

Probably she did not hear all he said, for, wonderingly, she was searching his face. "At one time, Adam," she began at last, "I thought I were beginning to be able to weigh you up. But I were wrong . . . I can't. Oh, it's hard to explain what I mean—I don't think I really know myself, excepting that . . ." her slight smile was perplexed, "I'm a right silly, aren't I?"

"Keep just the way you are, lass," he said.

Her troubled look lingered a little longer on him. "Good night, Adam," she said eventually.

When he was shutting the gate she had already gone indoors, and as he turned up towards Dolly Bridge, Adam was fervently cursing himself for the dilemma in which his wild fancies had placed him.

"But, just because I've got a maggot in my head, I can't tell her why I want to work for th'East Side Company," he grunted. "For that matter, either, I can't brag that if Reuben Nattrass ever seriously touched me I could make him wish he hadn't been born."

A few minutes later, still pondering, he was staring at the Skew, now reduced to an insignificant stream flowing between broad slopes of rounded, river stones, when he nearly bumped into Ambrose Pedley, a frantic figure.

For several days the behaviour of Agnes's father had been so peculiar that the thought of seeking fresh quarters crossed Adam's mind. But there was Agnes to consider and, in any event, he was seldom in the house, often eating either at Low Bands or Badger Hall.

"Stretching your legs afore bedtime?" he asked the wild-looking groover. "It's a nice night for it, anyhow."

The expression in Ambrose Pedley's eyes was that of one who is meeting a total stranger, not a young man who is becoming distrusted.

"Aye, I'm walking," he shouted, arm shooting out, pointing finger moving along the darkening line of the tops from Lovely Lady to Virgin Hill, "walking till I can walk no more, walking till I've made my peace wi' Him . . . as near to Him as I can get. Aye, I'se walking."

Distraught, collarless, he left Adam without another word, a small man in breeches and knitted woollen stockings who, clogs scraping on the gritstone of Jom High Road, disappeared into the twilight.

"If he doesn't take care of himself he'll go cracked," was Adam's thought.

As he expected, Agnes had gone to bed and so, after changing clogs for slippers, he was contemplating rummaging in the pantry, when very faintly he heard her call. Even from the stairs' foot, while she told him about the milk and custard tart, it was difficult to be sure of what she said.

"Are you all right, lass?" he shouted.

"I've a bad headache, that's all," she whispered.

"Would a drink of tea do you good, Agnes?" he suggested. "I can soon make some an' bring it up."

He heard her then, easily enough, the screeched : "No, you mustn't." But she calmed enough to add: "I . . . I don't want owt, thank you."

It was not the moment to press her. "All right then, lass," he said.

As Adam sat down to the simple repast, he was reflecting on what an unhappy house this was and must always have been. Later, however, strolling along Middle Sorrow to smoke a last pipe, his thoughts were exclusively about Cherry, her uncle, and her uncle's problems. His own assessment was that the West Side Lead Mining Company would be fortunate to survive very long. The New Drift was absorbing the money made in the two ore-getting grounds and if either of these had a set-back the whole organisation would probably collapse. Peace of mind for Titus Alderson in the near future seemed very unlikely.

6

The Blenkirons' haymaking took place in the large meadow behind the Smithy. It began on the Thursday and, the weather accommodating, ended on the Saturday.

Adam, now wielding a scythe with reasonable competence, was one of the mowers, cutting the green-brown swathes alongside Matt Tiplady, who had wound up his business engagements at Flout Level after netting a clear profit of fifteen pounds for himself, this after he and his partner had paid the analyst's fee and delighted Mary Jane with pie-dishes *and* pans.

Matt's solemn-faced small daughter, who in the light of household duties treated school attendance carelessly, heard her father mention the latter.

"Right nice pans an' all, Adam," she intervened, illustrating with her hand. "They start wi' a small 'un and get bigger an' bigger, like a family that's had 'em regularly standing in a row."

Adam just averted a laugh. "That'll be useful, love."

"Useful, I should say it is!" she proclaimed. "Why last night, wi'out having to ram it in, I stewed a——"

Her father coughed. "Walls have ears, lass," he advised her.

Mary Jane, following his glance, saw Mr. Blenkiron talking to Luther Thwaites at the roadside. "Eee, I deserve to have my tongue chopped off," she chided herself. "But . . ." her voice fell to conspiratorial depths, "have you asked him yet?"

Father and daughter then jointly requested Adam's presence on the evening of the 'Twelfth,' in approximately six weeks, when he would have placed before him a grouse prime as any of the gentry might hope to eat.

"Aye, I'll be there, Mary Jane, dead on time, you bet. Backsliding into your bad ways, Matt?" Adam chuckled.

It appeared, however, that this and future lapses from grace would be strictly non-commercial, for, as they steadily advanced to cut down the pink clover and tall grasses before them, Matt Tiplady confided that he and his present partner, with three others, had arranged to begin a really big adventure by opening up a mine at Gull Scar, below Silver Seat.

That was Thursday; Friday was far less laborious, though hot enough for cattle above to gather beneath the ashes for shade. But Hannah Batty, who from the kitchen window of Malaga had frequently been watching haymakers who were not making too much of a toil of it, subsequently advanced across the sun-drenched field to acquaint them with her views.

"Of all th'idle lot!" she scoffed. "Hand me that rake, Cherry lass, and I'll show you how to get on wi' it."

"There isn't any right need for us to hasten, Hannah," Fronick tried to explain. "The weather's settled an' Mr. Alderson isn't lending us the horses till to-morrow."

Mrs. Batty, black-bonneted, ignored all interruptions. With arms swinging vigorously, stiff, black skirt flying to disclose elastic-sided boots, she proceeded with her demonstration, not silently either.

"Why," she informed all and sundry, "when I were a lass, we thought nowt o' step-dancing through the night till it were time for the young men to start off to t'mines an' for us lasses to scurry home an' change into summat more suitable for scrubbing the dairy floor. I've no patience——" She glimpsed the blacksmith and his son, both grinning broadly. "Aye, you can laugh, Richard, an' you too, Wingy my lad—anyroad, what are you wasting your time here for while Her Majesty's mail-bag is slung round your neck, wi' a parcel fro' Corvy of corsets for your sister sticking out?"

"She's recognised the label," Dinah giggled. "But if she'd learnt her letters instead of dancing all night, so as when she looked closer——"

"Which you've seemingly done, miss," Mrs. Batty remarked with relish.

Fronick, scarlet-hued, would have been wiser to join in the fun at Dinah's discomfiture. "They're not for me, Hannah," she jeered. "So there . . . an' don't you be so clever again."

Old Hannah's eyebrows went up. "They're noan, lass? In that case to-morrow morn you'll do well to get somebody to lace you up about three inches tighter. A young girl like you, bulging as if you'd getten a horse-collar round your middle."

Richard Blenkiron, after swiping at a buzzing insect, remarked with a chuckle that when the exhibition ended she might welcome a cup of tea.

"Aye, I should, lad," Old Hannah agreed. "That is, if Grace hasn't misplaced the caddy."

Haymaking on the Saturday, with not a great deal to do, was another holiday, when all the young people were present with the exception of Ward and his cousin who, on the rising land above their grandfather's house, were engaged in secretive mining operations.

Mazy Bill rode Polly down from the mine, his countenance lightening only twice that day, on the mare's delightedly rolling herself between the windrows, and when, hearing Ben's whinny as Adam led the galloway from Yew Tree House, she cantered amongst the haycocks to meet her friend.

The last sled-load was loaded by six o'clock, but before then the young ladies were thoroughly tumbled, especially Annamaria Rutter who, on the strength of the farm-work she did at home, comported herself as the sole professional.

"Now then, chaps," Arthur Nattrass guffawed, "it's about time these lasses were tossed about a bit. Ready, Adam lad. Wingy——"

Tactically ill-placed, he bit the dust under a concerted attack by the girls from behind, when his shirt was enthusiastically stuffed with hay. That started reprisals, Adam eventually cornering Cherry after a spirited chase.

"No, you don't," she said breathlessly. "Adam," she screeched as he picked her up, "we're not going to be put under a mountain o' ——"

A dozen yards farther back she began to laugh, this regrettably at a friend, though Bart's amazed expression may have been a contributory cause. Fronick to-day certainly sported a very definite waist-line, but she was suffering for it.

"You can't run so far?" the clerk ejaculated. "Whatever for?"

Fronick dragged another breath from the depths. "Because . . . well . . . because I . . . I can't. It's too hot."

Bart eyed her more closely. "I say, love, you're noan i' some sort of pain, are you?"

"No!" Richard Blenkiron's rather prim daughter shouted.

When the girls were released after the 'burial,' the mound of hay beneath which they had been disciplined was placed on top of a sled partially laden. To this height, to ride in state on the final trip, Cherry, Dinah, Fronick, Annamaria and Mary Jane were hoisted, Agnes alone excused on the grounds that for some days past she had been poorly. Polly pulled the sled, with Ben escorting her, the young men acting as ceremonial guards during the short homeward journey made close to a hedge gay with creamy Lady's Fingers.

Soon afterwards, Mr. Blenkiron's haymaking had been completed. The door of the haymew was shut and then, Fronick bringing out soap and towels, the young men dusted each other down and washed themselves in the trough outside the back porch.

Mrs. Blenkiron was a descendant of the skilled miners introduced into

England from the Tyrol, at the instigation of Queen Elizabeth, to improve the mineral output of the country. Some notable relics of her forbears were in the parlour: a cypress chest with a lock and key, a copy of Dr. Martin Luther's 'Table-talk,' and a beautiful copper kettle.

Adam inspected these various objects, watched by the mistress of the house as she came in and out, the more closely whenever he was in conversation with Agnes. Gossip about the two cousins was on the increase, but the married ladies who, in the kitchen of Badger Hall, heard Mrs. Robert William Alderson's vicious attack, had decided to suspend judgment. Once or twice before, Ellen Alderson had sprung surprises proving more phantom than fact.

"They came to Cumberland, Adam, an' started real big lead an' copper mines there," Cherry explained. "And do you know, they went back to Germany for their holidays, in them faraway days, mind you. *All* that way, and they had to sneak through t'Spanish armies that were occupying the Low Countries."

"That'd be when a General Alva were there," Adam nodded. "I've heard Spaniards talking of him as if it were three years ago, not three hundred."

Fronick, fetching a chair, joined in. "That's why I'm called what I am, Adam. It's an old family name."

"Yes, an' for the same reason I were christened Annamaria," Miss Rutter said. "Anyhow, maybe it suits the face I've got."

If she expected some suitable comment from her young man she was to be disappointed. At one and the same time Arthur Nattrass leered at Dinah, uttered a ripely insinuating laugh, and dug Adam in the ribs.

"There's more to a lass than her face, what say you, Adam lad?" he began. "No . . ." he suddenly became aware of a chilliness in the ladies' demeanour, and in particular, of his betrothed's icy eye. "Yes, sweetness o' disposition——"

"And what's wrong wi' my face, Arthur?" Annamaria demanded.

"Wrong with it, love?" Arthur Nattrass exuded virtue. "Nay, lass . . ."

Altogether there was considerable uproar, but the mistress of the house, whose husband was casting a glance over a table not very lavishly spread, at last made herself heard, when the party trooped into the kitchen.

Mrs. Blenkiron indicated where they should sit, deliberately placing Adam and Agnes together, in such a position that if there were any hanky-panky under the table she would not miss it.

"Aye, all of you shove your knees under t'groaning board," her son said, adding less loudly: "And well it might groan an' all."

"No *there*, Dinah lass," Grace Blenkiron was smiling. "If the chair's too near the wall—what was that you said, Clarkson?" she demanded, but did not wait for a reply. "If your mother can't provide well enough for you, you can go elsewhere."

The postman retorted that he would if he could get a young lady. "It's noan that I'm choosy, either," he complained. "Owt 'ud do for me, and to tell you the truth I've been thinking, as a last resource of course, of sounding either Cherry or Dinah in t' matter."

These two young ladies, charms publicly despised, simultaneously went into action. But hostilities were not allowed to continue, for Mrs. Blenkiron still stood at the end of the table holding the teapot which, to attract his attention, she pointed at her son.

"I'm noan having you evading th'issue, Clarkson," she snapped. "What you said were downright insulting, and——"

A trickle of steaming tea, in transit, passed from the seed-cake to the scones.

"An' what do you think you're doing, lass?" Richard Blenkiron inquired. "Watering your plants?"

Mrs. Blenkiron's mouth opened in dismay. "Why didn't you tell me what were happening?" she asked furiously.

"Nay . . ." her husband laughed.

Sad to relate, the mistress of the house was once more involved when, glance roving as though over a grandiose buffet crowded with delicacies, she asked them what they would take.

"We'll begin with t'youngest for a change," she said. "Now, Mary Jane, what would you like to start off wi'?"

Mary Jane was staring fixedly at a lump of cheese, pale-coloured and decidedly soapy in texture.

"If you don't mind, Mrs. Blenkiron, could I have a nibble o' that there afore I eat owt properly?" she asked very politely. "I've never tasted Kirn cheese, an' I'se been wondering as whether it's like Dinah's mother says."

There was one of those dreadful silences, when everyone leaves it to someone else to speak. The deathly stillness was ended only when Adam leaned across Cherry to inquire of his host about an important matter.

"How are your bees keeping, Mr. Blenkiron?"

Great shoulders shaking, Richard Blenkiron's deep-chested laughter persisted even when the young ladies, leaving their chairs, assembled in a bevy to thump his back. Time alone was the victor, however, when he was spent.

"Capital, Adam lad," he said, wiping streaming eyes with an immense handkerchief. "In the very best of health . . ."

"Which is more than you are, Richard Blenkiron, in your cock-loft at anyroad," his incensed wife proclaimed. "Whatever on earth made you go off like you did? Of all the things, and i' front of company and all."

The blacksmith held up his hands in surrender. "Right, lass," he smiled. "Now let's get on, shall we?"

After the meal, the ladies who were guests assisted in clearing away. On emerging from the kitchen later, they found the young men disporting themselves amongst the flowers and beads, ribbons, linings, and bonnet shapes of Fronick's workroom. Secured by an elastic beneath his chin, Adam wore a rakishly-brimmed, man-like hat with tulle streamer. Bart favoured a curly-feathered concoction turned back to show his fringe; while Wingy went in for a combination of flowers and velvet trimmings which inadvertently he had put on back to front.

Even Agnes, wan though she was, livened up. "Look at 'em!" she ejaculated.

Fronick pushed past her friends. "Take 'em off, all of you," she screamed. "You cheeky——" Just then she caught sight of Arthur Nattrass who, bleeding from pinpricks, the result of attaching ready-made fancy knots, was industriously creating a model founded upon a drawing in a Peter Robinson Fashion Book.

"My best threepence-ha'penny velvet!" she gasped.

Drawn by the hullabaloo, Richard Blenkiron arrived. There had been mention of a stroll up Sorrow Near, and his instructions were brief.

"Be off wi' you sharp," he said, "and don't stop overlong. We're having a sing-song to-night—Cherry's uncle's coming, Dinah's mother an' father, and . . ." He enumerated them all.

Peace then descended on the house and, while elsewhere the young ladies titivated themselves, the menfolk talked about the forthcoming Greets First Fair. From the window the whole of Town Foot was visible and, rising to stretch his legs, Mr. Blenkiron watched a couple in earnest conversation.

"Well, Adam," he remarked, "I see that Ambrose Pedley and his brother James have made it up."

"Why, have yon two nanny-goats had a row?" Arthur Nattrass asked.

The blacksmith laughed shortly. "When such as yon have a difference they don't omit to let all t'world know about the sins of the chap who's offended 'em," he observed. "No, for a while they've been cool wi' one another, nowt more than that."

Wingy eyed the pair, who were walking arm-in-arm. "They're friendly enough now, choose how. I expect they're scheming to expose somebody's wrong-doings . . . maybe that's why they've getten together again. Huh!"

"The Congregational minister up at Yorrel," Bart Hugill grinned.

Sounds increased in the house as the young ladies began to descend the stairs.

CHAPTER SEVEN

I

MAZY BILL still brought Agnes Pedley flowers, pretty pieces of spar, and pounds of butter from his mother's dairy, but, as if imprisoned in some gloomy cell of his own enfeebled mind, he had altered immeasurably.

It was doubtful whether Agnes, far from being well, was aware of this. She, too, was different, withdrawn as never before, which made it all the more extraordinary when, on the morning of Greets First Fair, she announced she would go after all.

"Champion, lass," Adam smiled. "You're sure you feel up to the walk there and back?"

She was almost feverish in her reply: "It'll noan harm me an' maybe . . . maybe it'll do me good."

"Why shouldn't it, lass," Adam agreed. "Anyroad you'll be in jolly company, and that'll liven you up."

A new shadow crossed her face. "An' you're noan young for so long, Adam," she murmured. "After that . . . there isn't any more fun, is there? It's soon over an' then . . . there's nowt but trouble and——"

"Hold on, lass!" Adam protested. "To begin with, you can have fun and pleasure whatever age you are. Take Old Hannah for example . . ."

That was as far in his assurance as he was able to go, for at that moment Ambrose Pedley arrived home for his dinner, and Agnes retired to the larder, where she stared unseeingly at stone shelves, which, thanks to Matt Tiplady's skill and generosity, were furnished as never before. But no sense of well-being comforted her when at last she picked up a dish of roast hare.

From the Old Cow Inn Annamaria Rutter had been watching for her friends and, as soon as the party from Winterings came into sight, she joined them. In common with the other young ladies, she was wearing a light, summery dress suitable to the occasion and to the warm weather.

It happened that, after greetings were over and the walk resumed, a line of magpies, long tail feathers streamed behind, flew over the Dutch elm in Half House grounds.

"That's the last," said Cherry. "Four of 'em altogether. 'One for sorrow, two for a birth——'"

"No, it isn't, love," Dinah interrupted. "'One for sorrow, two for *mirth*, three for a wedding, and——'"

"'Four for a birth,'" Annamaria said with determination. "An' I can name who it is an' all. She's noan far from here either."

"Hush, lass," Cherry whispered.

"Hush nothing," Miss Rutter retorted. "But if it'll save the blushes of them chaps they'd better drop back a few yards."

Dinah jerked her head towards Adam and his companions, Len Rukin and Hugh Bearpark. "You hear what she says," she told them, valiantly trying to carry off an embarrassing business. "That's it, you can all hang behind for a bit."

"Once Annamaria's got summat to tell," Cherry sighed.

Thereupon the auctioneer's daughter, in several trenchant phrases, rounded upon the girls. It was not, she declared, gossiping for gossiping's sake about an unmarried young woman at Barfoot who already was showing signs of pregnancy. "It's t'coming baby I'm considering," she insisted. "You see it's one of them cases where nowt else but public opinion——"

Shouts from behind startled them and, spinning about, they saw Adam and the other two hastening back, while Bart Hugill, who had scrambled over a wall, was running across a meadow to the river. Meanwhile, looking thoroughly alarmed, Fronick Blenkiron was supporting Agnes who, sitting on a bank amidst reddish-purple cranesbill, had either fainted or was not far from it.

"What's the matter with her, Fronick?" Dinah gasped when the three girls reached the scene. "Did she go off sudden?"

Fright lent edge to Fronick's tongue. "If you lot hadn't been making so much row you'd have seen for yourselves," she snapped. "We were close on your heels when she began."

While the young woman attended to the girl, dabbing her face with Bart's wet handkerchief, the young men tactfully withdrew.

"Lucky you did," nodded Hugh Bearpark, when the clerk graphically described how he had caught Agnes before she fell. "She might have hurt herself real badly."

"Yes," Len Rukin agreed with the carpenter, "it could have been worse. You'll be taking her back home now, Adam, eh?"

"Aye," said Adam, "it's the best place for her."

When Agnes Pedley came round properly, she would have none of that, however. Stubbornly she insisted upon continuing, and on Adam trying to dissuade her the retort she made aroused Cherry's wrath.

"You needn't think, Adam Brunskill, that because you're my cousin, an' 'cause you're older," Agnes was saying, "that I shall take t'slightest notice——"

"He's only concerned about you, for your own good," Cherry interposed.

"You're noan my keeper either, Cherry Dinsdale," Agnes replied shrilly. "So you look after your own affairs."

Cherry flushed with annoyance. "All right, I will, but I'm telling you first that you're being both a silly and an ungrateful little thing," she said. "Your cousin's been kindness itself to you, but th'only coin seemingly in which you can repay him——"

The culprit's flood of tears stopped further criticism and, when the long-sustained outburst had spent itself, no one was in the mood either to scold her or to offer any more objections. In the event, Agnes improved rapidly, the transition really astonishing, from melancholia to spirits curiously high.

Greets First Fair was one of the major days in the Skewdale calendar, and the approach to the village was so congested that Annamaria luckily did not perceive the tankard which her young man, Bull Waggott alongside him, flourished from the doorway of the B.G. Inn. Arthur Nattrass was in great form and, attaching himself to Adam, described the fight he had had at the same fair two years before with a tough customer from Kettlewell in Wharfedale. The bloodthirsty account was punctuated by illustrations.

"No," he declared, fists weaving dangerously as they proceeded along the crowded roadway, past Greets Hall and the Vicarage, "I'd tapped t'claret all right, and he didn't ask for any more at after that. I slipped him one under the heart, an' then hooked to his jaw wi' my right——"

His vicious swing almost connected with an elderly lady who, rightly, was angered.

"You ought to be more careful, Arthur," Annamaria said when his near-victim had gone off after relieving outraged feelings. "You might have laid her out."

"Adam hasn't been to a big do like this afore, love," her young man said, red to the ears after his recent upbraiding. "An' I were nobbut trying to show him what can happen."

That led to another thing, the absence once more of a girl who, since early schooldays, had always accompanied his young lady to the Fair.

"Well, wherever she is let's hope she's enjoying herself and isn't filled wi' remorse about the trick she played on her best friend," Annamaria remarked, a shade tight-lipped.

"Aye, at least she could have written you, lass," Arthur agreed.

"If she'd had owt about her she'd have telled me she were going, instead of sneaking off like she did," Annamaria snorted.

Arthur Nattrass winked at Adam. "There's always one good reason why a young woman betakes herself out of sight of everybody, love."

"That wasn't it, anyhow," Annamaria snapped. "I were mates too long wi' Margaret Pedley not to know her better nor that."

In front, doggedly and clumsily, Bull Waggott was doing his best to entertain Cherry, Dinah and Agnes, young ladies of a type not very familiar to him. But Adam, on hearing that name, forgot his amusement.

"You and my cousin Margaret were friends then, Annamaria?" he asked.

She tossed her head. "I'd always reckoned so, but if she'd thought much about me she'd have sent me a letter saying where she were."

"You haven't any idea?" Adam next inquired.

"No, I haven't," Annamaria retorted. "An' I'm not going to talk any more about her either." Nor did she.

On the Green, a large oval of grass had been roped off, and there a horse-show was being held. This was not the sole attraction, for the Market Place drew as many people, while there was also a constant traffic to the pasture behind the Friends' Meeting House, where cattle and sheep were being judged.

Adam's party was greatly reduced. George Nattrass, from the parlour window above the shop, had beckoned in Arthur and his future daughter-in-law; the other young men had disappeared on their own affairs, and so had Fronick and Bart. This left Adam with Cherry, Dinah and Agnes, whom he accompanied while they examined lace handkerchiefs, ribbons, purses, baskets and sundry goods on offer.

Dr. Seaton's house and surgery were at that side of the Market Place, next door to the workshop and residence of Mr. Thomas Plews, the clock-maker. Both these gentlemen were visible, the diminutive doctor, astride his big horse, barking out demands for a passage through the throng, Screw Tom surveying the scene through steel-framed spectacles from his private door.

Mr. Plews, a director of the West Side Company, was a man whose high-domed forehead and narrow head were accentuated by a grey beard which, of the same width, appeared as a tail-piece to his face. Immediately she saw him, Dinah pushed Cherry into a space between the stalls.

"I know what he'll start on about if he sees you," she said, tartly.

"So that's Screw Tom, is it?" Adam murmured to his cousin.

Increasingly overwrought about the signals Cecil Waggott kept making her, Agnes jumped. "Yes . . . yes, that's him, Adam," she was gulping when Nathan Wharton, the sawyer, lightly slapping her shoulder from behind, bade her a jovial: "Good afternoon, lass," which startled her again.

Cherry and Dinah had decided that this would be an excellent opportunity for Adam to visit Leise Abbey, acquainting him to this effect on his return from buying brandy-snaps. The ruins were not very far off, over the bridge and then across a few fields alongside Greets Beck.

"Right," laughed Adam, holding out the paper bag. "Suits me, so you'd better lead the way."

With the exception of Agnes, who suddenly looked desperate, they were all enjoyably crunching as they pushed through the good-natured crowd towards the Grafton Arms and the main road to Corvy. Dinah Skidmore led the file and, in hastily avoiding Arthur Nattrass's elder brother, Alice's George, collided with a young man she detested. Reuben Nattrass's dark-eyed glance was only for her friend, however.

"Well, well, well, Cherry lass," he began. "So you're here, are you? An' these lot 'ul be more congenial company for you than I should have been, eh?"

Cherry's red lips curved with disdain. "Much," she said.

"You heard that, Brunskill?" Reuben Nattrass grinned. "Now tell me this—you're a chap who's getten a vast experience of the great world, aren't you?—what would you do if a woman insulted you that road? Would you clip her on t'lug to bring her to her proper senses, or what?"

"On the contrary, Cousin Reuben," Adam remarked with extreme deliberation, "I think I should betake myself off as sharp as I could."

Nod-nodding first, Reuben Nattrass replied to that. "Aye, maybe you're right, Brunskill, maybe you're right i' believing these matters are best argued out when other folk isn't present. But . . ." his mouth acquired distinctively aggressive lines, "I don't know as how I care to hear a chap advise me to make myself scarce."

The moment was quite inopportune in one sense, but it was characteristic of Agnes Pedley that she chose then to tell her cousin about a girl whom she had known years before.

"I'll look out for you here at after, but if I happened to miss you in t'crush I'd wait up at Town Foot till you came," she said breathlessly. "You see, I *would* like to have a right long talk with her instead o' going to th'Abbey."

"You do then, lass," Adam smiled.

Reuben Nattrass was eyeing Agnes as if he had never seen her before, which, changed by attractive clothes, was essentially the case. He was a renowned personality, and so it was natural she should be overwhelmed, but she revealed such astonishing recuperative powers that the glances of the two young ladies with her met.

The East Side Company's agent bent until his curly, black side-board was not far from her smooth cheek. "Haven't you a word for me, Agnes lass?" he chuckled. "You're noan frightened o' me, are you?"

Slowly and shyly she raised her head, veiling china-blue eyes with long lashes. "N-no," she stammered, but then, gathering confidence on perceiving the effect she was having on him, went on, prettily bold: "Why should I be frightened of you?"

"Aye, why should you, lass?" Reuben Nattrass winked.

Adam intervened. "You'll be missing that friend of yours, Agnes. You'd better be off, hadn't you?"

She tripped away, a slight but very well developed little figure whose retreat, watched speculatively by Reuben Nattrass, was commented upon by him in two words only, though he invested them with some significance.

"My, my," he nod-nodded as he began to saunter off. "Well, I'll noan detain you three from the rollicking time you'll have inspecting th'old ruins of the Abbey. But . . ." he jabbed a finger towards them, "I'll be seeing one or two of you again i' due course."

Dinah's brown eyes flashed. "Not if I can help it," she said.

Lazily Reuben Nattrass half-turned to eye her up and down. As always she was smartly dressed, her appearance suggesting much that she was not. "Of the three on you, lass," he grunted, "I were not referring to you. You see I'se not so partial to women as gives promise but doesn't perform."

"Cousin Reuben . . ." Adam started, "another——"

The general hubbub and the fact that Reuben Nattrass was several paces distant aided Cherry Dinsdale, or otherwise two powerful young men might there and then have entered into violent conflict.

"Come on, Dinah," she cried desperately, "or we'll never get to th'Abbey."

"Him!" Dinah stamped, several minutes afterwards.

In the peaceful atmosphere of a roofless nave she calmed down and, with Cherry, recalled for Adam's benefit many stories, notably to do with a stone figure of a Crusader, the shield and crescent on the tower, and the long lost secret of mortar which still upheld enormous, overhanging masses of masonry by its bond.

Butterflies fluttered and, in these pleasant surroundings, treading fine turf and worn flagstones, the golden afternoon slipped by.

The decision about tea was taken out of their hands when returning from the Abbey, the invitation being given from the open doorway of a small, well-tended residence near Greets Bridge, where Titus Alderson would be spending the evening with a much older and greatly revered friend.

"No, Cherry lass, so long as you've not made other arrangements you're having your tea here," Mr. Guy declared. "Me and the missus has allus kept open house for t'First Fair, so in you come, t'lot of you."

James Guy was an old man with a ripe sense of humour and, when his bosom friend, old John Dougill, arrived later, Adam began to enjoy himself even more. The two retired mining agents were, of course, avid to glean all they could about Spanish lead-mining methods, but this allowed him subsequently to steer the talk towards a very definite objective: the strata on either side of the boundary between the East and West Side companies in the region in which he was particularly interested.

"But how do you know for certain?" he asked. "Mr. Guy's just said the two setts haven't been worked in that area."

Old John Dougill smiled. "There'd be indications if iron-ore were about, lad. Yes, you can take it fro' us that there isn't any."

"Not a trace," James Guy agreed. "Aye," he added, "if you can fin' any where you've mentioned I'll eat t'lot."

"Hold on, James," Mr. Dougill observed. "Iron-ore is poor bait, an' you mustn't forget we've a pact to walk behind Hannah Batty on her last journey."

His friend rumbled into laughter. "Thoo means, lad, that she's telled us she'll be at our gravesides when *we're* put away."

Attracted by the noise, Mrs. Guy glanced at them. A fragile lady wearing a lacy covering on her head, she promptly challenged both her husband and Mr. Dougill with an undue interest in Mrs. Batty.

The old folk made the most of the joke and the young ones enjoyed their sparring. Adam's underlying feeling on another matter was of dissatisfaction, however—dialling was a simple matter when carried out by an expert of Titus Alderson's experience, and if ironstone had not been the root cause of the error at the Short Cut he could not think of any other reason.

Failing to find Agnes after a second round of the crowded Market Place, Adam and the two young ladies tried the Green, now largely deserted. A quick glance beyond the jumps and hurdles revealed nothing of the missing girl, but they noticed that Mr. Henry Hird had been entertaining his sister. Sir Charles Grafton's mineral-agent lived in front of the stocks, near the Friends' School, and he was having a parting word or two with Mrs. Roberty Will before she stepped into the waiting trap.

Within the next few minutes it was unanimously decided that a further search was hardly worthwhile. Actually the conclusion was reached after withdrawing to the opposite side of the Green, near the Post Office, past which they were strolling when Wingy Blenkiron emerged. The postman was in his best Sunday suit, and had been calling for the canvas bag in which he had carried down the mail. He, too, had seen nothing of Agnes.

The Postmaster, standing in his doorway, *pince-nez* and broad, black ribbon well in evidence, at once took steps to forward one of his commercial preoccupations by pointing out to Adam, whom he knew by sight only, the wisdom of taking back to Spain one or two suits of English-made clothes.

"If you haven't the time now, I could show you t'pattern bunches an' measure you on my next journey up t'Dale," he said. "As for t'cut, I'll personally vouch for that."

Adam, who had begun to scratch his head, then made an offer the introduction to which had an instantaneous effect upon his friends—hastily Cherry turned aside to convert her bonnet into a screen, Wingy was seized with a disturbing bout of coughing, and Dinah, in the worst plight, desperately strove to avert one of her attacks.

"While I'm about it I reckon I might as well have three or four suits, Mr. Trotter," he said, after referring to a depleted financial position due to the drain of a lengthy holiday. "I'll send you the brass when I've addled a Pay or two back i' Spain——"

"Send——" Lodge Trotter ejaculated. "I don't do business on them terms."

"I hope you're not doubting my word, Mr. Trotter," Adam remarked stiffly. "Of course . . ." he relaxed somewhat, "I can see your difficulty, so suppose, to prove my good faith, I paid you a sovereign on account of —well, let's say a round half-dozen suits."

The Postmaster glared. "Noan while I'm in my right mind," he snapped.

Strutting into the Post Office, he missed the disappointment clouding Adam's face, but his rapid departure was providential for those who had listened to the negotiations. In lively mood Wingy and the girls, with Adam, started homeward.

Dinah was escorted the whole way to Badger Hall and then Adam and Wingy brought Cherry back to Town Foot where, after she had gone in, the two young men yarned with Bart until suppertime, when only a few stragglers were plodding up from Greets.

As it was most inadvisable to linger where Ambrose Pedley might notice him, Adam made a couple of long trips down the high-road, without success, but when returning on the third occasion, as he strolled round the bend beyond Malaga, he saw his cousin up at Town Foot, not without relief. Skipping swiftly to meet him, she then embarked pell-mell upon explanations, why she had come back by Sorrow Near and how the time had sped. Her eyes were sparkling and she was a totally different creature from the one who had left Winterings that morning.

"I were in such a stew," she giggled indistinctly, hairpins in her mouth, fingers busy straightening dishevelled flaxen hair. "So I ran and ran an' ran."

"Anyhow, all's well now," Adam smiled, "and th'important thing is that you've right enjoyed yourself with that friend."

For a fleeting space her face shut down. "Wi' that——" she gulped, before laughing shrilly. "It's these hairpins, I nearly swallowed one. Oh aye, we'd a real lovely gossip. 'Course I were sorry we weren't all together, us and you and Cherry an' th'others."

They were arrested by a soft whistle. Wingy Blenkiron, in nightshirt, leaned out of his bedroom window, from which he had glimpsed, on Middle Sorrow towards Silence, a pedestrian whose gait was surely that of Agnes's father.

"He telled me he were going up bank for a long session wi' my Uncle James," Agnes gasped. "But they generally talk an' pray together till a sight after this."

"You'll do it all right, love," Wingy consoled her.

Calling out thanks, the pair set off hastily, arriving in Back Lane amply soon enough for Agnes to be upstairs before her father joined Adam in the dreary kitchen.

2

Freestone John proposed starting work in Martha Level the day after Askrigg Fair, and so, the evening before that well-attended Wensleydale event, Adam visited Cuthbert Daykin's shop to buy a pair of cheap trousers.

On the way, he dropped in at Blind Kit's. Notwithstanding the unequivocal statements of Mr. Guy and Mr. Dougill, he was still not completely reconciled to their views. Only some adverse outside influence, he felt, could have affected Mr. Alderson's triangulations.

"Evening, Adam lad," Blind Kit welcomed him.

Spread before the cobbler were neat piles of money. As Treasurer of the Cow Club he was counting the funds, unerringly picking up silver and copper and hesitating only when a milled edge was worn exceptionally smooth.

"Evening, Kit," Adam replied, shifting thread and a ball of wax before seating himself on the bench. "I've popped in to ask you something that you might know because of all th'exploring you've done in the mines."

He then became blunt, partly because it was difficult to delude a man so super-sensitive to any inflection, partly because he was sure he could rely on his discretion.

"What I'm really after, Kit," he added, "is to find out th'exact nature of the strata just to the east of where Titus Alderson started to dial for his Short Cut. There's no way into it from the West Side

Company's ground an' I've been wondering if it can be reached from the east."

Blind Kit was fingering a sadly-scarred cheek. "Not by nearer than two hundred fathoms, lad," he said.

"As far as that?" Adam said, disappointed.

"Every bit, or more," the cobbler replied. "Fro' Bucker Level you can strike west through either t'Black Drift or Blind Trial Crosscut, and then i' both cases for a fairish distance farther through th'Old Man. But they're dead ends in due course."

"You've burrowed about a good lot, eh?" Adam murmured.

Blind Kit laughed. "I'll tell you what: when I've lessened that heap o' clogs, I'll take you up both Blind Trial Crosscut and t'Black Drift so as you can see for yourself." Gleefully he slapped his hand sharply down, setting a score of coins jingling. "Aye, I'd right enjoy it, though we'd better go when nobody'll be any wiser."

"It's a bargain," Adam said.

Very satisfied with this arrangement, he went off to Cuthbert Daykin's shop, where, in a corner hemmed in by tubs of lard, rolls of Swan Down, and door mats, he bought a pair of cord trousers for twelve and fourpence.

The receding-chinned Mr. Daykin, singer of heroic ballads, had many pretensions, his business acumen amongst these. He was wont to point to his windows, in which the small-paned frames had been removed, as being the sole example of plate-glass in Skewdale; he would bring the conversation round to his Patent Roaster which, once a week, made the premises fragrant with Jamaica Coffee; and often, to illustrate go-ahead methods, he would direct attention to a sign announcing a discount of tenpence in the pound for ready cash.

However, save with those of the district who already knew the sorry fact—and amongst these he rightly assumed Adam to be—the middle-aged bachelor was reticent about the wild plunge which had landed him, with one hundred and thirty shares, as the third largest shareholder in the West Side Lead Mining Company.

"Aye," he sighed, "let's hope you an' Freestone John light on summat real rich, and let's hope then that t'vein runs right under Winterings Gill till it reaches where I've got a lot o' brass."

"Whatever made you buy that number of shares?" Adam inquired.

Cuthbert Daykin shrugged. "I'm that road," he confessed. "Of course you can lose by it, but it's th'only way you can make big money."

"Aye," Adam murmured with some dubiety.

Perhaps sensing a reflection upon himself, Cuthbert Daykin's florid cheeks deepened in hue, and his prominent-eyed glance, after touring past eighteen-penny rolls of oilcloth and a tower of oatmeal packets, came slyly to rest on his customer.

"You're driving Old Hannah to Askrigg Fair, I hear," he remarked.

"I suppose," he coughed delicately, "you'll be taking your cousin Agnes wi' you."

Adam nodded. "Aye, I've two ladies in my charge."

While caressing the tip of his moustache between finger and thumb, Cuthbert Daykin awaited the outcome of the next shot.

"Agnes should think a lot about you, after all you've done for her, lad. For that matter . . ." he continued smoothly, wishing Emma Ann could hear the next telling instalment, "you must think a rare lot of t'lass yourself, eh?"

Adam had scant desire for a chat on these lines. His response cursory, he tucked the parcel under his arm and left the shop.

Since first taken as a baby in arms, Hannah Batty had made eighty-six consecutive trips to Askrigg Fair, and, for the last dozen years, Winterings folk had acquired the habit of seeing her off, congregating near the bow-windowed shop before starting out themselves.

That morning Agnes Pedley again looked strained, and on the way down to the village had little to say. In the livery stable's cobbled yard, however, she burst into vehement speech, this just after a lively group had hurried along Main Street to swell the assembly around Mrs. Batty's door.

"I've changed my mind about going," she began.

There were other people present, including William Nattrass's small granddaughters from Silence who, with their mother, were being driven into Wensleydale by Reuben Nattrass.

"What's made you decide that so sharp-like?" Adam ejaculated.

Her rising tone virtually caused a suspension of activity in the vicinity. In particular, Mrs. Ralph Skidmore, attracted by it, edged nearer, covertly studying the girl's appearance.

Agnes forgot both graciousness and gratitude while incoherently tendering her explanations. In essence these amounted to an allegation that neither the day at the Fair nor the journey with a garrulous old woman would be very entertaining.

Adam's mouth was stern. "If that's how you're feeling about it you'd better go back home, Agnes?" he said.

"Well, it is," she half screamed. "I don't want to go an' . . . an' I'm noan going, *noan* going." She was frantically running away before Adam's terse "All right," had fully left his lips.

Never before had Isa Skidmore spoken voluntarily to her cousin, but now, a strange light in her eyes, she did so. "Young lasses get that worked up," she deplored. "I expect she were put out because she were going to have to share you wi' Old Hannah."

Adam, angered enough, slammed the trap door. "What do you think me an' her are?" he grunted. "Sweethearts?"

Too delighted by a wonderful opportunity, Mrs. Ralph Skidmore, bony features illuminated by a foxy smile, did not take offence at his abruptness. "As to that," she replied, savouring the moment, "I couldn't say."

Picking up the reins Adam clicked his tongue and drove through the gateway.

Enjoying a last minute's smoke before her escort's arrival, Old Hannah, in the familiar, high, black bonnet, was gently rocking herself when Adam, the shop-bell's clamour dying behind him, entered the kitchen.

"I'm all ready, lad," she announced, promptly setting aside the stubby clay pipe. "Agnes'll be stopping in t'trap, I suppose—to prevent yon noisy lot outdoors fro' starting the horse bolting. *Seeing me off*," she scoffed.

Adam briefly told her this was to be a party of two only.

"It'd have done her good," Mrs. Batty commented. "Anyroad . . ." she chuckled while bustling about with all the zest of a girl, "anyroad, I like my chaps to mesen, an' I usually managed it that way an' all. I'd no use for rivals, Adam lad."

This was the second occasion within a few minutes that Adam had heard himself coupled intimately with his cousin. "Rivals!" he said. "So there's some talk about me an' Agnes, is there?"

Hannah Batty's lips were scornful. "Nobbut by them as likes making summat out o' nothing," she said. "If it were owt more serious you can be sure that such as Anthony Skidmore 'ud soon be putting a stop to you going about wi' their lasses."

The sheer idiocy rooted Adam. "Well, I'm damned," he muttered.

"I should think so an' all," Old Hannah agreed, dismissing the business in favour of instructing him to locate in her bundle of cards the one with 'th'emporium' drawn in the corner. "Everybody knows I'm off," she stressed, "but there's nowt like being official i' these matters."

Duly Adam found the desired notice, with its picture, copied from some renowned London establishment, of a lengthy range of lofty buildings whose many imposing entrances were barred with iron gates. By then Mrs. Batty had completed her final task, a saucerful of milk placed on the sill for the well-being of what she termed 'her visiting cat.' This done she went through the shop and into Main Street, a very erect figure.

Seated in the trap, she was the centre of a storm of banter. "Aye, them as isn't going can look after theirsen for this once," she proclaimed with relish. "If any of 'em is taken bad they'll have to make out t'best they can wi' Doctor Seaton."

Richard Blenkiron winked. "Leaving 'em to his tender mercies, eh?"

Latterly, widely-reported, there had been considerable conflict of opinion between the Greets doctor and the old lady as to the correct treatment of a case.

"Him an' his new-fangled methods!" Old Hannah remarked with supreme contempt. "*Drugs* for a bairn. Who ever heard o' giving a little lad belladonna for bed-wetting? Of all t'nonsense . . ."

The roar of laughter which arose terminated the old lady's send-off. Grinning broadly, Adam flicked the reins and, followed by a few traps, dog-carts and wagonettes, started out at the head of a procession. Others, on foot and on horseback, struck out for the fells and the trods, the short-cuts over the tops. The weather promised well and, although the majority of pockets were scantily lined, high spirits abounded.

On her eighty-seventh Fair outing to Askrigg, Mrs. Hannah Batty distinguished herself by not reaching Winterings again until well after midnight. She had revelled in every minute, and was still in full but rather more circumspect voice as the lamps of the trap lighted up the parapet of the Brig, hymns now replacing the slightly dubious songs which, on lonely stretches of moorland, had convulsed her companion.

At this stage, with the Plug and Feathers in darkness, she broke off to say that, after leaving the horse and trap at the stables, Adam must return for a pot of tea.

"But you're noan stopping long, lad." Her bonnet nodded emphatically. "I can remember, if you can't, that you're beginning grooving wi' young John Raisbeck in t'morning."

"I know what you're afraid on . . . folks suspecting you've had a chap in the house till all hours," Adam sneered.

Her cackle echoed in the narrow alleyway between the façade of the derelict Fleece Inn and the house opposite.

Adam, too, had had a most enjoyable day, as he reflected when, William Nattrass's property handed over to a sleepy yard-man, he walked beneath the bracket lamp at Nick Turn. Taken here and there by Old Hannah, he had been made welcome in a dozen homes, but, most profound satisfaction of all, he had met Cherry and Dinah, both of whom would have heard the rumour linking Agnes and himself. He was quite convinced they were untouched by it.

"Yes, if the lass you care for . . . an' your friends, ignores such ill-natured scandal, I've no need to bother myself either," he decided. "Though . . ."

In his absence, while coaxing the newly-lighted fire with thin kindling, Hannah Batty was also thinking. She knew her own folk, and came to the conclusion that, unless the rumour died quickly, it would be undesirable for Adam to remain beneath the same roof as his cousin.

"Aye, he could lodge here," she pondered. "Wi' the calls I have for nursing I shouldn't be able to look after him as I'd like, but he's off at th'end of the year, so he wouldn't come to much harm."

She was pouring boiling water into the teapot when he entered and, as soon as the kettle was replaced on the hob, she told him her views.

"Yes, I've been chewing the cud on the same lines myself during the last few yards," Adam admitted after warmly thanking her.

"Well, watch how things go, lad," Old Hannah said. "But come whenever you feel inclined."

From then until he left the conversation was gay. In the short interval, however, before he returned with a card impressively marked: CLOSED FOR ANNUAL HOLIDAY, which he had removed from the outer door, Mrs. Batty had been cogitating anew. Pointing to the bottles on the shelf close-by a peep-hole into the shop, she started off: "You know, lad, it's a fairish while sin' Agnes stopped off coming here and I noan think it'd be a bad idea if you sent her to see me. Maybe a herb tonic 'ud put her on the right road."

Adam gladly accepted the suggestion. "I'll be on to her to-morrow," he vowed.

Much relieved, he was in especially good heart as he stepped briskly through the dark village.

* * * *

Before leaving home for work, it was Ambrose Pedley's custom to pay a visit 'round the corner.' As soon as he had gone Adam seized the chance to speak to his cousin, who appeared darker-eyed and more ghost-like than ever as she handed him a package of food.

"Agnes," he began, "you're noan so well, are you? Now pop along to see Old Hannah, will you ? I were talking to her last night an'——"

Fear of her father overhearing was the one restraining factor, but otherwise Agnes Pedley conducted herself as though nearly demented. Blue eyes sharp with fury, her small figure quivered as she spoke.

"You'd no call to discuss me wi' her," she said between her teeth, "You're nowt but an interfering——"

"Hold on, Agnes," Adam interrupted her. "What were said you could have listened to yourself."

"I'm t'best judge on that," she retorted. "An' as for seeing Hannah I'm noan, so there. And you keep your nose out o' my affairs in the future. Just because you bought me some clothes you think you've got a right——"

Adam immediately checked her again. "Do you really believe that's the reason I'm speaking to you like this?" he asked.

"Yes," she answered defiantly.

Sorely tempted to spank her, Adam fortunately resisted an impulse which, in any event, would have been difficult to explain to her father, who came in a moment later.

Ambrose Pedley had been queer for days, but now, in addition, he seemed abnormally jumpy, and so the walk up Sorrow Near to Mine Road was far less pleasant than others made it, especially the three ungainly Coopers and Cyprian Metcalfe, the squatly-built engineer, all of whom were joking noisily about an incident at Askrigg. In these circumstances it was a relief to Adam when, high up Winterings Gill, they reached a piece of waste ground colourful with willow herb. Martha Changing Shop was a short distance beyond this, and there, the new boy, he was jovially greeted by all, with one exception.

"So you're here, friend," Freestone John smiled. "An i' good fettle, I hope."

James Pedley began to pray, pale eyes lifted devoutly towards the roof beams. "Lord God Almighty," he said mournfully, his humble request largely extinguished by a hum of cheerful conversation, "in Thy loving kindness lend Thy grace to such as him . . ."

"I could be livelier, John," Adam confessed as he glanced at the Pedley brothers. "But," he started to unbutton his coat, "I'll pick up soon."

The changing shop was a white-washed apartment in which, at night, a banked-up fire dried working clothes to some extent. There were a few crude pieces of furniture: a deal table and benches, hooks and lockers.

When Adam had shifted into ancient hard hat, ragged coat, patched shirt and the new trousers, he and Freestone John went along to the store and office where they drew and signed for candles, powder, fuses and tools. Next, the equipment not heavy enough to require a wagon, they lighted candles within the tail of Martha Level and, donning hats again, advanced into the horse level.

About two hundred fathoms from the tail, at Old Wife Shaft, the tramroad forked, one branch running up to the profitable working ground at Jenny Incline. After a spell underground, two candles provide a passable light, and so Adam was reasonably able to see the clanking donkey-pump in the fathom-deep sump at the shaft bottom which, driven by a hydraulic engine on the surface, drained the low portions of Jenny Incline. This was the piece of machinery, he remembered, about which Droughty Tom eternally felt aggrieved.

"Aye, that's it," the Quaker said as they continued, splashing through deepening water in a section of the level known as Martha Water Gate, some distance along which he paused to point out a drift leading off. Abruptly abandoned long ago, Lone Crosscut had an uncanny reputation —durk wagons were often alleged to be heard creaking along in it, and the sounds of striking and shovelling were occasionally reported by those passing through the main gallery. "An ill place," he commented, shaking his bearded head.

Fifty-eight fathoms from the surface, Toft Rigg Whim Shaft came next, where the level divided, the right-hand bend leading up to Sun Hade Ground. In a man-hewn chamber a waterwheel rotated steadily, driven by water draining from Sun Hade to the east, the flow in the last few yards confined within a stone-built channel at the side of the waygate. Unlike the majority of those outdoors, the wheel was not overshot: its lower part was immersed in the dark-flowing canal and, on the perimeter, the overshot waterwheel's buckets were replaced by paddles. Eighteen feet in diameter, and seven feet in width, it was a powerful piece of machinery.

"For raising bouse an' deads to the top, I suppose?" Adam said. "I were wondering how stuff from Martha Forehead Ground and Sun Hade Ground was got out. It were plain that Martha Water Gate prevented any tramming out that road."

"Aye, it's all drawn up t'whim shaft here." Freestone John spoke over his shoulder. "Of course everything fro' Jenny Incline Ground and back yonder is hauled straight out to the tail."

Taking the left-hand turn and proceeding westerly, they arrived at their destination in just over a quarter of an hour. Percival's Rise was not far distant from Martha Forehead and, grasping the rungs of its ladders, they mounted steadily until they were able to step off into the Common Rully Gate. At the remote end of the drift, while coats were discarded and the clay-ball candle-holders stuck on to the rock face, Freestone John explained what he proposed to do.

"Right!" nodded Adam, spitting on his hands. "We drive out a crosscut for a few fathoms. Then study it over."

From then until midday, apart from a ten minutes' break, they laboured without intermission. Ventilation was bad, the candles burned dimly and smokily, and speech was conserved. Occasionally, when a shot was fired elsewhere, a rumbling volley was heard and a sharp waft of air was felt, but otherwise the only sounds were made by themselves—the jar as the point of a poll pick glanced off a great body of limestone inadvertently struck; the scrape of the borer as it was given a slight twist before the next blow was delivered; the in-drawing of breath as each, taking turn and turn about, prepared for a mighty effort with the big sledge-hammer, and the quick gasp at the termination of the stroke. In due course a face of rock became a doorway-like recess and, just before noon, the recess was showing all the appearance of the heading of a drift.

"A good morning's work, friend," Freestone John proclaimed rustily as, carrying food and drink, he started off to find a place where the air was fresher. "Aye, nowt to complain on."

Wearing tattered coats to offset the effect of the pervading chill upon shoulders and chests trickling with sweat, they ate their bait at the top of Percival's Rise. A little before a resumption of work was to be expected,

Adam excused himself to the Quaker on the very reasonable grounds of desiring to explore the extreme end of the mine.

Descending the ladder to the level below, he went past Martha Air Shaft, then over a small and over-brimming collecting-sump, and so to Martha Forehead. For several moments, removing his hat to bring the candle closer when needed, he studied the limestone face, a blank wall of rock beyond which, not so very far away, was the corresponding forehead of the West Side Company's Mary Level. There was no sizeable hole in the forehead, but the multitude of small cracks absorbed the shallow flow which unendingly slid past his clogs.

"Maybe it doesn't get to Mary Level," he soliloquised. "But . . ."

On his way back he decided that, if he were in Titus Alderson's shoes, he would initiate further tests to establish effectively whether or not the West Side Company was being penalised by inroads of the neighbouring company's water.

By the middle of the afternoon Freestone John had gauged his companion's capabilities, and from then the pair worked in a harmony which, if luck favoured, promised respectable results. Since bait-time their activities had altered somewhat—shots were being frequently fired, necessitating a temporary withdrawal before safe return could be made to a place choked with fumes. Neither spared himself, despite an atmosphere at times causing the wavering flames of the candles to diminish to little more than an uncertain red glow. Shortly before three o'clock there was an interruption, heralded by a vague glimmering of yellow in the slowly-moving smoke.

"How do, Adam lad," Arthur Nattrass coughed. "You an' John there seems to be kicking up the hell of a reek." Acting as assistant to his cousin, measuring chain looped about his arm, he carried a surveyor's three-legged candle-reader whose light, a candle screened on three sides, served as a focal point on which to train the sights of a dial when measuring angles.

Reuben Nattrass came next into view, bearing dial and tripod. "Well, well, well, so th'important chap fro' Spain has gotten himself down to some hard graft at last," he guffawed. "The question is, is he doing his share, John?"

Adam took upon himself the onus of replying. "Trying, Cousin Reuben," he said, undisturbed. "But a bit soft-muscled as yet."

"*No!*" Reuben Nattrass exclaimed. "But never mind, you'll improve i' that respect if . . . *if* . . . you can stick it out for two-three Pays."

He seldom loitered when engaged in essential operations and, the sally dispatched, turned away more quickly than was to the liking of his cousin, who had been eyeing Adam.

"All t'same, Reuben lad," Arthur Nattrass was saying, very much the connoisseur, "he doesn't strip all that badly. No, he's——"

"Hasten wi' you," Reuben Nattrass bawled, "and set the candle-reader up at t'first bend on the way back. We've still got to plumb that sump at after we've finished here."

With their departure the two partners resumed, at a pace which, about an hour later, was responsible for Freestone John putting aside his shovel with some deliberation. With sober humour he announced he was taking a rest.

"While I wet my mouth wi' what I've getten left in my tea-bottle," he explained. Very much as Arthur Nattrass had done, he noted his companion's rippled chest and powerful shoulders. "Soft-muscled, eh?" he snorted.

Adam laughed. "I'll suffer for it to-morrow, John. Stiff as a crutch, you'll see."

Just then the Quaker had only one idea in his head. "Soft-muscled," he scoffed as he selected a seat on a convenient boulder. "Thoo's nearly finished me off, friend."

It was not in Adam's plan to remain on the Pay Bill of the East Side Company longer than was essential, and therefore it was wise to make the most of any opportunity. So, while his partner refreshed himself, he wandered into the Common Rully Gate, where he knocked over the surveying tackle left there by the Nattrass cousins.

Attracted by the clatter Freestone John peeped out. "I'se rather under th'impression that you're one as can take care on himself," he remarked after spitting out the tea he had been swilling around his mouth. "But i' passing I might as well tell you that there tripod leg were broken by a wagon wheel, an' the trammer as were careless spent ten days in bed as a result of the crack Reuben gave him."

Adam picked up the dial stand, one of whose legs, he noticed, had been spliced with a length of wood different from the original. The foot of this leg, to prevent wear, had been heeled with a millwright's hexagonal nut.

"No harm done, John," he reported.

Soon they started again, continuing until Freestone John, extracting with some difficulty a watch from the remains of a pocket in his ragged coat, declared the day's work at an end. Tools were neatly stacked before they walked along the Rully Gate to Percival's Rise, where, feeling for foothold on the crude, vertical ladder, the descent to Martha Level began.

In the main level and up the crosscuts and drifts, bobbing little lights could be seen, carried by men who, in due course, reached the tail of Martha Level and the blinding glare of late afternoon.

In Martha Changing Shop, when Adam and his companion entered, a brisk discussion was under way concerning the trial stubbornly pursued by the company at the other side of Winterings Gill. For this once Titus Alderson's ability was not being questioned. The argument was merely whether or not, assuming Jamie's Mint were reached, there would be worth-while ore in that ancient place.

3

One evening in late July, Reuben Nattrass, a well set-up young man spick and span in his best suit, sauntered across Town Foot to join Titus Alderson and his pretty niece at the gate of Yew Tree House, where, like many others, they were awaiting the arrival of the Fair.

"Evening, Mr. Alderson, evening, Cherry lass," he said. "Heard owt coming yet?"

"Evening, lad," the old mine-agent replied, smiling. "No, I haven't, but this young lady here makes out she has."

Reuben Nattrass held his head sideways. "An' I believe she's right," he grinned. "Her ears must be better at their job than yours or mine, even if they are a sight smaller."

Fortunately for Cherry, her uncle began to talk about mining matters, this discussion continuing until gaily-caparisoned horses, hauling gold-and-red painted carts, came into view on the bend beyond Malaga. Trumpets were shrilling, and every youngster in Winterings was trotting alongside dusty artillery wheels.

"I suppose you an' Dinah Skidmore 'ul be jaunting to the Fair together?" Reuben Nattrass inquired, turning to her.

Cherry was smiling, enjoying the scene and the excited cries of children who were swarming round a noisily-chuffing, brass-mounted steam engine.

"Yes, I expect so," she said, very much on her guard.

To her surprise, however, nothing resembling an invitation followed. "A nice lass is Dinah," he remarked gravely. "Aye, me an' her always seems to scrap every time we meet, an' I'll own I'se oft rapped back at her in a fashion as I shouldn't. But all t'same her sharp tongue has been used to help her mate, and that's summat, I reckon."

The rumble and the cheering grew louder, drowning all else. Teams of horses and heavy vehicles lumbered past, wheels setting up a bigger din when they reached the cobblestones. The cavalcade proceeded on Main Street as far as the opening between the end of William Nattrass's cart shed and the alehouse opposite Edmund Kearton's house, the entrance to a plot of waste ground above the Skew upon which, in November, the village bonfire was lighted in celebration of Guy Fawkes's Day.

* * * *

For several years Winterings folk had been warned by the showmen that, unless receipts improved substantially, they and their children would soon be denied even a stand of one day. Nothing much could be done about that, so, Skewdale people not being temperamentally inclined to meet trouble half-way, everybody for miles around squeezed the last ounce of fun out of the Fair.

Agnes Pedley did not participate, refusing her cousin's invitation both for afternoon and evening. Before leaving Back Lane after dinner, however, Adam acted upon the decision at which he had arrived earlier. The task was repugnant, but someone must assume it if Ambrose Pedley, who latterly had become even more overwrought and peculiar, were too wrapped up in himself to heed the disastrous change in his own daughter.

"Agnes," he began, "your father's just gone off to wear himself out still more with poring over t'Bible, so I'm going to speak to you about summat."

"What?" she asked swiftly.

Shocked by a pair of eyes far more miserable and haunted than they had been when he first came to England, Adam tried to be very gentle. "You know, lass," he said, gazing at the rock roses gathered by Mazy Bill the previous evening, "it bothers me seeing you like you are. Now if you won't go to Old Hannah, why not let Dr. Seaton look at you?"

"I'm not, I'm not," she gasped. "Why should I? There's nowt wrong with me. Excepting my headaches I'm as well as t'day."

"No, you're not, love," said Adam.

"Yes, I am. An' why shouldn't I be?"

As she demanded this, her expression was momentarily so strange that Adam, his emotions chaotic, felt as if he had been touched with an icy hand. From then he realised he must be more direct.

"Are you in some sort o' trouble, Agnes?" he asked.

Lips quivering, she defied him. " 'Course I'm not. What sort o' trouble should I be in? If you're so clever you'd better tell me that."

Adam pressed lightly on her shoulders, until she was sitting on the stool. "There's all kinds o' troubles you could be in, lass, some small an' some so big that you can't spot any road round 'em, however you twist and turn. No . . ." he checked her, "don't say again that I've no business to interfere, because I know I haven't. All I want to make clear is that if you're in trouble, whatever it is, I'll do th'utmost in my power to give you a hand."

She must have inherited an unbalancing proportion of sheer foolishness, or else she could not have missed the profound concern in his eyes. Instead she rose abruptly, resentfully said: "I've telled you," and then noisily heaped dirty plates one upon another.

Adam attempted nothing further and, deeply anxious, left the cottage.

That afternoon another man was thinking almost entirely about Agnes Pedley as he prowled about the Fair. "When t'horses stop I've a good mind to ask Brunskill where she is," Bull Waggott muttered, staring at the blaring roundabouts. "It's getting bloody funny, I reckon . . . why she's never out."

But the opportunity to draw Agnes's cousin aside did not offer then, though later, making no bones about listening, he heard the mistress of Silence inquire about her. Mrs. Ralph Skidmore, chatting with Dinah and Mrs. Peacock, rather surprisingly addressed the chap who was probably best informed.

"Eee, I did think it a shame when your cousin ran out o' my father's yard," she opened disarmingly. "On t'morning of Askrigg Fair, I'm meaning. Missing a treat like that is all the harder for a young lass."

"Aye, it were a pity," Adam replied.

"An' she's noan here to-day either, is she?"

Adam shook his head. "No, she's not. These headaches of hers fair fetch her down."

Isa Skidmore's scanty eyebrows went up. "Headaches, is it?" she wondered. "Yes, they can be nasty things, specially when they hang on like hers seem to do, poor thing. T'doctor's attending her, of course?"

Perceiving the malicious trend, Adam was very easy. "As a matter o' fact he isn't, Cousin Isa," he smiled. "But you'll know better than me what girls can be—full of whims."

Mrs. Ralph earnestly enlisted the aid of the little group, increased now by Mr. and Mrs. Harker. "All t'same, she ought to have a doctor, oughtn't she. I mean, you never know what it is, do you?"

The discussion became more general, a difficult phase passed, but Adam was in no doubt about the danger looming ahead.

Mrs. Peacock invited a few people in to tea and, with Titus Alderson setting a sprightly pace with her, took the lead. On reaching the Plug and Feathers, where the other guests, including the youngest, Mary Jane, went inside, Adam and Cherry amused themselves with a game of quoits. While the spirited encounter was fought out Cherry confided to her opponent the belief that in their young days Lucy Peacock and her uncle had been sweethearts, supplementing this with an opinion that if the West Side Company had prospered at all recently they might have been married by now.

Exercising a woman's privilege, Cherry was being rather casual in her observance of the game's accepted rules. "But I don't think there's much chance yet," she remarked after gleefully clapping the brilliant outcome of her own effort. "Uncle Titus is noan one to hang his hat up, which is what it'd be at present."

"He's different fro' me then," Adam murmured.

Cherry dimpled. "Who's the heiress, Adam?"

Adam shot out an accusing arm. "Oh, there is one, an' she's worth her weight in gold. But . . ." he thundered to the astonishment of a throng of Fair-goers, "I'll have to teach her one thing, an' that's to play square. Aye, you can gape, lass, but the next time you have a go, don't bother to do any throwing—just stand on top and drop the thing on."

"I didn't . . . not quite anyhow," Cherry laughed. "Besides," she endeavoured to look aloof, "you're getting mixed up between her an' me. I'm no heiress."

Adam eyed her steadily. At least she had the grace to blush.

The servant girls were laying the table for tea in the dining-room of the Plug and Feathers, where a most professional confabulation was in progress between the inn's mistress and Mary Jane, with frequent allusions to 'basting,' 'toast and melted butter,' and 'bread sauce and gravy.'

In the depths of a comfortable chair Titus Alderson started to chuckle. "Well, Lucy lass, last Twelfth Mary Jane gave you a hand in the kitchen wi' the gentlemen's dinner, but seemingly this time she'll be able to take charge of the whole caboodle herself."

Mrs. Peacock laughed gaily. "An' I don't think she'd make a bad go on it either, Titus," she said. "Oh yes, she'll be here again to do her share, I expect, won't you, love?"

It was a poser for a very truthful little girl. She certainly attempted to reply, but, after one sentence, her solemn-eyed regard was switched towards Adam, who had just entered. He did not fail her.

"The fact is, that me an' Mary Jane have a long-standing appointment for that evening," he said, adding with severity: "An' don't try to worm it out of us what it's about."

Cherry deplored this explanation by murmuring a shocked: "Right carryings on," and Lucy Peacock commented critically with: "She's begun walking out soon enough, choose how." Mr. Alderson was more encouraging, however, with his: "Never you mind, Mary Jane. You keep your secrets *and* your young man to yourself."

Various emotions crossed Mary Jane's grave face and it was obvious she was bursting for these her friends to learn about the feast.

"No, lass," Adam's lips curled. "This lot's mouths are like pillar-box slits, an' they'll be babbling all over."

Reluctantly Mary Jane accepted this advice, but she made one point clear. "Me an' Adam isn't courting, Mr. Alderson," she said. "For one thing I'se not quite old enough, not just yet."

"An' what's the other, love?" Cherry asked.

There was a tinge of regret about the little girl as, after glancing at the young man towering above her, she firmly relinquished him.

"He's noan a farmer, you see, Cherry," she said. "An' it'd be a mortal shame for me not to take every advantage of all that Mrs. Skidmore's teached me about t'dairy an' such-like."

"That's settled my hash," Adam remarked with gloom.

Mary Jane unwinkingly surveyed him. "I think you're pretending, Adam," she declared, "'cause you an' Cherry's always making sheep's eyes at each other. But——"

"We're not!" gasped Miss Cherry Dinsdale, simultaneously with Dinah's joyous squeal.

"But . . ." Mary Jane resumed relentlessly with her afterthought, "if Adam had been a farmer, an' owt grievous had happened to you when I were older——"

Titus Alderson's pointed beard shook violently. "Not content wi' marrying him off, she's to be his second," he guffawed, to which Mrs. Peacock, tears streaming, added sepulchrally to a scarlet-cheeked young woman: "I suspicion, Cherry love, she's shortly going to dispatch you i' child-birth."

Unmoved, Mary Jane regarded them with big, grey eyes, waiting until their transports were over, when she had a request for her hostess.

"Mrs. Peacock, as soon as you're ready could I pull the bell-rope for you, to tell t'girl to bring in the tea-pot?"

Dabbing busily with a handkerchief, Lucy Peacock's usually strong voice was weak. "You can do it now, love," she nodded.

Mary Jane danced to the fireplace, seized the tassel, stood a pleasurable moment, and then with a gleeful "There!" tugged the cord, her sedate little countenance transfigured with joy.

That provided the keynote for the tea-party, a jolly and lively meal. There were intervals, of course, when the discussion was more sober, for shortly the mistress of the Plug and Feathers would be embarking upon the most onerous weeks of the house's year. For a fortnight or so onwards from the Twelfth, and for lesser periods in the months following, every bedroom was reserved by Mr. Hesketh: the Liverpool cotton-broker who employed Will Skidmore as keeper finding this arrangement far more advantageous than maintaining a shooting-box.

Smoke from the engine and steam from the deafening mechanical organs drifted through the bright light of sizzling naphtha torches. Chocolate-and-gold roundabouts whirled, netted-in boat-cars rose to heights suggesting that, near the top, they were hovering as if uncertain whether to complete the circle or return, and the barkers' stentorian cries, vying with each other, put in the shade the performances of afternoon and early evening.

Within the noisy throng the necks of several young men and women were bent back while they gazed upwards at two of their party. Over them the small swings swung to and fro, none more so than that in which

Arthur Nattrass was treating his young lady to a ride. Despite Annamaria's screams, arising partly from fright and partly because she was furiously conscious of revealing her underclothing to many a grinning male below, he continued to heave energetically on the plush-covered end of the rope, the luckstone on his watch-chain dancing wildly with his efforts, disaster nearly occurring when once he raised his hat to those underneath.

Reuben Nattrass, pushing through on his way to keep an appointment with Richard Blenkiron at a lofty, bell-capped erection whose attendant invited all and sundry to: "Try your strength, lads, aye, an' the ladies, too," paused long enough for a word with Cherry. "I'll bet Arthur hears summat fro' Annamaria when she gets out, Cherry lass," he laughed as he left.

The outcome was not as expected. Annamaria, queasy-stomached, was too forlorn to express herself and, fussed over by the girls, was taken nearer the river for a breath of reviving air, Arthur Nattrass, now decidedly alarmed, sheepishly accompanying them.

Adam, in their absence, withdrew into a less crowded part to light up the dottle in his pipe, and, while slapping his pockets for the box, was offered a match by Bull Waggott. At first the conversation was quite general, and then the groover made a remark which set his hearer's thoughts racing.

"Agnes! Oh, she's having a lot of headaches," Adam replied.

Bull Waggott sucked through a gap in his teeth. "Nay, it's noan a matter that's of interest to me. It were nobbut that I always used to see her wi' you at outings, and I haven't done o' late."

With brows slightly knit, Adam watched him saunter away, until the burly figure was lost to sight.

"Mmm . . ." he frowned, "it looks as if it were no casual meeting in Sleety Slape. The daft little thing that she is if she's playing about with a chap of his sort. But if there were owt wrong as flashed across my mind —and as cousin Isa is on th'eve of hinting—you'd reckon Agnes 'ud be after him, not the other road about. That is, if she were normal, which she isn't."

"Talking to yourself now," Miss Cherry Dinsdale remarked.

Startled, Adam did his best. "In my dotage, lass."

Cherry sucked her finger. "The shies'll be too much for you?"

Promising to shake off a few of his years, Adam took her arm, the prelude to another round of the Fair. They visited the many stalls, rode the roundabouts again, patronised the shies, ate sweets and brandysnaps, and tried their skill at the shooting gallery. But all good things come to an end, as Albert Gibson, the policeman, uneasily reflected when he discerned 'Less nor Nowt' Cooper in that stage of intoxication which is the forerunner to becoming a public nuisance.

A solid body of young men, whose number never diminished, escorted the girls of the neighbourhood to their homes. Dinah was attended to Badger Hall by a large party, and, at Yew Tree House, where Adam handed over a coconut, a showily-attractive bangle and a stuffed doll, Cherry received a chorus of good nights, as did Fronick and Annamaria when, making neither head nor tail of it all, they slipped into the blacksmith's house.

Then began the serious work, Wingy Blenkiron silently opening the Smithy door. "Now chaps," he whispered, "we'll noan be able to start operations yet, but we've got beer in here so we'll be all right."

A couple of hours after that a crowd of young fellows armed with spanners and wrenches walked cautiously up Main Street.

* * * *

Spaced widely and irregularly along the edge of the first great terrace of land on the north side of Skewdale were cottages which, in days gone by, had housed groovers conveniently close to their work. The majority were now empty, but at Kettle Dub one was occupied by an old groover who, to support himself since broken wind and rheumatism had caused his retirement, ran the sole milk-round in the district.

In all probability it was he, Chesty Geordie, who was the earliest to spot the mischief. Starting painfully towards the village, he did not immediately notice certain additions to the landscape. When he did he nearly tumbled into a patch of rag-wort, back-can as well.

"Well, I'se damned," he wheezed. "There'll be hell popping soon."

His smile broadening, he stared again across the steep-sided valley towards Middle Sorrow, along which a line of wooden horses was strung out, as if marching to Silence and Snorr. On barns and walls adjacent, perched at crazy angles, were the crocodiles and cockerels to which roundabout patrons had clung the previous day. Lower down, in the river, the orange beak and white-painted breast of a cow-sized swan faced the shallow flow.

Bolting breakfasts, Winterings folk laughed that morning until their sides were sore. But it could not be expected that the proprietor of the show, whose horse teams and thundering engine had before them a toilsome journey over rough mountain roads to the next pitch, would view the incident similarly. Unerringly he put his finger on the ringleader and, bent on vengeance, paid a call at Ash Grove, taking along with him a brutal-visaged Lithuanian Balt, six and a half feet in height, developed elsewhere proportionately.

It chanced that William Nattrass was leaving the house. "Our Reuben? Why, he's nobbut just set off for t'mine," he said. "But who," the folds of his chin quivered with sudden anger, "who the hell are you to shout at folk?"

The enraged showman started off again, followed by a crowd augmented as every house and cottage was passed, the noise of clogged feet carrying ahead. Thus groovers entering Sorrow Near halted to discover what was afoot and Reuben Nattrass, who had called at the Smithy on business, came to the doorway.

The preliminaries were over in a few seconds.

"Aye, you can bloody well laugh, Nattrass," the showman shouted. "An' you can make out you'd nowt to do with it."

"Which he hadn't," Wingy Blenkiron chimed in.

Reuben Nattrass's hand jabbed out. "Keep your mouth shut, Wingy, I'se interested to hear what this chap an' Silly Billy wi' him reckons they're going to do to me."

The showman's thumb jerked sideways towards the Russian. "He'll show you, Nattrass," he said thinly. "Oh aye, I know you're a bit on a champion at such places as Brough, but this chap puts his dukes up on Newcastle Town Moor an' at the big fairs . . . Nottingham Goose Fair and——"

"Well, well, well, I *never*," the East Side Company's agent mocked. Then, dark eyes narrowing, his mood changed. "In that case," he bellowed, "t'sooner him and me gets set-to the better. I'se work waiting, an' I'll bloody well see it's noan waiting much longer."

Roll of blue linen survey paper, book and coat were tossed aside, caught gladly by those who deemed it a privilege to hold their champion's possessions. In no time the two men faced each other.

To call it a fight would be a misnomer. True, Reuben Nattrass received a vicious crack on the cheek-bone which rocked him to his heels, and a steam-hammer drive to the midriff which made him gasp. But that was as nothing to the cruel punishment meted out by his flailing arms. Relentlessly the bigger man was beaten to pulp until, eyelid slit and nose and mouth streaming blood, only another decisive blow was needed.

"Now then, the fancy o' Nottingham," Reuben Nattrass exulted.

Deliberately lessening the force of his attack, the deep ranks of the throng opening to allow him passage, he contemptuously smacked his opponent into a retreat from the Roe to the old Bait House, and thence step by step backwardsway to Dolly Bridge, where he finished him off.

"Well, I reckon this man-eater'll be best brought round wi' a sup of water," he remarked, prodding the recumbent figure with his clog toe before hoisting him. "An' his manager an' all," he promised, when the stricken Balt disappeared over the parapet.

Hemmed in, the Fair proprietor had not a chance to escape, and another dozen fights would have begun if his men had attempted to interfere.

"I'll have the law on you if you lay a finger on me," he shouted.

The winner's eyes glittered. "Suit yourself, mister," he said. "But t'law 'ul ask who started all this, an' I've a few witnesses. Anyroad . . ."

Advancing, he silenced his victim with a vicious swipe across the mouth, and then, gathering him up, bundled him to the same fate, a considerable drop into a pool which, fortunately, was always a yard or so deep.

Cuthbert Daykin, collarless and with egg-stains on his moustache, liked to be considered a wag. "It's all very well, Reuben," he complained, "but i' Winterings the spot as we shove offenders over is the Brig."

The mine-agent grunted. "Let's know what you've been up to then," he said, wickedly amplifying this on glimpsing Cyprian Metcalfe, Emma Ann's husband, with: "Maybe we could have a public competition . . . to guess which of t'Commandments you've broken, lad."

As the showman and the Balt began to crawl feebly through the shallow water of the river, housewives, tradesmen, and groovers started to disperse, one and all still full of the bloody encounter.

"Aye, he's a rare scrapper is Cousin Reuben," Adam murmured to himself. "But noan quite in the class of my old friend Humphrey."

Just as racing men estimate form by comparisons Adam Brunskill might by such means have speculated upon the outcome of a clash between himself and the all-conquering mine-agent. If he did so, he showed no apprehension.

4

About a fortnight before grouse shooting would begin, Will Skidmore asked Adam if he would be a beater. For generations, as at haymaking, sporting-minded groovers had gladly exchanged the mines for a few days on the high moors.

"Aye, I'll be glad to, Will," Adam promptly accepted. "I know Freestone John's hoping to be in at it an' all."

This was below Badger Hall, when he and the keeper were walking down the riverside. It was peaceful and lovely; the Skew rippled soothingly, bee orchis brightened chalky pastures with pale purple bloom, and, surrounding dells of close-cropped turf nearer by, rabbits' playgrounds, gently waving mauvish-blue harebells pleased the eye.

Despite working daily in the Common Rully Gate, Adam was not neglecting farming, and although there had not been much to do this particular evening he had helped to load one of George Nattrass's carts with Mrs. Skidmore's famed cheeses, the first collection of that cheese-making season.

Suddenly, recalling the negotiations with the gipsies, Adam chuckled. "I'm thinking of your father, Will," he said.

The weather creases at the corners of Will Skidmore's blue-grey eyes deepened with amusement. The more filthied wool, rotten and befouled with urine, droppings and dirt, was not permitted to compromise that of superior quality and, after shearing, was put aside to await the annual call of the potmen, with whom his father enjoyed nothing better than to dicker.

"For nowt more than a few coppers at that," he grimaced. "Aye, an' he'll go on bargaining for an hour or more yet."

Soon they were over the three arches of Snorr Bridge and walking up the flower-narrowed pathway of the pretty cottage in Blenk Bottom Lane. In a tiny kitchen polished to perfection Mrs. Will was entertaining the schoolmaster, whose outflowing tail-coat virtually hid the cane-back chair in which he was sitting. Alice and her brother, Walter Heseltine, were there, too, in nightclothes ready for bed. Their faces shone with soap, but it was most unlikely, as their father remarked, that their air of rectitude arose from cleanliness.

"All the same, they've done very well, Will," Susan Skidmore told him proudly.

Will Skidmore found the weak spot. "Yes, but what about our Bob?" he grunted. "Let's see his."

It was the custom of the Committee of the Wesleyan Day School to send out their accounts quarterly, Mr. Kidd delivering them personally. Each bill was a folder, and on the opposite side were details of attendance and the master's comments.

Plump Mrs. Will looked a thought apprehensive as her husband's lips began to move. "Extras; Exercise Book, a penny; Wordsworth Excursion, three ha'-pence; Reading Book, half-price, three ha'pence; Copy Book, a penny; Geography o' Yorkshire, tuppence. Mmmm . . . Writing, good . . . Arithmetic, bad . . . Spelling, worse . . . Reading, defective. By " he growled. "Times late, *fifteen* . . . Times absent, *four*——"

The sheet was flung aside. "*Four* times absent, an' he's never had a finger-ache, so what's he been up to?" Will Skidmore stormed. "An' here's me forking out tuppence ha'penny a week for him, *and* sixpence a week betwixt the three on 'em for coal for the school-room when it's cold enough. But wait till I get hold of him."

There were people older than Agnes Pedley capable of doing the wrong thing at the wrong time. Retrieving the bill from the drugget-covered floor, Mr. Kidd's puffy forefinger underlined a passage, copy of the report which Her Majesty's School Inspector had appended to the Master's certificate after visiting the school.

"This . . . er . . . apropos of myself, is not without interest," he boomed, clearing his throat to start anew. "'*Mr. Kidd*,' it begins, '*taught with precision and good judgment, and the results of his lessons are very satisfactory*.' Signed, '*R. T. Benson, M.A.*' Master of Arts, that is."

"Satisfactory, eh?" Will Skidmore snapped.

But he soon lost his ill-humour and the sole indication later that he had been ruffled recently betrayed itself in the tap-room of the Royal Alfred when his brother-in-law limped in.

"Hey, Matt," he beckoned, "it's noan the Twelfth yet, but there's already plenty o' prime birds about. Keep off 'em."

Matt Tiplady, who was tapping the counter with a coin, preferred to address himself to the piebald bitch at his feet. "Seemingly, Floss lass, there's folk as takes me for a poacher, instead of a well-to-do 'venturer wi' a stake in a decentish-sized mine. But they'll look right silly in a year or two when maybe I'm renting my own moors."

Adam grinned. "An' how's it going at Gull Scar, lad?"

"Well, we're nobbut opening up yet, lad," Matt replied. "But never mind that—what's Will getten t'black dog on his shoulders for?"

"He's seen Bob's school report," Adam said.

Matt Tiplady began to shake with laughter. "Young devils, him and our Ward, aren't they? Mind you," he held up a finger oracularly, "that's noan going to prevent me tanning the hide off my lad if t'schoolmaster's writ as bad about him as it sounds he has about Bob."

"Yes, you've got to drill summat into 'em," agreed the gamekeeper.

No doubt this was acted upon, the first of two severe hidings the cousins received within a few days.

* * * *

On Saturday afternoon Adam was sauntering round the bottom of Jom High Road when he met Cherry returning from the village with a shopping basket. They started to chat against the yews, and probably were each of the opinion that they had not been dallying more than five minutes when Richard Blenkiron, who had seen them there for over a quarter of an hour, sent a jovial hail resounding across the road.

"Now I reckon you two 'ud be more comfortable if I brought a couple o' chairs for you," he suggested.

Cherry's cheeks flamed delightfully, so the young man near her thought. "No thank you, Mr. Blenkiron," she remarked with dignity. "I'm just going in as it happens."

"You are, love?" roared the blacksmith.

She put out her tongue at him. "Yes, clever-clogs."

Tickled by this and even more pleased about the success of his own artifice, Richard Blenkiron rubbed his hands. "In that case, Cherry lass, I think I dare ask Adam if he's any time to spare. With him now being," he added innocently, "at a loose end as you might say."

"As you've seen to, Mr. Blenkiron," Adam said, chuckling.

" He's after you to help i' carrying the hives, Adam," Cherry explained. "He were sheeting 'em up afore I went on the street."

Taking advantage of the nearby presence of the moors, there were two varieties of honey in Skewdale, that nourished upon the garden flowers of early and mid-summer, the other from the purple moors when summer was declining. The former was whitish and clear, the latter, heather-honey, much more esteemed, brownish and thick.

Bart Hugill, calling for Fronick, had naturally been roped in by her father, the other assistant so far garnered being Edmund Kearton who, incidentally, had not for a long while spoken a civil word to the blacksmith's latest recruit.

"Now we can make a start," Mr. Blenkiron declared.

Each hive was suspended at the middle of a lengthy pole shouldered at both ends, Adam and Bart bearing the first and the older men the second. The hives were to be taken near to Sweet Tarn on Noggin Moor, the initial part of the journey up walled-in Sorrow Near. However, not more than two hundred yards of the climb had been accomplished when they were arrested by a sweet but imperative voice from below.

"It's Cherry!" Adam exclaimed. "I wonder what's up?"

Manœuvring their burdens in the narrow alleyway, the two pairs of porters swivelled around until they could look downhill. Skirts fluttering, Cherry hastened upwards to acquaint one of their number with what Mark Iveson's wife had shouted to her from above Dolly Bridge.

"She's says it's like a river, Mr. Kearton," she cried breathlessly. "And that it must be running somewhere near the back of your house."

When he had heard further details, Edmund Kearton's lantern jaw dropped. "A lot o' water streaming down t'pasture. But where could it be coming fro'?"

"We'd better get back sharp to see," Richard Blenkiron grunted.

The hives were lowered and, in a trice, three men were galloping down Sorrow Near. Adam, however, had other ideas. "I've a fair notion who's responsible, lass," he grinned. "But let's go and make sure."

He helped her to the summit of the lofty wall and then, climbing over himself, caught her as she jumped at the other side. Hand in hand they scampered across the steep slope beyond until, Cherry even more breathless with laughter, they came to two small and disconsolate boys and a scene of havoc: the dam which had burst its turf embankment.

"An' so this is the hush, is it?" Adam remarked.

Ward Tiplady's snub nose wrinkled. "Aye, but it got out o' control, Adam."

"More trouble," Cherry said sympathetically.

"Aye, lass." Bob Skidmore knuckled his square chin. "I don't know how it is, but me an' Ward seems to land i' more bother than's our proper share."

In a telling silence the four of them eyed the desolation. The main flow had ceased, but nothing could prevent another three or four thousand gallons of water from sliding down the channel torn in the ground by the early onrush.

"Well . . ." Bob sighed, "we'd better be off to face t'music. An' I'm that sore to begin wi'."

Ward winced slightly as his hand strayed behind. "Me an' all, Bob lad," he admitted. "My father didn't half lay it on."

Gallant to the last, they took the most sheer and dangerous route down the scar, Adam and Cherry adopting a more prudent course.

If it were desolation at one small point in a pasture high above the village, the outlook was even more devastating below. Main Street in places resembled a river; buckets were in brisk use as balers, and stones, gravel and water were being besomed out of doorways to either side of Mr. Kearton's premises. It was a strange whim of fate, however, that the culprits' grandfather suffered the worst damage. The stream, entering a passage at the back, had swept irresistably from there through the joiner's shop; the front doors were burst off their hinges, and a vast amount of wood and other stock, blind cord, chair webbing, cabinet paper, and so forth, was being salvaged outside.

"Proves the power o' water, doesn't it, lass?" Adam said. "And that were nobbut a little dam really."

"I've never properly understood before how those big gashes in the hills were caused just by hushing." Cherry shook her head. "But I do now."

While others aided the man who had sustained the bulk of the blow, Mr. Kearton himself, rolled up trousers revealing skinny shanks, was engaged in a bitter dispute with the Schoolmaster, his grandsons standing meekly by.

"Well, are you flogging 'em or not?" he shouted. "You're the one as is responsible for teaching 'em good behaviour."

"In school, yes," Mr. Kidd retorted. "But this didn't take place in school. And for that matter," he put in slyly, "the school doesn't re-open till Monday."

Incensed by the Schoolmaster's scarcely veiled triumph, Edmund Kearton's voice reached new heights. "I'm noan one as rows outdoors," he bawled, "but are you whipping 'em? Just say."

Mr. Kidd forsook subtlety. "You're grandfather to both of 'em," he roared. "Get on with the job yourself . . . instead of measuring me."

"Or leave it to their fathers, or onnybody, as *you* would," scorned Mr. Kearton. "An' how do you mean, *measure*?"

Bob glanced sideways at Ward. Their signals must have gone amiss, for they spoke together. The gist of their jumbled remarks was a request that the punishment should not be left hanging over their heads.

"So you reckon I can't hit as hard as your fathers can," their grandfather snapped.

"Do you look as if you could?" Mr. Kidd jeered. "All teeth and e'en."

"I'll crack 'em as hard as you pound t'piano keys," Edmund Kearton retorted. "Mind you," he continued aggravatingly, "that's considerable. I've oft wondered why you an' th'instrument didn't go through the floor of the Literary Institute the road you raced an' banged away."

Touched on a sore point, Mr. Kidd drew a deep breath and the contest raged on, neither elderly gentleman willing to concede an inch—until they saw most of the village grinning around them. Upon that a compromise was speedily reached: the Schoolmaster fetching his big ruler.

Positioned with tips of fingers on the iron toe-plates of their clogs, the boys received six strokes from each. As a matter of personal prestige, neither of the executors spared himself.

Decidedly pale after the ordeal, Ward straightened up. "Well . . . well, that's getten it over with, Bob lad."

Bob Skidmore bit back a groan. "Aye, it has, Ward lad," he nodded shakily. "An' that's summat."

"And now you can help to clear up some of t'mischief you've caused." Their grandfather pointed. As obediently they did his bidding, a couple of boys who meant somehow to keep the tears from their eyes, a glimmer of pride crossed Mr. Kearton's lean face. "An' then maybe at after, *maybe* I say, you can come into t'house an' have a good tea," he called after them.

It was an exciting afternoon for everybody and, for the wives and families of those who worked for the East Side Company, a most welcome afternoon. This was the Saturday of the company's monthly Pay.

The White Hart at Winterings was not occupied but, for a small sum annually, Mrs. Robert William Alderson allowed the two local mining companies the use of one of the ground-floor rooms to disburse the Pay. The hour of the Pay varied according to circumstances, but on this occasion Reuben Nattrass and the clerk, a young man from Greets, seated themselves behind a dusty table at six o'clock.

Adam and Freestone John had come out fairly well, but the brothers Pedley and their partners, whose leader succeeded the Quaker at the Pay table, had a very sorry draw: twenty-eight shillings it worked out at for each man for the month.

"Well, Ambrose," guffawed Nowt Cooper, "thoo'll have to get a tip or two fro' that lodger o' thine on how to do better."

Only one curly side-piece and a bruised cheek were visible as Reuben Nattrass groped for five shillings' worth of copper in the yawning-mouthed, leather bag at his feet. "John's had a right expert as a partner," he mumbled from this position. "Makes all t'difference."

"Aye, persuade him to put you in t'way o' things, Ambrose," someone cackled.

Either of the Pedleys would gnaw a bone with any dog. In any event, Agnes's father for some days past had been in a condition bordering on frenzy.

"I'll persuade him nowt," he responded shrilly. "Anyroad, how do we know he hasn't been tinkering wi' the nick-sticks?"

Until Freestone John's voice rang out, not a word was spoken. There was no offence more heinous than to tamper with the slender pieces of wood in which notches were whittled to record numbers, whether of wagons of bouse, shots fired, or bings of ore.

When the Quaker's stern admonition had ended, a man at the back expressed the general feeling. "Don't be so bloody daft," he growled at Ambrose Pedley, "an' thank your stars that Brunskill hasn't knocked your head off. And . . ." he caught sight of James Pedley's movement, "an' *you'd* better keep quiet for once or maybe both John and his partner'll set about you."

Nothing further took place, so business was resumed, men coming and going, others drawing to the side to split up the money received. Outdoors, Adam awaited Agnes's father, stretching out his arm when he appeared on the outer step.

"Don't you drag me about," Ambrose Pedley screeched. "If——"

"I'm nobbut pulling you out of the way to tell you summat," Adam said curtly. "It's this: that I'm leaving Back Lane."

The older man licked his lips. "Leaving," he muttered. "No . . . no, you mustn't, you mustn't. I'll own I were sinful i' what I came out with, but it were because I were nettled. I'll pray to th'Almighty to forgive me, and——"

Adam shook his head. "At the end of the month. It's final."

Ambrose Pedley's burning glance darted everywhere, rat-like. "At th'end of the month," he whispered, lips continuing to move as if already he had either begun to pray, or were calculating. "Well, I can't stop you . . ."

With that they parted, Adam walking with Freestone John towards Town Foot, neither of them making more than a bare reference to a charge which left a nasty taste in the mouth. On the other side of the street, too intent to notice them, Hannah Batty hurried along towards a cottage near Blind Kit's shop. The Postmaster of Greets bustled to the same door a minute or so after she had entered.

"Bothering folk when they're i' sore trouble," Freestone John complained. "But Lodge Trotter 'ud do owt to pocket a guinea."

How this precisely related was not clear to Adam, but he was better informed before he and his partner separated. It was the Quaker's surmise that Mr. Trotter's call was in the nature of a reconnaissance upon an old man taken gravely ill, with ultimate objective the drawing-up of a testator's Last Will and Testament.

Friends would not be coming out yet, and so, ruminating about the Secretary of the West Side Lead Mining Company Ltd., Adam retraced his steps, avoiding the many deep pools for which Bob and Ward were responsible. The grey village street was settling down to ordinary Saturday evening preoccupations, although some refurbishing was in progress in anticipation of the shooters' arrival within a few days. In William Nattrass's yard horse-gear was being looked over, and at the shining-windowed Plug and Feathers a man was varnishing the artistically grained front door.

* * * *

Sunday afternoon was very warm and many householders on the north side of Main Street brought outdoors chairs and stools on which to laze in the bright sunshine. It was just after half-past one and, beyond the Black Bull, now only an off-licence establishment, Adam and Wingy heard children scurrying along the flagged pathway from the Sunday School. The teachers followed much more circumspectly, Bart, Cherry, Dinah and Fronick amongst them.

Invited to tea at Annamaria's, it was decided to go there by the long way round, the postman advocating a prompt start. As Librarian of the Sunday School he should have been present, and had no desire to be interrogated by the Superintendent.

The first stage of the walk was easy, up the main road to the Royal Alfred, then along Sorrow Far almost to Bloody Sigh, and so to Legatt's Way. At a point about four hundred feet greater in height, on the culvert crossing Foul Syke, Fronick insisted upon resting. Her plump cheeks were deeply flushed with the long ascent and, apart from the heat, she was worried about her brother's failure to attend to Sunday School duties. Always susceptible to what other people might be thinking, this may have been why she began to probe about Agnes, concerning whom a whisper of scandal was now travelling on the wind.

"But she never comes out wi' you like she did, Adam," she said fretfully, tucking under her bonnet pale gold hair which was moist at the roots. "It's so queer, isn't it?"

Bart Hugill, reddening fiercely, loudly drew Adam's attention to the nearby tower of the South Smelt Mill's flue. While Fronick remarked that he had not "the manners he were born with," the clerk told Adam the flue had received its periodical sweep that morning. In his embarrassment he explained to a young man far better informed than himself just how valuable the soot was—lead volatilised freely when smelted, he said, and in the absence of suitable traps as much as two-thirds of its weight might be lost in the form of fume. The interposition between ore-hearths and flue of condensers packed with brushwood and pebbles, over which water dripped, substantially reduced the loss, but even when these were provided much of the mineral was carried forward in the smoke.

"And that's the reason for th'immense length of the flues, Adam," Bart wound up his exposition. "To catch as much soot as is possible . . . you see it's rich in lead and when it's roasted again yields a rare rich haul. An' . . ." he jeered at himself, "listen to me jawing to such as you, lad. I'm a reight fool, aren't I?"

"And you're rude an' all, Bart Hugill," Fronick wailed.

Wisely the others left the pair to settle their differences, but when out of earshot, on the stretch of Legatt's Way which ran undeviatingly amidst ling, bent and rushes to Smiddy Bridge, Wingy Blenkiron referred to his sister:

"Eee, our Fronick!" he despaired. "I wish she were more inclined to stand to her own guns. And weren't Bart upset when she started tittle-tattling? He must have been, for I've never heard t'mention of a smelt-mill flue pass his lips voluntarily since his brother's tragedy."

"That was how it happened, Adam," Cherry said. "Sweeping down the soot one Sunday."

Graphically Wingy portrayed that sad Sabbath for the Hugills. How, his mate sending word of sickness late on Saturday night, Bart's elder brother had tackled the job by himself at cock-crow, working downwards from the octagonal tower at the outward end of Bucker Smelt Mill flue.

"When sweeping is being done, as you'll know, Adam, a stream o' water from high up in the hills is turned into the top of the flue, and this carries along wi' it the fume soot that's brushed from the side walls and arched roof. Anyhow, your foot-hold isn't all that secure in a steep, slippery-bottomed channel, and it seems likely that an extra spate o' water washed him an' the sooty water right down into the closed-in tank alongside the condenser—almost all t'way to the ore-hearths, that is."

In a few more telling phrases, until the young ladies closed their eyes and exclaimed in horror, he described how the doomed young man, choking and nearly drowned, must have struggled back up the slimy flue towards the tower a mile away, his sole means of escape. Bucker Smelt Mill flue, unlike others in the Winterings' setts, was not provided with manholes.

"No, it doesn't bear talking about, nor th'outcome either," he muttered. "When he went in that morning he were lively Alf Hugill, but when he clawed himself out of the top he were Rive Rags, that's all."

For a while, saddened by the fearful disaster, they were silent, but when Fronick and Bart came nearer, a fresh start was made up the Roman road. Leaving tumbledown Smiddy Bridge behind, and passing Martha Air Shaft and Toft Rigg Whim Shaft, they kept straight along the turf-carpeted track as far as the source of Heugh Syke Gill, Yorsall Moss a deep green island amidst a sea of purple heather away to the left, the soft blue of the sky reflected in the plate-glass surface of Sweet Tarn below to the right.

"Wheel down here," Wingy directed them, nodding towards his father's bee-hives, "past yon lot an' down the gill to th'Old Cow Inn, where we'll see what's to offer, though I don't think the prospects are over bad, ladies and gentlemen. My Uncle Martin may be near, but whatever else he's noan skinny enough to interfere wi' Aunt Jennie as to what she sets on the table."

Dinah Skidmore screwed up her face for Adam's and Cherry's benefit only. "I don't consider that's the right spirit to go out to tea in, Clarkson," she remarked primly.

"Hallo! Hallo!" Wingy guffawed. "Our Fronick to the life, eh?"

The pair were obviously destined to wrangle amiably, and gradually Adam arranged matters so that he and Cherry bore away from them, meandering with her amongst a wide spread flock whose woolly lambs, untouched by clipping-shears, looked appreciably more bulky than the semi-naked ewes they trotted alongside. Since the previous evening's Pay there had been no opportunity to let her know he was leaving Back Lane shortly, but he did so when, sharing an entrancing view, they stood against a clump of rowans and silver birch which leaned over the beck just before Heugh Syke's thin stream shot sheerly downhill to Juniper Wood.

In her relief, Cherry's gloved hands were clasped tightly together. "Oh, I'm right glad, Adam," she said.

Adam was watching her. "Why, lass?" he asked. "Because there's been some talk associating Agnes wi' me?"

She turned quickly to him, but, woman-like, did not reveal her true fears: that half-hints could lead to a scandal which, though disproved by the passage of time, might leave its mud splashes on him. Instead, to spare him, she tried to convey how, in a sparsely-populated countryside, gossiping is a pastime, and often less harmful than the outsider would imagine it.

"But this is summat worse than the latest tit-bit that lasts only until the next one arrives, isn't it?" Adam said.

Cherry swallowed. "Well . . . well, it's noan improving things when Isa Skidmore is going about making a mystery of why Agnes won't have the doctor."

Adam spoke very deliberately. "Cherry, lass," he asked, "you've thought of what Cousin Isa is hinting at?"

Colour flooded Cherry's smooth cheeks, but then, as she forced herself to meet his glance, the colour as swiftly ebbed away. "Yes," she replied, almost inaudibly. "But . . ." her voice strengthened, "she's just being *wicked*, for no one in their right senses would ever think of Agnes doing owt . . . owt like that. I'll own she's surprised me an' Dinah once or twice, but being a bit arch isn't a sin in any lass . . . and for that matter I don't reckon Agnes even realises she's being arch. Yes, it's ridiculous, Adam, and more than that."

The remainder of the party were below, in the scrub surrounding Milton Hall, but indifferent as to whether he were seen or not Adam lightly put his arm around his companion's slender shoulders.

"Yet you're pleased I'm leaving Back Lane, lass," he suggested.

"Yes, I am," Cherry murmured, wishing this beautiful moment could be prolonged for ever. "Because there's Agnes's father an' all—it's all over the place what he came out with at the Pay, about you tinkering with nick-sticks."

Adam nodded. "Well, I shan't be under his roof at after the month end. I wish now I'd said sooner, but I didn't."

Still remaining there, a clean-shaven young man bronzed by the fiercer sun of the south, with his arm resting across the shoulders of a young woman whose lovely eyes were filled with joy, they stared down into the distant dale, at sleepy fellside hamlets and grey, isolated farm-houses screened by trees, all a-shimmer in the heat-haze.

"As soon as possible after I'm settled in at Old Hannah's," Adam's free hand waved impatiently, as if shaking off the complications in which his relatives had involved him, "I want you to come with me to a spot like this, Cherry. You see, I've a lot of talking to do, and . . . and I've summat to ask you, too."

Gently he turned her until, instead of lower profile and side of shady bonnet only, he could see more of the sweet face. "You'll come, will you, lass?"

From the day she first met him, Cherry had always been affected when a smile so amazingly transfigured his stern expression. "Yes, Adam," she promised shyly.

"Ah!" Adam muttered, which might have been, as indeed it was, an exclamation of satisfaction, as though one important obstacle had been bridged. To this extent relieved, he went on to confess that already he had put the cart before the horse. "I didn't tell you t'programme in the proper order, lass. It's *before* I talk a lot to you that I've summat to ask you. If——"

There and then, Cherry Dinsdale, a tender and affectionate girl, became an out-and-out minx. Though her heart throbbed and her red lips were parted with happiness, she resolved that, if she were to receive the one proposal that mattered to her, it would be at a single wonderful session, not in instalments.

"Well, you'll be able to tell me everything when the time comes," she observed with great dignity, feeling very cruel. "Whatever it is," she added, a clever stroke, she thought.

Their friends were a long way below, not far from Half, in a wooded ravine where about sixty geese and a number of ganders, aroused by the invasion, began to prepare themselves, with dyspeptic animosity. The swift passage of fluttering skirts was the call to action when, great white wings outspread and feet barely touching the ground, the birds furiously chased the intruders along the gill.

When Adam and Cherry arrived an army of vociferous and enraged creatures was drawn up in battle array athwart their path.

"I think, lass," Adam remarked, "that discretion——"

"Up the side o' the gill," Cherry said hurriedly.

In this way, clambering on the high verge, a conflict was avoided and, beyond catching their clothing on brambles, they rejoined their companions without damage.

"Who'd live in Half?" grinned Bart Hugill.

The young women were preparing themselves for a social call. Bonnets were adjusted, gloves smoothed out and, although the Old Cow Inn was but a few paces distant, sunshades were ceremoniously opened before a ladylike advance was made, when never more than a tip of a toe peered out from beneath the hems of summery dresses.

5

The Twelfth began early for beaters, each finding his own way across Water Ling Moor to the rendezvous up Yorrelgrain, where, under the direction of Luther Thwaites, the Lord of the Manor's keeper, they took up stations for the drive. Before eight o'clock, too, a dozen saddle-horses from William Nattrass's yard were pawing the cobbles in front of the Plug and Feathers, with three or four Skewdale ponies in attendance to carry up, pack-beast fashion, the provender provided by Mrs. Peacock. In due course the cavalcade set forth, turning up Sleety Slape towards Mill Bridge, where the riders dismounted, both men and horses cautiously climbing the track alongside Joss Foss. Then, strung out in a long line, the shooting party proceeded for three miles across the wastes, finally to reach, over a beck and beyond a band of rough scree, an old wall upon which at regular intervals numbers were painted in white. Here Will Skidmore, who the previous evening had gone through the arrangements with his employer, showed Mr. Hesketh's guests the positions assigned to them.

The day was fine though blustery, making conditions less than ideal, but, advancing over far-extending stretches of heather upon the bloom of which bees were feasting, it was an experience Adam Brunskill would not have missed. All too soon for him the morning ended.

The midday meal was taken below Deer Pot, the gentlemen refreshing themselves in a small wooden luncheon hut, the beaters and loaders eating at the margin of a boggy area reddish-hued with sundew.

"Aye . . ." Nick Pratt observed, his shapeless fingers making short work of opening a bottle of beer, "even if there were no pay t'victuals 'ud tempt me here by themselves."

Ned Mason who, standing, dealt with a tumbler and two heaped plates as effortlessly as one of his Breton ancestors might have held himself when dizzily high on the Keep of Corvy Castle, flicked a dark eyebrow. Craftsmen of Nick Pratt's occupation were somewhat more prominent in the masonry hierarchy than dry-wallers, who seldom lost an opportunity of redressing the balance.

"I should have thought you were too throng arching," he remarked.

"I'm throng enough," Nick Pratt replied, poker-faced. "What wi' that an' racking my brains how best I can invest t'dividends fro' my West Side shares."

Adam was disturbed as groovers, dressing-floor men and smelters roared with laughter. Fascinated, he had been closely watching an insect which, alighting on the sticky surface of a round leaf of sundew, was held there long enough for the tentacles of the plant to close remorselessly over it.

"So you've some shares in t'West Side Company, Nick?" he asked, smiling.

"Sssh!" hushed the archer to the others, adding comically under his breath: "I've got a customer, lads, so keep quiet. "Aye . . ." he turned expansively to Adam, "an' you can have all ten of 'em at a bargain price. You needn't pay me owt, for that matter."

"You hang fire a bit, lad," Adam's neighbour advised him. "Afore you can say ' knife ' he'll be offering you a bit o' brass if you'll relieve him of 'em."

An elderly man shook his head. "Aye, an' there's plenty more wi' shares who'd do the same gladly if they could find a big enough mug."

"Yes, and the transfer 'ud go through, too," remarked another. "The West Side directors' permission hasn't to be asked, as I'm telled is usually the case."

"Aye," Adam's neighbour spat, "Lodge Trotter can contend he arranged it deliberately, but I reckon he made a reight slip."

Adam soon gleaned that the Postmaster of Greets had drawn up the Articles of Association of the West Side Company, in return for which services he had been presented with a number of shares and appointed Secretary. It was not until many weeks later that he learnt at first hand how Mr. Trotter, in usurping the functions of a lawyer, was responsible for an omission of the utmost magnitude.

The afternoon's drive extended from a desolate, cliff-like edge overlooking Foul Syke to a line of permanent butts on the crest between Dagger

Gap and Mirk Gutter, at right-angles to a pack-horse track still marked by crumbling wooden snow-posts.

To Adam, as the thin crackle of shots ahead became stronger, the second half of the day was as satisfactory as the first. It was a well-organised shoot, too, and not of least interest was the quiet efficiency of dogs whose backs, black and white, and liver-coloured, he now and then glimpsed weaving amongst the heather. When the bag was counted it proved to be up to the average, considering the number of guns and the conditions.

"Two hundred and twenty-two and a half brace . . . nothing to complain of, Skidmore," remarked Mr. Hesketh, a gentleman in his forties. "And see the beaters and loaders have the usual."

"Right, sir," Will Skidmore nodded.

Adam, a brace of grouse swinging below his hand, walked down the moor with Ned Mason similarly laden. At Doomsday High Shaft they paused to watch Hugh Bearpark and Sam Kirkbride securing or pulling away all loose gear at the eye of the hopelessly decrepit shaft so that, when at last the New Drift connected with the sump, no one below would be injured by fragments of stone or timber falling from the top.

"Well," the engineer said, "a chap 'ud get more nor a bad headache if he were hit by an eight-inch bolt tumbling this distance."

Adam began to test the depth in what Hugh Bearpark termed "t'lads' way," by dropping a stone, listening as he did so. There were no bunnings, the wooden resting platforms fitted throughout shafts in regular climbing use, and so the rock fell without interference, though he believed he heard a sound before it struck the sump, as if the crumbling side-wall had been touched. Such diversion from the vertical was commonplace and, out of his own experience, he knew that, though there was no worthwhile explanation for it, a man falling down a deep shaft is invariably drawn to the eastern side; in wood-lined shafts the body was usually recovered some way up from the bottom, wedged in the timbers, on that side.

"Round about five seconds," he murmured, stowing watch away.

"An' how much does that make it?" Hugh Bearpark grinned.

"Oh, say a hundred an' thirty-five yards," Adam replied.

The joiner looked surprised. "By, but you're noan far off," he exclaimed. "It's sixty-four fathoms . . . a hundred an' twenty-eight yards."

Sam Kirkbride's dismal expression lightened. "Multiplies real well, does Hugh," he said, a remark which caused some joking before Ned Mason and his companion left.

Though not the shortest route, Adam preferred to continue with the wiry mason along the purple-flanked trods to Dubbing Quarry so that, parting from him there, he would be able to feast his eyes on a creeper-clad farmhouse at the foot of Winterings Common Pasture. This plan went awry, for, on rounding Chesty Geordie's lonely cottage, where the view of the 'bottoms' opened out, there was a promising diversion. The distance was too great for Francis Harker's voice to be heard, but, as he ran across a meadow where the 'fog' grass of after-haymaking growth was sufficiently deep for fattening up livestock before autumn, there was no mistaking the raised fist shaken towards the walled-in pinfold opposite the Royal Alfred, into which Ralph Skidmore, with the bullocking assistance of Hey! Thoo! was driving a flock of thirty or forty sheep.

"Maybe they've been straying," Ned Mason laughed. "Ralph's on t'Pasture Committee an' he'd sooner report to them than pass the word to his neighbour."

A quarter of an hour later Adam and the angered tenant of Low Bands Farm were walking down the highroad towards the Brig.

"It's noan the fine of a penny apiece I shall have to pay t'Pasture Committee as bothers me," Francis Harker exploded. "It's that he could do such a thing. Why, dammit, I'd nobbut left 'em there till after milking."

"He's noan like the rest of the Skidmores, choose how," Adam remarked.

The farmer, still boiling, was prepared to extend the conversation, but Adam did not dally. At Old Hannah's, when he presented her with the grouse, there would be at least an appreciable interval of lively gossip, and he considered it only proper to have sufficient time in hand at Back Lane to dress himself as immaculately as possible before appearing at the house of a young lady who had invited him for the evening.

* * * *

With another meal in prospect Adam ate only a light tea and then, hearing Mark Iveson feeding his poultry, seized upon this as excuse to leave a kitchen which, always depressing, had never been more so. Ambrose Pedley had intermittently rocked and moaned the whole time he had been at the table, and Agnes's wraith-like behaviour was that of one to whom nothing matters on this earth.

The previous night, Adam had told his cousin he would not be lodging there after the end of the month. She had reacted neither one way nor the other—the fact that he was going elsewhere shortly seemed to pass just as completely over her as his offer to provide her with a nice winter outfit at the end of the summer.

More and more shocked by the deepening stains beneath her eyes and the aura of fixed apathy encasing her, Adam then made another attempt to bring her to her senses. Tactfully he began by saying she could not possibly continue in the state she was, the one-sided conversation ending immediately he tried to coax her into seeing Dr. Seaton. To that she responded without question, instantaneously, in a feverish and savage flow.

That was why, on the evening of the Twelfth, Adam Brunskill was not sorry to be outdoors, peacefully discussing with the shepherd the merits of White Leghorns.

Evening chills, harbingers of the long winter, came early to Skewdale, and a bright wood fire burned in the tap-room of the Plug and Feathers, where Mr. Hesketh and his friends were treating the company before sitting down to a dinner whose appetising smell permeated the house.

Adam's entrance fortunately coincided with one of Mrs. Peacock's hasty visits to the bar-counter, and from her he bought four Romeo and Juliet cigars. The drinks which were to be his contribution to Mary Jane's efforts he obtained farther along, at the Royal Alfred, two quart bottles of ale and a stone jar of ginger beer.

Approached across a patch of ground rioting with fluffy, white meadowsweet, Matt Tiplady's cottage at Lane End was upstream from Badger Hall, on the edge of the river, where the bank was cut-away and high. It was a neat little house, with stone slates mossy green through the influence of an ash whose branches spread over the low-pitched roof. The garden was small and tidy, the low wall in front sprouting reddish-purple Herb Robert backed by fine, fern-like leaves.

The Tipladys were attired for the occasion, and Adam's reception, Ward and his father shaking hands with him, was very formal, this much to the gratification of Mary Jane, who, delighted her instructions had been so faithfully followed, straightened to smile at the guest. She was clad in a workmanlike white apron, and her face, after bending over the oven, was beetroot coloured. "I'll noan be so very long now, Adam," she told him. "So you just have a crack wi' my father for a bit."

Matt Tiplady waved grandly towards a chair. "Take a seat, Adam," he said, to which, politeness still to the fore, Adam responded with: "With great pleasure, lad."

A wink or two passed between the men, signals in which the third male was participating until peremptorily dispatched to the stick-place for a few pieces of bark "to hasten th'oven on." Ward went willingly enough and, not many minutes after his return, Mary Jane was able to announce all was ready.

"Now Adam and our Ward sits opposite each other, an' my father goes to t'top facing me, like the master and the missus does," she said. "An' be careful wi' the plates, because they're right hot."

With Ward acting as assistant, the first course was quickly served. "Now come on, Adam lad, tuck in," Matt Tiplady said, grasping knife and fork.

"You've forgetten summat, Father." The stern reminder arose from the "missus's end."

"Eh!" the poacher ejaculated. "Oh, aye . . ." Bending his head he repeated a Grace during which, in the passage rendering humble thanks to Him who had provided the food, one of his hearer's was guilty of a mumbled aside with a suspicion of laughter in it. Ward's sequent "Ugh!" may have been due to a sisterly kick.

"Right!" Matt Tiplady exclaimed.

Ale gurgled from a bottle, and ginger-beer foamed from a light-brown jar, prelude to the attack upon a meal which astounded Adam. It began with trout fried to perfection, caught by Ward and his cousin long before leaving for school. Then beautifully roasted grouse, with boiled potatoes, green peas, bread sauce and gravy. Finally, on blue-and-white plates recognisable as Hannah Batty's, there was blackcurrant tart with an abundance of thick Badger Hall cream.

"Well, Mary Jane, love," Adam remarked at the conclusion, "I'll bet the shooters haven't relished their grub to-night any more than I have."

Mary Jane's lips pursed slightly. "T'pastry weren't all it should be," she demurred. "My hand weren't as light as I like it."

In his chair Ward had slumped spectacularly. "It were champion, lass, an' I'se as full as a fitch," he groaned. "I nobbut wish Bob had been here to get as well lined."

Their father coughed. "In t'circumstances . . ." he said, glance passing to the remains of a grouse.

"Oh aye, it could have been awkward for t'lad if Uncle Will or Aunt Susan had asked him questions at after," Ward agreed. " 'Course he understands."

At the foot of the table Mary Jane was looking pleased. "For that matter I wish as how Grandfather Kearton could have come. But . . ." she gave her attention to the guest, "but him an' my father has never hit it off, Adam. It's one of them things that does happen i' families, even in t'best regulated 'uns. Ah well, there it is, but talking about such stuff'll noan get the siding-away done, will it?"

"Me for washing t'pots," Ward elected, promptly to be put in his place. "No, you're doing the drying, lad," his sister said. "You never shift t'grease off properly. An' you chaps light up your cigars."

Father and guest did as they were bid, both involuntarily smiling now and then, once when Ward, picking off the floor a plate licked to quite unbelievable cleanliness by Floss, declared it could be stacked on the crockery shelf as it was, and again when Mary Jane, remarking to herself apparently, "What th'eye doesn't see, the heart doesn't grieve," heaped upon the fire every remaining scrap of grouse.

With this Ward laid a rabbit skin. "You can't tell owt then," he said to his sister. "My Uncle Will couldn't, nor anybody."

Mary Jane nodded. "I know, lad," she agreed. "I've been out afore now to niff t'chimney smoke, an' t'rabbit fur hides everything."

"They're well trained, Matt," Adam chuckled.

Matt Tiplady leaned nearer. "To be fair honest, lad, it's them who's trained theirsen."

When household duties were completed, young Ward changed his clothes to go out, while Mary Jane, after fluffing up any cushions within sight, took off her apron and, bringing out work-basket, settled upon a hassock to knit, Floss stretched out at her feet.

"How do you like that, lad?" Matt Tiplady pointed his cigar at the hearth. "Mary Jane has been in a rare sweat to get it finished afore to-night."

"Grand," Adam replied, inspecting a rug in which cloth-clippings of black, red and blue formed an attractive pattern. "And who taught you to do this, lass?"

"Eh, lad," Matt Tiplady chortled, "she's trailed day after day to th'Old Cow Inn for just that purpose."

His daughter appealed to Adam. "If you're going to learn you might as well be teached by them who's the best at it, mightn't you?"

"You might, Mary Jane," Adam smiled.

"Well, it's nobbut commonsense," she said, her gaze earnest. "An' Jennie Rutter has a name second to none for her rugs."

"We're noan differing with you, love," her father grinned.

Until Ward came in the talk was general, but then Mary Jane went upstairs, returning a little later in her nightdress to say good night. She kissed her father and Adam, a little girl who at that moment of bedtime was not a day older than her years. Ward followed her, and they heard the squeals as brother pushed sister up the steep stairs.

"Get on well, yon two, Matt," Adam laughed. "And Bob seems to fit in with 'em an' all."

"They both think t'world o' Mary Jane," declared Matt Tiplady, before recounting a story of how the pair had fought a couple of boys bigger than themselves for jeering about her housewifely qualities. "Aye, they gave 'em such a pasting that their fathers came to complain to me an' Will, and *we* damn near had to take us coats off to *them*."

"Aye . . ." Adam smiled.

It was cosy, a peaceful room in which to put thoughts lazily into words. Topics ranged wide, lightly about Greets Last Fair, Skewdale's last day of general holiday before the mists and snows silently crept along; with poignancy when Matt Tiplady, confiding as he seldom confided, spoke about his wife. Operations at Gull Scar were reviewed, too, and also Adam's own work.

"Freestone John tells me you're leaving Martha Forehead Ground an' going to Sun Hade for your next bargain," the poacher remarked about eleven o'clock. "Well, you'll nobbut have to do a spell at Jenny Incline and another in Bucker Level to be knowing all there is about th'East Side's sett."

"Nay, Matt," Adam expostulated. "There's around seventeen miles o' drifts and levels in Martha Level alone, not mentioning th'Old Man."

"Aye, right enough," Matt laughed.

Half an hour later, Floss standing behind him in the soft yellow rectangle of the doorway, he saw his guest into a starless night.

The wind was blowing more strongly, and leaves, green as yet but soon to change, blew occasionally into Adam's face as he went along the riverside. It was very dark, without a window glowing anywhere, and he never knew his precise bearings until, eyes attuned to such scant light as there was, he reached the top of the steep hill on Middle Sorrow, where an owl hooted in the rotten scrub-larch above Silence before gliding, unseen and unheard, above his head.

"Aye, I'll have to carry a lamp like everybody else when th'autumn comes," he mused. "It makes you realise what it can be here in the depths o' winter if it's like this now. Well . . ." he smiled, "maybe I'll see for myself."

With that hope in his heart he stumbled along the rough track towards Pewitt Pillar and Back Lane

CHAPTER EIGHT

I

On the afternoon before Greets Last Fair, Freestone John knocked off work in Sun Hade Ground sooner than usual so that he could complete a hearth-stone. Before that the partners had been discussing the West Side Company's New Drift, now more than a month overdue in reaching Doomsday High Shaft. Already it was being freely hinted that the gallery had been driven eight or ten fathoms longer than should have been necessary, which meant that direction was inaccurate.

"You're dodging nowt, John," Adam shouted as the Quaker's candle disappeared up the ramp-like slope of a slant. "No, I'll just stack these deads an' then I'll be off myself."

The groover's voice rang hollow along the way-gate. "Well, I'm noan so suited about leaving you to do my share," he grumbled.

Adam set to with a will. Luckily there were areas of the Old Man in the vicinity, and these made convenient stowaway places for useless rock, saving much labour and time otherwise required to tram out.

"Aye," he murmured to himself about an hour later, bringing his watch face into the light of the candle on his hat-brim, "everybody 'ul be out by now, so here's my chance to explore a bit more."

From the higher end of the Slant he proceeded along a drift whose timbering plainly revealed the white fingers of dry-rot, and then, taking to the ladders in a draw-shaft, climbed to Martha Level. A durk wagon filled with his and Freestone John's bouse stood at the top, but he continued easterly in the level, towards its outermost limit.

At Sun Hade, Martha Level dipped, so preventing natural drainage, and thus the only method of removing water was to lift it directly to the surface, where motive power was supplied by a twenty-seven-foot waterwheel placed on Heugh Syke Gill a little above Sweet Tarn. Seventy-four fathoms deep, Sun Hade Pump Shaft was unusual in that, instead of rising vertically, it haded about fifteen degrees to the south.

"Nowt special here," he muttered.

On returning, he pushed the durk wagon down to Toft Rigg Whim Shaft—indicated, as he came nearer, by the groaning noise of the waterwheel—and there, in readiness for hoisting by the banksman, tipped the bouse into a kibble, an iron receptacle the shape of an egg whose top and bottom have been cut off squarely. Pulling from his pocket the partnership nick-stick, a pen-knife and chalk, he traced Freestone John's tally on the kibble, and along the edge of the thin stick whittled out another notch.

"An' that's that," he remarked.

Before leaving he examined the machinery—the ponderous waterwheel whose foot-diameter axle turned, through gearing, the flanged driving drum; it was provided with clutch, reversing motion, brake and a tell-tale showing the changing position of a load in the shaft. There was also a two-way signalling apparatus connected at each end to clappers, metal plates so mounted as to create the most noise. Above the lever, in cast lettering, was the intimation:

1 *Stroke=Stop;* 2 *Strokes= Wind up;* 3 *Strokes=Lower.*

Outward bound again, Adam splashed along Martha Water Gate, but halted at a trial of ill-repute, Lone Crosscut. "We'll have a squint up here," he muttered.

Some distance along the widely-shunned working, as he discerned an old gimp-sided lantern and the frame of a wooden wagon half-buried amidst the pile of good mineral in which it had rotted away, the smoky flame of his candle-stump swilled violently and went out. But, as he stood in the impenetrable darkness fumbling for another candle in the cord-strung candle-box over his shoulder, he heard nothing more grisly than an occasional drip or the soft sound of slurry slipping down the side of a heap. No striker drove a plug between feathers nor, when the new candle burned, did invisible spectres leave their visibly-moving shadows on the rough sides of the drift.

"Well, there's one thing," he thought gravely, as he picked up a chased-brass tobacco box, on the green top of which a chaw of mouldy twist still rested, "they left here in a hurry all right."

There was nothing else worth delay and so he went back to the main gallery, thence to Old Wife Shaft, where he decided to branch sharply left to Jenny Incline, three hundred fathoms distant. Attaining this ground, one of the East Side Company's best, he swung on to the ladders in sumps and rises driven in the vein, but as nothing remarkable met his eye, soon turned about, to bear for Old Wife Shaft once more, where he descended a shallow collecting sump in which a powerful modern pump clanged away.

"Aye . . ." he said to himself when upon the sole of the level again, "I can understand Droughty Tom not wanting to throw money away by fetching this pump out, but if he ever did," he stared at flowing water which submerged sleepers and chairs of a tramway, "he'd shut down Jenny Incline quick enough."

From Old Wife Shaft outwards to the tail the gallery was of standard horse-level size and so he was able to step out with reasonable speed.

At Martha Changing Shop he shifted into old but cleaner attire and spread sodden working clothes before going outdoors, where he followed the track down Winterings Gill. When passing the East Side Company's office he was hailed from across the beck. It was Hugh Bearpark's turn to cook the evening meal and Len Rukin was taking his ease on the threshold of Notion Level Changing Shop.

"You're going to miss t'procession, lad," the groover bawled.

Adam funnelled his hands. "What procession, Len?" he inquired.

"Why . . ." Until he glimpsed a faint grin, the dark-jowled young man looked completely astonished. "Why, when t'Circus from Greets comes up to Winterings to—an' this 'ul cost you a pint of ale, Adam lad, to compensate me for my injured feelings."

Increasing distance ended the banter, and soon Adam was striding down Mine Road and Sorrow Near. Town Foot was almost deserted, with only two persons in it, one of them an individual, white at both ends, top-hat and canvas shoes, who was posting a lurid-coloured bill setting out the various attractions to be enjoyed at Greets the next day. The other, Luke Close, the Council's roadman, was energetically sweeping up, in his own time, the horse manure which always accumulated outside the Smithy, a somewhat astonishing devotion to duty explained only by the fact that he was holidaying the next day. It was scurrilously said of the ex-miner that wherever he might die the chances were at least even he would do so leaning on a broom handle.

In the kitchen at Back Lane Adam at once noticed two almost infallible signs that nobody was at home. The Bible was not on its usual shelf, nor did a bonnet hang on the hook at the foot of the stairs. The marble-patterned oilcloth on the table was bare and so, philosophically reflecting that there was nothing novel about getting his own tea ready, he took a towel from the line below the mantelpiece and, hunting out a more respectable pair of trousers in the cupboard recessed beneath the boarded-in staircase, went through the larder into the end-place. This was a small, stone-flagged room with a draining grate in the corner; underneath a small window a stone trough was fed continuously by spring water brought from a point just up the hillside behind the cottage.

After fastening the door he stripped and then, working up as much lather as carbolic soap and ice-cold water could furnish on the flannel, started to wash himself from face and chest downwards, ending by squatting in the trough where, using an old pan, he sluiced himself with clean water. Then, stepping on to the flags, he towelled himself until his skin tingled.

Hitherto, in splashing and hearty song, he had made a great deal of noise, and it was not until he was finally rubbing down that he heard distraught sobbing above his head. Every movement arrested, outstretched arms holding the towel across his shoulders, he listened intently. "That's Agnes, an' she seems in a bad way," he muttered. "I'd better see what's up with her." Hastily pulling on trousers and tying the braces round him, he went as he was, bare from the waist upwards. In the kitchen, from the bottom of the stairs, he called to her, but as this was without avail ran up the steps and knocked on her door. "What is it, lass?" he asked anxiously. "Agnes! *Agnes!*"

Momentarily the cries became more alarming before they died away; then she moaned and, once, it sounded as if she were choking. Utterly distracted, she seemed completely oblivious to his near presence, and although doubtless it would have been wiser to seek Mrs. Iveson's assistance, Adam Brunskill had for too long been accustomed to assuming his own responsibilities. Realising further appeals were futile, he entered the bedroom, the ill-balanced door latching behind him as he stood over his cousin who, limbs and body quivering, was huddled face downwards, clad in her petticoat. "Now come, Agnes," he said. "Try to calm yourself and then, if you like, tell me what's the matter."

There was brief silence. "How . . . how *dare* you push in here?" she then asked, her voice muffled by the blankets. "Into a lass's bedroom."

"When you hear somebody in sore trouble you want to help, don't you?" said Adam as, sitting on the edge of the bed, he attempted to turn the rigidly-resisting little figure.

Twisting free, she half sat up, her lips thin with purpose. Just as suddenly she screamed: "I'll never live down t'shame of this, never. Get out!"

"Steady," Adam said. "If you'll nobbut control yourself and——"

Her scream was even more piercing. "Get out on here, get out on——"

"That'll do, Agnes," Adam checked her. "I'm not intending . . ."

Without the least intimation previously of footsteps, the bedroom door crashed open, to disclose Ambrose Pedley on the threshold, slack mouth twitching, his sallow cheeks darkly flushed.

"So I've copped you red-handed!" he screeched. "Aye, noan only catched you in an innocent lass's chamber unbidden, but catched you at after I'd heard her begging you to leave it."

"Enough o' that," Adam said sternly. "I'm here nobbut because——"

Flecks of foam dribbled down the older man's chin. "An' who are you to tell me to be quiet?" he asked shrilly. "Do you reckon t'Lord Almighty 'ul noan protect His servant against him who's defiled his roof? Aye, I name you for what you are, a . . ."

"Agnes!" Adam's tone was imperative as he grasped his cousin's shoulder, "tell your father I hadn't been in more than a minute, an' tell him I haven't harmed you in any way."

But his appeal failed, and the more urgent one with which he followed it. The noise in the little room was deafening, Ambrose Pedley's frenzied requests to his Maker to strike down the seducer as sustained as the shattering cries from the bed. So, confronted by their hysteria, Adam took the first step towards ending it.

"You'll noan touch me," Ambrose Pedley screamed, darting to the window, where he tugged at the stiff, lower sash. Thrusting his head sideways through a narrow opening he sent out a demand for help, so much startling a couple of women in Dirty Bottom that they spun about sharply. "Tell Albert Gibson to come here quick," he yelled. "Go to t'policeman's house, woe to me . . . I'se found out as I've been nurturing a snake in my bosom, an' I'm having him out on here . . ."

Adam's face was carved in grim lines. "You've no need to bother about Albert Gibson," he said. "I'm losing no time myself in shaking the dust o' this place off my feet."

"Aye, a lecher," bawled Ambrose Pedley, "that's what t'lodger I've had is. One as rapes the gentle . . ."

Before leaving, Adam attempted once more to compel Agnes to say the few words only that were necessary. She was no longer screaming, but when he touched her she started again, and so, chilled to the heart, he went away to collect his possessions. After dressing, he stuffed clothing into his carpet-bag until the drawers of the old chest were emptied, when, ready to go, he picked up dial and tripods. For the last time, to satisfy himself nothing else remained, he glanced round the bedroom, from drooping wallpaper to bed with its straw mattress. Slowly, holding his luggage fore and aft, he descended the narrow staircase.

That evening Mrs. Iveson had been visited by an old friend from Barfoot, but, when the strains of a band were faintly heard, the caller thought it would be pleasant to stroll down to Town Foot. Both, of course, were aware of strange happenings next door, but it was not until they went into Back Lane, where Mark Iveson was standing aghast, that they learnt the reason.

From an upper window Ambrose Pedley was doing his utmost to leave no room for doubt, but exhaustion was telling its tale. "The Lord 'ul take vengeance on him if I can't," he sobbed. "Oh aye, he were going to satisfy his lustful desires i' comfort——"

"Hold on," snapped the shepherd. "There's ladies present now."

But, fascinated by the spectacle, they still gaped at the head with its tangle of whisker and beard squeezed sideways below the sash.

"He'd closed t'bedroom door," Ambrose Pedley continued unabashed. "An' he were on the bed, and——"

Mrs. Iveson and her friend were about to walk away hastily when the door nearest to them opened. For a while they stared at one another, the tall young man who was well burdened, and three very shocked people.

"Well . . ." Adam remarked evenly, "you'll have heard what's supposed to have been going on."

Mark Iveson's kindly face was most unhappy. "Aye," he muttered.

"Now I'll tell you my story," Adam was resuming when Ambrose Pedley brushed past him. "It's just this—I were drying myself off after a wash all over when I heard Agnes crying her heart out, an' so I hastened upstairs. I went in to her when she wouldn't reply——"

Ambrose Pedley found new strength. "Thanks be, O Lord," he exulted. "Out on his own mouth th'evil-liver has condemned himself. There he were, fresh fro' the end-place as he's admitted, driven to t'virgin's couch by his gross desires, stark naked an' all."

Vastly excited, Mark Iveson thrust out a challenging arm. "Just a minute," he rapped out. "The lad had his britches on, I saw that for myself as I were coming up from t'Hippy Stones."

"He were as naked as t'day he were born," Ambrose Pedley shouted.

The shepherd's jaw took a more determined set. "Chaps i' my job have quick enough eyes, Pedley," he said. "I made no mistake, not I."

Comfortable-looking Mrs. Iveson chipped in hotly. "He's making one though," she declared. "A fat lot o' good it'll do Agnes him howling out to the world such awful things. Whatever may have occurred it's nowt but lunacy to——"

"Nowt's occurred, Mrs. Iveson." Adam interrupted her. "But perhaps we'll get the truth if you'll go in and talk to Agnes yourself. There's no greater favour you could do me, as you'll understand clearly enough."

His voice had deepened and, possibly because of this appeal, possibly because her husband had been so flatly contradicted, Mrs. Iveson inclined her head towards her friend as if fully determined to get to the bottom of the affair.

"She'll noan!" Ambrose Pedley violently nipped the project in the bud. "Th'only one as can bring comfort to a lass is her natural protector."

"What harm will it do for t'missus to have a word with her?" the shepherd demanded.

"It might do a lot," Ambrose Pedley hissed. "You Ivesons an' him has always been as thick as thieves, but I'm noan allowing you to concoct summat to cover him up. You might be willing to 'low a poor lass to——"

Rightly incensed, Mark Iveson jumped forward, his attack frustrated only by the joint efforts of the ladies. That ended the bitter battle of words. Ambrose Pedley, leaving another threat lingering in the air, went into his home, slamming the door behind him, while in Back Lane a growing awkwardness descended upon the small party.

"Well, I'll be on my way," Adam said.

"Aye . . . aye," Mark Iveson mumbled. "Yes, I'm sorry about this business. You know . . ." he shook his head, "he'll screak his tale fro' top to bottom o' Skewdale, as he says."

Possessed by this vexatious thought, Adam walked ahead of the others to Town Foot, where the crowd was intent upon what would soon appear on the bend beyond Malaga. A few people scrutinised him certainly, but that arose entirely from the strange sight of the carpet-bag, overcoat, and surveying equipment he was carrying, and, with the exception of a group at Calvert's Wynd, it was the same throughout Main Street.

In this fashion Adam reached the little bow-windowed shop not far short of Winterings Brig.

Hannah Batty's shop-bell rang twice in fairly rapid succession, as Adam entered, and when Mrs. Hastwell, summarily dismissed, left with her purchases: a gill of vinegar, four nutmegs, and a pint of raspberry wine. As the concluding reverberations faded away, Old Hannah's shrewd glance passed from the carpet-bag, placed between stone bran-tub and a roll of diaper, to the grave face of the young man.

"Summat up, Adam, isn't there?" she remarked. "I thought there were an' that's why I got rid on Puke's missus. Is it serious, lad?"

Adam nodded. "It's so serious, Hannah, that this stuff o' mine is stopping out in the shop till you've heard about it."

Mrs. Batty nodded, too. "In that case we'd better have a crack in t'kitchen, lad. And it'll be as well if we're noan interrupted, either."

She thumbed through the pile of cards which served her in so many ways before finding the picture she needed, that of a gentleman in a frock-coat intently listening to a trumpet-like appliance whose narrow end was pressed against a patient's heart. When this notification had been hung outside the shop door, informing passers-by that the establishment was CLOSED FOR FIFTEEN MINUTES—CONSULTATION ON, she led the way into the small room at the rear. There she pointed to a rocking-chair nearby the swinging pendulum of the Dutch clock, seating herself in a wing chair at the other side of the hearth, a strategic position with back to the window.

"Well now, lad," she said, "let's hear what it is."

Never missing the slightest change in his expression, she attended carefully to the story, interspersing a few thoughtful "Mmm-mmms" and nodding again, at least a dozen times, at the conclusion. Then, briskly but somewhat indirectly, she delivered judgment.

"Your bedroom door faces the top o' the stairs, lad, so take your things up there—you'll find t'bottom two drawers in the tall-boy is empty, 'cepting bags o' lavender and you've to leave them be, choose how you think you'll smell like a lass at after."

"Aye," Adam protested, "but you haven't said a word about——"

Mrs. Batty cackled. "I should have said plenty if I'd thought there were owt queer in your tale, lad. But never mind about that . . ." Unaccustomed furrows lined her forehead as she inspected the wing chair. "And he's bigger than James were," she mused aloud, a reminiscent smile illuminating her face. "No, we can't have him, when he fancies a lark, squeezing into this an' then setting off to t'Plug with it stuck to his bottom, as James did. Yes," her voice became businesslike, "yes, while you're upstairs hug th'other down."

Adam grinned. "What other?"

"My words," Old Hannah laughed. "I must be getting on, mustn't I, talking to mesen an' so on. It's my husband's old chair, lad, right comfortable for a big chap, and it's in the little room next to your own."

Shortly afterwards Adam was standing in a fragrant-smelling bedroom whose small-paned window looked towards roan Shorthorns feeding upon pastures steeply rising to Notion Bridge. In it he felt the same friendliness which was so much a part of the house and, as he lifted the carpet-bag on to the heavily-corniced Tudor bedstead, his gloominess had lessened.

Unpacking did not take long, nor the search for the broad-seated horsehair chair he carried downstairs, where he was able to eat a plateful of ham and eggs before gaudily-habilimented horses and gilded chariots thundered by. A little later the bell rang and Old Hannah bustled off, leaving airing problems for the moment.

From the kitchen Adam heard nothing save an indistinct murmur in the shop, though the colloquy flared at the end. On her return Mrs. Batty did not attempt to deceive him. Conscious she had dealt efficaciously with a scandalmonger, she was holding herself especially erect.

"You're going to find out, lad," she opened without preamble, "that a sight too many folk 'ul take notice o' what Ambrose Pedley says, 'cause they're made that road. But I think you'll also find that them as really matters isn't going to credit what's said about you by a chap who's getten spittle trickling down his whiskers when he's maligning you."

"So it's begun already?" Adam remarked.

Most obviously her thoughts were elsewhere. "Aye," she muttered, "somebody such as me or Katie Iveson 'ul have to get hold on that lass t'minute we can . . . in fact I'll walk up to Back Lane to-morrow morn myself, when her father's off. She'll be frightened to death of him, as they all were, but she's got to be made to understand, for her own salvation in the hereafter, that she must clear you o' this cruel charge, lad."

Adam's breath escaped in a sigh of profound relief. "You'll tackle Agnes then?" he said.

That the vilification had spread as rapidly as a prairie fire he realised on stepping into Main Street. And in the Literary Institute Reading Room his neighbours at the stands to either side glanced inward, a trio on the varnished pine benches along the wall went into a whispering huddle, and now and then, cautiously, thick-lensed spectacles peeped above the remoter slope of his own stand.

A visit to the tap-room of the Plug and Feathers was merely a continuation of these unhappy circumstances and anger began to rise in him when he went out again, so that, as he paused near the mounting-block, he was hardly aware of the lay figures on the inn's quoits-court, whose faces turned with curiosity, or those across the road who had ceased to play hand-ball since sighting him.

"No," he told himself while striding towards Nick Turn, many a nudge and aside marking his progress, "I mustn't act as if I'd summat to be ashamed on, but all the same you can't expose nice lasses to t'company of a celebrity of the nature I've just become."

As luck had it, Cherry was at Town Foot, talking to Fronick outside Smithy House, and, as he drew nearer, it struck him how much in recent days worry about her uncle's affairs had caused the soft bloom in her cheeks to decline. But, if the girl he loved were pale, Fronick Blenkiron rapidly acquired more than enough colour for two immediately she perceived him. Incoherently ending the conversation, the blacksmith's daughter fled.

"Well, I reckon that amply serves as a suitable introduction," Adam began when Smithy House door banged as if to intimidate any rampaging deflowerers of virgins. "As things are, it'd be as well if I didn't go to t'Fair with you and Dinah, lass."

Cherry's cheeks started to glow. "Suit yourself," she told him.

If anything, Adam became a trifle too paternal, but his greater error was in missing the storm signals. Cherry's over-bright eyes were not innocent of flashing occasionally and her toe tapped the cobble-stones.

"It's not a case of suiting myself, lass," he said. "I'd like to go all right, but until this affair is squared up properly——"

"What sort o' friends do you think we are?" she interrupted furiously. "Fair weather?"

As she turned to follow Fronick, whose bulbous eye was positioned behind the mesh of the parlour curtain, Adam was reflecting with some discomfort that he was by no means enjoying an easy passage with one he sought to shield from any stigma. But Cherry still had something to say, and she did so very aloofly.

"You can please yourself, of course," she said. "But if you're noan here in the morning I'll never speak to you again."

Adam found tongue again before it was too late. "Nay, Cherry, I'm nobbut trying to do what's best."

From the step of Mr. Blenkiron's front door, chin tilted disdainfully, she surveyed him. Regrettably her icy response was not grammatical enough to have won Mr. Kidd's approval.

"I've telled you," she pronounced. "An' I'm noan telling you again."

Until her slender figure was hidden by the door Adam stayed there. Then he started along Main Street, so contented by this proof of her trust in him that for a few paces he forgot the reason which might have caused distrust. In this more cheerful mood he never hesitated on reaching the cobbler's shop on the corner of Calvert's Wynd, but went straight inside, where silence at once fell upon the company gathered there.

"I've just popped in, Kit," he said, "to see if that job's still on that you're doing for me one evening."

"Aye, I think so, lad," was the hearty response from the bench.

"Champion," Adam said.

All of which was a decidedly ambiguous method of confirming that the arrangement still held for secretly exploring certain workings running westward in Bucker Level, the leased property of the East Side Company.

Adam eyed the faces of those about him—Richard Blenkiron, Puke Hastwell, William Nattrass, Edmund Kearton, Matt Tiplady, Martin Rutter, Nathan Wharton—some coldly hostile, some friendly, and some embarrassed.

"Well, I'll be away, Kit," he added. "There's a ripe young lass somewhere upbank as keeps house for her father. He's usually out boozing till late of an evening."

As he passed the array of clogs, slippers, and ladies' cloth boots in the window on Main Street he heard the hubbub within, voices raised in expostulation and deep-chested laughter, too.

2

The morning of Greets Last Fair was oppressive, but the clammy heat had nothing to do with spoiling the day for a few young people. Trouble began at Town Foot, when Fronick glimpsed Adam near the Wesleyan Day School. She grabbed her young man's arm and, his face growing redder with every step, dragged him down the main road. Seeing this, Wingy lost his temper, making such remarks about his sister as would have sent her into hysterics had she heard them.

It was no more pleasant at Half. Arthur Nattrass had walked up from home and he and Annamaria came out of the Old Cow Inn together. Where most young women would have considered it expedient to keep a still tongue in their heads his young lady preferred otherwise.

"You shouldn't be pleasuring wi' nice lasses just now, Adam Brunskill," she began. "Not till what happened with your cousin is explained properly."

Cherry flew battle colours. "There's nowt as wants explaining,

Annamaria Rutter," she said. "And Adam's with me and Dinah, not wi' you."

"He's noan with me," declared Miss Rutter.

A high-pitched laugh created a diversion. "Eh, Adam lad," scoffed Arthur Nattrass, "you must be a right May-gosling. I well remember one o' the times I landed myself into a bit o' woman difficulty myself——"

Annamaria quickly disposed of his pretensions. "And that were with Scald Wiseman's eldest," she announced. "But as every other chap i' Greets had been with her afore you the only difficulty you were in were which of 'em to select to lay t'blame on."

"We're not listening to any more of that," Dinah cried desperately.

"You're noan listening to me any more, choose how," Annamaria snorted. "Not while *he's* with you an' Cherry. Come on, Arthur."

Dinah, too, had her tale of woe, which she told as Annamaria and Arthur Nattrass, still warring bitterly, drew farther ahead, towards the heather-covered brow crossed by the main road before descending to Greets.

"Mrs. Roberty Will came specially to our house last night, at *after* a quarter to ten," she gulped. "An' . . . well, she carried on awful about Adam. I'd a real set-to with her and my mother and . . . and if it hadn't been for my father this morning I wouldn't have been 'lowed to come."

Adam's mouth was grim. "I seem to be making a rare mess o' things for you lasses," he said.

"It's others who's making a mess, Adam," Cherry reminded him.

"To hell wi' women," Wingy Blenkiron exclaimed unexpectedly.

That relieved the tension, and from then, in outward appearance at least, a happy little party climbed the dusty highway. Adam, however, had his own particular cross to bear, the knowledge that the problem might take much longer to solve than he had imagined in moments of optimism the previous night.

Mark Iveson's news early that morning was responsible for this. The shepherd had called at the shop to buy tobacco and to leave a plucked fowl. Hearing one portion of a very weighty discussion Adam had left the kitchen to inquire—his first glimpse of the grave faces of Old Hannah and her customer-supplier told him as plainly as words that something was gravely amiss.

"What's up, Mark?" he asked.

The shepherd preferred to report in his own way, the narrative including details of the idiosyncrasies of his dog, who hated tramps.

"It were just starting to be rosy in th'east when he began barking an' snarling, so I gate out o' bed," he went on. "But it were no Weary Willie, Adam, as I soon saw when I popped my head out o' the window. There were Agnes carrying a bundle, with her father hurrying her towards Jom High Road. My idea is that he were taking her to relatives—he's plenty, in every one of t'Dales."

Old Hannah made a remark not wholly relevant, associating Bible-thumpers with those who spawned "worse 'an old Nick." Subsequently she said: "Aye, an' if so, she'll take some getting at if he's warned 'em. No, Adam lad, I can't say this has improved matters."

That, and more, was what Adam was thinking about as he looked down on Greets, a patch of soft grey amidst vast stretches of browns and purples, sole touch of vivid colour the gaily-striped marquees which, with the throng about them, hid everything of the Green except the mighty elm thrusting its head above.

Gently Cherry touched his arm. "We're nearly there," she said.

He smiled down at her. "Aye," he nodded.

Quietly talking, they went down the winding road, past clumps of ripening bilberries towards the turnpike's Bar House and the merry-making beyond.

* * * *

Usually sunny-dispositioned, Wingy Blenkiron's humour was never other than uncertain throughout the day. Nothing earned his approval, neither acrobats in tights and spangled dresses, strong men, dwarfs, conjurers, the fat woman, nor the boxers in the booths. And, in the menagerie, bumping into his sister, he had such a quarrel with her as to bring him also to loggerheads with his best friend, Bart Hugill. He insisted upon an early tea, taking a perverse delight in pointing out the black clouds piling up to the west.

"A damned nice outing it's been," he said irritably. "I might just as well have carried t'mail down myself as have arranged for old Chesty Geordie to do it for me." Just then he noticed Arthur Nattrass and his young lady. His eyes gleamed and, with the quick temper of his gingery-bearded father, he dashed off.

While Annamaria responded in full kind to his furious assault, Cherry and Dinah decided it would be wise to return as soon as possible—there was the threatening storm, and circumstances anyhow had robbed the day of much it could have been. Adam, too, was not reluctant to leave, and so, when Wingy came back, in a much better mood, a prompt start was made.

Both girls were good walkers, and soon the B.G. Inn was well behind, the sky ahead ever darkening behind the point where the highway curved over the ridge on Hart Moor. From this summit, the portents in front more menacing still, they started to run-and-walk down the slope towards Half, but once halted fleetingly while Cherry pointed out to Adam the site of a baile-hill, a crude and ancient means of smelting consisting of a low wall built in a circle, with vents on the west side to obtain draught from the prevailing wind.

"We've improved since then," she dimpled. "Just think of the North Mill . . . and in Spain you'll have smelt mills a lot more up-to-date even than that."

This reminded Adam of a surprisingly chatty letter from Simon in which, after a budget to do with the affairs of family and acquaintances, he wrote about the magnificent smelt mill shortly to be built by his employers.

"I've summat right amusing in my pocket you must read, lass," Adam laughed. "The first part that is," he amended on recollection, "the rest is nowt but technical stuff."

From then it became a helter-skelter race, a wild pursuit of Dinah and Wingy, who already were a couple of hundred yards ahead. An occasional spatter of rain met them, but although the drops were steadily more insistent at the ornamental gates of Mr. Wade's residence the real deluge did not begin until they had tumbled into the Groovers Welcome. From behind the counter, Jonas Cottingham, the West Side Company's chief smelter, was talking to Luther Thwaites, the Lord's keeper, who lived next door to Freestone John in a row of cottages across the road.

"Two glasses of ale, and two bottles o' lemonade," Adam ordered.

Jonas Cottingham's thin lips curled as he complied. "So you're patronising me, eh?" he remarked. "Well, you'll find this is noan one o' them fancy houses like t'Plug, as is frequented by such as you . . . or as *were* frequented I should say, for I can't imagine even Lucy Peacock, a queen amongst money-grubbers——"

"What are you serving me for then?" Adam demanded.

Jonas Cottingham laughed. "Under th'Act, my lad . . ."

Leaving him to explain Licensing Conditions to anyone who might care to listen, Adam made a couple of journeys to the settle in the corner, where Wingy was endeavouring to console Dinah.

"She's frightened o' thunder, Adam," Cherry whispered to him. "And it is getting bad, isn't it?"

The heavens, in support, resounded with a gigantic crash.

The thunderstorm was destined to be remembered for many years in upper Skewdale. Tremors constantly shook the ground and, as if desirous of prolonging vicious joy, the ear-splitting detonations which rent the stifling air close above the chimneys continued to rumble snarlingly amongst the folds of the hills. In the semi-darkness blue-white lines of awe-inspiring brilliance forked in the black sky, tearing down towards Silver Seat and Virgin Hill, each flash coating with an eerie pallor the upturned faces in the bar of the Groovers Welcome. Then suddenly, as if to mock the present heavy downpour, the cloudburst came, obliterating everything save the very near landscape. Raindrops, drumming on the stone slates of the cottages opposite, which hitherto had had a single splashing identity, were lost to form part of a whole, a foot-thick thatch of steam-like vapour clothing the length of the roof.

"I think it's passing, lass," Adam reported three-quarters of an hour afterwards. "The sky's lifting an' there's a break or two up dale. Anyroad, it's getting lighter, and maybe you can see Simon's letter."

So Cherry Dinsdale, a smile often playing about her mouth, read stories about Bessie, who remitted exactly seven kisses, gossipy paragraphs obviously dictated by Jane, and an inquiry from Daniel as to why he had not heard more of his Aunt Ellen. There were other matters, too—Simon's long conversation with Mr. Phillips, the manager, who had mentioned that Jim Calvert might be retiring sooner than expected. . . .

"That's the lot, lass," Adam broke in. "It's nobbut about work an' such like at after."

Cherry flushed vividly. "I didn't know there was owt private," she said.

"There isn't really, lass." Adam floundered a little. "It were nobbut that . . ." Impulsively he returned her the pages she had thrust at him. "Finish it," he asked.

Her red lips were mutinous. "I shan't."

Quietly he put out a sensible plea. "Cherry lass, there's enough bother about just now without you an' me adding to it. Read it, won't you, while I go off to the others?"

She swallowed. "All right and . . . I'm very sorry."

Adam smiled. "It's noted, lass."

Since the beginning of the storm, Wingy keeping her company, Dinah had been hiding, and when Adam had gone, to talk to them beneath the stone staircase, Cherry read a letter whose concluding lines reflected Mr. Phillips' high regard for him. For a moment, as she refolded the sheets, her expression was contemptuous, while she considered Reuben Nattrass, who had decried the capabilities of a man held in such esteem by the manager of a great lead-mining company; but her face soon grew wistful when, once again, she wished Adam were grooving at the other side of Winterings Beck, when perhaps he could have helped her uncle in these crucial days.

The rain had completely ceased, and a watery shaft of sunlight was brightening the brown-grey crags at Gull Scar as the party left the Groovers Welcome. Heugh Syke nearby roared down the gill, boulders grinding along its bed as the pressure forced them forward. The swollen beck, instead of being amber-tinted as with normal rain, was black with fine peat carried down from the moors.

"By!" Adam ejaculated. "But water can rise fast here."

Cherry was glancing up bank, above the turbulent area where Heugh Syke entered the Skew. "The river's out an' all," she said. "They must have had it bad round Yorrel."

Wingy was remarking that if the centre of the cloudburst were higher up more water had still to come, when Dinah pointed to a tottery old man working with a dog in the bottoms. "He's driving out stock yonder," she said anxiously. "Oh, I do hope everything's safe at home. And wi' nearly everybody down at the Fair. Let's be off quick."

With skirts held above their ankles the girls led the way, picking a path amongst the pools and jumping or being helped over gullies scored across the road. The fellsides were traced with silvery threads, innumerable feeders of a river already spreading from its channel. Near Malaga the bodies of sheep were being carried by the muddy flood, a pathetic sight which increased Dinah's fears.

"You'll get back just as sharp, lass . . ." Wingy was advising her when, from the front door of Malaga, they were hailed by the residence's full-bosomed mistress.

"Hey, come here!" Mrs. Roberty Will shouted. "You . . . Cherry Dinsdale."

"Well . . . it can't be a torrent getting in," Cherry said, startled. "I'd better see what she wants, but don't wait."

She ran through the gateway to the house, but paused beneath the pediment until brusquely bidden to enter. Then she went along the hall, passing a line of sacred pictures, before turning into a room where, not invited to sit, she stood between a glass-panelled bookcase and a claw-footed loo table.

"Are you out on your senses, girl?" Titus Alderson's wealthy sister-in-law demanded. "What are you doing wi' that Brunskill? You've heard th'awful thing he did last night, haven't you? An' afore this, I've telled you what he was, haven't I?"

"But you were wrong, Mrs. Alderson," Cherry retorted. "An' he did nowt last night as he shouldn't."

The gold locket on Mrs. Alderson's black bodice began to heave. "Don't you answer me back that road, miss," she said.

Cherry's lips trembled, but she managed to retain an undaunted front apart from that. "I wasn't answering you back cheekily, Mrs. Alderson. But he hasn't done owt wrong, an' it'd be me who were behaving wrongly if I acted as if I were condemning him."

"You were there, were you," stormed the older woman, "when he bullocked his way into Agnes Pedley's bedroom?"

"No," Cherry replied with quiet dignity. "And I think I'd rather not talk about it any more."

Mrs. Robert William Alderson quivered. "Well, I shall be doing some talking, young woman. An' it'll be to your Uncle Titus."

"You must do as you please," Cherry said, excusing herself.

When walking along the curving, gravelled drive she decided that she would *never* allow herself to be coerced, but unhappily for this brave resolve the choice was not left to her, for Adam had been doing a great deal of thinking himself since morning. He was pacing in the road as she emerged and, between there and Town Foot, told her his conclusions.

"It's just commonsense and I ought to have realised it last night," he admitted. "Till this affair of Agnes's is cleared up I mustn't go about with you and Dinah."

"But, Adam . . ." she protested.

"It's best, lass," he said gravely. "And it'll make it all the better on that day you an' me clamber up one of the hillsides, for the talk I mentioned that Sunday we went to tea at Annamaria's."

Conscious of a scalding feeling in her eyes, Cherry gazed towards the old paving-stone quarry beyond Rachel Shafts, up Jom High Road. "All right, Adam," she said, her throat strangely dry.

Relief from an agonising situation came almost immediately. Wingy and Dinah had been talking to Chesty Geordie, who had not dared to start for Greets with the mail-bag. The rheumaticky milk vendor had told them what he knew.

"Yorrel Bridge gone, washed completely away, and th'water's near the top of the middle arch of Snorr Bridge," the postman shouted, before they met.

For a space they stared at one another in silence, until Cherry made a proposal. "I'll tell you what," she said. "Dinah 'ul come in with me for a quick cup of tea, Wingy, while you an' Adam hasten to the Brig to see if Badger Hall's all right. If it is, don't bother to return, but do what you think you should."

"Aye, that's sound enough," Wingy agreed. "Listen, though," he nodded emphatically at Dinah, "you mustn't go up to t'Royal Alfred an' risk Snorr Bridge, lass."

Cherry was firm, too. "I shall go back with her myself on Middle Sorrow, if Dolly Bridge is safe. Ben's in the stable, I know, so we can ride on him together."

Without delay, the two young men began running along Main Street, encountering not a soul from end to end. But, when racing past the waste ground on which Winterings Fair was held, they glimpsed a line of eight or nine geese sweeping down on the river towards the dam-stakes above the Wood Yard.

"It's as bad as when there's been a sudden thaw i' winter, when th'ice has packed up on the top side of one o' the bridges," Wingy panted.

Just how much worse it was they were able to perceive more accurately from the higher land up Sleety Slape.

Facing westwards, their glances intent, Adam and Wingy scanned the scene of desolation. The flood bank on the near side of the river had burst, and from just above Modesty to beyond the Royal Alfred not a wall was visible nor much of the main road. Will Skidmore's cottage in Blenk Bottom Lane showed its upper storey only, and at the opposite side of the dale, though Matt Tiplady's cottage was still unharmed, water was lapping against the doors of the Masons and the Waggotts. Tiny waves broke over the parapet of Snorr Bridge, the three-arched giant which at most times seemed absurdly large for its duties.

"They're all serene at Badger Hall, Adam," the postman muttered, his eyes narrowed. "It'd have to rise three or four feet more to touch anything, an' I shouldn't reckon it'll do that now."

Before them, studded with the roofs of byres and barns, a yeast-coloured lake stretched, the course of the river through the middle marked by a darker and swiftly-flowing ribbon which, bearing timber, trails of hay, and things far more pitiful, whipped the lower branches of trees along its furious route.

"Looks as if t'water is starting to move right over at this side, Wingy," Adam remarked. "Is there owt else that could give way?"

"No," Wingy frowned. "Unless—aye, by God! Skulldug, where a lot o' gentlemen dug up reindeer bones and flint arrowheads when I were a lad. The river used to come round this way hundreds o' years ago, and the old chaps always declared that th'excavators had damned near trenched it back to its former course."

"If owt remotely approaching that happened just now, any beasts at Low Bands 'ud be in a bonny plight," said Adam.

"There is some there," the postman observed briefly.

With one accord the two young men started to run down Sleety Slape, near the bottom of which they were drenched by the spray thrown out from the maelstrom above the Brig. Winterings Beck was in savage spate, and, as it leapt over the third and lowest fall, it shot far forward, curving down only when within a few feet of the side of the bridge.

If hardly-won possessions had not been in danger, no one would have known that, the serving girls given holiday until eight o'clock, Titus Alderson and the mistress of the Plug and Feathers had been hoping to enjoy themselves peacefully together. These two elderly people were standing as far as possible up the main road and, as Adam and his companion arrived, Mrs. Peacock turned back to prepare rooms for any who might be homeless.

Titus Alderson looked dreadfully ill, his face sunken. "Now then," he warned them, after hearing Wingy out, "I've telled you. Right enough livestock is precious, but human beings are more precious, and if you go over yonder . . ." he pointed to Low Bands Farm, surrounded by water, "maybe you'll noan make t'return journey."

"It's fairly shallow, Mr. Alderson," the postman replied.

Again the trembling finger pointed, at the water sliding past their feet. "It's noan that, it's this *here*," the mine-agent shouted. "When it really shifts you'd be cut off by a channel scoured out as much as the river proper."

"We'll take care, Mr. Alderson," Adam promised.

Accompanied by Wingy, he entered water which, in the last stages of their trip, was only knee-deep. At the farm they assessed what must be endeavoured—hens perched miserably on cart-shafts, geese paddling happily, a flock of about thirty fat sheep squeezed together on a knoll, and three milk cows, no glimpse of daylight beneath their bellies, lowing feebly under an ash tree. Meantime the shippon shook with roars made even more stentorian by fright.

"Francis's bull, the pride on his heart," Wingy muttered. "An' a heller," he added wryly.

"He'll noan be any more agile in this stuff than we are," Adam said. "Anyroad, let's make a start, lad."

The upper storey of the haybarn was used as a refuge for the hens and cocks, but the geese were ushered into an outbuilding to which, previously, Wingy had been attracted by a whimper. On investigation, Mr. Harker's dog was discovered, swimming and nearly spent. He was placed on a stack of bracken.

Steadily this work of rescue proceeded, a cow being left behind to act as lure for the bull. But the stream below the highway flowed faster and the passage was much deeper when Wingy helped to hoist the last sheep on to Adam's back. Both then were aware that the worst was still to come, but, on Adam's return after another difficult journey, the postman flatly refused to cross until the bull had been released.

"Oh, I'm nobbut half a man, I know, just good enough to stick at this side to lend a bit of a hand while you've carried animal after animal over t'water, but I'se bloody well staying with you until that bawling chap's let out," he snapped.

Without more ado they struggled to the ash. It was a strange business driving a beast while water was often up to the drovers' thighs, but they brought their charge without mishap to a point opposite Titus Alderson, who stood anxiously against a tree stump to which was attached the safety rope thrown across earlier. The cow was tethered, the chain fastened under water to a small elder.

The bull proved easier to deal with than anticipated. When the shippon doors slowly opened, as if lock-gates, he bellowed a mighty challenge and put his head down. Defeated by the hold of the water he stumbled in his attempted rush, ultimately to emerge clumsily, when, small red eyes darting wickedly, flanks heaving, and twin jets of vapour spurting from quivering nostrils, he suffered a stout cord to be inserted into his ring. Trouble arose then, but, scenting the lady ahead, he became more amenable, even eager. In due course, a dozen yards behind the cow, he was secured to a stone gatepost.

"Well, I'll get to th'other side, but I wish we'd some more help, Adam lad, so's we could be sure of holding you and a beast," Wingy grunted as he moved into swiftly-running water. "It's still rising."

Adam was eyeing the broad crossing, a dark brown surge promising many trials to a man sadly handicapped. "Aye, I wish to t'Lord we had, Wingy," he agreed devoutly. "Anyhow, let's begin with t' cow."

Carefully the postman advanced into the torrent, which rose quickly towards his armpits, when he lost his foothold. For a few harrowing seconds nothing of him was visible except a hand clutching the straining rope, but then by some miracle he recovered and, battered by drifting wood but safe, at last seized Mr. Alderson's hand and climbed out.

Unloosing the end of the rope, Adam took it to the cow.

Many portions of the main road were impassable, but, either by detouring, or lifting vehicles over obstacles, help was coming up the Dale. Every horse was stretched to the utmost, and every trap, dog-cart and wagonette which had gone down to Greets that morning was occupied by coldly-sweating men and women who knew from experience that, though the rain had ceased, little trickles on the high moors were still joining together to make greater trickles, and that those trickles, from half a million acres of ground, would maintain the swollen Skew yet awhile.

So, in course of time, Main Street rang with the passage of iron-rimmed wheels, and the hand-ball court against the Bridge Inn and the space in front of the Plug and Feathers became packed with conveyances and saddle horses. Strings of folk ran across the hump of Winterings Brig, to be brought to a stark halt by the fearful spectacle—a far-extending sea, a new river, and, beyond dark tumbling water flying like a mill-race, a young man and a thick-necked beast, lone figures well immersed.

Richard Blenkiron pushed forward. "Hey!" he shouted. "Fasten another good rope round a rock an' fling it to him—he'll know what for. Then some o' you take this end and be ready to pull 'em in as soon as they've gone downstream to the full extent of the rope he's already getten round t'bull's neck—and some more o' you grab *that* . . . you'll have to hang on like grim death or that pair 'ul be mangled on the dam-stakes."

Reuben Nattrass's finger jab-jabbed towards one strongly-built man and then another. "Aye, an' you four get ropes about your middles, an' others of you hold the ropes from the bank side. What's wanted is a few of us on the spot, for when t'bull is in the deepest of the swill he'll take some dragging this road. Now look bloody sharp, you lad."

A heavy face became even more lowering as ostentatiously great hands were thrust into trousers pockets. "Bugger yon fellow," Bull Waggott growled. "Let them as wants volunteer, but not me."

"A chap as is scared 'ul do no good, choose how," the mine-agent grunted, before bellowing, hand at side of mouth: "Oy, Cyprian! Come here quick."

On the opposite slopes of the Dale, near Droughty Tom's cottage at Pewitt Pillar, three people silently awaited events. Cherry Dinsdale, as pale as death, sat sideways on Ben, Dinah behind her; Anthony Skidmore was there also, on Prue, whom he had ridden bareback from Greets.

"It's washed them away!" Dinah gasped. "Oh . . ."

Her father shook his head. "No, they're being checked, lass, wi' that rope whanging on t'water. But how long they'll be able to hold 'em . . ."

Hardly breathing, they stared at a battle of fluctuating fortunes in which the young man on the outer flank of the bull sometimes gained a couple of feet only to lose part of it again, the current rushing at man and beast forming a V-shaped wake on their lee. The climax passed suddenly, but as to what happened the impotent onlookers could not be sure. Adam's head almost disappeared in the water, while simultaneously the bull rose several inches and, as if violently thrust, rapidly moved an all-invaluable yard or so sideways. Then other heads began to bob in the raging stream and in five minutes the business was done.

"He's . . . he's safe," Cherry said to herself, trembling.

Dinah gulped. "I feel . . . feel right sick."

Pulling out a bandanna, Mr. Skidmore wiped his brow. "I've never seen a human life hovering on t'brink like that afore," he muttered. "An' I never wish to do again either."

There was no need to linger, and indeed good reason for them to go their own ways, and so, after Dinah had slithered to the grassy track, Cherry said good-bye, reining Ben to face homewards. The brown galloway went his own pace, tears of relief trickling down his rider's cheeks as he ambled along.

A powerful beast, frenzied by fear and discomfort, is a difficult customer to pilot across a broad stretch of raging water, but Adam's greatest test arose quite near the roadside, where the shelving bank torn out by the torrent sloped steeply. The turning point came unexpectedly, however, through the jamming immediately up-stream of an uprooted tree whose butt end, with the riven roots, swung round to press against the bull's chest. Ashore a woman screamed as, overborne by the extra force, the sweating men on the tail end of the main rope began step by step to yield ground, but the change miraculously gave Adam his opportunity. His feet found secure hold on an outcrop of rock, and he was enabled to stoop and use the full force of his shoulder, the elm clearing as he did so.

Danger still lurked, in chest-high water swilling furiously over a slippery bottom, but assistance was at hand. The first of the helpers was the raven-haired head agent of the East Side Company, who efficiently knotted a rope round Adam's waist.

"Useful if you're swept away," Reuben Nattrass grunted. "Now let's see . . ."

Crouching, every muscle of Adam's body was in play. "Thanks," he said. "Now can you keep him propped up on your own while I bend lower?"

"If you can manage it," Reuben Nattrass laughed, "I reckon I can do t'same without any undue trouble."

Adam had undergone many trials during the past fifteen minutes. "Let's see you then, Cousin Reuben," he remarked, spitting out a mouthful of water.

It may have been fortunate for Mr. Harker's cherished possession that acceptance of the implied challenge was prevented by the appearance at the other side of the bull, now gathering new life and bellowing ferociously, of Cyprian Metcalfe's head and immensely wide shoulders. Other powerful helpers were on the spot shortly afterwards.

"We'll leave him as he is, facing t'flow," said Adam. "But as soon as he can dig in his forelegs it'll be best to switch him so as he can clamber out on his own."

Stations were taken up and then, under a concerted effort, the operation went as planned until, scattering water and onlookers, the bull scrambled on to dry land, where within a respectably-distanced circle of spectators he halted, the rise and fall of a great chest and the twitching of bloodshot little eyes his sole motions.

Wingy Blenkiron's back had been clapped by the grateful owner of the animal until it was nearly sore, but now Adam's hand was wrung with a like disregard of time.

"Me and t'missus 'ul never be able to thank you enough, lad," Francis Harker said, blinking. "Never i' all our days."

"No, we'll noan, lad," Mrs. Harker chipped in through her tears. "You know we lost all them sheep and——"

"Keep him a bit longer," Lucy Peacock intervened tartly, "an' you'll be able to show your gratitude wi' an expensive wreath."

Then Adam, amongst many other men whose clothing was dripping, squeezed through an excited throng and squelched across Winterings Brig.

In Old Hannah's kitchen certain preparations had been made. From the spouts of two huge kettles steam spurted, and, matting and hearthrug pulled back, a tin bath stood on the flagged floor before a roaring fire.

The old lady issued her instructions: "Doff every stitch you've getten on, and into that wi' you in two jiffs."

"Eh!" her lodger ejaculated.

"You heard what I said," Mrs. Batty rapped. "Now look sharp."

"Aye . . . but . . ." Adam muttered.

"I've summat better to do than stop here to watch you, if that's what you're thinking," she scoffed. "But if I did you'd noan be the first grown man I'se seen wi' nowt on." With that, she bustled into the shop, but left a touch of the macabre behind her, calling back: "Or the first dead 'un either, lad. An' upstairs straight off when you've finished. I'se bringing you a hot brew out o' one of them bottles of mine."

The combination of hot water and the fire's red glow warmed Adam's chilled bones and, in bed later, he drowsily drank off a most nauseous draught. About half an hour afterwards Mrs. Batty went upstairs again, carrying broth in a feeding-cup. Her patient was sound asleep, but she listened carefully to his breathing, and then murmured: "It's free enough, and I don't think I'll waken him. Aye," she bent again, searchingly to look at his face, "he's Jim Brunskill's lad all right."

Profound satisfaction in her, she tip-toed from the bedroom.

* * * *

The next morning the Skew was not far from becoming once more a clear little river singing its purling song, far too innocent-seeming to be accused of the mischief it had wrought a few hours earlier. Nevertheless, for mile upon mile in the bottoms, walls had been flattened, barns wrecked, and bridges gravely damaged. In places holes roomy enough to hide a horse and cart yawned in the ground—when conveniently sited they served as burial vaults for the sad carcases stranded here and there. But the sun shone, flood waters were ebbing away, and the folk of upper Skewdale, familiar with the elements' extremes, began with a will to re-do all that had been so mercilessly undone.

3

If the dalesfolk settled down in due course after the flood the same was not so with Adam, who suffered the relentless vilification of the Pedley brothers without possibility of response. The whereabouts of Agnes, the key to the situation, was a complete mystery, and although Adam was not without supporters it was not very consoling to realise that the overwhelming factor in their championing of him was his performance at Low Bands Farm, not the moral question. Meantime, the former serenity of his stay destroyed, he steered clear, without being discourteous, of the young women of his acquaintance, and associated only with those men of whom he was absolutely sure.

One Saturday night, after milking, he and Blind Kit sauntered upwards past the junction of Sorrow Near and Mine Road, Adam commenting with amusement upon a bevy of cows who, contrary ladies indeed, jostled strenuously to browse a clump of hazel, though thereabouts limestone rose close to the surface and the grass was the sweetest and greenest in the district. Beyond Bucker Grinding Mill, however, the cobbler paused to listen carefully while his companion scrutinised the rough road and the grey, silent buildings of the North and South Smelt Mills across the beck.

"No, not a soul stirring," Adam reported.

Blind Kit nodded. "Right, then up to t'tail o' Bucker sharp."

The small arched entrance to Bucker Level was situated in a narrow offshoot of Winterings Gill. Heading along the tramway emerging from the dark opening, they were soon a few feet within the level's concealing shade, where Adam lighted a candle.

"As they say afore you get wed," the cobbler chuckled, "two can live as cheap as one, an' one tallow dip does for us two, eh? 'Course I've to prove it."

As unerringly he did when leading the foray, his back illuminated by brief splashes of light from a flame shielded by Adam's hand, faltering once only in the vast labyrinth, when a fall of roof had necessitated the driving of a gallery new since his time.

About four hundred fathoms from the tail Blind Kit halted at a turnrail, to point at a branch on the left, running towards the west.

"There's t'Black Drift, lad," he said. "But we'll leave that until we're coming back. We've still a fairish way to go forrard."

A hundred and ninety fathoms farther north they left the main level to proceed along Blind Trial Crosscut, a working continuing of the accepted description as far as a caved-in sump. Beyond there the excavations became aged and confused, sometimes lofty but at others so low that, in serpentine passages hewn in solid rock, crawling was the sole means of moving forward. In this part—' Freezeland ' Blind Kit called it —the air was less still, and the reason for this Adam learnt when, after entering a burrow which looked precisely similar to several more burrows which were its close neighbours, he emerged into a crypt-shaped cavern. There was a wooden-sided ladder at the opposite side, whose iron rungs were gradually lost to sight in the gloom above.

"Whistling Shaft," the cobbler said. "Th'eye is a bit higher up Winterings Gill than Glory waterwheel, but well on this side, of course."

"So we're still some distance from the two companies' boundary?" Adam mused. "And this is as far west as we can get fro' Bucker Level?"

"Through Blind Trial it is," Blind Kit said. "And we'll noan get much farther, if any, through th'other road as we passed back yonder."

"We won't," Adam muttered.

If the cobbler sensed his companion's disappointment he did not refer to it, but began to explain how, long before his grandfather's day, Freezeland had earned its icy-sounding name. Whenever the wind was around north-east the normal up-cast in Whistling Shaft was reversed, and groovers below were chilled to the marrow.

"But," he smiled broadly, "I'd better cut short my reminiscences or we'll never do t'Black Drift."

Afterwards, in the Black Drift and beyond, Adam's experience was very much the same as it had been along Blind Trial Crosscut, modern workings progressively degenerating into regions of old and shaky drifts and slants, low and askew. From Bucker Level they had gone to the fore end of the Black Drift, thence along a barrow-gate to Rise Foot, the beginning of an intricacy of water-gleaming passages which, after Rise Top, brought them to a heap of rusty kibbles in the sump of Wild Goose Shaft, a damp, echoing chamber.

"You'll know where Wild Goose is up Noggin Moor," Blind Kit remarked. "Maybe half a mile fro' Smiddy Bridge."

Adam was thinking hard. "Aye," he told himself with little elation, "and that makes this spot every inch as far from t'boundary as the other was."

As they retraced their steps he meditated upon the hopelessness of ever attaining the strata adjacent to both the Short Cut and the New Drift on this side. Without a physical examination it was impossible either to prove or disprove the presence of ironstone, and that left him as vaguely dissatisfied as before.

"Cherry's uncle is noan addle-pated," he frowned, "and I still can't believe——"

A muffled exclamation escaped him as, doubling to pass beneath a massive rib of the Red Beds, pinkish limestone, he saw a clear-cut impression on the sole of the drift. Sinking down, he peered at a small six-sided hole.

"Looks as if a nut had been trodden in an' then dug out," he marvelled. "The ground's firmish, but for all that it couldn't have been done so long back because t'mark wouldn't have lasted. Now why should a modern engineer's nut be dropped here in the Old Man? Still squatting, he tried to find an answer but, as often happens, a far-fetched but credible explanation came in a flash, when reasoned conjecture had run its course.

"By God!" he ejaculated, springing up so quickly that he bumped his head, "Cousin Reuben's tripod leg, the one as was heeled with a nut."

Nothing was visible of Blind Kit as, far along the gallery, his clogged feet stopped a few rungs down a crazy ladder. His voice sounded thin and remote in the sump. "Owt up, Adam lad?" he shouted.

In the short space before rejoining him, Adam had determined upon searching the area by himself, in the hope of tracing to where the mark left by dialling led. "Nay, I lighted on summat as made me wonder who were last here afore us, Kit," he replied.

"I should reckon it were years ago," the cobbler said, the rays from Adam's candle falling upon his scarred face and sightless eyes. "Leastways," he amended, resuming the descent, "until you muttered sharpish-like an' I heard t'crack of your knee as you went down."

Unless he were to reveal entirely what was in his mind, Adam's only course was silence. As it was, however, Blind Kit drew nearer to the matter subsequently when, outside Bucker Level again, they sat for a smoke on a pile of beech planks near the dressing-floors, facing Winterings Gill and the rich hue of afterglow.

"Now, Adam lad," he began, "it doesn't require acute perception for onnybody to realise as you're chafing . . . because you can't credit why a certain grievous mistake i' mining were made. Is that so?"

"Dead on the nail, Kit."

Nodding slowly, the blind man continued: "All reight then. Well, I'll tell you one thing, though whether it's concerned either wi' the Short Cut or the New Drift they're wagering about I can't say. It's just this, Adam, that for months I've been conscious that summat unusual were in th'air. I've never been anywhere near to putting my finger on what it were, but t'feeling has been with me."

For a while longer, without gaining any ground on this particular point, they discussed mining problems and then were agreeing that a visit to the Plug and Feathers would nicely wind up the evening when the cobbler had an afterthought.

"Harking back to th'other matter, Adam, though I can't conceive there's any relation," he began, "I've just remembered a little incident as occurred noan so very far from here, one night last winter when I were tramping home after preaching at Stone Gayles, away over the tops beyond Great Barg. It were a real raw night, and late an' all . . ."

Vividly he described the journey through the clouds—over exposed mountainous shoulders to trods skirting bogs. At Joss Foss, where frozen mist had glazed the surface of the steep path alongside, he had been compelled to sit down and, Bible and Prayer Book tucked beneath his arm, shuffle downwards from top to bottom.

"Sound travels on nights like that, Adam," he laughed, "an' at Notion Bridge I stopped, to count Greets Church clock striking eleven, and to brush off the bits o' shale and muck plastered on my behind. "But . . ." he sobered, "I heard summat besides the clock . . . first a chink o' what I took to be metal, an' then voices."

"What did you make it out to be, Kit?" Adam asked.

"To begin wi' I thought it were some of the Cooper lot, trying to nick old brass bearings," the cobbler replied. "But it weren't . . . I heard all three of 'em when I reached the village—they live i' Dirty Bottom, you know, th'other end of Calvert's Wynd fro' me."

"Aye," said Adam. "And did you do owt then?"

"Just listened carefully," the blind man told him. "But I never heard another whisper."

"At eleven o'clock on a Sunday night." Adam frowned. "About what date were it, Kit?"

"The first Sunday in November," the cobbler answered without hesitation. "I'se always planned for Stone Gayles Chapel then."

There seemed little likelihood of a sinister connection between the mining projects of the West Side Company and stray voices heard through the mist of a November night. But as it happened Adam was aware that Titus Alderson had, on Guy Fawkes' Day the previous year, taken the first practical steps towards starting the Short Cut, a survey about which many others would have known in advance. As he and his companion walked down Sleety Slape he was considering these things.

4

On the opening day of September, not sufficiently appeased by the delivery of one shattering blow in the morning, fate launched a second crushing stroke against the West Side Lead Mining Company. By evening, Main Street hummed with news, rumours, and surmise about the two-fold disaster: the flooding of the North Sun Vein Ground as a result of the final collapse of the old pump at Maybe Shaft, and the decision to suspend further driving of the New Drift, a trial soon to be known more generally as 'Alderson's Folly.' It was reported at first-hand that Titus Alderson, when discharging the drivers of the Folly, had admitted a mistake in direction.

In the Plug and Feathers, where Mrs. Peacock was more watchful for misdemeanours than ever before, the winners of bets boisterously celebrated from their spoils. For others it was no festive occasion, every West Side man appreciating that, with only Mary Forehead Ground producing ore, their Company was in a desperate plight. It was widely realised, too, that Mr. Wade, the chairman, meant exactly what he had said a year before, when he vowed that never again, under any circumstances, would he provide additional capital. The general body of shareholders, each liable for a call of eight pounds on every share, shivered in their shoes.

* * * *

The next afternoon, unexpectedly, Adam met his cousin, coming face-to-face with her in the midst of children who were swarming round a ragman's handcart at Nick Turn.

"You've got back!" he ejaculated. "An' aren't I glad to see you."

Agnes Pedley looked worse than before, the purple shadows beneath her eyes more pronounced. When he spoke she shrank back, retreating so far into the weed-overgrown, junk-bestrewn quoits-court of the Golden Lion that, rather than escaping it, she attracted attention, becoming a figure of interest to a group of West Side groovers, dressing-floor and crushing-mill men, assembled there to discuss the situation.

"Well, now then, lass," Adam resumed when she halted, "I want to talk to you about myself, an' then we'll deal with your troubles if you'll let me. You remember the last time I saw you, when I came into your bedroom . . ."

She closed her eyes and, swaying a little, rested her cheek against his arm, an action causing an ore-picker lad to snigger.

"I *am* tired, Adam," she murmured.

"I'm sorry, lass, but I'll soon get this over," Adam sympathised. "In fact we can finish my part off in a twinkling if you'll go wi' me to Old Hannah and tell her exactly what happened that night."

"I'm not," she said swiftly. "Why should you take me to anybody?"

Adam became more imperative, with consequences far from those he intended. "Listen, lass, there's a lot o' folks believes——"

Drawing a deep breath, she broke in: "I'm noan staying here any longer, Adam, an' if you've got to talk to me it'll have to be where it's right quiet. If my father caught me wi' you he'd . . . he'd make me take all my things off and . . . and he'd slash me with his leather belt."

"He'd what, lass?" Adam asked, aghast.

She was edging away. "So if you want to meet me it must be somewhere where he never is. He's going to my Uncle James's, to-night, I do know."

"Bloody Sigh then, at half-past seven," said Adam.

"I daren't," she shivered. "Juniper Wood 'ud be better."

"That'll do," Adam nodded. "I'll be there, lass."

Piteous entreaty filled her blue eyes. "Will you go afore me, Adam? So as nobody'll be any wiser."

"All right," Adam promised. "An' we'll take all care, so don't be so scared, lass."

He stayed behind sufficiently long to ensure she was well out of the way, and then returned to Main Street, where every massive stone chimney was occupied as a post of vantage by a swarm of loudly chattering starlings.

In the shop Old Hannah was reckoning up the monthly bill of a woman whose most remarkable feature was a thin and excessively prominent nose. "Now there were the sovereign as I loaned you, Connymarie, an' offen that is four dozens' worth of eggs you brought in," she was saying. "Then there's t'goods."

Adam loitered, as much as ever unable to understand his landlady's method of accounting. One thing only had he gleaned, that the emblem she first drew represented the customer's identity, in this instance the head of a curlew with long, narrow beak.

"Aye," she murmured, finger pausing now and then upon the slate, against scrawled little pictures: amongst them a beech leaf, candle-snuffer, sheep's horn with brand, pig of lead, and a monk's ewe-milk cheese. "Aye, sugar crystals, oatmeal, Turkey Rhubarb, an' Candy Lemon. Then . . ." her lips framed numerals, sometimes everyday ones and sometimes those used by shepherds since the Celts withdrew to the hills. "Then a quarter stone o' currants, that's a pussycat an' a half wi' a button off . . . Syrup, that's a lad's taw, making altogether a couple o' Hanover Georges wi' a button off . . . mmm, a quarter o' figs—did they shift her, Connymarie?"

"They did that," affirmed the customer.

"Nowt like 'em, them an' prunes," Old Hannah nodded.

When the balance was struck at twenty-nine shillings and fourpence ha'penny, with the coppers off 'for luck,' Adam went into the kitchen, slightly better informed perhaps.

"Yes," he smiled, "I think a ha'penny is a button, and Hanover George is a recruit's shilling. But I'll listen again."

The shop-bell rang and, as its echoes died, Mrs. Batty briskly entered the kitchen. Over tea, he told her about Agnes, but she did not pronounce until later, when he was smoking in her husband's comfortable chair and she, sucking bull's-eyes, rocked opposite.

"Daft, you having to trail right up to Juniper Wood, but I can well see that if you'd over-pressed her she'd maybe have screamed her head off. Yes, you go, Adam, and quietly persuade her to come back wi' you an' tell the truth to a few folk."

"Aye," Adam sighed. "The trouble is that she's in a mortal funk about her father, and," there was quick anger in his eyes, "I'm noan surprised."

Severity clothed Hannah Batty's face. "Maybe so, lad, but justice to others comes afore owt else. Perhaps she will catch it, though we'll do us best to restrain Ambrose Pedley——"

The shop-bell clanged but, before the carrier's cheery voice rang out, Old Hannah had spied his vehicle through the peep-hole. With ample time before him, Adam assisted in lifting indoors kegs of lard, boxes of soap, tins of mustard, and other stores.

Up Sleety Slape, some distance below the West Side Company's octagonal-shaped Powder Magazine, a massive, stone building whose windows were permanently walled-in, Adam rose from a grassy bank. Before continuing upwards, he gazed once again both at the glowing red expanse of creeper covering Modesty and at a wall which at close hand revealed its many hues, the limestone and freestone in shades of grey from pale dove to medium, in tints of pink to browns ranging from light buff to sepia, a harmony embellished with the verdant tones of mosses and lichens.

"Full o' colour," he murmured, glancing at clusters of bright red berries alongside Winterings Gill. "But nowt sticks out somehow . . . it's soft, an' even when there are splashes, like on that rowan, they fit in."

It was a lovely evening, an evening when there should have been as much harmony amongst men as there was in the beauties of nature, but as Adam reached the traps and horses tethered near the South Smelt Mill there was unpleasant discord. It was evident that the special meeting of directors, hastily called to deliberate the disastrous position of the West Side Company, had had a protracted sitting. But the movement of feet suggested that business had been completed, this being borne out by the appearance at the office door of Mr. Wade, Mr. Rutter and the Company's Secretary, Lodge Trotter. Behind them were the agent, a Greets clock-maker and Mr. Hird, the single outsider.

Officially business might have been completed, but this did not prevent recrimination being heaped on Titus Alderson's head outdoors by Henry Hird and Screw Tom. As Mr. Plews continued the tirade Adam glimpsed the ashen face of Cherry's uncle.

"If that pair doesn't leave off," he growled, "they'll have summat on their conscience. If ever an old fellow is near dropping it's Mr. Alderson."

Across Winterings Gill, as he left Mine Road to take the trod which followed closely beside the edge of the tall scar stretching to Heugh Syke Gill, Adam began to think of Titus Alderson's problems and, to a much more concentrated degree, about incipient suspicions of his own.

The evening was balmy, the light golden. In a pasture below, a sheep-dog was rounding up cattle, flying in quarter-circles behind to snap at each pair of heels, keeping his charges on the run until, half a field's length from an open gate, he sat down, tongue lolling, permitting the beasts' stampede to slacken lest, in the jostle of thrusting through a narrow passage, a horn might be broken against a stone gate-post.

Slowly, cogitating about Reuben Nattrass, Adam went forward again, gradually drawing nearer to a track down the scar which led to Milton Hall and the low wood of juniper surrounding it, renowned and favourite place of courting couples for generations.

Though her father was fully aware of what she was doing, Agnes Pedley very nearly dropped the forbidden mirror she had withdrawn from a crack in the floorboards of her bedroom when he shouted to her.

A few seconds later two frightened people were staring at one another, the girl at the top of the flight of steps and the man at the bottom. Both faces were in semi-gloom, Ambrose Pedley's a pallid blob which caught such light as there was on fevered eyes and moist lips, his daughter's, doll-like as ever beneath its canopy of palest gold, shadow-etched with new lines, of sharpness and resolve.

"I'm going now," Ambrose Pedley said, a tortured groan slipping from him as he fumbled for a cap. "I'll . . . I'll noan be back till late."

As the outer door closed Agnes was trying to view herself in a totally inadequate piece of silvered glass. Next, the twisting and contortions ended, she liberally sprinkled perfume on her coat and in the opening of her bodice, shuddering as the cold drops trickled down the valley between her upthrusting breasts; and, as afterthought, she raised her long skirts, to shake the scent on her drawers.

"There!" she said, spots of excitement colouring her alabaster-like cheeks as she inspected herself again, "I shouldn't shame anybody, not even t'lasses in Spain, them whose fathers addle real good money every Pay." Her expression changed when, unseeingly, she stared out of the window. "I must, I *must*," she murmured, her fingers clenching tightly. "I must make it so he has to take me back wi' him, away from here."

When, after a while, her breathing became quieter, she left the desolate bedroom and went determinedly down the stairs.

If a young girl, the subject of considerable gossip, reappears as suddenly as she has been whisked away, it is natural she should be scrutinised. Still more is she likely to be remarked about if, on an evening when no social event offered anywhere, she walks out in her most precious finery. Even more extraordinary, it was seen by quite a few people at Town Foot that the promenade took her along the lonely highway to Greets.

She was observed in Half, too, by the families of Luther Thwaites and Freestone John. And, last but not least, she was perceived from Half Common by a young woman milking there. When the well-turned-out little figure began to climb a rough and precipitous track Annamaria Rutter's reaction was prompt. She picked up pail and stool, to scurry home, where her voice carried everywhere in the Old Cow Inn. "Arthur, where are you, lad? I want us to go out right off . . ." At that moment Mrs. Rutter intervened, with news that her future son-in-law had gone to inspect Jonas Cottingham's pigs. "Pigs be hanged!" Annamaria retorted. "He'll be propping up t'bar of the Groovers Welcome, but I'll have him out in two shakes of a lamb's tail."

At Milton Hall, Adam, interestingly occupied since the trilling of birds had ceased suddenly, did not hear his cousin's approach over the soft turf. Following the glance of a wren whose bright and tiny eye searched the sky for the enemy, he had rolled on to his back. In that position he discerned the black speck floating above, and caught the hoarse cry of the marauding raven.

"I never heard you, lass," he said, sitting up to ejaculate a surprised: "Well . . ." at her grand appearance.

Agnes smiled sweetly. "That hill!" she protested. "It's like climbing a mountain."

"Sit you down, lass, an' get your wind," he invited her.

She took her time, arranging her skirts carefully after finding a comfortable spot close to her cousin. Gradually she leaned nearer to him, a faint but blissful sound passing her parted lips.

"Eee, I am cosy, Adam," she whispered, looking sideways through long lashes. "It's so nice to be up here wi' you, just us two."

Adam, astonished enough already, was roused by a piercing whistle. "Well, lad." Arthur Nattrass grinned, obviously prepared to stop, until Annamaria savagely jerked his arm. "Enjoying yourself, eh?"

"Go on wi' you, Arthur," Agnes pouted. "Interfering thing that you are."

As the couple disappeared along a pathway leading to Sorrow Near, Annamaria's tight mouth implicit of her belief, Adam turned to his cousin, his face at its most disquieting.

"Now what do you think you're up to?" he demanded.

"Me, I'm up to nowt," she replied. "'Cept to enjoy myself."

"But I'm not here to enjoy myself, lass," Adam retorted. "I'm here to talk to you about——"

Roguishly she glanced at him. "We can talk about that later, can't we, Adam? Why shouldn't we have a bit o' fun aforehand, like a young man an' a young woman does when they're out together. Oh aye, I'm a woman now, Adam, whatever you think, an' . . ." gulping in another supply of air she went on, even more rapidly, "an' I've right looked forward to being wi' you to-night . . . why have I put on all my nice clothes if it weren't for you? Everything you bought me."

His mouth even more grim than before, Adam eyed her. He was convinced he had estimated the situation, and that left him with a very sickly feeling.

"You have, have you?" he commented.

"Everything," she declared, loosening her coat to display the scented bodice, raising skirts appreciably to show her stockings. "Yes, everything, Adam, including th'underclothing you gave me. But . . ." she added tantalisingly, " that's summat you haven't seen, isn't it?"

"It is," Adam agreed.

She gazed at the toe of her shoe, which she started to waggle. "Leastways not *on*," she murmured, a secretive smile on her lips.

"Nor at wash-day, to my knowledge, either," Adam said briskly. "Now no more o' that, Agnes, and listen to me. Do you know your father's saying summat took place between you an' me that night in your bedroom? Well, it is so, and that's why I want you to tell one or two folk that nothing did."

Her tone became less soft. "I'm talking to nobody," she proclaimed.

Adam was now standing. "Why not?" he asked.

"Because nobody believes a young woman i' things like them, because it's nobbut to be expected she'd deny 'em."

"I see," said Adam. "In that case what would you do if you were me—leave everything be?"

She was perfectly still, the only sign of emotion a slight flush. "No, I shouldn't," she admitted.

"What would you do then?" Adam persisted.

The pause was even longer. "I . . . I think I should do what everybody reckons I have done . . . if the lass were willing, that is."

"Aye," Adam nodded. "An' would you be willing?"

In less cruel circumstances Agnes Pedley's prim reply would have been laughable. "That's noan the way a chap should go about things with a young woman," she informed him.

Adam Brunskill's voice cracked like a whip. "Get up," he ordered her. "I'm taking you straight to Back Lane."

For a brief spell, until the completeness of her failure sank home, she stared at him. "I'm noan going," she screamed then, her eyes wild. "I'm noan, noan going."

It was the beginning of a nightmare journey. For periods she was quiescent, but at others unrestrained. Where the byway curved through coarse grazings before joining Mine Road, she refused to budge and, nothing else left, Adam used force. That was when, his eye caught by a striped poplin dress, he glimpsed Cherry and Dinah near Pewitt Pillar.

Down the walled-in part of Sorrow Near, Agnes was no worse than sullen, but, as if she had conserved her energy for the purpose, she gave a superb exhibition at Town Foot. Screeching, beating her fists against Adam's chest, the progress of the couple towards Jom High Road was watched by a round dozen people.

From the middle of Dolly Bridge, Adam saw Cherry and Dinah crossing the Hippy Stones. "They can't abide going through Dirty Bottom, so they must have seen this carry-on—and be avoiding me," he muttered. "All right," he promised himself, "when I've got shut o' this little devil my first call's at Yew Tree House."

In Back Lane, Mark Iveson was sitting outdoors and never were two men more relieved than when Mrs. Iveson, a few minutes later, arrived from the village and persuaded the girl to enter her own home.

Adam's limbering walk soon took him to Town Foot, where a throng now four-fold greater heard Mrs. Roberty Will, outward bound, try to arrest his further progress at the gate set between lofty, tapering yews.

"If your calling here has owt to do wi' that young woman as house-keeps for my brother-in-law I can save your legs," she snapped. "She wants nowt more to do with you."

"I'd prefer her to tell me so herself," Adam retorted.

Accompanied by Sambo, who had been taking his usual evening airing, he went up the flagged path. After rapping with the gleaming knocker, he was left to cool his heels awhile before the door opened. Cherry's cheeks were pale and it was evident she had been crying.

"Can I come in to talk to you, lass?" Adam asked.

She gulped, made an effort to say something, then shook her head. "No . . . no," she managed at last. "I . . . I can't ask you in."

"That 'ul do for me," Adam said, swinging about.

On the footpath, immediately outside the gate, Reuben Nattrass pulled him up, to advise him to keep away from that house and from the young woman who lived there.

"Have you authority to speak for her?" Adam growled.

The mine-agent cogitated. "Strictly speaking, I can't say as how I have, but——"

Seldom did Reuben Nattrass's words fall upon thin air, but on this occasion that occurred. Adam was already striding through a crowd of people who instinctively opened their ranks on seeing his expression.

The same expression caused Hannah Batty to push aside the ingredients for the herbal cough mixture she had been contemplating preparing for winter demands. "Noan gone so well, has it, lad?" she inquired.

"Neither for me nor that cousin o' mine," Adam replied. "You see, for her, I wasn't inclined to start what a lot o' folk supposes I've already done."

Mrs. Batty, though deeply grieved, did not appear wholly surprised. "Human nature's queer, isn't it? You never can tell how they'll behave, can you?" she murmured.

Adam sat down. "Seems I'm in a bigger mess than even I thought."

The old lady stirred. "Is she wi' child, do you think?"

"I've wondered," Adam answered.

Old Hannah snorted. "I shan't be wondering as soon as I've set eyes on her. An' then if it's necessary we can begin going into t'question of who's getten her into trouble."

"Aye, there's that," Adam muttered.

Over supper of buttered currant tea-cake, cheese and jam pasty, with cocoa, thick and very sweet, he pondered about the situation in general. Once the question had been whether his future should be in Skewdale, but now incontestably he must remain until he had cleared himself, which might well take months, and consequently raised another matter. It was September already and if he were not returning to Spain when expected he was under an obligation to inform his employers.

The shop-bell rang twice, to announce the arrival and the quick departure of a very late customer. When Old Hannah returned Adam mentioned his thoughts.

His landlady was incensed, but in another direction. "Two penn'orth o' treacle, indeed," she scoffed, blowing at the taper she had carried out. "For nobbut else but to quiz me about you. I asked her who she thought she were stuffing an' I sent her off to buy her treacle where she always does, fro' Cuthbert Daykin." Having relieved outraged feelings, she told him he was welcome to lodge with her as long as he wished.

Fetching writing materials from his bedroom, Adam wrote three letters on the kitchen table, the first, of a few lines, to the London office of the London and Andajoz Lead and Silver Mining Company requesting them to transfer all his funds, both lodged with them and at the mines, to Messrs. Richardson & Storey, at Corvy. The remaining two were addressed to Spain, one to Mr. Phillips regretfully tendering his resignation for private reasons, and the other, the longest and most difficult, to Jane Sunter, for herself, Simon and Daniel, explaining bluntly why he must stay in Winterings for an indefinite period.

"Well, that's the beginning o' that," he muttered, sealing the envelopes. "Nowt much more I can do about it just now, but there is another affair I can start doing summat about.... I say, Hannah, have you any objection if I'm oft out in the night? I'll use the back-door. The truth is that I've got some sort o' vague idea about the cause of Titus Alderson's troubles, an' I'm of the mind to look into it."

Old Hannah glanced over the bowl of her pipe. "You have, have you? An' so that's why you've been in a trance. Aye, you can be a night-rake as much as you please so long as you don't disturb me when you come in. I reckon it's due to taking care," she went on with some complaisance, "that I'se as I am."

"Yes, you're one for coddling yourself an' troubling about nobody," Adam laughed. "Anyroad," he became serious, "I'm off to-night. My farming clothes 'ul do for me till I can bring my others down from the changing shop."

"You're stopping for th'East Side Company?"

Adam nodded. "As soon as I've finished my bargain with Freestone John. Aye, I've plenty to do otherwise . . . have you any groovers' thread, by the way?"

Once there had been a constant inquiry for this yarn and Mrs. Batty believed she might still have a few hanks in stock. Adam was advised to take the lamp and rummage in an old box supporting one end of the board on which the biscuit tins were piled.

When he returned, his search successful, a beam of pure pleasure had settled on Old Hannah's face. "No, I'm sickened enough for your sake about th'Agnes business," she explained very sincerely. "It's nobbut that what wi' one thing an' another I reckon I've yet another thrill or two afore I totter through t'white portals. Oh, I'll keep it all to mesen, don't you forget, an' I'll noan ask you any questions about your notions to do wi' Titus Alderson either. And you're really going underground to-night?" Rising concern dispelled some of her animation. "You'll be all alone, too. My words, lad, do be careful."

An hour and a half afterwards, the only sounds those of night creatures, the stirring of a horse, or the distant lowing of a beast, Adam Brunskill slipped through the darkness to the tail of Bucker Level.

Every minute of the day had been wretched for Cherry, her heart aching for her uncle. After tea she went to Badger Hall, where, the dairy swilled out, Dinah was at liberty. As it was such a fine evening they sat in the battlemented garth until it was time for Cherry to leave, when her friend decided to walk with her part way on Middle Sorrow. Just before reaching Droughty Tom's cottage Dinah remembered that her sister-in-law was at Mr. Kearton's, cleaning down for him, and so it seemed sensible to go round by the village to call for her. In a trice, though, she changed her mind.

"I'm *perfectly* all right, silly," she replied, still flustered, when questioned. "Nay, it's nobbut that I think I'll turn back after all. But you come with me, say as far as Silence."

Cherry was plainly perplexed. "Are you sure there's nothing up?"

" 'Course there isn't," Dinah retorted, too loudly.

The first impact of shocking discovery can be brutal. Cherry, the little colour she had in her cheeks fading, breathed a faint "Oh!" when, chancing to glance across the narrow dale, she noticed Adam. Before the couple passed from sight she saw that he was holding his cousin tightly to him.

"Let's go back, lass," Dinah begged.

A dogged argument began, in which Cherry's resolution ultimately won the day. Dinah, however, would not abandon her friend, but her nerve failed entirely near Back Lane. "We shall meet him wi' her, Cherry," she gasped. "Come on down to the river an' cross the Hippy Stones."

Her brown eyes were so imploring and the tug she gave Cherry so imperative that a tired brain refused to function as well as it might. But in Calvert's Wynd, against the weed-overgrown Roman Catholic graveyard, Dinah made a remark which brought matters to a head.

"I couldn't bear to look at him," she explained, "not after we've stuck up for him as we have. And they'd been at Milton Hall I'm certain."

Great trouble reflected itself in Cherry Dinsdale's vivid face. "We've made an awful mistake, Dinah," she faltered. "He'd spy us from Dolly Bridge and guess we were dodging him."

"But . . . but," Dinah stammered, "you don't believe in him now, do you?"

"Yes . . . yes, I do." Cherry bit her lip. "There'll be an explanation, you'll see. You know, Dinah, it's a long way from Pewitt Pillar to where they were and you couldn't properly tell."

Nevertheless, at Town Foot, much that had been observed at close quarters was being related greedily within earshot of the two girls. Fronick, from her workroom window, had watched Adam, as she termed it: "hugging his cousin i' Jom High Road." But the outstanding informants were Annamaria Rutter and her young man.

"That's just how it were, Reuben old cock," Arthur Nattrass guffawed, slapping the mine-agent's shoulder. "Just how it were."

"I've never had a doubt about yon two," Annamaria bragged.

"They're lovers all right, so let's leave it at that, lass." Arthur Nattrass summarily dismissed the episode but continued to talk about it. "Aye, lovers, Reuben . . . you get what I mean? If you could have heard how Agnes sort of let me know that two's the best company, like . . . phew!"

Cherry glimpsed a dignified but rather top-heavy figure emerge from the gates of Malaga. The largest shareholder in the West Side Company, with a hundred and seventy-five shares, Mrs. Robert William Alderson had virtually lived in Yew Tree House since the disasters of yesterday. After this latest and most terrible thing it was more than Cherry could endure to listen to her again. Hastily whispering good night to Dinah, she slipped away.

Anxious when her uncle did not respond, Cherry peeped into the office, called upstairs, and then, surmising that Ben might be receiving his nightly sugars, hurried outdoors by the back way.

Eventually she found Mr. Alderson in an outbuilding behind the peat-place, beyond a studded, oaken door she had never seen open before. In front of him, in three piles, soft-gleaming pigs of lead were stacked, each pig with a hart in relief upon it, the signature of the long-forgotten Hart Mining Company, predecessors of the B.G. Mining Company of Greets.

"Now then, love," he smiled, "this'll be a surprise for you. The family fortune, eh? It's part o' what my grandfather left. You see, lass, in his day th'old groovers distrusted the banks, and so they put their savings into lead an' kept it beneath their own roofs. Aye, and I've never thought of selling till this year."

"Are you going to, Uncle?" she asked.

After a while, heavily, he replied: "No, lass, it's too late now. Last week I were, after me and Sam Kirkbride agreed that th'old pump at Maybe were on the point of dropping to bits. So I divided the pigs into three—there's over fifteen ton altogether—one lot that 'ud never be touched, to bring you a bit o' brass when owt happened to me, another to have by us for emergencies . . ."

Cherry saw the drawn face and the tired shoulders. Eyes pricking, she remembered how his savings had been used to one unselfish end while he, whose honourable retirement should not have been far away, allowed himself only a few pennies for pocket money, insufficient to gratify even his simple pleasures. Only dimly did she hear him say that, since the beginning of the year, lead had advanced in price from thirteen pounds to seventeen pounds a ton, which, for a third of the pigs, would fetch a little above eighty pounds when expenses were paid.

"Wi' that, lass, I were going to order a brand new pump," he said. "And buy other small necessaries."

"Why don't the directors do summat, instead o' leaving it all to you, Uncle?" she asked.

Titus Alderson's smile was tortured. "Because I'm the man wi' all the confidence. Oh, they've been above board enough with their opinions."

She slid her arm through his. "Don't take on so, Uncle. You've still plenty of good and true friends."

"Aye, I have, Cherry lass," he said. "But when a chap who's always been proud of his profession knows his reputation is sullied for ever . . . there's nowt much left for him."

His eyes welled and, as a tear-drop slowly lengthened on his grey cheek, Cherry quietly began to cry, too, dispirited by the cloud shadowing him, gnawingly oppressed about Adam. Closely they remained together, a nautical-bearded old captain who was watching a loved ship sink beneath his stricken sight, and a slim girl who was the first to fight out of despair.

"Well . . . well, I feel a lot better for that, Uncle Titus," she declared, busy with her handkerchief. "But I reckon it's time we went back into t'kitchen, don't you, and behaved ourselves?"

Heroically he endeavoured to follow her example. "It's me who ought to be ashamed, lass, a grown man blubbering. Now then, you'll noan tell on me, will you?"

Cherry tossed her head. "It depends on how you go on now."

Shocked, Mr. Alderson clicked his tongue. "So you're holding my weakness over me, are you? A nice thing that."

She left him then, and was able to complete her preparations in the kitchen before he arrived. His chair had been drawn up, and on a table alongside were a tobacco jar, churchwarden pipe, tumbler, glass jug filled with water, and, hitherto sternly hoarded, peaty-coloured Scotch whisky.

"Well . . ." he murmured. "Aye, I think I will for this once, lass."

"I've gone extravagant all of a sudden," she announced. "But if I run short I shall know what to do. If you see me staggering out wi' a pig of lead tucked under each arm . . ."

Unfortunately, in arranging for her uncle's comfort, Cherry forgot the one essential, privacy, and so, while liquid gurgled from a bottle, Mrs. Robert William Alderson was able to enter without hindrance. She interpreted the scene in a single comprehensive glance.

"Drowning your sorrows i' drink, I see," she remarked. "Well, it's more than some poor folk wi' shares in t'West Side Company 'ul be able to do."

But her visit, primarily anyhow, was concerned with Adam Brunskill, about whom she brought her brother-in-law fully up to date.

"Well, you've had your lesson even if you've had to weep afore learning it, young woman," she said, rounding on Cherry. "Maybe in the future you'll noan be as anxious to speak to him as you have been."

Cherry's deathly pallor far more than a sip or two of whisky may have emboldened Titus Alderson. "No lass who thinks owt of herself 'ul have anything to do wi' a young fellow who, as now seems likely, has done the terrible thing to his cousin we've heard of," he said. "But let it drop, Ellen, because I want no more on it."

In a fine tantrum at this snub, Mrs. Roberty Will's first trenchant stroke was a reference to a conversation she had had with her brother, who, she bitingly reminded them, would fulfil his duty to Sir Charles irrespective of the loss she might sustain.

"Oh, yes, even though he knows I'd have to sell two-three good farms to pay for a total call on my shares, for that's what it may come to."

"Mary Forehead Ground's still working, Ellen," Titus Alderson said.

"Mary Forehead!" his sister-in-law shouted. "If you'd bought a new pump instead o' wasting brass in dead-work, the North Sun Vein wouldn't be flooded to-day, an' that's better than Mary."

Titus Alderson was breathing with difficulty. "I did what I did because the Company needed a good big new discovery. And you seem to forget anyroad that in th'early days I provided some of the money for driving the New Drift out o' my own pocket."

"Yes, an' how much?" Mrs. Roberty Will laughed.

"Maybe not much . . . to you . . . Ellen, but a fairish bit for . . . a chap like me," Mr. Alderson gasped.

"And how were it t'New Drift missed Doomsday High Shaft?" his critic demanded.

Feebly he shook his head. "I don't know, Ellen."

Sweet mouth and lovely eyes furious, Cherry was about to intervene when the older woman, her harangue ended, flung towards the passage door. Mrs. Roberty Will, however, left an ominous hint behind her.

"Well, somebody may have a go at finding out," she rapped. "Henry says as Lodge Trotter were talking about t'question of proceedings against you for negligence, *criminal* negligence."

When she had gone Titus Alderson shakily set aside pipe and drink, alike tasteless to him. With his head resting against the antimacassar, he lay back. After a time he whispered: "Criminal proceedings . . . an' neither she nor Henry Hird realises that even summat awful like that doesn't make me sweat . . . because I'se so hurt within myself already that I'm nearly dumb."

Gently Cherry touched his shoulder. "Come on, Uncle Titus, sup up t'rest of that whisky and——"

The knocker resounded, a sharp signal which roused him from his apathy. "Go see who's there, lass, but . . . but don't let anybody in, whosoever it is," he begged. "I'll be better in t'morning but just now I can't stand owt else, whether it's nastiness or sympathy."

"I won't, Uncle," Cherry soothed him.

She hastened across the red-striped matting, using her handkerchief to remove, as she hoped, any stains remaining on her cheeks.

What she said at the front door when confronted by the tall figure of Adam Brunskill she never afterwards properly recalled—all she clearly remembered was a broad back moving away from her in the declining light, towards a gate beyond which a crowd of curious folk waited, with raven-haired Reuben Nattrass at their fore.

"Adam . . ." she cried, but the words died in her throat.

Brokenly she closed the door and, as if dazed, walked down the long passage to her uncle's office. In this seclusion, burying her face in her folded arms, she wept anew, against the cold wall.

* * * *

The next evening when Adam returned from the mine, Old Hannah told him she had been to Back Lane.

"But Agnes has vanished again, lad, just like she did afore."

"I'm not surprised," Adam replied. "I heard one of Ambrose Pedley's partners say he hadn't turned up."

After tea, before snatching some sleep in the chair prior to starting out again on his self-imposed task, he thought longingly of Cherry. The previous night, soon after leaving Yew Tree House, he had become conscious that in his touchiness and haste he had not given her a chance. But now, as he sombrely concluded while staring at the fire, it was all to the good that subsequently he had resisted an impulse to return to her.

Bad as the position had been, it was becoming infinitely worse. For Cherry's sake he must go to extremes he had never contemplated, to the extent, that was it, of deliberately avoiding her.

CHAPTER NINE

I

TOWARDS DAWN on the second consecutive night that Adam trespassed in Bucker Level he traced to their outer limit a line of hexagonal nut-marks. This was in an old working, a cavern with an Old Man's rise out of the roof, and a sump, crumbling sides supported by black, rotting timbers, in the sole. The light from his candle dimly illuminated the place, but carried sufficiently to two tramrails at the farther side of the sump, upon which his glance was riveted.

"Well, there's my ironstone," he growled. "An' there's the most cruel trick a man could have played on him. Aye, they'd attract Mr. Alderson's dial needle, an' throw it off pointing correctly."

Still a shade spellbound, he cautiously walked round the brink of the yawning sump, meantime from the rise, disturbed by vibration, particles tumbled upon his shoulders. On inspection, he soon realised the tramrails were not of standard pattern, neither the solid eighteen pounders used in horse-levels, nor the ten pounders which were adequate for drifts.

"Maybe bought for economy and neither one thing nor the other. But . . ." his mouth momentarily set hard, "good enough for *this* dastardly job."

Crouching groover-fashion, he came to the conclusion that he was assuming too much. The winding route he had followed made impossible an accurate estimate as to how near he was to Titus Alderson's first disastrous essay.

"No, I'll have to dial it to find out, as somebody's had the need afore me," he thought. "An' by!" the twists, turns and other difficulties came to mind, "it'll take some doing, single-handed. Then . . ."

After the survey, he would need to plot the calculations on to a plan in which both Bucker Level and the West Side Company's Notion Level figured. Only in this wise could he establish where the two rails were in relation to the Short Cut.

"I'll have to get plans somehow," he was musing when, in the gloom, he discerned the imprints of many more rails, evidence which brought him quickly to his feet, face again excited. "Why, there's once been a sight o' rails here and they've been shifted. For why? Well . . ." his eyes became steely, "one answer could be that after they'd done their dirty work here they were moved to do dirty work elsewhere, say a spot where Mr. Alderson's dial needle would be affected when he were laying out for the New Drift."

With nothing to detain him further he started homeward, muttering: "Aye, I'll bottom that, too," before edging through a partially collapsed drift, from whose fore end he followed his line of yarn through an eerie wilderness until he reached a cross-cut. There he picked up the thread on the sole and, breaking it, began to wind the remainder into a ball as he progressed. Once he paused to examine an old powder-can with measuring cap on top, but otherwise did not dally.

Up to a point Blind Kit had been absolutely right in his statement that, from Wild Goose Shaft, no advance westward could be made. The outlet was some fifty fathoms farther back and, as Adam drew nearer to the Black Drift, he resolved that when in due course he attempted to strike out from Blind Trial Crosscut he would seek first an outlet at the beginning of Freezeland, not from Whistling Shaft in the middle.

That morning he had less than two hours in bed, and Old Hannah showed her caustic side at breakfast, when she thrust a steaming plate of porridge at him. "If you'd rather have brown Demerara wi' it you can fetch it from t'shop. An' how long are you going to work night an' day?"

"This finishes it," he promised.

He had enough wisdom not to indulge in an outsize yawn until the shop-bell rang above his head as he set off for work.

Adam's last day with Freestone John was quite uneventful until he and his partner were knocking off work, when the clapper at Toft Rigg Whim Shaft sounded a frantic alarm. The clevis-man, the hooker-on of kibbles, had been drawn about forty-five fathoms up the shaft, possibly the result of standing with a foot inside a bight of rope while shifting the clutch-lever of the waterwheel. He was hanging upside down, held only by a turn around one ankle, and his cries were becoming faint. As starting the machinery might jerk him free, men with ropes and timbers suspended from their belts swarmed up the climbing-way. Eventually he was secured and hoisted out of the eye.

Adam and a few more had arrived late at the scene, their nerve-racking part that of impotent onlookers.

"Well, friend," Freestone John remarked as he, in company with a small crowd, splashed along Martha Water Gate, "that's ended better nor it might."

One other must have been intolerably affected by the suspense, for, as Adam replied, bright steel flashed past his head and a pick-point shivered in the side of the level. Spinning round, he grasped his assailant before another attack could be framed. "Now then," he said, "what's all this about?"

"You!" Ambrose Pedley screamed. "You as never so much as sunk on your knees to pray for that chap, you who's brought my poor little lass to ruin. Aye, I've known since this morning."

"Known what?" Adam snapped.

From a clay-joint in the zinc air-pipes in the roof of the level there was an insistent hiss. Against this background someone laughed harshly. "What a few more knows, Brunskill. If you're all that ignorant you an' him should have a talk together, private like."

Adam saw the hostility in the faces about him.

"Seemingly so," he agreed. "Well, we've a retreat here that's handy." Undeterred by warnings more awed than threatening, he rushed Ambrose Pedley into the nearby cross-drift, the candle flames on their hats laid horizontally with the speed. Along its bends they went until far removed from intrusive spectators.

"Lone Crosscut!" the older man gasped. Glance darting from side to side, mouth open, he stared affrightedly. "Lone Crosscut," he repeated.

"Why don't you call on the God you so oft invoke against others?" Adam inquired. "Surely he'd protect you against a Partnership o' spectres going about their endless trials."

A long shuddering sigh escaped Ambrose Pedley, his head dropped. "O God, help me, give me succour, Jesus . . . protect me, Joseph, the husband o' Mary, Mary th'Immaculate, th'Immaculate, *Immaculate*," he whispered before fainting.

Adam carried the lay-preacher back to Martha Water Gate, staying there with him until he had revived. Then, his jaw relentless, he trudged towards Old Wife Shaft and the tail of the level.

In the changing shop, where sudden silence fell upon his entry, he singled out the individual who had been spokesman below. "Pedley weren't able to explain," he told him. "So you'd better."

"Get somebody else as is willing to speak to you," the groover growled.

Adam took a step nearer. "I said . . . *explain*. What is it he's known since this morning?"

"That he's t'father of a lass who's carrying your child," the other shouted.

"Who's telled him that?" Adam demanded.

Fatal words dripped into the attentive air. "She did."

Quietly Adam changed and, bundling mine rags, went into the dull evening to search for the clerk, who was checking the loading of one of William Nattrass's carts with pigs of lead. At the opposite side of the gill there was activity also, for, whatever the fate of the West Side Company might be, steps had been taken to ensure that a season's supply of fuel should not be lost. Carts were winding down the tracks on Water Ling Moor and, in the long-extending, open-sided Peat House, men on ladders built summer-dried, hard blocks of peats into tall stacks.

"Well, this business of Agnes's is the last straw," Adam grunted, setting down the tools he was returning to store. "But . . ." his grey eyes glinted as he peered through the open door-way of the East Side Company's office, "this seems to be a golden opportunity in another matter."

Casually entering, he immediately selected a tier of broad drawers for search, finding in them an old plan of Bucker Level, one inch to twenty-two fathoms, with invaluable Ordnance Map references. It was heavily backed with linen, rolled and about four feet long, but Adam, stifling a surveyor's instincts, folded and refolded it into a bulky, square package. Slightly pot-bellied in appearance, he awaited the clerk's arrival.

Later, on Notion Bridge, he met Mazy Bill, down whose cheeks tears steadily streamed.

"He knows about Agnes apparently," Adam murmured. "Aye, an' so does somebody else," he continued when Bart Hugill, who was locking up the West Side Company's office, hastily went inside again. "Well, if friends are going to shun me I've a rare time ahead." Weight was added to this melancholy forecast by four or five persons in Sleety Slape, all ignoring him.

Old Hannah had a visitor, an old gentleman who had met Adam in the Spring. Peg Stephen got up to shake hands. "Well, lad," he said gravely, "I've been looking forward to seeing you again, but I'm sorry it's under . . . er . . . such circumstances, like."

"You've heard then?" Adam said, turning to his landlady.

Old Hannah, who was slicing bacon, pointed a fearsome knife at the scissors sharpener. "I'se heard," she nodded. "An' I'se heard summat else fro' Peg an' all. Your cousin Agnes is wi' kin either at Smollock or Bardy."

Peg Stephen coughed. "I got it offen a game-watcher at t'top of High Straits. I telled you, lad, I knew everything that were going on. Aye . . ." his face screwed up as if he had drunk a sour draught, "aye, an' I telled you a lot besides, didn't I?"

"Never mind that," said Old Hannah, putting essentials first. "You'll be off to see her, lad?"

"First thing in the morning," Adam replied.

"You're stopping in to-night, then," Mrs. Batty declared, wagging the knife again. "You've a rare lot o' rough walking afore you."

While Peg Stephen manifestly withdrew from any participation in the deliberations, she told Adam, with precise instructions about certain hazards, where Smollock and Bardy were, the former at the head of a little fold on Outer Snorr Moor to which Far Yorreldale sent up a narrow green tongue, the latter in the wastes to the east of Virgin Hill. Both were small and poor farms.

Peg Stephen shifted his feet. "He can't go wrong wi' them comprehensive directions," he remarked.

Hands on hips, Old Hannah surveyed him. "What were it I interrupted you i' saying, Peg lad?" she inquired.

His response was airy. "Just summat an' nowt."

Old Hannah laughed. "We know it'll be nowt, lad. But what were it?"

Until chairs were pulled to the table the pair rowed with zest, but then the 'educator,' eyes sparkling at a heaped plate, referred of his own free will to a joke against himself.

"There I were, Hannah, teaching lead-mining to this young fellow. You must have thought me a right know-all, lad."

"What I thought was that I were enjoying myself, Peg," Adam smiled. "My opinion's still the same."

"Aye," Peg Stephen said.

"Now he's your friend for life, Adam," Old Hannah jeered.

The war of words was resumed between the old man and old woman. They were still contending when Adam, much leeway in sleep to make up and an arduous day before him, went to bed.

2

The previous year, at the second collection, George Nattrass was so disturbed by the quality of a proportion of cheeses received into his warehouse that he decided, where certain remote suppliers were concerned, to be on the spot henceforth when his wagons were loaded. On duty for this purpose one morning at a lonely farm, he did not see his dead sister Mary's son until the young man was approaching through a flock of short Scots sheep which, fattened since midsummer, would soon be rounded up for selling. The sight of his nephew, unacknowledged hitherto, crystallised a lugubrious reverie.

"He'd do, and he's never so much as entered my head," he muttered. "A chap who's tried to get half a dozen suits o' clothing for a sovereign down isn't worth much more than what he stands up in, just t'sort to jump at a five-pound note . . . aye, an' I'd go to ten."

George Nattrass, in common with other shareholders of the West Side Lead Mining Company, had disagreeable realities to face, and knew, by favour of his brother William, that the directors were calling an Extraordinary General Meeting.

"H'mm." He scowled. "Yes, no harm in putting out a feeler. Though why ever I were such a dafthead as to take up fifty shares . . ."

In remarking thus George Nattrass overlooked a tendency in himself, which was always to go one better than his older and less successful brother. Until there was an opportunity to speak to his nephew, he brooded upon his predicament.

After an interview sharp on both sides, Adam was leaving the little farm when, round a corner on the dairy side, he met a relative who, to his astonishment, began to speak movingly about the delights of early rising. It was a far cry, however, from the beauties of nature to the matter of negotiating a transfer of shares in a moribund mining company, but, perceiving the gist, Adam cut short the circumlocutory display.

"Now what you're saying is this, isn't it?" he asked. "You'll pay me five pounds if I'll take the shares off your hands?"

"Pay *you*?" George Nattrass's eyebrows went up. "Nay, I were nobbut speaking generally, lad, though of course——"

"Works out at two shillings a share," said Adam. "And for that you'd be relieved of a liability that might, at the worst admittedly, involve you for eighty times as much."

"Eh, lad, that'd be my side," the cheese-factor laughed. "T'other side is that some chap will get brass for nowt, that's what you've to consider."

With many miles of hard walking still before him, Adam was not inclined to linger. "I haven't time to consider owt just now," he said.

His forehead slightly furrowed, George Nattrass watched the young man lithely climb a winding track which led within a couple of hundred yards to the purple-brown edge of the moor above.

"No, he's not so simple, yon," he murmured to himself. "Knows how to behave when it's a question o' raising t'price. Aye, I daresay I should have to go to four shillings with him."

A call of one pound was the smallest of which George Nattrass had ever heard when lead-mining companies were in difficulties, and when he mounted his horse to ride from Smollock, leaving the carter to cover the loaded cheeses, he was very satisfied. Soon he would have extricated himself from an extremely awkward situation.

For nearly three hours Adam did not see a soul as he strode across wild moorland, the only living creatures about him winged game, sheep speckled of face and leg, the curlews whose bubbling cries sounded in the blue sky. The weather was beautiful and, in ideal conditions, he made good time. At one o'clock in the afternoon, on the last high terrace below Silver Seat, he paused awhile to obtain bearings and, this done, stared at the dark gap in the centre of Yorrel Bridge, far away and below.

From there his progress was downwards, and soon he reached old mining regions. On the next great expanse, the purple of which was declining, some sense told him he was not alone. Glancing behind he recognised an old friend padding at his heels, a piebald bitch of multitudinous sporting strains.

"Floss, you old thief in the night," he chuckled. "Where have you come from, eh? And where's your master?"

Together they continued to a deep, narrow gill where, in the beck below, a waterwheel patched with new wood was geared to a drum mounted in a shallow pit. From the winding-drum a rope extended to a head-frame over a shaft up the steep hillside beyond.

"Gull Scar! Looks as if they've finished with the levels and are making trials in real old workings," he was muttering when Matt Tiplady came into sight waving an oil-can.

The poacher shook his head at Adam's question. "Nowt so grand, lad. The fact is, I think, that we've nearly shot us bolt. Anyroad," he suppressed a sigh, "where have you come from, an' where are you off to?"

"Smollock," Adam answered. "I'm on my way to Bardy now."

Whether the other guessed his purpose he did not know, Matt merely remarking that, at this stage, a pot of tea would be welcome. Ten minutes sufficed for the halt, and then Adam, refreshed by the warm sweet drink and the ham sandwiches Old Hannah had made for him overnight, resumed his journey.

Following Matt Tiplady's countrywise directions, he struck upwards towards the line of snow-posts at the summit of Jom High Road. About four o'clock, delayed by a mishap in boggy peat hags, he sighted a small herd of shaggy, Highland cattle. The home of Agnes Pedley's great-uncle was beyond, at the foot of a grey, rocky scree, its pastures despite their poverty an oasis of green amidst the darker moorland hemming them in.

From then Adam used what cover there was, walls if they served, and gullies when available. That morning he had had one experience of the implacability of his cousin's kin.

An elderly woman was in the dairy, repression carved in every lineament of her face. Cautiously Adam withdrew, tip-toeing in his clogs past cow-place and haybarn, which were a continuation of the main structure, until he reached the end of the farmhouse. The first window into which he peered at the front revealed a sparsely furnished parlour, with mildew on the wallpaper; the kitchen was next, where small flames in the grate licked round a log. At first he thought the room untenanted, until he perceived his cousin kneeling on the floor, black-leading the boiler-front. Silently he entered and, once inside, as silently latched the door behind him.

" Agnes," he whispered.

Startled, she jumped up, blue eyes dilating. Her breast heaved and, rising and falling with it, the soiled hand she had placed there.

"Don't be frightened, lass," he told her, keeping his voice low. "I've nobbut come for a quiet talk with you about the situation I'm in and your own . . . well, trouble."

"I . . . I don't know what you mean," she said.

Adam had firm hold of himself. "Let's begin at t'beginning, Agnes," he said. "You're having a baby, aren't you?"

Her lips quivered. "Yes," she gulped.

"Right then," said Adam. "Now, have you told your father as I were responsible?"

She hesitated perceptibly, then shook her head, unable to speak.

"Are you sure you haven't?" Adam persisted.

"Yes," she faltered.

Whether she were lying he could not be sure, but, that avenue unprofitable anyhow, he tried other means. "Anyroad, lass, somebody's responsible, an' so I want you to think of me just as if I were that big brother you once wished I was, so as I can look after you. Who is it, Agnes?"

He just caught her whisper: "I shan't tell."

"But, lass," he urged, "you can't be left to bear the brunt o' this on your own. Some chap should be standing by you, helping you to make t'best of it. Aye . . ." his grimness drew even the stricken girl's attention closely to him, "and I'd see he did, too, or I'd know the reason why. Now won't you tell me his name?"

"No." Her lips framed the word.

"It's Bull Waggott, isn't it, lass?" Adam asked.

It seemed as if a frozen and sorrow-stained face melted into softness. Her eyes closed, she smiled pitifully. "Cecil," she breathed. "No, it's noan Cecil. I . . . I nobbut wish it were."

Whatever had gone before, Adam knew then with full surety that she was speaking the truth, nothing else. "Then who is it, Agnes?" he resumed after this set-back. "You must tell me."

"I shan't say, an' who says I must?" she retorted childishly.

Adam made another effort. "Come, lass," he coaxed her, "we shan't get any forrader at this rate, shall we?"

Already he had had her to himself for longer than he would have believed possible when starting out on the quest that morning, but this privacy now ended. The door-latch clicked sharply and the old woman he had glimpsed in the dairy entered the kitchen, a white-bearded man behind her.

Whitfield Littlefair's thumb jerked towards the yard. "I saw you fro' t'moor, and you'll be that Brunskill," he said. "Get you gone fro' under my roof."

"Not just yet, if you please," Adam replied. "Not until my cousin here says more than she has done."

Without another word of protest, Whitfield Littlefair stretched his hand to a rack, from which he unclipped a shot-gun. When the weapon had been loaded the barrel swung until it trained on the young man, a gnarled trigger finger in position.

"We've been warned as you could bend her to your will to make her say what you wanted," the old man began harshly. "But you're noan doing it while she's in my charge. I'se ordering you to leave. Are you going?"

"No," said Adam.

"He's ordering you," Mrs. Littlefair shouted.

Whitfield Littlefair hugged the butt beneath his arm. "When a man no longer has t'strength to guard the decency of his own home by ordinary means," he said threateningly, "he has to use what method he can. In my case it's wi' this gun, what I shoots worse vermin than you with. Now I'm getting on i' years an' if in my justifiable wrath and fear I happened accidentally to fire, I don't think either my Maker or them who judged me 'ud condemn me over hard."

Adam eyed him. "If that's your mind, Mr. Littlefair, you've th'opportunity of proving for yourself what a jury 'ud do. I'm not going, not yet."

As if hardly comprehending, the farmer stared blankly at Adam and then at the shot-gun, the overwhelming arbiter which had failed.

His wife recovered first. "Oh, an' when do you reckon you *are* going?" she inquired shrilly.

"When my cousin has answered just one question I'm putting to her afore you," Adam replied. "If she answers as I trust she will, then, as honest, God-fearing folk, you'll be glad for truth's sake you've let me stop."

Man and wife looked at each other, the sole sound that of Agnes Pedley's sharp intake of breath as she stepped backwards. The old man broke the silence. "If it's nowt else but a plain question you can ask it."

Quietness reigned briefly again. Whitfield Littlefair's hard-eyed glance was directed towards the young man, while his wife's much harder glance rested unwaveringly upon a pretty little creature who had become a fallen woman, who stayed as she was, shoulders strained against the wall, bosom tumultuous.

Adam began gently. "Agnes, when you answer will you do so as you've been taught at Sunday School and Chapel, as your own conscience must tell you you should? Will you, lass?"

She swallowed. "Yes," she whispered.

For Adam, as he knew so well, the next few seconds might either leave him forever under a dreadful cloud or allow him henceforth to travel unhampered towards the girl he loved. His voice strenghtened when he next spoke.

"Agnes," he said, "this is what I'm asking you, afore your great-uncle and aunt . . . and afore God. Am I responsible for t'baby you're having?"

For a short while, only her lips trembling, she remained rigid, and then her face crumpled as she covered it with blackened hands.

"How could you ask me such an . . . an awful question?" she sobbed.

As she fell to the floor, the barrel of the gun swung round towards the door, Whitfield Littlefair's head jerking in the same direction.

"She's said nowt yet," Adam protested grimly.

The old farmer's mouth thinned. "She's said enough," he growled.

Pale beneath his tan, Adam looked down at his cousin, who, writhing in the corner, alternately moaned and mouthed incoherencies.

"Yes, I reckon she has, for such as you," he retorted savagely.

Without another word, he left the house, and, hot with anger, filled with apprehension as to what this terrible thing would mean, started across the moor, following any sheep-track heading more or less in the desired direction, wholly absorbed in personal affairs while passing from wastes to common grazing lands, pastures to meadows, until, upbank from Half, he reached the Skew.

Near a run of water highly esteemed by fishermen the Vicar of Greets was stridently endeavouring to quarrel with a close friend. "Your damned dressing-floors," he raged. "Enough dangerous muck comes down from 'em to poison every fish there is."

Mr. Wade waved a plump hand. "There'll be less pollution in the future," he remarked with some significance. "From the side of Winterings Gill that I'm connected with, anyhow."

Mr. Penrose laughed uncharitably. "Hope your infernal mining company comes to grief, hope it costs you thousands, *thousands.* Here we have some of the finest fishing in Yorkshire—what do you think I accepted the living of a dead hole like Greets for? Eh?"

Dolly Bridge was the nearest point to cross the river, and so Adam, barely noticed by the two fishermen, turned upstream, his thoughts dwelling exclusively upon the one problem. He was absolutely sure Bull Waggott was not to blame for Agnes's misfortune—her poignant wish that the groover had been came too much from the heart for that.

"But if not," he scowled, "who the hell is it? Could it be Mazy Bill for instance? No girl would like to admit she'd been got into trouble by a crazy lad like him."

It seemed highly improbable, he decided. Next, while mentally ticking off the young men she knew, he was diverted by the memory of a little scene in the Market Place of Greets—Agnes's astonishing coquetry with Reuben Nattrass, and how, when she tripped away, a blossoming little figure, the mine-agent had closely watched her.

"All t'same, I don't reckon it's him either," Adam murmured. "But it's somebody. . . . Wingy and Bart are out of the question, I should say, but there's Puke Hastwell's two lads—she oft talked to them. And I remember once seeing her scuffling with Luther Thwaites's youngest brother . . ."

In the days after the cloudburst many people had seemed glad of the company of the man whose determination had been mainly instrumental in saving the stock at Low Bands Farm, but that no longer counted. Feeling certain he was ostracised by his former friends it was fortunate there was important work to occupy Adam's mind. That night he dialled to the west of the Black Drift, and the following night did the same, but left Sunday free.

After Sunday dinner with Old Hannah, Adam sauntered to Bloody Sigh, where in the semi-gloom beneath a belt of oaks he wandered past the moat and cairn before crossing the sorry pasture adjoining, tufty and run to seed because tenants had seldom remained long upon land so ill-omened.

Regaining the path winding along Yorrel Side he met Blind Kit, who, preaching at an outlying hamlet that evening, invited him to walk with him for a while. Climbing the hill together the topic principally on folks' tongues soon was mentioned: the difficulties of the West Side Company, not the more commonplace wronging of a young woman.

"Aye, it's a pity about stopping Titus's New Drift," the cobbler said. "If they could have got to Jamie's Mint it might have made a difference."

"You believe there's ore there?" Adam asked.

His companion laughed. "Well, a groover's allus optimistic. Anyroad, I'll bet this, that if ever your cousin Reuben gets t'West Side under his control as well it'll be the first ground he goes for. Even a smallish discovery 'ud put more solidity behind his company's shares than they enjoy at present."

"Mmm," Adam murmured, thoughtful.

When they reached a point where, on the land sloping towards Yorrelgrain below, cloudberries grew profusely, Blind Kit halted. "Afore my accident, Adam," he said, "I always used to have a breather here, to look fro' Lovely Lady to Silver Seat yonder. It's wonderful, isn't it, lad?"

"Nowt more so," said Adam. "It must be awful not to have your eyes, Kit."

"There's no gainsaying that, lad," the cobbler agreed. "But I have my compensations, you know," he added, smiling. "I always remember things when they were at their very best . . . t'landscape the purest white everywhere . . . or the heather just at its most beautiful . . . a waterfall glittering wi' icicles . . . t'sun sinking over the high moors an' the sky so lovely as to bring a lump into your throat."

Brightened by friendly companionship, Adam eventually turned homewards, glimpsing in pasture, garth and at roadside as he descended evidence that it was the Sabbath. Everywhere, the hour advanced to allow chapel-going, milkers were peacefully occupied.

After tea he washed and brushed himself up.

"You're going then, lad?" Old Hannah asked him a little unhappily. "It's nobbut Lodge Trotter as is preaching."

"I shan't get scalding brimstone thrown at me then," Adam remarked. "Anyway, I'm not hiding from anybody."

"No," his landlady observed. "But it can be awkward for folk o' that sort."

When Adam entered the chapel a host of necks twisted towards him. Previous to this he had been ignored by the Rutters and Blenkirons, young and old, but Cherry, though the pain in her face tugged at his heartstrings, gladdened him with a lovely smile. Later, in the gloom outdoors, while not far away the evening's preacher spoke knowledgeably about the desirability of obtaining in due course a Putative Order in Bastardy, "*In re* yon Brunskill," Adam was encircled by a throng twelve deep who eagerly listened to Agnes Pedley's father and uncle.

"For t'last time are you wedding my lass?" Ambrose Pedley shouted.

"An' you still insist you've noan had carnal intercourse wi' her?" James Pedley persisted, jumping his turn. "Would you swear that on t'Book . . . aye, here it is, take it in your hand. Will you swear now?"

"Aye, I'll swear now or anytime," Adam replied.

James Pedley's breath hissed in horror. "I hope as th'Almighty, in His stern judgment, 'ul cause your hand to rot off for that, t'lying leper as you are."

"Judge not that ye be not judged," Adam remarked. "And good night."

"Aye, go . . ." the Pedleys shrieked.

Using his shoulders, Adam was soon free of the press. When crossing Main Street he passed close to Cherry and her uncle in a darkness relieved only by the dim light from the chapel windows, the candles in houses nearby, and such faint illumination as came from the lamp at Nick Turn.

* * * *

By post the day before, shareholders of the West Side Company had received an official letter from the company's secretary, Lodge Trotter, notifying them that an Extraordinary General Meeting would be held on Thursday fortnight at Half House. In such circumstances many worried people accosted Titus Alderson after Chapel in the hope of gleaning a crumb of comfort. Others, anxious breadwinners, wished to know when there might be a prospect of resuming work.

Near Nick Turn, Mr. Alderson had a conversation which, in deference to the sanctity of the Sabbath, was strangely worded by William Nattrass, who was opening the gate of Ash Grove. "Evening, Titus," he wheezed. "Well, another week starts to-morrow, doesn't it?"

"It does, William," Mr. Alderson said. "Aye, it does."

"Yes, to-morrow horses an' carts 'ul be 'livering coal up to t'mines, taking timber about, bringing machinery parts fro' Corvy station, an' carrying pigs o' lead there an' all," the proprietor of the stables soliloquised.

"An' what about it, William?" the old mine-agent asked, his tone suspicious.

William Nattrass's chins wobbled as reprovingly he shook his head. "Nay, this is noan the day to speak on business matters, Titus," he said. " 'Course, if it'd been to-morrow I could have telled you I wanted my account paying without further delay, an' that I were doing nowt else for you excepting it were cash in advance."

Titus Alderson sighed. "All right, William," he muttered.

Cherry contained herself as long as she could, which was as far as the uninhabited White Hart. "Aye," nodded her uncle when she had expressed fully her feelings about hypocrites. "But when one wolf scents owt, the rest soon gathers round. Nobbut yesterday Henry Hird were at me about the Wood Yard bill. An' he knows we can't keep even Mary Forehead Ground going without timber."

That was Sunday night.

Monday was wash-day, thrice as hard as usual because of the weather's tantalising tendency to promise fair, and then rain sharply awhile.

On Tuesday Mr. Dougill and Mr. Guy drove up from Greets to pay a call upon Titus Alderson. The three friends had a jolly talk, perhaps over jolly, for underlying their seeming high spirits was the knowledge, embarrassing to the visitors and humiliating to their host, that the Directors of the West Side Company had engaged the two seniors to make a report.

On Wednesday it rained again, with obliterating squalls and a wind so fierce as to try frayed nerves. During one of the dry intervals in the late afternoon, Cherry hastened to bring in kindling and peats. She was closing the stick-place door when Nathan Wharton whistled softly from the Saw Mill.

"Watch yon hen-hole, lass," he whispered. "A rat went in just now, an' if it does what it did yesterday . . . well, you'll think I'm t'biggest liar there is unless you see it for yourself."

In due course his veracity was completely established. The rat emerged with an egg, which it energetically rolled with nose and paws.

"Unbelievable, lass." Nathan Wharton grinned, before going his way. "I laugh my sides sore every time I think o' the way it's robbing Puke."

Cherry, her heart nearly breaking, had not smiled much of late, but she was smiling when she heard a thin cry. Curious, she walked towards the river, reaching the tail-race of the waterwheel as the faraway call was repeated. After a while she discerned a figure silhouetted against the dull sky, on the edge of the scar extending from Slackrigg to the moor gate on Jom High Road.

"Mark Iveson! An' here I'm dawdling because he's shouting to his dog," she told herself with disgust as she returned for the buckets.

Mark Iveson's dog, head sideways and bright eyes eager with inquiry, stretched near his master, who was glaring down in exasperation at Pewitt Pillar, where Droughty Tom continued to fill a limekiln with alternate layers of rock and coal.

"He'll noan hear me if I bawl my head off," the shepherd muttered, definitely uneasy. "A thousand to one it's a false alarm, but wi' lasses like her you never know."

Clambering down the scar to the fringe of moor, he set course towards a sloping pasture studded with juniper whose chips had once commanded a good price for fumigation in times of plague. His destination was the Rachel Shafts, in the vicinity of which he had last seen Agnes Pedley.

Mark Iveson had noticed the girl when he straightened after examining a lamb stricken with maggot. Immediately his keen, far-seeing eyes had picked out his neighbour's daughter. She was walking slowly, almost dragging herself along, from the cottage towards the junction with Jom High Road.

"So Agnes is home again," he thought. "An' noan long back either, for she hasn't lighted a fire yet. Maybe off shopping first."

An onrush of flat-driving rain drove both him and dog to shelter behind a boulder of limestone, but the blast was soon over and, as visibility improved, he took a more general view of the Dale. It was only by chance that he glimpsed the same figure in a strange locality, trudging along the line of dead heaps marking old Rachel Shafts.

"Why, she's comed uphill," he puzzled. "An' what in the name o' goodness is she doing i' that spot?"

A wall of cloud racing from the west within a minute brought blinding rain. When the all-concealing curtain at last sailed away he looked at the lengthy line of shafts. Nowhere was Agnes Pedley in sight. He started to shout to Droughty Tom.

Latterly Titus Alderson had been less a man of routine than ever before, so Cherry was relieved about half-past five when she heard the clatter of Ben's shoes. A few minutes later her uncle entered the kitchen.

"What sort of an afternoon have you had?" she smiled.

"Oh, I've been hunting through th'old machinery stored at the Great Deep," Mr. Alderson replied as he tickled Sambo. "But I couldn't find owt that would serve as a makeshift pump for Maybe Shaft."

"Well, never mind your mining problems now," Cherry said. "Just look on the table at what Mrs. Peacock's brought us back. She'd to make an early trip to Corvy."

Titus Alderson rubbed his hands. "My! Soused herrings . . . aye, I reckon I can do justice to them. For that matter," lightly he pinched his niece's soft cheek, "you're fairly partial to 'em yourself, eh, lass?"

Whatever appetite Cherry might have had for this savoury meal she lost within the next moments on learning that Agnes Pedley was missing after returning home by herself from her great-uncle's farm out at Bardy.

" 'Course, she could easily have slipped off somewhere else," her uncle observed, breaking a piece of bread to mop up the tasty pickling liquid. "But if there isn't any news on her soon they're talking about searching t'shafts."

There was no further peace for Cherry that evening, and during the night, while clusters of lanterns along the rake of Rachel Shafts moved now and then through the downpour, she slept only fitfully. Her worst fears were realised next morning, when Wingy Blenkiron delivered a letter. His face told everything.

"Aye, she's dead all right," he said sombrely. "And there's somebody else as owt to be dead an' all, that chap Brunskill."

"He's no more guilty of what's being said of him than you are," Cherry declared with sudden vehemence.

Wingy Blenkiron gave her an expressive look. "Now listen, lass," he said. "I know we've all liked him, as often you can like wrong 'uns, but her death's at his door an' nobody else's."

"I think I'll take this letter to my uncle," Cherry remarked with icy dignity. "He likes to have 'em as soon as they come when he's in."

Titus Alderson was spending the morning in his office, but she did not go to him at once. Shakily she closed the front door and returned to the kitchen where, her limbs unsure, she sat down. After a while she got up and looked at herself in the mirror, where she saw a pale young woman whose eyes were almost as shadowed as Agnes Pedley's had become. There was little to be done about the stains beneath her eyes, but, before going along the passage, she vigorously rubbed her cheeks.

"A letter, lass?" Titus Alderson said.

He drew out a crackling sheet covered with exquisite copper-plate. It was from the Bank, stating the amount by which the West Side Company's overdraft exceeded the figure guaranteed by Mr. Wade. Politely but firmly Messrs. Richardson & Storey appended the warning that, unless monies were deposited or other satisfactory arrangements made, the monthly Pay cheques would not be cashed excepting against the railway company's voucher denoting that pigs of lead to an equivalent value had been received into the Lead Warehouse at Corvy Station.

"Will it be all right for t'next Pay, Uncle?" Cherry inquired.

Mr. Alderson nodded. "We shan't feel the pinch just yet. Anyroad, even if no bouse is being won in the North Sun Vein Ground, at least we shan't have th'expense o' driving the New Drift, shall we? That's how to look at it, isn't it, lass? Making the best of things, eh?"

"Yes." Cherry tried to smile.

While going back she sternly resolved that, if she really were to be a support to her uncle, she must take herself in hand. A heavy programme of work might enable her to forget Adam's dire entanglement with the tragedy of this terrible morning, and, to this end, she was planning turning out every room in the house as never before when Reuben Nattrass walked into the kitchen, unbidden. But he was preoccupied, not arrogant.

"Nay," he mumbled when she told him he could go through to her uncle, "I nobbut want him to oblige me wi' some Low Moor iron, but that can wait. Till then I'll sit me down wi' you, lass."

Never before had she seen him behave so strangely. Lost in introspection, he was gazing at the fire, a film of moisture in his dark eyes; slouched in the chair, he fidgeted ceaselessly with his big hands.

Eventually he started to explain: "I've just got Agnes Pedley out and it's given me a rare turn. She were over thirty fathoms down, enough to have smashed her to smithereens, but there weren't a bruise on her face. When my dip-light fell on her, there she was, like a little lass waking up, wi' her eyes open—right blue they were an' all—and that fair hair of hers barely tumbled. I can't forget it somehow."

Feeling horribly sick, Cherry's glance sped to the kettle. "Would you like a drink o' tea?" she asked. "I'm . . . I'm having one myself."

"Nay," Reuben Nattrass shook off disturbing memories and grinned broadly, "I'se noan all that bad." After that he closely watched her lift crockery from the cupboard, but spoke again as she was spooning tea from the caddy: "There's all sorts o' lasses, isn't there? Lasses that are easy wi' everything including their virtue; lasses that hasn't any backbone as Agnes Pedley hadn't; and lasses such as yourself, who's as bonny as any of t'others but——"

"You're not talking to me like that," Cherry said determinedly.

Jabbing a finger, he checked her quite good-humouredly. "All right, lass," he said, "your next lesson shall be about chaps, because there's chaps of all sorts, too. Take myself, for instance. . . I'se known plenty o' young women of t'frail variety, but I've always taken damned good care not to land myself wi' one of 'em. You see, they weren't the kind as I wanted to find waiting at home for me of a night, the kind as I intended were to bring my youngsters into the world."

Cherry's foot stamped. "How dare you talk to me in that way, Reuben Nattrass."

The mine-agent chuckled, unrepentant. "Because you're the lass I have i' mind, so I'd give it plenty o' consideration if I were you."

Imperiously Cherry rejected the proposition. "I won't hurt your feelings by telling you how much consideration I shall give it."

Lazily he rose, laughingly making his last remark but one when sauntering out: "Aye, the sooner you get into your pretty head th'idea of being Mrs. Reuben Nattrass the better it'll be."

His clogged feet clattered a few paces along the oilcloth of the passage, the sound ceased, to be renewed as he returned. Around the door-jamb he bent, only his head visible with its dark eyes, fight-broadened nose, and ear over which raven black hair curled. Nothing but relentless purpose was in him now.

"For *that*, lass," he said before disappearing finally, "is what you're going to be, an' afore so long."

With fearful happenings to contemplate, Cherry's annoyance swiftly sped. From the rain-streaked window of Yew Tree House she could glimpse more and more people assembling, their faces shocked and angered. In life Agnes Pedley had caused great mischief to her cousin Adam; in death the damage she had done him might be irreparable.

3

For four nights, beginning after supper on the Sunday evening the brothers Pedley assailed him, Adam dialled steadily from the most westerly station in the Black Drift plotted on the plan he had stolen in the East Side Company's office. At four o'clock on Thursday morning he was so near completing the task as to think it worthwhile to finish the remainder.

"Aye," he said to himself, "I think I will, even though Hannah gives me another wigging."

Levelling the instruments, measuring with a copper-linked chain, the job was infinitely slow single-handed, innumerable the journeys between the tripods for candle-reader and dial set up at every surveying point, to sight the dial until a bead was drawn on the yellow candle-flame ahead, to obtain a back draft on the candle then taken behind.

"Well, it's kept me at it longer than I thought," Adam murmured when at last, in the Old Man's cavern where two rails rested near the edge of a sump, he noted in a columned dialling book the final particulars: *South sixty-nine East twenty-nine. Distance from preceding station, fifty-three links.* "H'm," he continued, pulling out his watch, "half-past eight. Well," his lips quirked, "they'll be nicely at work in t'Black Drift by now. Look surprised they would, if I went out that road. Well . . . I can't carry this stuff in daylight."

He wrapped the equipment in a gutta-percha cover, hiding the whole beneath a pile of small rock. "Shan't want that lot again here," he told himself, "but I'll pick it up the first convenient night. In any event my next job's in Blind Trial Crosscut, to see if I can come across any of Cousin Reuben's hexagonal impressions there."

He was soon stumbling over the old kibbles tumbled in the sump of Wild Goose Shaft, where he took to the sixty fathoms ladder. Apart from the absence of bunnings to rest upon it was not a difficult ascent, the only hazard a trapdoor about two-thirds up which was much more awkward to open from below than the hinged door at the eye.

"Raining again," he muttered. "But noan so much."

Wild Goose Shaft was in the midst of as wild a stretch of landscape as there was in the district, and from it Adam struck southward down Noggin Moor, maintaining more or less the same distance from the tips of rowans and birch trees marking the course of Winterings Gill. Eventually he crossed three smelt mill flues, Smiddy, Martha and Bucker, and scrambled over an artificial watercourse covered in by woodwork to guard against the blocking tendencies of heavy snow. By then it did not matter if he were seen and so, the rain a little more insistent, he sheltered in the tail of an old level, idly wondering why he was unable to hear the thunderous rolls of Bucker Grinding Mill.

The spot he had chosen had a commanding view across the dale, but visibility was far from good and he had settled himself comfortably, with pipe pulling freely, before he noticed a number of people moving slowly above Middle Sorrow, four men in their midst walking in unison.

"Might be a gate they're carrying," he muttered. "An' if so somebody's hurt. I hope Ward and Bob haven't been playing about at Rachel Shafts."

Using short-cuts, he soon was speeding down Sorrow Near to Town Foot, where he met Fronick Blenkiron, who was on an errand to buy mourning trimmings from Emma Ann Metcalfe in anticipation of funeral orders.

"What's the matter up yonder, Fronick?" he asked.

"It's . . . it's your cousin Agnes," the milliner replied, greatly taken aback. Later she told her young man how Adam had been sent scurrying, but all she added then was: "She's gone afore . . . killed herself."

Old Hannah, in black coat and bonnet, was starting out to perform a sad and necessary duty. One of her door-cards lay face upwards on the kitchen table, the little pictures on it those of a basin and a few folds of winding-sheet, the caption: THE LAST DRESSING-UP, A SNOW-WHITE SHROUD.

"Now then, lad," she greeted him, smiling gently.

"This is an awful affair, Hannah," Adam said.

For a while she was busy, placing in her waterproof bag a clean towel, soap, strips of linen, a tight roll of cotton fabric, flannel, hairbrush, and comb. "An' now where's t'pennies for her eyes?" she murmured to herself, answering him only when the preparations were complete. "Aye, it's terrible, lad, an' I'se just praying that she's left behind summat as she's writ to clear you, or telled somebody, but I'll find out. Now get yourself some breakfast while I'm off."

To Adam Brunskill it seemed a long, long time before she returned. She shook her head gravely as soon as she saw the inquiry in his face.

"No, lad, there were nowt and I don't think she saw onnybody to say owt to either."

Despite his protests, she shooed him off to bed where, the effect of endless application underground gaining supremacy over present worries, he slipped into sleep.

In the early evening Adam sat in front of a bright fire with Old Hannah, who was saying that Ambrose Pedley was not in the Burial Society.

"Why, lad?" she asked. "Were you thinking o' giving a bit on a helping hand?"

"Nay, I were just wondering," Adam murmured.

When the old lady spoke she admitted to doubting whether St. Peter's smile would be very genial when he saw her trudging towards the white portals to which occasionally she referred.

"To tell you the truth, Adam," she resumed, "I were thinking: 'Why, should he—you, I mean—considering th'awful position she's left him in?' But now I don't know. Mind you, I always shall blame her for not doing what were right in the beginning, but maybe at th'end she were too muddled for owt. Aye, if you've a mind, lad, I'd see to her being put away decently."

It was wet and dark in Main Street when Adam went outdoors. Few people were about and nothing more serious happened than that, beyond Nick Turn, two or three stones whizzed harmlessly by him, thrown by boys who, sheltering in an alley, had seen him passing beneath the lamp.

A light shone behind the dusty window panes of Mr. Kearton's workshop, but the undertaker, as the door opened, did not immediately look up from the oak varnish he was mixing. He straightened quickly enough, however, on hearing Adam's voice, and from then the caller could not complain of any lack of attention. Mouth tightened, Edmund Kearton uncompromisingly measured him up and down, lean face become even more austere before the process ended.

"So you think you'll save your soul by paying for a bit better quality coffin for your cousin, eh?" he demanded.

"It hadn't occurred to me," Adam replied. "An' instead of breaking your own rule, which I've heard you say isn't to bandy words wi' people, I'll be obliged if you'll answer my question, a civil one."

Mr. Kearton's Adam's apple bobbed alarmingly. "Aye, I'll answer it," he shouted, "by saying I'm noan taking instructions fro' such as you, not unless Ambrose Pedley is agreeable."

"I'll see him then, an' let you know, Mr. Kearton," Adam said.

He walked along in the downpour to Town Foot, where raindrops on a pair of tapering yews glistened in the shaft of light from the open door of the Smithy. Richard Blenkiron was treadling a grindstone, but, though Adam perceived the golden sparks, his thoughts were elsewhere, inside a kitchen whose lamp-lit window was on his right. In this mood he paused on Dolly Bridge, to listen to the menacing hiss of a river steadily rising, to peer over the parapet into inky gloom, faintly to see below, borne swiftly on the flood, the foam and bubbles carried down from the dam-stakes.

"Well, I'd better get on," he muttered.

A solitary dip shadowed deeply the depressing, uncurtained room he knew so well in Back Lane, but when he knocked the candlestick was picked up and the shadows, as seen from outdoors, assumed even more grotesque forms as the light moved. Then the wavering flame disappeared, to reappear when the door opened held high above an unkempt head.

"You!" Ambrose Pedley recoiled a step. "W-w-what——"

Briefly Adam explained the reason for his call. "So if you approve, I'll let him know," he ended.

"Aye," the older man said faintly, "you can tell . . . Edmund Kearton."

"Right," Adam said, turning away into the darkness.

Though silent, the Smithy was still illuminated, and as Adam swung round the corner of Titus Alderson's garden a burly figure lessened the beam of light from the broad doorway. But such ray as remained was sufficient to allow Mr. Blenkiron to identify the passer-by.

"I thought I recognised t'footsteps," he growled, brawny arm silhouetted as he beckoned. "Come over here, Brunskill."

Adam's temper was wearing thin, but, restraining the impulse to respond just as curtly, he obeyed the order. "Well, what is it, Mr. Blenkiron?" he asked when inside.

The big blacksmith was an angry man, but, for all his anger, he plucked thoughtfully at his beard before replying. Then, nodding to himself, he began to blow the slumbering embers on the forge, his whole attitude implicit of the belief that his few words could not be other than final.

"Don't go near my lass again, Brunskill," he said gruffly. "If you do I'll throw you fro' here to the West End."

"That's summat you couldn't do, Mr. Blenkiron," Adam retorted.

The blast of the bellows ceased and ruddy colour flooded the smith's cheeks. But as yet he was too astonished for his powerful voice to reach its full dominant strength. "What were that you said?" he choked.

"What you thought I did," Adam told him quietly. "Now, Mr. Blenkiron, I'm in enough trouble as it is——"

"So I can't throw you fro' here to t'West End, can't I?" Richard Blenkiron observed, wiping his hands on his leather apron. "Well, I'll show you what I can do . . . maybe I can't land you as far as t'Brig, but by God you're going through that doorway a damned sight faster than you walked in . . ."

Arms outstretched, he strode forward to grasp his opponent, the weight of the initial onslaught driving back the other. But after that, save insignificantly, Richard Blenkiron did not move again, his hands held in a vice-like grip from which he could not free himself. While his colour deepened alarmingly and sweat increasingly trickled down his forehead, he attempted to force Adam's arms farther apart; as a pulse throbbed more plainly on his temple and veins stood out ever more starkly, he sought to break the relentless hold. Great chest heaving, breathing laboured, he utterly spent himself, until only the painful gasps of impotence and exhaustion were heard.

"I'm sorry about this, Mr. Blenkiron," Adam said, releasing him.

Richard Blenkiron sat down abruptly on the anvil. "You've bested me," he muttered. "Fairly and squarely bested me."

"You can't expect to do what you once could," Adam reminded him.

The pulsating cords pillaring the blacksmith's mighty neck were subsiding when, with the back of his hand, he wearily wiped away the moisture blinding red-infused eyes. As if collecting himself by the sight of familiar objects, his glance slowly roved, passing from the ratch drill and screw stocks and dies, to forging mould and the tongs he used for picking horse-shoes from the fire. Only twice did he linger in this appraisal, once on glimpsing the fourteen-pound sledge hammer he could swing so effortlessly and next when, in the gloom behind the cooling trough, he discerned a couple of solid iron spheres joined by a round bar.

"Weight-lifting . . . by t'Bask way," he murmured, a wry twist to his mouth. "So at after all you *were* gymnasting wi' the real 'uns at Mayday, weren't you?"

"Yes," Adam said.

Richard Blenkiron soliloquised as he stared again at the spheres. "No, there never were a time I could have done t'tricks as you did wi' that. An' even when I were at my best," a leonine head was shaken, "I should have been nowt much more nor a baby in your hands," he confessed with moving simplicity.

"Well, I'll be off now, Mr. Blenkiron," Adam said, "so good night. An' I'll noan trouble your Fronick any more."

He went along Main Street, calling in at Edmund Kearton's on the way to Old Hannah's, where, after supper, he changed into mine clothes before starting out.

His first mission when underground was to retrieve the surveying instruments he had secreted. "An' now for what I hope'll turn out to be number two knavery," he grunted, eyeing the pair of rails at the side of the Old Man's sump before leaving. "Yes, if I can nobbut locate the marks o' Cousin Reuben's tripod in the other spot . . ."

Returning to Bucker Level, he continued towards the forehead as far as Blind Trial Crosscut, striking along that to the west. Beyond an old String, where all modern workings ceased, he began to search, methodically penetrating the many tortuous galleries leading off on either hand, each with its host of minor members, a maze on the fringe of Freezeland whose intricacies could aptly be compared to the tunnellings of some mammoth worm-like creature. Unfortunately he was under a two-fold handicap: in many parts the sole was rock, and in some places knee-deep water flowed silently along, a consequence of the heavy rain, usually felt in lower workings within twenty-four hours.

Nevertheless, despite the absence of positive results, the second half of his self-appointed mission had been begun, and he was by no means dissatisfied when, in Old Hannah's kitchen later, he fried breakfast rashers for himself and his landlady, whose footsteps he had heard upstairs.

In the late afternoon, when Adam woke, he heard the murmur of voices downstairs. In due course Albert Gibson served him in the kitchen with a coroner's warrant to attend the inquest the following day.

"The funeral's not till Monday," Old Hannah said when the policeman had gone. "You see, she's a rare lot o' relatives on her father's side, an' it gives 'em time to make their arrangements."

Adam, who had been comparing his watch with the open-pendulumed Dutch clock, remarked that *his* arrangements were simple. "Just a black tie," he said. "I think I'll nip along to buy one while it's quiet. There'll be a deal o' excitement here to-morrow, I should imagine."

Old Hannah's eyes widened. "Aye, won't there just?" she exclaimed. Then, repenting this outspokenness, her lips met firmly, but shortly opened again as the outcome of her deliberations. "So you're 'tending t'funeral an' all, are you?" she inquired with some grimness.

"Agnes is my cousin, Hannah," Adam pointed out.

"An' you're that fond of her . . . *still*?" the old lady snapped.

"No," Adam agreed.

More than once since the girl's death, Mrs. Batty had kept close guard on her tongue. She relaxed somewhat now. "You're going to show folks, aren't you?" she demanded. "Show 'em you're noan afraid."

"What else can I do, keep out of the way, or bolt?" Adam asked, a cold intentness in his deep-set eyes she had never seen before. "I'll bet already," he added, "that there's one or two saying I'll soon be making myself scarce like my father did, eh?"

His companion observed, not quite so easily as she would have liked, that in life there were always thorns in the flesh. "But even so, lad," she went on, "you can't fight the whole community."

Neither Adam's promise nor his manner reassured her. "I'm noan meaning to," he said. "If they leave me alone I'll leave them alone."

"You're going to see this business right through to t'bitter end," she persisted.

"Aye," Adam nodded as the shop-bell rang, engaging himself also, beneath his breath, in another direction. "An' a second piece o' business an' all, a real dirty bit o' business, too, I'm almost certain."

During the next twenty minutes Old Hannah had a rush of customers, but, while supplying their needs, must have been doing a great deal of cogitating. She epitomised her thoughts when she again sat down in the kitchen.

"Well, I'd better order t'timber for the barricades."

Adam chuckled. "Think it's necessary, Hannah?"

Mrs. Batty stretched for her pipe. "No, hardly," she cackled. "But, mark you, there's nowt like being prepared. Why, for over forty year I've had a nightshift all ready i' my third drawer down—for somebody as 'ul have to lay *me* out."

"That'll be a sad day," Adam sighed. "But not so bad maybe for Mr. Dougill and Mr. Guy down at Greets."

Old Hannah sat up. "Them two dodderers!" she ejaculated. "I'm seeing both o' them under t'sod and don't you forget it, lad."

In a lighter mood they chaffed and bickered, but, before Adam went outdoors his landlady's humour sobered. "Take care o' yourself fro' now on, lad," she warned him. "When folks get worked up you can't be sure what'll occur."

It was still raining and the roar of the waterfalls above the Brig was thunderous. As on the previous night, few people were abroad and, from there to the little shop beyond Nick Turn, Adam met no one.

From behind a counter heaped with glass plates, boxes of men's handkerchiefs, boys' fronts, and a flower-stand upon which a spotted muff and boa were draped, Emma Ann Metcalfe looked up, her welcoming smile quickly vanishing.

"No," she dithered, "I'm afraid I don't stock gentlemen's mourning."

"I'll try my luck with Mr. Daykin," Adam told her.

As he stepped on to the wet pavement Mrs. Metcalfe burst into a gay trill, the reason for which he guessed when, cooling his heels next door amongst elastic-sided boots, lamp-wicks, the sticky treacle jar and canisters of BEST TEA, he heard a subdued hum in the kitchen behind.

Ladies' shawls and gingham squares dangling perilously above the paraffin bin danced giddily when Cuthbert Daykin, entering his shop, forced a passage between a side of bacon and brushes and pans hanging from a beam. A man of many fears, he was always fearful of his plate-glass windows when cattle were driven through the village or a wayward horse showed temper, and he was relieved that this customer had not arrived in daylight.

"Mrs. Metcalfe, real neighbourly she is, were kind enough to tell me what you were after when she popped round hurriedly just now to let me know my gutter were choked wi' leaves," he vouchsafed with uneasy aplomb while reaching for the required box. "Very good quality these ties, but," confidently believing that Emma Ann was still within earshot he conceived a telling sally, "but you're noan wanting it for your cousin's funeral, are you?" he inquired, raising his eyebrows.

Adam glanced at him. "I'll have this one—what about t'discount for cash?"

Reddening perceptibly, Mr. Daykin blurted out what should have been a witty allusion to the ample financial resources naturally assumed to be those of a young man who can afford to travel abroad for the best part of a year. "'Course one lives an' learns," he blustered, fingering his waxed moustache, "but I shouldn't have thought a chap such as that would have quibbled about t'difference betwixt elevenpence ha'penny an' elevenpence."

Adam pocketed the change. "Every copper counts when you might have to flee from a place. Maybe you'll learn that for yourself one day."

"Me!" the shopkeeper squealed.

Adam's voice sank. "Things get out," he said darkly.

Of Cuthbert Daykin's many fears two were paramount just then, one that Cyprian Metcalfe might find out, the other as to what would happen to the West Side Company. He was still far from recovered when the customer who had shocked him was passing the annexe of the Literary Institute, an arm's length behind whose door lay the stiffened body of a girl.

CHAPTER TEN

I

THE INQUEST upon Agnes Pedley opened with all the decorum proper to an ancient form of legal inquiry, but, long before its termination, the proceedings degenerated into a heated squabble between the Coroner and the Postmaster of Greets, who, sitting next to Mrs. Robert William Alderson, jumped up frequently to pose questions pertinent and impertinent. In due course, aware that the gratuitous harrying of witnesses by an unqualified know-all might leave grave gaps in their evidence, the squirely Corvy lawyer lost his temper and so far forgot himself during the summing-up as immediately to return a verdict of Death by Misadventure, without referring the matter to Sam Kirkbride, the foreman of the jury. This omission, however, was subsequently rectified.

"Outrageous," Lodge Trotter shouted, fired to a fresh step by the anger upon his client's face. "It's again t'weight of evidence and I warn you, Mr. Coroner, as I shall have to think seriously about drawing up a memorial for quashing th'inquisition."

"Stuff and nonsense, sir," roared Mr. Miles Buckle, and roared again when the postmaster, his manner sinister, named the Memorial's destination: the Chambers of Her Majesty's Attorney General. "You can send it to——" he checked himself not very adroitly, to resume on a tack more in keeping with the circumstances. "Another word from you, Trotter, and I'll commit you for contempt."

Ineffable scorn filled the Postmaster's face as, holding his lapels, he rotated slowly, eyeing through the plum-shaped lenses of his *pince-nez* an audience much too small for the telling rejoinder he proposed to deliver before sitting down.

"For what's noan an indictable offence?" he queried when satisfied his words could be heard. "Nay, Mr. Coroner, really for a chap who's supposed to have had some education in t'law you——"

"Another word, Trotter," Mr. Buckle rapped, so obviously meaning business as shortly to be able to wind up the matter in a more seemly atmosphere.

Once monthly, during the winter, the members of the Winterings Mutual Improvement Society gathered in the Institute's library and had not a great deal of space to spare. That afternoon almost twice their number were present, jurymen, witnesses, and certain privileged spectators, who now were treated to a difference of opinion between Mark Iveson and an elderly lady who, indirectly, had been as much a nuisance to Mr. Buckle as her representative.

"But I'se sworn to it," the shepherd said, exasperated. "He had his britches on and——"

"That's noan of any real importance," Mrs. Robert William Alderson declared.

"Not of importance!" Mark Iveson yelped. "Well, what is, then?"

"Agnes Pedley herself," Mrs. Roberty Will retorted, "because she were that simple she could have imagined——"

"Nay . . ." Mrs. Iveson protested. "Not unless——"

"Summat o' some sort took place between 'em all right," Mrs. Alderson persisted. "An' her partner's got her death on his conscience . . . him, that chap yonder."

Arthur Nattrass was squeezing towards the door. "Well, he's going to pay for it," he promised. "I seldom lets myself go all out, but on this occasion——"

"Now we want no disorderly conduct, Arthur," the mistress of Malaga remarked with severity. "Times have changed, lad, and the hand o' the law stretches farther, you must remember. Maybe that's why young chaps are tamer nowadays, thank goodness—my words, they were hot-blooded i' my time, and if owt like this had happened——"

Anthony Skidmore had been listening with rising annoyance to his wife's greatest friend. "What do you think you're up to, Ellen?" he asked, adding very pointedly: "An' if there has been changes, hasn't it occurred to you it may be because a lot of our best blood went elsewhere to carve summat out for theirsen?"

"Nowt of t'kind," Mrs. Alderson replied, quite amused.

"*Tamed!*" Arthur Nattrass' scowl was ferocious. "Of all——"

As the general hubbub of conversation faded his voice, too, trailed into silence. All heads were turned as Adam Brunskill edged towards the doorway into Main Street, where a big crowd waited in the rain. At the forefront were twenty to thirty men who, if they acted upon arrangements privately entered into, could hardly have been considered any less wild than their redoubtable forbears.

The morning had been filled with tension. Saturday tidying-up for the week-end had been scamped in most houses, and the men of both mining companies, after drawing the weekly Lent-Money of four shillings advanced against the next Pay, hurried to Town Foot instead of home.

Of the many groups gathered in the vicinity of the Smithy, one huddled for shelter at the foot of Sorrow Near especially had a purposeful air. When dispersing at dinner-time, many a nod pledging joint action and secrecy was exchanged.

Wingy Blenkiron's face was white with intent. "Right," he said as he went in. "As soon as he comes out at after th'inquest."

"At him in a rush," Jonas Cottingham gloated.

"An' then away to t'Brig wi' him," Cyprian Metcalfe grinned.

"The beck's real out," Nathan Wharton said, not wholly at ease.

"Deeper t'better," snapped Bart Hugill.

Reuben Nattrass chuckled. "Well, if you find you want some help . . ."

Ned Mason's vehemence of feeling about Agnes Pedley's seducer very nearly involved him in a row. "If a score on us can't handle him, then us'll call for your valuable services, Reuben," he said tartly.

At one o'clock in the afternoon, Albert Gibson took his post at the door of the Literary Institute; half an hour later the throng in Main Street numbered more than a hundred and was approaching twice that when, a few minutes short of two o'clock, Adam Brunskill joined at the tail of those who, permitted or required to attend the inquest, were being passed inside one by one.

When, at a late phase in the inquest, in response to a dig from an elbow, Lodge Trotter bobbed up again, Mr. Miles Buckle's blood-pressure soared and his fist banged down upon the table. "I will not tolerate these interruptions, Trotter," he shouted. "So long as I am entrusted with the conduct of——"

Mrs. Roberty Will's agent, in an aside, forecast that the Corvy lawyer might shortly lose one of his present emoluments unless he mended his ways, namely, his Coronership.

"What did you say?" Mr. Buckle glowered.

"Merely summat as is outside t'scope of this present inquiry, if it pleases you." The Postmaster smiled offensively. "But what I were going to submit—*in re* a certain witness's depositions, were . . . er . . ."

"He wants her cousin cross-examining again," Mrs. Robert William Alderson interposed with scant patience. "Him as wouldn't wed her even though he were responsible for t'child she'd conceived."

"Madam," Mr. Buckle began awesomely, so engrossed that he failed to perceive the piece of paper Dr. Seaton was waving at him. His officer, however, touched his sleeve and onlookers watched while coroner and doctor put their heads together in a lengthy, muffled colloquy. It would not be too much to assert that, when Mr. Buckle subsequently addressed the jury, his demeanour, changed strikingly, was that of a man who has a rod in pickle. He began by pointing out that their duty was to ascertain how a girl had come to her death, not her morals.

"Doctor, if you'll be kind enough to testify once more," he observed with relish. "Thank you, sir . . . Now sir, you described earlier the nature of the injuries which had caused the deceased's death."

"Aye, I did," Dr. Seaton confirmed.

Mr. Buckle's preliminary cough blew out his ruddy cheeks before the next weighty question. "Now sir," he resumed, "in your examination of the body did you notice symptoms consistent with the state you have heard affirmed by deceased's father and uncle—and by others more irregularly?"

With praiseworthy caution the medical witness asked for the question to be clarified. This was done and then, every eye on him, Dr. Seaton replied with a very proper sense of theatre, withholding his vital pronouncement for a few telling moments.

"No, sir," he said firmly. "The deceased girl, Agnes Pedley, was *not* pregnant."

Pent breath was released, the only other sound that of rain splashing against panes. For a brief spell this silence held, but then Lodge Trotter, once again usurping Mr. Buckle's function, started a commotion which raged on even after the Coroner had closed his file, though its tenor changed when Mrs. Roberty Will and Mark Iveson had a difference. It died quickly when Adam Brunskill pushed forward towards the library door and the outer lobby.

A few seconds afterwards a new noise began, the revengeful roar of a crowd. Under the onslaught of a horde of angered men the victim, who fought with his back to buildings whenever possible, was forced little by little along Main Street, towards the mist of spray clouding the hump of Winterings Brig.

Meantime jury, spectators and witnesses tumbled out of the Literary Institute. "We must stop 'em," Edmund Kearton gasped. "They're in a terrible mood."

Puke Hastwell guffawed. "I didn't know you were a supporter o' his."

"I'm noan," the joiner snapped. "But if he loses his life the ringleader 'ul swing if t'police can put their finger on him, an' at the best three or four of our lads 'ul do penal servitude. Come on, Richard."

The blacksmith had a son prone to take a leading part in most events. "Aye," he said, clearing a path. "We'll have to be sharp an' all."

Running in pursuit when free of the press they passed the casualties of a bitterly-waged struggle—Arthur Nattrass, doubled with pain, vomiting on the doorstep of the Fleece; a West Side groover spitting out teeth on the handball court; Nowt Much Cooper staggering about, his jaw broken.

"By God!" Richard Blenkiron muttered with unholy delight. "But he can scrap. He'd have made Reuben Nattrass more nor a sparring partner if he ever gets fixed up to battle wi' Gipsy Joe."

James Pedley, on top of the stone post from which young ladies dispatched the runners for the Maidens' Garland, screamed in exhortation, his piercing voice just audible in the roar of falling water. "He shall be driven fro' light to darkness. . . . Cast him in, th'evil-doer . . ."

"That's enough, Pedley," Blind Kit shouted.

A wild figure, matted hair dripping, pale eyes venomous, James Pedley took no heed. "Prepare to meet thy God," he screeched.

The struggle was indeed ending, but, though hemmed in at the peak of the bridge on the river side, Adam dealt out plenty of punishment to attackers hampered by the closeness of their ranks. From a half-circle flailing fists struck at him, Bull Waggott in the middle of the ring, bloody-faced and dazed, but with enough sense left to desire to hurt again and again the destroyer of the little lass he had truly favoured.

"Hey, Anthony!" the blacksmith bellowed. "Come on, Edmund, Francis . . . Here, Mark . . ."

The elders made a concerted effort to get forward, an attempt at intervention which might have been successful had not Reuben Nattrass vaulted on to the parapet at the bridge's approach and, clogged feet twinkling, run up the narrow line of sharply-rising masonry until, near the hump, he was twenty or more feet above the fast-flowing water. Without pause he launched himself in the air, his momentum and the direction of the unexpected assault unbalancing the common victim. A heap of bodies writhed on the muddy ground, but soon there was a slow upheaval as, three or four pairs of hands hanging on to each limb, a tall and powerful figure was rolled on to the parapet.

"Ho'd on," Anthony Skidmore bawled. "Don't, you damned fools, she weren't having a baby."

It was too late. Remaining grip broken by a savage kick from a clog, a united thrust accomplished the rest. Adam dropped into the peaty flood below, whose embrace whipped him towards the junction with the Skew, not far distant, sweeping him downwards past green-lichened boulders protruding above the frothed waters.

A few boys, hoping for an exciting spectacle on reaching the river's bank, tore along a winding path through the hazels, ashes and thorns lining Winterings Beck at its lowest part. Their voices did not carry well, but the gestures they made, no less than the sudden dread on young faces, told a story all too clearly.

"He's gone over t'dam stakes," Edmund Kearton said bleakly.

The undertaker's antipathy towards a young man who within the next minutes might be dead was well enough known by his hearers. Quite a number of hearts, hitherto stimulated by passion, became heavy as lead.

Fortune favoured Adam during his racing passage in the furious waters of the Skew. He shot over the dam stakes at the one place where the undertow beyond was weak, this enabling him to escape the sucking intake of the saw-mill race. Farther beyond he entered a stretch of comparatively slack water where, blessing the experience acquired in one of the most turbulent rivers in Spain, he struck towards the bank, aided immeasurably just past Dirty Bottom and the unseen Hippy Stones by a mysterious shoreward surge. Eventually, not a dozen yards upstream from the place where the river narrowed irresistably for a flying rush under Dolly Bridge, his feet found bottom. Slowly he struggled uphill, finally to rest upon an old oil barrel.

"Well," he muttered, gulping in deep breaths, "if you've a fancy for excitement . . . visit t'place . . . where your own folk has lived for generations. And this'll mean a new suit," he ended incongruously.

About then he heard the urgent patter of feet and, glancing over his shoulder, saw Cherry running towards him, her head bare, white apron fluttering behind her. "Oh, Adam," she cried, "are you hurt bad? I . . . I saw you from t'staircase window, scrambling out."

"I'm all right, lass," he reassured her. "Nowt but a few cuts and bruises here and there."

She seemed oblivious of the rain falling on her soft hair. "They've thrown you over t'Brig, haven't they?"

"Aye, but that's finished everything, hasn't it? Or so I remember once being telled," Adam said. "Once you've paid the penalty you're not supposed to be punished again, are you, eh?"

Her red lips quivered. "It's never happened i' my time afore," she said. "But when it did I think them who got out always left Winterings sooner or later. I believe one or two tried to stick it out, behaving very carefully, like, but in the end they had to go. It . . . it were better for 'em."

Savagely determined not to be driven away for something of which he was innocent, Adam stirred. His aggressive train of thought carried him to the quiet but tangible challenge he would offer. His jaw tautened, he smiled grimly.

"Well, I'm stopping, an' I'm noan being humble either. In fact . . ." he glimpsed her pale and frightened face, and tried gently to comfort her. "It's all right, lass, I can look after myself."

"Yes," she whispered, quite unbelievingly, her eyes exceptionally bright.

"And now you pop off indoors," Adam said. "Or you'll soon be as soaked as I am."

Tears welling, she turned away, taking her own sorrow to a home already overburdened with despair. Shivering a little, Adam waited until she had gone from sight and then, bent upon implementing the idea which had occurred to him, sprinted towards Puke Hastwell's house and the Wood Yard gates, past the thirty yards long saw-bench in the mill and scanty piles of English and foreign logs, durk drift sleepers and groove timbers. Main Street was deserted as far as Nick Turn, but when he rounded the corner a tremendous stir passed through the throng at the Brig.

Old Hannah was standing at her door. "Thank God you're safe, lad," she said, sniffing. "And," she scrutinised him thoroughly, "you haven't got pummelled all that terribly."

"I've a long reach," Adam grimaced. "Useful when a chap's a rare conceit about his face."

"Nowt to try to be funny about," she said. "Now come you in sharp——"

"I'll be back i' no time for that mustard bath I'll bet you're shoving me into," Adam broke in ruefully. "But I want to see Mr. Buckle first."

Old Hannah's eyes widened. "He went into t'Plug two-three minutes since. But what is it you're after, lad?"

He grinned wickedly. "Tell you later."

Watched by many in whom cold apprehension about possible consequences had rapidly been translated into lively bellicosity both by his reappearance and levity, Adam continued to the inn, where Mrs. Peacock, at first stiffly inclined to refuse, ultimately showed him into the dining-room, in which Mr. Buckle was standing with his back to the fire.

Gazing with frank curiosity, the lawyer listened to his caller's request. "Yes, I shall be at my office throughout Market Day," he agreed, his manner guarded. "What is the nature of your business, Brunskill?"

"A matter o' farm property, Mr. Buckle," Adam said. "But in t'meantime it'd do no harm if you made a few inquiries about me on Monday, fro' Richardson & Storey's Bank. Might save time."

Straddling his feet wider, Miles Buckle visibly expanded. This, after all, was a client, not a young fellow who, as the result of unofficial but severe castigation, wished to make embarrassing revelations after an inquest had ended.

Nevertheless the lawyer's first thoughts were those shared for much longer by many Winterings folk. It was everywhere openly stated that Adam had visited the coroner to confess that while under oath he had lied. Nicely spiced, the same topic provided entertainment for the men who, the following morning—certain necessary activities were allowed on the Sabbath—climbed Jom High Road with muzzle-loaders under their arms, their objective a vagrant, sheep-worrying dog roaming the fells.

Still further embroidered, the tale was in active currency on the grey Monday of Agnes Pedley's funeral, when a cloudy vapour obscured the peaks of the hills, and water dripped endlessly from faulty gutters and browning leaves. By then opinion had crystallised, following closely upon Mrs. Roberty Will's reasoning. It was held that, in her ignorance, the dead girl might easily have imagined she was with child, but sound cause she must have had for the belief. Few people in the district were other than convinced that intercourse had taken place between the cousins.

* * * *

Pitifully entreated by Mazy Bill, Titus Alderson granted permission for Polly to draw the simple, two-wheeled farm-cart which bore Agnes Pedley's remains to their last resting-place. As with all obsequies for which Mr. Kearton was responsible, the funeral procession started at the precise time appointed, and, despite the drizzle, moved forward at the exact crawl he invariably insisted upon. In the front, a crazed, grief-stricken lad kept level with the grey head of a beloved mare whose luxuriant mane was tied with bows of black crape, as were the shafts of the springless vehicle and the spokes; immediately behind Polly's glossy rump the coffin rested in a soft bower which quivered constantly, a green, red and mauve bower of spruce, rowanberries and Michaelmas daisies. Farther behind came mourners sombrely clad, a long-extending company of relatives and others, Winterings signifying its regret with a very full representation.

Slowly the *cortège* proceeded, into Jom High Road, over Dolly Bridge, and then, along a street in which every blind was down, to the West End, where a most unseemly disturbance was quashed only by the quiet violence of Mr. Kearton's reproof to the dead girl's uncle. James Pedley's beliefs would not allow him to attend the funeral of a suicide, but he had chosen to appear there for one purpose only, to renew his assault upon Adam.

Another incident did suddenly occur, however, as the coffin was being borne into the chapel, when Polly backed viciously, the protruding tail-end of a through-shaft striking a stone gate-post with shattering force, Bull Waggott escaping by a hair's breadth.

"My, but he can count hissen lucky," Francis Harker gasped.

"Never known her to do owt like that afore," Titus Alderson affirmed. "Have you, Bill?" he went on, addressing the trammer who, standing by his horse's head, was shaking like an aspen leaf. "Now it's all right, lad. . . . Bull's noan hurt. It missed him."

"M . . . missed h . . . him," Mazy Bill chattered through his teeth.

"No damage, lad," the policeman said officially.

Thereafter everything went smoothly: the service in the Chapel and the last poignant offices in the graveyard when the coffin was lowered from sight.

When Nick Pratt, who acted as Mr.Kearton's assistant in these matters, began to fill the grave, closely watched by many children, Richard Blenkiron and others walked towards Town Foot. At the Wood Yard they halted, sheltering in an open shed for a smoke before changing into workaday clothes. As was natural their talk was concerned mainly with recent events. It was considered that Adam Brunskill would leave Winterings within the week, but gossip about this was rudely disturbed when Hugh Bearpark, scarlet-faced after his run, arrived with the news that Big William had broken down.

"Just one segment, you say, lad?" Titus Alderson inquired anxiously. "If it's more it means ordering a complete set."

Richard Blenkiron overheard. "I'll get up there straight off, Titus."

"Aye, do, lad," the old mine-agent nodded. "We can't smelt a bing from the one ore-producing ground we've left unless he's turning."

Reuben Nattrass began to commiserate, declaring as he steered Mr. Alderson towards the pit of the great circular saw, fortunately for hearing stationary, that the West Side Company was experiencing nothing but trouble. "An' that's why I'se wanting to talk to you, about both us companies. Mind you, I haven't any authority to speak about what I am, but my directors listen to me an' they've got confidence in me." Bluntly he then advanced the advisability of some form of amalgamation, pointing out that the pair of them could work in accord, and that for his part he was very willing to shoulder most of the burden. He remarked, too, that age tells its tale, as he would find out for himself in due course.

Undeterred by bright spots of colour clearly tingeing the older man's sunken cheeks, he continued: "Now you needn't say what I reckon you're going to say. But it would be different if it were a family affair, wouldn't it?"

"How do you mean a family affair?" Mr. Alderson exclaimed.

"If me and that niece o' yours reached an understanding."

"Cherry and you!" Titus Alderson ejaculated. "Why, I don't know as how she's showed any signs o' fancying you."

Reuben Nattrass paid tribute. "She's fruit as wants picking, noan like a windfall as tumbles off a tree. But you can leave that part to me."

Nearby, in the muddy yard, oak framing for wagon repairs was being loaded for the East Side Company, timber which Puke Hastwell had for weeks past vowed there was no prospect of obtaining. But the old mine-agent, still bewildered, gazed without anger at this patent proof of discrimination. After a while, however, he spoke about his niece.

"Whenever she wants to get wed I shan't stand in her light, so long as it's a decent chap," he said slowly. "But even if you an' her make a match on it I'm having nowt to do wi' this amalgamation you've mentioned. I'm against that, an' if it comes up at t'Extraordinary General Meeting I shall fight it tooth and nail."

"It'll come up, I'm afraid," Reuben Nattrass said with a flavour of regret. "You see, it's summat I believe in, and as I've a few shares in t'West Side Company I shall bring it up myself. Nowt like being straightforward wi' you, is there?"

"No, there isn't," Mr. Alderson said. "You stick to your guns, lad, but don't expect me not to stick to mine. Of course," he smiled wryly, "th'Extraordinary General Meeting may recommend dispensing with my services, and then you'll noan have my opposition."

"Nay, I think not," Reuben Nattrass laughed.

Little more could be said to advantage by either of them, and so, each with arrears of work to make up and one with a new care about an all-important waterwheel, they went their separate ways.

2

On the day after the funeral, Adam walked to Greets, where, at the Grafton Arms, he hired a hack to ride to Corvy. Before this he learnt a little more as to how he was regarded. When passing the Wesleyan Day School in Winterings the children, ignoring Mr. Kidd's furiously rung bell, lined up to watch him, and he saw, but was not seen by, Wingy Blenkiron who, mail-bag slung over shoulder, had just negotiated a gill on a fallen larch, not a stone's throw from the main road below Malaga. Still farther along, beyond geese enlivening the deep-cut ravine of Heugh Syke, Ned Mason was pointing the lodge of Half House, but the keen-eyed mason, who usually had a cheery word for everybody, was another too preoccupied to notice the pedestrian.

These incidents were all negative in character, but in another Adam had been the target for very positive action on the part of Annamaria Rutter, and only considerable agility enabled him to avoid a rampaging bull.

"A dangerous trick, that," he remarked as bull and sheepdog receded rapidly towards Winterings. "The trick of somebody without a ha'porth o' sense."

Annamaria flushed angrily. "Even if you'd been badly hurt there'd have been no tears fro' me, not even crocodile 'uns."

"Maybe so," Adam nodded. "But perhaps you'll have more feeling if youngsters are savaged. Say a few tots picking brambles at t'road-side."

Her colour vanished. "Are there bairns up yonder?" she gulped.

"I couldn't say *now*," he told her in all truth.

Domineering and capable, she could nevertheless lose her head. Panic-stricken and remorseful, she scuttered up the road, thought better of it after fifty yards, stopped, climbed over a wall and, when last seen by Adam, was frantically endeavouring to round up a horse.

"Serve her right," he muttered with some grimness.

On arriving in Corvy he went to the Bank, where, despite the pressure of Market Day, the precise-featured senior partner found time for a chat about lead-mining. Mr. Storey was extremely pessimistic about the West Side Company, but expressed the opinion that the concern, under really *vigorous* management, could become a feasible proposition, an estimate which caused Adam to frown when once more in the thronged Bull Ring.

"I wonder if his lot is just biding their time?" he mused.

He was wandering in the alleyway between kerb-side stalls and buildings when he met the master of Badger Hall face to face. "I've been wanting to see you," Anthony Skidmore announced, drawing him from the traffic current on to the steps of a Georgian residence. "Wanting for a bit now."

Adam was terse. "If it's Dinah you can save your breath, Mr. Skidmore. I shan't be bothering her."

"Just as well for the time being," Dinah's father remarked. "But that weren't what I were going to say." Never one for half measures, he hesitated appreciably before resuming, distaste evident in his fine-boned face. "Well, there it is and I nobbut hope I haven't offended you," he wound up, still ashamed. "You're welcome to spend what time you want wi' me on t'farm, but keep clear of the house. As I've said, that's the missus's province . . . and as far as Dinah is concerned—she's a young, unmarried lass so I need say no more about her. I'm sorry th'invitation is such a miserable——"

"Never mind that," Adam restrained him. "The main thing to me is that you don't believe I've any responsibility for my cousin Agnes."

"I don't, lad," Anthony Skidmore declared. "An' I never have for a moment . . . as I've argued more nor once."

They arranged to meet at the Saracen for the one o'clock Ordinary and then Adam, immensely invigorated, departed for Groat Alley, Mr. Miles Buckle's place of business beneath the shadow of the castle's Norman Keep. Several brass plates gleamed outside the lawyer's door, one amongst them: 'Steward of the Manor of Greets,' and another: 'Registered Office of the East Side Lead Mining Company, Limited.'

In the waiting-room Adam prowled around examining bills of sales and cartoons of legal luminaries. He was not detained long, however, and this, coupled with the welcoming wave of Mr. Buckle's plump hand, rather suggested that inquiries at the Bank had proved satisfactory.

Twenty-five minutes afterwards there was deadlock. Mr. Buckle was willing to let Modesty for twelve months from Michaelmas, with option to purchase at the expiration of that period. The figure for the latter was the stumbling block, exactly fifty pounds dividing them, Adam not budging from a sum which, by devious means in months past, he had ascertained as fair.

"Well," Mr. Buckle said with overpowering gloom as he ushered his visitor to the door, "I'll obtain the owner's views."

After dinner at the Saracen, for which Mr. Skidmore insisted upon paying, Adam went to a tailor recommended by his host, where he was measured for a suit. Later, to cover any needs which might arise, he embarked upon a round of shopping the nature of which would have transfixed the inhabitants of Winterings. From a saddler's he bought a commodious wallet with strong leather strap, and elsewhere he acquired a groover's hammer, sets of borers and drills, dynamite, a coil of fuse, and cartridge paper for plans. Armed with these, he collected his horse from the William and Mary and, leaving the busy little town, took the winding and ever rising road up lonely Skewdale, reaching Greets just after nightfall.

George Nattrass's big shop was separated from the Grafton Arms by a private house of some repute because, in the earlier days of John Wesley's attempts to convert the Dale, the floor of one of its rooms, beams below partially sawn through by a fanatical opponent, had collapsed beneath a company of his adherents gathered in holy meeting. The frontage of this house was narrow though, and so Mr. Nattrass had no difficulty in recognising from his shop door the young man who, after handing over his mount to the ostler, came striding out of the stable-yard of the inn. "Evening, lad," he called out and, when they were together, continued to speak of something and nothing until he realised with asperity that if he did not refer to a certain matter his nephew would not do so either. "Well, have you given any thought to what I mentioned out at Smollock? About shares," he snapped, on Adam's blank stare.

Adam was enjoying himself. "Shares . . . Oh, aye, I remember, you offered me two shillings a share to take 'em off your hands. Aye," he laughed, "two shillings."

Swallowing his annoyance, George Nattrass touched upon the ties of blood which, in the light of a tragic event, had persuaded him to increase the amount to four shillings. "Your poor mother were my sister after all," he lamented. "An' a bit extra brass 'ul help her lad to get on his way. Moreover it could come to more than you'd suspect. I've one or two friends as might join in, an' all told t'number o' shares should add up as high as a hundred."

Adam, far from being moved, chose to remark that the transaction was not the sort to redound much credit to either side. "Anyway," he loftily announced, "my good name is worth more to me than twenty pounds."

"Your . . . your good name!" Mr. Nattrass gasped.

"Mind you, Uncle George," Adam promised, "I'll give t'proposal serious consideration."

The cheese-factor remembered before it was too late that a nephew shortly leaving for Spain was far away his most suitable outlet. "All right then," he said, subduing a growl. "You can let me know, but I'm noan keeping th'offer dangling. There's others who'd jump at it."

Hiding a broad grin for a safe distance, Adam set off across the Market Place towards the Green. The moon was rising as he climbed the moor road beyond the B.G. Inn, and in Winterings it was quite light. At Town Foot, from behind the security of the Bait House, a lad shouted: "Do you know where you ought to be, mister?"

"No, tell me," Adam said.

"Where Agnes Pedley is," came the triumphant reply. "Under t'sod."

Comforted by Anthony Skidmore's support, Adam dismissed the incident as easily as he dismissed the fact that voices were hushed as he passed. Many people were walking towards the Literary Institute, where a company of strollers was giving a performance of Hamlet, and, nearing Nick Turn, he drew level with a party of former friends and acquaintances. They, too, quietened, all except Arthur Nattrass, who made a loud demand:

"How much more have we to do to you, Brunskill, to show you as you're noan wanted here?" His next remark was so offensive that Annamaria jumped forward. "Now you give up, Arthur," she said. "You've seen for yourself how Nowt Much Cooper's bandaged up. An' don't talk that nasty way either."

Arthur Nattrass glared at her. "Are you trying to make me look small or summat? Why, if I once demeaned myself by setting about a chap like him——"

Left hand shooting out, Adam grasped a fistful of clothing about his cousin's middle. At full stretch, he thrust him at the lower, ornamental arm of the lamp bracket which, finding passage beneath the coat-vent, did not appear again until it burst out at the collar. Fore-end suspended horizontally in the position of a swimmer, Arthur Nattrass' sulphurous comments were accompanied by a series of tiny reports as the stitches in his attire parted. Then Adam went his way, leaving behind new sounds, Fronick's wails of embarrassment, Annamaria's screeches of anger, and Wingy Blenkiron's gusty laughter.

Old Hannah glanced up inquiringly when he entered the kitchen. She had been very understanding when he broached living at Modesty by himself. Scolded he had been and charged with vanity, too, but, as always had been her belief, people had the right to make their decisions for themselves.

"How did you get on, lad?"

Over a late tea which she shared with him, he gave her an account of his interview with Mr. Buckle, but, more notably, of his meeting with Mr. Skidmore.

"Aye, Anthony's no fool," she was remarking when a customer arrived. "An' that reminds me o' summat I've been chewing over, but I'll tell you when I'se finished in the shop."

It was a very peculiar item, Adam thought. "Nay, I'se been wondering if it were possible to discover why it were your cousin Margaret left home," she said ten minutes later. "You know, somehow I'd like to have a talk to t'lass."

"My cousin Margaret!" he eyed her closely. "What's the connection?"

The old lady would not commit herself, guesses in such a matter being as wicked as they were unhelpful, she vowed. Adam, however, did hear a year-old tale, at fourth or fifth hand, that Margaret Pedley had been seen in Newcastle wheeling a baby. "The story went as t'carriage were a real expensive 'un," Mrs. Batty continued, "an' fro' that you'd be inclined to think she were a nursemaid pushing somebody else's child ... not her own."

"You would, aye," Adam agreed, very thoughtful.

When they left the table for a pipe apiece at each side of the hearth, his landlady initiated a very lively discussion. "Well, I hear you've started, lad," she observed.

"Started what?" Adam exclaimed.

She cackled. "Arthur Nattrass on t'lamp bracket at Nick Turn. It's gone round like wildfire."

"Oh, that," Adam laughed.

"Aye, just that," the old lady smiled. "Nobbut that."

With a companion of Old Hannah's proclivities it was impossible not to be amused when she was in the mood to give them play. Until he left for a stroll the tiny kitchen resounded with Adam's hearty laughter.

Main Street was deeply shadowed at one side but brilliantly illuminated on the other. Adam's walk took him first to the Brig, where the terraced waterfalls danced in the silvery light and the windows of a little farm-house shone dazzlingly.

"Aye, it's vanity all right, as Hannah insists, wanting to shove my defiance down everybody's throat," he murmured with a last look at Modesty, smiling faintly. "But at the bottom there's summat else ... aye, I'm after getting hold o' that spot so that if ever all the 'ifs' came out right I should have that and all."

Enjoying the night, he turned back along the village street, meeting Matt Tiplady as the trustees of the Chapel were emerging from a meeting. Mr. Kearton surveyed both of them with disapproval, but his disapproval was no less when a lady in the Literary Institute, for whom the actors' realism was too much, screamed piercingly.

"Coming, lad?" the poacher grinned. "I'm away to them pastures below Silence. Rich feed there and hares oft comes down from the peat-hags."

It was exhilarating higher up and, when they reached the desired place, a thirl-hole in a wall, Adam feasted his eyes on the beauty of moor and fell, a gracefully-crumpled tapestry whose folds and patterns were bestrewn with a soft sheen. Meantime his companion fixed a net over a rectangular hole whose legitimate purpose was to allow sheep to pass from one field to another. This done, he touched Adam's arm.

"We'll go up t'wall a bit," he whispered. "Off, Floss lass."

The piebald bitch disappeared and, perhaps four minutes later, Adam again felt the pressure of fingers. Keeping quite still he shortly picked out the hare in leaping flight, its quick turns always headed off by the dog, steadily driven lower. On perceiving the thirl-hole, it shot forward like an arrow, to end up crying as a hurt child, enmeshed in the loosely-attached net, a dark bundle which somersaulted a dozen yards.

"No, she's wi' young," Matt grunted as he unwrapped the trembling creature. "Of you go, lass, an' take greater care in t'future, or your family'll be going wi'out."

For a while, Floss squatting at their feet, the two men talked, Adam warmed again by the sure knowledge that here was another sincere friend. Then, as he wished to return to Old Hannah's to change, and as Matt had important affairs to deal with on the high moors, they separated.

Towards eleven o'clock, keeping within the shadow of the trees, Adam climbed Sleety Slape until he came to the mine buildings at Notion Bridge, silent and eerie in a wild landscape lighted by the moon. From there he was soon at Bucker Level, where, with candle burning, he proceeded through dark workings until he reached Blind Trial Crosscut and, along a narrow drift striking to the southward from Freezeland, the end of the piece of groover's thread he had left there.

That night he had his first success since starting to explore this area, discerning an hexagonal mark on a patch of powdery shale.

"Looks as if there's been knavery here an' all," he muttered.

Taking off his hat to mount an extra candle, he renewed the task with vigour.

3

Shortly after dinner on the day of the West Side Company's Extraordinary General Meeting, Titus Alderson completed the Ore Count End at the bouse-teams outside Mary Level, a regular monthly duty, that of supervising the weighing of the various partnerships' ore. He next went across to Mary Dressing Floors, where he spent an hour straightening out minor troubles.

Putting away notebook and pencil, he started off again, along the double tramway leading down the gill to Notion Bridge. The clouds were very low, and, as they drifted, the gill and the moors surrounding were often blanketed by a chilling mist from which a curlew once silently appeared, a phantom being.

The North and South Smelt Mills were completely enveloped, but, in such conditions, the splash and groan of Big William should have carried far. Fearful of further misfortune Mr. Alderson hastened along, to find the waterwheel standing it was true, but only for the short interval required by Richard Blenkiron to re-check the soundness of the pinion wheel toothing into the new segment.

"Yes, it's all serene," the blacksmith muttered, putting hand at side of mouth to bellow to Harry Blaydes who, towards the foot of Joss Foss, waited at the sluice-gates. "Right as a bobbin, Titus," he said when the old mine-agent suddenly came out from the grey cloud.

"Well, now," Jonas Cottingham remarked as if he had been delayed for hours, "maybe we can get going again."

From seventy feet above splashes fell down, the advance guard of water which, released by Harry Blaydes, rushed along watercourse and elevated launder to spill into the uppermost bucket. Big William began to move and, bucket after bucket filling in turn, it soon attained its maximum dignified rate of five revolutions to the minute, when fans nearby set up a scream which never quite drowned the chattering in the compressor house, where a double-cylinder pump once more forced high-pressure air into the reinforced wrought-iron receiver supplying the air-pipes of Notion Level. That noise also hid clattering hoofs.

Both the old mine-agent and the blacksmith smiled, each of them showing the affection of their kind for a fine waterwheel.

"Well, he's off again," Mr. Alderson said.

"Aye," Richard Blenkiron grunted, stooping to pick up a portion of the fractured segment, which he threw amongst the wash grates, wheels, and broken lead pans on the scrap heap. "An' a rare grand 'un he is."

"Easy for him, isn't it?" Jonas Cottingham pointed, referring to the smith's effortless trip with a piece of metal weighing a hundredweight and a half. "That comes o' being the strongest man in t'Dale."

Richard Blenkiron paused. "You think so?" he said laconically.

"You haven't acknowledged as Reuben Nattrass is your master, have you?" the chief smelter jibed.

This question remained unanswered because of Bart Hugill's arrival with the information that Henry Hird had called. The clerk, convinced that very soon he would be without a job, looked profoundly downcast.

Sir Charles Grafton's robustly built mineral agent was sitting near the office fire. His introductory statement when Titus Alderson entered was substantially the same as that he made on leaving very much later.

"Well, there it is, Titus," he said, at last rising. "I thought it nobbut fair to let you know that wi' Mr. Wade's permission I shall be at th'Extraordinary General Meeting to-night. What I'll do at after that depends on what I hear, but I'll noan conceal fro' you that I'm all but positive I shall advise Sir Charles to instruct t'lawyer to protect his interests . . . even though that means seriously hurting one o' my own, my sister, that is."

Titus Alderson was a very tired man, so there was peace. "Well, I think that finishes everything, Bart," he murmured as the horseman disappeared. "Fetch Ben on for me, lad. I've to wash me an' change when I get home, and I want to do a bit o' studying afore I start out for the meeting."

When alone, he glanced around an office he had known since the Skewdale Lead Mining Company was a virile undertaking. Used for rough work, the room had never been other than comfortably untidy, and the battered sloping desk was a familiar friend. There had always been a dusty but fascinating heap of pieces of rock and mineral: glazed spars, black flints, cuprous pyrites and quartz, sometimes unique in coloration. Samples had the habit of remaining there, too—pick shafts, specimens of fuse, two or three types of socket shovels. The box holding agents' candles, so often dismissed to the Candle Place with the groovers' candles, had a habit of straying back—it always had, convenience saw to that.

Titus Alderson's expression changed—it was as if he knew he might never see these everyday objects again.

As he intended walking to Half House for the meeting, Mr. Alderson stabled Ben for the night and then entered Yew Tree House by the back kitchen, shouting a jovial: "Now then, lass." To this, before passing into the kitchen proper and seeing the two visitors, he added that he would write up his rough notes before tea.

"Well, Reuben," he said with surprise. "Wanting summat?"

The young mine-agent appeared ill-humoured, but he replied agreeably enough: "Nay, I were passing so I thought I'd look in."

"Oh," Mr. Alderson murmured, a little vaguely until he remembered the conversation in the saw mill. "An', now, Mistress Tiplady," he laughed, bending over a young lady who was extremely busy with her slate, "what's t'problem . . . five Skewdale cheeses, best quality—sixty-four and three-quarter pounds at fourpence ha'penny a pound."

Mary Jane, glancing up, earnestly explained ready-reckoners. "But Mary Harker o' Low Bands mislaid hers one day an' she telled me how mortified she were—a special customer as she sells odd cheeses to had called and it took her ages to make out the bill. And she finished up eighteen pence on t'wrong side at that, an' all for a twopenny book."

"Penny wise and pound foolish, love," the inquirer observed.

Solemnity itself, Mary Jane nodded. "I were going to say that myself, Mr. Alderson. It were on the tip of my tongue."

For the first time for many a long day Titus Alderson really brightened. "I'll bet you were, lass," he chuckled as he left.

Mary Jane stared after him, but then, dismissing the peculiarities of the aged with a shrug, her slate pencil once more began to squeak.

Reuben Nattrass lost no time with Cherry. "Well, what of it, lass? An' remember this, I'll stop any bother for your uncle if you'll say yes. And that, mark you, is a question I'se never asked another lass."

Cherry was under the necessity of keeping her voice low, which made her even more furious. "I should have been more honoured if you'd asked me when somebody else weren't there," she said.

"You've taken damned good care not to give me th'opportunity," Reuben Nattrass scowled. "Anyroad, you're noan bothered about that little lass, are you? She's too throng wi' her own affairs."

Just then, as if unconsciously supporting his contention, Mary Jane sighed loudly while ferreting out a mistake. Through Mrs. Harker's embarrassing misfortune she had become aware that her education in certain practical directions was being neglected and, casting about for the best teacher, had selected Cherry, whom she visited twice weekly.

"You wed a chap for other reasons than some you've named," Cherry was saying. "But I'm talking no more to you about——"

Quickly Reuben Nattrass slipped his arm around her. Dark eyes excited, he held her tightly. "For love, eh?" he demanded. "Well, for that matter——"

"Give over," Cherry gasped. "If you don't——"

He laughed, but, as they struggled, he pulled her even more close, pinioning her arms helplessly as he lifted her off her feet. But she was free elsewhere and made desperate use of what weapons she had.

Kicked on the shinbone with all the force of an infuriated young woman, Reuben Nattrass yelped as he dropped her. "You damned little spitfire," he growled.

Hair tumbling, cheeks brilliantly flushed, and eyes sparkling, Cherry Dinsdale's breasts heaved tumultuously. "You'd better go," she told him, still finding breathing difficult.

His mouth was ugly. "Aye, I'll go, but nobbut because I've to dress me for th'Extraordinary General Meeting, where I were going to do the best I could for your uncle."

"He'd a sight rather you did your worst," Cherry declared proudly, "than say things you don't mean just for ulterior motives."

At the passage door he turned, his smile grim. "Oh, I'm noan going to do my worst, lass. You see I'se coming back here again afore so long . . . in fact I'se coming back till I'se mastered you. An' when that occurs, my love," he nod-nodded before leaving, "you're noan going to find it all that bad."

Trembling with anger, Cherry arranged her hair at the mirror, finishing as Mary Jane's pencil squeakingly drew a line. This time the sum had been done correctly, which meant that lessons were over, and so Matt Tiplady's daughter settled herself for a womanly chat.

"If he'd gone on I were going to get t'carving knife," she announced. "He were awful, weren't he?"

"He wasn't so nice, love." Cherry smiled.

Mary Jane's slow head-shake was ripe with knowledge. "If chaps behave like that aforehand what will they be like when they've getten you?" she deplored.

"Yes, what will they be like?" Cherry agreed lightly.

Mary Jane, if this reply were not entirely satisfactory, politely stifled curiosity and chatted gaily enough on other matters until she heard the footsteps of the master of the house, when immediately she got up.

"Men don't like outsiders about when they're sitting down to their tea," she explained. "An' thank you very much, Cherry love."

Titus Alderson was quite cheerful throughout the meal, but, as the minute hand of the grandfather clock neared half-past six, when Cherry was helping him into his coat, he made one remark which was to cause her a great deal of heartache.

"Cherry, lass," he began while she was straightening his collar and pulling his lapels, "is there owt betwixt you an' Reuben Nattrass?"

"No," she answered, startled. "For why, Uncle?"

"Nay, I nobbut wondered, lass," he murmured.

"Oh!" Cherry's lips just moved.

Concerned, he held her away from him. "My words, love, by th'expression you've got I reckon you're of the opinion I'm trying to get shut o' you. Well, I'm not . . . only . . ."

"Only what, Uncle?" she asked swiftly.

He shook his head. "We seem to be getting into deep waters, lass. All I'm thinking is that, when t'right young fellow comes along an' you get wed, I shall sorely miss you, but . . . well, I'm noan any younger, love, and in the position I am it'd be a comfort to see you happy in a home of your own."

Whether or not he meant he would not be ill-pleased if she were more accommodating about Reuben Nattrass's wooing, Cherry did not know. But the mere suspicion of it depressed her inordinately while she cleared the table and washed up, and when, to pass the anxious time, she put the iron on the fire to press a few clothes which might well have waited.

At nine o'clock, too restless to sew any more, she put on her mantle to walk to Half.

The clouds had thinned appreciably, the moon behind shedding a pearly light upon shareholders of the West Side Lead Mining Company who, on foot, on horseback, or in vehicles, streamed down the drive of Half House towards the Dutch elm near the main gates.

Cherry waited on the grassy verge opposite, just far enough from the Groovers Welcome to escape the notice of Jonas Cottingham and his customers, who had taken post in the tap-room to miss nothing. She soon saw her uncle and, when Mr. Rutter turned into the Old Cow Inn, she slipped across and took his arm.

Beyond telling her that no real conclusion had been reached at the meeting other than that if possible the company would keep operating for a while, Titus Alderson said little, obviously too worn out to talk.

Very slowly, and largely in silence, they walked home, where Cherry quickly blew up the fire with the bellows. Soon she had a pot of tea ready for him with a few of his favourite ginger biscuits.

"That's been very refreshing, lass," Mr. Alderson remarked as he pushed cup and saucer aside. "Well, I've got a rare lot o' writing-up to do in th'office, so you go off to bed when you're ready."

"You'll light the fire, won't you?" Cherry insisted. "It's laid."

He patted her hand when he got up, and bent to kiss her fondly. "You're a good lass," he told her, voice not too sure. "Done all you could for th'old uncle who everybody tells has made such a mess o' things."

"Were they awful to you?" she asked.

Very much as he had done at the mine office, he glanced about the bright room, from the display of his mother's china in the corner cupboard to the clay pipes by his own chair. "Well, t'young fellow I were inquiring about afore I went weren't one of 'em, choose how," he told her. "Bear i' mind, I didn't agree with any of Reuben Nattrass's arguments about th'advantages of the two companies joining forces—if his would consent, that is—but I will say this, he never uttered a single word o' criticism about me. In fact, he did his best to stand up for me while some of th'others were being . . . well, noan so nice."

"Try not to worry, Uncle," Cherry begged.

Titus Alderson's smile was grotesque as he walked towards the door. "I believe all the talk at the Plug last night were about them English folk who's been murdered i' Cabul, but to-night I've the privilege o' being the talk of t'district. Yes, that's how it is, but don't you fret. Remember, love, all's for the best."

During the very few steps he took before passing from sight Cherry could think of nothing to bring him a vestige of consolation.

That evening Matt Tiplady had called at Old Hannah's for a yarn, consequently Adam was extremely late in setting out for a glass of beer before changing and climbing Sleety Slape to Bucker Level. The Plug and Feathers was crowded, and his advent was not marked by the company either with a scowl or other sign of non-acceptance, itself an indication that more exciting matters were under deliberation. A friend told him what these were. Both Mr. and Mrs. Harker, for reasons not wholly sound, had been Adam's champions ever since the gravest of his troubles started.

"Aye, th'Extraordinary General Meeting of the West Side Company," Francis Harker said. "I was there myself, Adam, and there's been a real row."

"And what about Mr. Alderson?" Adam asked.

The farmer was swilling the remaining contents of his tankard. "Publicly censured for bad mining," he replied succinctly before drinking off. "Never heard owt like it i' my life," he added. "Th'awful things as were shouted at that poor old chap."

Elsewhere Richard Blenkiron raised his mighty voice. "Why should Reuben be able to make all that difference to t'West Side Company? When all's said, he's noan doing so grand with his own, and——"

Nathan Wharton interrupted him. "Anyroad, a lot o' shareholders sounded as if they'd agree to owt which 'ud defer th'evil day. Talk about throwing Titus Alderson to t'lions . . ."

Adam leaned nearer Mr. Harker. "How were Mr. Alderson?"

"Like . . ." Francis Harker frowned, "like a chap as were going to his death—I mean when he walked out at th'end. He fought like a black aforehand."

The Plug and Feathers kept only the best beer, but Adam disposed of what he had with scant regard to its prime quality. On stepping outside, he turned along Main Street, his long striding gait soon taking him beyond Old Hannah's and Nick Turn.

"I'll place afore him such evidence as I have as to what may have been happening," he reflected. "It's noan conclusive, but . . ."

The lamp was burning in the kitchen of Yew Tree House, but, his pace slower, he continued past the green gate as far as the Bait House, pondering how he might disarm curiosity if others were present, who certainly would wonder about the errand of someone no longer a welcome visitor to the house. This particular dilemma was solved for him as he turned back, when he glimpsed a thin slit of light peeping round the blind in the agent's office. A few seconds afterwards he was tiptoeing closer to the window in Jom High Road.

Through the narrow gap he saw Mr. Alderson, not more than five feet away. The old mining-agent's haggard face was ineffably sad as, lips moving, he read the Bible. Close by his elbow were several envelopes and, so out of place on a neatly-kept desk, a coil of sump rope.

"I don't like the look o' this," Adam muttered, slipping to the side door, which he knocked. To begin with there was no response, but then dragging footsteps came nearer and the knob turned. "I'm sorry to trouble you, Mr. Alderson . . ." he began.

Titus Alderson peered uncertainly. "It's noan . . . *you*, Adam Brunskill, isn't it?" he said. "An' what is it you want wi' me?"

"To talk to you, Mr. Alderson. And I must."

So near to the fulfilment of a dread purpose Titus Alderson forgot that the young man was largely ostracised by the village. "Any other time, lad, any other time gladly," he whispered. "Not to-night . . . not . . ." A spasm of pain contorted his face, his hand went to his side. He moaned and, eyes closing, swayed.

Adam caught him before he fell and, shutting the door with a backward kick, carried him inside where, lips blue, he lay unconscious.

"He's real bad," Adam muttered. "But afore I fetch anybody I'm looking on that desk."

His surmise correct, he collected the betraying evidence: letters addressed to Cherry, Edmund Kearton, and Mr. Miles Buckle, Coroner. These, together with the rope and a card inscribed: 'Bolted inside—Fetch Richard Blenkiron to open this place,' he had just stuffed into a cupboard seldom used, deep beneath dusty old copies of the *Mining Journal*, when a latch clicked.

"What are you doing here?" Cherry asked, and then flew to the chair. "Uncle Titus!" she cried. "Oh, Uncle Titus . . ."

In a brass candlestick a stump of candle remained and, after striking a match, Adam touched her arm. "Light me to his bedroom an' I'll sam him up," he said. "Then if you've got some brandy in the house, get it."

With scarcely a word passing between them they did their various duties. Adam undressed the old mine-agent down to his flannel shirt and, when Cherry was in the kitchen filling the stone hot-water bottles and heating bricks, continued with the moistening of her uncle's lips with spirit. After a while, though his colour was acutely ominous, a faint but shuddering sigh escaped him.

"I'll be off sharp for t'doctor," Adam said.

Cherry, deathly pale, had fought through the shock and was a competent young woman. "Take Ben," she said. "The lamp for the stable is in t'back kitchen, hanging up."

Arousing an animal not used to night jaunts, Adam quickly saddled and led him out by the side gateway into Jom High Road. Town Foot was deserted, but from within the gloom at the foot of Sorrow Near Adam heard a slight scuffle, and so crossed the road.

A feminine shriek answered his call, but a young man stepped forward determinedly with fists clenched. "What the hell's your game, Brunskill?" Bart Hugill growled. "And . . . an' what are you doing wi' t'galloway?"

Adam's head jerked. "Run as fast as you can to Mrs. Batty's an' tell her Mr. Alderson's been taken bad and that I'm off for Dr. Seaton. And get Fronick to go and keep Cherry company till Hannah comes."

Conditions for the ride were tolerable as far as Half, but, even where the highway rose across the moor beyond, the promise of the moon to dissipate the fine cloud was never fulfilled and, man and horse swathed in bright silvery vapour, Ben's instinct was always preferable. Over the summit it cleared, however, and Adam was able to speed down towards the few lights still twinkling in the village. Shortly he reached Greets Hall, the Green, and the northern side of the Market Place.

The doctor was visiting patients, but returned within a few minutes. He barely heard Adam out before he was roaring for Mighty Joe to be brought round, meantime blasphemously struggling into the ruins of a many-caped garment which accorded ill with natty checked breeches and resplendent leather leggings. Simultaneously he flamingly and repeatedly declined to listen to a middle-aged, stubborn-featured domestic whose theme was: "But it's on t'table, if you please, sir, an' it'll noan tak' long to swallow summat, an' anybody 'ud think you were daft, they would really."

"What you hanging about for?" this much-engaged gentleman flung at Adam. "Be off with you."

Adam's next sight of Dr. Seaton was on the Green, near the big elm. A mad drumming of hoofs heralded his coming and then he swept by, a little man, in an extremely formal hat, upon a gigantic horse. Adam was under the impression that the wild rider was eating a veritable doorstep of a sandwich.

After settling Ben, Adam entered Yew Tree House from the back as Old Hannah was on the point of going upstairs. She paused to tell him that Mr. Alderson was conscious but very weak.

"I'm stopping here t'night, lad," she went on. "An' if I'm noan home by breakfast time put out a card for me, will you? The one wi' the picture of a bed-pan."

Adam waited in the kitchen until she reached the end of the long passage, when quietly he took the same course as far as the foot of the stairs, where he slipped into the office, in which the lamp still burned. Immediately opening a cupboard, he began to search through the plans stacked upright in it, rejecting dozens before coming across what he required, one in which Notion Level and Old Joss Main Level were set out, with the Short Cut and the fore-heading of the New Drift also shown.

"Now with this and th'other I got I can lay my survey westward from t'Black Drift, using the measurements and dialling particulars I've already booked," he mumbled. "*Then* . . ."

His deep-set eyes gleamed as, re-rolling the plan on its wooden roller, he opened the door into Jom High Road and placed it outside for recovery later.

These matters had been nicely accomplished when Cherry left her uncle's bedroom. At the foot of the stairs she was turning along the passage when she remembered the lamp which until then she had been too busy to extinguish. At the sight of the tall young man in her uncle's office her breath caught.

"I've startled you, haven't I?" Adam apologised.

Expressionlessly she looked at him. "Did you startle my uncle as well? What were you doing in here when I found you with him?"

"I'd wanted a word with him, an' I saw his light here," Adam told her.

She was the inexorable judge, passionless. "So you did startle him then? But you wouldn't have done if you'd come to the front first, would you? Like others do when on a private call."

Adam's voice rasped a trifle. "All right, I startled him."

"But if you hadn't, he wouldn't be where he is," she continued with cold logic. "Lying helpless and in pain."

There are better medicines than those of the doctor, and Adam believed he had one which might revive even a very sick old man. "When do you think he'll be able to see anybody?" he asked.

That broke her calm. "I don't know whether ever . . . I don't know even if he wants to get better."

"But that isn't because I startled him," Adam said.

The flush ebbed from her cheeks, the flame was spent. "No, it isn't." she murmured. "An' I'm sorry I've spoken to you as I have. And . . . and I'd like to thank you for what you did at after."

"Aye . . ." Adam nodded. "Well, it were all I could do, and as apparently it's all I can do now I reckon I'd better be off."

She seemed to accept this as quite final, and he left.

The same night, Adam worked on Hannah's kitchen table re-scaling and transferring to a sheet of cartridge paper the two plans he had purloined. This tricky job done, he drank a bottle of beer and smoked a pipe before returning to quadrant, divider and rule.

"And now for th'easiest part, and," he promised himself without fear of contradiction, "the most interesting part."

Slowly the dots representing each dialling station began to extend westward from the Black Drift, the zig-zagging line eventually crossing the two companies' common boundary. Soon he had established his theory beyond doubt, when an infinitesimal strip of virgin white paper separated the place where Titus Alderson had started the Short Cut from the last plotting point pencilled: that indicating the position of two tram-rails.

"Aye," Adam said exultantly, "there's nobbut a very few fathoms between 'em, close enough for the needle of his dial to have been affected. Yes, this is number one knavery all right. But as yet I haven't any valid proof linking Cousin Reuben with t'business. A few hexagonal nut marks wouldn't count, and what I want is evidence that could stand up in a court of law if needs be."

The next two nights he spent in Freezeland, where already his route was immeasurably longer than the first survey he had completed. Between whiles he saw Hannah Batty occasionally, who gravely told him the sick man was neither better nor worse.

On Sunday, anxious to speed with the job, Adam set off for Bucker Level in the late afternoon. The weather was not pleasant, with frequent showers of cold and fine rain which in the bottoms lent rawness to the air, and higher up the fells froze in a thin film upon rocks and hard places.

Several hours later, some four hundred fathoms from where he had begun this section of his search, he entered an extensive cavern whose remote cheek was cut in solid chert. As he glanced upwards the light of the candle on his hat illuminated the roof of the gallery, but the shadow made by the brim, its edge a crescent, darkened the sole. Almost inevitably the soft yellow glow would have shone on the pile of tram-rails, but the clink of his toe on metal allowed him an earlier intimation.

"They're here!" he ejaculated, bending closer. "And a rare pile an' all." Mouth harsh and eyes angered, he counted twenty-two, of the same bastard pattern as the others. "Well, I've still to dial and measure to here," he muttered, "and it's going to take me a fortnight or three weeks at the best. But I'll bet now that somewhere noan so far beyond that face o' chert is what they've christened Alderson's Folly."

Without instruments there was nothing further he could do then and so, his face stern, he started back. To save himself a long walk underground, he headed for the old ladders in Whistling Shaft. Miner-like, as opposed to sailors and others, he held the iron rungs and not the wooden sides, the stiff soles of his clogs giving secure foothold. This once, however, pliable leather would have been better, for, perhaps thirty-five fathoms up, the regular rhythm of his legs and arms, a ten-inch lift each time, was rudely altered on reaching a length where the rungs had been set an inch wider apart, an alteration frowned upon by law. Insecurely grasping the next rung, he lost balance, his clog irons skidding off a rung icily coated by the combination of rain and freezing downcast. Candle long before blown out by the draught, he swung sideways in the darkness, hanging on by two fingers, but on the return recovered, the sole damage a sharp scrape from a wall-plate.

"That's summat I'd better watch out for i' future," he warned himself when, the stars coldly scintillating above, he stepped from the eye.

Following trods discernible in the starshine, he strode freely along until he was nearing Smiddy Bridge, when he heard footsteps on the hardening surface of the Roman road. A powerful voice was being permitted full scope in the Calvinistic *Rock of Ages* and, from behind an outcrop of rock, he watched Richard Blenkiron go by. The blacksmith crossed Winterings Beck and then turned down the track winding alongside the gill, the sound of the hymn dying away as the distance increased.

"Been preaching somewhere," Adam thought, just as he realised his right hand was warm and sticky. "Must have cut myself when I slipped."

That night Mrs. Peacock was taking turns with Cherry to sit up with the invalid. This allowed Old Hannah a night in bed, where she was when Adam entered her little kitchen. The wound, rather deep near the elbow, was oozing only slightly when he examined it after washing away dried blood, and it felt quite comfortable after he had bound his arm with a couple of strips of snowy-white linen kept by his landlady for emergencies.

Very satisfied with the outcome of the night's work, he poured a cup of coffee from the brown pot which latterly it had become Old Hannah's habit to leave on the grate.

4

On the night after Adam's narrow escape in Whistling Shaft, Matt Tiplady was caught poaching in a well-organised trap, gamekeepers and gamewatchers from outside having been brought in secretly. This news might well have kept Winterings agog for longer had not Mr. Wade's angry retort to Mrs. Robert William Alderson in Blind Kit's workshop become public property. The spinner had declared that while he was chairman of the West Side Company, "which God help me I am," no decision would be made about the company's future until its head-agent's illness was resolved one way or the other.

As talk went, Mrs. Roberty Will threw prudence to the wind, but she had her brother's support. "The one thing as should be done, Mr. Wade, is to approach th'East Side Company as soon as possible," she was supposed to have said. "Henry here isn't sure, of course, but he seems inclined to believe they might pay attention. An' if you've any regard for your shareholders you'll do so, if you're a businessman, that is."

This piece of news reached Yew Tree House shortly before the wife of a groover in Mary Forehead, troubled by another rumour, called to ask if it were true that her husband would not be on the Pay until his partnership's ore had been smelted into lead and the proceeds received.

"Worried or not," Old Hannah pronounced downstairs, "she oughtn't to have come wi' a silly tale like that. Not when there's serious illness."

Cherry touched the old lady's arm. "Is he going to get better, Hannah? Tell me really what you think."

Slowly Mrs. Batty shook her silvery-white head. "I don't know, lass. You see your uncle's noan trying."

"It's because he's broken-hearted," Cherry told her.

"Aye, I reckon so," Old Hannah sighed, noting the girl's peaked face.

Out of the blue she then became an old woman with a grudge. Had she always to be working herself to the bone for others? Would she soon have another patient on her hands? As outcome, Cherry was bundled off in bonnet and cape, under strict instructions to visit Dinah at Badger Hall, where she was to chatter about anything except ailments and people's troubles.

At Sun Hade Pump Shaft on Heugh Syke, where the waterwheel was geared to a pump of six-foot stroke, Reuben Nattrass had been making an inspection with Cyprian Metcalfe. New gland packings decided upon, the East Side Company's agent started down the beck towards Sweet Tarn, where he found Richard Blenkiron looking at his hives, now overdue in being taken back to Smithy House garth. As the means for carrying were there, he offered to shoulder one end of a pole and so, a hive swinging between them, they marched in file down the moor, arriving at Town Foot as Cherry turned up Main Street.

A single-purposed young man, Reuben Nattrass caught her up before she reached Calvert's Wynd—he also warded off several people who wished to inquire about her uncle. Busy with persuasions, he even waved his father aside. William Nattrass, who was driving four cows, winked knowingly at Cherry, his jowls quivering at the sight of his son so engrossed in a young woman.

At Ash Grove Reuben Nattrass detained her while he summed up: "Now I've already showed my good faith, haven't I? At th'Extraordinary General Meeting didn't I up to my feet to speak for your Uncle Titus?"

"Yes, and I'm grateful, an' he was, too," Cherry said wearily. "But that's nothing to do with me marrying you."

Sharply he pulled her to face him. "Love again, eh? Isn't what I've telled you enough? Well, if it isn't . . ." he flushed slightly, "then here goes—I love you."

Cherry shook her head. "I'm sorry, but you see I don't love you."

"But you soon would, when we were wed," he urged. "Leastways you'd either do that or you'd hate me . . . and I don't reckon it'd be that, not wi' a full-blooded lass like yourself."

"I won't listen any more to such horrid——" Cherry was beginning furiously when he interrupted her to remark that he had little use for mock modesty. "Why, in country like this," he added, "with all th'animals, there's always mating going on."

"But I'm not an animal," Cherry retorted. "An' I'm *not* listening to anything else. It's noan decent, it isn't."

The pair of them, not unreasonably, had attracted attention, but his good-humoured smile became an ominous glare when he noticed the ever-curious Cuthbert Daykin making the most of posting a letter in the pillar-box built into Mrs. Metcalfe's wall.

"All right then, lass," Reuben Nattrass conceded as the grocer scurried inside, "but maybe you'll listen to this. If . . ." he pointed at her in his customary style, "you'll promise to wed me I'll have things well i' train for an amalgamation of the two companies afore you've getten the gold ring on your finger. An' I'll work it that your Uncle Titus is still kept on as chief agent. Could you give him any better tonic than that?"

"There's only one tonic that would help him," Cherry murmured. "To be able to wind the clock back and start over again . . . and not to make the mistakes he has."

"He'd forget all that in due course if he were associated with twice as big a company," Reuben Nattrass assured her. "An' I can do it, lass. If you want to know why . . ." he rubbed forefinger and thumb together, " it's because I've got Mr. Storey like that. So you'd better think it over again, lass."

"I've nothing to think over," Cherry said.

Reuben Nattrass pushed open the gate of Ash Grove. "Oh yes, you have, lass," he grunted. "Your uncle's well-being. But that seems by the way, doesn't it?"

"To do with what you want . . . yes," Cherry replied.

"It's in your hands anyroad," the mine-agent countered. "I'se heard as how he is, so don't tell me he wouldn't begin to mend if he were told his services were wanted in a grand scheme that were afoot."

Cherry never succeeded during the rest of her walk in shaking off the impression these words made. Leaning on the parapet of the Brig she hardly saw the quaint acrobatics of a water-vole perched upon a half-submerged rock, or the valiant efforts of a trout to surmount the waterfall in search of a breeding ground. Lovely colour was before her, the rosy rays of a sinking sun lighting up the purplish bark of alders and the saffron and cinnamon marks on the smooth, silver-grey stems of birches. The trees had thinned out and the full glory of autumnal change had passed, but much breath-taking beauty remained—the dusty green of Scots pine and the deeper green of spruce; the pale, yellow green of ash and the guinea gold of elm; the shiny green of holly separated from browning larches by the big blowsy leaves of the sycamore.

"Oh, God," she whispered, "please make Uncle Titus have a real turn."

Filled with foreboding, she started off towards Blenk Bottom Lane, barely noticing the young rabbits who played spirited games beneath the flood bank, but, nearing Snorr Bridge, she was roused from her abstractedness by the sound of youthful voices, and from the crest she saw a sad *cortège* passing the Waggotts' cottage.

Wearing a black wide-awake hat which rested on his ears, Ward Tiplady walked in front, immediately before Walter Heseltine Skidmore and Nancy Skidmore, who jointly pulled the rope fastened to a piece of board covered with black cloth upon which, becoming a trifle plump, Nell reclined placidly, apparently in the guise of the dear departed. Next came Mary Jane, whose face was buried in a black-bordered handkerchief, just ahead of Alice and Harriet, secondary mourners. Bob Skidmore kept station alongside the hearse, he and Ward constantly bickering about the pace, very much as their grandfather differed with parson and mourners on such occasions.

At other times Cherry's eyes would have crinkled with amusement, but now, because of that unquiet in her, they welled. Unable to face either the children or her friend, she turned abruptly, blindly to run past Susan Skidmore's little house lest she should be beckoned in for a talk.

From Middle Sorrow, at the top of the hill by Silence, her retreat in the declining light was seen by the tall young man who was striding there.

When the weather was good enough Adam usually got up in the early afternoon, and as a bracer for the coming night's work took a brisk tramp. That afternoon, always preferring higher ground, he had crossed the Hippy Stones to Back Lane and Middle Sorrow, pausing near Silence to glance at the pasture below where Ralph Skidmore, Hey! Thoo! not far away, was leading a sled-load of stone for drain building. From there he glimpsed Cherry.

"Still blames me for her uncle," he murmured. "Well, that's summat that can be straightened out eventually, I hope."

At the foot of the deeply-rutted hill, the children had finished their game. They viewed him with considerable solemnity.

"My mother says as we haven't to speak to you," Nancy began, not uncoquettishly.

"You *were* speaking to him," her sister complained.

"This comes of 'lowing them to join in, Ward lad," Bob grumbled. "Anyroad, you an' me 'ul speak to him, won't we?"

"We will that, Bob lad," Ward confirmed. "Aye, we're with you."

"To t'last inch, Adam," Bob added.

While gravely thanking the cousins, Adam pulled out his watch in response to Mary Jane's request. On hearing the time she pointed towards the village and, in terms obviously borrowed from some mother with a vocabulary highly suited to dispatching unwilling children on shopping errands, directed the boys to be off at once.

"That's right," she screamed, when Ward expostulated, "cause me some more bother . . . as if we hadn't enough trouble as it is."

"But we'll go in two-three minutes, lass," her cousin Bob promised.

"You'll go now," the shrew announced. "Because I can't start cooking until you get back an' . . ." her lips quivered and big grey eyes began to fill, "and I wanted my father to have summat real nice afore . . . afore he went to prison."

At that, both Bob and Ward comforted her, but, the finest way of all to make amends, they tore over Snorr Bridge on their mission.

Adam walked with her to Lane End. "Your father's only going afore the magistrates, love," he told her. "He's noan going to prison."

"He is, Adam," Mary Jane replied with absolute surety.

At the little cottage sheltering beneath a far-spreading ash, Adam stayed with her until long after she had become her chatty, informative self, but, as her father did not appear, went up Snorr Beck, where Anthony Skidmore was sawing or lopping off with a bill-hook the branches of a small larch he had felled. Matt Tiplady and Floss arrived some time later.

Bidding the farmer good night they strolled to the Royal Alfred, where Will Skidmore acknowledged Adam with an almost imperceptible nod before once more tackling his brother-in-law as to how he should comport himself in Corvy.

"Now when you get there," he urged, "ask Albert Gibson to take you to t'Manor office. Mr. Buckle's a decent sort, an' if you act civil, an' apologise——"

"Hark at him," Matt jeered. "Ever heard this, Will lad?

> '*Lambs are killed by the butcher's knife,*
> *Ducks by the hand of the farmer's wife,*
> *But Game lose their life by t'Quality.*'"

Will Skidmore remained patient. "Never mind about that, Matt. See Mr. Buckle——"

"Like hell I will," Matt Tiplady remarked amiably.

"Well, if you won't . . ." the gamekeeper said. "But for the Lord's sake don't start airing your views to t'magistrates, or it'll noan be a question of a fine."

"It's a chance I've been waiting for, is this," the poacher gloated. "By, but I'll let 'em have it."

Elsewhere in the tap-room old Luke Close and his friend of a lifetime, Chesty Geordie, were discussing with three or four groovers the prospects of the West Side Company's survival. One of them was observing that, whatever Henry Hird's advice might have been, Sir Charles Grafton had not as yet made a decision adverse to the company.

"Maybe going in line wi' Mr. Wade," he continued. "Doing nowt till it's seen how Titus Alderson gets on."

Adam paid a great deal of attention to this conversation, which ended just before Matt Tiplady, who had promised to be home early, limped to the door. Outside, Mary Jane's father made his position finally clear.

"There's occasions, Will," he said, his expression almost visionary, "when a chap has to speak out bold about what he believes. I reckon t'moors are still what they used to be called: 'wastes and commons,' and by commons it means that any chap——"

"You'll get fourteen days at t'best," Will Skidmore groaned.

The pair were still arguing when Adam wished the poacher 'good luck,' but thereafter they may have agreed to differ, for soon Matt Tiplady's superb baritone was raised in Blenk Bottom Lane.

The wind was increasing and, towards Winterings Brig, Adam heard the rattle of tins which Francis Harker, in preparation for winter, had fastened on the outbuildings of Low Bands Farm to scare away foxes driven down by hunger.

At Old Hannah's supper awaited him, but he was not allowed to sit down to it then.

"Doff that coat and roll up your right sleeve," she ordered him with appreciable grimness. "That arm o' yours has been getting stiffer an' stiffer. What have you done?"

"Nobbut cut it a bit," Adam excused himself.

"Now let's see," she muttered as she prodded the wound with a finger-tip. "Puffy . . . I reckon t'cleaning balm first. And you're noan going out to-night, lad."

The cut was thoroughly washed in very hot water, plentifully salved, and then bandaged. After a while Adam began to feel a little more comfortable, but he was glad enough to stay indoors for once.

Two days later he knew he should not have indulged himself; with shattering force he realised that from then he must pursue with all the energy he could muster the undertaking he had assumed.

5

The afternoon was perishingly cold and the children were being sent home from school an hour earlier. Mr. Kidd, whose voice boomed much less since he had become starkly apprehensive about his West Side shares, was emphasising that delivery of the coal for the schoolroom fire was promised before evening, which meant that prayers and hymn-singing would start without fail the next morning at nine o'clock sharp.

"So you're all to be here," he told his charges, clapping podgy hands. "An' it'll be the ruler afterwards for them who doesn't heed what I've said."

Boys and girls scattered happily, those from outlying farms running to the Skewdale ponies tethered opposite, others with shrill cries dashing along Main Street. Amidst these youngsters and purposefully plodding horses Adam walked along, overtaken now and then by a rough-coated animal which, heavily cantering, seemed as glad to be homeward bound as the family party on its back.

Adam's errand was to Richard Blenkiron, who, after examining Old Hannah's broken grate, said what was necessary and no more: "Aye, I can mend it. It'll be ready on Saturday if you call."

Town Foot was rather thronged with the influx of children and other activities. Whips cracked as a load of mine wood, drawn by three horses, entered Sorrow Near for the stiff climb to Notion Bridge; four more horses were hitched by the Smithy door, two waiting to be shod, the other pair to lend additional support to the team just arrived from Corvy with a wagon laden with explosives. One of the kegs was faulty and two boys, Ward Tiplady and Bob Skidmore, disappearing down the highway, were retrieving grains of the fine trail of black powder.

Between the houses beyond Edmund Kearton's workshop and the policeman's cottage a strip of pasture reached down to Main Street. As Adam returned he noticed a sharp-nosed hedgehog whose bright, dark eyes watched him.

"That's summat else I can tell little Bessie about." This reminded him again of a somewhat strange letter from Bessie's mother. "It's noan like Jane to be so vague," he murmured, re-reading. "But you might almost imagine she and Simon were thinking o' bringing Bessie over to see Nell and Ben and all th'other animals. But surely they'd never make the trip to arrive i' winter."

As he folded the two pages, in which there was a slight but consoling reference to the misfortunes he had written about, he saw George Nattrass crossing the street. They met against a much-prized plate-glass window, Adam's eyes gleaming momentarily as he came to a standstill.

"Well, Uncle George," he began with great solemnity, "I've been devoting a real lot o' thought to that proposal, but I somehow can't reconcile my conscience to it. And even if I could, the brass weren't all that tempting either."

The cheese-factor's sneering: "Ha!" cracked out so loudly that Cuthbert Daykin slipped from behind his counter to arrange more artistically a pyramid of potatoes at the top of the barrel outside the door. While uncle and nephew were within range he picked up enough to send him hastening inside again, where, in the room behind the shop, he burst vehemently into *Come with me to Fairyland*.

"So the conscience you vaunt has a price, eh?" Mr. Nattrass snapped before then. "In that case you'll be glad to hear I'm fixing t'price at an all round figure, five shillings."

Adam looked pained. "I don't know as how I should put it quite that road, Uncle George."

"Put it how you want, t'fact is that you're after more money," the cheese-factor said nastily. "Anyroad, as it happens I can meet your demands handsomely, because there's more than I thought on who'd be willing to follow the line I took. All told it'd amount to two hundred an' seventy-five shares. Now, how's that conscience o' yours feeling?"

"Dulling," Adam admitted with regret. "Course it'd depend on what I were paid for each of t'shares, wouldn't it?"

"But I've just named it," George Nattrass growled. "Didn't I . . ." he glimpsed Cuthbert Daykin's half-opened mouth and changed irritably to: "Come on down t'street, there's too many nosy folks about here."

Against the big gates to his brother William's stable-yard entrance the essentials soon stood revealed. "Five shillings is the limit," he said.

"But it's noan mine," Adam retorted.

Flushing with temper, the older man strove to contain himself. "How much do you want? Go on, let's have it."

"Nay, you've put th'idea forward," Adam hedged. "But I'll tell you this, I shan't do any serious thinking till ten shillings is mentioned."

"Half a sovereign apiece!" the cheese-factor glowered, before flinging away. "I'll rot first."

Highly tickled by still another of these encounters, Adam was starting off towards Nick Turn when he was cautiously addressed by Cuthbert Daykin, who, arrayed in white apron, stood back in his doorway. Mr. Daykin, conscious of initiating a conversation with one at whom the majority of his customers looked askance, was extremely hurried. "Hey!" he hissed. "If you arrange owt wi' George Nattrass I'll be willing to come in on t'same terms."

Astounded, Adam had hardly begun to speak before the grocer brushed aside any possible objections.

"Here, hold on." Adam at last stemmed the tide, when with real curiosity he asked a question: "Do you mean you'd pay the same as my Uncle George, without even being consulted?"

"To t'penny," Cuthbert Daykin confessed. "George Nattrass is an astute 'un, and what he'll agree to pay 'ul do for me. Now then, you'll give me the same opportunity?"

Adam got out of that by saying: "If the occasion arises." Lost in reverie about an individual the hollowness of whose pretensions to be a self-confident tradesman could not have been revealed more clearly, he was proceeding along Main Street when jostled by a young woman far more bemused than himself. Brown eyes horrified, Dinah Skidmore was running, but the impact shook her out of herself. Recognising Adam, she forgot all that had happened in recent weeks.

"Adam," she gasped, "I've been to ask Cherry if she could manage to drive with us to Hawes Bull Fair——"

Mrs. Ralph Skidmore had been shopping and, incredulity and anger mixed in her expression, she tugged her young sister-in-law's arm. "What do you reckon you're doing, Dinah, talking to *him*?" she asked. "Come you away or I'll be off to tell your mother."

"Please yourself," Dinah said. "Go anywhere, in fact, so long as it's out of my road."

Mrs. Ralph spluttered, remarked wildly that "someone 'ul suffer for this," and then marched off, her angular face colouring alarmingly.

"What's up, lass?" Adam asked Dinah.

Miserably she looked at him. "Cherry's wedding Reuben Nattrass," she gulped. "Soon."

Adam's throat felt dry. "Wedding him?"

Dinah nodded. "Oh aye, and she's going to see Rosie Caygill about a real nice dress, an' Fronick'll be making her a special bonnet. Of course," she mimicked, "it's time she were settling down. Yes, that's what she telled me, *me*, her best friend. But I'm sure she's doing it because she's got it into her silly head that that big bully can help her uncle . . . as if he could."

Pallor crept beneath Adam Brunskill's tan. "So it's all fixed?"

"In under a month, at t'Chapel on the third Saturday in October," Dinah announced. "And I'm to be a bridesmaid, *and* Fronick an' Anna-maria, even though she hasn't had much to do with either of them since —well, for a longish while. Oh yes, it's going to be a grand big wedding."

Slow tears were escaping from her eyes when Wingy Blenkiron stepped pugnaciously across the street. "What's he been saying to you, lass?" he demanded.

She spun on him with quite unnecessary venom. "Nowt as calls for your assistance, though even if it did you wouldn't be able to do much about it, would you, not when you've an arm missing? It's a rare handicap i' life, isn't it?"

Watched by the two men, she fled towards Winterings Brig, neat ankles flashing.

"She's very upset," Adam remarked, turning towards the bow-fronted shop.

"Nice bloody thing to say to a chap," the postman growled.

Old Hannah found Adam extremely uncommunicative during tea, but let him be. After the meal, contrary to recent habit, he immediately changed into mining garb.

"Aye," she mused when he had gone, "he's a dangerous customer now. Well, you can't wonder after what I'm sure he'll have heard. T'lad's always favoured that lass."

News travelled fast in Skewdale. For some hours she had known that Cherry Dinsdale and Reuben Nattrass were to marry shortly.

CHAPTER ELEVEN

I

AT DAWN, on the fifth day before Cherry Dinsdale was to become Reuben Nattrass's wife, Adam climbed painfully out of Whistling Shaft, the conquest of every rung a feat of balance when hindered by an arm almost useless. At the eye, after stepping on to solid ground, he dashed sweat off his forehead before sitting on an old wind-machine wheel.

A sigh escaped him. "It's no good," he thought. "If I'd another pair of hands I could finish the dialling within a night, but as it is I'll be a week or more, an' I'm getting slower. In any event I've discovered nowt else that's conclusive."

Moor life was awakening—a single grouse cried harshly, and then another, until the air resounded with whirring wings as the cocks circled, chattering to the hens. As the light strengthened, flocks of sheep came into view, busily nibbling.

"Well, I'll have to do summat," he muttered.

He got up, to follow the trod winding round the edge of Swallow Bog, whose innocent-looking surface was clothed with the creamy-white flowers of the starlike Grass of Parnassus. Below Wild Goose Shaft he halted, to stare at the sun rising in the gap between Usha Beacon and the fells to the south of Greets, and then, reluctant to return to Old Hannah's until he had formulated some plan, lay down on springy growths dried by the Indian summer of the past days. Wearied by more than a fortnight of physical and mental strain, he dropped into sleep. When he awoke it was after eight o'clock.

By now an adept in crossing the moors undetected, he slipped past several people unobserved—Francis Harker cutting bracken for bedding; Will Skidmore baiting with rabbit the delicately-balanced flagstones of Samson traps whose fall would bring instantaneous death to weasels and stoats; Reuben Nattrass, more and more cock-a-hoop with himself lately, joking with the men cleaning out a watercourse.

At the foot of Noggin Moor, Adam sat down again. From there he had a commanding view of the lower part of the Dale.

"But what can I do?" he puzzled, unsmilingly watching a pair of squirrels who, from branch to branch in a copse in the pasture below, were swinging in search of acorns. "Except tell about what I've already found."

His glance roamed up-bank. The two little girls from Silence, bound for school on their white horse, were passing three carts taking new-dressed stone for the repairing of Yorrel Bridge. Women everywhere had put up clothes-lines and many were starting to hang out washing.

"Except tell what I've already found," he repeated, staring keenly at the strip of ground between Yew Tree House and the river, where a young woman was similarly occupied in Monday's time-honoured task. "And *that's* what I'll put in train . . . within the next hour, too. Old Hannah's at Titus's, I know, so I shan't be detained arguing about t'breakfast I ought to be having."

Acting upon this resolve he rose, to head for his lodgings, where, after changing, he made himself a pot of tea.

Not ten minutes later, gaped at no less by Fronick Blenkiron at Town Foot than by Puke Hastwell in the Wood Yard, he approached Cherry as, taking the last clothes peg from her mouth, she spread one of her uncle's night-shirts on the line. She did not hear him immediately and, in the brief space before, he noticed the thinness of her face.

"Adam!" her breath caught. "Meet you where it's very quiet . . . to do wi' Uncle," she added wonderingly, when he had come directly to the point. "To-night?"

"If possible," Adam said.

She swallowed. "Mr. Blenkiron's sitting with Uncle this evening," she said. "You see, I were going to Dinah's for a bit."

"By yourself?" Adam inquired.

"Yes," she replied, colouring.

"Will you meet me then?" Adam asked.

"Yes," she whispered.

Adam nodded. "Right . . . leave Dinah's early and when you get to t'Royal Alfred, cross into Sorrow Far, and start walking up to Bloody Sigh. Nobody dares go there, and I'll be with you," he added when she shivered, "long afore you reach it."

Saying good-bye to a young woman whose limbs felt as though they were as weak as water, he returned to Main Street, through which, on the way to the morrow's market at Corvy, a flood of lambs poured, gay with their markings of red and blue. Joined by a gander who, tinkling bell around his neck, had been wandering about the village, Adam took refuge near the door of Edmund Kearton's house, where he talked with Mary Jane. Matt Tiplady, who had expressed his beliefs disastrously to the magistrates, had still several days of his month's sentence to serve, and while he was absent his daughter kept house for her grandfather,

Mary Jane enjoying herself immensely as the mistress of a larger establishment. She was conveying as much to Adam when Mr. Kearton, from his workshop, frowningly noticed them.

The joiner's intervention had not the happiest repercussions for himself. "Now love," he temporised, "you've no need to carry on like this."

Her face outraged, Mary Jane continued to unfasten her apron. "I'm no man's slave," she announced. "He's a friend o' mine as I'se fond on, and——"

"Don't bandy words in public, love," Adam murmured. "Think of the good example your grandfather always sets you."

Edmund Kearton glared. "Are you insinuating as . . ."

However he may have regarded himself there is no doubt that a few hours afterwards he was perilously near to disgracing himself openly. But then his grandsons' past mischiefs were a very different matter from their present stubborn lie. Loudly, from Main Street, he bawled for the schoolmaster.

"So you've been given holiday, have you?" he warned the boys meantime, his glance piercing. "An' why hasn't th'other scholars as I can hear reciting up there?"

This took place about a quarter of an hour after Winterings had been aroused by an explosion which blew down the remainder of the roof of a ruined cow-house behind the Roe, a building which had caused much anxiety to mothers of children who played there. Cherry, shaking her uncle's pillows before hurrying off to do some shopping, endeavoured to brighten him from the window with a description of the appearance of Bob and Ward—dishevelled as though they had been part of the explosion, black-faced and grinning.

"They must have got some gunpowder somehow, Uncle," she ended.

Titus Alderson looked very frail. "Maybe from outside one of t'magazines," he said. "Oft a little is spilled when t'groovers' powder-canisters are filled from the kegs of a Monday morning. But . . ." he summoned up a smile, "don't fail to bring me all the news about it."

Cherry laughed. "You're an old gossip."

When she left the house a few minutes later she met a woman who everlastingly felicitated her on her good fortune while seeming jealous of it. Isa Skidmore, on her way to Smithy House, rushed across Town Foot to add a bit more to what she had previously said on the matter of mint sauce, which Reuben preferred very, very sweet.

"An' another thing you must never forget either, Cherry lass," she told her future sister-in-law. "He's partial to mint sauce even when you're having beef—to put on his Yorkshire pudding."

Too remote from the immediate present to be distressed by this domestic reminder of her future, Cherry nodded understanding when necessary and, in due course, still palpitatingly remembering she was meeting Adam that night, continued along Main Street, where, for the same reason, she was unable to share to the same extent the amusement of a small group who were listening to the stupefied Mr. Kearton outside the Wesleyan Day School.

"But it's a simple enough question," the undertaker was shouting. "Are these grandsons o' mine lying or aren't they? Did you or did you not give 'em permission to absent themselves?"

"Sssh . . ." Mr. Kidd said, tapping his lips with a sausage-like finger. "If I can have your ear for a moment——"

"Have my ear!" Mr. Kearton marvelled. "Why should you have it?"

Grasped by the sleeve, he was compelled to listen to sibilant outpourings which, on his comprehending them, were responsible for his expression becoming that of one whose enemy has been delivered into his hands. "Well, seemingly I owe these two lads an apology," he proclaimed loudly. "So you've getten a distinguished visitor to t'school?"

Wingy Blenkiron helped things along. "Aye, and who would that be, Mr. Kearton?" he inquired with interest.

"Oh, nobbut a gentleman to report on the scholars' progress," Edmund Kearton shrugged. "And t'certificate is bound to be better if you keep them youngsters who isn't all that good away fro' school. But don't raise your voice, lad, or he might hear—t'School Inspector, I mean."

Mr. Kidd's shamefaced: "I protest in the strongest manner at the worst breach of confidence as I ever heard of," was overshadowed by Nathan Wharton's comment: "Aye, but you've got to agree, haven't you, that it highers t'standard."

"Certainly, Nathan," Mr. Kearton observed. "Yes, apparently we've to be congratulated for having as us schoolmaster a chap who can manipulate matters like these wi' a very light touch . . . the only pity is that he hasn't the same touch on th'ivories, instead of bursting our ear-drums every time he brays away at the piano."

For Mr. Kidd this was the last straw, and, long coat-tails flapping, he jumped forward. "You'll withdraw that," he roared. "If you've owt against my technique an' execution——"

"Owt against your execution!" Mr. Kearton laughed to high heaven. "Not me . . . I'm i' favour of it."

"A hoary jest, you stupid fool," the Schoolmaster bellowed. "As old as when George Frederick Handel came to——"

Mr. Kearton's stringy grin vanished. "Stupid fool, you called me, eh?"

Friends ensured that the dispute did not go as far as once it seemed likely: to fisticuffs. The heavily-breathing schoolmaster was escorted to the school-gate, the tight-faced joiner to his workshop.

About a quarter to seven, as Cherry carried down a tray from her uncle's bedroom, spirited hoofs clattered to a standstill at the gate. The dog-cart was driven by Reuben Nattrass, who, freshly shaved and in his best suit, was attending a smoker at the Grafton Arms.

Smouldering fire lurked in his dark eyes when he entered the kitchen, but, to begin with, he contented himself with speaking about general matters. In view of Mr. Alderson's illness, he and Cherry would be living at Yew Tree House after the wedding, but it had occurred to him that Modesty might suit them later. The rent would not be large and, farming it in a small way, he could still see to his work at the mines.

His next remark came abruptly. "I'se been telled as you an' Brunskill were talking together this morning. For why were that?"

Cherry coloured at his sharp tone, but her eyes were a little mocking as she replied. "Oh, he wanted to see me to-night in some real quiet place, and of course I were willing enough," she said, glancing at the grandfather clock. "Bloody Sigh it's to be, and I shall soon have to be getting ready."

His mouth took on an ugly twist. "Less o' your lip," he growled. "An' think on i' days to come as I'm noan having my wife gossiped about by all and sundry because she hasn't a proper regard for herself."

Uptilted chin and resentful eyes must have shown Reuben Nattrass, who in the past fortnight had experienced her mettle, that he must bide his time, and, on leaving, his lips merely brushed her cheek instead of greedily fastening on her mouth in one of the sustained kisses she had schooled herself to bear.

From then, as the minutes ticked by before her meeting with Adam, Cherry's excitement grew.

After crossing Legatt's Way where it began to dip towards the river-ford, Cherry became less bold. Ill-omened Bloody Sigh was not far off—a soft breeze moaned through the trees and often there were most uncanny sounds.

"I'm here, lass." Adam's voice came out of the inky gloom.

Startled by the scraping of leaves, Cherry gulped: "It's me."

"Well now, we'll go somewhere where we can talk naturally instead of whispering," Adam said.

Sensing nervousness, he took her arm and soon she was settled in a ferny bower in the lee of one of the burial mounds. Without further ado, starting with ideas about ironstone, he brought her to date with what he had found and done so far underground.

"It's . . . it's terrible . . . an' wicked," she gasped. "But . . . but, Adam, you must guess as I'm guessing who's responsible for these cruel things."

He restrained her. "I know only what I've told you, nothing more. And, as I've mentioned, I can't be sure where the big pile o' tram-rails stands in relation to the beginning of your uncle's New Drift."

She touched his arm. "Couldn't I help you with the dialling? So's you can let my uncle know properly about both places when you see him?"

"*You*, lass!" Adam exclaimed, aghast at the thought of a dainty young woman in the Old Man, though he could hardly help thinking that here was the second pair of hands for which he had hankered. "Nay . . ."

"You talk as if I'm made of sugar an' spice," Cherry indignantly over-ruled his objections when he made them. "Oh, do let me, please."

"It means being out with me all night," he pointed out gravely. "And if anybody got to know——"

Passion in her, she interrupted him. "Do you reckon that bothers me?"

Adam knew that he must let her have her way. "Right, lass," he said.

For the next few minutes they discussed details, deciding to take Old Hannah into their confidence, so that someone would be with Cherry's uncle during the night. The final arrangement was about the meeting-place the following evening, a short distance up Sorrow Near being chosen, round the bend from Mr. Blenkiron's cow-place.

"That's finished then, lass," Adam said, finding her hand as he rose, to help her up. "Now t'sooner you're in home the better. And by the way, you ought to wear some old clothes of your uncle's for our trip, not forgetting a hard hat. Skirts are far too awkward and dangerous for where you'll be going."

There was a brief silence. "You think I ought?" Cherry faltered.

Adam's response was matter-of-fact. "A groover's garb is the only thing, lass."

Ancient workings have many perils, but Cherry's thoughts, as she walked towards the Royal Alfred, dwelt entirely upon appearing in them clad as she had been informed she must. However, nearer the main road, when a faint glow from the inn fell upon her companion's face, she recalled another duty.

"Adam," she whispered, "afore I leave you I want to say how sorry I am about my behaviour on t'night Uncle Titus collapsed. You'd gone to his office to see him about these things you've been telling me, hadn't you?"

Adam nodded. "Yes, but never mind about that now. You be off sharp . . . I'll be there to-morrow night."

For precious seconds their eyes met and then, anxious lest some unforeseen nightfarer should perceive them, he gently pushed her on her way.

2

It had been a quietly eventful day in Winterings. The women had been interested in turning over the ribbons and fancy materials taken from door to door by a pedlar, while the more sober-sided were pleased with the news that a stronger leader of the Wesleyan class meeting at Barfoot had been appointed. There were other incidents to report—a horse at Yorrel had bolted; a groover in Hart Mine had been seriously crushed; an old woman at Carling had fallen down the stairs; a sheep had been rescued from a pot-hole on Outer Snorr Moor by a boy lowered by rope; and at Corvy an old man with a bag of sovereigns beneath a flagstone had hanged himself for fear of poverty.

These excitements combined, however, were less than that shared by two women, one young and one extremely old, in the back kitchen of Yew Tree House.

Old Hannah prowled round once more, to examine Cherry from front, back and both sides. "Well, love," she pronounced, "there's one thing I'm sure about—if I were a lass again I shouldn't quiver all over if a lad like you doffed his beaver to me."

Cherry's trousered legs were so tightly together as to seem as if she were practising offering a picture of the lower part of herself in a skirt. The relics of her uncle's coat drooped from her shoulders, the opening filled in by a muffler, and a dinted gent's hat perched upon a mass of hair. Her cheeks were scarlet, partly at the thought of meeting Adam when so habited, partly because Old Hannah's comments were causing her nearly to burst.

"So I don't make much of a young man?" she dimpled.

"Not you," Mrs. Batty said. "Every inch of you stands out as a lass."

Cherry's eyes widened with alarm. "You don't mean——"

"No, I don't," Old Hannah chuckled. "Now I've left the tea-caddy out for when Adam takes you to t'shop to show you his plan, an' there's some pieces o' pasty . . ."

"You're a grand 'un." Cherry smiled.

"And another thing," the old lady nodded, imperatively. "Try to persuade that lad to have his arm seen to . . . th'inflammation's still gaining an' I can't do owt else. But he's that stubborn about finishing this job."

Firmly waved away, Cherry left by the back door, from there cautiously advancing to Town Foot, where, after satisfying herself no one was about, she darted across to Sorrow Near.

Adam was waiting, carrying a leather wallet over his shoulder, but though the night was slightly misty he did not light the lantern he had brought for her convenience, a precaution which served them in good stead when, high up Mine Road, they heard voices.

"Stay here, lass," Adam said into Cherry's ear.

On returning he grasped her hand, guiding her towards a line of old levels, the first few fathoms of which were often used for protecting wagons from the weather. At least one level possessed a frightening reputation and so Adam, taking a couple of dips from his candle-box, placed one on the leader of five coupled wagons, the other on the hindmost.

"There's three of 'em, hunting for whatever they can pick up," he muttered to Cherry. "But we'd better try to shift 'em from here."

Started off with a powerful push, the train moved down a winding track, never fast enough for the candles to be blown out. They watched the pinpoints of light lessen and then disappear altogether where the rails curved behind a dead-heap. Next they heard a high-pitched yell, more shouting from others, and clogged feet in frantic retreat down the rough road.

If Adam could have glimpsed his companion's lovely eyes he would have seen they were shining with admiration, but, on arriving at the tail of Bucker Level, where he lighted her lantern and a candle for himself, Cherry had other preoccupations.

"You . . . you go first," she stammered, flushing vividly. "It'll . . . it'll be better."

Adam eyed her impassively. "A sight, lass," he agreed.

"What do you mean by that?" she demanded.

He seemed surprised. "A sight better if you're behind me," he explained.

"Oh . . ." she said. "Well . . . well, let's start."

"Right," he said.

Her feelings extraordinarily mixed, and her doubts by no means allayed, she followed him along the tramway sleepers.

After showing Cherry the pair of rails, Adam made a remark she did not understand till later. He was glancing from the crumbling sump at their feet to the unsure-looking rise above their heads.

"I'd really like to seal them rails off," he told her. "But the whole spot is so shaky that I might bring it down an' lose 'em altogether. Anyhow, there's the others."

By now Cherry was so interested that she blushed only when she imagined he was staring, and indeed became more forgetful still in Freezeland, when the serious work with the instruments began. Survey station by survey station they penetrated farther, ever progressing until Adam, straightening from the dial sight after taking a back-draft, did not ask her to bring the candle-reader forward.

"Well, we've done," he said, pulling out his watch. "Not bad either, nobbut two o'clock. Now here's th'other rails . . ."

After being shown the pile, she was very astonished when, presenting her with a bag of Old Hannah's broken toffee, he told her she must be patient for a couple of hours. From his wallet he removed a hammer, various sizes of drills and borers, a coil of fuse, and strange-looking cartridges.

"Blowing in a thirty fathoms length!" she gasped after curiosity had got the better of her. "But you won't be able to bring anybody to see that heap o' rails."

"No," he replied, eyes steely, "and them that's put 'em there won't be able to get 'em out either . . . not without spending more money than they can afford, or giving themselves away. But," he pointed, "if just beyond there is t'beginning of the New Drift, it'll be possible to cut through to 'em from *that* side when the time is ripe."

Her lips parted. "I see," she breathed.

Adam started drilling a series of holes, an undertaking less awkward than it might have been because of the ability he shared with every good miner to strike as strongly with the left arm as the right. Nevertheless his single-handedness gave Cherry the opportunity to urge him to visit the doctor as soon as possible.

After a while she began to wander about the Old Man, making several interesting finds, including a length of larch rail of the era before iron tramways. But when her lamp-beam shone upon the whitened bones of a sheep which had tumbled down some unguarded shaft on Noggin Moor, she hastily retreated towards Adam's flickering candle-flame.

Inquiring if anything were amiss, his eyes were a little crinkled as he glanced down at her, a young woman in baggy masculine attire whose face was as dirty as that of any groover who had done a full shift.

Her slowing pace became even more negligent. "No," she said. "I nobbut thought I'd look round at this end for a change."

Suppressing a smile, Adam resumed his work until, the last hole cleaned out with a copper scraper, he knelt on the sole of the working, examining cartridges, primers and caps. Very intent, he was cutting off lengths of fuse, calculated at thirty seconds to every foot, when a scream startled him.

"What's t'matter, lass?" he ejaculated, jumping up.

Wild with excitement, Cherry held up a light-coloured, strangely veined half-circle which, when whole, must have been about the size of a small wedding ring. "I found this just there, near these tramrails," she gasped. "It's Arthur Nattrass's luckstone, part of it, anyroad. The one as he boasts he always wears. . . . I know it as well as the day, Adam, an' I couldn't be mistaken about the markings."

"Then we're a bit farther along the road, lass," Adam said.

Her face fell. "But this is proof, isn't it?"

"It might have been dropped at any time, mightn't it?" Adam explained. "Or he could say so."

While they searched vainly for the missing portion, he was able to cheer her up, and soon she recognised the discovery for what it was: a counter which might one day serve admirably.

Then came final preparations. "It's dynamite, isn't it?" Cherry asked. "Terribly powerful, I've heard say."

"Aye, six times as strong as black powder," her companion replied, "but six times as safe, lass."

When the fuses were sizzling he joined her in a distant retreat, where huddled together they waited. Soon there was a bright flash; then came a fierce gust of dust-laden air and reports which echoed and rumbled in faraway parts of the old workings.

"Well, that's finished it, lass," Adam murmured when, back at the scene of destruction, they peered through slowly-swirling clouds. "So now we can be off."

Carrying between them tools and surveying instruments, they began to return, at last leaving behind stretches where progress was hard. Once in modern workings their speed increased and quickly the tail of Bucker Level was reached. From there, in a misty world of their own lighted by Cherry's lantern, they crossed Notion Bridge and Mill Bridge, eventually arriving in Old Hannah's kitchen after tip-toeing from the Brig.

First drawing the blind and blocking the peep-hole into the shop, Adam lighted the lamp. Before Cherry had cleaned the banked fire he was busy with dialling book and plan, and when the tea was ready he had already plotted two points of survey.

Much later, after surreptitiously glancing over his shoulder, she made another brew, and, as she lifted the teapot, he slowly put down a pencil, his task done.

"Yes, lass, it's the same there," he said. "Nobbut a rib of hard rock betwixt that pile o' rails and where your uncle dialled for his New Drift."

Bending over the table to look, she began to tremble with rage. "If you murdered . . . murdered the one as were responsible, you'd be hanged. But what's been done has nearly killed my uncle . . . an' I think he would have been dead but for you. You see . . ." her lips quivered, "I've suspected that on the night of the Extraordinary General Meeting my uncle . . . intended to take his life."

Firmly he grasped her hand, the gesture that of a friend. Holding her so, he advised her not to delve into the past any more, but to think of the future. "That's what I'm doing, about . . . about everything," he continued. "As to this business, well that's summat in front an' all, to be attended to, as attend to it I will, till I've nailed th'individual as is guilty."

Before they separated it was arranged he should call at Yew Tree House that evening. "But don't tell your uncle what it's about," Adam went on. "Is Reuben Nattrass likely to pop in, by the way?"

Cherry shook her head. "He's going to Greets again . . . something to do with his Uncle George. But . . ." her lips curled, "as to him seeing me, except once——"

"No, lass, you mustn't do owt until I've gone into things with your uncle," Adam broke in. "Even then Cousin Reuben mustn't be told why you're . . . doing what I imagine you will be doing."

Solemnly Cherry answered him. "Yes, that's what I shall be doing, but I won't let on about anything that matters."

His eye caught by the Dutch clock, Adam pulled the blind to one side. "By Jove, lass!" he said.

In daylight Main Street was too risky and so Cherry left by the back door, to slip along the pastures behind the houses. Beforehand, however, there was one thing she had to say, the thanks that came from her heart.

"Hold on, lass," Adam smiled. "Or I'll have to have my hats specially made."

She was pale in her earnestness. "Well, it is so," she insisted. "For me it's relieved me of summat I . . . I dreaded, and for Uncle Titus it'll be t'greatest miracle that could happen to him."

Quite plainly Adam was inspecting her, from head to foot. "Anyroad, even if I didn't have my hats made for me they'd fit at least as well as that one you've got on," he commented. "An' as for that suit o' clothes——"

Fiery colour flooded her cheeks and, utterly unable to meet his eye, she fled from him, her heart thumping joyously as she scrambled over walls on the way to Town Foot. From the snicket adjoining the Roe she ran across the highway, the side wall of her uncle's garden muting the hoofs of three heifers who, leisurely walking from Dolly Bridge in front of their owner, were on their way to be sold.

At the sight of the flying figure, Hey! Thoo! raised a noisy alarm. The sheepdog leapt forward, but his master's feet were rooted on glimpsing the apparition. The permanent furrows on Ralph Skidmore's forehead deepened and multiplied. Various emotions, from bewilderment to censure, chased across his lean face as, fingers scratching beneath cap-band, he gaped at Yew Tree House.

* * * *

Later that morning, when Adam returned from delivering groceries to the Plug and Feathers, Old Hannah told him of a rumour brought from Greets by the postman. Like many rumours, it was hopelessly discredited within twenty-four hours, but for that day it raged unabatingly in the upper Dale.

"Aye, Sir Charles is supposed to have given it straight to Mr. Wade against t'Market Cross," she said. "That he were instructing his man o' law about t'West Side lot. Nowt but villainy, is it?"

"Eh!" Adam exclaimed.

Mrs. Batty's unexpected remark referred, however, to information confided to her earlier on, and as she spoke she was glancing at a rolled plan. "The scoundrel ought to be chucked over t'Brig for a start. Anyroad, never mind that," she chided herself, "because there's a letter for you, lad. It'll be fro' Mr. Buckle, I suspect, trying to cozen you into splitting t'difference."

For once she was wrong. The lawyer wrote in quite definite terms: the owner of Modesty had agreed to let it for twelve months with an option of purchase at the price Adam had originally stated.

In high fettle Adam went to Low Bands after dinner. Francis Harker, astride a rectangular creel upon which his two helpers stretched sheep out, first one flank up and then the other, was salving his stock to prevent scab and to kill ticks. With a finger-tip he opened out long partings in the wool, rubbing along the centre line a greasy mixture of Norway tar and cheap Irish butter, the partings so closely adjacent that in due course every inch of skin was covered.

Meantime Adam smoked and discussed such problems as jointly interested them: the best time to shut up meadows, when to open pastures, the average yield of a dairy cow, and the amount of winter feed she would need.

Mr. Harker, with a milker's hand blemished by warts similiar to those found on cows' teats, cuffed an unruly sheep. "Roughly about three loads o' hay for every beast," he cogitated.

"H'mm," Adam murmured, turning over with his toe the carcass of a rat killed by a weasel. "You don't keep records, do you? Written ones, I mean."

Francis Harker laughed. "Nay, we're noan clerks, Adam lad."

The cloudy mist still persisted. It was wet and permeating, and as he could not take any active part in the noisome undertaking, Adam did not stay much longer. On the way back he saw children gathering acorns, too busy to notice him, and, very clumsily, her complexion that of a peony, was avoided by Mrs. Will Skidmore. But, beyond the Brig, he was hailed by a relative.

George Nattrass's face was thunderous. "There's a private little meeting at Mr. Plews's house to-night," he snapped. "If you're of a mind to do owt about them shares you'd better be there."

Adam sighed with regret. "I'd like to do summat for someone who's so eager to do me a good turn, but I've weighed it up, Uncle. It'd be a pound a share if I lent myself to it."

The cheese-factor made a few lurid observations about his nephew's parentage, calming down very suddenly, however. "Don't talk so bloody daft about a sovereign apiece," he said. "But we might go to a shilling more than I spoke of to you—or maybe two."

Adam moved out of the path of a donkey bringing milk down from the Common Pasture. "Fifteen shillings is t'least I could consider, Uncle."

George Nattrass laughed derisively, but that was before he again recalled how much he would have to pay if Sir Charles Grafton's threat materialised. "Don't think you can bamboozle me," he said. "Anyroad, you'd better present yourself at Mr. Plews's."

Adam sighed again. "I hardly think it's worth it."

"It's summat for nowt." The cheese-factor's pent-up exasperation was almost released. "An' I've said we might go a bit higher."

Livened still further by this brief conversation, Adam continued to his lodgings, where he speedily lost any desire to grin. Old Hannah gave the suppurating wound on his arm the most excruciating poulticing he had as yet endured.

By chance in Richard Blenkiron's wake, Adam was leaving the Plug and Feathers as Reuben Nattrass entered. The mine-agent, who was spruced up, grabbed him by the coat-collar.

"I'se nobbut the time for a brandy or two an' noan to attend to you," he growled. "But think on in t'future not to push yourself on to my young woman, or I'll put you on your back for a week. Can you remember that?"

Mildly Adam met the quarrelsome dark eyes. "Every single word."

Contemptuously Reuben Nattrass thrust past. "Hear that?" he inquired of the company. "For all t'way he cracked Nowt Much Cooper an' threw my cousin Arthur about he takes care of his skin when he's up again a real chap, doesn't he?"

In the restricted space on the ochred doorstep outside, two big men eyed one another in the dim light, Richard Blenkiron fighting an ache to which he succumbed. "Why didn't you belt him?" he blurted out. "You could, easily."

"I keep out o' scrapping if I can, Mr. Blenkiron," Adam replied. "And I've an arm that's not as good as it might be."

"Aye, your arm . . . yes, I've heard about that," the blacksmith muttered, plucking his beard. "Festering or summat, isn't it?"

"It's noan healing up as it should."

As the other seemed disinclined to say anything further, Adam started up Main Street, carrying a rolled plan. Beyond Nick Turn, where his tall, striding figure was silhouetted against the lamp, he was recognised too late by a shopper leaving Cuthbert Daykin's. Ambrose Pedley dived towards the dark alleyway alongside the Queen's Arms, but his line of retreat was too confined.

"I could almost think as you were trying to avoid me," Adam said.

"Aye, I were," the groover croaked. "Because I'm noan wanting to risk brushing against one whose . . . whose flesh is *tainted*."

Thoughts lie fallow for a long time. Hardly of his own volition Adam made a remark the effects of which were astonishing. "Never mind about my flesh, think of your own instead. Aye, what about that cousin o' mine, the one I've never met?"

"Cousin?" The inquiry was higher-pitched.

"That's her, my cousin Margaret." Adam pressed home his advantage on perceiving it. "I've heard recently as she's i' Newcastle, and as soon as it can be managed I'm seeking a talk with her."

Ambrose Pedley's breath rattled. "Talk to her, talk to her," he spat. "You'll be well suited, because she's evil and steeped i' sin like you are. She's a liar an' all, allus has been, never known t'meaning o' what were truth since she finished wi' baby lisping."

"That's summat I'll judge for myself," Adam said as he turned away.

Until reaching Town Foot, this encounter was in the forefront of his mind. He had all the feelings of a man on the eve of a most repugnant discovery.

"Old Hannah's instincts were right," he muttered. "There's summat as wants looking into . . . or does it? Aye," his face saddened, "these terrible things do happen an' maybe that's why Margaret ran off, why she couldn't tell anybody what for."

Only as he lifted the brass knocker on the door of Yew Tree House was he able to put the matter aside.

However much the young man who stood in Titus Alderson's bedroom might be held in disrepute, he had certain credentials of considerable appeal to the sick man. As soon as Cherry closed the door on leaving them, her uncle referred to these.

"That night, lad," he said feebly, "you must have done summat wi' them letters on my desk or I should have heard."

"I hid 'em safely away, Mr. Alderson," Adam explained, striving to hide his shock about the invalid's appearance. "But later if you like I'll destroy everything for you."

"Aye, do," Titus Alderson muttered. "Of course you'd notice who one of t'letters were to. Aye——"

Adam's tone was brisk as he unrolled the plan. "Do you know, Mr. Alderson, I shouldn't be surprised if in another few minutes you were trying to nip out o' bed to borrow a shotgun."

Momentarily, in the physical sense, Titus Alderson reacted badly to the disclosures, and Cherry had to be called. But in spirit he soon became a new person, and his strength improved, too.

"Yes, I can appreciate why I can't be cleared straight off," he said. "But . . . but it'll come, lad, I hope."

Adam nodded. "It *will*," he said. "But before we act we need real proof, an' even that half of Arthur Nattrass's luckstone as Cherry found isn't enough."

"Cherry!" the old man ejaculated. "Has she been in th'Old Man with you?" When he learnt that this was so, he stared wonderingly at them, blinking back tears of weakness. "My, but . . . but I've summat to thank you two for, I have an' all," he ended tremulously.

For the next quarter of an hour there was a conversation in which all shared. Adam contended that, for everything to work out right, the West Side Company must somehow be kept in being, while Mr. Alderson's firm view was that, so long as a modest number of pigs of duty lead were received each month, Sir Charles would not, despite all rumour, close down the company. Certain essentials towards this end were then thrashed out and, before long, Cherry's cheeks were glowing with pleasure and excitement.

"Aye, it needs a vigorous chap to run t'job," Titus Alderson affirmed, brighter than he had been for many weeks. "An' if you'll take it on, lad . . ."

Adam's eyes gleamed. "Gladly, from to-morrow if you like—no, the day after 'ul be better for me as I've to go to Corvy. In the meantime I reckon it'll be advisable if we keep th'appointment to ourselves. But what about the directors? Won't they object when this is sprung on 'em?"

"They may," the invalid replied. "But a chief agent has always t'privilege of choosing an assistant. Now there's the question o' wages. . . . I've nobbut been drawing a pound a week, but I've the means to——"

"That can be left over," Adam intervened. "What's important now is how best we can do two things: put a bit more life into the company and nobble whoever is responsible for what's been done to you."

"If you could nobbut bring th'outrage home to Reuben Nattrass," Titus Alderson said wistfully. "Oh aye, you've noan charged him, but . . ." His mouth opened, he tried to speak, and for a space failed. Then, a great concern in him, he turned towards his niece. "Him as you're going to wed this week, lass. And till now I've been so muzzy wi' delight that it's never so much as entered my selfish head that he'll be your husband on Saturday."

"He'll not, Uncle," Cherry cried, sinking her face into his breast. "And I couldn't tell you how thankful I am."

Titus Alderson gently stroked her hair. "So you were doing it for my sake, lass?"

Adam decided to remove himself from the intimate scene, pleading that it might be of advantage for him to examine the mining records below, an excuse the old agent interpreted in his own way, nodding with significant understanding.

And so, in the office, Adam's first task was to burn a few letters. That done, he began to take down the files hanging on nails driven into the wall, briefly leafing over their contents before transferring his attention to a row of books, in one of which he came across a couple of sheets of foolscap containing a list of the company's shareholders. This he studied closely, for it could be useful to know whom he might be up against in his capacity of assistant-agent. As the information was not dated, he thought it worthwhile to ascertain if there had been any change.

"Nobbut except with mine, lad. I took up another seventy-five shares to help things along," Mr. Alderson told him when he went upstairs again. "Yes, them's the folk who's been stopping me in t'street."

The old man was very tired and Adam did not stay. But, before leaving, he asked Cherry, whose eyes were wet with tears, if it would be much trouble for her to make him a cup of coffee.

"No, of course it won't," she smiled mistily.

Soon she was downstairs, where, while she busied herself, Adam continued to stare hard at a list of shareholders whose holdings, he totted up, amounted to one thousand and fifty, including Mr. Alderson's extra seventy-five.

"Here's your coffee, Adam," Cherry whispered, surprised by his air of concentration. "And there's the fruit cake by your elbow."

Mumbling thanks, Adam started to pencil again. "Two hundred and seventy-five shares that Uncle George and his cronies are anxious to be relieved of, and the hundred and thirty I'm positive Cuthbert Daykin's just as eager to be shut of, which makes four hundred an' five," his reverie went. "And that," he thought impishly, "'ud put me as the biggest shareholder. Aye, wi' them and Mr. Alderson's we should have five hundred an' thirty shares, a tidy lot that'd enable us to say our say nicely."

Suddenly he jerked upright, gazed intently at Cherry, muttering: "By God, it 'ud do more, because we could outvote the rest and so have control." Then he laughed, a deep-chested and unexpected bellow which caused Sambo to fly from the hob into the sanctuary of the back kitchen.

"Whatever's the matter, Adam?" Cherry gasped.

"Nobbut that me and your uncle may be in for some right fun." Adam still was shaking. "That is if I'm not too late to arrange t'gamble. But I'll noan borrow Ben to-night, because it might give too much away." He chuckled anew at her completely bewildered face. "You'll hear about it afterwards, whichever way it goes," he added.

"Well . . . well, that's summat," Cherry murmured.

He gulped down the coffee and, before she could help him, slipped as quickly into his overcoat as a painful arm would allow. "Cherry," he said then, quite soberly, "that cup of coffee were an excuse to get you alone. I wanted to tell you that to-morrow I'm fixing up to rent Modesty, with the option o' purchase. You see, lass, I'm just about minded to be a cow keeper and shepherd . . . to farm there some day."

"Oh!" Cherry whispered.

While she stood by herself wondering whether she were on her head or her heels, Adam sprinted along Main Street to the livery stables, where, after protracted argument clinched by silver coins, the yard man consented to leave his cottage to harness an old horse into an even older trap.

Some considerable time later, in a squeaking vehicle from whose lumpy seating horse-hair protruded, lighted by a single lamp the candle of which showed through splintered glass, Adam drove past the gateway into the village street.

The weather was too unpleasant for many people to be about, but the battered equipage was seen by Mrs. Emma Ann Metcalfe, who, from her shop door, was peering out in search of any last-minute customers before putting up her shutters for the night.

When a young man's call was announced a measure of relief was fleetingly revealed on the faces of the gentlemen assembled in Mr. Thomas Plews's parlour. In due course Adam was ushered in, the whole of the company present being known to him except for the Master of the Workhouse and two others.

High-domed Screw Tom impatiently silenced the Postmaster when that individual began to address the newcomer. "I'll deal wi' him, Trotter," he barked. "Now then, Brunskill, it's late, an' we know why you're here, so there's no necessity for me to go into that."

"Not a bit, Mr. Plews," Adam agreed. "It'll save time, too, if I tell you what my terms are for the two hundred an' seventy-five shares, and they're final. It's fifteen shillings each, for all or none, an' cash on the spot, to-night."

During the ensuing minutes several persons calling for bottles at Dr. Seaton's surgery paused to listen. In the early stages Reuben Nattrass roared: "Bloody well not likely," and Screw Tom charged the common opponent with being "a fornicator and a rogue," to which Adam replied that at least he was not a pillar of rectitude taking advantage of a quack lawyer's slip to escape moral obligations.

Commonsense prevailed when Adam picked up his cap. After that, price and mode of payment cholerically conceded, the problem of obtaining a large sum in cash created a fresh outburst. Here Lodge Trotter got some of his own back, observing: "Why, Tom, it's everlastingly been your boast as you allus kept five hundred sovereigns in the house. Were there nowt to it? Anyroad, I expect George has summat put by for an emergency, an' if you're unable . . ."

Eventually, after much argument as to who should pay back whom and when, the necessary forms of transfer were drawn up and signed. Soon, weighted with clinking yellow coins, Adam bade farewell to those bereft. It was not surprising his cordial ' good night ' hardly evoked a gratifying response. In fact William Nattrass expressed the hope that he would be drowned when voyaging back to Spain.

As he drove round the side of the Market Place towards the Green, Adam laughed, amused by the thought that the disconsolate party he had just left were providing money with which the West Side Company could launch out a little. "That's what it'll be used for," he said to himself. "I'll lend it as it's needed. That'll be the best road."

On the way home he had a passenger. Droughty Tom's business in Greets had also been at Screw Tom's, to collect the movement of a grandfather clock, which he was carrying out of the B.G. Inn in a butter-basket.

"Aye, gladly," was the answer grunted in reply to Adam's invitation. "For that matter I'd ride with t'devil to save myself fro' walking up yonder."

"A gentleman like you ought to have a trap of his own," Adam suggested.

"Aye, and t'sixty pound for that pump I were tricked into buying 'ud buy one and more," Droughty Tom complained.

Between slapping the reins and the aged horse's laggardly acknowledgment, Adam explored other possibilities. Then casually he inquired if the lime-burner had anything to show that the East Side Company refused to admit ownership of the pump.

"Haven't I just!" Droughty Tom snorted. "I've two letters on their billheads, an' in one of 'em they'd the neck to tell me I were at liberty to take it away if I wanted."

"You're caught properly," Adam said. "I reckon I shall have to buy your rights to see what I can do in t'matter."

"Is that a firm offer?" his companion asked with exaggerated guile. "If so, I'm taking it."

"Done," Adam grinned.

In the early weeks of his arrival in Skewdale he and the old man had often endeavoured to best one another. And so when, at Town Foot, Adam turned the horse up Jom High Road, Droughty Tom guessed the change of direction to be part of the gullery, even though he privately considered that for various circumstances the moment was unfortunately chosen. But he did his share. "Always carry as much as sixty pounds on you, lad?" he quizzed.

"I like to have a bit o' loose change handy," Adam retorted.

The lime-burner smiled in the darkness. "Oh, nowt like being prepared," he agreed. Determined not to be beaten, he invited the young man into the cottage at Pewitt Pillar, and, in the same spirit, brought out the receipted invoice for the pump and the East Side Company's two letters. Only when Adam wrote out a few lines of assignment and counted out sixty sovereigns did he realise he was wrong. But he was an honest man.

Adam glanced up from the table. "It's all right, Tom, I know what I'm doing. But keep everything to yourself, that's all."

In a decided daze, Droughty Tom completed his side of the strange transaction, and then saw Adam to the door. Through a break in the low cloud the moon shone, heavily halo-ed, and absentmindedly the lime-burner remarked that it was "wadeing." But his faculties improved before he said "Good night."

"I may have all the law in my favour, but you can bet your boots I'll be as mum as t'grave," he muttered. "If this got out, as likely as not hell 'ud be let loose."

That was not to be Adam's last engagement of the day. As he drove into William Nattrass's yard, a thickly-swathed figure stole out of the shadows.

Cuthbert Daykin was blue with cold. "Have you been settling that affair wi' your Uncle George?"

"Aye," Adam admitted.

"Come round to my house when you've handed in t'trap," the singer of romances croaked. "To the back door."

In this wise Adam acquired another considerable holding in the West Side Company, with an undertaking for payment to be made to him at eleven o'clock the following morning in Corvy. Unexpectedly, too, he obtained twenty shares he had not reckoned upon, these from Emma Ann Metcalfe who, while the arrangements were being made, stood at the back of her neighbour's kitchen outside the direct rays of the lamp; her attention was divided as she tried to listen to what was going on and for the first intimation of her husband's unsteady footsteps as he staggered home.

Fingers uncertain, she began to fold a share certificate. "I . . . I haven't fifteen pounds," she faltered. "So I'd better be off in home."

Adam enlisted Mr. Daykin's support, remarking that in view of the big deal they had entered into he thought the lady's shares could be transferred without any question of money passing. With this proposal the grocer gallantly but hoarsely concurred.

"Oh, Cuthbert dear, you sound bronchial," Emma Ann exclaimed. "I do hope that——" She bit her lip, blushed painfully as, with pathetic dignity, she spoke to Adam. "Mr. Daykin's got a very wonderful voice . . ."

Cuthbert Daykin was just as upset by the slip. He made no mistake. "Mrs. Metcalfe's a rare fusser where artistes is concerned," he explained. "It doesn't matter who it is, she's allus the same is Mrs. Metcalfe."

"I quite understand," said Adam. "Now, shall I write out another piece of paper to cover your shares, Mrs. Metcalfe?"

Her worn face brightened. "Oh, if you would," she said.

Mrs. Batty had gone to bed when the shop-door bell rang at her lodger's entry. Usually most considerate, he was singing so heartily that, suspecting much, she tripped downstairs, immediately to be seized and waltzed madly.

"Well!" she gasped. "You . . . you great barmpot."

"You once said I'd started summat, didn't you?" Adam grinned. "Well, I hadn't . . . but I have now."

Severity in her expression, Hannah Batty pointed to her husband's chair.

"Sit you down there, lad," she ordered. "An' you're noan getting up again till I've bottomed this. Now what have you been up to?"

With a knitted night-cap upon her silvery-white hair, an old coat over her nightdress, and a pipe in her mouth, she toasted her feet over the fire while making him repeat in detail his story again and again. It was nearly two o'clock when the pair of them climbed the stairs.

3

While Adam watched the jackdaws on the keep of Corvy Castle, Mr. Miles Buckle droned through the particulars of that highly-desirable property, Modesty . . . one messuage . . . pastures . . . meadow fields . . . intake . . . close . . . garth . . . common rights on Water Ling Moor . . . twenty pasture gates in Winterings Common Pasture.

"For twenty cattle that means, one cow to a stint," the lawyer murmured, looking up. "There's an . . . er . . . sort of conversion table, five sheep to a stint and so on, which enables you to use the rights for mixed stock."

"I understand, Mr. Buckle," Adam nodded. "Now is there anything else, sir?"

The lawyer was prejudiced slightly in favour of his new client, who had stood up well to a merciless and unfair hammering at a recent inquest. "Only to hand you the key, the option, and the receipt for six months' rent in advance, for which, incidentally," he smiled beneath beetling brows, "I did not ask you. And should you decide to complete the purchase I shall be delighted, on receiving a deposit of ten per cent, thirty-five pounds, to proceed with the conveyance. You can, if you desire, employ another lawyer to act on your behalf, but it is not in the least necessary . . . I frequently act for both seller and buyer, with some pecuniary relief to each when the bills are presented."

"And no financial loss on your part, I trust?" Adam observed.

Mr. Buckle's squirely person swivelled a trifle. "I think not," he replied, after satisfying himself no impertinence was intended. "Shall we say a little advantage to all parties?"

"Aye," Adam laughed, shaking hands.

The lawyer, before re-entering his snug office, contemplated the young mining man who was walking away. "A good type, far superior to the prize-fighter Storey's taken up so wholeheartedly these past months," he soliloquised. "First rate at his job I should imagine, too."

At the bank Adam drew some money, placing this in his clothing separately from the large sum Cuthbert Daykin had given him earlier. Dinner at the Saracen occupied nearly another hour and then he went round the second-hand dealers, buying chairs and an iron bedstead, a kitchen table, and a big dining-table suitable for spreading large scale plans upon, rubbish which would serve his purpose until the time came for it to be thrown away. An ironmonger was visited for a good lamp and various utensils, and, last of all, after browsing for a little while, he acquired a few books on farming, one an old but interesting volume devoted to the Western Dales.

These enterprises ended, he sought a carrier willing to start out at once. Long before dark he was perched at the front of a dray. His new belongings piled behind him, he rode up Skewdale.

The news of Adam's possession of Modesty sped like wildfire that night in Winterings, as did his subsequent activities, none of which was missed. It was known everywhere that at the three shops he had dealt extensively in groceries, lamp-oil, candles, brushes, crockery, blankets and such like. Almost every able-bodied soul in the village walked to the Brig despite the rain, to stare at a house each window of which was illuminated, one brightly and the others lambently from the waxing and waning glow of applewood fires whose pleasant smoke, as it drifted from the chimneys, mixed with the prevalent tang of peat.

In the Plug and Feathers, where nothing else was talked about, Edmund Kearton emphasised by repeatedly banging his glass. "Defying t'lot on us, that's what yon's doing."

"Aye, and he's two-faced an' all," William Nattrass bawled. "Setting up here wi' other folks' brass instead o' getting back to——"

"What's that, William?" Blind Kit queried. "Which brass?"

But Adam's uncle, who had repented of his loquacity, anyhow, was immediately engaged by Francis Harker. "Well, William, you Nattrass lot 'ul have to swallow your words," the farmer pointed out. "He didn't run off an' seemingly he isn't going to, like you made out his father did an' as he would as well."

"There's more to that young chap than some o' you would credit," Richard Blenkiron observed profoundly.

The Wood Yard foreman laughed. "He's shown us that, hasn't he? Of course you may be one of t'singular exceptions who considers him a white sheep so far as his dead cousin is concerned."

His face vaguely troubled, the blacksmith was less forthright than usual, "Well, he's noan behaved as if he were guilty, Puke," he said.

In all its aspects the controversy was raging when Adam came in, grimy after finishing a throat-parching job, sweeping down the floors of his new home. As he edged to the bar, voices died away one by one, and silence was absolute when he asked Mrs. Peacock for a glass of beer.

"Aye, lad," she smiled. "And it's going to be on the house . . . to mark th'occasion of you moving into Modesty."

The warmth of her greeting nonplussed Adam until he recalled that since Titus Alderson's illness he had often seen her either leaving or entering Yew Tree House. If she had been there that day she would probably have learnt a great deal.

The remainder of Lucy Peacock's hearers were even more nonplussed about the change in a woman normally most taciturn. Reuben Nattrass, however, was eager only to come to grips with a man whom he dimly suspected as responsible for a lack of ardour in the girl he was to marry.

"Well, well, well, I never," he taunted. "So you're reckoning on settling down among us, eh?"

"Aye," Adam nodded. "And Modesty's a grand little spot, too."

The mine-agent's eyes darkened. "Aye, it is," he growled.

"A chap has to live where his work is," Adam explained as he put his glass down and thanked the landlady. "And Modesty's specially handy for me."

This announcement so stupefied the company that Adam's tread was the only sound as he walked towards the door.

Reuben Nattrass caught him just in time. "Hey, you, Brunskill, what's the job you've getten?"

"In my own line." Adam turned in some surprise. "Lead-mining of course, on t'management side."

"Where at?" the angry mining-agent shouted. "There's no company here as wants anybody."

"You've forgotten Mr. Alderson's illness," Adam deplored. "Yes, fro' to-morrow morning I'm taking charge of the West Side Company—under him, naturally."

The stillness lasted almost until the latch of the swinging door clicked home, when a babble mightier than ever broke out, during which Lucy Peacock, in the interests of a secret which must be closely guarded, had to keep a tight hold on herself. Otherwise, for language vehement but no worse, Reuben Nattrass would have been ordered out of her premises forever.

Meanwhile Adam, who was to sleep at Old Hannah's until his new bedding was thoroughly aired, toured Modesty to make sure the fires he had built, from logs found in the stick-place, were safe to leave.

"Well, I think everything's all right," he murmured, setting down the lamp in the room to the right of the front door, which he had chosen as living-quarters. "So now, as I want to be at t'mine early, I might as——"

He heard a faint squeak and, moving quietly, walked along the passage. In the gloom near the kitchen window he perceived a movement, and the flash of something bright.

"Who's there?" he called out, but, obtaining no response, struck a match, glimpsing in the flare the thin figure of Mr. Rutter's crazed son. "Oh, it's you, Bill, is it? Why don't you come in properly instead o' hanging about like this?"

"Light," Mazy Bill muttered.

"I've nobbut come to-night," Adam explained. "You'd be surprised that somebody was here?" Cautiously, ever alert to an aged but freshly ground hunting-knife, he drew the trembling youth towards the lamp-lit room. "What are you doing round here, lad? Oughtn't you to be at home?" he asked.

Spittle trickled. "Kill . . . hurt Agnes," the trammer choked.

"Yes," Adam said, watchful. "But who hurt Agnes? Do you think it were me?"

"Not y-you," Mazy Bill gasped.

"No, it wasn't me." Adam spoke very softly. "In fact it wasn't anybody. Do you understand that, lad?"

Violently Mazy Bill shook his head. "Killed Agnes, killed Agnes," he said, bubbling at the mouth as he stabbed the air. "K-kill him, *I'll* kill him."

Patiently Adam attempted two things: to persuade the youth that no one had killed Agnes, and to glean whom he suspected. Failing lamentably, he tried to instil another idea into the demented mind while gently releasing the fingers gripping a fearsome weapon.

"I'll take care o' this for you, Bill," he promised. "And another thing, lad, if ever you've got it in for anybody, don't bother with a knife or anything else. Just clench your hands and smash his face . . . it hurts a sight more."

A frothy string connected Mazy Bill's jaw with the torn lapel of his coat. "Kill him," he moaned.

"No, no, battering with fists is best," Adam insisted. "If you have to do owt like that, try it my road, it's much better, if you really want to make 'em suffer."

The youth's hysteria was subsiding and a little time afterwards, quite submissively, he left the house with Adam. Together they crossed the

Brig, where the waterfalls were noisy but unseen in the rainy mist. At Old Hannah's they parted, Adam entering the shop, the stricken Mazy Bill continuing to stumble along the street, the light of the lamp at Nick Turn revealing the tears which flowed down his hollow cheeks.

4

Within an hour of taking charge of the West Side Company, Adam was encouraged by slight co-operation in some quarters and not unduly depressed by opposition in others. The first strike in the history of Skewdale lead-mining occurred, too, though its duration was not more than twenty minutes.

"What's these chaps after?" Adam muttered, rubbing the steamed window to watch a group of men crossing the Mill Bridge. "Better find out an' let me know."

Bart Hugill's sustained glare was entirely lost upon the figure bending over the ore-dressing costing book. The clerk shifted his feet irresolutely, but in the end, a rude retort hardly beneath his breath, went outside. On returning, his manner a mixture of sullenness and excitement, he reported that the smelters, whose complaint was that the ore contained too much sludge—often a bone of contention between them and dressing-floors men—were demanding an increase upon the standard rate of six and eightpence a ton.

Adam, who was bringing himself up to date with the company's affairs, looked round. "Tell 'em to get inside the weigh-place out of the rain and I'll be with 'em shortly . . you be there, too. And by the way, I suppose you keep some brass here, to buy bill-stamps and for oddments?"

Bart Hugill's lip curled. "If you're here much longer you'll learn it's never a case of having owt much i' hand."

Gravely nodding, Adam took out a soft leather bag from his pocket, and counted out ten sovereigns. "Here you are," he said. "Make out a receipt in my name for this, and use it as you're accustomed. Let me know as soon as it's down to two pounds."

It was a long time since the dinted cash-box had held so much money, and the bemused clerk was still staring at the coins when Adam, after calling in at the furnaces and slag hearths, entered the North Mill's vast open-hearth chamber. There he examined the ore in dispute, but found it reasonably clean.

"Mmm," he murmured, his glance alighting on the assistant smelter. "Where's Cottingham?" he shouted.

Harry Blaydes, who had been surreptitiously watching, turned with a not very convincing start. "He's gone to listen to t'fun. That is . . ." he floundered, "he's——"

"I suppose you're able to take full charge here when you're left alone?" Adam asked.

Receiving a satisfactory reply, he mentioned the change he proposed, adding that the wage would be adjusted accordingly.

"Me . . . t'master smelter fro' now on!" Harry Blaydes stammered.

Adam was laconic. "Aye, and that means no more sweating with shovelling out hot slags, you understand, and no more wheeling barrows in the rain. Your job's on the spot, as oft as not supervising from one of t'benches in front of the hearths and furnaces."

When, a moment later, Adam had gone, Harry Blaydes, a middle-aged man, wasted of face and curved of back, meandered past great chimney-place ore-hearths. He spoke aloud once: an affrighted "Jonas!" but his panic soon subsided and shortly his reflections were those which, more and more in the months ahead, represented the feelings of the bulk of Winterings folk. The tribute to the new assistant-agent was not without its terrible reservation.

"No," he cogitated, "he may have sent a little lass to her grave, but he's noan one as is scared. He'll tackle Jonas unless I'm mistaken."

This was precisely what Adam did in the weigh-place, singling out the chief smelter to inquire why, when the ore complained about referred only to one hearth, so many had left work elsewhere.

"And why didn't you come to me yourself first?" he wound up.

The underlings were favoured with a wink from the drooping-mouthed object of this stern onslaught. "Nay," the host of the Groovers Welcome drawled, "I think they preferred to meet t'boss theirsens . . . that's if it's noan stretching things too far to term you that."

Adam's smile was grim. "I take it you don't accept me as that?"

"Is it likely?" Jonas Cottingham laughed. "No, I'll answer to——"

"I'm noan your boss, you're right about that, Cottingham," Adam intervened, turning to Bart Hugill. "Get his money worked out, to th'end of the Pay, and give it to him."

The chief smelter's breath hissed. "Eh! What's this?"

Adam was brief. "You're sacked. And get off the company's property as soon as you've been paid."

"Get off . . ." Jonas Cottingham bawled.

Glum-faced Sam Kirkbride joined in. "You ought to have had more sense, Jonas. The company's hanging up by nowt much stronger nor a daisy chain, an' if Titus Alderson's seen fit to——"

"You shut your bloody trap," the dismissed smelter said savagely. "And as for you," he rounded on Adam, "aye, I'll be off all right, but the first business I do i' Half will be at th'Old Cow Inn . . . Martin Rutter'll damned soon put you in your place, by God won't he?"

Silently watched by a number of men whose countenances had changed greatly, he flung off. To them, Adam said a few words: "Get back to your jobs, lads. If there's owt to be rectified it can be done later, but don't hold things up now. It's just as Sam says, an' I'm nobbut doing what I can."

Not very long afterwards he and the engineer saw that this piece of advice had been acted upon.

"Now I'm off up to Mary Dressing Floors," Adam said. "But when I've finished there I'm going to Mary Forehead. Will you meet me there and arrange for Len Rukin and Hugh Bearpark to be with you?"

"Aye, I will," Sam Kirkbride rumbled.

Following the tramway past Notion Level, Adam strode up the winding gill, which now was taking on a winter appearance. Overhead, rain squalls howled, but the steep sides of the ravine afforded protection from their worst blows.

At Mary Dressing Floors he made a cursory inspection, walking quickly from the crushing-mill to the slime pits, where, as he fingered a small parcel of lustrous, blue-black ore, dug out from the upper and richest band deposited upon a cone-shaped, wooden buddle, he could not but reflect that the floors were not being employed at even one-tenth of their capacity. For the present, however, he had a more pressing matter to consider: the influx of water at Mary Forehead. A test, if stringently conducted, would establish the facts, but he doubted whether Reuben Nattrass would agree. In that case there was only one thing to be done.

"Aye, an' I'll put it in hand," he said when climbing the side of Winterings Gill, whence, head ducked down, he tramped across the moor towards Great Faith Shaft, which, sunk to the Great Deep Level, intersected both Mary and Notion Levels. "But I'll give Cousin Reuben th'opportunity of refusing a trial."

With one arm useless, it was awkward but nevertheless a pleasant surcease from buffeting wind and lashing rain to descend Great Faith, down which he paused on the first bunning to light a candle. From there he soon stepped off the ladder on to the sole of Mary Level, where, held up only once when taking refuge in a safety niche to avoid an oncoming horse and wagon train, he made good progress. Until he drew nearer to Glory Shaft it was very quiet, but in the sumps and rises of the forehead ground there were a few indications of groovers at work: the thudding of tools, a distant glow of light on the cheek of a drift, many an echo, and acrid fumes.

At Glory Shaft Adam looked at the spear rod in the shaft, which, moving up and down in guides, was connected to the arm of the pump in the sump. Designed to lift three hundred gallons of water every minute, the shuddering motion denoted strain.

"It'll make a lot o' difference to it if I can cut down what it's got to do," he muttered. "And it'd increase the production of ore hereabouts if the working places were drier."

A dim triangle of lights in front told him that Sam Kirkbride had done his part, and so he splashed through the oncoming flow to join the men at Mary Forehead, nodding to Hugh Bearpark and Len Rukin on reaching them.

"I want to make provisional arrangements for a strong stemming here," he began right away. "To block the water that's flooding down to the pump."

"Block it?" the groover ejaculated.

"Up to a point, Len," Adam confirmed. "Hold it back till it's five feet high, say. What are your ideas about the best road?"

The trio glanced stealthily at one another, but, whatever their private thoughts, they were soon animatedly arguing methods. At that particular spot the level was driven through solid rock, and it was decided that slots nine inches deep must be hewn out on each side, the bearing face of each dressed off smoothly. Five-inch thick oak planks, stretching from side to side, were to be placed one upon another, all joints to be stuffed with sheep's wool and tar.

"Yes, and on t'water side we can bank up wi' small peats as will choke any gaps," Sam Kirkbride brooded. "I could send Mazy Bill wi' Polly up t'moor for a few loads fro' the hags."

The carpenter frowned. "The timbering's easy enough," he said. "But oak's expensive . . . will t'Wood Yard let me have it?"

"I'll arrange for that wi' Puke Hastwell, Hugh, as soon as I know we're going on with the stemming," Adam promised. "Meantime get everything measured up in readiness for the word go. I shall know afore I get back to the mine office, an' if you'll pop in, Sam . . ."

For some moments Len Rukin had been rubbing the profusion of black stubble on his chin. "You know, as soon as t'water at the far side rises to five feet, just as much 'ul spill over the top an' come this way as it is doing now," he muttered.

"It will," Adam agreed.

Leaving three men who, when he was out of earshot, started to puzzle about the reasons for the undertaking, Adam went to the tail of Mary Level. The East Side Company's office was opposite, but as the beck was running deep he was compelled to go down to Notion Bridge and walk up the gill at the far side.

Reuben Nattrass was coming away from Martha Bingstead when he glimpsed Adam and, omitting the usual preamble, he spoke his mind, dark eyes narrowed angrily. "I can flaming well see I'll have to watch you a sight more than I thought," he announced. "You've getten my brass off me, an' you've nipped in for Modesty afore me. Is there owt else you're wanting? Or is that bloody well more than you'll be kind enough to tell me?"

"Not at all," Adam grunted. "What I'm after persuading you to do is to increase your pumping eastward of Martha Forehead, and to make sure also that all tail-race water fro' the waterwheel at Toft Rigg Whim Shaft is directed down Martha Water Gate. You see, I'm wondering if the water we've to deal with at Mary Forehead comes from your side of the boundary."

Reuben Nattrass's face suffused. "Not a bloody pint," he roared. "It's been tested for that matter."

Adam nodded. "Aye, by oil, but that's a surface test only. Anyroad, be that as it may, the best test of all is to stop everything at your side. It's better than having summat forced on to you, and we'll know properly."

"Nobody'll force owt on me." Reuben Nattrass's teeth bared in a nasty grin. "Including this bloody business o' yours."

"Is that final?" Adam inquired.

For the first time then Reuben Nattrass's finger jabbed. "Aye," he nod-nodded. "And hop it, afore I put you out on here neck an' crop."

A peculiar smile occasionally lightened Adam's face as he walked down Winterings Gill. If there were substantial percolation, a five feet stemming at Mary Forehead might have serious repercussions for the East Side Company. The water, backing up, would rise in Martha Level, with unpredictable consequences.

Sir Charles Grafton's mineral agent, fiery complexioned, awaited him at the office. As for Bart Hugill, his demeanour was that of one who gleefully expects to hear an interloper put in his place.

"Good morning, Mr. Hird," Adam said as he hung up his coat. "I hope you haven't been here long if you're wanting to see me on business."

"Th'only business I have is to ask why Titus Alderson has put you in his room while he's badly," the royalty agent barked.

"That's summat, Mr. Hird, you must inquire of Mr. Alderson when he's well enough." Adam was firm but polite. "And as that's all you've come about, perhaps you'll excuse me if I get on with my work."

Observed spleenishly, he dipped a pen to begin drafting on a bill-head a letter to the East Side Lead Mining Company Ltd. expressing regret for their agent's refusal of that morning to take precautionary measures relative to the possible movement westward of water from Martha Level forehead. The last paragraph intimated that, in certain circumstances, the liability of the East Side Company for damages might thereby be onerous.

This communication was handed to Bart Hugill, together with a pencilled note instructing him to damp off two copies, one to be retained, the other to be posted, covering letter attached, to the East Side Company's Registered Office at Corvy. The original was to be delivered by hand to Reuben Nattrass.

"Aye," the clerk mumbled, looking up.

Events were beginning to have their effect upon him. Head bent, long hair tumbling, he avidly re-read the assistant-agent's uncompromising lines, quite forgetful that these were hardly his affair. He was still more shaken when Sam Kirkbride popped his head round the office door.

"The word's 'go' all right, Sam," said Adam, anticipating the engineer. "I'll leave it to the three of you, and the main thing is speed. Get all the extra men and tackle you need, and keep 'em at it as long as you can."

"Extra time?" Sam Kirkbride inquired.

"Aye, or through the night if you can arrange it," Adam said.

"Right." The engineer nodded before withdrawing.

As Sir Charles's agent, Henry Hird had come to believe his authority supreme. "Well, now," he boomed, "maybe you'll be good enough to enlighten me as to what you've just telled Kirkbride to push on with?"

"Just ordinary mining business, Mr. Hird," Adam answered.

Henry Hird reddened again. "That's no reply."

A minute or so later, when his attention was most certainly not on what he was doing, Bart Hugill trapped himself in the letter-press. But, as he sucked his thumb, he admitted that the pain was worth it.

Adam had been courteous throughout. "So that's how I look at t'position, Mr. Hird: you as representing the royalty owner, an' me doing my best for my company. Where our respective functions overlap I shall be only too pleased to listen to any advice you care to offer, but otherwise what I do is my concern. In the present instance it's nobbut a matter of day-to-day mining practice, and as such it's noan summat I ought to trouble you with, as I trust you'll agree."

Far from being mollified, Henry Hird began to shout. "So that's your attitude, eh? Well, I'll——"

Before the mineral agent got into full stride Adam mentioned the timber he would require both immediately and in the future. In response, Mr. Hird vowed that, ready cash notwithstanding, the Wood Yard would not supply the West Side Company until the overdue account had been settled.

Adam Brunskill's deep-set eyes glinted. "If that's so, I'm off to see Sir Charles this afternoon."

"Nobody can interview Sir Charles on mining business except through me as th'intermediary," Mr. Hird bawled. "I've to be telled aforehand why . . ."

While he ranted, Adam had an aside with the clerk. This was to ask Bart to arrange for Hugh Bearpark to be at the agent's office that afternoon soon after one o'clock, to ride down to Greets.

"Greets!" the mineral agent roared. "I've warned you, haven't I?"

"I'm seeing Sir Charles if I can, Mr. Hird," Adam said quietly.

The mineral agent temporised. "If it's about wood . . . you spoke o' paying in advance, didn't you?"

Adam was not to be dissuaded. "In any event, now I'm deputising for Mr. Alderson, I reckon it'll be nowt but civil if I show myself to Sir Charles," he observed.

There was another reason why Adam should meet and, if possible, be approved by the royalty owner. But this he did not learn until shortly before he and Hugh Bearpark, on Ben's back, ambled out of the yard of Yew Tree House.

Still another ill-humoured encounter had to be borne by Adam that morning. On leaving Notion Bridge a little short of midday he walked down Sleety Slape to Modesty, where he did one or two small jobs before continuing to Old Hannah's for dinner. As he was hurrying across Winterings Brig, reflecting that by the week-end he would be sleeping under his own roof, a furiously-driven trap clattered on to the cobbled forecourt of the Plug and Feathers. The driver, Martin Rutter, brandished a whip.

"You, Brunskill," he yelled. "What the hell do you mean, I say what the hell do you mean, by giving Jonas Cottingham his notice?"

"Because he's an obstructionist an' noan above causing bother," Adam retorted.

"What Titus Alderson's been thinking on to start you in his place I can't imagine, can't imagine I can't," the auctioneer snapped. "But you've made a right beginning, haven't you?"

"If you're meaning Cottingham, yes," said Adam.

Mr. Rutter drew another breath. "Playing ducks an' drakes with t' Company . . . you that hasn't owt at stake, not a single share. But I'll put a stop to this, put a stop to it I will."

Bending forward, Adam spoke evenly. "So long as I'm in charge, Mr. Rutter, Cottingham's done for."

That sank in, but Martin Rutter's volubility increased as a result. "Is he, is he?" he rattled on. "If I hadn't a farm-sale to arrange about this afternoon I'd be off to Mr. Wade at Greets Mill about this here impertinence, but I'll be at Half House to-night. Aye, you'll hear in the morning, hear in t'morning you will."

"Then we'll leave it till then, Mr. Rutter," Adam murmured.

On the way to the bow-windowed little shop he had time to meditate. "Well, who's going to be next?" he asked himself.

This question was answered after dinner, immediately he unlocked the agent's door in Jom High Road. The voices of Cherry and Mrs. Robert William Alderson, who stood just within the front door of Yew Tree House, were perfectly audible.

"Well, Lucy Peacock's oft upstairs with him," the mistress of Malaga was complaining.

"Mrs. Peacock's been helping to nurse Uncle," Cherry replied. "And she doesn't disturb him with business matters."

"I daresay not," Mrs. Roberty Will said. "But all the same he's got to be telled quick that I'm noan having that Brunskill kept on as his assistant. I'm the biggest shareholder in the company, and . . ."

Making no bones about listening, Adam heard a series of threats. There were dark references to a demand for a general meeting of shareholders, and a few remarks not wholly complimentary to the Chairman of the Company.

The older woman was becoming a little over-excited. "Oh, yes," she declared, "if needs be I shall go straight to the fountain head. In th'ordinary course of things Sir Charles doesn't interfere, but he's the lessor of t'royalties after all, an' if I inform him the West Side Company's going to be wrecked beyond redemption . . ."

As Hugh Bearpark tapped on the office window, fresh-complexioned face close to the pane, Adam heard Mrs. Roberty Will's next effort: "I shall be here after tea again and I shall require a reply then. If it's no, if your uncle's so much out of his senses as to say no . . ."

In consideration of the double burden, Ben was allowed his own gait to Greets. Perhaps not entirely strange, Henry Hird was in the vicinity when the snuff-brown galloway ambled past the B.G. Inn.

Taking refuge with Ben beneath the castellated garden wall of Greets Hall, Hugh Bearpark watched the two men walking up the rear drive, the new assistant trying to forge ahead but thrown off balance now and then by his companion's restraining clutches.

"Well, I don't know how it'll end," the carpenter grinned. "But that chap's stirred things up so far."

Meantime, great splashes from water-laden silver firs dropping upon them, Adam and Henry Hird passed the stable belfry to turn towards the back door of the house.

Adam was singularly fortunate with both Sir Charles Grafton and Mr. Joseph Wade. As regards the former, it was a stroke of supreme good luck that Sir Charles already had knowledge of first-rate references to his professional ability. The testimonials were indirect, and, of all people, through Mr. Hird: in a letter James Calvert had written from Spain a couple or so months after Adam's departure.

"Yes, yes, I remember quite clearly, Hird," Sir Charles said a trifle testily. He was an elderly gentleman whose clothing was decidedly shabby. "James wrote in exceedingly high terms of this young man. Surely you recall showing me the letter and why—the remarks he made about our cutting water in the Great Deep."

Henry Hird was grudging. "Vaguely, Sir Charles, just vaguely."

Priding himself on an excellent memory, Sir Charles's rising annoyance was plain enough, but Adam's appreciative observations about the Great Deep Level kept everything harmonious. The talk for the next few minutes' ranged animatedly upon the problems attending such an undertaking, and, at its conclusion, Sir Charles wished the young man the best of adventuring.

"Thank you, sir," Adam said. "And there's just one other matter I'd like to mention while I've th'opportunity . . ."

Soon afterwards Mr. Hird's cheeks were of a hue as vivid as his big nose, when his employer offered to allow the West Side Company three months' credit for their timber, a mid-way accommodation between cash on delivery and the half-yearly account formerly granted. Moreover, Sir Charles was agreeable that a note should be penned there and then to Puke Hastwell so that, on presenting it, Hugh Bearpark would be able to obtain a few oaken planks urgently needed.

Hugely delighted with this outcome, Adam handed the letter to the carpenter when he got outside, with orders to return at once to the Wood Yard.

"No, I'll get back all right later," he laughed. "You be off, lad."

Whether inspired or not by the new times, Hugh Bearpark started Ben at a rare gallop towards home, while Adam, unmindful of mud and pools, speedily reached Greets Mill. The proprietor was at business and soon his visitor faced him across a desk. As with Sir Charles, Adam opened by identifying himself as the man who had been thrown over Winterings Brig, but, likewise, the admission evoked no substantial response, Mr. Wade merely muttering disparagingly about the brains behind mob law.

So Adam began his story and, after a time, his face a picture, the yarn-spinner's aldermanic front started to swell. "The damned scoundrels—paying you to escape their moral obligations!" he exploded. "And from that, young man, you'll appreciate the prudence of not suggesting I should consider a similar transaction."

"What I'm here for, Mr. Wade," Adam said, "is to tell you that Mr. Alderson has appointed me his assistant, an' that I'm having a shot at running the mines while he's ill."

Joseph Wade barked: "You'll get no money from me for that either. Not a pennypiece more will I invest in lead-mining."

Adam hit back. "I don't want you to, sir. All the Company needs is a little to grease the wheels, like. I'll provide that myself, on a day to day basis, reimbursing myself from every payment received for lead."

"Out of money received from these dishonest rascals, eh?" the older man snorted.

"Could it be used for a more suitable purpose?" Adam demanded.

Momentarily that checked the yarn-spinner. "No," he conceded.

"But," he pointed triumphantly, "you're going to ensure that you get it back as soon as you can."

"Who's shouldering t'risk on the shares?" Adam asked. "And there'll always be a carry-over in the brass I've lent, won't there?"

Mr. Wade's thick neck thickened further. "It's a gamble," he roared. "If you win you're in clover, if you lose you've nothing to lose."

"Ask Richardson and Storey about that," Adam retorted.

"And what then?" the other scoffed.

"You might apologise," Adam grunted. "It'd be about th'only thing a gentleman could do after as good as telling a chap he were a rogue."

A throaty cry heralded Mr. Wade's upheaval from his chair and a subsequent promenade with his hands bustling out the tails of his coat. Once or twice his shrewd glance slid to the caller, but it was not until he had been standing awhile in the window, staring at the waterwheel, that he spoke.

"Who are you?" he asked, his tone without offence. "You'd better tell me that . . . and a few more things, too. They'll occur to you."

The lights in shop windows and houses were glistening upon the wet pavements of the Market Place when he ushered the young man to the door of his office.

"Well, Brunskill, I think you've bitten off more than you can chew," he declared. "But, whatever else, you may be assured I shall not be swayed by anything Mrs. Alderson or anyone may say."

In the passage an elderly clerk stood aside to allow them to pass. To him, Mr. Wade, his expression suddenly stern, issued certain commands —William Nattrass's account for carting was to be closed, the same applying to George Nattrass, from whom no more fodder must be bought henceforth, and Lodge Trotter was never again to be permitted to buy job lots of yarn.

"That disposes of those gentry," he remarked with a tight smile. "And only one thing remains now, Brunskill, and that is for me to ask you a question which has been on the tip of my tongue."

"Yes, sir, what is it?" Adam said.

Mr. Wade was very bland. "I rather think it will have occurred to an astute young man like yourself that, together with Alderson's holding, you and he have sufficient shares to kick me out of my chairmanship if you wished. Why didn't you . . . er . . . hint at it when I was a thought awkward?"

"Well, for one thing I don't reckon you'd have cared," Adam said, his solemnity increasing as he added: "For the other, by working myself into your good graces I might some day be able to do you down for thousands. I've drawn quite a bit for nowt recently, and it gives an enterprising chap big ideas."

The yarn-spinner's amused guffaw not only arrested the attention of passers-by but brought Mr. Thomas Plews to a standstill, the clockmaker recognising Adam too late. "Now then, Mr. Wade," he observed, "what's up, eh?"

Joseph Wade drew himself up to his full height, not very imposing. "You cheating, Sunday-praying shark," he thundered. "For two pins——"

Screw Tom's jaw dropped. "I don't understand, Mr. Wade," he gasped. "But if that evil-liver with you has been saying owt to my detriment, him as is a liar and . . ."

By grandfather, son and son's son, the fortunes of the Wades had been raised from penury to their present modest plenty. The virility of Joseph Wade's ensuing language revealed in part why his family, refuting the adage of clogs to clogs within three generations, had not declined within that commonly accepted space.

The inner man comfortably lined with roast beef and pickled walnuts, Adam was leaving the dining-room of the Grafton Arms when he bumped into his cousin Arthur, dressed for the pleasures of the evening. Resilient always, Arthur Nattrass had explained away in his own manner how he had come to hang ignominiously from the lamp-bracket at Nick Turn, and so, seldom cherishing enmity, he had not held that episode against Adam. But the considerable sum paid out by his enraged father had changed the complexion of things.

"Doing yourself proud, eh?" he jeered. "Well, you'll noan be short o' brass now."

"I'm very nicely placed, lad," Adam conceded smugly. "In fact, so bursting wi' cash that my first idea was to stand you a few drinks."

His cousin's light-coloured laugh greeted this intimation. "Then you thought better, is that it?"

"What I thought, Cousin Arthur," Adam smiled, "were that you hadn't a stout enough head."

Arthur Nattrass reacted strongly. "Why, I could sup such as you under t'table afore I'd really wet my whistle," he said, following this up by quoting figures of consumption that sounded impressive enough to float the Channel Fleet in beer.

"A real seasoned toss-pot," Adam remarked. "Still, I wouldn't object to taking you on some night, but it's a bit late for a session now, isn't it?"

The mild appeal produced the effect desired, and Arthur Nattrass post-haste pulled out his watch, the chain of which Adam took pains to examine.

"Aye, it's too far on," Adam murmured. "By the way, I see you haven't got that luckstone o' yours, Arthur."

His challenge declined, George Nattrass's groover son was in the ascendancy. "Eh, you chaps as imagine you can knock 'em back," he chortled.

"You haven't lost it, have you?" Adam inquired with concern. "It were a bonnie thing, too."

Arthur Nattrass was surprisingly short. "Never mind dodging th'issue. An' that's beer."

"Aye, beer, wonderful stuff," said Adam, preparing to move. "Take my advice, Arthur, and gulp down as much as possible while you can. Think o' Matt Tiplady, put away where he can't touch a drop, poor chap. Which reminds me, he's released to-day, isn't he?"

"And why the hell should I be put away like Matt Tiplady?" Arthur Nattrass asked breezily. "Me, a law-abiding citizen, as everybody knows, eh?"

"I oughtn't to have compared a poacher with a ripsnorter like you, lad," Adam confessed. "No, when *you're* taken away it'll noan be for a minor offence. I'm noan gifted wi' second sight, naturally, but if I had to guess I should say that when you're shoved on the tread-mill it'll be for years an' years."

Arthur Nattrass licked his lips. "What the hell are you jawing about?"

"Penal servitude were what I were trying to describe, lad," Adam replied in surprise. "Anyroad, how ever did we come to be discussing it?"

"Matt Tiplady." Arthur Nattrass breathed more easily.

Adam frowned. "Aye," he cogitated. "Maybe so, but I'm more inclined to think it started through you mentioning you'd lost your luckstone."

"I didn't say as I'd lost it," his cousin snapped.

"Well, have you?" Adam persevered.

"What's it matter if I have?" Arthur Nattrass demanded.

A rising sense of unease possessed him as in vain he endeavoured to assess the unfathomable expression in his cousin's searching grey eyes.

"That 'ud depend, wouldn't it?" Adam said, moving nearer the door. "But supposing a bank had been robbed an' a luckstone as easily distinguishable as yours were found in the vault——"

"Well, I haven't robbed any bank, lad," Arthur Nattrass retorted, his smile a travesty. "So——"

"No," Adam nodded, his hand on the knob. "But there's all sorts of thievery. You can rob a man of his purse, for example . . . and you can rob him of his good name."

The door opened and closed, leaving within a gangling young man who, for an appreciable while, remained rooted as he was, pallid, tremulous of lip, and chilled to the marrow. Then, when he had pulled himself together, Arthur Nattrass went to the bar, his gait less swaggering. Adopting for this once the taste of a cousin of whom he had always been in awe, he ordered a double brandy.

The Doctor's lamp, at the opposite side of the Market Place, reflected in a thin red line upon the wet cobblestones, passing close by the Market Cross before stretching to Adam's feet.

"Aye, while I'm here," he muttered.

In due course he was sitting in his shirt sleeves while the wound in his arm was probed. Dr. Seaton's comments were often obscure, ranging from calling Hannah Batty "a murderous old female," to claiming her as a stouter ally than the entire College of Surgeons in certain complications of child-birth, but his last pronouncement was commendably clear.

"Newcastle Infirmary," he said, as he completed the dressing. "I'll write to-morrow . . . be ready to go in three days . . . no time to be lost."

"I've a lot to arrange an' I'll have to stay here all next week, doctor," said Adam. "How long shall I be off?"

Dr. Seaton shrugged. "Ignore medical advice . . . perhaps for ever. Where would you be buried—here amongst your dear friends and relatives?"

Adam grinned. "They don't think much of me, do they?"

"Think less of you if you lose your arm," the little doctor crowed. "The Lord's vengeance . . . His visible sign . . . rotting limb . . . dropping off. Ha!"

"What!" Adam ejaculated, the meaning of one or two strange remarks becoming apparent. "Do you mean to say as I'm supposed to be visited by the wrath o' God because of this?"

Dr. Seaton was standing, too, but he had to look up a long way. "Just starting," he observed with unimpaired cheerfulness. "Sweeping the Dale . . . raging by week-end."

"Well, I'm damned," Adam grunted. "Is there owt else you can tell me? For instance, the why and wherefore of my cousin Agnes?"

The inquiry caused the doctor infinite amusement. He chuckled, slapped his knee and, on straightening, took a nip of whisky from the bottle neck. "Simple . . . unnatural coupling . . . that's all."

Adam's brow darkened. "I've wondered if it was that, doctor," he said. "Does th'awful truth ever come out in cases of that nature?"

But Dr. Seaton was off on another tack. While shoving his patient none too gently towards the door he irritably explained he had a round still to make before sitting down at the Vicarage for a hand at cards. Twice, before he could stem the flow, Adam was compelled to repeat the all-important question.

The doctor's face saddened. For a brief space he became a quiet-spoken, shrewd and understanding man. "Best to be plain," he said, tired eyes kind. "Large families, yes . . . many witnesses . . . court cases . . . cross-examination. Otherwise, no."

Oppressed by the confirmation of his worst fears, Adam walked up the dale highway, overcoat sleeve flapping, his arm much more comfortable in the sling. Again and again he turned over in his mind the one thing that mattered, but his conclusions were always the same: to hope for the best, to keep pegging away in all he had undertaken.

Abruptly he forced his thoughts away from Cherry and, as the light in the Smithy came into sight, he had decided he would re-dial the New Drift for a cross-drive to the sump of Doomsday High Shaft. When started, this would necessitate an adequate stock of the most vital tools and, in view of his impending absence, it would be advisable to put all the arrangements in hand as quickly as possible. With the intention of speaking to Richard Blenkiron, he bore to the right.

Two heads turned inquiringly at the sound of footsteps. Matt Tiplady's delight at seeing a friend was very evident, but the blacksmith was hardly in the same position. It became a conversation in which only two participated.

"Aye, no worse for my experience, lad," the released man grinned, replying to Adam's question. "And all agog to get down to business. I've got to keep Will an' Luther Thwaites up to scratch, haven't I?"

However Matt Tiplady might be maligned in many quarters, Adam was quite certain he could be trusted. Ascertaining whether his own connection with the West Side Company were known to the poacher, he then referred to the important operation in prospect: "So instead o' snickling game, will you come back as a groover? I'm beginning this new drift within a day or two, and I want chaps who will really belt away in t'forehead."

"A proper job, lad?" Matt said. "Noan of this grubbing for a bing or two o' bouse?"

"No, it's right graft, an' for many a week," Adam promised.

Eagerness to take part in the enterprise warred with the knowledge of one used to the disappointments of lead-mining. "I'd like," the poacher muttered. "But think you the Pay 'ul be enough for me an' the childer just to manage on?"

"Yes," Adam nodded. "But how about being at Notion Bridge to-morrow morning to talk it over?"

"I'll be there, lad," Matt Tiplady said.

Meanwhile, his attitude as though he were half-inclined to join in, the blacksmith remained in the background. It was his nature to itch to be in at anything exciting and, since early afternoon, when odd snippets of news had begun drifting down from the mines, he had scented lively times ahead.

"And there's summat *you* can do for me, Mr. Blenkiron," Adam said. "About making extra drills and borers an' such like." He went on to say that he meant to link with Jamie's Mint with all dispatch, and, as suitable men became available, the shifts would be increased to two or more, the ultimate objective a twenty-four hour day for six full days. "But I shan't want 'em to be held up for owt."

Richard Blenkiron seemed slightly dazed as he remarked that, if so much were being contemplated, he would have to open up the forge at the North Mill. "There's noan much octagonal bar, though," he murmured. "And the foundry hasn't been all that willing to 'liver."

"If you'll let me know to-morrow what you'll require I'll deal with that, Mr. Blenkiron," said Adam. "An' you'll see we're all right in the way I've spoken of?"

"Aye, I will," the blacksmith mumbled.

"Thanks," Adam said. "Well, I'd better get off to report to my boss. Good night to you both."

Slowly he crossed towards Jom High Road, engulfed by another of the bouts of nausea with which latterly he had been afflicted. The wave of sickness was beginning to recede when, at the door of the agent's office, he fumbled single-handed for key and matches, but, though rapidly improving, he was still not sufficiently himself to take much notice when a gate was violently slammed at Town Foot.

Before entering, Adam paused to take a few more restorative breaths of fresh air. By then the green-painted gate of Yew Tree House had ceased to quiver and, in the kitchen, Reuben Nattrass savagely confronted the girl who had jilted him on the eve of their wedding.

* * * *

That same afternoon, after swilling out the dairy at the Old Cow Inn, Annamaria Rutter scowlingly announced that, before milking-time, she would ride up to her Aunt Grace's, rain notwithstanding.

"There's summat fishy about this wedding, Mother," she declared. "And I'se going across to tackle Cherry Dinsdale, I am that. She can't pull wool over my eyes."

Wrapped in an oilskin cape and mounted on a broken-winded animal, one of her father's rare bad bargains, she went up to Smithy House, where the conversation between herself and her cousin pursued similar lines. From the workroom window, too, they saw Dinah Skidmore hurrying up the flagged path opposite.

"We'll go over now," Annamaria decided. "To find out what's the latest about t'blessed nuptials."

Fronick giggled. "An' have you heard the to-do over the West Side Company . . . About Adam Brunskill being given charge?"

"Aye," scoffed her companion. "By, and isn't my father in a paddy."

After satisfying Mrs. Blenkiron as to just why they were going out, a quick dash took them to the front door of Yew Tree House. In the kitchen, their first glimpse of Dinah's spellbound face prepared them for something extraordinary.

"Hallo!" Cherry greeted them. "Now take your things off——"

"The wedding's off," Dinah burst out. "She's chucked him."

Annamaria snorted. "Come to her senses, has she, the silly dafthead?"

Lips protruding in a perfect circle, her cousin's eyes goggled. "Ough, but I'm not blaming her," Fronick explained. "But think of all t'gossip there'll be. It's to-morrow . . . I . . . couldn't look at folk for weeks an' weeks at after if it was me."

"Well, I could," Annamaria said. "Owt 'ud be better to me than wedding Reuben Nattrass. I'd as soon mate wi' a gorilla and live with it in its cage."

Thin cheeks flushed, and happiness and relief in her shadowed eyes, Cherry Dinsdale stood surrounded by her bridesmaids. The later comers plied her with questions, and, though she fenced off the more inconvenient, enough was extracted to cause Miss Rutter suddenly to nod in triumph.

"I've getten it!" she exclaimed. "There's been a whisper as the two companies might be joining forces—I know my father were that fed up he'd have agreed—and you promised to wed him because on that, for your uncle's sake, didn't you?"

"Oh, Annamaria," Cherry begged, scarlet, "let's let it drop."

Annamaria stared. "All right then," she conceded after a while. "But I think as I ought to tell you straight out that your Uncle Titus's latest move isn't going to help him, because my father is dead against yon Brunskill being th'assistant agent."

"Need you come out wi' stuff like that now?" Dinah demanded hotly.

Checked for the second time, Annamaria Rutter surveyed the two friends. "You have to face up to what's what i' life, haven't you?" she asked, patent disgust in her tone. "Nay, I never thought you and Cherry were shrinking violets like Fronick here, who colours all over if her skirt lifts an inch."

"I don't," Fronick said.

Annamaria smiled broadly. "You don't, lass? Well, I'll bet you would have if you'd heard what some of t'lads said when you started the Maidens' Garland three year ago."

The milliner gasped. "What did they say?"

"Same as they say every year," her cousin replied. "You can't expect to stand on the pillar at the end of the parapet o' Winterings Brig without showing summat, can you? Besides, even if there isn't a wind there's always an up-draught from the gill."

Dinah screeched. "That's what they were laughing at me about. I knew it, too."

Hand on heart, Fronick Blenkiron might have been the wronged woman in a palpitating stage drama. "What could they see?" she asked tragically.

"Your drawers, what do you think?" Annamaria chortled. "Red 'uns they were an' all. I remember that because I'd all on to keep a straight face when I overheard Bart say summat about 'red for danger.'"

"He said that!" Fronick breathed.

Even Miss Rutter perceived something amiss. "Aye," she soothed. "But it were afore you an' him were walking out properly."

Bulbous eyes hard, Fronick promised a warm reception for her young man. "Wait till he comes to-night," she said.

Annamaria chuckled. "So you an' him discuss things like that, do you, Miss Prim? *Underwoollens.*"

"That we never," Fronick rounded on her furiously.

"You've admitted it . . . or as good as," her cousin pointed out.

After a time the cousins' dispute petered out, but, as Annamaria was leaving she made a remark which caused more trouble. It had crossed her mind that there could be another reason why the wedding was not taking place, and she popped her head around the door-jamb to say so.

"Hey!" she smiled. "Are you sure, Cherry love, as it's you who's given Reuben Nattrass the go-by, or is it t'other road about?"

Amazed, Cherry laughed nevertheless. "No, it was me, Annamaria, though I'm noan boasting about it. But why ever do you ask?"

Annamaria explained. "Nay, there's one o' those daft rumours going about as you were seen wearing men's clothing somewhere. And if Reuben Nattrass heard as how his future wife——"

In the midst of a fit of the sulks Fronick's trill was decidedly unexpected. "Nobody but you, Annamaria, 'ud ever be so silly as to credit such a ridiculous tale," she proclaimed.

"I didn't say I believed it, did I?" her cousin expostulated.

"As if any decent lass 'ud be immodest enough to wear trousers," the milliner jeered.

"What about red drawers, love?" Annamaria twitted her.

The corners of Fronick's mouth drooped, her lips quivered, and within a moment she was blubbing lustily. Blotchy-cheeked and red-eyed, she was eventually taken home by her cousin.

In the kitchen of Yew Tree House, two girls looked gravely at one another, the gravity of Cherry's friend the greater. "I've . . . I've heard that tale and all, Cherry," Dinah murmured. "At first-hand, too. Ralph and Isa came home specially to tell my mother and father. I vowed it couldn't have been you as our Ralph saw in a chap's suit o' clothes."

"It was, Dinah," Cherry nodded. Instinctively her glance went to the ceiling and then to the grandfather clock. Lucy Peacock was sitting upstairs and she saw it was not quite time for her to leave. "I'll tell you all about it," she whispered.

As the account of her friend's adventure in the night unfolded, Dinah Skidmore grew more and more enthralled, and at its conclusion her brown eyes were as round as saucers. "It's . . . it's like a fairy story, Cherry," she gasped. "But I'll never let on a word to anybody, 'cause I can understand how important it is that it's kept secret." Raptly she pressed question after question, but soon realised that present needs were more urgent. Sure that Reuben Nattrass would shortly arrive at Yew Tree House she offered to hurry home and back, so as to be in support when he came. "He'll be like a wild man, I'll be bound," she ended.

"No, lass, you needn't," Cherry smiled. "I'm not frightened of owt he can do or say to me. I'd rather have telled him to his face, of course, but with being tied with Uncle, and with to-morrow being Saturday, I thought I ought to let him know straight off. That's why I wrote a letter this morning and asked Wingy to deliver it at Ash Grove. I said to him, Reuben Nattrass I mean, that it were no use him thinking he could change my mind, but if he preferred to hear from my own lips he could come."

"As he will." Dinah shivered. "You're certain, absolutely certain, love, that you wouldn't feel better if I were with you?"

Cherry nodded. "I'll be perfectly all right, thank you, lass."

From then onwards, when her friend left, she busied herself with household tasks, slipping upstairs now and then to her uncle's room. The question of Mrs. Roberty Will was dealt with after she had taken up his tea-tray.

"Well, whatever the consequences—and she's a rare determined woman is Ellen when she's thwarted—there's nobbut one answer possible, lass," said Titus Alderson. "Of course she'll cause grievous trouble, and do all——"

Cherry had just mended the bedroom fire and was on her knees sweeping up the hearth. "We'll meet things as they come, Uncle," she said firmly, adding with severity: "And you get on with your tea."

Titus Alderson smiled. "Aye, well, strength goes in at the mouth, doesn't it? And I've summat to fight to get better for now."

The late afternoon sounds of Town Foot were dying away. From the Smithy the last horse to be shod that day clattered off, and the last groover returning from work clumped out of Sorrow Near. At Yew Tree House there began a period of waiting, both uncle and niece striving to maintain a semblance of bright conversation. The grandfather clock in the kitchen struck seven, then eight, and it seemed an age beyond that before Cherry heard the click of the gate, just as the earliest of the supper-beer fetchers, can rattling, ran along to the Roe. She hastened downstairs.

In the kitchen Mrs. Alderson did not speak until Cherry turned up the lamp. Then, holding a hand to shield her eyes from the bright light, she said one word: "Well?"

"Will you sit down, please?" Cherry asked.

The range of movement of the mistress of Malaga's bosom extended. "I'm noan going to be here long enough for that," she said harshly. "All I need is a plain yes or no as to whether he's getting shut of yon Brunskill. Which is it?"

"No," Cherry replied.

Initial shock stupefied the older woman, but she was rapidly making amends until silenced by a gate crashed open as though by a madman, by clogged feet tearing up the flagged path, by a front door flung back so viciously that the screws holding its hinges shrieked in protest.

"He's not, isn't he?" Mrs. Roberty Will stormed. "Well, I'll soon learn him what going counter to my wishes means. I'll——"

She stopped, cut short, notwithstanding her anger, by the nearing indications of an enraged man's violent progress.

Dark eyes glittering, Reuben Nattrass filled the kitchen doorway. He came slowly forward, his glance never leaving a white-faced but proudly erect young woman.

"So you reckon you've jilted me, do you?" he shouted. "Jilted me on t'very day afore we were going to be wed."

"No, I think nothing of the kind," Cherry told him quietly. "All I think about it is what I wrote in my letter . . . that I didn't love you, as I've never hidden fro' you, and that I couldn't wed you . . . and that it were better for both of us for it to be broken off when it's that road. I'm sorry it's been so near to-morrow, right sorry, but——"

Savagely Reuben Nattrass's thumb jerked sideways. "Starting already to try to make me t'bloody laughing-stock o' the village, are you, talking that way afore her? Oh aye, I know your game, but it's noan coming off. Right enough, you sent me a letter, but even if you hadn't I should have been round here to-night, and if you couldn't have proved your innocence to th'hilt in summat I should have asked you about . . . well, well, I shouldn't have been waiting for you at t'Chapel to-morrow. No chap in his right senses is going to wed a lass who's immodest as you've been."

Mrs. Roberty Will's mouth had been open a while. "What's she done?" she inquired eagerly.

"Ralph Skidmore spied her i' trousers early one morning," the mine-agent growled. "What she'd been up to I don't——"

"*Trousers!*" Titus Alderson's sister-in-law gasped. "It's noan true, is it? No one but t'most shameless hussy——"

Cherry's foot stamped. "I'm having no more of this from either of you," she cried. "Do you hear what I say——"

In the brief interval while she gulped another breath Adam wished them: "Good evening" from the passage doorway, one sleeve of his overcoat loose. Three heads turned and the glances of two pairs of eyes, as had that of Richard Blenkiron a little before, travelled to the bulge beneath the coat.

"Evening, lass," Adam smiled. "How's your uncle?"

"He's . . . he's a lot better," Cherry replied, her breath now uneven for another reason. "Dr. Seaton were very pleased with him."

"This is his house, isn't it?" Adam observed somewhat surprisingly. "Why not pop upstairs an' ask permission to order these two out?"

"I'se bloody well beginning to see summat else now," Reuben Nattrass swore. "He's getten my brass, he's getten Modesty . . ."

Firmly Adam escorted Cherry to the door, waiting there until she had reached the far end of the long passage, by which time his cousin was repeating himself.

"And what were that about my woman, Cousin Reuben?" Adam inquired.

"As you've getten off me an' all, what the hell do you think I mean?" the other roared. "Well, you're welcome to her."

Adam shook his head. "There's nowt like that ever passed between us, I can give you my solemn word."

Reuben Nattrass laughed coarsely. "I could name one thing as has passed between you, t'same as passed between you an' your cousin Agnes . . ."

With incredible speed Adam's left arm flashed out, his fingers sinking deeply into the speaker's windpipe. Caught utterly unawares, Reuben Nattrass was hurled backwards, his head striking the wall with a sickening thud. His arms flailed, but, the relentless grip never relaxing, his strength became more feeble as he was forced to the floor.

From the chair on to which she had sunk, Mrs. Alderson mutely watched. Her eyes terrified, she saw Reuben Nattrass slowly pull himself to his feet.

"I . . . weren't . . . on guard," he croaked.

"Neither were your tongue," Adam retorted.

"Of all t'disgraceful assaults!" Mrs. Roberty Will found voice. "If you want a witness as he nigh throttled you, Reuben lad . . ."

Irritation was distinguishable even when cloaked by hoarseness. " 'Course I . . . bloody well don't," he snapped. "I'll settle this on my own, won't I just."

"Don't use language like that to me," Mrs. Alderson shouted.

Adam was reminding her of the sick man when Cherry returned. The message she conveyed did nothing towards smoothing troubled waters.

"Oh, I'll go," Mr. Alderson's sister-in-law said venomously. "But he'll rue this night, I'll see to that."

"No, he'll rue nowt, Mrs. Alderson," Adam was very grave. "Because you've lost all power to harm him as you imagine."

Reuben Nattrass, who had gingerly been feeling his throat, brought the hand away to jab a menacing finger. Huskily he delivered a passionate threat. "Which is more nor I have about you, Brunskill. You were thrown over t'Brig, weren't you, and that didn't shift you out o' Winterings. But I will, an' afore so long—I'll have you skittering out on t'Dale like your father did. Oh, I'll own you're a tougher customer than I'd ever given you credit for, but you'll noan catch me wi' my britches down another time."

The two men were confronting each other, one with raven black hair who shook with fury, the other, in whom the pallor of ill-health was displacing tan, sure and quiet, self-contained.

"All right, Cousin Reuben," Adam sighed. "But I wish you'd consider th'audience you've got."

Reuben Nattrass's lips curved cruelly. "Never mind them so long as you understand what I mean. Fro' now on it's going to be another Nattrass again another Brunskill, an' by hell I'll see t'result's the same." Abruptly he started for the door. "Trust me," he threw over his shoulder.

When Mrs. Alderson followed him out, kindly peace seemed to steal back into the pleasant kitchen.

"I . . . I want to forget about it as soon as I can, Adam," Cherry said, shaky after the storm. "But what happened when I were upstairs? Reuben Nattrass's face were nearly blue when I came back."

"His breath caught," Adam said lightly. "But don't let's bother about either o' them any more, lass. So your uncle's a sight better, is he?"

She hesitated as if inclined to pursue the subject, but eventually replied: "He's different altogether, Adam, and he slept real well last night. He didn't the night afore, after you'd gone, but that were only to be expected, with him being so worked up."

Adam laughed. "He'll do some tossing about to-night. But wait till you hear."

With a quick movement he shook himself free from the overcoat which, when it fell upon the red-striped matting, he picked up and hung on one of the line of clothes hooks in the passage. Meantime he was severely interrogated about his visit to Dr. Seaton.

"Oh, I'm so glad you've been to him," Cherry said, a profound relief in her. "But I *knew* it was summat worse, because you're looking so badly."

"Nay, it's nobbut a matter of scraping a bone an' getting it cleaned up properly," Adam objected.

"What's that except a right operation?" Cherry demanded.

Above, Titus Alderson began to thump the floor with the walking-stick he had that morning insisted should be placed near his bedside. The knocks were both forceful and frequent.

"He's mending," Adam grinned. "Well, unless we make haste the ceiling 'ul tumble in, so come on, lass. That is," he amended solemnly, "unless you're noan wanting to be wearied wi' tedious business talk."

Cherry's eyes danced. "Try to stop me," she invited him.

Smiling, they walked side by side along the passage, Cherry holding the candlestick. In the narrow stairway she took the lead.

"This reminds me o'summat," Adam soliloquised, as a much trimmer figure than the one he next hinted about climbed before him. "Yes, that's it . . . when we were dialling in that slant noan so far short of the second knavery."

She stopped suddenly, rosily-flushed cheeks plainly revealed in the light of the candle. "And what do you mean by that?" she asked.

The picture of innocence, Adam stared back. "Nowt but that it were steep like here," he remarked, "and you were i' front of me just the same. Whatever did you think I meant?"

Cherry's red lips parted, but fortunately for her the invalid's resumed onslaught with his stick saved her from the perils of countering an ingeniously pointed question.

As they had been for the past hour, Cherry's cheeks were blooming with excitement when, across the bed, she sent a discreet signal.

"Yes, I think that's about all, Mr. Alderson," Adam said, responding. "And so if you'll excuse me—I want to be on t'job early to lay out the ground for the new drift."

"Aye, if we can nobbut get to Doomsday an' then on to Jamie's Mint," said Titus Alderson, shuffling himself into a more comfortable position. "As for the stemming you've set afoot at Mary Forehead, I think you're right. For the last few months I've wondered in my heart whether water were seeping through, but at after the disaster with my Short Cut I were frightened of making a fool of myself."

"We shall soon know anyhow," Adam said, rising. "Well, I shan't be seeing you again till Monday or Tuesday . . . I'm dialling to-morrow, an' during the week-end I shall be plotting the figures on to paper."

Titus Alderson sighed with happiness. "I can't believe it yet, lad. You and me the unquestioned masters if we've a mind . . . and about two hundred an' forty pounds to get things moving with."

Grimaced at sternly by Cherry, Adam was edging towards the bed-room door, but this statement reminded him of an important omission in his narrative which, owing to many eager interventions of uncle and niece, he had quite forgotten.

"Aye, an' I'd sixty pounds more than that, but I used it to buy Droughty

Tom's rights in the donkey pump at Old Wife Shaft," he explained. "I reckoned it might be a suitable trump-card to have by us."

Ministering duties forgotten, Cherry gasped. "You've bought that?"

Her uncle was longer in finding tongue. "Trump card, lad, I should think it is. You know it drains all th'East Side's Jenny Incline Ground?"

"A first-rate pump, too," Adam said. "I've examined it."

"Oh, it is," Titus Alderson agreed. "Aye, I've oft envied 'em and wished we had it at Maybe."

Adam's eyes glinted. "It'd have done for Maybe, would it?" he said.

"Just the ticket," Mr. Alderson replied, "even to t'pipe connections. Why, one like that 'ud shift all the flood in the North Sun Vein Ground in no time"

"We shall have to see about providing ourselves with one then," Adam said very non-committally. "But that can be gone into when I'm back fro' Newcastle."

Chancing to catch another of Cherry's signs to Adam, Mr. Alderson was declaring that, doctor's orders notwithstanding, he would not forever remain on his back, when they heard the rattle of the front-door knob. Then Mrs. Peacock called out.

"Cherry love, you run down and stop her fro' coming up just yet," her uncle ordered. "An' you, lad, hand me t'scissors out of the top drawer there an' set that swing mirror i' front of me on the bed. I've a reet story to tell Lucy and I'm noan going to resemble an unkempt tup while I'm telling it."

Amused glances passed between Adam and Cherry before she hastened downstairs to detain the mistress of the Plug and Feathers while her uncle restored a white beard into its pointed, nautical style. In due course Mrs. Peacock was allowed to ascend to the bedroom and Adam went down to the kitchen, where he burned a small, newspaper-wrapped parcel of hair trimmings.

"They're so fond o' one another," Cherry smiled.

"Aye, an' let's hope all goes well for 'em," Adam said.

Before leaving he went along to the office, to scan the Company's Mining Lease, and on his return they talked awhile. Then Cherry helped him into his overcoat, promising to undertake a commission out of the half-sovereign he had given her: the purchase of a joint of beef when the butcher's cart arrived. She also arranged to cook this for him so that he could take it on to Modesty.

"I shall be very grateful, lass, but . . ." Adam coughed, "don't suggest doing owt else for me. It gets awkward for a chap when he's overwhelmed with offers from young women."

This once Cherry was not caught. "Mary Jane," she dimpled.

Adam grinned. "Aye, Mary Jane, an' so far she's alluded to washing, cooking, darning, spring-cleaning and the Lord knows what. But I fear she thinks nowt of my furniture, though she did say she would do her best to make the place presentable."

"With a deep sigh?" Cherry laughed.

"Aye," Adam chuckled. "Well, lass, I'd better be off so that you can nip upstairs to join your uncle and Mrs. Peacock and go over everything two or three times more."

Indignantly she repudiated this, which was certainly why, when the front door closed behind him, Adam chuckled again as he heard her footsteps beat out a tattoo on the oilcloth-covered floor of the passage. With eyes as yet unaccustomed to the darkness he went down the path to the gate.

As he stepped on to the pavement he was struck simultaneously from right and left, a swinging hook to the mouth and a hard punch behind the ear. The suddenness of the attack and the physical disability he suffered rendered his chances hopeless. It was a quiet fight, merely the light patter of clogs and the quick breathing of two men inflamed by spirits. Each blow carried a sting in memory of a woman lost as Reuben Nattrass and his crony relentlessly battered their opponent until he slithered against the low wall, to fall prone on the muddy ground.

Head whirling, Adam slowly clawed himself up and, legs and feet unsure, began to stagger homeward. As Blind Kit's workshop was for the older men a place of meeting so was the blacksmith's shop for the younger, and hazily, after a boastful remark shouted into the Smithy doorway by Bull Waggott, he heard the turn-out. An unknown voice growled: "Serve t'bugger right," but then he was sick, supporting himself left-handedly against the end wall of a cottage beyond the Roe.

A match flared close to his face, and an awed "God Almighty" was breathed on him. "Well, I think nowt o' this, whatever he's done, Nattrass," Wingy Blenkiron went on. "He's handicapped and it's been two to one . . . a right bloody way o' scrapping, I don't think."

"We were teaching him a lesson, noan scrapping," Reuben Nattrass swallowed painfully. "You nobbut *fight* chaps as is sound and whole."

Dizziness overwhelmed Adam again and he was hardly conscious of the hand propelling him or the postman's aside: "Fetch a bucket o' water, Bart, an' get some clean rags from the house. We'll have all these chaps away and all."

He remembered nothing more until, clear-minded but very chill, he opened his most serviceable eye. Before him he saw Wingy Blenkiron and Bart Hugill.

"Are you all right?" the clerk asked.

"I could be livelier," Adam admitted thickly. "But sound enough to get on to Old Hannah's."

"You're sure?" the postman insisted.

"Aye," Adam nodded carefully. "But I'll just dab my face wi' water again."

"You'd better take a piece of this linen with you," Wingy Blenkiron suggested. "You're still bleeding fairish."

Watched silently by the two friends he bathed himself, their glances following him as he walked stiffly across the Smithy.

"Thanks to both of you," he said from the doorway.

"You're welcome," the postman replied gruffly.

At Calvert's Wynd a light shone in the cobbler's workshop, where Blind Kit was knocking out a dint in his back-can. "H'mm, that'll have to do or I'll waken all t'youngsters," he decided, feeling the rounded surface of the metal. "Aye, it's all——" Head on one side he listened to erratic footsteps, and then muttered: "Sounds like yon young fellow, but . . ." A little proud of an unerring faculty, he unlatched the shop door, where soon he satisfied himself that his ears had been accurate as usual, guessing also that the mishap was due to a fight.

"Well, never mind about t'bashing I've had, Kit," Adam said. "What I'd like to do is to tell you summat very private like."

"Come on in then, lad," the cobbler said. "But afore you start I'll slip through to the back to see if t'missus has a sup of owt warm."

Later, sitting on a bench near the iron stove, Adam sipped steaming coffee and told his tale. "What I'm going to say, Kit, really begins as far back as when I used to be inquiring off you how far west it were possible to get fro' Bucker Level. Anyroad, here it is . . ."

Interrupted frequently by bursts of wrathful indignation from a rapt listener, he recounted everything he had done and found up to the moment of plotting on his plan the situation of the pile of rails.

"Never heard of such terrible doings i' my life, lad," Blind Kit declared at the conclusion. "So seemingly I weren't wrong in everything . . . there were some foundation for that betting as t'New Drift would never hit the sump of Doomsday. Somebody knew, eh? Well, poor old Titus."

"Aye," Adam agreed as he got up. "Thank your wife for the coffee, will you? It's right refreshed me. And good night, Kit."

As yet a little unsteady he walked slowly towards Nick Turn and then along to Old Hannah's, where, rather to his surprise, he sighted through the bow window the soft illumination of the peep-hole. The bell ringing behind him, he crossed the shop to enter the kitchen, Mrs. Batty, whose silvery-white head was bent over a pan, not at once noticing anything amiss.

"No, I haven't gone to bed yet, lad," she said, stirring away, "because I thought as it were your last night here we'd have a bit on a crack. Mind you, even when you're under your own roof, I shall expect you coming here regularly, for summat to eat occasionally, and," she laughed at herself, "to keep me posted wi' what you're doing at t'mines."

Needs must, Adam spoke out of one corner of his mouth: "Makes you wonder whether all women are born inquisitive."

As a jovial rejoinder it fell flat. Old Hannah turned, stared hard, pushed him nearer the lamp, and muttered: "So summat else has started." Then, at closer range, she scrutinised his face, nodding to herself at each feature—the torn lip, a cheek cut by a signet ring, the closed eye, the livid bruises, and the crimson line oozing from his nostrils.

"Just t'usual," she remarked cheerfully. "What they call superficial. Aye, some sticking plaster and a few daubs o' my salve . . ."

"Not that stinging stuff as makes you want to jump into t'Skew," Adam protested.

"Of all the babies!" Old Hannah jeered. "No, it'll be one o' my cooling ointments."

While washing and dressing his many injuries, she crowed about his visit to the doctor. "Newcastle, eh? I telled you that if I couldn't do owt for you he couldn't, didn't I? And for t'Lord's sake keep still, I'se noan hurting you."

When patched up to her satisfaction he was installed in the big chair, and given a spoon, a smallish one, and a basin of bread and milk. This eaten, he was summarily ordered to bed.

CHAPTER TWELVE

I

THE FOLLOWING morning Winterings buzzed with gossip about a broken-off wedding and an intended bride who, hitherto regarded as a nice lass, was brazen to the point of shamelessness if the allegations about her had any foundation. Next, also in the limelight, the chap from Spain, who, thrown over the Brig, had so little learnt his lesson as to rent a house in the village. Evidence of the severe thrashing he had received was seen when he went to the Wood Yard, where, the information speeding from Town Foot to the West End within minutes, he ordered a load of coal for immediate delivery to Modesty. Speculation that morning, too, rose to a peak as to what might be the disorder in his arm, and many people cast a morbid eye at Adam's sling. Finally, it was bruited generally that the new assistant-agent of the West Side Company, with the financial backing of a sleeping partner, had bought all the company's unissued shares, marking this assumption of authority by dismissing Jonas Cottingham. Additional information was gleaned, however, as the consequence of two encounters which did not escape attention.

On this Saturday morning which should have been Cherry's wedding day it was an ordeal for her to go along Main Street. But, apart from those who cold-shouldered her or stopped to pry, her walk to Cuthbert Daykin's was made infinitely worse by Nathan Wharton, who told her all too realistically about Adam's beating.

Mrs. Ralph Skidmore, entering the shop, came face to face with Cherry as she was leaving. Eight or nine other women were about, which made quite a little crowd. Reuben Nattrass's sister began rather indirectly, mentioning the pains she had taken with Nancy's and Harriet's dresses for the wedding.

"But even if they wouldn't do for owt else an' I had to throw 'em away, it's worth owt to know our Reuben has seen his folly i' time, afore he'd wed a trollop like you," she said, warming up. "To think on a grand fellow such as he is . . ."

Cherry was in no mood to hear herself wickedly traduced and Reuben

Nattrass lavishly praised, but, no match for a screaming virago, began to withdraw with dignity as Cuthbert Daykin anxiously pushed out to request the throng not to press against his window.

"I nobbut hope that afterwards you don't remember all the disgusting things you've come out with," she said, undaunted but very pale.

Lost to all reason, Mrs. Ralph made the situation worse. "Aye, go to him as I'm positive you've bedded wi' . . . . him, yon Brunskill, who's getten brass off my father on th'understanding as he were leaving straight—"

William Nattrass's wheezy bull-bellow from the gate of Ash Grove was strong enough to arrest his daughter. "What the hell are you opening your big mouth for, Isa?" he bawled.

The village was furnished with further food for thought when Mrs. Robert William Alderson caught Lodge Trotter on his insurance round near the Wesleyan Day School.

"I've finished wi' you," she was shouting as a small assembly formed. "Moreover I'm having one o' them accountants up fro' Corvy to examine your books."

Pince-nez tumbling from his nose, to dangle from broad, black ribbon, strutting little Lodge Trotter shook with rage and vexation. "If that's an innuendo as I've done owt as I shouldn't, it'll go into t'Courts," he snapped.

"If it goes into t'Courts you'd better be seeing about a lawyer to act for you," Mrs. Roberty Will retorted. "For *you* know nowt about law, whatever your pretensions. Nobody but a jackass 'ud draw up Articles of Association so as to leave a loophole for any Tom, Dick or Harry to have shares handed to him without t'directors giving permission first."

"It's got its advantages," the Postmaster roared.

Mrs. Alderson's familiar gold locket see-sawed even more extensively. "Maybe for you and the quick-witted cheats you hob-nob wi', but it's noan got any advantages for me. Me . . ." she stormed on, "me, who were the largest shareholder."

This tit-bit, together with other items, such as the news that Mr. Wade, whip in hand, had chased George Nattrass out of the mill yard at Greets, was effective in channelling wide conjecture into narrower lines.

Meantime, in Old Hannah's, Cherry was with Anthony Skidmore, who, in the temporary absence of the shop's owner, had taken tobacco and matches, chalking these up on the customers' slate as a reminder to himself when next he came in.

"Oh, I don't think he's all that bad," Mr. Skidmore remarked. "Any-road, he's walking our way this afternoon, so he must feel up to it."

"Nathan Wharton telled me such an awful tale," Cherry shivered.

"He looks a right sight, of course," her friend's father said, "there's no getting away fro' that. Anyway I must be off, lass, but tell your uncle I'm popping in to-night. I'll be seeeing you afore then though, shan't I? You're coming on to tea, eh?"

Cherry laughed. "Me an' Dinah's one or two things to talk over."

Anthony Skidmore chuckled. "Never knew you two when you hadn't. However . . ." his voice lowered as gently he nipped her cheek, "I've summat to tell you, too, lass . . . it's that I'm fair suited I'm noan in my best clothes at t'Chapel to-day."

When Mrs. Batty bustled in a few minutes afterwards, Cherry had ferreted out for herself everything she required except three washing powders. "You're looking pale round t'gills, lass," the old lady remarked. "Now it's noan exactly the time for 'elevenses,' but what say you if we put t'kettle on for some 'tenses'?"

"Well . . . well, I wouldn't mind sitting down for a bit," Cherry confessed.

Old Hannah's wink was of the outsize order. "Just long enough for us to let th'other know what's happening at us own end," she chuckled.

Over coffee and a slice of Madeira cake each, the couple had a most entertaining tittle-tattle.

While the first of these events was taking place, Adam examined the stemming at Mary Forehead, where seven men were making excellent progress. Len Rukin, standing knee deep in water on the east side, inspecting the latest caulking of wool and tar, announced the job would be finished by early afternoon.

"Aye," he said, "I should be up to my chin if I stayed here till nightfall."

"That's th'idea," nodded Adam. "And I've summat else now . . . meet me in about an hour at Noddy John's Rise, will you?"

"Right," the other said. "I'll be there."

Before leaving, Adam issued one important instruction. From Monday all sump partnerships to the west were to be terminated, the men to be shifted to new places higher than the sole, a precaution against the breaking of the massive stemming.

This understood, he turned about to keep the appointment he had just made, the condition of his arm necessitating the avoidance of ladders. In due course he reached the tail of Mary Level, to be treated to catcalls and many inquiries as to the state of his face from the smelters and dressing-floors men of the East Side Company across the beck as he started down Winterings Gill.

After a lengthy trudge through Notion Level he came to Noddy John's Rise, where Len Rukin, Matt Tiplady and Sam Kirkbride awaited him. Bart Hugill had arrived also, carrying the surveying instruments, but the clerk was at once sent back, entrusted with the paying-out of Lent

Money, a responsibility for which he tried hard to conceal his gratification.

"I'm wanting to dial afresh Mr. Alderson's New Drift," Adam explained. "So let's get through the Short Cut here an' go on to Old Joss Forehead."

Of the main workings driven within the past eighty years Old Joss Level, for long disused, was the oldest. In stretches boot-deep in sludge, it had all the defects of an abandoned gallery: where arched and walled it often bulged ominously, and where timbered the rot had set in many decades before.

Through this depressing working the four men walked, but soon, with dial, candle-reader and measuring-chain, they were well employed and, given such capable assistance, Adam completed the task shortly after noon. Owing to the nearby—though unseen—presence of a pile of tram-rails the procedure departed from the normal, but none of his companions referred to this, probably assuming it to be a mode more up-to-date.

"Right," Adam said as he put his dialling-book away. "If it's in the Main Limestone all the way through, how much speed do you reckon we'll make . . . durk drift size'll be big enough?"

Squatting on the sole, Len Rukin transferred his quid of tobacco into the other side of his mouth. "On t'basis of six men, I'd reckon seven fathoms a month."

In Spain, Mr. Phillips had everlastingly drilled one rule into his subordinates on the management side: never to spoil by over-interference the enthusiasm of trustworthy men. It was a policy which, both now while details were hammered out and in the future, Adam tried to follow.

"About t'deads," Sam Kirkbride proposed. "If the sole is sludged out cleaner, we can get a horse through an' save any amount o' time . . ."

"Aye, I'll ask Freestone John if he'll make the third chap to be at t'Forehead wi' me and Len," Matt Tiplady said. "It were lucky I had that talk wi' him when I were homeward-bound fro' quod. Anyway, he didn't seem at all suited with th'East Side lot, but as winter comes on there's nowt much i' quarrying, and he'll soon be looking for a bargain somewhere."

"Well, I think we've got everything clear, lads, for a crackaway, stop-for-nothing job," Len Rukin remarked to his two colleagues subsequently, "Yes, you can take it as being cut an' dried, Adam."

"Champion," Adam approved. "Now as to the price per fathom, we can fix that up on Monday morning. I'll be here first thing to give you t'bearing of the new cross-cut and whereabouts in the New Drift it's to be started from. 'Course, as soon as we can we'll put more shifts on, and my idea is that the three chaps who are in at the beginning should split up and . . . well, sort of captain your own teams . . ."

As he walked away through the level and down to the office he felt immensely encouraged by their eager attitude. With such support, especially if the influence spread, much might be done. Capital was extremely limited, but, by offering the bait of extra discount for quicker payments and in divers other ways, a swifter turnover might be arranged and this, in its turn, would provide the funds for a more rapid opening out of the ground.

Mineral mining prospects always have a considerable element of chance in them, and it had also been Mr. Phillips' firm view that a bold onslaught, allowing a much earlier withdrawal to pastures new if unsuccessful, was infinitely preferable to eking out the agony.

Adam intended to pursue that same vigorous policy.

* * * *

A long period of mist and storm on the high moors had had its effect upon the sheep, fourteen of which, quite blind, had been brought down to the garth of Badger Hall. As part of the treatment to remove the thick, sight-destroying film, Mark Iveson and Mr. Skidmore were pouring a spoonful of white sugar into each eye. Adam was there, an exceptionally indolent onlooker, now fully feeling the consequences of the brutal usage of the previous night. His arm had been re-dressed by Dr. Seaton, but wisely he was deferring the drafting of the New Drift until the next day, when he hoped his many aches and pains would be less nagging. Cherry and Dinah, too, had appeared from the courtyard at the back of the house for a few minutes, both to be horribly shocked by his disfiguration.

"Aye, and you'll be a bigger scarecrow by t'middle of next week," Mark Iveson remarked after the girls had gone.

Adam laughed twistedly. "That's the stuff . . . give me all the encouragement you can, eh, Nell lass?" he said.

She was becoming portly, not far from her time. "Still wanting one of the pups, lad?" Anthony Skidmore inquired.

"More than ever," Adam promptly replied. "But with th'irregular hours I shall be having at the mines I'd be obliged if you'd keep it here for a while."

"As long as you like," Mr. Skidmore said heartily. "She can run wi' her mother and learn a few good manners."

The shepherd was less reticent. "Sounds as if you're noan off back to Spain as soon as you'd reckoned."

"No, I've too much on," Adam said, leaving it at that.

Tea-time was not far off and so, to avoid the awkward moment when the master of the house was called in, he left with the shepherd. As they were crossing Snorr Bridge, Mark Iveson began to talk about his neighbour, whose queer condition he experienced difficulty in describing.

"Nay, he behaves as if . . . as if he were frightened of his own shadow."

"Strange, isn't it?" Adam murmured. In point of fact he was wondering whether he were responsible for that uneasiness. If so, Ambrose Pedley would have additional cause for disquiet on hearing he had gone to Newcastle.

Near Winterings Brig, he and the shepherd parted, Adam turning towards the garden gate and the path leading up to Modesty. As he entered the hall-way, hammering resounded on the back door and, going through, he found that Chestie Geordie had not forgotten his promise of early morning. But he was compelled to listen to a stiff lecture on the advantages of putting the milk-jug out on the window-sill in future. Next, both upstairs and down, he replenished fires he intended to keep burning until a house so long untenanted was properly dried out.

"Well now," he said, this done, "I'll get summat to eat, and then it's going to be a quiet evening for me . . . by, and in my own home."

Handicapped as he was, the preparation of a satisfactory meal was not easy, but when at last the place was redolent with the savoury smell of bacon and eggs, the scent of freshly-scalded tea, and the aftermath of toasting, the effort had been worthwhile. Slipping his arm out of the sling to grasp knife and fork, he ate the main dish with relish, finishing off with jam, a currant tea-cake lavishly buttered from the pat Mr. Skidmore had given him, and a couple of slices of ginger-bread loaf, the whole attended by four cups of strong tea.

The evening was to be less solitary than he had conceived, and within half an hour of washing up, eleven people in all crowded the front room, their contributions to the house-warming piled on the table: eggs, jars of jam and honey, fruit cakes, cheese, and much more.

Francis Harker and his wife were the first callers, the farmer shouldering a fine, two-stone ham.

"Yes, you're having it," Mrs. Harker declared, overruling objections. "Nay, at after what you did for us, we're noan taking a refusal."

Others followed: the Ivesons, Mary Jane Tiplady, Old Hannah and Cherry. Mrs. Peacock was last, accompanied by Matt Tiplady and Blind Kit, who carried between them, on her behalf, a case of bottled beer.

It soon appeared that the ladies had another purpose: to arrange that until Adam left for Newcastle he should, in rotation, accept their hospitality for his meals. They had their way.

A light-hearted conversation then began, this continuing until the womenfolk one and all remembered, and did not fail to point out, that lounging about was not for them.

With their departure the men drew round the fire, a couple of boxes easing the problem of seating accommodation. The room was warm and, tobacco jar at call and beer available when required, there was little disposition to face the keen easterly wind which now and then shook the windows.

All five men contributed to the talk, farmer, cobbler, mining-agent, poacher and shepherd, and good talk it was, too, sometimes sober and sometimes gay, but always the reflections of those who had learnt much in their various humble forms of life.

"Aye, it's been grand," Adam smiled when, his guests gone, he paused at the long staircase-window on the half-landing to peer into the darkness. "Yes, let's hope it augurs well for my future here . . . in this house, for that's where it's going to be."

Just within the bedroom doorway he paused again, his glance passing over a chamber furnished meagrely with a broken-down bed, a tottering table, and a strip of second-hand carpet. But the rosy glow from the fire was kindly, revealing a low-ceilinged oblong of good proportions, an inviting window-seat with small panes above it, and walls lined with panelling demanding nothing more than a coat of paint.

"A real lovely house, as any man could be proud for his friends to come to," he murmured. "And whatever I'm supposed to have done, and whatever Cherry's supposed to have done, we've got friends of the right sort, an' what more nor that can you have?"

Warmed by this truth, he was asleep soon after his head sunk on to the pillow.

Meantime in the dark hours of the night, relentless inch by relentless inch, water continued to rise in the East Side Company's Martha Forehead Ground.

On Sunday afternoon, before starting out to Yew Tree House for tea, Adam could have finished both the re-plotting of Mr. Alderson's New Drift and the setting-off of the new cross-cut, but, to make assurance doubly sure, he worked again with ruler and instruments on coming back to Modesty, so that he did not finally put aside his pencil until mid-evening. The upshot was disappointing, but proved how much Titus Alderson had been led astray by a pile of tram-rails.

"A rare long way," he mumbled. "Even wi' three shifts it'll be Christmas afore we can reach Doomsday."

How driving might be speeded up preoccupied him until supper-time, and again on his return from Old Hannah's. But, lacking the right materials and men seasoned in other methods, he was not able to solve his own question.

Putting aside mining problems before going to bed, he read *The Vicar of Wakefield*.

2

Every Monday morning Bart Hugill unlocked the octagonal-shaped Magazine, where he weighed out and delivered into the groovers' canisters quantities of black powder not exceeding four pounds to each man. After that, leaving the sheltered fold in which the Magazine had been built for safety, he climbed the rough pasture towards the South Smelt Mill, accompanied by the last few men whom he had supplied. The remainder awaited him outside the Candle Place and Store, where he handed out the various tools and candles for which they asked. On returning to the mine office, he fair-copied from his notebook: routine week in and week out on the first working day.

It was less ordinary for smoke to be trailing out of the house-like chimney of the forge at the North Mill where Richard Blenkiron was taking off, in batches of three, pick-heads strung up by wire threaded through the hole for the handle; each blunt point was heated, hammered out, sharpened and then tempered to the utmost of his cunning and skill.

Apart from this slight change, the affairs of the West Side Company were being conducted, as far as the eye could discern, very much as usual. It was soon to be strangely different for the mining concern at the opposite side of Winterings Beck.

Three men outside the North Mill forge stared up the gill, fascinated by the spectacle of groovers pressing round the office doorway of the East Side Company at Martha Level.

"It's that stemming as has done it," Sam Kirkbride muttered.

The blacksmith turned an amazed face to his future son-in-law. "And Arthur Nattrass telled you himself, Bart? That Martha Level were flooded that bad?"

"Aye," the clerk nodded. "The forehead is four foot deep, an' enough water has backed up to stop the tail-race water from the water-wheel at Toft Rigg Whim Shaft, which means they can't raise bouse to the surface."

"An' more nor that, lad," Richard Blenkiron grunted. "It means that both Martha Forehead Ground and Sun Hade Ground are done for for many a day. My, but there'll be hell to play about this . . it'll be a nasty crack for th'East Side lot if they don't do summat quick."

"There's nobbut one thing they can do," the engineer observed laconically. "Go cap i' hand to our new assistant. Yes, I'll admit I wondered if Brunskill knew what he were up to, but by God he's proved where t'water came fro' at Mary Forehead. Len Rukin says so an' all, and it's his job more nor mine."

Bart Hugill shook his head. "What's Reuben Nattrass going to do about it, eh?"

Richard Blenkiron's strong voice deepened. "I don't know, lad. But there's one thing as is already becoming plain, that Brunskill means to do his best for t'Company, an' when it's that road such as us ought to rally round—an' forget for t'moment whatever he's supposed to have done wrong in the past."

"If he ever did owt wrong," Bart Hugill blurted out.

The older men's faces were expressive of inquiry rather than surprise as they stared at the clerk, who immediately attempted to explain. "Oh, I've been against him as much as anybody," he confessed. "But, looking back, I'm noan so sure now. He's never flinched about anything and he's noan doing now, even though he's pretty badly, as more than me has seen. What I mean is that if he'd done owt to Agnes Pedley, I think he'd have stood by her."

" 'Course, having guts is one thing . . ." Sam Kirkbride was remarking as the groovers at Martha Level began to walk in twos and threes to the changing shop. "Still I'd like to think he weren't guilty about his cousin."

"Aye," rumbled Richard Blenkiron. "Well, I've plenty o' work waiting for me down at t'Smithy without idling here."

"Them steel bars you want 'ul be here by Wednesday, Mr. Blenkiron," Bart told him. "For extra drills for the new cross cut."

"Has it been started yet?" the blacksmith inquired.

"Oh, I expect so," the clerk replied. "Brunskill took his bait in there first thing an' said he wouldn't be coming out to the day again until it were time to meet Henry Hird for weighing the duty lead."

"He'll have summat to chew about . . . his high and mightiness, that is," Sam Kirkbride growled.

Bart Hugill grinned. "I'm not missing that if I can help it."

This was repeated by Richard Blenkiron a few minutes later, though it referred to quite another engagement: the fight he felt sure must eventually take place between Reuben Nattrass and Adam Brunskill.

"Aye, an' I'm not missing *that* if I can help it," he muttered to himself, a smile of the most unholy glee lighting up his face.

At the drive-off from the New Drift, great sledge hammers thudded on to the mushrooming heads of borers, candles flickered, the wheels of wagon-trains droned, and the acrid fumes of explosions filled the air.

Freestone John had been relieved by Matt Tiplady at the narrow face when Adam tapped his shoulder. "I'm off now," he shouted. "Keep her just as she is, seventy-eight west o' south, an' I'll be here in t'morning for another check."

The Quaker nodded understanding, but, sweat running off him, did not speak until Adam began to collect the surveying gear, when he restrained him by saying that he and his partners would take the tackle to the office at the end of the shift. "You've all on to get out a match when your candle dies on you," he said gravely.

"Well, it'll be helpful, John," Adam admitted. "Especially as I'm wanting to have a look at t'North Sun Vein."

In the once valuable North Sun Vein Ground, where he waded seventy or eighty fathoms along the main horse level, the flood never rose higher than the side pockets of his ragged coat, but the light of his candle, reflected in black water, showed that cross-cuts and drifts everywhere were similarly inundated. "Noan so bad as it might be," he mused. "If I get Droughty Tom's pump installed, we should be able to clear the ground very quickly."

With just enough time in hand to reach the office and exchange soaked tatters for drier clothing before Henry Hird arrived, he began to splash towards Maybe Shaft.

Every sixth pig of lead, after passing over the scales in the Weigh Place at the South Mill, was put on one side, the property of the royalty owner. Each shining bar, with the setting sun emblem of the West Side Company moulded on top, theoretically weighed one hundredweight, the surplus or deficiency noted for clerical adjustment subsequently. The pigs, class letter and smelting number called off first, were lifted on to the scales by two men, when the balance was agreed between mine-agent and royalty agent before entry.

"Well, that seems to be the lot, Mr. Hird," Adam said.

It was an observation offering a splendid opportunity for a sarcastic rejoinder, but, as Bart Hugill that evening told the Blenkirons, father and son, Henry Hird was after bigger game.

The mineral agent began immediately upon entering the office. "Well, Brunskill," he jeered as he sat down, "you've made a right mess with your cleverness, haven't you? What are you going to do about that stemming you've putten across?"

"Nowt," Adam replied.

A turkey cock enraged, Henry Hird swivelled in the chair. "Nowt!" he exploded. "Do you know as Reuben Nattrass is asserting you've destroyed t'delicate poise of water underground, and . . ."

During the next few seconds Bart Hugill's nose sank lower over the Lead Book as he struggled to ward off laughter when, at some considerable length, the assistant agent admitted to being overwhelmingly surprised that the other had thought it worthwhile to pass on a postulation so untenable.

Livid, Sir Charles's agent stumbled to his feet. "I didn't say as how

I supported his idea," he bellowed. "Anyroad, is that all you've getten to say?"

Most seriously Adam disassociated himself from that. "On t'contrary, Mr. Hird, I'm requesting you to take the steps mentioned in the parchment lease."

"Steps!" the older man ejaculated. "What steps?"

He was reminded of the clause providing that in the event of a dispute between the mining companies sharing Winterings Gill, the Royalty Owner or his agent should appoint 'two indifferent persons as arbitrators' if called upon to do so by either side.

Plainly Sir Charles's agent hardly knew what to say next. "Aye . . . aye, but it means a lot of arranging, and I don't know as I'm justified. After all, if you get rid o' that stemming——"

Intervening, Adam expressed regret, but his next words left no room for misunderstanding. "I can appreciate your difficulties, Mr. Hird," he said. "But as I've my own, maybe it'll be best if I notify you here an' now that I'm requiring you to see to arbitration, with as little delay as possible."

Henry Hird glowered. "I'll study it over."

"Thanks, Mr. Hird," Adam said warmly. "I shall, by the way, be sending you a formal letter repeating th'essentials of what I've already said, so maybe that'll assist to keep the details fresh in your mind."

After the mineral agent's blundering departure, during which he made a remark not very complimentary, normal work in the office was resumed, Adam starting to write the letter he had mentioned, Bart Hugill at last to begin the entry of Weigh Place particulars. The clerk, who would have enjoyed a gossip on the matter, wondered how he might broach the subject to someone with whom he was on strained terms. Apart from that, it was sinking into him that Adam Brunskill had become a somewhat different individual from the chap who had laughed and larked in the spring.

In the end he said nothing on this, but as his senior was leaving brought up the question of a piece of chicanery he suspected that a durk drift partnership at Mary Forehead contemplated. It was a species of trickery often tried by the less scrupulous upon a new agent, consisting of deliberately by-passing a place rich in ore, bidding for and obtaining it at the next Bargains at the high rate paid for presumably poor-pay ground.

Adam knuckled his chin thoughtfully, and then inquired of the clerk how he would deal with such a situation.

"Tip another partnership aforehand, a decent lot of chaps, and then knock it down to 'em afore t'other lot know what's what," Bart Hugill said eagerly.

Adam nodded. "Aye, that 'ud salt their tails," he smiled. "Well, I'll have a good look round out of working hours, to-night I think."

Reddening, the clerk diffidently proposed himself as a companion. "Wi' your arm being as it is," he muttered. "They'll have hidden the good place somehow, maybe by piling deads, an' they'll have to be lifted to one side."

"It'll be a grand help," Adam responded. "Would seven o'clock do for you here? Unless . . ." he paused before closing the door, "you call for me at Modesty on t'way up."

"It'd save both on us hanging about unnecessarily, wouldn't it?" Burt said gruffly.

During the next few minutes the expressions of both these young men depicted a satisfaction which, in one case, arose from feelings still strangely mixed. In the other's, Adam's, there was no doubt.

"Aye, they'll all back me up i' due course," he told himself as, in the fading light, he walked down Sleety Slape.

Donkeys supporting cans on either flank were daintily picking a path down the rough track from the Common Pasture, and a score of milkers, the majority women, made the same journey, back-cans harnessed on their shoulders. Many were the whispered remarks passed as Adam went by and, although his disfigured face came under discussion, that was only as prelude to estimating how much more he would be battered shortly when the East Side agent got at him again.

The same thing was being animatedly debated later that evening at the Plug and Feathers when Reuben Nattrass clumped into the tap-room to announce that, after breakfast next morning, the horn would be sounded for a hound-trail. To the surprise of everyone he did not seem to regard the issue between the two companies as warranting personal conflict between himself and the rival agent.

"Why should I knock Brunskill about?" He glared at Puke Hastwell, who, extremely anxious, had been inquiring about prospects. "He's in for enough bother as it is without me doing owt, ruining his own company as he has. Anyroad, plenty of my chaps has nowt to do to-morrow, so we're having a bit o' sport. We shall enjoy it all the more because it'll be at th'expense of the West Side lot in the long run."

For a few seconds there was silence. The truth was that the vexed question of the stemming had already been decided by the most experienced groovers in the village.

"Don't be so daft, lad," an old man on the long-settle eventually declared. "Keep such rigmarole for them who's simple enough to listen."

With an effort the raven-haired young man contained himself. "You were never owt but a groover, Ned Kate," he retorted. "But if you'd had the education and read t'books as a mining agent has to——"

Ned Kate received support from a neighbour. "Eddication, nowt," this hoary gentleman scoffed. "All Brunskill's done is to set up a stemming i' one of his own workings, as he'd every right to do."

To the regret of all, Mrs. Peacock came from the kitchen, coldly to inform the infuriated agent that the servant girl from Ash Grove had run along with a message, to the effect that his father and Uncle George were waiting for him.

"You're to go home sharp," the mistress of the Plug and Feathers reported faithfully, adding on her own account: "Well, as two directors of th'East Side Company are together, I should imagine they're wanting to discuss the muck you've made."

Before he could reply to this unpleasant reminder, Droughty Tom's rumbling laughter drew everyone's attention. "He'll be in a bigger mess, will Reuben, afore long," the limeburner chuckled. "Aye, I somehow reckon he's up against a chap who'll allus be one move ahead on him."

Reuben Nattrass lost control. "What the hell does a bloody old muddle-head like you know about it?"

Head turned slightly sideways, Lucy Peacock patted a coil of dark, shining hair. But, before she was able to deal with the disturber of the peace, he banged out of the tap-room.

There was much amusement in the Plug and Feathers that evening, the only non-participants in the general hilarity either shareholders in the East Side Company or groovers who were now idle. It had been rib-tickling enough to know that a number of local personalities, as the result of paying out good money to free themselves of a dangerous liability, had lost valuable business connections; but it was even funnier that they were still as closely as ever involved in the fortunes of a mining company whose position was now no better than that of the company from which they had taken such sly pains to escape.

* * * *

At Town Foot, hounds, owners and followers were assembling for the contest, while in the distance above Kettle Dub, as Adam saw when climbing Sleety Slape, two young men with turpentine-soaked rags were laying a trail.

Two very much younger men, Bob Skidmore and Ward Tiplady, were nearer. They also carried a bottle and dragged along fragments of cloth by a length of twine, but otherwise the similarity ended, for it seemed that a section of the official scent was being obliterated and a new one provided. This led into the Great Deep Level, and as Adam drew closer candles had been lighted and a piece of stick substituted for the cord, presumably so that the wall at the side of the level, just above the outflowing water, could more easily be brushed with the impregnated rags.

"Busy, apparently," Adam remarked. "Another visit from t'School Inspector?"

Both boys laughed, but their explanations, supplementing one another, were more serious. A trail was held all too seldom, and, at the last one, a record of two hours and ten minutes had been set up.

"So we thought it'd noan be a bad idea if we tried to arrange for a record for the longest back home, didn't we, Bob lad?" Ward said.

Adam grinned. "The pack'll be late all right if it streams into the Great Deep."

The cousins nodded. "That's what we thought, Adam," Bob Skidmore said with infinite satisfaction.

Amused, Adam continued upwards to Notion Bridge, where, after calling at the office and looking round the smelt mills, he visited partnerships underground. In the early afternoon he spent some time at the New Cross Cut, and also measured with Bart Hugill's assistance what little Dead Work there was in readiness for the Pay.

Towards four o'clock, when he was in the office, his cousin Arthur arrived with a sharp message.

"How did the trail hunt go?" Adam inquired, ignoring the peremptory demand to present himself at the East Side office. "Who was th'owner of the winner?"

"Winner!" Arthur Nattrass spat in disgust. "Why, t'damned lot has disappeared, an' they've had to cry off all bets. It'll be a bitch or a hare they're after."

"Maybe so," Adam murmured. "Now, as for Reuben, I'm here if he wants me, but you'd better warn him I shan't be able to spare him long."

Arthur Nattrass glared. "There's some chaps, like Reuben an' one or two more as I won't name, that it's noan so prudent to reply to like that."

"I daresay, lad," said Adam, stretching for the inkwell. "But things can't always remain the same, and so Reuben and the other chaps you hint about 'ud do well to get used to the change. Anyroad, a change is as good as a rest, as Mary Jane Tiplady telled me when I caught her doing a few jobs for me, but whether you'll find picking oakum a pleasant change——"

Considerable noise ensued, as Arthur Nattrass flung a chair to the side, kicked Bart Hugill's unoffending stool, and upset a bottle of gum.

"Now, I'd enough of that bloody nonsense down at t'Grafton Arms," he bawled. "An' I'll tell you this, a chap who relies on another chap's good nature because he's disabled is no bloody sportsman, if you understand what I mean."

Steadily Adam eyed him. "Aye, I reckon I do, lad," he said dryly. "Now you be off and tell Reuben exactly what I've said. Don't spare owt to save his dignity, either."

"I'll noan that," the other snapped.

As Arthur Nattrass crossed the front of the office, Adam nodded. "Yes, he'll crack, will yon . . . I've only to keep at it."

Long after he had completed the extraction of the smelters' current production from Harry Blaydes's Rough Pig Book, Bart Hugill fretted about the ill-luck which had detained him in the North Mill while, across the Mill Bridge, the East Side Company's agent, pale with suppressed fury, threw open the office door.

Reuben Nattrass laughed harshly. "Well, Brunskill, seemingly you're the chap I have to deal wi', so I'se going to tell you for your own good what the position is, and never mind what some o' these crackpots has to say about it."

For an analogy of what he intended to demonstrate he spoke of a double-limbed, U-shaped thermometer, asserting that, if pressure were introduced into the lowermost part of the tube, the levels in each stem would rise, but not necessarily evenly.

"An' that's what's happening betwixt Martha Forehead an' Mary Forehead," he declared, pounding his fist on the desk in the middle of the room. "You've altered the pressure wi' your bloody stemming, an' it's going to cost you West Side lot dear if you don't act quick."

"It's an interesting notion," Adam conceded. "But if it's leading up to me removing that stemming I'd better tell you I shan't do it."

Mouth ugly, Reuben Nattrass restrained himself with an effort. "All right then, but instead o' being highfaluting, let's get us feet on firm ground. Now I'se still bent on skittling you out of t'Dale, but in the meantime you an' me is neighbouring agents, an' neighbouring agents always has to work together to some extent. Well, just now you're the new broom as is sweeping clean, but to-morrow or next week it may be you who's wanting the favour, because there's nowt as is sure i' lead-mining, now is there?"

"There isn't, Cousin Reuben," Adam murmured.

"Look you here then," his cousin began again, forcing the words out of himself, "if you'll take the stemming down nobbut a board at a time, an' let me put an extra pump into Glory Shaft at your side, I'll tell you what I'll do when Mary's right clear . . . I'll divert down t'Water-gate any water as remains running an' I'll put a little pump down Martha Air Shaft so as t'forehead always keeps absolutely dry."

Adam stared out of the window at a cart rumbling over Notion Bridge with barrels of Gallipoli oil. Much hardship to many a family could easily have been avoided had such a proposal been made earlier, but despite that he might have acceded to it had it not been for the damning recollection of hexagonal marks underground and their sinister meaning.

"That wouldn't either prove or disprove whether water passes from one forehead to th'other," he said, stern lines of resolve in his face. "Which is what I'm after knowing."

"You're going ahead then wi' this bloody arbitration Henry Hird's nagging at me about?" Reuben Nattrass said thickly, jabbing his finger. "You ken as all the main directors 'ul get to hear?"

"I should think that's likely," Adam agreed.

Reuben Nattrass breathed hard. "I'se tumbled to it . . . you're blasted well hoping to show me up, that's what. Go on, then, have a bloody try. Aye," his dark eyes narrowed and his lips thinned, "they tell me you're off to Newcastle wi' that arm. Well, don't put your nose back here at after, because if you do, and if you're noan crippled, I'll level it with your face the first minute I see you. And if you're still crippled I'll bide my time till you're right, and then do t'same to you, with a few extras as 'ul make you eager enough to betake yourself elsewhere. Oh aye, I can be sharp myself and I'se noan going to give you the chance to make out at afterwards as you were not fit to stand up to me, which is what a sharp-witted 'un like you would say. No," he wound up before slamming the door, "Winterings is going to watch me smash you to bloody bits when you haven't a ha'porth of excuse."

When Bart Hugill, much too late, hurried back to the office, he received instructions to write out a couple of notices inviting experienced durk drift drivers to present themselves at the Bait House on Saturday. With the East Side Company in the doldrums, this was throwing down the gauntlet with a vengeance and the clerk shaped his lips as if to whistle. "Did you come to some sort o' terms with Nattrass?" he asked dubiously. "I mean, were he more moderate, like?"

"Not noticeably," Adam said.

Bart gave up, but nevertheless dipped his pen with gusto. Business life had taken a welcome and stimulating turn, and, as he had told his not too responsive young lady the evening before, nowadays he never knew what excitements the next morning would bring.

In the early evening Ned Mason and Cyprian Metcalfe, two men who had little in common, were standing beneath the lamp-bracket at Nick Turn discussing the sorry outcome of the trail. Wearily resting at their feet were their respective hounds, the last couple home. Each dog, head, back and flanks, was plentifully plastered with a reddish mud, and the matted hair carried traces of a grey, mineral slime.

"Well," the mason muttered, "mine's going into t'river for a swim. The missus 'ud have seven fits if he went indoors i' that state. What the hell can they all have been up to?"

"Grooving, I should think," the other grunted. "Maybe this chap's . . ." his voice thickened as Adam approached, "let 'em a bargain."

Ned Mason failed to follow this up. "I see he's posted a notice for drivers."

The squatly-built engineer shifted oak-like legs the better to glare at the passer. "He'd better noan steal any o' our men," he growled.

Adam did not heed the provocative remark and, his thoughts busied otherwise, continued along Main Street to Yew Tree House, where, on hearing Cherry's call, he joined uncle and niece in the bedroom. To begin with, he reported Reuben Nattrass's attempt to seek a compromise.

"He's overplayed his hand, that's why, lad," the invalid declared, thumping the bed covers.

Adam agreed. "The test'll decide, but for myself I reckon it's a foregone conclusion."

"An' what's to be done next?" Cherry asked eagerly. "You know, to make him sit up. I mean in a business way, nothing else."

Both men were chuckling about her thirst for anything short of blood when the arrival of Edmund Kearton interrupted a most promising conversation. Cherry went downstairs, but Adam stayed in the bedroom until her uncle's visitor came up. The joiner's nod to him was the bleakest imaginable, but fortunately Titus Alderson did not notice this.

Dinah called, too, and in the kitchen Adam inquired as to how she was faring with Isa. "Oh," Cherry laughed, "I think the tide of battle has passed over her. Mr. Skidmore didn't half give Isa a sharp talking to."

Voice sinking unbelievably, Dinah said: "But that were nowt to the dressing-down our Ralph got from him. He said he should have spoken to Cherry first instead of spreading his . . . well," she laughed, winking conspiratorially, "ridiculous tale, as my father naturally thinks it is."

Work awaited Adam on his big drawing table at Modesty, but he remained long enough in Mr. Alderson's chair for Sambo to consider jumping on to his knee, meantime Dinah, in the red-cane rocker, held a skein of wool while her friend wound.

Before leaving, Adam asked Cherry if she could spare an hour on Saturday afternoon. "You see when I'm at Newcastle you could help with a few things if you would."

Cherry's pretty face flushed with pleasure. "Oh, I'd be real suited to do anything," she said.

Adam smiled. "Well, I'll go into it with you on Saturday. It should be more peaceful then."

That raised the question about which the whole district was now agog: how soon would arbitrators investigate the crucially serious dispute between the companies? As Adam told the girls, the issue was too important for Henry Hird to take any risks, and he fully expected to hear from the 'two indifferent persons' the next morning.

In assuming this Adam was wrong and it was not until the night afterwards that Mr. John Dougill and Mr. James Guy interviewed him at Old Hannah's. The delay, he then gathered, had been due to Reuben Nattrass's stubborn attempt to prevent a finding being sought in the precise manner provided by the mining leases.

Mrs. Martin Rutter was spinning out pleasurably the purchase of rice, currants and a pint of ginger wine when she was almost paralysed by the casual disclosure that the object of her inquiry sat in the kitchen beyond, the door to which was wide open.

"No," Mrs. Batty continued loudly, blind to a frantic signal, "I should say that an arm that's been infected naturally comes off by t'surgeon's knife, but when it's been struck by th'Almighty—like you mentioned, Jennie—the devil-tainted flesh 'ul probably drop off a bit at a time, like th'ash on a gentleman's cigar."

Leaning across the crowded counter, the auctioneer's wife made a desperate effort. "He'll hear, Hannah . . . you left t'door open."

Brow knitted, Old Hannah absentmindedly removed the glass lid of a sweetmeat jar and popped a humbug into her mouth. Cheek swollen out, she gazed fixedly at the lettering on a bag of yeast.

"It's noan oft you can see owt as has been defiled by the Prince o' Darkness," she went on, achieving a terrific facial contortion as she poked her tongue into the crevice of a tooth, "so come you into t'kitchen wi' me, lass. I'm noan saying he takes a pride i' displaying Belial's handiwork . . ."

Mrs. Rutter hailed from a remote hamlet lost in the fells to the north of Great Barg, and populated almost entirely by those of her maiden name. The Allisons of Scrow had married amongst themselves over much.

"I didn't say as how I believed the tale," she trembled. "An' I'd better be off . . . Martin's driven me up and he gets that impatient——"

"Nay, I'll get him to bare his arm for you," Old Hannah said generously.

But the much-tried auctioneer's wife was departing as quickly as she could, watched ironically by the old lady who, as soon as the shop-door closed, hurried into the kitchen to join the big young man who lolled in an outsize armchair which was still kept there for his use.

Adam chuckled. "You've talked about white portals once or twice to me, Hannah, but I'd better warn you as t'way-gate is becoming narrower for you."

"In that case, lad, I ought to attend Chapel on Sunday night," she grimaced. "That is, if you'll take me."

"I will," Adam smiled.

Probably arising out of Mrs. Rutter's behaviour, Old Hannah then remarked how often people were burdened with primitive fears. "But to me, Adam, t'wonderful thing is how oft when they're at the point of death," she was continuing when the shop-bell rang, "they seem to forget them sort of absurd dreads. It's as if summat sustains 'em in t'last minutes, and—I'll noan be long, lad."

Adam had cause to listen again. As soon as the old lady entered the shop her voice rose scornfully, her comments such that he half rose to glance through the peep-hole, when he recognised the two broadcloth-clad visitors as Mr. James Guy and Mr. John Dougill of Greets.

"Aye, he's here, so come in," she cried. "An' how did you two manage to get up to Winterings? I haven't heard tell as we've getten one o' them ambulances in t'Dale yet."

Mr. Dougill laughed. "Oh, me an' James can still keep us feet moving when we've a likely lass in prospect."

Beckoning peremptorily to Adam, Old Hannah observed that, although his arm might be in a sling, he must vacate the big chair in favour of those in greater need. "Which of 'em 'ul have it I can't say," she said. "Th'one I expect as is able to stagger that far."

The badinage lasted a few minutes longer, but then both old mine-agents became exceedingly solemn. Inquiry was made if Adam had any objections to them as arbitrators and, quite satisfied on this, he was asked if ten o'clock the next morning would suit him for the test. Finally he was told how it was proposed the trial should be conducted, a matter not so simple having regard to the flood. Fortunately Martha Air Shaft was fitted with a climbing way, and so the colouring matter stipulated by Adam could be introduced into the level at a point about a dozen fathoms from the forehead.

"Aye, James is going down there wi' the permanganate o' potash, an' I shall be at your company's side, at Mary Forehead," Mr. Dougill explained.

"It'll be timed, I suppose?" Adam queried. "Flow and distance?"

"Aye," said Mr. Guy.

John Dougill and James Guy had many friends in Winterings and so, before leaving for home later that evening, they paid several calls, the Plug and Feathers and Blind Kit's amongst them, both admirable places for the dissemination of news. As a result, a large number of people decided upon a jaunt up to Notion Bridge the following morning.

3

Shortly before ten o'clock on the blustery but dry morning of an all-important test, the throng in the vicinity of the South Smelt Mill was considerable. Meantime the serious business of the day had begun elsewhere. On Noggin Moor, Arthur Nattrass, representing his cousin Reuben, had descended Martha Air Shaft, forty fathoms deep. Soon, on the bunning recently set up just above the water flowing at the sump, he was joined by James Guy. Len Rukin was the third to reach the temporary stage, there as an onlooker on Adam's behalf.

"Well, I'll first measure how fast that water's moving," Mr. Guy muttered.

A simple trial established the speed at approximately three-quarters of a fathom each minute. Next the gear was finally checked—a small tin can the sides of which were perforated with a multitude of tiny holes. This container, filled with dark purple crystals, was weighted with a piece of lead, and a stout cord fastened to it.

"Five to," the old mining-agent murmured, peering at his watch. "You're both agreed on that?"

At ten o'clock precisely the tin was lowered into the flood. Dozens of colourful streamers started to move westward towards Martha Forehead, soon to mingle with and darken the flow.

Behind the stemming at Mary Forehead a galaxy of not less than twenty candles stuck against the rock face by clay daubs, together with an assembly of some consequence, made the event seem much more important than that on the bunning in Martha Air Shaft.

The directors of both companies were there in force, Mr. Storey especially noticeable in a scare-crow rig-out at least as decrepit as the sorriest working garb worn by any Winterings groover. His company was on trial, but despite this the pale-faced banker plainly enjoyed his role and, in the period of waiting, oblivious to the scowls of Reuben Nattrass, genially pursued a point of difference with a rival concern's assistant agent.

Nearer the stemming, across the top board of which a stream of water poured as over a weir, Bart Hugill, timed by John Dougill, filled at minute intervals a glass jug, this subsequently being held in front of a candle. "Still as clear as a bell," the retired mining agent remarked.

Spurred by his cousin's palpable resentment, Adam took even more pains in handling the East Side Company's chairman, who, upon an abstruse problem of geology, was expressing a very definite opinion with an ease belonging only to the enthusiastic and unskilled amateur.

"Ha! You're not tripping me up, Brunskill," the banker crowed. "The hanging cheek and the lying cheek of a vein, eh?"

Adam smiled. "That's it, Mr. Storey," he admitted. "After all——"

The tatterdemalion shook his head, infallibility written all over him. "I can't accept that, my boy . . ."

For some moments Reuben Nattrass had been glaring at Adam, but his gaze, becoming patently derisive, switched to the chairman of the East Side Company when that gentleman once again began to expound omnisciently. The banker, however, was not destined to complete a supposition which would have raised the hair of any self-respecting groover.

"It's here, Mr. Dougill!" Bart Hugill yelled. "You can make it out even without holding up t'jug."

"Keep it still, can't you?" the arbitrator snapped. "I'm wet enough as it is without you slopping it all over me. Aye, it's there all right," he said, examining the jug before taking out his watch. "Just short o' twenty past."

A strange silence fell upon the group, unbroken until the chairman of the East Side Company stepped forward, his tone now quite different. "So," he remarked bleakly to no one in particular, "there is a substantial percolation after all."

John Dougill spoke next. "Me an' Mr. Guy 'ul have to consult together, but if you gentlemen will be kind enough to foregather in t'West Side Company's office, we'll be along as soon as possible to acquaint you with our finding."

A long file of candle-bearers began to move along the level. At the tail end of the strung-out procession, dropping steadily farther astern, was Mr. Joseph Wade, his rotundity made even more striking by the two capes, of cloth and waterproof, he had evidently thought fitting to wear over shooting clothes. Stumbling and splashing into pot-holes, tripping over tramway sleepers, he lost his candle twice. At the metal lobby near the turn-rail close to Great Faith Shaft, he sat down, profanely announcing this intention to Adam and Mr. Rutter, who were a little ahead. "An' how much God-damned farther does this grand tour continue?" he snorted. "I thought the internal tunnel was never ending when we came in, but why the devil have we to return by a longer route?"

"We're not, sir," Adam soothed him. "It's just the same."

"Don't believe a damn' word," the spinner retorted, raising his candle to glance about. "Not a damn' word."

The halt within the uncanny seclusion of an underground gallery enabled Adam to discuss with his directors the line to be taken when Messrs. Guy and Dougill had delivered judgment.

"Not a doubt but what it'll be, not a doubt," Mr. Rutter observed.

"Yes, it looks very much as if you've been right, Brunskill," Mr. Wade rumbled. "If so, they'll have to put in a pump or something, which means," he chuckled, "that that romantic figurehead, Storey, will have to unloose the strings of his money-bags, though he'll nearly tear himself in two first."

"Ha! Ha! Ha! Aha! Aha!" Martin Rutter laughed. "Aye, he's a cut, is Mr. Storey."

Suppressing a grin, Adam pursued his theme. "Mr. Storey will have to cough up for more than a pump, if you'll 'low me to explain."

Granted permission, he referred to damages, but suggested that a claim too onerous could bring about the downfall of the East Side Company. If that occurred, waterwheels and pumping gear would be unattended, to the detriment of their own affairs.

The gentlemen to either side of him, each with a face of unaccustomed filth, listened with a growing attentiveness. At the conclusion, Mr. Wade gruntingly pulled himself up. "Out of our depths, Rutter," he said. "If you're agreeable we'll leave it to him."

"But you'll start the ball rolling, sir, like we've gone into?" Adam reminded him.

"If I ever arrive," the chairman replied.

On this, the trio started off again, their progress just as sedate as before.

The verdict of John Dougill and James Guy had been the only one possible and, as soon as it was delivered, Mr. Wade cleared his throat to inform the quivering Mr. Storey of the grave situation which had arisen.

"I deeply regret this, Wade," the chagrined banker said. "Had I inspected the rock face myself instead of accepting assurances, I do affirm that steps would have been taken to mitigate the influx."

Ham-like fist clenching and unclenching, Reuben Nattrass made another bid to reinstate himself. "Aye, you're rarely informed on t'strata hereabouts, Mr. Storey," he said. "But if you remember we'd once summat at Sun Hade o' the same nature, when neither on us were at all certain."

"Tch!" the banker said.

Mr. Wade then gave notice to the East Side Company's directors that steps to terminate the abuse must at once be taken. With this notification he also coupled Sir Charles Grafton's mineral agent.

"Oh, certainly, Mr. Wade," Henry Hird agreed hastily. "You can rely on me not to miss a day i' keeping an eye on how they're rectifying matters."

Portly Joseph Wade smiled tightly. "That's pledge enough, Hird," he boomed. "I had thought I ought to see Sir Charles, but your very explicit undertaking is sufficient." His company had suffered many pinpricks, and a suspicion of satisfaction still persisted in his shrewd eyes as he invited Adam to carry forward the deliberations. "I can't tackle these matters as . . . er . . . expertly as you would, Storey," he explained with extreme courtesy. "An' so Rutter and myself have thought it expedient to . . . er . . . instruct our agent to deal with the technical issues involved . . . er . . . past and present. All right, Brunskill."

"Thank you, sir," Adam said.

His first point, on the main claim for long-term seepage, caused a lively upset. "Don't be so bloody daft," Reuben Nattrass bawled. "How the hell can you show you've lost owt till you've proved th'ore were there to win?"

"Where a nuisance has been established, a certain latitude has to be allowed the wronged party . . . and is," countered Adam before drawing Mr. Storey into the argument. "You'll support me, sir, when I say that's the accepted practice?"

The banker's reply was rather confusing, caution warring with an eager desire to air mining knowledge. The mixture was too much for Mr. Rutter, who, a humourless man extravagant in his few waggeries, startled the close-packed throng with a howl only partially choked.

Mr. Storey's guess may have been not wide of the mark. "What the devil is the matter with you, Rutter?" he snapped.

"Summat tickled me," Martin Rutter gasped. "Nowt to do wi' this affair naturally, nowt to do wi' this affair nat——"

"Bloody parrot," Reuben Nattrass growled.

The exercise of his profession had made Mr. Rutter's ears sharp. "What's that, what's that?" he stormed.

This particular difference was never resolved, Mr. Wade's fog-horn trumpeting drowning all else. When the spinner emerged from behind a big handkerchief it was to suggest, in a weak voice, that essential business be resumed.

Adam next referred to the sump partnerships at Mary Forehead, who, for safety reasons, had been removed to places much poorer in ore. Here, after making allowances, the loss could be accurately computed.

"It's eight pounds every working day until the water as comes through fro' Martha Level is stopped entirely," he said. "Moreover I think it only fair for this portion of the claim to be back-dated to when I confirmed my regrets for the refusal I'd received . . . a letter," he went on, noticing several blank faces, "I sent up to th'East Side's office after I'd failed to arrange summat amicable on this question."

"What letter is this, Reuben?" George Nattrass demanded.

"You've no call to adopt that tone with t'lad," William Nattrass wheezed. "It'll be nowt as were worth mentioning to us."

Since young manhood Reuben Nattrass had ridden rough-shod over almost everyone he had encountered. "It were about nowt, as my father said, Uncle George," he chafed.

"Where is this letter?" the cheese-factor snarled.

"In t'beck, I expect," his nephew retorted, pent-up. "Where I usually chuck rubbish."

A dog with a bone was irresolute by comparison with George Nattrass when rooting out another's deficiencies, but he was sternly anticipated by a gentleman who hitherto had taken little part in the proceedings. Mr. Miles Buckle fixed Reuben Nattrass with an unwavering eye.

"That is not so, Nattrass," the lawyer said. "The communication set out in a civil manner the salient points of an important interview."

The younger man's jaw dropped, and slowly he licked his lips. "Well . . . well, I suppose in a way it referred to what he'd seen me about," he muttered. "But, wi' all respects, it were noan o' real value."

Temper rising, Mr. Buckle informed him that a precise copy of the letter had been received at the Company's Registered Office. "So no more evasions, Nattrass," he concluded severely. "Through your arrogance and your crass idiocy you have placed your own company in a most unfortunate position."

Even as he spoke Reuben Nattrass's glance moved to the man he rightly believed responsible for his humiliation. "Have you owt else to say while you're about it, Mr. Buckle," he inquired, dark eyes savage.

Made foolish by the underling he had supported, Mr. Storey was in no mood to be liberal. "Not now," he intervened tartly. "*That* can be left until we reach our own office."

Before the visitors departed Mr. Wade addressed a few kindly words to them, their substance that it was not his company's intention to crush a struggling little undertaking.

"Why, dammit, latterly we've produced four times as much ore as you," rapped the banker, cut to the quick. "As so we shall again."

Mr. Wade seemed gratified. "Glad to hear you expect continuing, Storey," he said blandly. "I wondered whether——"

"If," Mr. Storey interrupted with notable scorn, "*if*, Wade, you'd a ha'porth of the true adventurer's blood in your veins, you wouldn't have to be told that the lead-miner must be prepared for ups and downs. Good gracious, man, of course the East Side Company will rise superior to this——" He checked abruptly. "All this, I hardly need add, Wade, will depend on your interpretation of fair limits for the damages. I warn you I shall personally scrutinise the figures you submit."

"Quite," the spinner said, unperturbed.

Shortly afterwards the crowd occupying the strip of ground from the South Mill to Notion Bridge were treated to the spectacle of a well-to-do banker leading co-directors and agent to their side of the gill, his purposeful stride and the blustery wind so much opening out the many vents in his mudlark attire as to expose areas of very white flesh expansive enough to cause some dismay amongst the womenfolk present.

Meantime, in the West Side Company's office, the two arbitrators, with Mr. Wade and Mr. Rutter, lowered the bottle of rum thoughtfully provided by the assistant agent.

"Bart," said Adam, when his seniors were comfortably settled, "you nip off to Yew Tree House and let Mr. Alderson know that everything is all right—couldn't be better i' fact."

Mr. Wade's chair was quite near. "And tell him also, Hugill," the spinner added, "that I'm looking in on him before driving home." Leaning towards Martin Rutter, he went on to propose that, as they were together, a directors' meeting might as well be held on the spot. "And while you're in the village, Hugill," he resumed after obtaining the auctioneer's consent, "run along to Mr. Kearton's workshop. Give him my compliments and say I should be obliged if he could come up here at once."

Later, after Messrs. Dougill and Guy had set out for the Plug and Feathers, Adam escorted his directors through the many compartments of the North Mill, when he acquainted them with what he had done so far in the company's interests and what further extensions he had in mind on returning from Newcastle. All in all, much that was relative to the directors' meeting had been reviewed when Mr. Kearton arrived at the mine office.

Whereupon, Bart Hugill left for the store, where, amidst pick-shafts, smelters' ladles, hilted shovels and bags of bray nails, he picked up a self-imposed task of taking stock. Here and there in the men of the West Side Lead Mining Company Ltd. were signs of a new spirit abroad, and the events of the day had not lessened them.

Edmund Kearton accepted the post of secretary made vacant by Lodge Trotter's resignation, and after freely expressing his opinion about those who had abandoned the company, next dwelt upon the chairman's offer about remuneration. "I want nowt except out-of-pocket expenses, Mr. Wade," he declared, jerking a thumb towards Adam. "Not when such as him can refuse a wage for t'moment. 'Course he's done well for himself, hasn't he?"

In considering the joiner as a shareholder suitable for office, the spinner had not expected to be met with antagonism in this form. "Yes, he certainly owns many shares," he agreed. "But I trust he does not imagine their possession will now impel me to move his appointment as a director."

"If he were a director I wouldn't be associated wi' the company as secretary," Mr. Kearton snapped.

"We've all to work together," Mr. Wade reminded him. "If we're at sixes and sevens the company will be the sufferer."

The joiner's stringy face remained hostile. "That's as maybe . . . but I wouldn't be t'secretary if he were a director."

"All right," the yarn spinner said testily. "But possibly you'd do well to defer judgment, defer judgment . . . damme, I'm getting like Rutter."

"*I* beg your pardon, beg your pardon," the auctioneer said, ruffled.

"Oh, hell!" growled Joseph Wade. "Anyhow, you Brunskill, now let's have your contribution to the prevalent discord."

Little by little Adam and the chairman were coming closer to obtaining the measure of one another, and the younger man, rightly or wrongly, believed he was being encouraged to tackle Mr. Kearton. Acting on this instinct, he stated categorically that he was not seeking a directorship and would not accept one unless Mr. Alderson were similarly invited, a suggestion which had an uncanny effect upon the undertaker.

"If anybody here is going to speak up for Titus Alderson, I'm t'chap," he said, flushing dully as if personally affronted.

"Yes, but would you speak up for him in that connection?" Adam asked. "You're cool with his niece because you must believe all the scurrilous tales about her, and isn't it likely also that you've swallowed everything you've heard detracting from her uncle's professional ability?"

Trembling, Mr. Kearton rose. "I've been Titus Alderson's friend since we were lads together an'——"

Brusquely Adam broke in. "Would you vote for him as a director of a mining company?"

"How could I?" Edmund Kearton shouted. "I'm as sorry to say so as anybody, but he's made terrible mistakes, hasn't he?"

"Then you're in no danger about t'secretaryship, Mr. Kearton," Adam said, smiling a little queerly, "because obviously Mr. Alderson is unfitted to be a director, and that as I've telled you, puts me out of the running, too."

After this, assisted by the rum bottle, such business as remained to be done was conducted in harmony.

"Ah, well," the yarn spinner remarked, wiping his mouth, "I think that's everything, gentlemen, except that we might pool our wits about damages. Brunskill informs me that without any hocus-pocus the total could be very high indeed, but for reasons we all know it would be inadvisable to overtax our forlorn friends."

"Then we've to think up what 'ul be t'largest figure we can squeeze out without causing 'em to throw in their hands," Mr. Kearton observed.

"Aye, and to do that, we've to try to put ourselves in their shoes," Adam concurred.

Joseph Wade chuckled. "Yes, I agree our best plan is not so much to think in terms of damages as to estimate the limit of new capital they, or rather Storey, will provide."

"One under two-fifty, five hundred or a thousand, them's his favourite amounts," Mr. Rutter said obscurely. "A sovereign above an' William Storey leaps out of his chair as if he'd been stung, leaps as if he'd been stung he does."

Various negotiations had made the auctioneer familiar with the banker's idiosyncrasies, and his succeeding contributions were invaluable.

"This is lead-mining," the chairman summed up dryly. "So for our purposes we'll assume the middle figure, say something short of five hundred. Anyhow, how does that strike you, Brunskill?"

"Around three hundred for the claim, sir," Adam said. "Leaving 'em enough to buy a new pump, with a bit o' spare brass over."

Joseph Wade chuckled again. "A variation of cutting the coat to suit the cloth, eh? Can you let me have details before you set out for Newcastle?"

Adam undertook to do so and then, making sure he was no longer required, excused himself. Watched through the office window by the three men, he walked towards the Mill Bridge, their tongues not loosening until he was level with the splashing buckets of majestically turning Big William. After that, for quite ten minutes, the directors and secretary of the West Side Company devoted themselves to the subject of their assistant agent. Opinions about him varied extraordinarily, but it was rather illuminating in that on one or two essential aspects the views of these gentlemen coincided.

* * * *

On Friday the drivers of the New Cross Cut were split into two shifts, Len Rukin taking charge of one, Freestone John and Matt Tiplady sharing responsibility for the other, an arrangement which would stand until suitable men were found for a third.

After Lent Money had been paid at Saturday noon, Adam had dinner with Mark Iveson and his wife in Back Lane, and in the early afternoon let the Bargains at the Bait House. There, thanks to Bart Hugill's tip, he sadly confounded a partnership already counting the rich spoils of the next but one Pay, this wholly to the pleasure of a crowd of groovers who, guessing trickery had been nosed out, almost blew off the remnants of the roof with their laughter. And when the last take had been put up, bidden for and knocked down, he engaged four first-rate drivers recently in the employ of the East Side Company.

Subsequently a meeting was held in the office up Jom High Road, when Cherry was present. In effect the gathering was a committee which in all practical matters would carry on the mining operations of the West Side Company while Adam was away. Explaining that similar meetings of agents and deputies were held weekly at the Spanish mines, he announced that the same system would be continued on his return, this palpably to the satisfaction of everyone.

Duties were assigned to Cherry: she was to fetch wages from the Bank, assist Bart with the Lent Money and Pay, and ride up daily to the mines, taking messages and bringing down the post.

"Right, that disposes of the New Cross Cut," Adam enumerated in due course. "Three shifts from Monday, and a full six-day week. But that's all paying out, all Dead Work, so what about winning some extra bouse? Mary Forehead's the spot, isn't it, as soon as it dries out properly?"

It was resolved that when conditions were safe the sump men should be started, and at least half a dozen fresh partnerships encouraged elsewhere. By then a thick blue haze of tobacco smoke filled the room, although the fireplace was littered with match stalks, the consequence of rapt speakers allowing pipes to go out all too frequently.

The extensive preparatory operations required to reinstate the North Sun Vein Ground were next dealt with. After a round table talk it was determined that the pressure pipe line from Deer Pot to Maybe Shaft should be surveyed for faults; the stripping down and re-building of the hydraulic engine and compressor in the Engine House at the eye of the shaft was also listed for attention.

"Aye, an' as for a new pump the exact timberings can be got ready an' put into position," Adam said.

"I shall have to know what kind on a pump," Hugh Bearpark pointed out.

"A standard Davey No. 2," Adam replied immediately. "Bart can write to t'manufacturers for blueprints."

Flushed with excitement at the novelty of entering a world of men's affairs, Cherry's eyes were on him. She knew just what this meant, but somehow, though she would always be fearful of what Reuben Nattrass might do under a blow more awful than the one he had recently sustained, the old feeling of panic was passing as she witnessed the keen and thoughtful deliberations of Adam and those he had gathered about him.

"A standard No. 2!" Sam Kirkbride ejaculated. "Why, that's what th'East Side's getten at Old Wife Shaft, the one Droughty Tom goes on about."

"Aye," Bart Hugill muttered, making a note, "I'll get a letter off to the makers."

This concluded the business and, in a few minutes, a general upheaval began, heralded by the stirring of feet and the scraping back of chairs.

"I'll tell you what, Adam," Matt Tiplady suggested, "I could call in at Modesty first thing on Monday morning, so as if you've had any last minute thoughts about anything you can tell us."

"A good idea, lad," Adam nodded. "But what about Mary Jane coming on and making breakfast for all on us, Ward as well?"

"She'd like that," grinned her father.

Solemnly, one by one, the men shook Adam's hand. Four left by the side door, but Freestone John, Matt Tiplady and Sam Kirkbride were taken upstairs to visit Mr. Alderson.

On Cherry's return Adam was finishing a letter to Daniel Dolphin. "He's a real crackerjack wi' dynamite and I'd like his ideas on how to train men as isn't used to it," he explained. "You see if we could substitute it for black powder everything would be speeded, including the new Cross Cut."

She dimpled as she put him right. "It's not just the new cross-cut . . . it's Brunskill's Cross Cut. Both Matt and Sam Kirkbride called it that when they went in to my uncle. 'Course it's oft done, to name a working after the chap who's planned it."

"Aye, lass," Adam said slowly. "And sometimes such ventures are renamed by popular consent."

For a second or so she looked at him. "Alderson's Folly," she half-whispered.

The contents of Adam's inner pocket crackled as he tapped his breast. "I've got the damage claim here, an' that's why I must be off straight-away, lass. What will bring the truth out I don't know, but I can't help thinking that the more pressure we can shove on in every direction the sooner it'll emerge."

"They've had plenty lately, Adam," Cherry said. "I heard tell that Reuben Nattrass has been almost a madman since he lost the award."

She did not detain him, but waited in the doorway until he reached Town Foot, her face lighting up as she responded to his wave when he swung into the highway.

It was a steely afternoon, with a light but chilling breeze creeping from the north, and so Adam, whose bodily condition tended to make him feel the cold, stepped out freely past Malaga. Round the bend he paused to watch two irreconcilable tups, the mating season not far distant, waging relentless battle. Time after time the animals withdrew a few paces from each other, once again to lower their heads and charge forward in tourney array, their bony foreheads meeting in a sickening crack.

The tinkling of polished metal and the dainty clip-clop of high-lifted hoofs announced the approach of a turn-out beautiful both as to fine, varnished dog-cart and skilfully groomed horse. "Afternoon, Brunskill," Mr. Wade shouted. "On your way to my place, I suppose. Wait until I've got this lively fellow as near still as he'll ever be and then climb up."

The drive was exhilarating but brief, a fly-away gallop down the main road and a breath-taking lurch through the gateway of Half House on to the carriage-way beyond.

After an encouraging hour in the spinner's study, Adam was in a very happy mood as he walked back to Low Bands for tea with the Harkers.

* * * *

On Sunday morning Adam pottered about Modesty, doing little save packing his carpet-bag. "And that's another thing," he muttered, stuffing in a dazzlingly white shirt. "Whatever Hannah asserts I reckon somebody younger ought to do my washing in future." If his rueful smile meant anything it was that he had doubts as to whether he would be able to impress this view upon his former landlady.

He had dinner with Cherry, a meal of interruptions and friendly disputes as successive courses were carried to her uncle's room. Later, until it was time for him to start out to Old Hannah's for tea, he sat with the old mine-agent.

"Well, I'd better say good-bye now, Mr. Alderson," he said in due course. "An' as I've telled you, Cherry 'ul be in touch with everything and she'll keep you up to date."

The invalid pushed back against his pillows. "So a bit on a lass wi' no experience 'ul keep me up to date, will she?" he snapped. "Now look here, lad, isn't it commonsense that I should be doing some superintending for you while you're off?"

Cherry quashed that. "Well, you can't, Uncle Titus. Every day you're steadily improving and . . ."

Titus Alderson continued to urge his case, promising moderation. Interviews could be over the kitchen fire and so forth. "And I'd give a solemn assurance as I'd noan ever dream o' going to Notion Bridge unless summat desperately urgent happened . . . not that it'd hurt me to ride up on Ben."

Outraged, Cherry took a deep breath. "Go on," she said, dangerously persuasive. "Let's hear how much more you can give yourself away."

The combination, wrathful niece and mutinous uncle, had a powerful effect upon Adam. Unfortunately he chuckled aloud.

"Aye, an' you're in league with her," Mr. Alderson stormed. "In fact you're all i' league together, you, her, Lucy Peacock, and . . ." he nearly choked, "that damned doctor, him that isn't the height of two penn'orth o' copper."

They tried to coax him into a better frame of mind, but if he were more amenable when Adam left the change was hardly perceptible.

The Yorrel preacher planned for Sunday evening service at Winterings had been taken ill during the afternoon, but Adam and Mrs. Batty did not hear that James Pedley was deputising for him until they were passing the bowl of chrysanthemums on the table just inside the Chapel.

"Well, lad," Old Hannah looked up inquiringly, "what do you think?"

"We'll stop," said Adam, adding not very hopefully: "Maybe another brainstorm at the sight o' me will finish him off for good."

In the moments after the last line of a martial hymn had thundered to the rafters, before the opening of the address, there was that stirring of expectation not unnatural amongst a congregation awaiting a preacher whose notoriety rested upon an ability to chastise a culprit whom he fearlessly named. About ten minutes later heads surreptitiously started turning towards the young woman who sat with her friend in the Skidmores' pew.

James Pedley, however, failed to earn the kind of triumph gratifying to his soul. Glimpsing the young man who had ruined a previous peroration, he at once abandoned the abominations zealously culled from the Book in witness against the woman whose fair face hides sickness and rot.

Hand outstretched, he pointed. "Look at him yonder, him as swore on Holy Writ as he hadn't deflowered a virginal little lass."

Old Hannah leaned nearer Adam, whose sadly-battered appearance enhanced to a malevolent degree the anger burning in him. "Better you nor her, lad," she whispered.

The preacher's tone became higher. "And I were t'Lord's chosen vessel as confronted him outside the Chapel here and telled him I hoped his flesh 'ud turn foul for the false oath he'd sworn. Well, look at him now, th'evil-doer as the Lord has struck."

But if denunciation at a more intense pitch were expected, he disappointed, for he then made clear that the Miracle of Skewdale, as he termed the fearful penalty, could not be dealt with in an interlude. They would sit under him again, he promised, to listen to the account of God's manifestation upon the body of a lustful man.

This brought him back to the young woman whose conduct, he fervently declared, must be examined forthwith. "For inquire ye should have done as soon as my dear brother-in-t'Lord, Ralph Skidmore, reported as his shamed eyes had fallen on her indecently exposing herself. There she is, wi' gay bonnet ribbons and senseless fripperies on her cloak. But it's unchastity an' noan vanity, brethren, as you've to catechise into. What were she doing? Had she been to the top o' Virgin Hill in the hope of spying her future husband when dawn came, as silly lasses has been known to do? Or were she up there as t'Pagan women used to be, worshipping the sun when it rose, dancing naked on the turf in wild orgy?"

In three separate parts of the Chapel there were sounds; at the back, where Adam, grey eyes hard, began to rise; in the Blenkirons' pew as sister scuffled with brother; and from the vicinity of the Skidmores' across the aisle—where Dinah hardly bit off a furious cry, and her father's fine-boned face flushed with quick fury as Cherry began to gather up her Prayer Book and gloves. The gallery's woodwork creaked, prelude to a spate of murmurings which eventually degenerated into a scene unparalleled in the history of Winterings Chapel.

Wingy Blenkiron, shaking off Fronick, started the decline. "Sit down, Cherry lass," he shouted. "And take no notice of him."

"Clarkson!" Mrs. Blenkiron screeched, "don't you know where you are?"

The ginger-haired postman was eyeing his sister, who, red-faced and with eyes closed, had collapsed against her young man. "Aye, I know all right, but I'm going to say some more—it's time somebody did."

Grace Blenkiron endeavoured to enlist her husband's support. "How much longer are you keeping on wi' your arms folded, trying to look as if nowt out of th'usual were happening?"

"Well, it is," her son observed grimly. "I'm about fed up wi' ravel-whiskers yonder, for he's always on about somebody or other. Now he's picked on as decent a lass as——"

James Pedley's thin neck jerked forward. "It's got to be proved she's noan a strumpet an' loose in her ways. For my part——"

The next interruption came from a source so unexpected that bonnets in scores turned towards one another, to be nodded meaningly. It was almost unbelievable that a man who had been jilted should defend the young woman who had made a fool of him, but there it was. Many a lady was guilty of whispering that the day would arrive when Cherry Dinsdale became, after all, Reuben Nattrass's bride.

"Another wrong word about her, Pedley," the East Side mine-agent bawled, "and I'll slit that slimy tongue o' yours t'next time you come to work. I'd do it now," he added with relish, "but I don't hold wi' butchering on t'Sabbath."

The commotion increased on this, but died away when it was seen that the Blenkirons, father and son, were differing with all the rashness of their hot-headed natures. James Pedley directed his talents to them.

"Richard Blenkiron, when are you going to bring to order that son o' yours who's defamed t'Chapel?" he demanded. "You're a preacher of Holy Writ like me, aren't you? One who through the Lord's mysterious ways has been raised above his fellows? Speak up then, man, as I charge you in th'Almighty's name."

"Aye," the blacksmith coughed to clear his throat. "I don't know as this is a suitable spot to kick up a row."

"You don't need to select the spot when it's a matter o' sticking up for what's right," Wingy argued. "We're under God's roof, true enough, but it's yon pale-eyed goat who's making the place stink, though maybe he doesn't appear to you i' that light."

The preacher's arm shot out. "Richard Blenkiron," he screamed, "the child as sprung from your loins is bespattering me, t'Lord's servant . . ."

The blacksmith was more concerned with his son's impertinence. "Of course I think he's a pale-eyed goat," he roared. "I've eyes in my head, haven't I? But that's no excuse for you being sarcastic-like about preachers."

"Nay, don't let your side down," Wingy snorted. "You and him is raised above your fellows, remember."

Feeling a little foolish, Mr. Blenkiron forgot himself even farther. "If you say owt else I'll fetch you one on th'ear-hole."

"Aye, an' I'll invite you to step outdoors," his son shouted.

"Now . . . now then, both on you," Mrs. Blenkiron gasped.

"An' if you do, I'll damned well go," Richard Blenkiron bellowed. "And I'll fight wi' one arm to keep matters even."

Wingy Blenkiron, looking as wild as his father, pushed past Bart Hugill and then his sister, who was roused sharply from her swoon when he trod on her toe. Father was following son when the men in the congregation as one individual came to their senses, the aisles darkening as pew after pew spilled its male occupants until each of the combatants was ringed round safely.

Meantime tears of joy streamed down Old Hannah's cheeks. "I'se sorry, Adam lad," she said, rocking. "It were terrible in the beginning, but th'end has been too much for me. An' I doubt the business 'ul have hurt that lass much, not as it's finished up."

"I don't think so either," Adam smiled.

When he and Old Hannah reached the shop door a small crowd had collected there, the Ivesons and the Harkers, Dinah and Cherry.

"Now what's this, Mrs. Batty?" Adam inquired.

She laughed. "Nay, I've made a bit on a plateful o' cheese-cakes and I thought we'd have a few folk in to eat 'em."

In due course her guests groped towards the kitchen in such scanty light from outside as found its way through gaps in the merchandise crammed in the bow window, the sole misfortune when Matt Tiplady and his family, latecomers with Blind Kit and his wife, upset a box of precariously balanced onions.

The peat fire glowed welcomingly, and if the seating accommodation were limited no one complained. Hymns and sacred songs were sung, with story-telling rounding off the evening: a pleasant send-off for the young man who would be leaving in the morning, Godspeed from his friends.

The ground was hard and the roofs of Winterings glittered with white frost when Adam and the Tipladys sat down to the very fine breakfast cooked by Mary Jane, who chattered constantly as to how she would improve Modesty with soap and water in her host's absence.

While the youngsters moved from bacon and eggs to prodigious slices of plentifully buttered bread and jam, their elders deliberated upon more important matters. Adam brought up the question of dynamite.

"Aye," Matt Tiplady said. "I'm sure both Len and Freestone John 'ul have a try with it, so long as you put us in t'way on it."

"We'll go into it when I get back," Adam said.

Before noon that day he had been kissed by four ladies, once when Mary Jane saw him off and again as he was leaving Old Hannah's.

At Yew Tree House Cherry had not yet started her washing and, as he reached the gate, she was throwing crumbs to a colourful party of chaffinches, robins and tits, closely watched from the topmost branch of one of the tapering yews by an elegant, light-waistcoated storm cock.

"Well, I'm on my way, lass," Adam smiled. "And how's your uncle this morning?"

Cherry tucked in her chin to deepen her voice manfully. "Just about all he's said is: 'Wait till that . . . that doctor comes.'"

"Summat stronger than that, I'm thinking?" Adam quizzed her.

"Yes," she was laughing when, perceiving the massive young man who was striding across Town Foot towards the gate, the brightness left her face. "Reuben Nattrass is coming," she said quietly, "but however he riles you don't do owt that might cause your arm to be worse hurt just as you're going off."

When he arrived the raven-haired mining-agent was brief. "You've taken four o' my best men offen me, Brunskill," he growled.

"I've started four chaps out on t'seven who applied to me," Adam countered. "And when I'm back I shall start as many more as I please."

Reuben Nattrass's mouth went tight. "Right, but think on what I said to you at Notion Bridge."

They watched him walk to Sorrow Near, but, before Cherry could ask what he meant Wingy Blenkiron marched through the gate, red with embarrassment, and bent on not forgetting his opening words. He started off by describing himself 'as a right bloody fool,' following this up by stating explicitly that he no longer believed Adam responsible for Agnes Pedley's misfortune.

"What's changed your mind, Wingy?" Adam asked curiously.

The postman's colour deepened. "I don't know . . . nobbut it's been coming over me for a while. Aye . . ." he said in desperation, "it's a rare lame tale, isn't it?"

"On t'contrary, lad, it's a grand 'un," Adam told him warmly. "What do you say, lass?"

Cherry glowed. "The same as you, Adam. Oh, Wingy, I am pleased."

Sheepish still, the postman held out his left hand. "We'd better shake on it, Adam lad, if for nowt more than that yours—for t'moment we hope anyroad—is one of the few handclasps about here that'll fit comfortably into my own."

As solemnly they shook hands, Cherry's eyes misted. She had always liked Fronick's brother and had taken his attitude hard. Five minutes later her eyes were misting more freely when she peeped round the gatepost before running indoors. The two young men were disappearing round the bend beyond Malaga, Wingy carrying a bulging carpet-bag, and Adam, point of slung elbow showing from behind, with Her Majesty's canvas mailbag hanging schoolboy fashion across his broad shoulders.

Adam had no compunction whatsoever in obliquely hammering a few more nails into Reuben Nattrass's coffin that morning at the Bank in Corvy, when Mr. Storey chatted to him as he drew five sovereigns for personal expenses.

"Maybe so, sir," he remarked respectfully when the banker's highly technical homily ended. "I agree a wide vein is seldom very productive, but, all the same, when beds are rising ore is often near."

"Decidedly so," the older man muttered, before reverting to a subject upon which already he had been foiled. "Anyhow, on that question of development up the Dale, what was it you had in mind? Merely a matter of interest, of course."

"Oh, I don't think I'd care to go into it more deeply, sir," Adam excused himself. "In any case my Cousin Reuben is a sight more competent to speak, knowing the particular problems of Skewdale lead-mining as he does."

William Storey's pale face became sour. The directors of the East Side Company had each signed a guarantee to provide additional working capital, and of the risk his was much larger than the remainder of the Board combined. "Your attitude does you credit, I suppose, Brunskill," he observed, "but frankly I think you're carrying rules of conduct to extremes."

Allowing this to pass without comment, Adam pulled out his watch. Then he stooped to grasp the handle of the carpet-bag, and prepared to move towards the door. "Anyway, sir," he smiled pleasantly, "anything I could say would be based on my experiences of . . . well, how things are done in a great mining company. Similar methods to do with organisation and so on might not apply here."

Mr. Storey appeared to be quite irritable. "Don't know about that, Brunskill," he declared. "Don't know at all."

Adam wished him good morning, and then went into the Bull Bing, where he bought half a dozen handkerchiefs. This left him with nice time to stroll along to the station yard, where, upon the strong double doors of the Lead House, he was able to decipher the names of some of the famous old Skewdale mining companies.

Corvy was the terminus of a single line, but the track was empty. However, after buying a ticket and stowing away his purse, matters not without difficulty to him, he heard the rumble of wheels and, on emerging from the booking-office, saw the long funnel of the engine speeding just above the low cutting outside the station. Shortly afterwards, brakes began to squeal and the train jerked to a standstill in a cloud of steam, when doors were thrown open and a surprising number of people descended.

Preferring privacy, Adam wandered along the platform before stopping at a suitable compartment. Placing his bag down, he opened the door and was turning back again when his glance fell upon a bright-eyed little girl of about three who was standing beside a well-stuffed, straw travelling case, hugging a doll in her left arm. Her right hand clutched the skirts of a tall and rather thin young woman whose plainness of face, like Mary Jane Tiplady's, was gloriously redeemed by a very lovely pair of grey eyes.

Adam's mouth opened wider. "Jane an' Bessie," he muttered. "And Simon and Daniel an' all!"

Simon Sunter looked a trifle worried as usual, and Daniel Dolphin, stocky and moustached, seemed the same lively fellow he had always been. Slightly dazed, Adam was still gaping when Jane Sunter's eyes met his.

She gaped, too. "Adam!" she cried, horrified.

Forgetful of his scars, all unconscious that they were dumbfounded, he kissed her, wrung the hands of Simon and Daniel, and received from Bessie several smacking salutes, this not until that young lady had coyly swivelled on a heel before relenting.

"Your face, Adam!" Jane Sunter gasped. "What *have* you been doing?"

"A cousin o' mine and a mate of his gave me a beating," he told her.

Daniel Dolphin swallowed. "What are they, mountains?" he ejaculated.

"And they gave you that arm and all?" Jane inquired shrewdly.

"No, I had that afore, lass," Adam said.

"Oh," Simon Sunter breathed as if this explained everything. "B-B-By jove, but they've knocked hell out of you, lad."

Daniel Dolphin's brown eyes flashed. "Aye, and we'll give 'em hell, too. Setting about a chap as——"

Adam was so very decided, so insistent, that they listened to him without raising an objection. "No, do nowt, except keep your eyes and ears open. But make yourselves acquainted with an old chap i' Winterings, Titus Alderson of Yew Tree House, and with his niece in particular—I mentioned her to you."

Jane Sunter smiled. "If she's called Cherry, I think you have."

"Well, that's her," Adam said hastily. "Give her what advice you can —I mean Simon and Daniel. It all sounds mysterious, I'll admit, but she knows you're right friends o' mine and she'll tell you everything."

Simon Sunter occasionally achieved a heavy joke. "Once we're s-settled, lad, our first visit 'ul be on this Cherry. W-Why, I shan't be able to sleep till I've bottomed t'mystery."

"H'mm!" Adam murmured. "And I've a mystery to bottom, why you lot are here. It wouldn't be, would it, because o' the trouble I've got into?"

Jane Sunter mocked him. "Hark at the chap. He's got a rare conceit of himself, hasn't he?"

In turn, Adam eyed them. "Well, we'll leave it at that," he remarked.

These friends stayed on the platform until he could see them no more, a little group of familiar and yet strange figures from the world of his boyhood and young manhood, a world in which he had always been respected. When the rising line of the embankment cut them off, Adam pulled up the window and, inexpressibly touched by their loyalty, sat reflecting in the corner until long after the massive Keep of Corvy Castle sank from view. After a while the expression in his eyes began to change, a glint portending future action driving out softer signs of reminiscence.

"By God, but now I can push on wi' the affairs of the West Side Company," he gloated. "Aye, with the grand chaps as I've already got, and now with Daniel and Simon . . . I'll make things hum."

The wheels of the train droned out all too slowly their regular rhythm. He was impatient to reach Newcastle, impatient to put an unpleasant operation into the past, impatient for the sound of train wheels carrying him back again—to Skewdale and to Cherry, and to the renewal of a fight in which he could pit his mining skill against that of his cousin Reuben, and, if it were forced on him, his bodily powers as well.

CHAPTER THIRTEEN

I

During Adam's absence Cherry was too occupied to heed very much the handful of hide-bound zealots who pilloried her. Fortunately these more fiery detractors were few, but perhaps the hurt she felt most was that the puzzled majority of Winterings folk, who should have known her better, preferred to stand aloof, suspending judgment. She found, however, new and staunch friends in Daniel Dolphin, staying with his Aunt Ellen at Malaga, and in Simon Sunter and his wife Jane, who, with their little daughter, Bessie, were living with Rosie Caygill at Yorrel. These, with Dinah, Wingy and Bart, formed her little social circle. She was kindly treated, too, by a few elders with whom she had been intimate since childhood.

Meanwhile Brunskill's Cross Cut was proceeding as fast as good men and black powder could advance it, and from Mary Forehead Ground, drier than for years, a rising output of ore was flowing from the fourteen partnerships at work. The great difficulty was the weather. Sunny but cold days succeeded one another, with hard frosts every night, and little by little the moorland becks dwindled. Water supplies were becoming inadequate for the dressing floors, and not only were the bouse teams outside Mary Level filled to capacity with unwashed ore, but wagon loads had also been tipped in the open alongside. As conditions worsened the ore, instead of being trammed out of the level, was heaped underground, where at least it would not freeze into a mass difficult to separate.

This state might have been disastrous, but happily the funds of the West Side Company, increased by the compensation received from the mining concern at the other side of Winterings Gill, were sufficient for the present.

One afternoon in the middle of the month, Cherry took her fancy clogs to be repaired before starting out to the mines. As she neared the Wood Yard gateway several grinning men were leaving the cobbler's shop, and inside both Blind Kit and Luke Close were chuckling. The old roadman, needles busily clicking, roared with laughter when she asked what they were amused about. Abandoning brush and shovel in favour of warming himself at the full-bellied stove, he had brought out his knitting, a long stocking, when comfortably seated.

Blind Kit's scarred face crinkled. "Nay, lass, we've nobbut been talking about Adam and how he drew brass fro' them who wanted to be shut o' West Side shares, and then, when he's the West Side's largest shareholder, he lands th'East Side so as they've to pay big damages, some on it out of the pockets of them as were so clever in the first case. George and William Nattrass, who'll have forked out both ways, 'ul never live it down."

"Enough to make a cat laugh," old Luke added.

Again Blind Kit was overcome. "I don't know about cats, Luke," he vowed weakly. "But a lot of folk in t'Dale is splitting their sides about it."

To appreciate a young man for tactics which have discomfited astute but not particularly popular people may be one short step nearer to personal liking and that was a possible outcome which comforted Cherry up Sorrow Near.

Bart Hugill was wearing most seriously his authority as a member of the 'committee,' and, at the mine office, he gave her figures, for her uncle's information, of the latest Metal Count End, with equal gravity mentioning that Big William could now drive the North Smelt Mill blast only for a limited period each day.

"The frost must have been cruel hard on t'tops," he remarked. "I've never known the water drop off so sharp."

Finally he requested her to take a message to Mary Dressing Floors, brushing back his long hair while pondering over its phrasing. Before she left, however, he relaxed sufficiently to suggest a visit to Joss Foss, and quite definitely smiled at the queer writing when she handed him Adam's letter to her uncle.

"With his left hand, of course," Cherry laughed.

"Aye," the clerk muttered. "Seems as if he's getting over his operation nicely, doesn't it?"

A few minutes later Cherry walked briskly up Foul Syke Gill to the foot of Joss Foss, a magnificent spectacle. Icicles thick and slender, closely together, extended from top to bottom of the falls, steely-white columns reaching upwards for almost eighty feet towards the cold blue vault above, the mighty silvery organ pipes of a celestial church. Water trickled upon and within the hollow, shining pillars, so that the whole presented a quivering light-palpitating effect, as if a glorious anthem silently ascended.

The numbing chill of the sunless depths of the gill was a small price to pay for such wonder, and Cherry lingered so long that she had to run back on her errand, pausing only to glance into the blacksmith's shop at the North Mill, where Richard Blenkiron was forging into chisel-shape the ends of four-foot lengths of octagonal steel bar. Sparks were flying as he hammered the red-hot metal into a cutting edge, and clouds of steam hissed upwards when, at blood-red heat, he plunged the tool into an iron water-tub.

"Well, miss," he inquired with sly deference, "any orders?"

Cherry eyed him severely. "Nobbut that you're likely to be behind-hand with them borers if you're noan quicker, Richard."

His snatch just missed her as, with a most unladylike squeal, she fled outdoors.

The day was very beautiful and the ground clean and hard, and so, her mission completed at Mary Dressing Floors, she continued up Winterings Gill, entranced by trees outlined in frost and terraced water-falls whose risers were a lacework of ice. On rounding the last bend before Glory Waterwheel, however, she saw Reuben Nattrass at Smiddy Smelt Mill over the beck. The raven-haired mine-agent at once started across the black-and-white mottled course of the stream, his passage tricky upon water-smoothed rocks glazed with ice, and hastily she abandoned the ravine to scramble up an even rougher offshoot, the beginning of a chase which did not end until she was in one of the loneliest regions of Water Ling Moor, at the edge of a shallow gully above Doomsday High Shaft.

"I've brought this on through my own silliness," she told herself with annoyance. "Why couldn't I have faced him wi' dignity?"

Nevertheless she was cautious as she raised herself on tiptoe to peer over the bracken-fringed bank, and a faint sigh of relief slipped past her lips when, well along the track winding to Foul Syke Gill, she perceived Reuben Nattrass's broad back.

"He reckons I'm going all that roundabout way," she was crowing when her foot skidded on the steep, hard-frozen surface. Slithering ignominiously, she came to rest at the edge of a small and newish hole made, she concluded, by a boulder which, breaking off from the scars of Little Barg, had bounded down the sheer slope. "Well," she laughed breathlessly, sprawled on all-fours, "I'm a right 'un to mention dignity." Instinctively she straightened her skirts, but her hand stayed suddenly when her eye was caught by small particles, coloured light brown to red.

"I've seen stuff like that afore," she murmured, brow knit.

Generations of groovers' blood in her, she delved into the hole to scratch out a small quantity of the friable substance, using the envelope of Adam's letter for a wrapper.

Since his dismissal by Adam, Jonas Cottingham had become the chief smelter of the East Side Company, and he and Bull Waggott, from the other side of Winterings Beck, were bawling for information about the whereabouts of their agent when Cherry reached the tail of Mary Level, from which Mazy Bill and his grey-headed mare had emerged with a wagon-train of spar destined for the dead heap. As she talked to the crazed trammer, the groover began to cross the stream towards Mary Dressing Floors, no doubt to pursue the inquiry nearer at hand.

The memory of a panic-stricken retreat still rankling, Cherry obtained little satisfaction from the thought of Reuben Nattrass now roaming vainly on Water Ling Moor.

"Well, I should think so," she assured Mazy Bill. "What could Polly have better than a hot mash when t'weather's cold like it is?"

Conversation with him was always a little difficult and, as so often, it ended abruptly, the shambling youth and his mare moving away without warning, leaving her, for all its familiarity, saddened by the encounter.

At Mary Dressing Floors, she had a chat with Sam Kirkbride and Hugh Bearpark, who were endeavouring to maintain the vital flow of water, breaking up the ice on watercourses and cleaning out launders so beautifully festooned as to appear like fairy bridges. The next haul of bouse-wagons would soon be starting off for Notion Bridge and, preferring company on the way, she idled a little, wandering from the silent Crushing Mill down to the jigging place, where, caught examining a pyramid-shaped pile of shining, blue-grey smitham, the smallest ore passing through the sieves, she was roundly teased by a washer-man.

Several minutes later, when she set off towards Notion Bridge, Bull Waggott was about a hundred yards ahead, nearing the end of the great dead heap looming above him on the right. Both she and the horse-trammer of the bouse train saw the cascade of spar flying down, her own scream and the driver's shout certainly checking the groover before he could be overwhelmed. At that, a lump of flint-like quartz, big enough to have brained him, whizzed closely past his shoulder.

"That were a near thing, lad," the trammer remarked.

For a rough customer, Bull Waggott was pallid and shaken. "Aye, an' that's t'fourth I'se had within a matter o' months," he mumbled. "Makes you wonder if you're fated, like."

"Why, have you had all that lot of narrow escapes?" Cherry inquired.

"Haven't I just!" the groover groaned.

They went together as far as Notion Bridge, Cherry afterwards walking by herself to Town Foot, where, in the failing light, she saw a cart emerging from Jom High Road. It was laden with a rubbishy collection of furniture, and, as it turned down the mainroad, Mrs. Iveson came round the corner. The shepherd's wife explained that Ambrose Pedley was leaving the village to live three miles below Greets.

"An' talk about being peculiar about it," she continued. "Why, he's behaving as if he never wants to set eyes on a soul he's ever known."

"But he's always been odd," Cherry remarked.

The usually even-tempered Mrs. Iveson snorted. "Aye, but he's being going on as if it were a matter o' life and death to be off, wi' every day counting. Anyway, lass, don't let's waste time on him."

The two ladies discussed Adam's progress in hospital. Both Mark Iveson and his wife considered it their prerogative to be told whatever news there might be of a young man whom they had more or less championed from the start.

After tea, before Nathan Wharton came, Cherry played draughts in the bedroom with her uncle, who more than once reverted with palpable regret to the decaying fragments Cherry had found on Water Ling Moor. "Gozzan, that's what it's called, lass, and it's generally th'indication of a vein coming up to the surface. Aye, a hundred years ago they'd have hushed it to prove if there were any worthwhile ore below, but of course that's noan allowed now because of t'damage it might do to property by swelling the becks all of a sudden."

"Couldn't it be dug out, Uncle?"

Titus Alderson was speaking about prohibitive costs when the sawyer shouted from below, and so Cherry was able to clear up a few household matters before Dinah arrived with her needlework.

Settled at each side of the fireplace the two girls chattered away, their subjects covering dresses for Annamaria Rutter's birthday party at the beginning of November—which Cherry after serious reflection had decided to attend—to the latest scandal inflicted on a greatly ashamed village by Nowt Cooper, who for weeks had stubbornly refused to maintain his wife and children while living under the same roof as they.

Daniel Dolphin came next on the agenda, Dinah colouring deeply when twitted. "Eh, I like him better than I did," she admitted, convulsing Cherry by adding: "But do you know at the beginning he treated me as if I were . . . well, a loose woman, lass. He kind o' leered at me, and . . ."

The front gate clicked when she was remarking that probably she had sent him on a wild goose chase that night. "He were at Susan's this morning," she giggled, "and I made out as you and me were going to Rosie Caygill's to see Jane. Anyroad, serve him right, t'cheeky thing . . . I hope it snows for him."

Cherry's second convulsion was due to her friend's expression when Daniel Dolphin, entering the kitchen, courteously wished her: "*Buenas tardes, señorita.*"

"Well, Dinah lass," he continued, ripely surprised, "so you're here, are you? We seem to bump into one another everywhere, don't we?"

"Sit down, lad," Cherry smiled.

Dinah glowered. "There's no need for him to, is there? You know very well your uncle gets real sharp if folk hang about downstairs."

Daniel sighed as he took off his overcoat. "As if visiting a sick man were nobbut an excuse. But there's one fortunate thing, Dinah lass," he brightened up, "you'll have company all t'dark way back to Badger Hall."

"I can manage by myself, thank you," Dinah exclaimed.

Daniel favoured her with a languishing regard before he turned to Cherry. "*Una cosa tan hermosa no se hace de balde*," he said with conviction.

"And what's that mean, pray?" Cherry laughed.

His voice was yearning. "Such a beautiful thing is not made for nothing," he translated. "Just that, Cherry lass, nobbut that."

Dinah was stony. "Daft-head," she said, but, oblivious to her hints, he remained with them until the sawyer left.

2

One cold and grey morning in the last week of the month, Wingy Blenkiron delivered at Yew Tree House a letter in which Adam announced he would be leaving the infirmary on the following Monday afternoon.

Now sitting up each day in his bedroom, the old mine-agent was drawn close to a blazing fire. "Aye, t'lad says as he won't be able to get back here the same day and so he's putting up for a night mid-way," he murmured.

There had been a great deal of commotion at Town Foot, the mad patter of small, clogged feet as youngsters ran about in search of a rumoured pig-killing, and the antics of a new horse, bought in flat country, which had required a string looping about its tongue before it could be forced to think of climbing Sorrow Near.

Her heart thumping, Cherry turned from the window. "When will he be here, Uncle?" she asked.

"About tea-time on Tuesday, he hopes," Titus Alderson replied.

"Well . . . well, I'd better be getting on," Cherry said.

In actual fact, quite apart from a desire to be alone, she had much to do if she were not to be late for the sewing-party at Badger Hall, with which Dinah's mother was celebrating the end of the season's cheese-making. There was the usual ride to the mines, and shopping afterwards, when she would tell Old Hannah the exciting news from Newcastle. She began to bustle with a will.

At Badger Hall, Nell was most accommodating in allowing her family of six to be inspected by a bright-eyed little girl and three young women, who exclaimed over and fondled a bevy of plump, uncertain-legged creatures before leaving. The departure from the barn was arranged diplomatically, but happily there were other attractions for Bessie: Mr. Skidmore, with Prue, bringing in a sled-load of timber, and Mark Iveson, who, refurbishing mole-traps in the garth, delighted her with an impression of the weekly carrier returning late at night. Next, driven by her 'Uncle' Daniel, the spanking arrival of Mrs. Robert William Alderson's trap, aunt and nephew laughing uproariously—there was no doubt, as everyone said, that her nephew's visit had immensely livened Mrs. Alderson.

But if the mistress of Malaga seemed in a good humour, Dinah knew how very quickly she could change. In dismay she whispered to Cherry: "Oh, I do hope it isn't going to make it awkward for you, lass, specially as they're both here. But I hadn't the least idea as how either her or Isa were coming."

For one reason or another the afternoon was not an unqualified success. Dinah's mother had taken a great fancy to Bessie, and, as Simon's aunt, she felt it would have been more fitting if he and his family had stayed at Badger Hall.

"She's been on again," Jane said under her breath to Cherry and Dinah in the parlour. "Talk about giving me what for."

As the party got into full swing she was engaged in conversation by Mrs. Roberty Will, who, remarking that this was the younger woman's first sight of Skewdale, added that the dalesmen were a much softer breed than formerly, an estimate from which Mrs. Ralph Skidmore immediately dissented. In reply, Mrs. Alderson willingly admitted that if there had been more men of Reuben Nattrass's kidney, Winterings would not now be disgraced by a seducer openly walking about.

"Yes, he's that an' a lot else," Isa Skidmore agreed.

"I'm noan so certain," Mrs. Blenkiron objected. "Mind you, I still think Ambrose Pedley should never have left 'em alone so oft on Sundays."

"All t'same, I'm not sure, either," Mrs. Skidmore chimed in.

Mrs. Roberty Will jerked forward. "Are you out on your head, Minnie?"

Her best friend stared coldly. "Not as I'm aware, Ellen."

"You must be, for it's as plain as the nose on your face," the mistress of Malaga rapped out.

"Then I'm another ugly sister," Mrs. Harker of Low Bands said. "Why, there isn't a ha'porth of evidence against him, as th'Inquest proved."

With considerable triumph Mrs. Alderson observed that *she* had evidence, obtained a long time before. "Of course George Nattrass is a chap wi' no morals," she continued. "Bear in mind I'm meaning morals of another sort—like him being t'ringleader in getting rid of shares in an underhand manner—but I believe him in this."

"That's champion," Isa Skidmore said cuttingly, forsaking an ally. "But I'll have you remember you're slandering an uncle o' mine."

"Anyroad," Mrs. Puke Hastwell brushed irrelevancies aside, "what were it you believed him about?"

"As yon Brunskill found t'brass for his cousin to buy herself *underclothing*," Mrs. Roberty Will informed the circle. "And there's no need for me to tell you what's going on when that happens."

A flush crept into Jane Sunter's cheeks and her luminous grey eyes were hot with anger. "Well, you'd better tell me, Mrs. Alderson," she said.

Mrs. Roberty Will lowered her voice, presumably in recognition of the presence of unmarried women. "Either that he's had his way wi' her," she shrugged, "or that he's getten things so as he'll noan be long."

"Rubbish," said Jane Sunter.

Mrs. Roberty Will's hackles went up, as did her tone. "Don't you speak to me like that."

"I won't, if you'll stop talking such silly nonsense," Jane retorted. "I wasn't here when all this happened, but you can't know a chap all your life without knowing him better than that."

"You can," shouted her elderly opponent. "If you haven't the wit you were born with."

"I've got eyes all right," Adam's champion retaliated. "And so has my husband and so has your nephew Daniel . . . they've been his closest friends since boyhood, and you can usually judge folk by t'company they keep. Of course you may think they're all birds of a feather, Simon, Daniel an' Adam . . . seducers were the word you used, wasn't it? Well, I'll vow to this, Mrs. Alderson, that if Adam Brunskill is one then you're harbouring another beneath your roof."

Mrs. Alderson's gold locket took a dizzy ride. "How dare you!" she choked. "Minnie, you're supposed to be the hostess, aren't you? Are you going to sit there while your nephew's wife insults me?"

Endeavouring to pour oil on troubled waters, Mrs. Blenkiron disastrously involved herself in quite another sense. With the exception of the bread and butter and the buttered fruit cake, which the mistress of Badger Hall would never allow to be prepared until just before the meal, she knew tea was already laid. Laughingly she proposed that while Mrs. Skidmore smoothed down injured feelings she would do whatever remained to be done in the kitchen.

"You'll do nowt of the kind, Grace," Mrs. Skidmore snapped.

The blacksmith's wife's smile vanished as she halted near the parlour door. "Certainly not if you don't want me to, though I can't say as how I like your manner," she said distantly. "But perhaps you'd be good enough to explain."

Mrs. Skidmore was annoyed about Simon and Jane, upset about the discord, and resentful towards Ellen Alderson, who had, she fully believed, inferred she was incapable of sound judgment and plain-featured into the bargain. It was the last straw to be tried by a niggardly friend's lavishness with other people's foodstuffs.

"I didn't churn so much butter last week, an' if you shovel it on I shan't make out," she blurted.

Flushing dully, Richard Blenkiron's tight-fisted wife drew an outraged breath. "I don't know as I'm in the habit o' shovelling butter on."

Mrs. Harker winked at her neighbour. "Nobody 'ud ever think of disputing you in that, Grace," she consoled her.

A ding-dong battle had started which promised to delay tea considerably, and so Cherry decided to slip away, partly because of her uncle and partly because she wished to avoid the embarrassment of Daniel's offering her a lift in his aunt's trap.

Thinking excitedly of Adam's return, she enjoyed the walk home apart from one incident in Main Street. While overtaking James Pedley and several of his austere brethren from Yorrel she became both sick and furious on hearing Cyprian Metcalfe's filthy language and the sound of blows. The party of hot-gospellers, sacrificing the morrow's earning, were on their way to Corvy to hold meetings in protest against the drinking and betting taking place during a three-day pigeon shooting-match. Recognising in the lamplight the young woman hurrying by, each was ardent in his desire to strike a shrewd blow for the Almighty.

"There's th'abandoned creature," James Pedley pointed. "Her who——"

In a fine rage Cherry spun round. "Instead of starting on at me, why don't you go into the shop there an' stop that brute beating his wife? Or are you too frightened?"

The mission to Corvy seemed more inclined to discourse on the charge than to take action which might bring them into conflict with the East Side engineer. In the main they spoke to empty air, for their accuser, her ringing "Cowards!" bringing the white face of Cuthbert Daykin a little farther out of his shop doorway, turned on her heel and left them where they were.

With account books under his arm, Bart Hugill called at Yew Tree House. His young lady was with him, sullen in manner as she refused to take off her coat.

"We've company to-night, Mrs. Skidmore's nephew Simon and his wife, an' we shan't be staying long," she ended stiltedly.

Cherry decided that the couple had had another of their quarrels. "Anyway you might just as well sit down, lass," she coaxed.

The clerk, already bending over the table, removed a pen from behind his ear and disgustedly tossed it down. Fronick must have suspected what was coming, but, undeterred by her warning, he said his say. In effect it was that, as the result of a scandalous tale, his young woman preferred not to mix with Cherry.

"I'll never forgive you, Bart Hugill," the blacksmith's daughter screeched, face puckering. "And you may as well understand I've done wi' you for good. An' you needn't think you can creep back and apologise, either. A chap who lets on things he's learned privately . . ."

"I make nowt of hole an' corner ways," Bart retorted.

Cheeks blotchy with mortification, Fronick seemed undecided whether to swoon or strike him. Ultimately, however, she burst into a flood of tears and, after blubbering a threat as to what her father and Clarkson would do, ran out wildly.

Urgently Cherry pushed him. "Be sharp, Bart. Go calm her down and——"

White but determined, Bart shook his head. "She can find somebody else to calm her down in t'future." Studiedly careless, he arranged the chair to his liking, closely examined his pen, and then changed the nib. "Now, let's get on, lass," he finished up.

About three-quarters of an hour later, Sam Kirkbride arrived with Simon Sunter and Jane, whom he had met along the street. As business matters were obviously afoot they went upstairs at once, returning when Bart was shutting the books. The lugubrious-looking engineer and Simon were in animated conversation about attempts to alleviate the water shortage, but it soon became evident that, in the presence of the old mine-agent, the whole story had not been revealed.

Simon Sunter stared, genuine horror in him. "You mean somebody may be t-t-tampering with your water supply? *To* the s-s-s-smelt mill?"

A man to whom smelting was more a calling than an occupation, his stutter grew worse, and he was still incoherently wrathful when he and Jane set out for the Blenkirons, Sam Kirkbride leaving at the same time.

"Mmm . . ." Bart Hugill mumbled a little while afterwards. He fingered the lobe of his ear, very much at a loose end, the more so as his best friend lived in a house at which it would be most awkward to call.

A tattoo resounded out on the brass knocker, just after Cherry's next attempt at mediation had been rebuffed. Despite this gay notification, however, Wingy Blenkiron's expression was the epitome of stern resolve as he marched towards Bart, to hold clenched fist in front of his face.

"See that," he growled. "And there's a good arm behind it."

The clerk stood his ground. "Well, what on it?"

"Nobbut this," the postman promised, "that I'll burst your nose if you're ever jackass enough to make it up wi' our Fronick."

Cherry conveniently forgot that she herself had been guilty of meddling. "Wingy!" she expostulated. "That's summat they'll have to settle themselves."

Doggedly, Wingy Blenkiron was remarking that he preferred Bart as a friend and not a miserable brother-in-law when, overhead, the ferrule of Titus Alderson's walking-stick banged down. For the time being that disposed of the two young men.

3

On the Saturday preceding Adam's return, the trousers of the groovers and dressing floors men were frozen like stove pipes when they entered the agent's office in Jom High Road to draw their Lent Money.

The weather was very much the same the next day when Cherry took her class at the Sunday School, her sole connection with the Chapel since James Pedley's denunciation of her, and not too pleasant at that. In the evening, while her uncle was holding court at home, she went with Jane and Simon Sunter to Greets Church and loved everything, from the service to the soft light from delicately-chased brass oil-lamps which dimly illuminated the old high pews and Jacobean pulpit and dealt kindly with the severity of plaster and whitewash.

Monday, as usual, was Washing Day. Clothes on the lines became as hard as boards before the last drips of water had fallen from them, when they had to be taken down, prelude to a disheartening struggle indoors.

Cherry, however, with Adam's homecoming only twenty-four hours distant, was not disheartened, and she was blithe even when, later on, she dressed in an ice-cold bedroom for Annamaria's party. Dinah called for her, bundled up like herself as if on a trip to the North Pole, and Wingy Blenkiron, who chanced to be leaving Smithy House as they started, rode down to Half with them. The Old Cow Inn had commodious outbuildings, and though already the animals of a dozen guests were comfortably stalled there was no difficulty about arranging for Prue's well-being.

"You two mummies get warm indoors, so's you can begin unwinding yourselves," the postman grinned, a dewdrop on his nose. "I'll take her out of her gears."

"I'd better give you a hand, lad," Dinah said.

In the wavering yellow light from the near-side lamp of the trap Wingy Blenkiron's frost-stung face was visible to Cherry. Fiery-tempered, he glanced sharply at her friend, the twist to his mouth portending words more violent than those he uttered.

"Don't you reckon I can manage by myself?" he asked.

Cherry acted with praiseworthy firmness. "Now I'm going to tell the pair of you summat," she announced. "To begin wi', Dinah, it's you as oft causes bother by making remarks which could be thought hinted about Wingy only having one arm. And as for you, Wingy, you go seeking slights so far as Dinah is concerned, which means you're ridiculously over-sensitive. If you weren't, you wouldn't have taken on t'postman's job after you'd had your accident, not when your Uncle Martin wanted to train you under him as an auctioneer . . . like he did, an' like he still is wanting to. No, you were nobbut fit to lug a mailbag about, or so you said, and you wouldn't even take into account as poor Bill were no use to his father or that Arthur Nattrass, who were the next most likely because he were courting Annamaria, weren't considered to have a good enough head-piece."

Conflicting emotions traversed the faces of the culprits. Once Wingy's mouth opened as though he were about to speak, and twice Dinah shot glances at her friend strangely compounded of fury and appeal.

The young man was the first to break the silence. "Well . . . well, at after that lecture, Dinah lass," he said with an effort, "I think th'only thing I can do is to ask you to help me out."

Fiercely Dinah Skidmore bit her lip. "And the only thing I can do is to stand over you an' watch you do everything yourself."

In due course Prue was led inside and the trap wheeled where it would not obstruct later arrivals.

For young and old, Annamaria Rutter's birthday party was going with a swing, and everyone seemed to be jolly with the exception of her brother, who, head to one side and shoulder slightly dipped, stole about like a lost soul.

Mr. Rutter was perfectly content with the Old Cow Inn as a residence, but it was his wife's greatest cross that he refused to make changes to hide its former purpose. Hence, in a room obviously once a saloon bar whist was in progress, while in the tap-room, to which the unerring eye of Mighty Joe's rider was attracted as he rode along the main road, a smoker was being held.

Warmed by a huge fire with a meshed guard, the former skittle alley was the preserve of the younger generation. There was dancing there, to music provided by Hugh Bearpark on the bassoon, with Nick Pratt and Nathan Wharton fiddling energetically, and Simon Sunter accompanying on the piano. Supper was at midnight and *Hide the Thimble* was played in the hour before, during which Arthur Nattrass's elder brother, Alice's George, was blushingly complimented on his near success by Fronick Blenkiron, who had been throwing her cap at him the whole evening.

It was Cherry's turn next, and while waiting for her call to return, she peeped in at the purposeful-faced whist players in the saloon bar, but stayed a little longer in the tap-room, where Dr. Seaton, who had decided to make an evening of it, was chilling his hearers' blood with a macabre account of a winter night he and a fellow student had spent in the dissecting theatre at Edinburgh.

Shivering a trifle herself, it could be forgiven of Cherry that, as she closed the door behind her and turned into the passage, she gasped on bumping immediately into the towering figure of a raven-haired young man.

"You've no need to be frightened, lass," Reuben Nattrass assured her. "But I'se been wanting a word wi' you for a while."

Quickly he bundled her into a small room where a wall-lamp lighted up corn and meal bins and cases of beer.

"Now listen," he resumed before she could protest. "I'm nobbut wanting to own I shouldn't have said what I did when I galloped into your uncle's house at after you'd chucked me."

"It doesn't matter . . . and I must go now," Cherry said.

"Not yet, lass, not till I've telled you that I still want you," Reuben Nattrass persisted. "I once said as you'd getten into my blood somehow an' that I were going to have you. Well——"

She shook her head. "I'm sorry, but it's no good."

He laughed. "Isn't it, by God? Well, well, well, but we'll see about that, we will that. If I don't tame you afore I'se done——"

Hitherto, realising that struggling would merely make things worse, Cherry had suffered him to hold her wrist. But now, angered, she made the mistake of trying to escape, and the more she fought the more his arm tightened around her, and the more he enjoyed himself.

Mazy Bill rescued her. Frothing from his lips he kicked up such a hullabaloo that speedily there was a rush of feet to the scene.

Daniel Dolphin appeared first. "What's this about?" he demanded.

Cherry tried to pass it off. "It's all right, Daniel."

"Is it?" Annamaria declared furiously. "Not while that orang-outang is in the house. An' who asked you to show yourself at my party, Reuben Nattrass? Because I didn't."

"Well, I can take myself off," the East Side Company's agent retorted, jerking his head to his cousin. "Come on a few yards down t'road to Jonas's, Arthur. You look as miserable as sin, but a brandy or two 'ul help you to tackle this sharp-tongued scold."

Arthur Nattrass gulped. "You . . . you keep off Annamaria," he muttered. "And I'm not going to t'Groovers Welcome either."

His cousin's dark eyebrows went up exaggeratedly. "My, can't she put the screws on you! Well, in that case, Arthur lad, I shall have to do without your company, eh? No ill-feeling of course."

Jestingly, it seemed, he punched Arthur Nattrass in the ribs. But though his clenched fist travelled only a few inches the blow was powerful, and the knuckles of his first and second fingers were protruding. His victim gasped, but valiantly tried to conceal that he was in pain.

Annamaria was not deceived, however. "That's right, you nasty bully," she shouted. "But instead of cracking at a chap weaker nor yourself why don't you have a go at a real champion, like that Gipsy Joe as I've heard tell on."

The mine-agent grinned at her while disclosing that, news to them all, he was booked to fight the pugilist.

"Next spring as a matter o' fact," he continued. "And if any on you wants to win a bit of brass——"

The throng packed at both sides of the doorway was rudely jostled when the master of the house plunged in from behind. Mr. Rutter remembered the mine-agent's ' bloody parrot ' at the adjudication.

Arm raised, he started off. "Get out o' here, Nattrass. Are you going, I say are you going——"

"What'm I bid, what'm I bid, aye, going, going, gone," the younger man derided.

His dark-eyed glance rested momentarily on Cherry. Then he thrust a passage outwards, to clatter along the stone-flagged floors, to slam the front door.

A chit-chat on the episode slightly delayed supper, but the gathering lost none of its zest either then or afterwards.

Farewells were said at three o'clock in the morning, when iron-shod hoofs, going up-dale and down, began to ring out clearly upon the frost-bound road.

It was a short night for those who had enjoyed the hospitality of the Old Cow Inn, and half an hour longer between the blankets would certainly have been permissible. But, for the ladies whose cheesemaking season had just closed, Market Day was not to be missed. They started out as usual, or even a little earlier, a very few hours later, one and all wishing to be home to share in the fun of Bonfire Night.

CHAPTER FOURTEEN

I

THE MILK cows, housed until the following year, were no longer dotted upon pasture and fell, and the landscape itself was changed, the towering hills more stark and yet more beautiful in their sombre magnificence.

With the exception of a bonfire piled as high as a cottage roof there was no change, however, in Main Street, through which, inquisitively eyed, Adam carried his bag to Old Hannah's, where he was pushed into the kitchen and bidden to sit down to a meal.

"Oh, it's noan because you'll be short at Modesty, lad," the old lady smiled. "You'll find so much baking's been done for you by t'good fairies that you'll have to get them mates o' yours to help lower it."

As might have been expected, she was most interested in hearing about his operation, and, after eating, he was ordered to roll up his shirt sleeve. "Aye," she said, touching the puckered flesh. "Now tell me again what t'doctor said yesterday. It'll be as sound as ever in three months, but you've to use it carefully. You mustn't knock it or you might lose it, eh?"

Adam wriggled a trifle. "I wouldn't say as——"

His interrogater blew up. "Do you think I've getten some green in my eye?" she inquired, putting her pipe down the better to castigate him. Her luckless prey learnt that she and Dr. Seaton had gone thoroughly into his case, the basis of their conference a letter written by the Newcastle surgeon to his colleague at Greets. "Now!" she whooped, so pleased that she thumbed through her cards, selecting one with the picture of a herbalist's mortar and the intimation: DISPENSING. DON'T DISTURB. This she hung on the shop-door, murmuring on her return: "Well, I'se dispensing good advice, choose how," before lighting up her pipe again.

Dusk was not far away when he left, but the light was sufficient on the Brig for him to see the loveliness of the ice-mantled falls, and even in Modesty the specialities of both Cherry and Mary Jane could be picked out in the array of newly-made tarts and cakes. Elsewhere were signs of thoughtfulness: fresh milk, a crisp loaf under a linen cover, warm embers in the bedroom grate, and a couple of lumps marking the position of hot-water jars beneath the bedclothes.

He was descending the uncarpeted stairs, a smile softening the sternness of his face, when Daniel opened the front door.

"Well, Adam lad," he breezed in, "inspecting what your womenfolk have done for you? Talk about . . ." He stopped, peered, and whistled. "By, lad, but it's fetched you down. You must have lost nigh on two stone."

They sat in front of a blazing fire and for a while chatted about personal matters. But in due course more serious affairs came under discussion.

"Aye, Cherry telled us everything," Daniel nodded. "And since then me an' Simon have been hobnobbing wi' that lot as calls themselves the 'committee.' Anyroad, as soon as we got your letter we went deeper into things with one or another of 'em, and betwixt us we worked out a plan that'll shove t'driving along in the way you outlined."

Adam's friends had indeed schemed well. Daniel, with Sam Kirkbride, had examined the McKean Rock Boring Machine stowed away in the machinery store-house at the Great Deep Level. It would drill a one and a quarter inch shot hole, needed a simple overhaul only, and if installed would complete in less than a fortnight the Cross Cut.

"I'll ask Sir Charles if we can have the loan of it," Adam rubbed his hands. "Well, that's champion, lad. Owt else?"

Daniel Dolphin chuckled as he described Simon's wrath when it had been proved that the diminution of Foul Syke, supplying Big William and the smaller South Smelt Mill waterwheel, was not due to frosty weather. Harry Blaydes, he added, was now quite certain that water was being diverted.

"I'll see him to-night," Adam observed grimly.

"See Simon instead," Daniel laughed. "He's itching to stop their little game."

"You're both on the Pay fro' to-morrow, lad," Adam grunted. "Mind you, it'll noan be much——"

"Nay, just bacca money 'ul do for us," the other said. "And we've got on all right with the 'committee.' They're a decent lot o' chaps, an' talk about keen . . ."

In a while they set out for a glass of ale. Already the sky was reddened by the glare of bonfires, but it was by the light of the bracket lamp that Adam recognised his cousin.

"There's Arthur Nattrass down yonder," he remarked. "The next time I meet him I'm starting things moving—you know what about."

"Don't I just," Daniel growled.

An encounter which might have been delayed for days occurred ten minutes later, when his friend's willowy cousin marched into the cosy bar of the Plug and Feathers to make the third customer there. Mrs. Peacock had greeted Adam with a beaming smile and would still have been talking to him had not a shattering crash of crockery sent her off to inquire into the misfortune.

"Well, you've won me a bet o' two shillings wi' coming back, Adam lad," Arthur Nattrass cried with hearty good-fellowship. "And not even an arm or a leg dropped off by t'way either."

Instead of replying, Adam looked with some significance at his companion, who, after a brief pause, favoured the newcomer with a cold stare.

"Well, my lad," Daniel Dolphin began, grave as a judge, "I'm i' lead-mining myself and my advice to you is to get hold on a few sovereigns as sharp as you can, to buy yourself a steerage ticket for anywhere far enough off."

Arthur Nattrass blew up. "Here, I'm noan standing another bloody chap talking t'sort o' nonsense as he does."

"Nonsense you call it," Adam remarked. "And did you think it were nonsense when you placed them tramrails so as they'd affect Titus Alderson's dialling?"

Cheeks utterly drained of colour, Arthur Nattrass stood rooted. Then, in a spate of words hotly spiced, he made plain he was weary of innuendo. "And what flaming tramrails do you mean?" he shouted. "And where the hell am I supposed to have put 'em?"

"Close-by t'Short Cut," Adam challenged him. "Wherever else would it——" His sentence died, his jaw dropped and he stuttered. "You . . . you haven't been on with that trick in another spot, have you?"

"What trick?" his cousin bawled. "Come on, out wi' it, and flaming sharp."

The mistress of the inn sailed in from the kitchen, her expression at its most forbidding. But Adam forestalled her. "This chap's just had a cruel shock, Mrs. Peacock," he said, "and you'll be doing a Christian kindness if you pour him a stiff glass o' brandy."

"I've had no shock an' there's nowt wrong wi' me," Arthur Nattrass said shrilly. "I want no brandy either, leastways," his smile was grotesque, "not because I'se badly."

Adam shook his head before turning towards the door. "Don't stick it out too long, Cousin Arthur," he murmured. "Because then it may be too late."

In Main Street again, Daniel at once asked why Adam had professed not to know about the big pile of tramrails Cherry had told them about, those near the New Drift. "Were you reckoning it might pay to keep that up our sleeves for t'moment?" he inquired.

"Summat like that, lad," Adam nodded.

For the remainder of the short walk serious business was allowed to lapse, and Adam listened to his friend's impressions of Winterings and its people, one of which was that Dinah Skidmore had all the appearance of a lass who would enjoy a bit of fun once she could be got into a dark corner. Emphatically Adam made representations to the contrary.

In the kitchen of Yew Tree House, with an overcoat over his night-shirt, Titus Alderson had almost talked himself speechless, and twice already his niece had reminded him that he must go to bed.

"Aye, in a few minutes, lass," he retorted when she tried again. "Adam's nobbut just back and while him an' Daniel's here together I may as well go into t'question of . . ."

Cherry's face was softly flushed, and although on the whole she succeeded in dividing her attention equally between the two young men and her uncle she was conscious of effort. Her glance, nevertheless, strayed often enough towards Adam for her to notice the few tiny scars left on his face. He was thinner, and pallor had replaced deep tan, but she felt certain he was much healthier than when last . . .

"I say, lass," her uncle broke into her thoughts as a rocket whizzed into the air. "We've forgotten about Ben and t'fireworks. Will you stuff up the stable window wi' some old sacking?"

Adam went with her, carrying the lantern, and, while the galloway crunched lump sugars, they were able to chat peacefully, about the mine and about their respective friends, chiefly concerning the affair between Daniel and Dinah, if affair it could be called. Afterwards, however, a chance inquiry by Adam led to sadness.

"No, I don't think owt else has happened," Cherry replied, keeping off Ambrose Pedley's departure, "excepting one thing." Briefly she related how, at Mary Level, Bull Waggott had narrowly escaped grave hurt. "It wasn't until later that I coupled it with poor Bill Rutter, and I wondered if he were getting incapable of doing his work properly."

Adam stared at her, his mind upon the circumstances of other incidents in which the groover had been involved. He remembered also a fearsome hunting-knife, and why Mazy Bill was carrying it.

"It could be summat worse, lass," he said at last. "Maybe Bill believes as it were Waggott who wronged my cousin Agnes. It wasn't though. I'm certain of that."

Cherry did not voice her depressing thoughts until after Ben's snuff-brown flank had received a parting slap.

"Do you think you'll ever find out who it were?" she asked.

Adam's tone was quiet. "I'm nearly sure I do already."

Her breath caught. "You . . . you know?"

He puzzled how he could decently explain. "I think so, lass, but it's one o' them terrible things as I wouldn't want to mention to you."

For a while, utterly perplexed, she looked mutely up at him until from the shadowy past there came into her consciousness one or two hushed allusions made by elders, those snippets imperfectly understood but recognisable as forbidden and evil by the young people whose sharp ears had picked them up.

Tightly, in horror, she closed her eyes. "Oh, Adam," she cried.

"Aye, lass," he said. "But remember there's a thousandfold more goodness in t'world than there is of abomination."

As a generalisation that may have been true, but it brought little comfort to the young woman who was with him.

The three whose faces were dimly illuminated by the glow from the kitchen grate in the Lodge of Half House rose simultaneously; Mrs. Blaydes to throw a piece of paper on to the fire so that she could see to thread a needle, her husband to open the door, and Adam because he was leaving, his departure accelerated by the goose which, from the day she had first been allowed indoors to sit on her eggs, had become a permanent inmate.

"Well, that's what they're doing at Dagger Gap, and t'marks of the planks are there, frozen stiff," the smelter repeated. "No question whatever about it, they're oft turning Foul Skye down Winterings Gill."

Powerful beak and long white neck darted out of the gloom beneath the table and, much to the amusement of the couple, Adam yelped when sharply nipped in the calf. "Hey, I'm off, Harry," he said, "and good night, Mrs. Blaydes. But think on to put that pet o' yours under lock and chain the next time I come."

"Pet maybe, Adam," Harry Blaydes chuckled, "but she's earned the bairns' clothes for this last year or two."

In Skewdale, bonfires were communal affairs, but the crackling pile at Half was a puny thing compared with the enormous erection in Winterings, whose fierce heat was of little comfort to property owners with panes of glass and paintwork to consider.

The Snorr bonfire, on the riverside below Badger Hall, was by no means a disgrace, and, as Adam neared, a blazing log tumbled into its heart, sending up a column of red sparks. A great tongue of flame followed, lighting up the umbrella-shaped tops of Scots pines and the white, ice-margined banks of the Skew.

He was kindly greeted by many people, but the party from Silence pointedly abstained. Mary Jane, who was having a very lively time pulling her grandfather's swallow tails, scampered to give him a youthful kiss, forerunner to an adult conversation on the domestic needs of Modesty. And Bob and Ward insisted upon taking him to the barn, to show him a sleepy litter snuggling against a soft-eyed mother. The boys were heatedly arguing the individual merits of the pups and a suspicion soon arose in both Adam and Mr. Skidmore, who looked in.

"Sounds as if you're noan having much say in t'selection," Anthony Skidmore laughed.

Potatoes were roasted, games were played, but when the fire was declining to a lurid glow and the last firework had fizzed into the air or thundered among the unwary on the ground, young and old trooped indoors. Mrs. Skidmore, with a pioneer's air, invited Adam.

While at the supper table Adam was involved in two matters of business, Jane Sunter telling him about the money she had received from the sale of his father's furniture. "An' we've brought the sea-chest, too," she said. "It's packed with your keepsakes just as you left it and I've got the key of course."

Rosie Caygill, who had been listening unashamedly, leaned across Cherry and wryly undertook to present him with another keepsake: twenty shares in the East Side Company. To her patent disbelief, he immediately offered to buy at ten shillings each. On this she took much convincing.

"No, I'll not run off my word, Miss Caygill," Adam promised. "But you'd better get proper advice first."

"If you really mean it I'd sooner settle t'deal now," the dressmaker said, pathetically eager. "You see, I've been wondering about a bit o' refurnishing, an' if I had the shares offen my mind I could tackle things wi' a lighter heart. Now take my front room carpet—of course I've a lot of callers . . ."

When a lady is garrulously-inclined it needs patience and time to bring her to the point, but eventually Adam succeeded in arranging that, on Friday week, Mr. Buckle's next day of attendance at the Plug and Feathers, they would meet there. The Corvy lawyer had seen to affairs when her father died.

Adam was not able to talk to Cherry about his latest interest in lead-mining until they were well on the way home, in Main Street, which smelled pleasantly of wood smoke drifting gently from the embers of the Winterings bonfire.

"Sort of to get a foot in the enemy's camp?" Cherry asked.

"Well, it might come in handy, lass," Adam agreed.

For the remainder of the walk to Yew Tree House they discussed Daniel, who, drinking Mrs. Skidmore's home-brew as though it were a light beverage and not a heady wine, had pursued Dinah to such purpose as to bring him within an ace of a fight, with Wingy Blenkiron.

* * * *

By eleven o'clock the next morning, Adam had completed a rapid trip round the principal workings and visited all the partnerships. A few minutes' conversation with Sam Kirkbride and Harry Blaydes in the office sufficed to initiate improvements in other directions, Simon and the smelter going off to the North Mill, while Daniel accompanied the engineer downhill towards the machinery store-house at the Great Deep Level.

This left Adam free to pick up the threads of affairs. The financial position was fairly satisfactory, but future prospects were less bright owing to the meagre amount of smelting which had been possible. But more than six hundred wagon loads of ore were stored in the mine, and so overtures to the big East Coast smelting concerns, with a view to selling to them as it was, seemed the soundest policy.

"It's oft done in Spain," he told Bart Hugill, who was much interested. "We used to ship thousands of tons of certain classes."

As he dictated, the clerk made a rough copy of the letter, and then noted down an order for dynamite, whistling both at the quantity and the price: two hundred pounds—at two shillings a pound as compared with black powder at fourpence.

"Now then, is there owt else, Bart?" Adam inquired. "I want to be down in Greets fairly early this afternoon."

The clerk produced a carriage account from William Nattrass, who, following the lead of the Wood Yard, had allowed credit, though to a more limited degree. The bill referred to the cartage to Corvy Station of pigs of lead, one of which had been lost in transit.

"I've deducted fivepence, that's t'charge for each pig," Bart pointed out. "The value of the pig at seventeen pounds ten a ton is eighteen and eightpence, but it's usual to leave that over till the next month, to allow 'em a chance of finding it." He received another surprise when instructed to deduct the larger item also, Adam explaining that on the way back from Newcastle he had seen Mr. Rutter, when it had been arranged for the auctioneer to buy two horses, so that the Company could make a start in carrying their own coal, pigs, timber and other requisites. "Another slap in the face for your Uncle William," the clerk grinned. "Well, he were soon demanding cash in advance when he reckoned things were worsening with us."

Preoccupied with ruler, pen and the deepening downstrokes of lovingly-fashioned figures and script, he failed to notice who was crossing Mill Bridge. Adam, too, was intently engaged, hence both looked round sharply when the rival company's agent stubbed his clog against the unfamiliar threshold.

Reuben Nattrass's stay was brief. He had called, he said, as a neighbourly courtesy between one mining-agent and another who had just resumed his duties. "And to inquire, of course, about that arm o' yours, Brunskill. I'se heard tell as it'll be a fairish time afore it's right shipshape again, and so I shall have to be patient. Yes, you're having no loopholes for excuses at after, an' all's going to be equal."

"That's very kind of you, Cousin Reuben," Adam smiled. "Aye, it'll be about three months if I'm careful.""

"Will it?" The East Side agent laughed derisively as he turned to leave. "All t'same, I'se a feeling as you'll noan be *too* careful, for I reckon you'll keep on dragging things along. Aye, the day as you'll admit you're i' fighting trim is a long way off, if it ever dawns, that is."

The office window had hardly been darkened by the passer when Bart burst out with a question: "Are you and him having a fight when you're better?"

"It's always been my rule, lad, to do my utmost to keep out o' scraps," Adam murmured.

The clerk's face fell. "Aye, I suppose it's wiser."

Adam was very solemn. "Takes all sorts to make a world, doesn't it?"

"Eh!" Bart ejaculated. He was left to sort that out.

The tradesfolk of Winterings were accustomed to entrusting to the local carrier monies for the payment of accounts with Corvy wholesalers, and when Adam entered the right-hand front room of Ash Grove, three people were there for that purpose.

William Nattrass's brusque: "Send young Hugill i' future . . . I don't want you here," secured precedence for the latest comer. It also meant that an audience was there to hear that the carrier had lost a customer.

"My words, William," Richard Blenkiron said sympathetically, "you an' George is having a bad spell just now."

The carrier's fleshy jowls quivered. "Do you think I care a damn about t'West Side lot's favours?"

"I never, *never* dreamed you'd take the blow so much to heart, Uncle William," Adam said.

William Nattrass's paunch, as he rose, tilted the table, sending an uncorked bottle of ink sliding to the floor. "Blow! It's no bloody blow," he roared. "An' you take yourself off afore I throw you out."

The blacksmith's sigh mourned departed youth. "We get older, William lad, and I doubt if you could. You were a rare 'un once, but I'se feared he'd make mincemeat o' you if you attempted owt."

"Would he, by God?" William Nattrass thundered.

To Richard Blenkiron's barely disguised disgust, Cuthbert Daykin advanced nonchalantly to remind the stables-keeper that a lady was present, "to wit, Mrs. Metcalfe."

"Oh, it's quite all right, Mr. Daykin," Emma Ann fluttered. "We all know some chaps is gentlemen and some isn't."

As Adam closed the front door he heard Richard Blenkiron, powerful voice overshadowing the triangular dispute, impatiently demanding attention for his affairs. The blacksmith sounded as if he had been cheated.

At the door of Yew Tree House Cherry was chaffering for a string of onions with a swarthy young man, and as Adam turned Ben down the main road he waved to her.

In Greets, he headed at once for a house opposite the stocks on the Green, but as Henry Hird was not expected home until evening he decided that, the courtesies fulfilled, he would return to Greets Hall. There Sir Charles was good enough to grant him an interview, with the very satisfactory result that he received permission to use the Rock Borer and any other machinery which would facilitate speedier opening out.

Well pleased, he rode in the gathering dusk to Winterings, where he watered and fed Ben before starting homeward. When approaching the Brig he glimpsed against the lighted windows of the Plug and Feathers an erect and well-known figure. Old Hannah was bound for Modesty and carried a gift, a roast chicken.

"Aye, I think I might as well go in wi' you," she agreed. "The shop-bell isn't exactly red-hot wi' ringing."

When Adam had lighted the lamp and stirred up the fire which, by arrangement, Bob and Ward mended on their way home from school, Old Hannah explained about the chicken, the fourth to be presented to her in four successive days, excluding the Sabbath.

"Folk give me a sight too much," she went on. "They do the same in a bigger way for t'doctor, leaving loads o' stuff when it'd suit him a lot better if they brought t'brass to settle their bills. Anyroad——"

Both glanced up when the back door banged and rapid footsteps resounded in the stone-flagged passage. Next, Daniel Dolphin appeared, grimy face scarlet with anger. "I've had a right row wi' my Aunt Ellen," he began abruptly, "because I said I were going to work regularly for the West Side Company."

Adam asked: "What were her objection, lad?"

"You," Daniel replied. "And if there's any crime in t'calendar of which you aren't capable she didn't name it. Aye," he eyed his friend with some grimness, "no wonder I oft grumbled to Simon an' Jane because you hardly ever answered my questions about her. How did the bother start between you, lad?"

Only after a prolonged struggle was Adam able to convince him that he had no idea, which further maddened the groover, who confessed he had hit back hard himself. "I told her I should damned well work where I liked, and to mind her own so-and-so business." He wound up by heatedly declaring that if his aunt remained in the same humour he would pack up and move in with Adam.

"Don't talk so daft, lad," Old Hannah remarked as she got up. "Why, it's nowt but a storm in a tea-cup as 'ul be over by to-morrow."

Staggered by this optimism, Adam twisted round to stare at the old lady who, having reached the doorway, was silencing Daniel most effectively. "Well, I hope you were exaggerating," she said through a narrowing gap. "It's nowt to boast about, speaking roughly to any woman."

With thoughts dwelling exclusively on her well-to-do niece, Old Hannah hurried down the path. On the Brig she muttered to herself: "The silly creature that she is," qualifying this with infinite pity: "Poor thing."

Some time later, after serving a customer, she returned to her warm little kitchen where, for a few seconds, she watched unseeingly the pendulum of the Dutch clock and its companion shadow on the wall. "Sometimes it's kinder to be cruel," she murmured. "Aye, I've let it go on too long."

An unpleasant decision made, she was able to relax, and the visiting cat, spending an evening with her, was invited on to her lap. She began to rock and he, claws slightly unsheathed until the motion became familiar, rocked obligingly with her in front of the fire.

With the routine operations of ore-getting, processing, and Dead Work under the responsible direction of trusted friends and enthusiastic colleagues of the 'committee,' Adam considered himself free to plan the next important move: the removal of Droughty Tom's pump. And so, after a very late tea, he unrolled a large-scale map and began to trace the most convenient tracks between Old Wife Shaft on Noggin Moor and Maybe Shaft on the opposite side of Winterings Gill.

"It's going to need a rare good team of horses to tug a heavy pump across there," he reflected. "Anyway, to-morrow morning I'll ride up as far as the lower slopes o' Spout Fell. From there maybe it'll be easier to pick out the best route."

This determined, he banked the fire with slack coal, and went along to Yew Tree House, where Cherry put aside the book she was reading and her uncle waved a churchwarden pipe in greeting. It was the old mine-agent's first smoke since his illness began.

"Now, lad, what's fresh to-day?" Mr. Alderson demanded.

"Nay, Uncle, wait till he gets that chair up," Cherry laughed.

The three of them were hardly settled snugly when Annamaria Rutter called. As she entered the kitchen Titus Alderson was heartily approving Simon's and Daniel's appointment, but, engrossed though he was, it was impossible for him to overlook her woebegone appearance. Eyes reddened with weeping, she seemed a young woman whose world had fallen round her ears.

"It's Arthur," she gulped, "an' I'm going everywhere to ask if anybody's seen owt of him, because he never went home last night. We . . . we were at t'bonfire here, and at after that we spent a bit o' time at Ash Grove with his Uncle William. Then he saw me home and came in for a short while . . ."

As she explained that on the walk to Half her young man had been even quieter than he had been latterly, Adam tried to catch Cherry's eye, succeeding in doing so when Annamaria, with a flash of her old spirit, spoke about her father in terms far from approving. It appeared that before leaving the Old Cow Inn Arthur had begged for a nip of whisky—according to Mr. Rutter afterwards the nip to which his daughter's young man helped himself had made serious inroads into a bottle.

"As if Arthur 'ud swig all that much," Annamaria said, up-in-arms. "But I can't help but think he must have felt poorly . . ."

Cherry followed Adam so shortly afterwards that, when she arrived in the office, the lamp had not been burning long enough to warm the glass chimney sufficiently for the flame to be raised.

"Cherry," he started off in the semi-gloom, "I've an idea that Arthur Nattrass may have tried to shift them two rails at that place we've sometimes called the First Knavery. In the Plug last night me an' Daniel gave him a scare about 'em."

Cherry shivered. "Do you mean he might have tumbled into the sump?"

"He may not even have gone there, lass, but as things are I shouldn't be comfortable if I didn't make a search," Adam said. "Now I'll have to collect a few oddments fro' Modesty and I'm wondering if you'd mind doing summat that 'ul noan be so pleasant—running on to Malaga and getting Daniel to himself somehow or other."

"Why, it's real important, so naturally I will," she replied with some indignation.

"Right, lass," nodded Adam. "Tell him I'll be waiting wi' candles and such-like as we'll need."

Cherry slipped out of the side door into Jom High Road, an old overcoat belonging to her uncle thrown around her shoulders. At the Bait House at the bottom she bumped into Mrs. Roberty Will's servant girl, dispatched to Cuthbert Daykin's shop. From her she learnt that Daniel was at home.

She quickly reached the semi-circular drive which led to the front door of Malaga. At that side the house was in complete darkness, but a shaft of light shone from the kitchen window. Puzzling about the best excuse she could make to speak to Daniel alone, her pace slowed, so that her approach was far too quiet to be heard by two women whose argument was rapidly drawing to a climax. From where she stood she could see the faces of Old Hannah and her niece, but although it felt dreadful to listen deliberately to the voices which carried clearly out of the larder ventilator, she soon began to think there might be some justification.

"That's noan the truth, Ellen," Old Hannah was saying sternly. "He'd always been a chap who went right to t'point when it were necessary."

"He didn't wi' me, choose how," her niece shouted.

Old Hannah never wavered. "Yes, he did, at least twice aforehand, an' he telled you again on the very eve of the wedding. But you swore you'd be waiting for him at t'Chapel the next day, because you thought that'd make him be there. Well, he wasn't, as he'd said."

"No, he were off wi' Mary Nattrass," choked Mrs. Roberty Will. "And I've hated him every minute since."

A black bonnet shook in dissent. "No, you haven't, lass," Old Hannah said sadly.

Furiously the younger woman turned. "Yes, I have," she gasped. "What do you think I've done?"

"Ached for him down t'years, Ellen," her aunt told her. "You were a bonny an' high-spirited lass all the young chaps tumbled over theirsen for, and you saw to it that Jim Brunskill did the same. But when he found out it were a mistake you were still determined to have him and thought you could bend him to your wishes, a quiet chap like he seemed to be. But that were where you misjudged him, just as lots are misjudging t'quietness of that lad of his as you've gone for tooth and nail ever since he came into t'Dale."

Mrs. Robert William Alderson was curing a ham. As if wearied of the subject she stretched for the rough salt on the kitchen table. "If I have," she muttered, "it's nobbut because of the sort he is."

"You went for him long afore you'd any chance to know what he were," Old Hannah replied. "An' though I can't pretend to explain why, I'se certain it's because he's the spit and image of his father . . . o' Jim Brunskill, th'only man you've ever loved."

Out in the darkness, the unseen witness did not hear the painfully whispered answer, but she saw Mrs. Alderson's quivering lips and heard Old Hannah's tender: "Now, love," which brought them clinging together, a silvery-white-haired old lady and an elderly woman with full bosom and a suspicion of dark down upon her upper lip, a woman whose sole remaining vestige of provocative young womanhood was a pair of passionate eyes.

A lump in her throat, Cherry stole away, towards the faint line of light she had noticed beneath the big double-doors of the coach-house. "So that's why she's always been so much against Adam," she mused, shaken by the poignancy of what she had seen and heard. "Course she's been wicked to behave as she has, but . . ."

Even as she talked to Daniel Dolphin a few moments later, she had not completely thrown out of her mind the tragedy of a woman who for always has lost the only man she could ever love.

The two candles burned sootily, but even in their dim light Adam perceived that the place had changed beyond recognition. From the Old Man's rise above, a thin stream of fine slither descended, dropping into a sump whose appearance was quite different, so broad at the eye that all the original margin had vanished, and with it the two tramrails which had been there. Arthur Nattrass, in the heavy sleep of exhaustion, trapped by two boulders which fitted round his ankle like a loose ring, lay on the sloping side, upon slackly jammed debris which might at any moment collapse into the remaining depths of the sump.

"He could have been suffocated," Adam murmured, a gleam in his eyes as he picked up a mine plan on linen. "A miracle nearly."

An increasing deluge from above gave peremptory warning that little time might be left. It was chancy work but they acted with the dispatch of men used to one another's methods: Adam, finding the best foothold he could, braced his back against the uppermost of the two big boulders and, when he thrust, Daniel dragged out the prostrate figure. Startled by the sharp awakening, Arthur Nattrass shouted incoherently as they carried him up, but, for a brief spell only, he was quite himself in the safety of the gallery.

From Adam he stared at Daniel. "Well, old cock-sparrow," he asked throatily, "who needs a few sovereigns now for a ticket to . . ."

He ceased abruptly, to gaze blankly at each of them before gaping with the widest of wide mouths at his surroundings, until a growing tumult made further retreat essential as hundreds of tons of rock thundered down.

The journey through the tortuous workings of the Old Man when so burdened was extremely arduous, but from the tail of Bucker Level progress was swift, to such purpose that shortly before midnight the rescued man was sitting in the front room of Modesty drinking a steaming glass of grog. While he sipped and looked vacantly into the leaping flames, the other two young men had a word together. It was decided that first thing next morning Adam would fetch Old Hannah, Daniel undertaking to go by a roundabout way to the mines, walking down to the Old Cow Inn to relieve Annamaria of her fears before climbing Heugh Syke Gill.

A moan from the swathed figure at the hearth attracted their attention. "How the hell did I get here?" Arthur Nattrass said feebly. "I'm . . . I'm a rare 'un for quaffing beer, but I've been mending my bad ways lately."

"Maybe we can bottom t'mystery if you tell us what you remember last," Daniel suggested.

"That's easy, lad," Arthur Nattrass grinned slightly. "Me and Annamaria wrapped up tight together in their passage just afore I kissed her good night . . . no . . . after that, just down the road, I hoisted my lamp to wave it at her afore she closed the door an' a few yards farther on I tripped over summat. It makes you wonder if I fell and injured my head, doesn't it?"

"And since then everything's gone, like?" Daniel murmured.

Arthur Nattrass's strength was visibly ebbing. "Aye, everything," he groaned, head beginning to sink. "It's terrible to lose your memory . . . but I'm noan in any state to . . . to discuss it now."

"Aye, the best spot for you is beneath the blankets, lad," Adam said. "And that's where you're off to."

Swiftly undressed and robed in a nightshirt belonging to his host, Arthur Nattrass was rolled into bed, to be joined a few minutes afterwards by a brownstone hot-water jar.

Downstairs again, his rescuers eyed one another. "He's foxing, you know," said Daniel.

"Yes, he's got shut of them rails all right," Adam remarked with some grimness. "But Cherry saw 'em when she were with me. Besides . . ." He pulled out a plan of Bucker Level and the ground to the west. The survey was stamped as the East Side Company's property and on it two lines of dialling points were plotted, their respective ends close to the Short Cut and the New Drift.

"By!" Daniel exclaimed, bending eagerly over the big dining-table, "that's damned useful evidence. His cousin Reuben's handiwork, eh?"

"Aye, I reckon we can say that, though it'd take more proving, I expect," Adam said. "But we'll keep all this to ourselves, including where we found him. Let him tell what tale he fancies—it'll rattle him all t'more if we're mum."

With an early start the next day in prospect it was as well to snatch as much sleep as possible, and Adam's battered horse-hair couch was already arranged as a bed when his friend left. Before then, however, Daniel had remarked wryly that his aunt would now have another cause for complaint, the disreputable hours he kept, but this he could well stand.

"On t'other hand," he went on pugnaciously, "if she goes on at me about that other matter any more . . ."

As it happened, Mrs. Robert William Alderson never again referred in terms of dislike to her nephew's association with Adam Brunskill.

2

The frost had eased a trifle and the fells to the south were becoming hazy, but the lower pastures were more clear. It was the mating period for the flocks, and, down there, a swirl of dingy grey movement, the tups were being allowed to the ewes.

On the high moors in the vicinity of Great Charity Shaft, Mr. Hesketh and several guests were out, but some minutes had elapsed since the last shot. The attention of all, the gentlemen no less than Will Skidmore and Luther Thwaites, was attracted towards a fight at Dagger Gap, where the East Side smelters had just broken ground. Scattering, the diverters of water ran to escape heartily-wielded sticks, none so frantically as their leader, Jonas Cottingham, determinedly pursued by Simon Sunter, who seemed to be making a very personal matter of it.

Two of Mr. Hesketh's friends were close to Adam, who, mounted on Ben, had been riding in great sweeps across Noggin Moor, to spy out from above the tracks along which the pump could be carried.

Mr. Joshua Crowther, one of the cottonbroker's intimates, chuckled as Simon Sunter, in an anciently-cut suit belonging formerly to Rosie Caygill's father, relentlessly followed his victim. "Aye, let him have it, lad," he remarked in a rich West Riding accent. "You know, Kit," he said very seriously to his neighbour, "I've known similar tricks when two or three mills drew water for their dams from the same beck. Some of 'em dry the next morning an' maybe just one suspiciously full."

The gentleman he addressed, a Mr. Ormerod, had lost two fingers when fighting with President Lincoln's armies in the American Civil War. Local people, however, were more interested in his fine house on the outskirts of Liverpool, from reports sent back to the Dale by a Yorrel family who had migrated into Lancashire. Such wealth contrasted strangely with another tale: of this friend and partner of Mr. Hesketh singing in the streets for coppers to support his wife and child.

"And what did the Crowthers of Bankdam do about it, Josh?" he laughed.

"Oh, it's never happened to us, Kit," grimaced Mr. Crowther, whose lively sense of humour was well appreciated in Winterings.

Frequent visitors, the two gentlemen knew a great deal more about the young fellow on the galloway than he would have imagined, and so, for a while, they talked to him with special interest. Then, in response to Mr. Hesketh's signal, Mr. Ormerod and his spaniels moved forward, while Mr. Crowther, muttering vaguely about "yon copse at the gill-side," put his gun down, seated himself on a tussock, and pulled out a small sketching-block.

From there Ben was headed towards the peat hags, where he was so mightily startled by the strident becking of a suddenly-surprised moor-cock as to become quite skittish until the North Smelt Mill was reached. There Adam paused for a few words with Daniel and Sam Kirkbride. The Rock Borer had been dragged up on round timbers from the machinery storehouse and they were stripping it down.

Adam next disposed of a matter with Bart Hugill, and then rode to Town Foot, where, without dismounting, he looked into the Smithy over the bottom half of the door. In anticipation of heavy demands, Richard Blenkiron was making ventilation pipes on a machine of his own contrivance which rolled the zinc sheets to the diameter required. Already a substantial number was stacked in a corner, together with the supporting brackets to be driven into the sides or roofs of workings.

The blacksmith seemed nonplussed by the invitation. "Aye," he muttered, combing his beard, "aye, I could be along at Modesty to-night. What exactly is it about?"

Adam apologised. "I'd sooner leave that over."

The older man hardly appeared satisfied, but made no further objection. "Anyhow," he rumbled, "how's that arm o' yours doing?"

"It should be as good as ever in a few weeks, Mr. Blenkiron," Adam told him. "And if it should ever be as I've to use it in a fashion you may have i' mind, I'll do my utmost to see you're present."

Before Richard Blenkiron recovered, horse and rider had wheeled about and were cantering along Main Street. Grinning broadly, the blacksmith resumed his task.

Adam's next calls were at Low Bands and Badger Hall, where, with Francis Harker and Anthony Skidmore respectively, he arranged to borrow horses for Sunday's big enterprise.

The first to arrive at Modesty were Len Rukin and Hugh Bearpark, but the other members of the Committee, together with Daniel Dolphin, Simon Sunter and Richard Blenkiron, were all there by eight o'clock. Within ten minutes Adam's hearers were all agog.

"But, friend," Freestone John protested, "if you've a legal right to Droughty Tom's pump, why go about it in this road?"

"What do you think 'ud happen to t'pump if it were announced we were taking it over in the ordinary way, John?" Bart Hugill inquired.

Sam Kirkbride nodded. "I reckon there'd be a nasty mishap at th'eye of Old Wife. Say a baulk o' timber tumbling down."

Richard Blenkiron had been cogitating about the proposition. His awed whisper, in one of his dimensions, was amusingly slight in volume. "Shifting without their leave a pump as 'ul shut down Jenny Incline Ground and play God's amount of havoc elsewhere! Why . . ." his feelings became too much for him, "why, Reuben Nattrass 'ul play blue hell about it, and his directors an' all. Talk about laughing here i' Winterings when they know . . ."

He missed Matt Tiplady's wink. "Nay, Richard," the groover censured him, "this is strictly business, but we can be sympathetic instead o' grinning."

Belatedly Mr. Blenkiron remembered that he, with Freestone John and

Sam Kirkbride, were of an older generation. "I'm sympathetic enough about the sad knock th'East Side's going to get," he boomed unblushingly, "but my duty comes first, doesn't it? I'm th'West Side's smith and as such I'll be needed wi' my crab and lifting gear an' so forth, shan't I?" He glanced irately at a company of men who, including his own contemporaries, were experiencing difficulty in keeping their faces straight, and must have realised that he had not carried them with him, for his voice rose. "But don't think I'm all that eager to be wi' you—as a matter o' fact I'se planned to preach in Greets, and I can tell you it's a rare sacrifice to give backword for an important engagement like that."

"Go on wi' you," Sam Kirkbride scoffed. "You wouldn't miss the fun if th' Archbishop were begging you to climb the pulpit i' York Minster."

When the laughter died away, which just about coincided with the fading of Mr. Blenkiron's sheepish smile, Adam got down to brass tacks. It was nearly half-past ten when the party broke up. The scheme by then had been worked out to the last detail.

* * * *

No one in Winterings during daylight on Saturday could have thought that anything unusual was in prospect. At the mines, before knocking-off time, the ' dries ' and changing-shops had their weekly swilling, and Lent Money was paid out in the ordinary way by both mining companies.

Inside Yew Tree House, however, the atmosphere was decidedly different in the afternoon. "Well, the wind's softish from t'west, so that means you'll have a bit o' bother with wheels sinking, lad," Titus Alderson was saying excitedly to Adam. "But the clouds are real low, so even if anybody were crossing the tops they wouldn't see the lights at Old Wife Shaft when you start lifting the pump to-night."

About then Mrs. Peacock arrived, and as the older folk began to talk together, Adam followed Cherry into the back kitchen, where she was making, for his convenience, a very early tea. While there, she told him what she had overheard at Malaga.

"Aye, and apart from her dislike of me, lass, it explains summat else as Hannah mentioned on my first evening here, the predicament my father were in," Adam murmured. "Of course he'd to run off that very night with my mother, when he knew for sure that Mrs. Alderson meant to be at t' Chapel waiting for him—to stop her finally. Well, I nobbut hope she leaves me alone fro' now on."

He left Yew Tree House as the light of the dark winter day was failing, and almost at once was accosted by Wingy Blenkiron, who abandoned a group silhouetted against the doorway of Smithy House to hasten across Town Foot.

"I can work through t'night if there's owt I could help with, Adam."

the postman said under his breath, but quickly added: "My father telled me, but I can keep my trap shut."

"Aye, you'll be useful, lad," Adam laughed.

Wingy, who looked delighted, then referred to a topic which was on every Winterings tongue, the strange misfortune of his cousin's young man.

"Have you ever heard owt like it? Arthur's mind a complete blank as to what he'd been doing!" he marvelled. "But what licks me most on all is why on all places he made his way to you at Modesty, Adam. That's t'next thing he remembers after leaving Annamaria."

"The brain's a peculiar piece of mechanism," Adam observed. "Any-road, we must trust that while he's been out of himself he hasn't done owt that 'ud land him in gaol."

Wingy Blenkiron guffawed. "Him and Annamaria's up to have their teas wi' us, so I reckon I'd better point out his danger."

Adam chuckled. "Don't give him the horrors by mentioning things like . . . well, treadmills."

"I don't know," the postman grinned. "There's nowt like drawing a vivid picture."

Smiling broadly as he pictured Arthur Nattrass's shock if, from a new and neutral source, such a suggestion were made, Adam went along to Modesty.

As full darkness fell upon Winterings, a handful of men slipped out of the village, to climb by self-chosen routes the pastures and fells until they came to the rendezvous on Noggin Moor.

When Cherry Dinsdale and Jane Sunter, a heavy basket of provender swinging between them, arrived at Old Wife Shaft, a good start had been made. At the sump of the shaft the donkey pump had been unbolted from its foundations and, in the glow from a cluster of lamps, they saw sheerlegs set up above the eye and a powerful hand-winch spiked securely to the ground.

Close to the point where the pressure pipe line from Sweet Tarn entered the hydraulic Engine House, an old building had been appropriated as a kitchen. A fire was burning briskly in an improvised fireplace when the two young women entered, and on it they quickly heated up an appetising stew of beef, mutton and potatoes, the main course of a repast to which everyone did full justice.

"Champion," said Richard Blenkiron, brushing crumbs of pastry from his whiskers. "Well, now you lasses have satisfied th'inner man of all on us I think we'd better get to work again. Adam, on second thoughts, I'd prefer the wire rope to a chain for reeving through that block."

Adam and Cherry were discussing arrangements about food for the next day, while Matt Tiplady earnestly warned Jane how much easier it was to deviate from a descending track than from one rising, particularly in mist or low cloud. She and Cherry, he insisted, must faithfully follow the grey gritstone however tempting another trail might seem.

"Or the last you'll see o' this earth will be from the level of your nose," he remarked gruesomely. "As you sink into a bog, I'm meaning."

"You're clear enough, lad," Jane shivered. "Isn't he, Cherry?"

"After that tale, we'll never dare shift a hairsbreadth to either side," Cherry agreed. "Anyhow . . ." she turned to Adam, "that's how we'll do it—Jane to-morrow morning and me th'afternoon. By then I think it'll be best if I make more or less for Maybe Shaft with the tea things."

"Well, we should be near by that time," Adam smiled. "Aye," he waved, "right-o, Mr. Blenkiron. And good night, lass."

Cherry smiled, too. "Good night, Adam, and good luck."

As the girls' lamp bobbed away into the darkness of the wild moorland, the yellow pinpoint of light quickly hidden by a swathe of cloud, the men resumed allotted tasks, down the ladders or on the surface. These efforts were maintained unceasingly until six o'clock in the morning, when the main body of the pump was hoisted on to a stubby, artillery-wheeled cart brought by Mazy Bill and Polly from Sir Charles' storehouse at the Great Deep. As dawn broke, other horses, in addition to the Company's, began to arrive: Mr. Harker in person led in two, and Bart Hugill came with three belonging to Anthony Skidmore. With the clerk was his brother, Rive Rags, who, however demented he might be, had recognised this as the Sabbath, the day he was taken out, and, although Bart got up in the middle of the night, his bed-mate had insisted upon rising too.

The cavalcade started out an hour before the bellringers of Greets ambled towards church, six pairs of horses strung out in front of the wagon. Sometimes the field of view extended a few hundred yards, but often the clouds so densely enveloped the company of horses and men that, on tracks abruptly winding, nothing else was possible except to wait for better conditions. In places the going was firm, elsewhere only the most strenuous endeavour prevented bogging-down, axle-deep. It was a see-saw journey, in which Richard Blenkiron was as often chaining wheels for sheer descents as he was risking his neck when inserting chocks to stop the wagon from slipping backwards on steep gradients.

By midday, with horses straining willingly and every spare shoulder bent to push when necessary, the pump had been taken to Smiddy Bridge.

Helpers and horses had left Maybe Shaft and the men who remained were those who would be actively responsible for lowering the pump. Tea was over and, pending Richard Blenkiron's return with extra gear from the North Mill, nothing much was being done. Sam Kirkbride, pipe stuck in his mouth, leisurely unloosed ropes holding the pump in position, and Simon Sunter busied himself with lamps, replenishing reservoirs and nipping off charred wicks.

At the side of a small but noisily bubbling beck, Adam was assisting Cherry in washing-up, but after rinsing the last pint-pot, he examined his watch. "It weren't so far from here, was it, that you found that gozzan, lass?" he asked. "We've time, an' I'd like to take a spade to the spot."

Windblown and flushed, Cherry looked radiant enough for the slight rings round her eyes not to be very noticeable. She had been very strenuously occupied lately, but the strain she was feeling arose much more from anxiety as to what Reuben Nattrass would do than from fitful sleep. Her fears about the East Side Company's agent were trifling compared with what they once had been, but never was she able to shake free from them completely.

A few minutes later they were higher up the moor, winding amongst the dead heaps and nigh indiscernible shafts of an ancient mine with an eerie reputation. For years it had been the tradition that hereabouts, on St. Thomas's Day, groovers could be heard shovelling bouse in the sump, eternal punishment for labouring at a holy feast.

At the opposite side of Worm Gutter, between that beck and Mirk Gutter, the next watercourse beyond, Cherry pointed to the hole she had almost slithered into when avoiding Reuben Nattrass. Without unduly taxing his right arm, Adam soon dug out a small heap of the reddish-coloured gozzan.

"Aye, it's here all right," he muttered, "cropping out o' the Crow Chert, I should think. But whether there's pay-ore or not is another matter. All the same, I'd like to hush it to find it, but . . ."

Standing together, the slight wind playing with tendrils escaping from his companion's bonnet, they stared down the fellside at the narrow ribbon of Winterings Beck. Instinctively, as if visualising what would happen if a great volume of water and debris tore downwards, their glances went farther along the gill, to the grey buildings of the East Side Company's dressing-floors and smelting mill at Smiddy Bridge below, just visible in the dying light.

"They'd take the brunt, and we'd have a claim for damages a mile long, apart from what happened lower in t'village," Adam said regretfully. "No, it's tantalising, lass, but we can't think on it."

Cherry laughed. "Why not turn the hush into one of these old shafts. Then nobody, neither the East Side lot nor the Lord, 'ul have anything to complain about."

"Some of the bargests as toils away in th'Old Man would," Adam replied, smiling. "How could they do a twenty-four-hour shift when their workings were watered to the roof?"

A mass of cloud obliterated their surroundings as they headed downhill, but the song of a waterfall gave them bearings, and thence they followed the course of the stream until the lights at Maybe Shaft suddenly loomed in front, their sole adventure throughout the descent an encounter with two or three languid creatures suffering from amorous excursions. But Cherry's stifled screech when her thigh brushed against a woolly but very bony skull persuaded the tups into action, and with a convulsive jump they disappeared into the gloom.

"Oh, Adam," Cherry breathed, releasing the arm she had involuntarily clutched, "that didn't half scare me . . . it's t'place, I suppose."

"Nay, lass," Adam said with disgust, "it were nobbut three of the Old Men up for a breath o' fresh air and a chaw of bacca."

"Less o' that, Adam Brunskill," Cherry said austerely. "Leastways till we get where there's some light."

They sparred until Maybe Shaft was reached, when it was ding-dong work for all, including Jane and Cherry, who prepared the men's evening meal.

Visiting preachers made happy use of Sunday jaunts to renew old friendships and the elderly groover planned for Winterings Chapel was no exception. Shortly before dusk he was sauntering along Main Street, after spending a pleasant hour at the West End, when he met Puke Hastwell against Blind Kit's. A trifle early for his appointment at the School House, to take tea, he was not averse to a chat, during the course of which he chanced to mention a matter to which he had given little thought at the time—in common with many other devout men, he believed that the Sabbath should be kept as a day of rest whenever possible, but had too much practical experience not to appreciate that mining concerns must sometimes depart from this sound precept.

The Wood Yard foreman, usually abundantly informed, tried to hide his surprise. He fished for further details. "But are you sure a Standard Davey pump were on t'wagon? You say you'd nobbut a brief glimpse through a gap in the clouds."

The old groover was tartly remarking that he had had over forty years in lead mining when one of the Coopers, Less Nor Nowt, clattered out of the alehouse down Calvert's Wynd. Sighting a probable informant, Puke Hastwell made inquiries.

"Well, we're doing nowt to-day, and I haven't heard as t'West Side lot is either. In any case they've noan got a Standard Davey to lug across Noggin Moor," the youngest of the three Cooper brothers replied. "Unless . . . " he revealed an irregular line of blackened stumps as he grinned, "unless that new agent o' theirs has done the trick t'same road as he gate all them shares." He was proceeding volubly with this theme, when suddenly, as he realised the feasibility, his eyes widened. "And he could have, couldn't he? By God, it makes you wonder."

"What does?" Mr. Hastwell snapped, anxiety about his East Side shares adding edge to his voice. "Come to t'point, man."

"I don't bloody well know," Less Nor Nowt retorted. "But I saw yon Brunskill and Droughty Tom wi' their heads together yesterday, an' Tom left all on a hurry afore nightfall—an unexpected call to one of his sisters, so he made out. But it rings damned queer to me, an' I'm off seeking out Reuben."

For that afternoon, by those careless of public opinion, a shooting competition had been arranged, and, the previous day, the targets for this, old wheels, had been taken to the juniper-fringed top of a steep pasture behind Middle Sorrow. But the cloud and mist varied chances so unfairly that the event had been abandoned; even with the best of visibility a good shot was needed to pepper a piece of paper tacked to a spoke when, in the speediest twenty yards of its run, a wheel bounded past towards Middle Sorrow and the Skew below.

Copious supplies of beer were provided for these occasions, and as soon as marksmanship became a farce, the company repaired to the most convenient barn. There Less nor Nowt took his puzzling news.

Though not on a drinking blind, Reuben Nattrass had taken enough liquor to dull his wits slightly, but, whatever his state, he would have had difficulty in entertaining the idea that anyone would ever have the audacity to treat him so. Nevertheless, while his companions argued, he thought hard. Conversant with the West Side Company's needs, he concluded that, if the incredible had happened, the pump would have been taken to one place only: Maybe Shaft.

"T'best thing is to find out," growled Cyprian Metcalfe. "One squint at the tail of Martha 'ul prove whether there's been any tampering."

"It's all bloody well," Nowt Much Cooper scoffed, "but some o' these blasted Bible thumpers rant so much about visions that it's as likely as not——"

"Martha Level first, lads," Reuben Nattrass said thickly. "That'll do for a start. Now let's sup up these other bottles and then we're off."

About twenty-five minutes later, Mark Iveson and his wife were considerably startled when overtaken by a number of men, who, after pounding over Dolly Bridge, shot across Town Foot to disappear into the gloom of Sorrow Near, their leader the big-built agent of the East Side Company.

A bellyful of ale is not the best preparation for arduous efforts, and it was an appreciable time before the party arrived at Martha Level, a score or more yards from which their ears told them all that was required to be known. The sounds of gentle water drainage, when the flow ripples softly over tramway sleepers, is very different from a steady outwards surge. Matches were struck, their brief light revealing the deep and dark volume flowing swiftly out of the level.

Reuben Nattrass's face was distorted. "Come on," he choked.

"By, but they've lifted t'pump out on Old Wife at after all!" Less Nor Nowt Cooper marvelled. "The water is almost to the height on a durk wagon, so what t'position is likely to be at Jenny Incline——"

In the darkness Reuben Nattrass spun round. "Keep your bloody mouth shut, Cooper," he bawled. "Save your flaming breath for what's ahead on us . . . you'll need it afore this roundabout tour's done."

It was a sound forecast. Cursing and floundering, the party ascended Winterings Gill, crossed the stream in swirling, waist-deep water, and then climbed on to cloud-blanketed, inky-black moors which were a nightmare even to those most familiar with them. The ground was treacherous, sometimes sticky with thaw, sometimes still ice-bound on the north-facing sides of gulleys, and ever was the fear of stepping too far into the engulfing arms of a bog. Lost more than once, it was seven o'clock when, appearing fleetingly as does a flash from a lighthouse in patchy fog, they glimpsed the yellow glow from an assortment of lamps about three-quarters of a mile away.

At Maybe Shaft there was quite a little crowd of men and their womenfolk in Sunday-best clothes. Grouped far enough from the eye as not to be a nuisance, they watched and discussed an operation which, known generally before evening service, had brought them hot-foot up rough tracks to the detriment of well-polished boots and trailing skirts.

Amongst the outsiders were Richard Blenkiron's daughter and Dinah Skidmore, who had been escorted there by Wingy. To the secret amusement of Jane and Cherry, who were packing crockery into a butter basket in readiness for returning to Yew Tree House, where Simon's wife was again spending the night, there had been differences between Wingy and Daniel Dolphin. These started quite good-naturedly when Daniel warmly thanked the postman for taking care of his young woman while he was absent. Wingy Blenkiron had replied in similar vein, but, as the banter proceeded, tones became sharper.

"*Adios*, and to hell with you," Daniel grunted, gesturing magnificently.

Wingy responded heatedly. "Aye, get on wi' thee, lad, and let's see what you can do besides jawing."

"I can do plenty," the groover from Spain rapped out. "An' if . . ."

With Adam, he was balanced dizzily on a plank spanning the eye of the shaft, his senior in the middle behind him, beneath the block dangling from the sheerlegs. It was hardly a position in which to gesticulate unduly, and the slender bridge was springing overmuch for the peace of mind of several nervous onlookers.

Adam glanced at his companion over his shoulder. "*Tenga cuidado con lo que hace*," he said, a plain command.

Daniel Dolphin bowed gracefully, but obeyed. "*Con muchísimo gusto, señor*," he murmured apologetically, taking care from then.

A wonderful voice was raised in *Under the Greenwood Tree*, but Matt Tiplady's song died abruptly when he was called to join the conference at the eye. A minute or so afterwards he and Richard Blenkiron disappeared down the timbered shaft, Adam's upraised hand, as he crouched trickily poised while gazing into the depths, checking the men who watched him alertly from the winch.

Just about then Freestone John picked up a piece of boarding and, the swaying ends each projecting six or seven feet, started to walk past the shaft. This, and the startled cry of a woman on the outskirts who first saw the wild face of the young man who raced by, was instrumental in saving both Adam and his friend. Daniel spun round, his hand diving to grasp the nearest weapon. Even at that he would have been too late had not Reuben Nattrass, deceived by uncertain shadows, collided with the wood carried by the Quaker. He recovered with amazing agility, but by then Daniel Dolphin's strong forearms were swinging viciously down.

Even the most savagely enraged man is chilled when his ear is brushed by a seven-pound sledge hammer wielded by one who knows that more than one life is at stake. Sobered momentarily, Reuben Nattrass recoiled. "You could have split my skull i' two with that, Dolphin," he roared.

"Aye, and us two could have been killed if you'd given either on us a dig wi' your little finger," Daniel retorted, sweat breaking out on his forehead. "Yes, an' more nor us, you God-damned lunatic. There's sixty-eight fathoms of air beneath here, and four chaps at the bottom who'd be pulped by owt heavy as fell down."

"What do you reckon you're doing?" Adam asked the mine-agent sternly, as a menacing murmur went up from a crowd shocked by the reckless onslaught. "Surely you've enough experience not to behave like a crack-pot when chaps are working in deepish shafts."

"Never mind about that," Reuben Nattrass snarled. "What I bloody well want to know is why you've shifted t'pump out of Old Wife Shaft. That's what you've done, isn't it?"

Quietly Adam explained that the pump had changed hands. "And as you've so oft telled Droughty Tom to take it out whenever he pleased, I thought I might as well do the same thing," he wound up.

Reuben Nattrass's mouth opened, closed, and opened again. "You mean as it's yours, Brunskill . . . as you've gone over the head of th'East Side Company and bought it offen him?" he said throatily.

"That's it," confirmed Adam. "And if you want proof as it's been done properly, I'll show it to any suitable person you care to name."

Adam's cousin was still too bemused for violent action to occur to him. "Maybe so an' maybe not," he muttered, licking his lips. "But there's one thing I'se certain you haven't bought, and it's the legal right to take t'pump out on Old Wife Shaft."

"That's summat as others more competent than you and me can decide," Adam remarked.

Reuben Nattrass's dark eyes began to glitter. He swayed backwards a trifle as if to prepare for a spring, but, keenly watched, was overwhelmed by a score of men, West Side men in dirty clothes and sightseers in broadcloth. Closely encircled, his glance never left Adam, who had taken no part in the fray.

"All right, Brunskill," he said, gulping in deep breaths, "you and me 'ul do the fighting another time. Aye, for this once I'll take a leaf out o' your copy-book . . . you're a dab hand at catching folk out wi' your letters, so this time I'll adopt similar methods. No scrapping . . . just lawyer's letters, that's all. An' by God, when you see t'claim for damages you'll get soon, as Miles Buckle 'ul send you . . . nay, what am I talking about . . . as he'll address to t'West Side Company at their registered office, you'll noan think quite so much of yourself in the future. No, you'll——"

"Oh, for Christ's sake, give over spouting," Bull Waggott spat prodigiously.

"Aye, we'll have to rouse 'em at the Roe afore *you've* done," Cyprian Metcalfe complained. "A nice evening's outing it's been, choose how."

With a thrilling story to relate, the throng soon started along the winding track across Water Ling Moor, and soon work at the shaft was resumed. It was thought that within a couple of hours the main body of the pump would have been lowered on to the bolts placed to receive it, a convenient stage at which to suspend operations for the night. Cherry and Jane, however, were sent home before that. Mounted on Ben, they rode down to Town Foot, where many small knots of people were talking in the darkness.

The next morning, before dawn, Reuben Nattrass galloped out of his father's stable-yard. Later, too bellicosely cocksure to convey complete conviction, William Nattrass allowed it to be known that his son had gone to Corvy, to be in attendance there when Mr. Buckle's office opened.

3

The mood of Sir Charles Grafton's agent was awkward rather than ill-tempered as, in the Weigh Place at the South Mill, the royalty lead was weighed. As each pig passed over the scales, he impressed it with his employer's mark, using a hammer the striking face of which was embossed, in reverse, with the initials C.G. and a boar's head, these signs of identity being contained in a circle.

"No, I'm noan saying your production isn't improving," he agreed with palpable reserve. "But it's nowt when all's said and done."

Bart Hugill glanced hopefully at Adam, who neither then nor afterwards permitted himself a rejoinder ranging on the provocative. Both of them knew that the real bone of contention was that Mr. Hird had not been notified in advance of the removal of Droughty Tom's pump. He reverted to this subject after stamping the last pig.

"Did you think I couldn't keep my own counsel, Brunskill?" he grumbled, as the men who had assisted in the weighing left.

Adam smoothed this over by presenting the alternative aspect. Would not the royalty agent have insisted upon less unorthodox methods, and might not some untraceable but absolute catastrophe have occurred to the pump?

Latterly Henry Hird had been more guarded in challenging the West Side Company's assistant agent. "Aye, it could have," he grudgingly admitted. "But don't get th'idea you're out of the wars, Brunskill. This is far beyond the question of a dispute betwixt the two companies . . . all Jenny Incline is flooded to the roof and it'll have to be made good. And you're noan bound to be in the right just because you've paid some brass to Droughty Tom. The law is funny, and . . ."

"I'd better show you summat, Mr. Hird," Adam observed with great gravity. "In strict confidence, of course, though naturally I've no objection to your mentioning it to Sir Charles."

Henry Hird brightened. "Oh, it'll be kept confidential," he promised.

On the evening Adam had justified at Modesty the exploit he proposed, the papers in that matter had been examined by all present, including Bart Hugill, who just then was checking against the royalty-agent's book. Despite this, he was impressively asked to leave the Weigh Place, on grounds that important information was to be placed at Mr. Hird's disposal. With set face, the clerk did as he was bid, but grinned from ear to ear when in the seclusion of the office.

Mr. Hird, distinctly placated by this deference, became more mellow. "Well," he murmured later, handing back the receipt for the pump and other documents, "well, I'm no attorney, but I should be inclined to say you've got everything tied up there."

"Anyhow, there it is," Adam said, not hiding his gratification. "Of course, I'll keep you fully posted about all subsequent developments."

"Do, lad," the royalty agent said warmly. But his expression began to change as he brooded about Reuben Nattrass's continued absence. "Well, I'd better be off, lad," he resumed abruptly, chafing under a sense of slight. "The day's getting on and I've still to talk to somebody at t'other side of the beck."

Adam accompanied him across the Mill Bridge and past Big William, beyond which, near Sam Kirkbride's house, he thoughtfully watched the royalty agent ride away. Gradually, he reflected, things were swinging to the advantage of his own company and to the detriment of the East Side.

"But I must shove on even more pressure somehow," he told himself. "Summat 'ul break if I do, and so long as I'm sure of my ground, it'll noan be us."

He nodded to himself, and then wondered where to go next before sitting down to prepare a report for presentation to the directors at the meeting in Half House that evening. Already he had visited the ore-getting places and the point in Notion Level to which the Rock Boring Machine, *en route* to the New Cross Cut, had been energetically hauled, and everything was proceeding apace in the vicinity of Maybe Shaft, where men were working like beavers, repairing the pressure pipe from Deer Pot, overhauling the hydraulic plant in the Engine House, installing pipes down the shaft, and putting the final touches to connecting up the pump.

"I'll see how Simon's getting on," he muttered.

Dust was thick in the air of the North Mill annexe where Simon Sunter, with five men labouring for him, was demolishing two ore-hearths to provide space for a more efficient one. The smelter, who broke off now and then to shout a word of guidance, told his friend the minimum necessary, obviously eager to get back to his job.

Well satisfied, Adam went outside again, where he examined a load of mine timber just arrived from the Wood Yard before crossing Mill Bridge to the office. He had hardly lighted up his pipe and taken foolscap from a drawer when a very young lady entered, her cheeks glowing with exercise and lovely grey eyes bright with excitement.

"Hallo, Mary Jane," Adam smiled. "Burnt Modesty down?"

"No, that's noan it," Bart Hugill grinned. "This is the day she cooks your tea, isn't it? She's up to remind you that if you aren't home on the dot everything 'ul be ruined."

Mary Jane surveyed them. "My, we are funny, aren't we?"

"Don't be too hard on us, lass," the clerk begged.

Miss Tiplady pointed out that it was full time that someone was hard on them. "You're both supposed to be working, aren't you?" she said. "Wi' pipes stuck in your mouths!"

Adam nodded. "Aye, men have it easier, love. Now with women . . . well," he coughed, "*their* work's never done, is it?"

Mary Jane drew an indignant breath. "That's noan t'first time you've picked summat up as I've said, Adam Brunskill, and imitated me at after."

Bart's bout of chuckling ceased immediately he heard her message. She and Adam started out at once, running hand in hand down Mine Road and Sorrow Near but separating at Town Foot, where Mary Jane went off on her own business. Clustered about the Smithy were a score or so of groovers and trammers whose working places were in Jenny Incline Ground; as the West Side's assistant agent crossed towards Yew Tree House a few scurrilous words were shouted at him. It was noticeable that even these were half-hearted—as once before, knowledgeable opinion in Winterings had pronounced in his favour.

The previous evening it had been quite late when Jane and Cherry rode down from Maybe Shaft on Ben, and still later when they went to bed, for Mr. Alderson had insisted upon every detail being repeated. Even then, when snug upstairs, the two young women continued to whisper, but the result was not that they overslept; both woke unconscionably early, so that Jane was able to set off to Yorrel much sooner than she had expected, and Cherry's Washing Day went so well that, aided by a good drying wind, she was ironing shortly after dinner. In this she was assisted by Mary Jane Tiplady, who had arrived slightly up-in-arms about her Aunt Susan—Mrs. Will continued to be adamant in insisting upon the Tipladys' weekly washing being brought to Blenk Bottom Lane.

Fully-dressed, the master of the house was sitting by the fire, partially hidden by clothing hanging from the rack. From this retreat, however, he was conversing with the visitor. "Well, if you're noan yet allowed to do your own washing, love, couldn't you have gone to school for a change?" he asked.

Mary Jane appeared through a gap. Carefully she made a nest in the fire for the reception of the second iron. "Oh, I think I know as much of t'three 'R.s' as I shall ever require, Mr. Alderson," she said.

"But how do you know what you'll require?" Titus Alderson smiled.

Bending over the kitchen table, which had been drawn nearer the window, Cherry brushed aside an annoying strand of hair. "Nay, Uncle," she protested, "surely you haven't forgotten what she's going to be?"

Fortunately Mr. Alderson remembered. "Of course . . . a farmer's wife, eh?"

Mary Jane barely troubled to nod. "Aye, and for that, if you've good cheese hands, an' know what to do wi' the hens when they're noan laying, and such-like, you'll noan go so far wrong, will you? 'Course you must be able to write out your bills and add up other folks', to say nowt of reading t'local news in the weekly paper of a Saturday."

Concealed by the dangling legs of a pair of lace-edged drawers, Cherry was fighting to stifle a giggle when her attention was attracted by the click of the gate. Glancing out of the window she saw Mr. Buckle and Reuben Nattrass walking up the path. Her thoughts first flew to the generous display of feminine underwear and, while Mary Jane went to the door, she darted between table, rack and clothes-line across the mantelpiece. And so, when the lawyer and his companion were ushered in, Titus

Alderson and his niece were ready to receive them, the former standing up and the latter richly flushed. Mr. Buckle, while civil enough, was plainly not in a good humour, but had not gone far when Mr. Alderson held up a restraining hand.

"I'm afraid I can't discuss t'matter except in the presence of my assistant," he said. "I'm behind him, of course, in everything he's done, but all to do with the pump is summat as he'll best explain."

"Where is he?" the Corvy lawyer inquired testily. "This affair is exceedingly grave, and I have been compelled to leave my office without a moment's notice—these *infernal* lead-mining heart-breaks and quarrels."

In the absence of Ben, who had been loaned to Richard Blenkiron so that he wasted as little time as possible when moving to and fro along the pipe line between Deer Pot and Maybe Shaft, it was not easy to get speedily into touch with Adam, and as a result, the next hour, while Mary Jane went for him, was insufferable to Cherry, who had to cope with a renewal of the persuasive attack in which Reuben Nattrass had been interrupted on the evening of Annamaria's birthday party. Her uncle had opened his last hoarded bottle of whisky, and he and Mr. Buckle settled down to an argument on the origin of certain customs peculiar to upper Skewdale. Throughout this, though keeping his voice low, the East Side's agent relentlessly pressed his pleas on her. She was unutterably relieved on hearing a familiar step on the path.

Within three or four minutes the representatives of the East Side Company had left. On learning their purpose, Adam simply handed to Mr. Buckle a few papers. Bending closer to the lamp lighted by Cherry, the lawyer carefully perused the documents before passing them back.

"The one which I imagine is your handiwork could have been more elegantly phrased, Brunskill," he observed bleakly, "but as a legal instrument I should pronounce it quite valid. Well . . . we won't detain these good people any longer, Nattrass."

Stupefaction, nothing else, showed on Reuben Nattrass's face. "You mean we can't do owt, Mr. Buckle?" he swallowed. "*Nowt?*"

"Nothing!" snapped the lawyer. "But don't think I hold you culpable in any way. The blame for this belongs to myself and the chairman, because we should have seen to the regularisation of a position clearly unsatisfactory. As a matter of precaution we ought to have investigated more closely the reports of your father and your Uncle George on their interviews with the owner of the pump."

As the gate shut, Mr. Alderson put away the bandanna with which he had been wiping his forehead. "Well, Adam lad, thank t'Lord that that's over," he murmured. "I don't mind admitting I've been sweating sin' Saturday as to what 'ud be th'eventual outcome. I think that's what kept me quiet while Reuben Nattrass were here."

It was too late to return to the mine and so Adam produced his rough notes for the directors' meeting. While these were discussed, Cherry ironed such innocent items as pillowslips and flannel shirts. Before the necessity arose of deciding whether articles of a more gentle and fancy nature could be smuggled in, she noticed the grandfather clock. The consequence was that Adam was somewhat startled on being firmly informed he must leave at once.

She dimpled at his patent astonishment. "Hadn't you to be somewhere . . . 'dead-on?'"

Adam stared before grasping her meaning. "By Jove, I'll have to skedaddle," he then exclaimed. "Any idea of what the feast is?"

"Chops," smiled Cherry. "And mince pies, warm. I think they're a sort of trial."

"So's she'll be able to do better when she makes 'em for Christmas," Adam grinned.

"Now then, that little lass does wonderfully," Titus Alderson reproved them. "So don't you two run her down."

This misinterpretation had to be dealt with. "We shouldn't think o' doing, Uncle," Cherry protested. "She's as grand a lass as . . ."

Adam left them to straighten out matters between themselves.

On the provisional quotations provided for them, the West Side Company's directors approved Adam's proposal to sell the accumulation of bouse, and he was empowered to treat with smelting firms at Stockton and Newcastle, setting out from Winterings for that purpose the following morning. It was decided also that the best means of transporting more than two hundred tons of ore to Corvy Station would be by traction engine and trailer.

Previous to this Adam had reported generally—production at Mary Forehead was still rising and, by the next afternoon, the New Cross Cut would be pushed forward by power borer and dynamite. The outlook for the re-opening of the North Sun Vein Ground was promising, too, and it would not be long before the pump purloined from the East Side Company was making effective inroads on the flood water there.

At this, Mr. Rutter was overcome at the thought of Mr. Storey, compelled to dip into scanty resources for a new pump at Old Wife Shaft. "Seven fits he'll have," he rocked. "Be up here putting things right, in them rags of his, i' them rags."

Mr. Wade was not much of a Christian either. "If they attempt to keep going, that is," he guffawed.

Officially speaking, the meeting ended shortly afterwards, but the yarn spinner, as he lifted a tray from the massive sideboard, took up the matter of the assistant-agent's loans. The balance, he said, would be cleared at once, and Adam was to be re-imbursed further, for what he had paid Droughty Tom.

"So you'll have got back all your ill-gotten gains, Brunskill," he laughed. "Moreover, as a mark of the directors' approbation of the vigorous fashion in which you are conducting the company's business it is . . . er . . . suggested that as from the next Pay you will receive a salary at the rate of a hundred a year."

"Thank you very much, sir," said Adam. "I greatly appreciate t'remarks you've made an' I'll do my utmost to keep on the same road."

The undertaker glared. "The labourer's worthy of his hire, isn't he?"

"I hope so, Mr. Kearton," Adam replied.

"There's no hope or question about it," Edmund Kearton persisted. "If a chap's doing his job——"

A cork plopped and Mr. Wade hastily wagged a bottle. "Kearton," he intervened hospitably, "you'll not refuse a drop?"

"I don't think I will, Mr. Wade." The undertaker's solemnity relaxed a trifle. "There's nowt like it afore a walk on a November night."

Mr. Rutter cackled. "Why, it's been one o' them close winter days when flies appear fro' nowhere. Warm as spring, warm as spring."

The undertaker dourly measured all that was visible of him above the table. "An' what are you insinuating by that, Martin?" he inquired at last. "Now don't hesitate—let's have t'worst. I'se a sot, is that it?"

Mr. Wade gesticulated fiercely at his co-director who, dimly perceiving he had blundered, at least had the wit to invent a line of appeasement.

CHAPTER FIFTEEN

I

As early as the Wednesday of Adam's absence from Winterings pumping operations at the North Sun Vein Ground were proceeding so satisfactorily that many members of East Side partnerships, out-of-work, made inquiries about places. Doubtlessly Reuben Nattrass was angered, but he said little either in regard to this or to do with Henry Hird's pursuit of him; nor did he comment much about the attendance he was compelled to dance daily upon his chairman. All this, so shrewd people asserted, was because he was still mightily relieved at not being blamed for the second misfortune his company had suffered. The East Side Company was indeed in a critical state, and shareholders' depression was not lessened by an advice of a Special General Meeting.

A smaller item of news was the death of Chesty Geordie's cow, a crippling blow which left the old groover with only the Provident Society's two shillings weekly. A whip-round to raise funds was suggested, but quite a few pointed out that, although willing enough in his mining days to pay one and fourpence monthly to secure himself if injured, he had stubbornly refused, since becoming a cow-keeper on retirement, to join the Cow Club, the small subscription to which would have insured him against his present loss. In the end common humanity won the day.

Adam's trip was quite profitable. He was able to come to fair terms with a Stockton firm of smelters, and fortune favoured him in the search for a disengaged traction engine. On his return to Winterings Mr. Alderson listed for him those who might be willing to hire out horses and carts to carry ore from the mines to Town Foot and, as sequel, a force of eleven vehicles began work the following noon. By that evening a respectably-sized mound of ore had been stacked at the foot of Sorrow Near, opposite the front door of Smithy House.

* * * *

For Simon's convenience, the Sunters had moved to his Aunt Minnie's, this greatly to her pleasure and secretly not unwelcome to Jane's Aunt Rosie, who had discovered that a small child can be something of a handful in a house. Miss Caygill, however, made rather a fuss outwardly, carrying this so far as to walk down to Badger Hall a day or two later to ascertain how little Bessie was supporting the change. While there, almost certainly the real motive for her visit, she mentioned to her niece's husband that the next day was Mr. Buckle's 'second Friday in the month.' Simon duly reminded Adam of this the next morning, as they sheltered in a doorway of the North Smelt Mill.

"No, n-n-not till six o'clock at the Plug," he said. "You s-see, Mr. Buckle's stopping overnight, b-because Mr. Storey's staying on here I suppose."

"I'll be there, lad," Adam bawled.

A fierce south-westerly gale whistled round the eaves of buildings and carried splashes from the upper buckets of Big William to the opposite side of Winterings Gill. Great masses of cloud scudded quickly from view, but as yet they brought nothing more incommoding than stinging splathers. The change came by early evening, when Adam, pursued by flat-driving rain, hurried over the Brig towards the agonised sounds made by the wildly-swinging sign of the Plug and Feathers, a sovereign bag in the pocket of his overcoat. In the peace of the inn, where the usual bright wood fire burnt on the hearth, Mrs. Peacock beamingly greeted him with the news that Rosie Caygill was in the dining-room.

The transaction was soon completed, the lawyer having already made it abundantly plain that, as opposed to advantage being taken of the dressmaker, the boot was on the other leg. This continued to disturb his client, who referred to Adam's friendship with her niece and Simon; he was a stranger to the Dale, too, she added.

"I hope as you'll noan regret it, lad. Th'East Side Company's in a mess now, and if at the Special Meeting——"

Adam smiled. "That's all right, so don't you worry, Miss Caygill."

"No," Mr. Buckle grunted, "you may be sure he's not doing it blindfold. Though . . . H'mmph!"

Solaced, the dressmaker eagerly pulled off her gloves, signed her name and then, clutching a bulging purse, tripped away happily. Whereupon Mr. Buckle with scant success endeavoured to discover why good money had passed for highly dubious shares.

"Well, there's noan so many, Mr. Buckle," Adam murmured. "If the worst comes to the worst I shouldn't have to stump up more than I could."

The lawyer sighed as he shook hands, heartily wishing his own liability were no greater.

The bar of the Plug and Feathers was lively with laughter when Adam re-entered. Puke Hastwell, chief collector for Chesty Geordie's fund, looked very pleased with himself, as well he might in view of the fact that the members of the shooting-party had contributed between them the balance required to provide the old groover with another beast. The shooters, too, as always when in the Dale, were in high spirits, despite a raging wind spoiling sport on their last day, and when Mr. Storey and Reuben Nattrass came in, both dripping wet, Mr. Hesketh and one of his friends started solemnly to pull the tatterdemalion banker's leg.

Solemn himself about lead-mining, Mr. Storey began to exhort them to buy a few shares in the East Side Lead Mining Company.

"Not as an investment I recommend—heaven forbid I should suggest that, gentlemen, but as a means of bringing a new and very unique pleasure into your lives," he urged. "There is nothing, *nothing*, so fascinating as lead-mining: the search for the fugitive mineral, the thrill of giving battle to elements which strive to deny you your way, the risk, the adventure, the comradeship of men with whom one joins in the hazard . . . one for all, all for one . . ."

The precise-featured banker was flushed with enthusiasm, and the excited pitch of his voice soon attracted attention, not least that of Mrs. Peacock, whose lips tightened on glimpsing his mouldering rags. Peremptorily she rapped a coin on the counter. "Mr. Storey," she cried sharply, "I mentioned summat to you when you came in last night, didn't I?"

The banker, interrupted in a piece of telling narrative, turned irritably. "My good woman," he snapped, "have you never seen a groover before?"

At this condescending form of address Lucy Peacock's expression became more alarming. "Never mind about that, if you please," she observed. "Instead, remember what I said about young servant girls being here."

The laugh which went up, not quite successfully smothered, thoroughly annoyed the banker. Curtly he demanded what was wrong with his attire.

"Nowt, in t'right place, but what do you reckon changing-shops is for?" the mistress of the Plug and Feathers asked. "And you're half-frozen anyroad."

This could hardly mollify a man who prided himself on a toughness in keeping with that of the great lead-mining adventurers of the past. The resentful reply was such that Mrs. Peacock turned her head quickly, in which attitude she began to pat a coil of jet-black hair.

"Good God, madam, here am I descending into the bowels of the earth every day, seeking exhaustively to find, if it be possible, the speediest method of putting men to work again, and what do you chide me about?" Mr. Storey raved. "A few trivial tears in my garments . . . yes, a paltry tear or so. Really, my good woman——"

"Now I'm noan one for vulgarity, Mr. Storey," Lucy Peacock intervened, "but I'm telling you summat as you've forced me into. Nobody i' Winterings bothers about a few tears, but——"

"Why all this commotion then?" her victim wanted to know.

The mistress of the house went on inexorably, "Because there's tears *and* tears," she replied angrily. "An' you've got one in a place as any gentleman 'ud do well to make sure were properly covered."

At this stage, with very great presence, she had the good sense to retire to the kitchen. For his part Mr. Storey, who looked horror-struck after a glance downwards, drank at one draught a glass of rum before retreating in not quite such good order. An overjoyed company behaved most commendably until the door closed, when shooting-party and locals alike rocked with mirth.

Within a matter of minutes two further incidents occurred, each likely to provoke subsequent discussion. Henry Hird stamped in, ill-humour in every line of his heavy face, promptly to single out Reuben Nattrass, whom he accused of avoiding him these last days. A short but sharp row ensued in which the younger man, who had suffered Mr. Storey's amateurish suggestions for almost the whole of the week, said a lot more than was discreet.

A party of eight men arrived next, the drivers and others of the afternoon shift at Brunskill's Cross Cut, every man-jack grinning broadly. Such an invasion could mean one thing only: a claim for the traditional reward of gin by those who had participated in the successful completion of a trial.

"Aye, we've hit the sump o' Doomsday High, Adam lad," Daniel Dolphin said delightedly. "Bang in the middle and all."

This was indeed important news, and passed quickly round the bar. Groovers, retired or active, pressed forward avidly for particulars, and Mrs. Peacock, good temper restored, served brimming and quite uneconomic measures in response to Adam's order.

Reuben Nattrass, whose black scowl derived entirely from Mr. Hird's persistence, endeavoured to shake off the royalty agent by ironically congratulating Adam, but was thwarted; Sir Charles's representative was difficult to deny once he had the upper hand.

The intersection with Doomsday foreshadowed the proving of Jamie's Mint, and, as the buzz of speculation continued, Adam secured a few private words with Daniel. "We'll follow this up during t'week-end, lad," he said.

"Aye, so long as I can have a couple of hours off, say after one o'clock Sunday School," his friend nodded.

"Summat on?" Adam smiled.

"In a manner of speaking," Daniel grinned. "Trying conclusions you might call it, in a little matter as has been baffling me for a while."

Knowing his companion of old, Adam did not delve, and, after making arrangements for the next day, left the Plug and Feathers. Driven on by the fierce wind he quickly reached Old Hannah's shop, where to his surprise and pleasure he found Cherry, bonnet and mantle discarded, sitting with the old lady in front of a fire roaring breast-high up the chimney. Both were elated with what he had to tell them.

"Uncle Titus'll be nearly out of his head," Cherry glowed. "And you're pushing forward this week-end to spy out what there is?"

"Yes, but that's between us lot," Adam said. "So far as your uncle's concerned we're noan beginning owt until Monday, an' by then I hope we'll have learnt all that can be learnt."

"Aye, excitement's noan good for him and that 'ud save him," Old Hannah approved. "Anyway, lad, sit you down an' we'll light up. You and me is having a big cigar apiece, out o' them Mr. Hesketh gived me."

While she cut off the ends of the cigars with the bread-knife, and Adam carefully made a narrow paper spill, the conversation was very light-hearted, but later became more serious, extremely so when Blind Kit joined them after calling in at the shop to buy snuff.

"Well, I nobbut hope you make a right good discovery at Jamie's Mint," Old Hannah said as she sat down again. "And what next then?"

"Get th'ore out if it's there," Adam stared innocently.

The cobbler's super-sensitive ears must have picked up more than the simple nature of the inquiry suggested. Carefully he put aside the glass of ginger wine he had been sampling. "I think, lad, she's wanting to know when you'll be able to take up t'question o' them rails," he said. "It sticks in both us gullets does that dirty business."

Cherry leaned forward. "Adam's idea, Kit, is that, important though it is, it has to take second place for the time being to putting the company a bit more on its feet. Uncle Titus agrees with him, though he naturally longs for the stain that's on him to be cleared as soon as possible."

"Think you'll be able to pull it off, lad?" Blind Kit asked.

"I don't know," Adam admitted. "But it's noan going to be many weeks now afore I have a shot, if we've a bit o' luck to help on, that is."

Old Hannah winked at Cherry. "He's a right 'un to talk about luck, isn't he?"

"Just jumps into everything haphazard, without a moment's thought aforehand," Cherry supplemented.

"Hey!" snorted Adam. "Are you two lasses seeking trouble . . ."

The cobbler did not take any part in the spirited rallies, thrusts and counter-thrusts which ensued, but his abstraction, quite noticeable, was explained afterwards at the end of Calvert's Wynd, as far as which he accompanied the young people.

"Well, Adam lad," he observed gravely, "all I can say is that I hope you'll nail that cruel trickery on to them who's responsible. And when you do, may God gird you so that t'wrong-doers are struck as low as they deserve."

Broadminded and far from fanatical, Blind Kit was nevertheless a very sincere believer in the value of condign punishment.

* * * *

The stricter of Skewdale's Sabbatarians had recently been considering what action might be taken against the West Side Company for too frequent desecrations of the Lord's Day. During the week-end following the break-through to Doomsday High Shaft these tight-laced folk had ample reason for further complaint.

About Saturday noon, Winterings was aroused by the thunderous sounds, echoing and re-echoing in the hills, made by a big traction engine majestically puffing up the main road. That afternoon and on the Sunday, despite the continuous rain, people flocked to Town Foot to inspect the fine engine; on both days sightseers saw Hugh Bearpark and Richard Blenkiron busily reinforcing the trailer to fit it for carrying ten tons of ore, fixing iron sheeting on the bottom and iron brackets at the sides.

That Saturday morning Adam went to the sump of Doomsday High Shaft, and from there, when Daniel had dynamited a passage, along a slant-rise. This upward slope brought the party to the head of Captain Tregoning's Stoping, an undertaking which, winning ore as it proceeded, had replaced the shaft sunk by the legendary Jamie. The stoping was a series of mighty steps, dropping sharply with the dipping vein. Hewn out of the rock, the steps were each about as broad as they were high, around five feet, and when Adam and his companions began to descend, the massed light from their candles failed to illuminate properly the lowermost.

Len Rukin bit off a heedless whistle. "I know what I'm puzzling about. If there is pay-ore there, how 'ul we get it up?"

Grimly Matt Tiplady agreed as he glanced up and then down the formidable terraces. "It'll be a problem, lad. Seems to me th'only thing to do will be to have a man on every stoping shovelling up to t'next one above him . . . which 'ud just about swamp all the profit."

At the foot of the stoping Adam stared at the narrow cavern stretching ahead. Jamie's Mint was about four yards wide, and perhaps a hundred yards long. If anything the thin strip of water was reminiscent of a lengthy canal lock, darkly roofed in. The most important factor was that the water everywhere was smooth, and only in one place did a small stream of bubbles reach the surface. The powerful onrush which had driven out resolute groovers in days gone by had ceased, and to lift out the water to ascertain what might lie in the sole was merely a matter of manual labour.

"Aye," Sam Kirkbride concurred when he mentioned this. "We could get hand-pumps into position by latish to-night, wi' outflow pipes running to the top o' the stoping."

"We'll do that," Adam muttered, peering at an old plan.

Daniel's head came closer, the candle on his hat adding to the lighting-up of a workmanlike job penned many decades before by some meticulous surveyor. He looked where Adam's finger had stopped, three-quarters of the distance along the gallery known as Jamie's Mint, on a circle marking a sump. "Bottomless Sump!" he exclaimed. "Sounds as if it might be real deep."

"I've heard my father speak on it," Sam Kirkbride said. "Of course he had it by hearsay."

"When we've got shut of the main body o' water, we'd better pump it out as well," said Adam. "The more we know the better."

Ten minutes' further conversation sufficed to cover most foreseeable contingencies, and then, each quite clear upon his part, they straightened from crouching positions. As one man, before clambering on to the tread of the lowest step, they stared up the stoping, necks craned back, when Matt Tiplady remarked that though it might be possible to hew out a tramroad bed up the middle of the terraced height, it seemed impossible to bring and apply sufficient motive power to such a distant point. Sam Kirkbride, however, preferred to leave the problem for the present; their immediate task, he declared, was to discover whether a decent body of ore were there.

"That's it," Adam agreed. "But if it is we've a rare tickler to solve. I know for t'moment I haven't the faintest idea as to how it could be managed."

Nor had he on Sunday morning when, in the shadow of Big William, he met Simon, on whose recommendation the South Mill was to be closed entirely, so that work could be more efficiently concentrated in the North Mill. The changes were being effected without intermission, another reason for the more fanatical servants of the Almighty to be affronted.

The smelter reminded Adam that he and Jane would be calling at Modesty late that afternoon, after an early tea. "We're picking up Cherry as well," he added. "She t-t-telled Jane she'd be ready in good time."

"So will I," Adam promised. "I'm going down to Freestone John now, and then I'm off back home. I've a real lot of old plans there and in the hope that we *shall* have to find means somehow of getting th'ore cheaply away from Jamie's Mint I'm intending examining 'em carefully—might drop on a line that road."

The elderly Quaker was in charge of that Sunday morning's shift at the trial and there was a touch of excitement about him when Adam jumped down the last step of Captain Tregoning's Stoping. Already the water had been lowered appreciably, at the rate of seven inches to the hour. Estimated by poling, it was thought the canal-like cut would be emptied before daybreak.

"But I'se summat to show you, friend," he beckoned.

Leaving the teams who ceaselessly kept moving the handles of the asthmatic, creaking pumps, Adam edged behind his former partner for about twenty fathoms. The Quaker than climbed down almost to the level of the water, where he scooped out a handful of flaky pieces of rock: decomposed limestone.

"Vamp, lad," he said impressively on regaining the narrow brink. "And I'se no need to tell you what that usually means."

"You'd better all the same," Adam suggested. "My mining weren't learned in these hills."

"T'presence of ore," the older man said. "So it looks as if it's noan all been imagination about goodly mineral being won down here."

That added urgency to Adam's further cogitations on a very tricky problem.

As deputy of the afternoon shift, Matt Tiplady relieved Freestone John at noon, so enabling his small daughter to rush along to Modesty to prepare dinner for Adam. He sat down to cold roast beef and mashed potatoes, creamy rice pudding, and a big jam tart criss-crossed with strips of pastry. With the main part of the meal he drank a bottle of beer, and the brown tea-pot was waiting for him afterwards.

The cook, while hanging up the apron she kept in the house, spoke heatedly about an oven which "no woman in her right senses 'ud put up wi'. Not unless she were wed to a good-for-naught like one of t'Coopers," she rounded off. "Then she'd be beyond caring what she slapped on to the table."

"You don't think I'm in the same class, lass?" Adam observed, troubled.

Mary Jane's grey eyes were kindly. "No, of course I don't, Adam lad," she said. "It were nobbut summat as occurred to me i' passing, as they say. Anyroad, I can't stand here gossiping wi' you. You've plenty on to look after two houses as I'se doing."

Before she left, Adam was told about tea, the boiled ham and the bread and butter which, already cut, rested beneath a suitable cloth. A clean nightshirt had also been put out for him, this because of the soiled towels she had come across.

"Our Ward," Mary Jane sighed gustily. "He'll run errands and shake rugs wi' me when I say he has to, but as for baths all over I just can't master him, I can't really."

Adam's smile lingered for a while after she had skipped away, but in due course his face became intent as he placed on the large dining-table plan after plan, the majority aged but some not more than a few years old. Time after time he shook his head, but, just after lighting the lamp, he made a discovery which might be of significance. It was that the Great Deep Level, driven so long afterwards, passed immediately beneath Bottomless Sump. The distance between the two was comparatively slight, but the strata in all likelihood exceptionally hard.

"I wonder if that's the answer?" he mused, absentmindedly grasping and re-grasping a screw of paper, an exercise recommended to him by the surgeon in Newcastle. "Sink Bottomless Sump to the Great Deep, and take th'ore out that road. Depends, naturally, if these plans are accurate . . . and on many other things besides—for instance, the difficulty of horse-tramming in a level that's carrying more water than the usual drainage."

In the middle of tea Daniel arrived,. nattily attired in a new hard hat, smart suit and overcoat. "I think I'll go down wi' you lot to Greets Church to-night," he announced. "No, I'll noan have owt to eat with you now, because Aunt Ellen's expecting me, but I'll meet you after."

Adam stared at him, his thoughts upon Wingy Blenkiron. Daniel might be turned out dashingly, but there was a blemish, a swollen lid and discoloration which promised to develop into a beautiful black eye.

"Been scrapping on t'Sabbath afternoon?" he inquired. "Or have you trodden on a rake and the handle's cracked you one?"

It was Daniel's turn to stare, which he did, suspiciously. "What do you know about it?" he demanded. "Anyhow it were a rake, but the handle were in a young woman's hands an' it were the business end that smacked me."

"Dinah?" Adam hazarded.

"Aye, an' dammit, I hadn't even kissed her," his friend snapped. "I'd nobbut slipped my arm around her waist when she went off at half-cock."

Adam grinned. "I warned you, lad."

Daniel was beginning to see the funny side of it. "Ah well, nowt like keeping on trying. Anyway, I'm off now."

Finishing tea, Adam then cleared away, washed the pots, washed himself, brushed his hair, and was spick-and-span when Simon and Jane called in the Skidmores' trap. At Town Foot, hitching Prue to the railings of Yew Tree House, the three of them went up the flagged path. Daniel, whose partially closed and rapidly darkening eye was very distinct in the mellow lamplight, had arrived before them and was explaining, with scant regard to the truth, a rather stupid mishap. Until then his audience had been Cherry, Mr. Alderson and Edmund Kearton, who had gladly assented to be watchdog that evening, so that no one could acquaint his old friend of what was occurring already at the mine.

Daniel's aunt had given him a message for his Uncle Henry, and, after service at Greets Church, he walked back to the Green, during which time Adam managed to detach Cherry from the others. The next morning, if all went well at Jamie's Mint, it was very essential that he should have a conversation on technicalities with her uncle.

"Oh, I do hope th'ore is there so as you can, Adam," said Cherry, clasping her hands. "And he'd be so pleased at being brought into things properly again. I'll tell you what, I'll light a fire in his office on the off-chance. . . . I've always the excuse it's getting damp, which it is, like most places here."

"Freestone . . . soaks up the moisture, that's what Nick Pratt says," Adam murmured. "But I don't think where I live is at all bad."

"Oh, Modesty's supposed to be built on the rock," Cherry told him. "It's a lovely house, isn't it?"

"Noan so bad," Adam conceded.

Cherry reacted. "It's a sight better nor that," she declared.

Truth to tell, the important affairs of the West Side Lead Mining Company were not again mentioned between them then.

* * * *

The mineral veins of Skewdale were more or less vertical, but the body of ore at Jamie's Mint was laid horizontally, in a freakish Flat. The groovers, gazing as if enchanted, were not held spellbound by an unfamiliar geological formation, however, but rather because of the mystery of a legend now demonstrably fact.

"Aye, there it is," Adam muttered, deeply stirred himself.

His companions shook themselves out of their abstraction, to listen carefully—the pumps were to be maintained at full strength to drain Bottomless Sump, where the water was already two or three yards below the sole of the lengthy cutting in which they stood; a small sump was to be hewn out at once, to absorb the flow of a tiny spring, and a single pump applied to it.

"Right," Len Rukin nodded. "We'll get on wi' everything."

Immeasurably pleased, Adam climbed Captain Tregoning's Stoping and from there steadily proceeded towards the day, along his own Cross Cut and Titus Alderson's New Drift to the heavy silences of honeycombed Old Joss Level, the light from his solitary candle never carrying far. From the junction with Notion Level to the tail his route was populous by comparison, and such trammers and groovers as were in that part pulled him up civilly but eagerly to hear the news, an experience repeated outside. It seemed as if everyone knew what had been afoot and, all the way down to Mill Bridge, he briefly told and retold the story to teamsters, outside trammers, dressing-floors men and smelters thronging the doorways of the North Mill.

Bart Hugill was waiting at the office door, Adam's nod sufficient to unloose his tongue. "By, Adam, but I still can't believe it," he chattered away, tossing his head back frequently, too excited for a determined effort to restrain his hair. "And fro' what you can tell there's a fairish amount of ore?"

Estimated by the yardstick of the London and Andajoz Lead and Silver Mining Company the potentialities of the new ground were modest, but in the Dale nowadays, where on the whole mineral was laboriously scratched for and poked out, the outcome rated much higher.

"Enough to help things along nicely," Adam told him.

While the clerk gloated over prospects, Adam reflected about what he must do before starting out to attend the East Side Company's Special General Meeting at Corvy. It was imperative to see Henry Hird, but fortunately Monday was his day, and if Bart hastened up Legatt's Way it would be possible to intercept the royalty agent as he rode down the Roman road.

"Take Ben, lad," he said. "And after you've telled him about Jamie's Mint arrange for Len to show him everything. Give him my compliments as well and say I'd be obliged if he'd then come to Yew Tree House."

This understood, Adam left the office to cross the two bridges. Down Mine Road, at Bucker Level Dressing Floors, where only a handful of the East Side men were at work, shovels and hoses were forgotten for the moment while inquiries were made about the trial, and exactly the same thing happened at Town Foot, where Richard Blenkiron, the loaders of the traction engine trailer and dozens of people who appeared to come from nowhere were all equally curious.

Washing flapped on a line stretched across a strip of ground above the river's bank, and, reminded by this, Adam changed course away from a green-painted gate. When he saw Cherry, she was perfectly still, clothes-basket at her feet, but his cheery wave and broad grin put life into her limbs again, though her eyes filmed and her red lips were tremulous.

"It's all right, is it?" she gulped. "There was some ore?"

Gently Adam squeezed her bare elbow. "A very nice quantity, lass," he said. "Aye, you can safely say that to your uncle while I pop along to Puke Hastwell."

Cherry swallowed again. "Apart from what you found out, this is the best news he's had for . . . oh, I don't know how long."

"Then you hurry and let him know," Adam laughed. "You see, somebody's got to tell him how he's been left in the dark this week-end, an' I'm all for leaving mucky work for others to do."

She smiled mistily, tried to speak, and then, turning sharply from him, made a bee-line for the back door of her home.

The house in the Wood Yard was extremely conveniently placed for Mr. Hastwell to slip away for 'elevenses' or other refreshment, and so Adam's business was dealt with by Nathan Wharton, who promised a load of horse-sleepers by the next afternoon. The sawyer expressed pleasure when told of the Flat, but nevertheless sounded pessimistic, apparently agreeing with the widespread belief that the ore, if ore were there, would never be brought to bank because of insuperable difficulties.

"Well, maybe we are o'er inclined to put two an' two together, not always correctly," he admitted sheepishly, when Adam had made some pertinent comments on the village. "But it adds a bit o' spice to life, lad. Anyroad, I'se glad it's noan so hopeless as has been made out."

Adam laughed. "Nowt on this earth could be as bad as that, Nathan. Talk about folk burying t'body afore the Reaper has put in an appearance . . ."

"Aye . . ." the sawyer muttered.

When Adam went into the kitchen of Yew Tree House there were suspicious streaks on Titus Alderson's cheeks and his hands still trembled. But he was recovering and, to begin with, gaily charged his niece and assistant agent with gross deceit. As soon as this sportive phase was over, however, he insisted upon a full account, plying shrewd questions which brought to the fore the real problem.

"That's what I came about," Adam nodded. "But if possible I want us to have evolved a sound method afore Mr. Hird shows up. It's a tough nut to crack though."

"Right, lad," Mr. Alderson said, overwhelmingly delighted to be associated once more with practical affairs. "But this is no place for serious discussion, and as it happens there's a fire in th'office."

Adam winked outrageously at Cherry. "Well, that's a bit o' luck to start with, Mr. Alderson."

Cherry stared stonily. "I don't know as how a wet patch on t'wall-paper can be called lucky," she remarked.

It was Adam's first proper experience of Titus Alderson as a mining agent, and he found him a thoroughly intelligent partner, capable, ingenious, and by no means frightened of contemplating novel methods. After hearing a precise description of the stoping he accepted the view Adam had reached, and his only doubts related to the estimated speed at which Bottomless Sump could be sunk to join the Great Deep Level. Even on that he was not pig-headed.

"No, lad, driving levels and drifts is more our kidney here, whereas sinking shafts is meat an' drink to chaps like you an' Daniel," he said. "So we'll take it, employing dynamite and tackle as I'm strange to, that it can be done as you state. But what when you've holed through to t'Great Deep—how is the ore to be got out that road, through a level as runs like a little beck? As you say, that's the stumbling block."

Within the next half-hour several schemes were thought of, but, although each might have sufficed at a pinch, none gave satisfaction to either of the proposers. The solution came suddenly, as the old mine-agent was speaking, when his words trailed off and his mouth remained open. Then his veined hand, extraordinarily soft and white, bunched into a fist and banged down on to the table.

"Little Punchard Gill in Arkendale!" he shouted. "Aye . . ." his voice rose, "and they did it up at Alston i' Cumberland and all."

"What?" demanded Adam.

"Why . . ." Titus Alderson spoke as if his thoughts had been outwardly expressed, "why, they made the levels into canals, of course, and carried th'ore out in boats. It'd nobbut mean walling up the tail of t'Great Deep about four foot high and letting it fill wi' water to that depth . . ."

Invigorated, arguing this and then that, they set to work with pencils and scribbling paper, and when Cherry announced Henry Hird's arrival the whole project had been planned: the locks to conserve flotation depth in a slightly sloping level, the rehabilitation of the Great Deep Level Waterwheel, to which a winding-drum would be fitted so that the boats, after their outward, ore-laden journey with the flow, could be drawn back to the loading hopper at Bottomless Sump; even the pattern of the boats themselves.

Unmindful of the caller in the kitchen, Mr. Alderson explained these matters to his niece. "Well," she gloated, "this is going to be one in the eye for a lot o' folk."

"It is," chuckled Adam, "so give the first one some stick, Mr. Alderson, Yes," he stressed, "*you're* doing the talking."

Mr. Hird had been mightily impressed with the Flat, but, affected by current opinion, had grave doubts also. Titus Alderson's slightly airy but nevertheless competent exposition made him decide to keep former reservations to himself. "Well," he boomed subsequently, "that seems satisfactory on all counts, Titus, and I'se fair suited you've been justified. And as for t'question Adam's just putten—you can take it as Sir Charles 'ul agree."

"Aye, it's better to be sure," Adam observed. "With both us and th'East Side Company having equal rights in the Great Deep."

The royalty agent's expression soured. "You'll have no trouble wi' them, lad," he growled.

Making his excuses, Adam slipped off to the kitchen, where Cherry remarked that it would be a change for him to listen to the deliberations at the East Side Company's Meeting.

"Nay," he fingered his ear, "I might make a few helpful suggestions."

Cherry eyed him sharply. "Helpful?" she queried.

"In a way o' speaking," Adam murmured. "I think that's the best road of throwing a bit more sand into Cousin Reuben's bearings."

The lines in his face were implacable, and Cherry's throat felt dry. "You're never going to let go of him, are you?" she asked.

He smiled faintly. "There's certain things as you and me know has been done. Would you compromise about 'em, lass?"

Despite a second's cold apprehension, Cherry replied honestly enough: "No, I wouldn't."

"You couldn't," Adam put it that way.

Outdoors his limbering gait soon took him along Main Street to Modesty, where, before sitting down to dinner, he washed and exchanged dirty clothes and snug clogs for a superior suit and less warm boots. Ben was in the stable, brought down by Bart Hugill, and in due course, mounted on the snuff-brown galloway, Adam rode down the main road. It was raining when he left Winterings, but, as so frequently happened, quite fine lower down, where the heights of the hills had lessened.

2

The East Side's Meeting was held in the Assembly Room of the William and Mary, and as Adam walked briskly under the stables archway he collided with a weedy young man who was quite lost to his surroundings, his Cousin Arthur, whom he had met only once since rescuing him in the Old Man. On that occasion, screwing himself up, Arthur Nattrass had eventually inquired why neither Adam nor Daniel had said anything to anybody about the night he had wakened to consciousness in Modesty—at which door he had appeared, and so on.

"Sorry, lad," said Adam. "I've noan hurt you, have I?"

Arthur Nattrass collected himself. "It'd take more nor that to damage such as me, old cock."

Adam eyed him dubiously. "I don't know about that, Arthur," he differed. "You don't seem all that grand. Nowt on your mind, is there?"

For a brief interval, teeth clenched and lips drawn savagely back, Arthur Nattrass really looked capable of delivering one of those flashing blows he often mentioned.

"Any more o' that cracked talk about letting t'cat out of the bag . . ." he hissed.

"All the same, I'm inclined to think you haven't dared tell Cousin Reuben what you were up to," Adam remarked.

"I didn't know where I'd been," his cousin snarled.

As if enlightened, Adam nodded gravely. "Then I know what you're worrying yourself sick about . . . whether you might lose your memory again, eh?"

"Well, I could, couldn't I?" he was asked sullenly.

Adam propounded pleasantly that that was a question for a doctor, but ended on a note of comfort, promising that in the event of a similar attack assistance would be rendered far more swiftly.

Very much on guard, Arthur Nattrass glared. "And what the hell do you mean by that?"

"Just this, Arthur lad," said Adam, "that I can put my finger on th'exact spot your poor mind would take you to."

With that he pushed upon the door, to be greeted by the warm, mixed scents of good cooking, cigars and drink. The Assembly Room was at the end of a broad passage, and there the atmosphere was made definitely less cheery by rows of glum faces.

The meeting began promptly, immediately after Mr. Storey and his co-directors had taken their seats on the musicians' dais. The proceedings opened with a report by the auditor, a statement not likely to assuage the fears of the nervous, but better things followed when the Chairman, in resolutely announcing that the Company would remain in business, disclosed that the Board were providing further capital, of which pledge the disgruntled expressions of Messrs. Miles Buckle and the elder Nattrasses, George and William, were effective token.

The storm broke when an intent audience was informed that, out of the fourteen pounds still uncalled on each share, the Directors had decided that all shareholders would be required to pay one pound. In the ensuing hubbub as many as half a dozen individuals simultaneously attempted to express an opinion, but a saturnine-looking gentleman, very knowledgeable, came off best. After vitriolically scourging the Board for their "criminal folly" about Droughty Tom's pump, he suggested the company would be better served if more were made of what material there was and less said about the manifold blessings which could be theirs *if* another company were absorbed.

Many were the furious outbursts, many the heartrending appeals, and not until late on was Adam able to catch the chairman's eye.

He began very diffidently, confessing that his position was embarrassing, holding as he did an important office with the West Side Company, to whose actions some of their own troubles could be traced. But, in reviewing matters as a newcomer saw them, he would strive to be as neutral as he could. There had been, he believed, other references to the two companies merging, and with such a proposal he sympathised. Smelting costs, for example, would be vastly reduced by his own company's concentration in their North Mill and, for a slight outlay, to throw a couple of tramway bridges over Winterings Gill, the whole East Side output could be carried across for processing at the same low rate, thus ending the uneconomic methods in force at Smiddy Bridge, Martha, and Bucker Dressing Floors and Smelt Mills, all small units.

"Hear, hear." The shout came from the back. "Go on, young man."

Amidst hints of mass approval, Adam next dwelt upon the ideal Board of Directors. "It should be composed as much as possible of gentlemen whose hearts an' souls is in lead-mining," he affirmed. "A combination of that and good management——"

The chairman's gavel rapped sharply. Mr. Storey was severe, but not too severe, as he requested the speaker to confine himself to present business, reminding him also that it was absurdly far-fetched to assume that the West Side Company might ultimately absorb them. Nor could amalgamation be discussed either.

Adam smiled wryly. "I must apologise, sir, for rambling on as I have. I don't know what I've been thinking of."

"Well, I'll bloody soon tell you," Reuben Nattrass roared, eyes redly suffused. Passionately roused, neither the chairman's commands nor the orders of his father and uncle could silence him. Words tumbled out as he accused Adam of scheming to oust him. "Aye, that's what yon cunning sod is after," he thundered, great arm outstretched. "Aye, him, who's stuck as fast as a thief about how to get out a passel of ore as his company's just getten to. And how much pay ore has he found for 'em on his own? Not a bloody bing. Every wagon o' bouse that t'West Side hauls to bank is drawn fro' places as were known long afore he showed up, and when they're done he'll be done an' all. Why, a dowser 'ud have a better chance o' locating lead in them Skewdale hills than he has."

The gavel held by Mr. Storey crashed down almost triumphantly. "A dowser might not perform ill, Nattrass," he said, informing agent and company impartially. "For centuries dowsers were employed in the discovery of minerals. Their art so far as water was concerned came long afterwards."

Nonplussed, Reuben Nattrass started to catechise. "You mean as a chap wi' hazel twigs goes seeking minerals? Seeking *minerals*?" Genuinely bewildered, he hit upon the most disastrous of solutions. "Somebody's been codding you," he muttered. "Of course wi' you not being brought up to lead-mining——"

"The facts are as I have stated, Nattrass," Mr. Storey snapped.

"Dowsing for lead!" Reuben Nattrass repeated to himself, aghast, his murmur heard only by those near, though his face told enough. "Of all t'bloody fairy tales."

"Nattrass," the banker inquired icily from the musicians' dais, "are you doubting my word?"

Worried though they were, the shareholders smiled, but Mr. Storey, with an important position to uphold, had too much sense to allow the situation to degenerate further. Soon afterwards the meeting ended, the directors and their agent leaving the big room.

Adam was buttonholed by a few shareholders, but after a little talk here and there was able to escape. Outside, in the broad passage, Arthur Nattrass paced to and fro, killing time until his relatives appeared. As Adam appeared, his cousin ignored him, but afterwards, on an impulse, spun round. "Reuben were right when he said you were a cunning sod," he blurted out. "You've planted some deadly seeds just now, haven't you? Aye, you got shares i' this company . . ."

"Deadly seeds?" Adam eyed him.

Arthur Nattrass gesticulated impatiently. "You know what I mean all right . . . but Reuben 'ul pay you back tenfold i' due course. Aye, he'll——"

"Do all he can," Adam interrupted. "And maybe it'd be as well if you did the same—so long as it's for yourself."

"On wi' that bloody nonsense again?" his cousin snarled.

Adam shook his head. "No, I'm bothering no more, and I mean that, Arthur," he said quietly. "All I'll say is that, though t'sands are running out fast, you've still time."

"Time!" the younger man repeated.

"Aye, time," Adam nodded. "Time to do what's right."

"Go to hell," Arthur Nattrass said viciously.

Instead, Adam went to the Saracen, where he enjoyed a very good meal.

* * * *

Throughout the next day, until the last bedside candle was blown out, the details of the special meeting were eagerly discussed in Winterings. A very real sympathy was everywhere expressed for those at their wits' ends about the call-up, but other aspects were commented upon less soberly, particularly the reported suggestion that if there were to be an arrangement between the companies the West Side concern would be the dominant member.

"Talk about turning t'tables," Mark Iveson chuckled that evening in the cobbler's workshop. "I nearly split my sides, Kit."

The shop door opened and closed quickly as the blind man made a laughing rejoinder. Sleet was driving heavily from the east, and the narrow canyon of Main Street was not a place in which to linger. Anthony Skidmore shook himself. "Well, what's t'latest? We're a bit out of the world at Snorr."

"The latest," said Mark Iveson, "is that I'se getten them three tups o' yours as were lost. They're penned safe enough now."

"I don't know how it is, Kit," Mr. Skidmore remarked, "but whenever Christmas is drawing nearish Mark always manages to produce some o' my missing stock."

"Nay, Anthony," the shepherd grinned.

"Well, never mind about that," the master of Badger Hall smiled. "Owt else come out about the meeting?"

This question, more or less, was asked by a dozen men who arrived at intervals during the next twenty minutes or so, and although the chorus of replies followed the same pattern, no one seemed bored by the repetition.

"Reuben were in t'Wood Yard this morning, and talk about Old Nick," Nathan Wharton, the latest comer, announced with relish. "No, I wouldn't like to be one of his sparring partners across yonder." He jerked his head sideways, towards the White Hart. "His training for the fight wi' Gipsy Joe starts to-night."

"I venture to observe," said Mr. Kidd pontifically, "that I would . . . er . . . be less pleased to be in the young man Brunskill's shoes."

Puke Hastwell was a man with a grudge. "What Nattrass ought to do, instead o' fighting anybody, is to try to pull his company round. A pound call on every share," he added with undisguised rancour.

"And they're having a bout or two in t'White Hart, are they, Nathan?" Richard Blenkiron inquired.

"Aye, you'd better be off, lad," Blind Kit chuckled.

There was good-natured banter on this, but, nevertheless, the blacksmith and several cronies darted across the street, to enter the hollow-echoing, front passage of the tenantless inn. In a room to the left, brilliantly lighted by four lamps and clusters of candles, Cyprian Metcalfe was spitting out fragments of a decayed stump, while Bull Waggott, head held back, endeavoured to stem the flow of blood from his broad nose. Meantime the youngest Cooper, Less Nor Nowt, was flatly declining to don the gloves.

"You're supposed to be having a work-out, Reuben," the groover grunted. "What you've done so far is to bloody well murder anybody who's stood up to give you a bit o' practice."

The East Side's agent was stripped to the waist, great chest and rippling muscles shaded by the light. "Right sportsmen you lot are," he growled. "Nobbut touch any o' you an' your legs are as tottery as a new-born calf's."

It soon became plain that, for want of opponents, training for that evening had terminated. The little party of spectators scampered back across Main Street in the stinging sleet.

* * * *

The West Side Company's activities were approaching a peak not attained in the Dale for years. Partnerships in the main ore-producing grounds steadily increased in number, thanks to a dryness never known before, and at Jamie's Mint preparations were quickly completed for ripping out the rich Flat as soon as the way-gate by Bottomless Sump and the Great Deep Level was finished.

The opening-out of the way-gate continued without intermission night and day. Bottomless Sump was attacked from both ends: by sinking in the Sump and rising from the Great Deep. Immediately on holing through it was seen that the junction was perfect, a tribute to the plan of a long-departed mining-agent. That, displacing the dynamite experts, brought a fresh batch of men, who, carrying plumb-line and level, swung sharp-pointed moils to carve out niches in the shaft, upon which stout lengths of timber were placed: supports for the temporary bunnings from which the more dangerous places in the sides would be repaired. These platforms also served for the installation of the hopper, a box-like wooden conduit into which the ore at Jamie's Mint could be shovelled, to fall upon a ramp at the bottom conveniently sited for loading the boats.

The small circular saw at the carpenter's shop at the North Mill never ceased buzzing throughout the hours of daylight, and the boats were built there too. They were of simple rectangular design, well caulked and tarred over-all, with watertight oil drums fixed fore and aft to supply extra buoyancy. The pressure on Hugh Bearpark and the two assistants he had now acquired was so great that the sluice-gates for the Great Deep had to be made in the village, Mr. Kearton cloaking his willingness by a disagreeableness which deceived neither his directors nor the company's assistant agent.

Simultaneously the necessary changes were effected at the tail of the Great Deep Level, where wooden mallets pinged home on the heads of wooden stakes, and those in authority slid one upon another the separate portions of measuring staffs before thumbscrewing tightly when the required dimension was obtained. Tradesmen of many descriptions were engaged here, including masons, who, instead of partially walling-in the tail, extended the sides at a height of four feet for a score of yards before closing the outer end, so forming a dock into which the ore-laden boats could come to rest, previous to being lifted out by a crane, to be powered by the Great Deep waterwheel, which groovers-turned-millwrights were improvising.

Fortunately adequate supplies of old plant and materials were available—sufficient lengths of cable which, when spliced together, were enough to reach from the waterwheel through the level to Bottomless Sump and back again, a mighty draw-rope; odd coils of smaller cable, hunted up in the stores, were used to connect waterwheel and crane, and the additions for the waterwheel itself, to cover these two different motions, clutch, slip-drum, brake, were picked up for a song in a district where so much machinery was rusting.

A considerable length of new tramroad was laid, by a circuitous route to avoid the steeper gradients, from the Great Deep Level to join the existing track ending below the South Smelt Mill. To save buying, rails were drawn from disused horse-levels in various parts of the mines.

By the end of the month the back of the work was broken, when less arduous but equally enthralling jobs were done. Novel arrangements for communication began to be installed, one of these a signal line operating both ways with Bottomless Sump, the other a method by which a banksman at the tail could control either draw-cable or crane without leaving his post, wires and pulleys stretching across to the waterwheel for that purpose.

On the first Wednesday in December the first load of ore from Jamie's Mint sailed down this waterborne route, the five coupled-boats greeted with a big crowd's enthusiastic applause on emerging into the day.

It was said approvingly that the West Side Company was reviving all the old customs—coffee for the smelters before tapping the molten lead, and gin as a gesture of appreciation when a trial had been successfully completed. The opening of the outer section of the Great Deep as a Boat Level, a major advance, strengthened this impression, when beef and mutton sandwiches, pastries, and endless mugs of steaming coffee were provided for all who cared for them.

The day was bright and the wind neither cold nor very strong on the ground, although higher up white clouds scudded at speed, the sun shining on them. Around the trestle-table from which Mrs. Peacock and Mary Jane Tiplady served food and drink brought up by donkey, a sandwich-chewing throng eddied. Little Bessie Sunter, perched up on Mr. Blenkiron's shoulder, noisily sucked goodies, and, at the banksman's control platform, in whose mechanism she was taking immense interest, Fronick Blenkiron's golden-haired head was in close proximity to Len Rukin's dark locks. Nearer the tail, scarlet-faced because she was unable to throw off the memory of days when she slunk past him, Susan Skidmore thankfully escaped from Adam after self-consciously telling him that the children, under Mr. Skidmore's tactful guidance, had selected his pup and named it, too.

"Well, Meg'll do for me," Adam smiled at Cherry. "Yes, very nice. Anyway, lass, we were interrupted just as you were going to say how it was you nearly missed the thrilling moment when t'wagon-boats popped out. Your uncle?"

Cherry's nose wrinkled. "I'd an awful job with him, because he said if he were fit enough to take short walks along Main Street he were fit enough to climb up here, so long as he did it slowly. I'd to take my bonnet off an' say I were stopping in myself if he behaved so foolishly."

"Aye, he's becoming a right handful," Adam laughed.

A few seconds later Sam Kirkbride bawled a warning and, shortly afterwards, the wheels of the crane began to turn. One by one the five boats, now empty, were hoisted into the water, where their short linking-chains were coupled together. Then another shout, the throwing over of another lever, when the slack in the draw-cable from the waterwheel began to take up. As the tow moved, cheering started which did not cease until the last boat had disappeared into the darkness of the level —the Great Deep as a boat-way had been publicly inaugurated.

Bidding Cherry good-bye as the crowd dispersed, Adam went up the moor, deliberately veering left to avoid company. He felt that this day, when ore had begun to flow from Jamie's Mint, marked the end of a very definite phase and the beginning of a new one. Routine work was in the charge of capable men, and at last he had breathing space to consider the other great duty he had for so long promised himself to perform.

At the octagonal-shaped Powder Magazine he sat down. "Now what exactly is it I'm after doing?" he mused, staring at the bright, winter landscape from the clear-cut lines of Lovely Lady to the blue and white sky over Silver Seat. "I want to nobble them who were parties to putting t'rails underground," he told himself. "And if I do that, beyond any question or doubt I shall end Reuben Nattrass's career as a mining-agent just as surely as he finished off Cherry's uncle, which is nobbut common justice."

Frowningly the journey was resumed to Notion Bridge, where, in the same abstracted frame of mind, he visited Simon Sunter and Harry Blaydes in the North Smelt Mill, where they were superintending the smelting of a parcel of soot lead which was somewhat erratic in its behaviour. Finally, after mooning between the Bingstead and the lengthy Peat House, he wandered back to the office.

Bart was elsewhere, collecting figures for the Quarterly Lead Account, and so Adam stretched himself out, with feet crossed on the top of the clerk's stool. "But how the hell am I going to do the job all that neatly?" he muttered. "Of course, what's required is a trap as can't be got out of."

He was no nearer a gratifying solution when the clerk came clattering in. Bart Hugill stared, recognised the symptoms, nodded a little gleefully to himself as if to say: "Well, who's t' next to be shaken up?" and then shifted his books to a waist-high desk, against which he stood to do his book-keeping, fully prepared to remain on his feet until it suited the other's pleasure to relinquish the stool.

CHAPTER SIXTEEN

I

EARLY ONE grey but fine morning a fortnight before Christmas a horn sounded in Winterings, hounds tore excitedly along Main Street to Town Foot, and by nine o'clock the members of the hunt, the majority of them men of the East Side Company who had nothing more profitable to do, were streaming into Sorrow Near. In the other direction, spectators hastened up Jom High Road, their destination the scar behind Rachel Shafts, from which vantage point a clear though distant view could be obtained of the sport in progress at the opposite side of the Dale.

A little before midday, from just above Worm Gutter, where he had been staring without inspiration at the spot where Cherry had found gozzan, Adam watched hundreds of sheep scatter frantically as the hounds, in full cry, headed for the close-cropped limestone turf below Deer Pot. Outstanding amongst the company widely strung out behind were Mr. Wade, Mr. Penrose, the vicar of Greets, Anthony Skidmore and other farmers, all of whom were mounted. Until lolling-tongued animals and panting foot-followers disappeared into a ravine he remained there, but then set off down the moor to the mine office, where he and Bart Hugill ate their midday bait and drank the strong tea brewed by the clerk. In the afternoon he was occupied in the vicinity of Notion Bridge, but, still plagued by the problem of the gozzan, returned home much sooner than usual, calling on the way at the Great Deep Level, where he paused while a wagon-train of bouse, pulled by two horses, started along the new tramroad winding up to the South Mill.

It was quite light even when Adam reached Modesty, where tea was laid, with shopping heaped neatly where he could not overlook it by the very young lady who was on his private Pay. After hanging the kettle over the fire, he went into the room at the left-hand side of the front door, where he vigorously pummelled a heavily-stuffed sack rigged up as a punching-bag.

Deeply satisfied as he buttoned up shirt sleeves and slipped into his coat again, he watched a cart crossing the Brig, heading down Dale. It was loaded with cheeses belonging to the more prosperous farmers, who, to take advantage of the superior prices ruling at the Christmas markets, always retained a few on their shelves instead of allowing the factors to clear them out completely in November.

"Yes," he muttered, a grin breaking out as he flexed his arm, "it'll be as strong and sound as ever it was afore long."

Dusk was falling when he went out again, but the easterly wind carried from Town Foot the thundering sounds of the traction engine as it started for Corvy with the last trailer-load of ore, the conclusion of a transaction which, in the New Year, would handsomely increase the West Side Company's bank balance.

A further supply of tobacco in mind, Adam intended calling at Old Hannah's, but the open shop-door, the animated chattering within, and the stool beneath the bow-fronted window outside, gave him another idea. And so, while Mrs. Batty and Mrs. Blenkiron discussed a case of sickness at Greets, he washed the small panes, the voices of the ladies perfectly audible to him.

"No, it's t'fever, Hannah," the blacksmith's wife observed mournfully. "And if another epidemic breaks out——"

"Eh, I never saw anything like you, Grace," Old Hannah interrupted. "Of all the dismal Jonahs, you beat the band."

"It's all right talking," Wingy Blenkiron's mother persisted, "but you haven't a lad who's i' Greets twice a day and might be smit . . ."

The conversation showed no signs of flagging when Adam with extravagant care tiptoed indoors bearing bucket and stool. In the same fashion, picking up the brass scales, he weighed two ounces of flake, chalking up the price under the symbol allotted to him, a circle indicating a Spanish onion. Just as cautiously, outward bound, he was sneaking from behind the counter when Old Hannah hailed him.

"Hey!" she demanded. "Haven't you a tongue in your head, lad?"

Adam oozed admiration. "Not in the presence of a real expert, Hannah."

"Brazzent, eh?" Mrs. Batty proclaimed. "Well, I see you've given t'window a cat-lick, but you'd have improved matters if you'd rinsed t'washleather more oft. An' how do you think the fanlight keeps clean—by prayer?"

"Sssh," hushed Mrs. Blenkiron. "If folk hear you talking that careless way, Hannah."

Old Hannah laughed uproariously. "Aye, Grace," she said with relish, "an' if folk heard you asking me if I'd knock off a ha'penny a pound if you picked out th'apples as were a bit bruised . . ."

Mrs. Blenkiron's outraged but dismayed protest was enough for Adam. Smiling as soon as he was out of her sight, he stepped along Main Street, his destination the agent's office in Jom High Road, where he lighted the lamp before settling down to examine a large-scale Ordnance Survey map. Cherry heard him enter, as did her uncle, who, some twenty minutes later when seating himself at the tea-table, suggested that the assistant agent should be invited to take pot-luck.

At that precise moment Adam's expression was dour, but it changed completely within the few seconds which elapsed before Cherry passed from the front door to the rear of the long passage.

"No, I've had my tea," he told her, his eyes gleaming, adding much too late: "Thanks, lass."

Cherry stared. "What's the matter, Adam?"

"That hush," he grinned. "I've just tumbled to how it can be done safely, and it's you who's given me the clue. Remember when we were up t'moor how you said for a joke as the hush water could be tippled down one of the old shafts? Well, that's what we'll do." Rapidly he thumbed through a range of mining plans, before pointing to the six-inch map. "It can go into Doomsday High Shaft, and from t'sump the only road it can run is along Old Joss Level. Now Joss Level dips in the middle, so the water 'ul gradually disappear into the Old Man at each side. Eventually it'll dribble out, but it won't hurt anybody —and it can't get up the slant leading to Jamie's Mint."

"It's . . . it's a wonderful way, Adam," Cherry said, delighted.

Adam smiled. "Aye, you've noan done badly, lass. But don't tell your uncle anything till he's had his tea or he'll be in here pell-mell."

Certainly Titus Alderson lost no time when, the meal over, his niece gave him the news. The whole proposal was then thoroughly dissected, the older man endorsing the main outline and adding several valuable contributions.

"By, but we're shifting now, Adam lad," he remarked in high glee.

Cheerfully would he have stayed there all the evening, but he was due at Edmund Kearton's, his first social jaunt since his illness began. Cherry, helping him into his overcoat and fussing with his muffler, was away from the office for about a quarter of an hour, when again she had occasion to stare at Adam, who was marching to and fro, between the desk and glass-fronted mahogany bookcase housing a local collection.

"Cherry lass," he halted in mid-stride, "*if* I can obtain one thing beforehand, I can kill two birds wi' one stone—the other is bringing the guilt home about them rails."

Her heart thumped violently. "How?" she asked.

He drew her to the lamp-lit table against the window. "Look, lass," he said. "When the hush water reaches the forehead of Old Joss I'll switch it through a drift cut to that big pile o' rails, which think on is *well within our boundary.* When the water pressure mounts up enough, that soft stuff I blasted down from the roof will give way like a cork in a fizzy bottle, and the whole flood 'ul run easterly, into th'East Side Company's sett."

Still Cherry did not understand, and it was only when Adam reverted to his opening remark that everything became clear, cold-bloodedly clear. "No, I haven't explained that mysterious *if* of mine," he laughed. "It's this—we must somehow get a declaration from the East Side Company that there's no way-gate of any description from their workings into our side. That, in the nature of things, will have to be vouched for by the only practical man they have . . . Reuben Nattrass. And he *daren't* refuse, lass."

Cherry's eyes were dark with excitement. "Because of the rails . . . because they couldn't have got there except through their sett? Yes, he wouldn't dare admit he knows how to get so far to t'west."

Discussing various aspects of the project, they stayed in the office until Dinah shouted from the front door, when a move was made to the kitchen and the comfort of a bright-glowing peat fire. Wingy and Bart arrived next, followed after a short interval by Daniel. Fronick finally made up the party, her appearance embarrassing to the young man who had courted her, though she was prettily pleasant with him throughout.

The dance at Greets they were all attending was talked about exhaustively, when a toffee-join was proposed. This wholeheartedly acclaimed, overcoats and mantles were donned prior to a scamper in search of the necessary ingredients to be bought, begged or borrowed.

The next afternoon Adam paid a visit to the office of the East Side Lead Mining Company, where he respectfully asked permission to penetrate as far westward as was possible in Bucker Level, so that the nature of the strata could be investigated.

"You couldn't get owt near the boundary fro' this side," the East Side agent growled. "Where is it you're bothered about, anyroad?"

"Around Old Joss Forehead, where it joins what's now known as Alderson's Folly," Adam replied mildly. "It's a usual civility, you know, Cousin Reuben, and I thought if you'd 'low me to go through Freezeland to——"

Reuben Nattrass's fist crashed on to the sloping desk. "I'se telled you, haven't I? Do you bloody well fancy you know more nor I do about my own ground?"

"In that case——" said Adam regretfully.

"In that case take your flaming hook," Reuben Nattrass roared.

Watched by two cousins from within the office, Adam leapt the slippery stones of the beck. When a particularly blinding squall concealed him as he turned towards Mary Grinding Mill, Arthur Nattrass made his first comment.

"It's rum he's interested i' where he says," he muttered.

"Rum!" Reuben Nattrass's lips were thin. "It could be bloody queer, is what you mean. Has a second pint o' ale started you blabbing or summat?"

His gangling cousin shot up like a Jack-in-a-box. "I'll let that pass," he swallowed. "But what the hell do you take me for?"

Reuben Nattrass eyed him. "I'll noan say, lad," he said cruelly. "But I do know this, that if you've let owt slip I'll break that long neck o' yours."

Until dusk, when all dressing-floors work ceased, owing to the impossibility of providing a bright enough illumination, Adam helped Simon with a refractory raff wheel on the rolls. Then, the sleet driving more intensely, they stumbled down the tramway, progress hazardous most of the way and welcomely easier round a bend where the fierce reddish-yellow glare from the North Smelt Mill lighted up the wild gill. Farther along, Simon turned into the engineer's shop and Adam continued towards Mill Bridge, passing doorways disclosing glowing ore-hearths from which a shower of brilliant sparks shot up whenever a smelter stirred with a poker as tall as himself.

Cap discarded and sodden overcoat draped before the office fire, Adam began to compose a vitally important letter. Though addressed to the Secretary of the East Side Company it was framed for Mr. William Storey, whom he was sure Mr. Buckle would consult. It was an innocent little document, designed to appeal to one who revered the traditions of the great mineral captains. The courtesies to be expected between mining companies were dwelt upon, with the hope that a recent decision of the East Side Company's agent might be reversed.

Notwithstanding the conditions, Adam whistled throughout the treacherous descent of Sleety Slape on his way home.

In the early evening, while traps returning from Corvy market splashed up the main road, he settled down with farming books. Modesty's acreage included a strip of moorland, and he was extremely interested in the possibilities of reclaiming to decent pasture by paring and burning.

* * * *

During the first part of a day eagerly anticipated by many young women at least, Cherry was exceedingly busy arranging her uncle's whist-party, to which Edmund Kearton, Sam Kirkbride and Blind Kit were invited. This entailed the preparation of a nice supper and a jaunt to Main Street, for bottles of beer from Mrs. Peacock and to call at the cobbler's to remind him to bring his special playing-cards.

Shortly after dinner she snatched time to sponge and press her evening dress, a black and white tarlatan skirt with separate tunic, which later she lifted off the line and, carefully spreading the two pieces along the length of her arm, carried them upstairs, where, after placing them upon the bed, she finicked with frills and ruches. Before going downstairs, she glanced out of the window. Town Foot, with teams of horses standing about, had been a scene of immense activity, but now the much awaited new pump for the East Side's Old Wife Shaft had vanished up Sorrow Near.

Daniel, Wingy and Fronick arrived just before half-past six, and they had barely wiped their feet on the mat when a two-horse brake driven by Simon pulled up smartly at the gate, his passengers Jane, Dinah and Adam.

The Parish Hall at Greets, brightly illuminated with lamps and scores of candles, made vivid contrast against the dark and chill outdoors, prettily decorated as it was with coloured streamers, the flames from the huge fires in the grates evoking responsive winks from striking tinsel-covered designs.

Cherry loved her evening, and, if it fell short of sheer perfection, she was acutely aware of the cause: Reuben Nattrass's dark eyes, which never seemed to leave her wherever she was.

On the other hand, Adam was quite unaware how often Bull Waggott glared at him. The extraordinary thing was that, if it were Bull Waggott's desire to use his big fists on Adam, as his manner indicated, the opportunity was afforded him the next afternoon. For the groover the result was ignominy, but, like better men before him, he kept his overthrow to himself.

* * * *

At midday it was freezing and, after completing the Ore Count End at Mary Level, Adam ate his sandwiches in front of the fire in the Changing Shop before mounting Ben. Higher up the moor, though the east wind was not strong, it was piercingly cold, and, on the bleak ground just above Doomsday High Shaft, he planned swiftly for the hush—the site of the turf-bank reservoir to be supplied from Worm and Mirk Gutters, the trench to be excavated along the line of the supposed lode, and the ditching near the shaft, with deep pit beforehand to retain the largest of the stones brought down.

Blowing through his hands to warm them, he watched a wedge-shaped formation of mallard winging effortlessly across the pale sky, and then climbed on to Ben again. Farther down Water Ling Moor he came across a coup cart leisurely drawn by Badger Hall's Prue. The vehicle, in which thirty or forty brace of grouse were tumbled, was proceeding up Legatt's Way to collect another consignment, the whole destined, on Mr. Hesketh's orders, for Christmas sale at Corvy Market.

Two men accompanied the cart: the Lord's keeper, Luther Thwaites, to whom Adam might not have existed, and square-jawed Will Skidmore, quite his old self.

"Well, we could have had more," Dinah's brother laughed, jerking his head towards the game, "but I fancy it'd have been less if Matt hadn't been respectable these days."

The distance between coup cart and horseman began to increase, and soon they were out of sight of one another. Engrossed in details of the hush, Adam allowed Ben to take him too far westerly, on to the edge of the desolate shelf of tableland through which Foul Syke hurried before leaping over Joss Foss. But the growing thunderous roar brought him to the present, and he pulled the galloway round. As he did so he glimpsed a movement, and, reining in, stared at the sloping ground beyond the deep defile, where, through dying grasses and ling, a man was creeping.

Another figure was slightly nearer, on the narrow, outward dipping track ascending alongside Joss Foss. The thin shoulders and a head permanently stiffened to one side were enough to identify this individual, but his actions were less easy to comprehend. Mazy Bill carried a bucket from which he splashed water on to the shaly surface of the path, at a point immediately above the jagged limestone rocks at the foot of the waterfall almost eighty feet below.

"It'll be a sheet of glass i' five minutes," Adam muttered. "By God, anybody going home over the trods that road . . . and that's what it's for."

The nearest level stretch at which he could put Ben across the gill was a good way off, and then there was hummocky ground dangerously pitted with rabbit holes. As he left the saddle Bull Waggott had grasped the shambling youth by the scruff of the neck, and great bunched fingers would have swung had there not been intervention.

"Now then, you murdering bastard," he was bawling. "Aye, it's been a bloody long time afore I tumbled as to why——"

"Let him go," said Adam.

The groover, and perforce the slavering creature he held remorselessly, turned to face the newcomer. "Like hell," he growled. "I'se whaling him till——"

"You can't do that to that lad, Waggott," Adam told him sternly.

The groover, whose wild rage made him look as crazed as his victim, flung Mazy Bill savagely aside, the youth rolling over before coming to rest, a quivering bundle. "Right, I can 'tend to him at after I'se dealt wi' you, Brunskill," he bellowed. "And I tell you this, I'll have more pleasure i' bashing a smooth-tongued lecher such as thoo than him. Aye, I'se been waiting for an opportunity to—but what the hell's t'good of me yapping?"

His left fist flashed; Adam leaned backwards, caught the extended wrist, jerked his opponent off balance and then, with the edge of his free hand, chopped him in the neck. A beaten man, Bull Waggott gurgled, ruddy cheeks invested with a greying pallor.

Never was Adam Brunskill able to deduce what good fortune guided him to utter the words he then did. It may have been the instinctive knowledge that bad blood between men is often dissipated by a fight.

"Bill," he said, pointing to the swaying figure, "this chap's your pigeon, so belt him while I fetch Ben. With your fists . . . *remember*?"

Froth trickling from his mouth, making animal cries, Mazy Bill rushed forward, his onslaught feebly parried by a man too stricken to see more than a few of the rain of insanely-furious blows. Two or three minutes later the groover was stretched on the ground, groaning, bleeding and senseless.

"Well, you've done it, Bill lad, done it for good an' all," Adam said warmly on returning. "You've taught him a lesson that you'll never need to repeat, haven't you just? And now you've managed it, where are you off to? Home . . . to have a tea as you've earned?"

Mazy Bill's lips trembled. "To . . . to Polly," he mumbled.

Heartily Adam approved. "Just the ticket, lad. And don't forget to tell her how you've settled your score wi' Waggott. You've somebody else to tell, too, haven't you? Somebody as 'ul be glad to hear you won't have to worry about it again . . . because up there she'll know better than either of us that you've now done all as is necessary."

Tears ran down the trammer's cheeks. "Agnes . . . will," he whispered.

Gently Adam squeezed a stick-like forearm. "Aye, she will, no doubt about that," he said. "So off you go, Bill lad."

He stayed until the youth had disappeared into the gloom, but swung on to Ben when Bull Waggott showed signs of stirring.

From there it was more convenient to reach Winterings by Legatt's Way and Sorrow Far, and slowly he rode down, pondering over what had occurred.

It was almost dark when he entered the main road at the Royal Alfred, but light enough for him to distinguish a vehicle strange to the district, a four-wheeled cart with high sides. This was standing against the pinfold, and two of the Tipladys, Matt and Ward, were piling bright-berried holly into it. Mary Jane was there, too, within the enclosure, where, her brow furrowed, she worked with pencil and paper in the glow of a lantern.

"A regular trade I do every year, Adam lad." Matt Tiplady laughed.

"Sssh!" said Mary Jane. "For heaven's sake."

From his commanding position on Ben's back, Adam was able to perceive freight of another description lining the bottom of the cart, the feathers faithfully resembling feathers he had seen not long before.

"I reckon," he murmured, "your customer 'ud take a bit extra holly —this corner."

Ward climbed up. "Might as well send a proper load, lad, eh?" he observed impassively.

"Saw your Uncle Will and Luther Thwaites Smiddy Bridge way," Adam mused.

"Aye," Matt Tiplady said with interest. "Gone that road, have they?"

Adam chuckled. "Yes, and I think I'll go mine . . . afore I'm soiled wi' you lot."

Ben started up the dark road, his shoes ringing out clearly on the hardening surface as he carried his rider towards the mellowly-illuminated windows of lamp and candle-lit houses clustered near the Brig.

2

One minute Main Street was tranquil, while in the next pandemonium had broken loose, the first just before Mr. Kidd dismissed his charges for the Christmas holiday, the second when the schoolroom door crashed open and children whooped into the chill air, some streaming along the village, others darting across the street to their big Skewdale ponies. Amongst the latter was Gem, who, immediately Nancy and Harriet Skidmore clambered on to his broad back, leapt forwards, dispatched by some young person unknown. Adam and his companion, breasting this sundry traffic, dodged the white horse, whose small riders were screaming more from liking the effect than from fright, and then returned to the topic of the weather.

Wingy eyed the leaden sky. "Looks like snow, lad, and yon lot must think so an' all," he said, nodding towards a long file of sheep, sinuously extended, which were winding down the lower slope of Noggin Moor. "That at the front must be an old 'un with a good headpiece, and wouldn't it save a lot o' worry if they were all that sensible. Well, good-bye for t'moment, lad."

To Adam's surprise, he had no need to use his key to enter Mr. Alderson's office in Jom High Road. In one of her huge mobcaps, Cherry was cleaning up the room.

Carefully closing the door into the passage, she whispered: "It's come," her hand mysteriously moving beneath print apron as she fumbled in her blouse. "I were real lucky, too, because Wingy brought another letter from one of my brothers in America, and so Uncle Titus didn't suspect I were keeping owt back."

Adam slit the flap of an envelope red-sealed with the imprint of Messrs. Richardson & Storey, but the billhead inside was the East Side Company's. Although William Storey wrote flamboyantly as one who desires to save a fellow-adventurer unnecessary adventuring, he stated categorically that his company's workings, at Bucker Level depth, nowhere even remotely approached the boundary. Moreover, the name of Reuben Nattrass was irretrievably coupled with this declaration.

Jubilantly Adam slapped the precious document with the back of his hand. "Read it, lass," he grinned. "We'll be able to get that cousin o' mine now. Aye, as soon as t'weather permits, I'll put everything in hand for the hush."

The snowstorm which began that evening precluded his taking any practical steps for the moment. Next morning, when he went downstairs, the back rooms of Modesty were greyly eerie, darkened by a drift as high as the middle sash of the windows. For the limited period of the fall, the snow was exceptionally heavy, and the shovels which the majority of people kept indoors for the purpose were invaluable. A neighbour of Old Hannah, whose solitary door faced up the fellside, was under the necessity of throwing back on to his kitchen floor a towering pile of snow before an exit could be won, and at Low Bands excessive cutting was required. The front part of Yew Tree House was no more than ankle-deep, such had been the vagaries of a swirling wind, and on that side, after calling to inquire, Adam had nothing more strenuous to do than knock off snow weighing the shapely yews. The story was different in the alleyway near the stable, and it was almost midday before Ben started to struggle up Sorrow Near.

At the mines the cleaning of choked launders and watercourses was a stern fight, and, after making the Metal Count End in the North Smelt Mill, Adam and Simon and their helpers left the stacked pigs of lead to lend a hand to the gangs engaged in clearing tramways and barrow-tracks.

The four-horse snow-ploughs, upward-bound from Greets and driving downbank from Winterings, met just before dark, but were out again the next morning to deal with the snow which had fallen again in the night. For Wingy Blenkiron the drifts were a nightmare on his long round, and for the disordered mind of his friend's brother they were a reminder of an accident in a smelt mill flue. On the Saturday afternoon, when Bart Hugill brought him down to the village, Rive Rags tumbled into a pyramid of snow heaped in front of the Plug and Feathers—his sustained scream filled many a heart with foreboding.

Low-running farm-sleds carried foodstuffs, fodder and family parties, and outlying farmers, saddle-bags stuffed with provender, resembled medieval men-at-arms. On Sunday, attempting to reach the Chapel-of-Ease at Yorrel to conduct the fortnightly service, the Vicar of Greets got as far as Snorr and no farther, but by Monday afternoon, when foxes raided poultry in daylight, stealing off with hens, and the grouse which had flown down from the moors to feed alongside them, conditions were easing. It was confidently stated that those wishing to attend Corvy

Market on the morrow—and who would wish to miss the bustle of Christmas market—could do so.

Therefore on Tuesday morning, the faces of their muffled passengers glowing with the keen tang, traps passed through Winterings, between roofs scalloped thickly at the edges with glistening white powder, the silently pounding shoes of the horses throwing back prettily-shaped pellets of light grey.

* * * *

The busy corner of Mercenary Lane in Corvy was not an ideal place for two ladies to chat, but there Mrs. Francis Harker and Mrs. Martin Rutter chatted, indifferent to Christmas shoppers laden with turkeys, geese and parcels. Apart from being jostled occasionally, their conversation was proceeding very smoothly until they noticed a well-set young man striding towards the Bank, carrying a leather bag which soon would be jingling with the West Side Company's next Pay. The auctioneer's wife at once remarked how pleased her husband was with the difference made by Adam at the mine.

"An' another thing, Mary," she said, "you can't forever hold his sin against him, choose how James Pedley keeps going on. Yes, I really think we shall have to consider asking him into our houses again."

"He's been welcome all along wi' us." Mrs. Harker tossed her head.

Wisely Mrs. Rutter avoided that dangerous lead. "Very quick in owt he does, Martin says. And he could easily be off back to Spain if we don't soon show as we recognise he's doing his utmost to reinstate himself."

"Well," Mrs. Harker smiled sweetly, "there's no gainsaying it's better for shares to be worth summat instead o' being a liability. Mind you, we've got nowt like the number as you have."

Her companion's face frosted. "I don't know as how that influences me, Mrs. Harker. To us t'matter is just one of Christian forgiving."

"You don't say," Mary Harker murmured admiringly.

All unconscious that he had caused a quarrel between two highly respected matrons, Adam went about his many affairs, but managed to join the Skidmores, who had Cherry with them, for the Ordinary at the Saracen, where there was hardly elbow room at the long table.

It was dark when Ben, after slithering down the hump of Greets Bridge, turned into the stable-yard of the Grafton Arms, a call saving his rider the trouble of preparing a meal on reaching home. In due course, warmly lined with a juicy steak, Adam decided upon a tot of whisky before facing the moor road. Seven or eight men were in the bar, amongst them the Nattrass cousins, but Reuben was leaving.

For a second the East Side agent's face hardened aggressively, but, controlling himself, he made a remark designed to dispel any idea that he had been flicked on the raw at the Special Meeting, which savagely he suspected might be generally thought. Overloudly he guffawed as they passed: "Well, well, well . . . now if there's any mining-agents here you'd better look out, for here's t'chap who's going to rob us of our jobs. Aye, this is th'expert. Anyroad, Arthur lad," he continued, abandoning Adam, "if you're noan coming you're noan. Shall I pop into th'Old Cow and give that woman of yours your love?"

A little later, when Adam had ceased to be the centre of interest for the company, he invited his younger cousin to a drink, mentioning that Christmas was not far away. Arthur Nattrass, on this occasion a dare-devil who pursued his own lone course, noisily accepted, but was exceedingly watchful nevertheless in the early stages. Their conversation in the main was about mining, for as lead-miners do each was accustomed to talking a great deal of shop. Only in the final phase was a matter in the forefront of the thoughts of both touched upon, when Adam referred to the strata near an old horse-level heading.

"Queer things happen in t'bowels of the earth, lad," his companion pronounced, picking up a third whisky. "And where were this, did you say, the forehead o' which?"

"Old Joss," Adam said casually. "Anyroad, I'm driving a small cross-cut in the New Year. That'll prove what's in the vicinity, eh?"

The other wakened up. "Aye, certainly it should," he agreed, voice rising a tone. "And which way are you setting t'drift . . . easterly, I suppose?"

Adam nodded. "A mining-agent has to know what's about him. Saves in the long run, doesn't it? And as Cousin Reuben's telled me you can't even reach t'boundary from your sett . . ."

"No, you can't," Arthur Nattrass confirmed, his colour ebbing. "Well . . . well, here's luck."

About the moment Adam reached the snow-padded brow of the moor road to Winterings his cousin came to a decision. Quietly the cheese-factor's stable-door was opened and a rough-coated mare saddled. In the darkness, taking to the whitened fields to avoid the village, Arthur Nattrass circled to gain the highway between the church and the B.G. Inn. Then he also put his beast's head up the Dale.

The newcomer's demand so flabbergasted the small party in the dimly-illuminated taproom of the Groovers Welcome, from Jonas Cottingham behind the bar to those in front of it, Cyprian Metcalfe, Luther Thwaites and several others, that the quips at the expense of Bull Waggott's lame excuse for his battered appearance ceased as if by magic.

"Well, Jonas," Reuben Nattrass said, grimacing at his chief smelter, "seemingly I'll have to use that ' snug ' o' yours for two-three minutes. Though why the hell you've the neck to call it a snug . . ."

In the small room to which the cousins went, as cheerless as had been hinted when a match was struck and a candle lighted, Arthur Nattrass told his tale. "So we've got to get them rails out to be on the safe side," he pleaded. "It doesn't matter about th'odd one or two left at the other spot, because they're lost to sight forever down that Old Man's sump."

Reuben Nattrass turned sharply. "How the hell do you know that?"

"Because I once went there, out o' idle curiosity it were." His cousin stared defiantly. "As a matter of fact I've been to th'other place as well earlier on, but nowt's happened there, naturally."

"Do you reckon Brunskill suspects?" the bigger man was ironic.

Arthur Nattrass licked dry lips. " 'Course he's never said owt to me, not a single word, but——"

Dark eyes eyed him contemptuously. " 'Course he hasn't, you bloody fool, because he suspects nowt. How the hell could he?"

"Be that as it may," Arthur Nattrass persisted, gulping, "it's nowt but commonsense to shift them rails afore he starts doing owt."

Reuben Nattrass need not have been a shrewd judge to realise that here was a young man terrified out of his wits. "By God, lad, talk about a cat on hot bricks," he remarked more moderately. "Aye, we'll relieve your anxiety i' due course or you'll be jumping atop of t'Plug mounting-block to confess your black sin."

"It's better," his cousin shivered. "An' now I think I'll shift some brandy. I'm that cold wi' my ride that I hardly know what I'm doing."

"Aye," Reuben Nattrass grunted. "But leave it to me when we go in to the others. Folks oft get close to t'mark with quizzing."

His method of deceiving the company in the tap-room was to march to the bar and demand of Jonas Cottingham the loan of a couple of sovereigns, grinningly declaring that nothing would persuade him to divulge the purpose for which they would be used. "You see," he said slyly, "when lasses give their favours . . ."

As a red herring the stratagem was efficacious. Fortunately the tale travelled in circles not frequented by Annamaria Rutter.

* * * *

The Monthly Pay of the West Side Company chanced to fall on Christmas Day, and so was advanced a day. When Adam left the White Hart after the disbursal, children pulling their sledges were scurrying towards Nick Turn, where Albert Gibson, officially clad, was interrogating Nowt Much Cooper about a goose he was carrying. At Emma Ann Metcalfe's he was kept waiting as the owner was looking after Cuthbert

Daykin's shop, but on her return she gave him the news that the long-expected black kid gloves had just arrived.

"Aye, three pairs, please," Adam nodded. "But as to the size . . ."

"Are they for three ladies or only one?" Mrs. Metcalfe inquired.

"Well . . one," Adam mumbled.

Emma Ann smiled. "Then I know t'size, lad."

This sidelight on local opinion kept Adam amused until he reached Mrs. Peacock's, where he bought bottles of whisky, gin and port for Old Hannah, and cigars for Mr. Alderson. Decorated resplendently with holly and mistletoe, the Plug and Feathers looked extremely Christmassy, and was made more so by the cheer stacked at the bar: Mr. Hesketh's presents to those who made his shooting parties enjoyable, tins of tobacco or snuff for the beaters, and turkeys and bottles of Scotch for the two keepers.

As Adam pocketed the tin of Virginia Flake which was his share, Cuthbert Daykin cut him dead, loftily averting his head. Adam had barely begun to wonder about this when he encountered a more vicious hostility elsewhere. This was something he could deal with, and so he joined Bull Waggott in the inglenook.

"Just listen a minute, lad," he said, restraining a savage objection.

As the story proceeded the expression on a bovine face moved from resentment to suspicion, from suspicion to wide-mouthed amazement. "Mazy Bill thought I were responsible for Agnes Pedley!" Bull Waggott ejaculated at the end.

"Aye, and you couldn't have drummed it into him it weren't so."

"Well, you'd know," the groover retorted, not too surely now.

"I did," Adam replied tersely. "I asked Agnes not long afore she took her life, an' I were certain she were speaking the truth."

Bull Waggott digested that. "It weren't you then?"

"No, it weren't," Adam said.

This time the silence lasted longer, an interval during which a burly, wide-nostrilled young man blinked several times. When he spoke again it was of things less poignant, to him anyhow. That morning he had met Mazy Bill, but the crazed lad had not seemed to notice him especially.

"If it's going to be that road, thank your stars, Bull," Adam insisted. "And let bygones be bygones."

The groover nodded. "No, I'll not touch him after what you've telled me."

Somewhat later Adam took his various purchases home, but came out again to buy wrapping paper. One of his calls was at Old Hannah's, whose little house was crowded as never before. This Christmas, as she boasted, seventeen of her descendants were sleeping out, two up on the previous year.

On Christmas Day morning, until Daniel drove his aunt off for dinner with the Hirds at Greets, Adam spent an hour in the stables at Malaga. Mrs. Roberty Will, carrying carriage rug and well swaddled, came out before he left. Her colour heightened as she responded to his greeting, but her constraint with him was apparently lessening.

Dinner was at Yew Tree House, and afterwards, insisting upon wearing the muffler she had knitted for him, Adam accompanied Cherry to Badger Hall. The intense cold persisted and, in Blenk Bottom Lane, they saw pitiful proof of its severity: four grouse frozen to death in a thorn bush. Beyond Snorr Bridge, while walking alongside the Skew into a bright sun which seemed powerless to affect the dazzling white carpet lying upon the valley and the enfolding hills, Cherry glimpsed Bob and Ward on the Waggotts' roof. A mammoth sphere of snow had been placed on top of the squat chimney, but this, as well as themselves, she sternly demanded should be removed.

"They're bad 'uns," she laughed, as the boys disappeared down the remote slope. "You've never been in a room, have you, when a real big snowball has been dropped into the middle of a hot fire? It's like an explosion, with clouds of steam, and soot and water over everything."

"Well, it's noan a trick for Christmas Day, lass," Adam chuckled.

Mary Jane met them a little farther on, and after kissing Adam for the sewing companion and Cherry for a quilted tea-cosy, brought the conversation to culinary matters at once. Her father, she said, had stuffed so much as to be unable to walk, and with Floss, likewise distended, was sleeping in front of the fire, an admission of gluttony affording her much satisfaction.

In the closing minutes before dusk, the garth at Badger Hall resounded with the shouts and screams of dismay peculiar to a mixed snowball fight, ultimately stopped by Mrs. Skidmore, who was becoming positively relaxed with Adam.

Nell's excited family was visited, rapidly growing but as yet woolly balls promising not the slightest resemblance to the slender-lined sheep-dogs they would become. Adam fondled his own pup. She was black, spotted white on breast and legs like her mother, Nell, who was taking an interest, too. "Now, let's see, lass, you're . . . aye, Meg, that's it. I always prefer to know these things," he murmured.

There was laughter at that, and it was good to hear, especially good to hear when shortly he would be going into a house whose friendly roof, apart from Bonfire Night, he had missed for a long time.

In Skewdale the Christmas holiday was just one day, but only a week-end intervened before the next general holiday, on New Year's Day, when Daniel, Cherry and Adam walked up to Miss Caygill's for dinner, picking up Simon, Jane and Bessie on the way. It was chilly again, but dry underfoot, though banks of snow ploughed to the side were still deep and the snow-line remained half-way up the fells.

On the temporary bridge at Yorrel, where the party paused to admire a heronsew of immense wing span gliding above the river, Daniel spoke for the third time. The previous evening, with other dark young men, he had gone round letting in the New Year, and was acutely liverish with the spirits he had drunk.

"I'm noan eating so much," he groaned.

His jaundiced appearance was responsible for an embarrassment at Rose Cottage, where Miss Caygill at once told them of her tragedy: the ravages wrought during the snowstorm by rabbits who had nibbled the bark from many of her small trees. At the door, standing aside to allow the young women to go upstairs to take off mantles and bonnets, she tactfully saw to social niceties for the men, too. "By t'look o' you, Daniel," she remarked, "you'd do with all the fresh air you can get. You two take him to where t'garden tumbles to the beck. Even in winter it's real bonny . . ." she coughed, "and secluded down where Yorrelgrain swishes past."

"Nay," Daniel deprecated, "I'm noan as bad as that."

Simon and Adam acted as one man. Before the flame of their hostess's confusion leapt too high, their astonished friend was removed elsewhere, where aspects of domestic regimen, appertaining to the private needs of visitors, were explained to him.

Later on, full stomachs suggested that a good tramp would be desirable. Climbing Yorreldale, the men in turn carrying Bessie, they struck eastward along a reasonably firm trod which ended at Kettle Dub. From there, above the quarry, a magnificent prospect was enjoyed. To the left below were the grey buildings surrounding Notion Bridge, while farther to the right and in the more distant bottoms the mullions and projecting wings of Badger Hall faced forward, the farm nestling amidst fields white-margined where narrow bands of snow still lay at the cold sides of walls.

Jane nudged Cherry. "How's Dinah, Daniel lad?" she inquired.

Daniel's noisy guffaw, abruptly cut short by a cry of anguish at the sudden pain in his temple, would have attracted more attention had they not all been startled by Simon's; "Hey! Look down yonder. Isn't that Reuben Nattrass going towards th'East Side Company's office? What's he doing there on New Year's Day? And who's w-w-with him?"

Their vigil was not prolonged, but the excitement of the loftily-placed onlookers did not really begin to increase until the Nattrass cousins, now dressed in tattered clothing, were hastening down Winterings Gill.

* * * *

For a man who had complained of the folly of a lengthy excursion in the Old Man it was a distinct surprise, when near the objective, to be confronted by a gallery blocked beyond redemption by ordinary means.

"Well . . . well . . . well," Reuben Nattrass said. "Looks as if we can't get to 'em. Cost a mint even if we could tackle t'job properly."

Arthur Nattrass's eyes seemed wild in the wavering yellow flame of the candles. "But Brunskill can," he gulped. "A drift like he mentioned——"

"Aye, an' if it were nobbut a shade out, it'd miss altogether," his cousin said impatiently. "Maybe he will needle eastwards, but he's no special place i' view."

Ignoring all soft matter as he scrabbled amongst the debris, Arthur Nattrass examined every sizeable piece of rock his scratched and bleeding hands encountered, searching for evidence of a borer having been used.

"So he's been here and blown t'flaming roof in to stop us reaching the rails, has he?" Reuben Nattrass asked sardonically.

The other jumped up frantically. "He's a bloody sight sharper nor you think, Reuben," he shouted. "You've been made a laughing-stock by him more nor once, choose how."

Reuben Nattrass, mouth vicious, raised his arm to strike. "No, I'll noan welt you, Arthur," he growled as his cousin jerked affrightedly away. "But if you ever say owt like that again I will . . ."

They stumbled back through the eerie mass of ancient workings, but, beyond Freezeland, Reuben Nattrass's glance rested momentarily on his companion. "Let's sit down for a chaw," he said brusquely. "You've getten yourself into a bloody fine state about nowt, haven't you? A rabbit's more nerve than you."

"I don't want us to be nabbed, that's all," Arthur Nattrass muttered. "It means . . . means 'prisonment if we are."

In silence they remained there a little longer, not enough to allow the permeating cold to penetrate. Then Reuben Nattrass spat, rose, hitched up his trousers by the belt, and made one incisive remark:

"If Brunskill starts driving, we'll go into their side an' take bearings. After that I'll concoct summat as 'ul stop his bloody gallop if it looks like being awkward, which it'll noan."

Mutely Arthur Nattrass nodded. Gleams from the candle he shielded with his hand now and then lighted up the massive, confident figure who led the way into the more modern parts of the mine.

3

The small gallery from the junction of Old Joss Level and Alderson's Folly was called, for want of a better name, Queer Drift. Driven in the toughest of the Cherts progress was slow, but a single daily shift would complete it in ample time to serve Adam's plans for the unmasking of those who had criminally led Mr. Alderson astray. One unusual feature was the step of rock, which could of course be blasted at the last minute, left at the entrance to the drift, without which all and sundry would have pointed out, quite rightly, that part of the hush water would flood into the new working.

Queer Drift was begun the day before Epiphany, and, about half-past eight in the morning of the Tuesday but one following, after Adam had bandaged a smelter of the midnight shift whose hand had been splashed by molten lead, he went to the New Trial, which was proceeding very nicely. Two secrets only had he kept to himself: when he would dynamite the forehead and his intention to divert the hush water that way. Otherwise the committee had been told the full facts.

"But don't forget, whoever's on, to keep tapping the face with a sledge," he reminded Matt Tiplady and his mate. "Stop as soon as it rings hollow. There mustn't be a hole through as big as your fist."

"We'll take care," Len Rukin promised, his expression hard. "Or . . ." he jerked his head eastwards, "yon lot 'ul make out the rails were put there fro' this side."

"Aye," Matt seconded as grimly, "we'll nobbut drill shot-holes so as it can be blown on t'day of reckoning."

Very satisfied, Adam returned to the office for a sandwich meal and then set off for Doomsday High Shaft and the moor above, where, the underground sights of the dial exchanged for a telescope, he surveyed for the hush, with Bart Hugill in charge of the striped rods. The sun was pallid and the piercing east wind numbing to the fingers. Teeth chattering, the clerk remarked that he could smell snow, but this forecast may have derived from the sight of Anthony Skidmore riding on Snorr Moor, Nell circling in great sweeps to round up sheep to be driven to lower and safer ground.

Despite the severe weather Henry Hird arrived as Adam noted down the concluding angle and measurement. The royalty agent was interested only in the production of ore, but as a matter of courtesy deemed it necessary to mention the proposed hush to the Lord of the Manor's Steward when next they met.

"But I'll tell you what, lad," he boomed. "It'd be in your favour if you wrote to Mr. Buckle explaining, and i' that case I won't say owt to him till you've getten your letter off."

"It's a very valuable suggestion, Mr. Hird," said Adam.

Henry Hird, greatly gratified, took a nip from his flask, and in due course kicked his heels into his horse. As the burly figure receded Bart Hugill's frozen face was a study. "Talk about the lion lying down with t'lamb," he smiled grotesquely.

The pair of them then thawed out on a bench before one of the ore-hearths at the North Mill, the clerk leaving a couple of minutes sooner than Adam, who was listening to Simon Sunter's proposal to break through a wall so that ore from the bingstead could be waggoned in instead of barrowed.

On the way to the office, as Adam approached the Mill Bridge, he noticed Bart and Wingy Blenkiron in rapt conversation. The postman, who delivered in the village all letters for the mines, was seldom seen in these parts. From his manner and breathlessness, something out of the ordinary must have happened.

"It has, lad," he grinned when asked, his powerful left arm shooting out to give Adam a hefty shove towards Notion Bridge, "and I'm advising you to dash off to hear about it fro' my father. Go on," he ended, very soberly then, "you'll find it's worth it, by God you will."

Filled suddenly with surety that whatever it was applied in the most personal sense to himself, Adam raced off without a word.

Meantime one friend pressed another for further details. "This death-bed confession o' Ambrose Pedley's," Bart marvelled, "now what were it again, lad?"

"Well, seemingly what took place were just enough for Agnes to imagine she was i' trouble in the most awful and hopeless way a lass could be, while her father got it into his Bible-addled head as it were another case of t'Virgin Mother . . . th'Immaculate Conception you know," Wingy said. "Mind you, it's such a mix-up that maybe I haven't got it correct myself, but the important thing is that Pedley knew at the bottom of him as he were responsible for her jumping into one o' Rachel Shafts, and so he owned up when his end weren't far off. The fever it were, an' for once, lad, it's done some rare good."

Both turned towards Bucker Level. But Adam Brunskill was out of sight, speeding between the high walls enclosing Sorrow Near.

The throng at Town Foot was in the main composed of women from the houses and cottages between the Roe and Calvert's Wynd, brought outdoors by Richard Blenkiron's stentorian demand, which, rising superior to the whine of the Saw Mill, had successfully attracted the attention of Nathan Wharton and Puke Hastwell. The blacksmith's excited bellow arose from a visit paid to the Smithy by Dr. Seaton, who, oblivious of the ethics of his calling, had revealed everything learnt from a patient living a few miles from Greets. The dramatic story was told in the presence of Mr. Wade's coachman, the roadman, several farmers, and the East Side's agent, who had come down with a small wheel to have its broken cogs replaced by pins.

Cherry, drawn by the gathering, came out, soon to become so sick with joy that she hardly knew how to regain her home. She was in this state when Reuben Nattrass saw her.

"Well, well, well, you seem right overcome to hear as Brunskill's a white lily," he began. "It makes me wonder if what I'se suspected once or twice is true." Though she turned away, he went on harshly: "But it's noan going to be, I might as well warn you, because in th'end, come what may . . ."

She was beyond hearing, blindly walking towards the green-painted iron gate of Yew Tree House.

When Adam sprinted round the corner at the bottom of Sorrow Near he glimpsed two things: the flutter of Cherry's skirts as she closed the front door and what appeared to be a sea of smiling faces. What he failed to see, however, was Richard Blenkiron's exultant swing, a swipe which sent him hurling, to end up on the ground near the Smithy, where sundry articles of wood and metal, previously leaning against the wall, clattered upon him.

"A bit too hard, lad," the blacksmith roared, vastly pleased. "Now come inside and hear summat."

Picking himself up, Adam did as he was bid, Wingy's father shutting the lower part of the door so that the three of them, himself, Adam and Dr. Seaton, could have decent privacy. In this wise did Adam Brunskill learn that he was cleared.

"Well . . . I can't thank you enough, doctor," he said huskily. "I sometimes thought there never could be a way out o' that mess."

Soberly Richard Blenkiron nodded. "It makes a lot of difference when a chap's on the threshold o' meeting his Maker, lad."

"Meeting Maker rubbish," snapped Dr. Seaton. "May have thought so . . . some people get crazy notions if finger aches . . . specially big strong men . . . blacksmiths."

Adam eyed the little man. "You wouldn't have helped him along wi' the notion, would you?"

The doctor sent up a howl surprising in one of his stature. "Monstrous allegation!" he yelled. "*Monstrous.*"

Quivering, he opened the door and tore outside, where he scrambled on to an up-ended barrel to mount Mighty Joe, whom he galloped towards Malaga before recollecting that patients in Winterings and beyond had not been seen. As he rushed through on the return, Richard Blenkiron was wiping his eyes.

"A grand 'un," the blacksmith chuckled. "One o' the best . . . and I shouldn't be capped if you were right, lad."

Adam had only one purpose, to get Cherry to himself. "Where's Mr. Alderson?" he asked.

"Courting, of course," the older man laughed. "Leastways he set off for t'West End a fairish while ago."

With peace in his heart, and an excitement too, Adam crossed the road, his progress towards the familiar yews interrupted once or twice by those who wished to shake his hand. But shortly he stood at the fore end of a long passage, quietly turning the knob of the kitchen door. Cherry was sitting near the fire, tears trickling down her cheeks, but, at the slight sound, she started, jumped up, and in a flurry tried to wipe her eyes.

Her lips trembled. "I . . . I can't help it, Adam. I'm so glad."

"Yes, and I'm glad an' all, so glad that I can't wait to tell you summat as I once said I wanted to tell you i' some place overlooking the Dale," Adam murmured. "Do you remember, lass?"

Her colour faded. "Yes," she whispered.

Adam was glancing round the bright room. "Yes, and I can remember t'first time I ever came in here, when you thought I were Peg Stephen. That, lass," he ended tenderly, "was when I fell i' love with you."

So they looked at one another, a tall young man whose grey, deep-set eyes were anxious, and a pretty young woman whose cheeks were now tinted gloriously.

"And I'm still in love with you," Adam said very distinctly. "Will you marry me, lass?"

Cherry tried to speak, but although at last she replied civilly enough, her sweet-voiced: "Oh, Adam, I'd like nowt better" was somewhat late in the permissive sense, for then she was in his arms and her red lips had just parted from his.

"Champion," Adam grinned. "Now I'm a busy man and I've a lot to say to you, so let's sit in your uncle's chair. If we're fairly close you'll not hold me up by missing owt I say."

Cherry soon experienced several unexpected but thrilling shocks, the first when Adam remarked that he would arrange at once to buy Modesty. "How'll that suit, love?" he inquired. "You an' me setting up to farm there?"

Her soft hair rested on his shoulder. She turned her head slightly more towards him. "The same as before, Adam love," she smiled mistily. "I'd like nowt better. It'll be wonderful."

Adam's involuntary chuckle, and what he said about the wherewithal for the purchase of Modesty, again astonished the young woman nestling on his knee. "Aye," he shook with mirth, "the brass I got in that share deal 'ul nearly pay for it, lass, and so I'll be all right out o' what I had before to stock the farm and so on. But let's get on, love . . . how soon do you think we can get the mistress of the house installed? I'd prefer it as sharp as we can."

"Me, too," his future wife whispered.

Next to be discussed was where to be married, Cherry averse to the Chapel for reasons that were natural. In between it was decided that only those who had stuck to Adam through thick and thin should be present at the wedding, with concessions for such as Wingy Blenkiron who had made amends. Greets Church, where Cherry had loved the services, was proposed and accepted.

"Right, love, I'm playing truant now," Adam announced. "I'll get my clothes changed, have my tea with Hannah as were arranged——"

"I'll go along with you, love," Cherry insisted. "So as we can go in and tell her together . . . about us, I mean."

Adam squeezed her. "Grand, lass," he said. "And after tea we'll foot it to Greets, to see t'Vicar and get fixed up."

"To . . . to-night!" Cherry gasped, but then she laughed contentedly. "I suppose I shall get used to you i' time."

They had had a very fair innings to themselves in view of the fact that Dr. Seaton, in spite of his indignation, continued to spread the news, as did others. In that manner peculiar to the Dale, Adam's whereabouts also were accurately known, and so it was not surprising that Titus Alderson and Lucy Peacock, the first of a stream, hastened to Town Foot to congratulate him. The congratulations became of a two-fold nature when the old mine-agent discovered his niece upon his assistant's lap.

"Aye," murmured Adam after thanking them again, his consideration so profound that his elders and Cherry stared. "Th'only blot on our happiness is Mr. Alderson, what's the best for him. Mind you, he'll be welcome enough at Modesty . . ."

By now Cherry was biting her lip, while Titus Alderson and Lucy Peacock surreptitiously eyed one another, both blushing.

"Well . . . well, you've no call to fret about me, lad," the mine-agent mumbled. "You see, wi' the West Side shares starting to have a bit o' value——"

Adam guffawed. "Aye, there's them an' all, love, and I've a good few," he said, an observation obscure to everyone save Cherry.

As *her* future husband was making heavy weather of it, Mrs. Peacock took the lead. She and Titus were to be married in due course, she said, and he would then reside at the Plug and Feathers. This broached, the pair became expansive, and, when the clatter of footsteps rang on the path, the young couple were being advised not to buy furniture until they had made sure of what they would like from Yew Tree House, where there were quite a few really nice pieces.

For the next few minutes Cherry was kissed and jollied, and Adam was clapped on the back and poked insinuatingly in the ribs. Immediately it was decently possible, they slipped away. Odd flakes of snow were falling in Main Street, where Adam was greeted with smiles and friendly words by people who had not acknowledged him since the closing days of Agnes Pedley's life.

In the tiny kitchen behind the bow-windowed shop, Old Hannah gazed with affection at the couple. "I've heard o' your good news, Adam lad," she said. "An' you've no need to tell me your other news, either, for it's writ on both your faces. Bless you, loves."

Cherry's brief call ended by her remaining to tea for, as Old Hannah firmly pointed out, Titus Alderson was well enough to look after himself for once, and it would do him good anyhow.

Much of the sting had gone out of the wind, but snow was falling thickly when Cherry and Adam walked to Greets, her hand warmly clasped in his overcoat pocket, he swinging a lantern at the other side.

"We're nearly there now, love," Cherry murmured blissfully as they passed the church. "Mr. Penrose's house is just up to the right."

Placing his lamp outside the door, Adam followed Cherry into the roomy Vicarage, where they were ushered into a study in which a comfortable-looking gentleman, pipe in mouth, was busying himself with catgut, hooks and colourful flies. Details about the banns and the wedding date were quickly arranged.

"February the fifth," Adam said, fumbling for pocket-book. "These things sometimes slip your mind, so I reckon I'd better note it, sir."

Cherry contained herself until she was outdoors, but no longer. "I think summat's gone to your head, Adam. As a matter o' fact," she rubbed her cheek against a wet sleeve, "summat's gone to mine, too."

"Aye, love," Adam chuckled.

That was the last thing they laughed at for a while. To Cherry's surprise, Adam, on reaching the main road again, drew her to the right, and from there they went to John Dougill's house on the Green, where, after a short colloquy, the bearded old mining-authority made light of the weather and accompanied them to James Guy's. For privacy's sake the conversation there took place in a fireless room, but Adam, dealing only with relevancies, was not long.

The deadening effect of the snow made the room seem even more quiet when he had done. "Well, lad," John Dougill said at last, "it's the most terrible story I've ever heard i' all my days o' mining. What you've said we'll keep strictly to ourselves and we'll noan let even a word slip out about our part if we come across this lass's uncle. And I think I'm speaking for James here when I say we'll do as you wish, to t'letter."

James Guy looked equally stern as he nodded. "You are, John," he began. "Yes, lad, we'll come to t'mine in the dark hours whenever you send the word, an' if conditions are owt like favourable enough, we'll ride us horses up the tracks northward to Usha Beacon. If we keep on t'moors nobody'll be any wiser."

Both Adam and Cherry thanked them and, as Mr. Dougill seemed inclined to stay behind with his associate, they said good-bye.

On the summit of the main road to Half, the snow was becoming much thicker, but progress as yet was not too difficult lower down. Beyond the Groovers Welcome they paused to listen to the whirring of a multitude of wings and the sounds of wild duck feeding on the Skew, and then continued along, closely together. So, in a little world of their own, clothed by a myriad snowflakes swirling in the light of the lamp, they gradually approached Town Foot near which, a pinpoint bobbing ahead and then strengthening, they saw the light of another pedestrian.

Cherry was too happy to bear enmity. "Good-night, Mrs. Alderson," she called out.

The mistress of Malaga peered, hesitating before she spoke. "I've heard tell as you two are to get wed," she began, raising her lamp until it shone on their glowing faces. "Well . . ." searchingly she stared at Adam, pain investing her dark eyes, "well, I wish you all th'happiness possible, lad, and as for you, lass . . . somehow I hardly think I need wish you it, for . . . for I'm sure you'll have it. Good night."

Abruptly she turned away, leaving them saddened by their glimpse into tragedy. Then on to Yew Tree House, for supper and a talk with a few friends assembled there, some of whom were quite shocked that they were to be married in church instead of at their own chapel.

Finally their parting, the last passionate kiss before Adam walked down a path still deepening in snow, and Cherry's wave as he closed the gate.

From the Roe, outside which there was a great deal of noise and laughter, Adam was boisterously hailed immediately on starting towards Nick Turn. Crossing, as cordially invited, his back was slapped by groovers, dressing-floors men and smelters, both on account of Cherry and himself and because of his own rehabilitation. But it was evident that another matter was responsible for the fun and excitement, a snow-race, the two contestants Cyprian Metcalfe and Daniel.

The pair came out at that moment, stark naked.

"Now then, you know what you're both to do," Matt Tiplady said to them. "To the Royal Alfred, where you snatch a tankard in t'bar—then back again and right down to t'Groovers Welcome, where you leave the tankard you've been carrying, and grab one of Jonas Cottingham's in its place. The loser pays for twenty-eight glasses o' ale to-morrow night and . . ."

A few seconds later the shivering athletes were silently off, difficult to see even three or four yards away. Adam went indoors for a brief spell, but, with Matt Tiplady, who delegated Nathan Wharton to declare the winner, then started off homewards. Wingy Blenkiron was leaving at the same time, a bundle beneath his arm in which trousers, necktie and shirt were certainly visible.

"I'd better take care o' Daniel's things," the postman explained solemnly. "Put 'em in a safe place, like."

Matt Tiplady guffawed. "What wouldn't I give to watch Daniel sneaking into Malaga stripped to t'buff later on."

That kept him and his companion amused as far as the schoolmaster's house, where they bumped into Puke Hastwell and his wife. The Wood Yard foreman was in the middle of saying a few appropriate words to Adam when Mrs. Hastwell's anguished scream disturbed a fine flow of eloquence.

"Two . . . two right queer things has run past!" she gasped.

The foreman's back was turned, and there had been little sound. "Now come, lass," he protested.

"I tell you they did, Puke," his wife persisted, sharpness in her voice. "They were like . . . like great knobbly white monkeys."

"Knobbly . . . *knobbly white monkeys*," Puke Hastwell stuttered dazedly, before he became a trifle stern. "Now come, Milcah."

"I did," Mrs. Hastwell reiterated shrilly. "I'm noan daft."

Adam and Matt, much in the manner of those who wish to withdraw from an embarrassing family squabble, made their excuses, an attitude which did nothing to reconcile the differences of Mr. and Mrs. Hastwell, whom they heard arguing steadily more fiercely as they themselves trudged along to Nick Turn.

In the light of the bracket lamp a grey shadow streaked across their path. Matt Tiplady was wiping his eyes. "A fox, lad," he said weakly. "I shouldn't be surprised if we're in for a right storm."

"And I just don't give a damn, lad," Adam laughed.

It was, he knew, the best day of his life.

* * * *

Next morning, from Modesty, Adam saw Ralph Skidmore riding in a serpentine course down Snorr Moor, his horse's hoofs treading out a track along which his flock would follow; and down at Low Bands Farm, where the snow had drifted, he glimpsed Francis Harker creeping on top of a high wall to reach the cow byre.

Throughout the day there were cold but bright intervals, but the snow between was sufficient to undo clearance at the mines, where gangs with greased shovels had been cutting roads.

In the evening Cherry and Adam struggled to get to Badger Hall. It was supposed to be an ordinary visit, but on arrival there they found a party in all but name, with themselves as guests of honour. On the way home it snowed again, and continued to snow without intermission for thirty-six hours.

4

Hundreds upon hundreds of sheep were missing between Greets and Yorrel as a result of the big snowstorm, and, as there was little Adam could have done at Notion Bridge save wield a shovel, he was amongst a party of farmers who, from Saturday morning until Wednesday evening, beat the moors. Anthony Skidmore was there, with Ralph Skidmore, Francis Harker and Mark Iveson, not forgetting Nell, Hey! Thoo! and the sheepdogs from Low Bands and Back Lane.

As a spectacle it was magnificent, vast white wastes in which every wall was buried. Certain patches near the bottoms were trampled and yellow-tinted, where sheep brought down to safety were eating hay anxiously removed from the hoarded supplies rightly needed to see the beasts in the cow-byres through the winter, and at the lowermost limits of the moor, in suitable places, Will Skidmore and Luther Thwaites worked desperately to bare parts of the heath so that mortality amongst the grouse might not be too severe. All this could be seen by those who, wherever there might be hope, poked and prodded into snow with sticks shoulder-height to a tall man. There was urgency in all, for if thaw came, their efforts would be too late.

Twenty-two sheep only were found on Saturday, but an hour after first light on Sunday Nell scented when working across wind and, more than a quarter of a mile away, eighty-four half-breds were discovered, to be dug out of a nine-foot drift. In the afternoon conditions deteriorated, a strong wind springing from the north-east. When facing the powdery but fierce-driving snow lifted from the ground, the eyes of searchers were no more than slits; ears and nostrils were filled uncomfortably, and the sting on cheeks was as of a hundred little lacerations. Long after dark, weary and worn, the shelter of Badger Hall was attained.

The remarkable effects of the wind were seen the next morning. Whole areas of snow had been thinned, but elsewhere was much deeper, and the horseshoe-shaped inlet of Dubbing Quarry, a hundred and twenty feet high at the back, no longer appeared to exist, filled as it was to the level of the moor. Seven different groups of sheep were dug out that day, all huddled against walls; though some of the wool was eaten from each other's backs, they did not seem greatly worse for their experience. It was a reward which sent tired men home happier, and earned for the dogs the specially good dinners increasing activities demanded.

Tuesday was still cold, and, while the Skidmore children tobogganed joyously down the steep lane from Slackrigg, their grandfather and his helpers were carrying on their shoulders half-breds too weak to walk, ferreted out from beneath an out-jutting ledge of freestone at the foot of Snorr Scar. Of them only two died, gruel pulling round the remainder.

The black-faced sheep were infinitely more hardy and, on Adam's last day before returning to work, a total of three hundred and sixty-two were released on Noggin Moor, the majority in reasonable health. That night the thaw started, a blessing to the horsemen who had been endeavouring to deliver provender to outlying farms, and a boon to such gallant souls as Nell and her kind, who by then could scarcely crawl home.

* * * *

Seen from the front windows of Modesty the higher slopes between Lovely Lady and Silver Seat were still clad in white, but lower down the hills were a network of streams, silvery at that distance but darkly peat-stained at closer quarters. The Skew, covering the Hippy Stones to a depth of ten feet, hissed down dale, and every waterfall was thunderous, that at the Brig filling the house with its tumult.

Painting and joiner's work already arranged, Cherry looked extremely pleased with herself when she shut the front door behind Ned Mason and the mistress of the Plug and Feathers. The mason had promised to fit a new kitchen fireplace within a week, and Mrs. Peacock, the best paper-hanger in Winterings, had undertaken to paper three rooms before the wedding, though only on the understanding that it was to be a present.

"Well now, love," Adam smiled, "afore I go back to the mine, what about the question o' furniture and furnishings, as I think they call 'em?"

That was disposed of fairly quickly. Cherry was to buy the curtaining, bed-linen, crockery, cutlery and so forth by herself at Corvy, where Adam would later help her to select furniture. As everything was being done in a rush they proposed to acquire the minimum, adding when Adam could spare more time.

They had hoped for a quiet evening to themselves at Yew Tree House, but Mr. Alderson and Mr. Kearton changed plans about, and unexpected arrivals were Dinah, who was supposed to be rug-making with her sister-in-law at Blenk Bottom Lane, and Daniel, for once genuinely surprised to see her. She ignored him, however.

A little after eight o'clock, when the undertaker's pipe was drawing badly, he gruffly dispatched the West Side's assistant agent to the joinery shop for a few feathers of a variety, he claimed, superior to those offered him by his host. As an *amende honorable* the errand took a great deal of crediting, but Adam was subsequently advised that in this fashion he had been reinstated publicly in Edmund Kearton's good books.

On his return, Adam had hardly been informed that he could have brought back a more representative selection if he had opened his eyes when, on the path outside, the tramp of many feet resounded.

When Cherry slipped back into the kitchen her expression should have been one of righteous indignation, not stupefaction. "Adam," she whispered, closing the door behind her, "it's James Pedley with a lot o' chaps and he's wanting to see you."

"James Pedley!" Titus Alderson growled. "Well, I know where I'd tell him to go if it were me."

"Th'hot shop," rapped out Mr. Kearton.

Adam, however, decided not to accept this advice, and so, as he reached the passage, absolute silence descended upon the room he had left. Despite straining ears, it was not possible to distinguish what was passing, but there was little doubt when a voice screamed supplicatingly into the dark night.

"Well, I'm noan missing this," Daniel grinned.

Squeezing alongside Adam at the front door he perceived, dimly lighted by the glow from the kitchen window, a semi-circle of extremely sober-looking individuals. At their fore was a hairy creature whom he took to be a dwarf until, more accustomed to the gloom, he realised it was a man kneeling in the slush.

James Pedley had quietened. "Aye, by t'Christian fellowship of a brother i' God, it's been specially arranged as I shall preach i' Winterings Chapel three weeks come next Sunday. And I beg you to be there, Adam Brunskill."

"Three weeks on Sunday, eh?" Adam murmured.

Rectangles of soft light appeared at Smithy House and elsewhere: open doorways. The listeners heard one more passionate appeal.

"Aye, I want you to hear me humiliate myself for misbegottenly charging you wi' a carnal offence, I want you to be present when, the Lord giving me all th'eloquence I'll require, I flail my brother Ambrose with my tongue . . ."

"Two o'clock or six-thirty?" Adam inquired.

"Eh!" James Pedley exclaimed. "Oh, th'evening service, that'll be the important one that day, when I——"

Adam's interruption was brisk. "Right, three weeks next Sunday, in the evening, Mr. Pedley, an' don't forget to change your britches when you get home. You wouldn't care for a stiff tot now?"

"Spiritous liquor——" James Pedley began.

"It does indeed, wards off colds like nowt else. Well," Adam went on genially, "all that now remains is for me to thank you for your attendance, as I indeed do, brethren."

"Amen," said Daniel.

A second later a small party of the Lord's most devout soldiers faced a closed door.

5

The smaller waterwheel at Mary Dressing Floors was slightly out of true, one inch down on the machinery side, and fairly early on Saturday morning, when Len Rukin hastened from the tail of Notion Level to the engineer's shop, Adam was completing arrangements with Sam Kirkbride to rectify the error during the week-end. The groover arrived with news that intruders had been in the vicinity of Queer Drift in the night. No damage had been done.

"We shall have to guard it in t'future," Sam Kirkbride remarked.

"If we do everybody 'ul wonder why," Len Rukin pointed out.

The gathering became almost an official meeting when Bart Hugill and Matt Tiplady joined in. Simon Sunter was the last to come—he had been to Deer Pot, cleaning the grates of the intake. A sudden increase in drainage often washed down choking masses of vegetation or the body of a lamb or sheep, and these could sadly affect water supplies.

Having regard to the subject of Queer Drift, the smelter was asked a question, at first sight irrelevant, about the snow on the moors. He reported that this was lessening quite nicely.

"Right," Adam nodded, "so now we can get on with the hush straight off, can't we? But . . ." twinkling, he eyed his colleagues, "I'm finding myself wi' qualms as to whether the hush water will do damage underground in places we wouldn't like. So we start doing what we can to make everything safe and secure. It's a big job, as 'ul require continuous shifts, of t'chaps who's on the committee and nobody else."

Matt Tiplady slapped his knee, delighted. "I'se getten th'idea, lad. Some on us always near Queer Drift, wi' a good excuse for being there. But what about t'drift? We can't drive it night and day or we'll be through too soon."

"Smoke your pipes . . . knit," Adam grinned. "Do owt you fancy."

The constructional work to be put in hand for the hush was then debated. Towards this, dam-building and the trenching of Water Ling Moor between the two Gutters, Bart ran back to the office, and there wrote out notices which he posted in the village before eleven o'clock. By noon Adam had engaged sixteen men out of the twenty needed.

Much was being done at Modesty that day, but on Cherry's insistence, Adam set out after dinner for Badger Hall, where Nell, surprised by his entrance through a seldom used gateway in the garth, near the grave in which half-breds crushed to death by the thaw had been buried barked twice before creeping forward abjectly on her belly to ask pardon for a rather stupid mistake.

A few sheep were there, lame, miserable and foul-smelling. The foot rot was treated with vitriol, the proud flesh destroyed by dropping the fiery liquid on to it, a nauseous job at which Adam acted as Mr. Skidmore's helper. The pair of them then thoroughly washed their hands, prelude to a smoke and a yarn in the sweet-smelling cow-byre where soft-eyed cattle stood in a row upon snug bracken bedding, their coats a little thin after being so long confined.

As Adam opened the front door of Modesty on returning he heard a number of young ladies chattering away against the sounds of vigorous scrubbing, and when he went into the kitchen he found Cherry and Dinah on their knees. A couple of visitors were there, too, their feet on gradually diminishing islands of dry flagstones.

Fronick Blenkiron, it seemed, had come to express her regrets both to himself and Cherry. As it happened, her cousin had always declared that Ralph Skidmore's story about the trousers was too silly to be entertained. "Oh, never mind such nonsense, Fronick," Annamaria snorted. "But if you must apologise to Adam, get it done wi', and let's be off. I can't for the life of me think whatever Arthur's up to till now of a Saturday afternoon."

"Well . . . I'm right sorry, Adam," Fronick wailed, busy with handkerchief.

"Of all t'cry-babies," Annamaria said disgustedly. "Well, you've brought it on yourself, lass. Didn't I tell you as there'd never been any need to apologise to him?"

Dinah's voice came from low down. "Eh! Annamaria, won't you ever learn?"

Miss Rutter stuck to her guns. "I'm suited enough as Adam's cleared, but you can't deny as it looked a certainty he were guilty," she asserted. "There were Agnes's underclothes for one thing——"

Fronick's elbow jabbed frantically, but it was Cherry who put an end to the discussion. "I don't want you to say any more about it, Annamaria," she said firmly. "*Ever*, if you please."

Grumbling about the "strangeness of some folk," Annamaria departed with her cousin, which allowed those left to talk about more pleasant subjects.

"Well, and how are you getting on?" Adam inquired. "Cruel hard work that, with dirt encrusted as it must be."

Dinah giggled. "I've an idea what he's going to say next, Cherry. As we mustn't overtire ourselves."

"And I can guess what he's after, lass," Cherry laughed. "Yes, we're making tea soon, lad."

"Ah!" Adam beamed.

Wingy, Bart and Hugh Bearpark arrived for the meal. The joiner, who was spending the evening at Modesty fixing up shelves, had got his bag of tools with him and, before sitting down, drew Adam to one side.

"I saw summat funny when I collected my tackle," he began. "You know what's just across Winterings Gill from t'carpenter's shop—up that deep gully?"

"Aye," Adam nodded, "th'East Side Company's magazine."

"Well," said Hugh Bearpark, enjoying the announcement, "Reuben Nattrass an' his cousin Arthur brought out enough black powder to blow up Winterings."

"Looks like as if we're stirring 'em up," Adam ruminated. "Anyroad, we've taken the necessary steps i' time, Len and John'll have got there now."

The joiner chuckled. "Freestone's taken his knitting. He says he's fully expecting to do a few pairs of long stockings afore t'gun goes off."

After tea work began again in earnest, Cherry and Dinah, additionally lighted by two borrowed oil-lamps, cutting out material in the front room and endeavouring to chat to the accompaniment of hammering and sawing; elsewhere, enthusiastic young men took up floorboards, freed window sashes, or raised flagstones in the hall to level them anew.

Shortly before nine o'clock, however, Modesty again became as silent as the increasing wind permitted. The two young women were going along to Yew Tree House to make supper, but on the gusty hump of the Brig, Adam slipped his arm round Cherry's trim waist. "I'm off into t'Plug for ten minutes, lass," he said. "I'd like to know if the seed that's been dropped has fallen on good ground."

"All right, love," she smiled.

Several items of news had reached Winterings that week—above Gayle in Wensleydale, Jimmy Metcalfe's body had been recovered from Wether Fell, where he had died in the snow; at the Old Gang Lead Mines in Swaledale, William Peacock's back had been broken when he holed through to water in an old level; Waller Heslop of Buckden in Wharfedale had been swept away and drowned in the swollen Wharf; and Noah Cherry and his wife, from Yorrel, had been killed in a railway disaster in America.

But in the Plug and Feathers that night these matters took a very secondary place to speculation about a hush for which the signal of full steam ahead had just been announced. Not a word, in Adam's hearing, passed about a drift called Queer.

* * * *

A few minutes before midnight on Sunday, as Reuben Nattrass pencilled a line on a soiled plan, his companion drew a quick breath, the slight sound lost in the incessant roar of the gale, whose furious assault whistled around the East Side Company's office.

"It's heading straight as a die for them rails," Arthur Nattrass shouted, wise enough not to move into the direct rays of a carefully-shaded lamp. "He must know summat about 'em."

Irritated, Reuben Nattrass swung round. "That drift's set dead east because it's a common practice to stick to t'principal points of the compass when you're nobbut probing. But I'll tell you this, if I once get a smell of an inkling he's summat like that i' mind, I know one road to stop him."

"How?" Arthur Nattrass asked, eagerness dispelling fright.

Reuben Nattrass laughed harshly. "Where it'll hurt most . . . getting hold o' that young woman as he's supposed to be wedding. Aye, he'd either throw his hand in then, or else . . ." He smiled a little, dark eyes becoming a shade darker. "Well, maybe an hour wi' her in a right secluded spot 'ud be worth what it might cost."

Arthur Nattrass's eagerness had gone. He looked a young man sick to the soul with apprehension. His dejection was further increased when, as they shouldered heavy wallets containing explosives and tools, his cousin referred again to a missing plan. "The proper one as I did i' ink," Reuben Nattrass snapped. "Have you no bloody idea where it were stuffed away? It's noan an article as wants leaving about."

The other sighed. "Which way are we going? We can't go up Notion because t'chaps as is getting ready for that flaming hush of Brunskill's 'ud sight us."

"By God!" Reuben Nattrass murmured with the exasperation of a strong man sorely tried, "have you forgotten as I know more of th'old workings hereabouts than anybody else alive?"

The climbing of Winterings Gill to Smiddy Bridge, in darkness and a howling wind, was unpleasant enough, but far more so was the passage across the heights of Water Ling Moor. A very real danger existed, however, in the descent of Old Joss Air Shaft, fifty fathoms of insecure hand and toe holes in shaky stonework with never a minute's respite. When he stepped on to the sump even the raven-haired mining-agent was breathing unevenly, and his cousin was in a parlous state.

"You stop here," Reuben Nattrass ordered, taking off his hat to snuff the candle. "I'll feel my way forward to spy out what there is."

His walk cat-like despite clogs, he disappeared into the blackness, to edge through way-gates and galleries. Ears alert, he checked himself suddenly, creeping round a bend until, in the distance, he saw the yellow glow of a candle and a man comfortably seated, jaws consolingly occupied.

At that spectacle, Reuben Nattrass returned to his cousin, the upward jerk of a thumb all that was necessary. Then the perilous ascent of the air shaft and the walk down to the office in conditions making speech impossible. Indoors again, the lamp was lighted and wallets removed.

"What was there?" Arthur Nattrass asked.

"A chap enjoying hisself chawing bacca." His cousin derided. "By God, but Brunskill must be bloody easy to hoodwink. Anyroad, there's nowt we could have done, but as it happens I've had the hell of a better idea . . . we're leaving everything alone for the time being."

"Leave everything . . . alone!" Arthur Nattrass ejaculated.

Reuben Nattrass smiled broadly. "Now listen, lad," he began amiably. "Nowt of any kind 'ul happen about t'drift or owt else just now, because they're occupied with this hush to th'exclusion of everything. Right, eh? Now the hush, as they've showed they fear, is bound to do a certain amount o' damage in the workings. But nobody can foresee how much. Well, you and me is going to add to it. On the very night after the hush, when nobody 'ul be there, we'll go down again. And for once I'se copying Brunskill's example—dynamite . . . plenty . . . for t'biggest blasting job as has ever been done i' Skewdale, which 'ul leave a trail o ruined workings from Doomsday High to Old Joss. Doomsday . . . aye, them rails 'ul be lost till then and long after."

"And where's all this going to finish?" Arthur Nattrass said shrilly.

"All what?" Reuben Nattrass asked.

The touch of contempt fired the younger man. "T'rails . . . grabbing Cherry Dinsdale . . . now this bloody blowing-up business," he bawled.

Reuben Nattrass bent down, to bring out a bottle of brandy from a cupboard. "Here, take a long swig o' this." He treated himself similarly, wiped his lips with the back of his hand, and leaned forward. "I'se inclined to think you haven't so much heart i' all this, Arthur," he said coldly. "But whether you have or you haven't you might as well know that you'll noan be 'lowed to backslide. And I'd better remind you that when them rails were carried you carried one end. You're in this wi' me, an' that's how you're staying . . . understand?"

Nothing further was said on the issue, and indeed little at all. From mining rags they changed into Sunday clothes before stepping into the darkness, Reuben Nattrass returning to Ash Grove by the pastures, Arthur Nattrass taking the trods to Greets, where, his future course of action determined, he climbed to his bedroom by a fall-pipe.

* * * *

On Market Day morning, as the Skidmores' Prue cautiously proceeded round Nick Turn, where once she had been involved in a collision, Adam and his young lady were waiting outside the gate of Yew Tree House.

"Well . . . well, it's your money, Adam," Cherry blushingly expostulated. "I mean you ought to decide, too."

"Now listen, lass," Adam smiled. "Whatever you'll buy suits me."

Dinah and her mother and father duly arrived alongside, when Cherry got into the trap, which started off down the main road. In Corvy, after disembarking the womenfolk, Anthony Skidmore drove to the premises of a coachbuilder to strike a bargain about the refurbishing of his best trap. As he came out, Arthur Nattrass was passing, dressed up and carrying a leather bag.

"Well, where are you off to, lad?" the master of Badger Hall inquired.

The young man jumped perceptibly. "Oh, it's you, Mr. Skidmore," he said wanly. "Nay, I'm off somewhere or other as my fancy takes me. Wandering o'er land and sea as you might say."

"Whatever for?" Anthony Skidmore exclaimed.

A pair of narrow shoulders shrugged. "It's in my blood, I reckon," their owner replied, his laugh, as always, a little light-coloured. "A rover, like."

Perhaps a couple of minutes later, utterly nonplussed, the older man watched a weedy figure swagger off towards the station. "Well," he muttered, fingering iron-grey beard, "if yon's a bold roamer, he's setting off wi' about the palest face I ever saw."

This strange encounter was duly related to the ladies over dinner at the Saracen. Cherry and her friend gleaned decidedly more at the Old Cow Inn on the way home, where Mr. Skidmore stopped for an important conversation about a bull. The girls, staying to straighten the many parcels in the trap, the majority Cherry's, were somewhat behind Mrs. Skidmore in entering the auctioneer's house. Just over the threshold they were arrested by a beckoning finger, and so turned into the former tap-room.

"It's about Arthur, isn't it, lass?" Dinah said.

Annamaria's eyes were red and swollen, her cheeks blotchy. "He's run away," she told them tragically. "I don't know what for except that it's summat awful. He . . . he wrote saying as he'd never be able to come back to Skewdale so . . . so long as breath were in his body."

"Did he give you any idea why?" Cherry asked.

Annamaria shook her head. "No, but I'm certain as it's summat to do wi' that big baboon of a cousin. And another reason why I think so," she continued after sniffing prodigiously, "is that Arthur said as I'd to tell you to take care, Cherry. He didn't explain why, but . . ."

Dinah nodded with severity. "We all know as Reuben Nattrass has never given up hope o' getting her, that's why."

"And it's silly, an' what could he do about it?" Cherry declared. "It's a free world, isn't it?"

This carefree attitude was far removed from that of her friend. Dinah was worrying when she went to bed, and the next day her troubled thoughts sent her along to Yew Tree House an hour before Dr. Seaton was due to start his lecture in the Literary Institute on 'Surgery and Superstition.' Near Old Hannah's, recognising Adam's tread behind her, she gathered up her skirts and flew to Town Foot. Fortunately Cherry was alone, and breathlessly she outlined her purpose.

"*Never* go out by myself!" Cherry laughed. "Oh, Dinah, you are funny."

"Funny or not," Dinah said, "you're promising."

"But I've to shop, and do lots o' things, like walking to the West End," Modesty's future mistress protested. "An' washing," she added.

On reflection, Dinah concluded she might be carrying things too far. She compromised by demanding that Cherry would never leave home by herself when it was dark. "And if you don't promise, I'm telling Adam," she threatened as the gate clicked. "That's him if you don't know."

"I promise," Cherry capitulated hurriedly.

"Cross your heart?" Dinah inquired, relentless.

"Cross my heart," Cherry nodded.

An inviolable oath entered upon, the two girls co-operated most loyally to hide from a young man that anything untoward had happened.

The day but one afterwards Cherry was again in Corvy, buying furniture with Adam, and smaller oddments, many of which they took back with them. The trap exceedingly well laden, Ben was not pushed along the road to Greets, where, near the elm on the Green, perceiving a gentleman in the light of the lamp over the entrance to the Friends' Meeting House, Adam pulled up for a few words.

"I see you've getten t'biggest trouble of your future wi' you, lad," Mr. Guy remarked jovially.

"I suspicion so," Adam laughed.

From then Cherry discerned a distinct turn in the nature of the conversation. "Aye, I've just been along to John Dougill's for a bit on a crack," James Guy went on. "About a little matter . . ." he cleared his throat, "as we've arranged to see to to-morrow night."

That was all, nothing much really, but Cherry wondered as they drove by the castellated wall of Greets Hall. At the foot of the hill beyond the B.G. Inn and the old turnpike Bar House, Adam reined in Ben and got out.

"Let me walk with you, love," Cherry said. "It'll be easier still for him then."

As she stood in the back of the trap he put his hands on her waist and lightly set her down. Tightly linked, they steadily marched up the moor road alongside the snuff-brown galloway.

"Well, love," he said fondly, "a week from now you'll noan be Miss Cherry Dinsdale."

"Oh, Adam, I won't, will I?" she said, almost choking with joy. "It's too wonderful to think on."

"Aye, lass," Adam's deep voice was contented.

They were much higher, and at least four kisses had been exchanged when quietly she asked a question. "Will it all be over by then, Adam?"

He knew what she meant. "By Tuesday afternoon, I reckon, love," he told her. "So long as we've no really hard weather."

She turned to him. "That were what you and Mr. Guy were talking about, weren't it?"

From the brow of the road the Dale stretched darkly ahead, a few twinkling lights marking the cottages of Half below.

"Yes, love," Adam said. "It starts to-morrow night at eleven."

The weather had been dull all day, but just then the clouds began to roll aside, stars appearing until a large part of the heavens was brilliantly studded, the soft starshine drawing a distinction between the far-extending lines of the fells and the sky. To Cherry it seemed a good omen.

CHAPTER SEVENTEEN

I

THREE-QUARTERS of a mile below Smiddy Bridge on Legatt's Way, sheltering in the lee of the big dead heap of Great Faith Shaft from fiercely driving sleet, Adam and Bart listened intently. This time each unmistakably heard the soft pad of hoofs, and so the clerk, holding the lamp aloft, squelched into the middle of the Roman road. Soon Messrs. Guy and Dougill, bearded and many-caped, were stiffly dismounting, Adam taking charge of their plans and mining instruments.

"It's been a rough trip for you," he said. "Came so suddenly, too."

"Ah, well, never mind, lad," James Guy grunted.

Bart, who was remaining with the horses, led them into the roofless winding-engine house, where their backs were protected with the sacking he and Adam had brought.

The party of three crossed a strip of Water Ling Moor before taking to the slippery ladders of Great Faith Shaft, stepping off these at Mary Level, along which they walked to Noddy John's Rise, descending this to Notion Level, where Adam ceased to sweat. Both old gentlemen, however, had been testy when he had suggested a longer but safer route.

From there it was easy to the New Cross Cut, where the committee waited almost in full force.

"Right," John Dougill said when, outer clothing discarded, he stood revealed in a tattered working suit. "We'll want two helpers."

Plans were unrolled, the corners pinned down by stones; the tripods of dial and candle-reader set up; measuring chain placed in readiness; extra candles stuck in clay daubs on the rocky sides. By two o'clock, Mr. Dougill and Mr. Guy satisfied themselves they were precisely positioned as Adam's plan stated and that the bearing and length of a very new gallery coincided exactly with the angle and dimensions he had ruled. Finally they assured themselves that the forehead of Queer Drift was absolutely intact.

Adam received permission to proceed. "Go ahead, Daniel," he then called.

In a secluded traverse off Old Joss Level, two old mining agents and the rest of the men waited, the talk desultory. At last it came, a tearing report assailing the ear-drums, echoes of it continuing in declining volume through the workings; candles died in gusts of dust; with aftermath the smell of efficiently exploded dynamite, not the characteristic odour of black powder.

None spoke on the return to Queer Drift, the forehead of which had been neatly blasted out. Gradually, as the haze settled, it was possible to see what was in front—an old working, contained at the back by the debris blown down by Adam months before, its sole seven or eight feet lower than the open door-like end of Queer Drift, with a pile of tram-rails in the centre.

"An honourable profession tarnished," James Guy sighed.

"Aye," John Dougill concurred. "But we must finish t'job properly . . . there's no telling where this may end."

The exact distance between the rails and the gaping end of Queer Drift was noted, and two of the rails were lifted out, ultimately to be stored securely. A small bright patch was filed at the end of each rail upon which, as a temporary measure, Mr. Dougill and Mr. Guy scratched their names.

"Well, I think that's all, Adam lad," the latter murmured. "You understand that fro' now this business is out of your hands?"

Neither gave any clue as to what their joint action might be, but started back at once, Matt Tiplady escorting them. When the sounds of retreating footsteps died, Adam pointed up Alderson's New Drift, down which the hush water would rush from Doomsday High Shaft. "Now then, lads, summat else," he said. "For about four fathoms back, and right through Queer Drift, rip out the sole about five feet deeper. Leave the step alone, but drill shot-holes in it, and arrange so as everything is ready by nine o'clock Tuesday morning."

A number of dumbfounded men stared speechlessly at him.

* * * *

While listening to Mr. Wade's observations Adam could not help reflecting how often he had been compelled to pledge others to secrecy while reserving a part of the secret to himself. On this occasion he was not able to mention the rails, although he revealed that the hush water might, under conditions he did not specify, move eastwards. He also produced a letter.

"Mmph!" The chairman blew out his cheeks. "Yes, I should say these lines of Mr. Storey's quite cover us, Brunskill."

"Gorilla, gorilla, impertinent an' all," Mr. Rutter snapped.

Initial bewilderment over, the others realised this surprising comment was intended for Reuben Nattrass, who was striding out of the Wood Yard gates. The East Side's agent, Adam concluded after scrutinising him carefully, betrayed just the slightest sign that the default of his cousin Arthur had shaken him.

"Well now, Brunskill," Mr. Wade said after this diversion, "before you leave us, I think I should say that you have our entire confidence."

Thanking them, Adam picked up his cap and went along to Modesty, where he changed and had dinner before setting out for the Bait House, where he put up the Bargains before a record attendance, accelerating the proceedings on noticing a passing cart loaded with furniture. Nevertheless when he reached the West End again, Daniel and Wingy were carrying into Modesty the last of the smaller articles. In the room at the left-hand side of the front door, which was to be the best parlour, Bart was lifting one end of a chiffonier while Dinah held the other. Cherry directed operations.

"Hey! Adam lad," the clerk groaned, "come and give me a spell." "We've tried it against two of t'walls so far, an inch at a time, mind you——"

"Bart 'ud stick it afore the fireplace if it were left to him," Dinah giggled. "He's that distracted by this hush——"

"Cherry's Hush, if you please, lass," the postman grinned. "Aye, that's what everybody's calling it."

"Which they should, lad," Adam reminded him. "Who found the gozzan, and who suggested using an old shaft?"

"But you planned it, love," Cherry insisted.

"By!" Daniel sighed forlornly, eyeing Dinah, "but it must be grand to have a young woman so passionately devoted."

"Depends on t'chap as well," Wingy Blenkiron said innocently. "Adam isn't like some whose eyes pop out on stalks whenever they spy the flutter of a lass's skirts."

"You seem to be looking hard at me, lad," Daniel observed.

"You have to take t'rough with t'smooth sometimes," the postman guffawed.

"Sharp as a needle, isn't he?" Daniel grunted.

Work awaited them, curtain pole brackets to be screwed into position, and oil-cloth to be laid. Then Ned Mason presented himself, with the devilish inopportuneness of timing shared by all masons, to finish off the kitchen fireplace.

Before separating for the evening, a walk the next day to Cherry's Hush was decided upon, "weather permitting," as Bart Hugill despairingly remarked.

However, though grey and chilly, Sunday afternoon was fine when he and the others went up Water Ling Moor, an outing during which he suffered a great deal of teasing. "Well, I do hope as it keeps fair," he expostulated. "And I'm noan th'only one as is eager."

He pointed to a distant skyline, where two tiny figures, wallets humped on their backs, moved slowly towards each other. Nowadays Len Rukin and Hugh Bearpark went home once a month only, but this day the time of rendezvous at the lonely place where they habitually met on returning from their respective dales had obviously been advanced.

The clerk rammed home his belief. "Aye," he went on, "and everyone o' you is as keen as me, t'lasses as much as us chaps."

In honesty, no one could deny what he said.

* * * *

As he descended the stairs early next morning, the light of Adam's candle shone upon possessions in the hallway—a green-and-gold iron bedstead bought for a guinea, and their greatest bargain of all, for half a guinea more, a French-polished mahogany card-table on turned legs.

"Aye, that right took her eye," he smiled, squeezing past a deal table supporting rolls of Kidderminster carpet and India check coco-matting. "But there's no doubt it's real nice."

While lighting the fire, he pondered about a very important responsibility, for which Freestone John was eminently fitted. "Yes, I'll talk to him this afternoon," he decided.

On the moors that morning, with the dam-builders and trenchers, he was exceptionally busy, but, after midday bait, returned to Modesty to meet Cherry, who was armed with cloths and a floor polish of Mr. Kearton's own making. Sundry domestic matters had been settled when Mary Jane arrived with Meg, who, if still bulging with puppy fat, was beginning to resemble her famous mother.

"I thought I'd bring your bitch, to get it used to t'place, Cherry," she explained when the puppy's exuberance had declined. "But I'll noan take her out too much because it wouldn't do if she got it into her head as I were her missus and not you, would it?"

"Well . . . well it might be awkward, love," Cherry, in certain difficulties, agreed.

The weekly weighing of duty lead was due to start in the Weigh Place before long, and so Adam, who also was trying not to laugh, said good-bye, picking up Cherry to kiss her. Before putting her down, however, he thought another inspection of Ned's fireplace might be desirable. Oblivious apparently that he was still bearing a burden, though absent-mindedly he swung it to cradle comfortably in his arms, he walked into the kitchen, the beginning of a tour which ended in the peat place, the crossing to which caused two rosy-cheeked girls to hang round a side window of the Plug and Feathers, where they goggled, delighted.

"Aye," Adam murmured, "a fairish stock. But another load or two o' kindling wouldn't come amiss. I'll tell Cherry I'm seeing to it."

That young lady whispered into his ear, as was very convenient for her to do. "I'm perched here yet, love. Or has it escaped your notice?"

Benignly Mary Jane had been watching this lover-like nonsense, and, as Cherry was put gently on the floor, she mentioned her own parents. "My father never lugged my mother all up and down t'shop like that, leastways not as I remember—of course . . ." she had an afterthought, "he might have done at the beginning, afore they were wed, mightn't he?"

Cherry did what she could to dispel a dispassionate acceptance of the decline in tender relationships of man and wife. "Your father and mother always thought t'world of one another, Mary Jane," she said.

"And make sure of a chap who is the same with you, love," Adam suggested.

Mary Jane's eyes acquired a soft and remote expression. "I'd like," she said, but became progressively more practical. "But it's all right me talking—you can keep a chap up to the scratch i' most ways, but noan at tossing you up to t'ceiling whenever his eyes light on you. But, of course, there's compensations like in owt else. When the childer start coming——"

"I'm off, Cherry lass," Adam grinned.

His young lady quite failed to meet his glance. "All right, love," she said confusedly.

In the Weigh Place that afternoon Henry Hird was good enough to remark, when he had impressed with his hammer the last encircled C.G. on the last pig of duty lead, that the royalty owner was very pleased with the steadily rising production, although he put it a little differently.

"Aye," he boomed, eyeing a respectably-sized stack of silvery shining criss-crossed piled pigs of lead. "I'm very gratified wi' what you've accomplished, Adam lad. And Sir Charles is an' all, of course."

The hush, a topic of eager discussion for miles around, was talked about until the agent mounted to ride down to Malaga, to take tea with his sister, and then Adam, who had seen Freestone John arriving, went to the office, where he told the Quaker what he required of him: to make sure the following morning that none of the East Side Company's groovers and trammers entered workings where they might be endangered if the hush water surged eastwards.

The dignified Quaker had no doubts. "Leave it to me, friend," he promised. "I'll be at the tail of Bucker Level early enough to stop 'em."

Detained in clearing up final details, it was approaching eight o'clock when Adam walked up the path to Yew Tree House, where lively voices carried to him from the kitchen. Cherry came out as he wiped his feet on the mat and, after he had kissed her, she made a face and whispered:

"Lots o' company to-night, and they aren't showing any signs of going, either."

"Who's here, lass?" he inquired, adding: "Aye, really?" when she counted off. "Now, let's see . . . if it happened to get into Hannah's head that she'd left t'larder door open and the visiting cat were on the rampage—and if your uncle started to have the notion that Mrs. Peacock—who oft seems to be needing a man's help nowadays—were having trouble with a barrel o' beer . . ."

Cherry laughed. "What are you up to now, love?"

When they went in the kitchen, Mr. Alderson was energetically declaring that nothing would keep him away from the hush. "Aye, I've arranged wi' Adam to have Ben, an' I shall be off bright and early."

"You're noan th'only one, Titus," Old Hannah crowed. "I were a little lass when I last saw a big hush an' I'm not missing this 'un. Oh, yes, I shall be there on the donkey as I've borrowed, wi' my attendants."

The minute hand of the grandfather clock was nearly upright, but, before the hour struck, Adam had succeeded in planting a doubt in Francis Harker's mind about the health of a prized bull, and Mark Iveson was puzzling about a wandering flock of sheep. Old Hannah's turn came, too, as did the master's of the house.

"There! That's all four of 'em," Adam breathed pleasurably when they had the place to themselves. "Not much after five past either."

"And how are you going to stop other folk coming for t'latest information about the hush?" Cherry wanted to know.

"They'll never come if they think nobody's in, love," he told her, shocked at her obtuseness. "So we'll see to that, eh?"

Cherry's bright eyes reflected the last glow of the lamp he had turned out. Until ten o'clock, unmolested, they once again shared a chair.

* * * *

The more distant travellers starting in darkness, walkers and vehicles of every description began to converge on Winterings, and by eight o'clock a never-ending procession climbed Sorrow Near.

About half-past eight, shortly after Old Hannah rode forward serenely from Notion Bridge on a donkey led by Bob and Ward, the West Side Company's clerk ran panting up Mine Road.

"Adam," he gasped, "that shimozzle outside the tail o' Bucker Level is getting worse. Th'East Side groovers won't go in, and Reuben Nattrass is that frenzied he'll fell Freestone John as likely as not."

Adam nodded. "Me and Daniel were going down anyway, so we'll be off, Bart. Catch Cherry as she comes up Sleety Slape and tell her to wait for me in th'office."

A considerable throng milled around Bucker Level, backed by scores upon scores of sightseers who had halted to listen to the row. As Adam and his friend came within earshot they heard the determined summing-up of a middle-aged groover.

"Take no heed of what a bloody fool like Freestone John says," Reuben Nattrass roared back at him. "How the hell could we be affected?"

Adam elbowed through, not seen by his opponent until he was quite near. "I want a word with you, Nattrass," he said sternly. "By ourselves."

The other swung round viciously. "Aye, and I want more nor a word wi' you. What's the bloody game you're up to?"

Steadily Adam looked at him. "That's summat I've come to tell you," he said. "And if you don't want it privately you can have it here . . . *now*."

Temper mounting dangerously, Reuben Nattrass stared back. For several moments they stood so, squared to one another, and then, with an impatient oath, the East Side's agent thrust towards the bingstead. Adam followed, restraining Daniel with a movement of his hand. Watched dumbly by the crowd, the two agents disappeared into the small building.

"Now, let's have it sharp, Brunskill," Reuben Nattrass growled.

"Well, this is it," Adam began crisply. "Barring a thin rib o' rock, I've driven a deep-soled drift out from t'New Drift to the pile of tram-rails you heaped for Titus Alderson's undoing when he were dialling. That step of rock is drilled for blasting and t'charges are in, and the choice is yours as to which way the hush water goes. But what you'll have to do afore I'll stop blowing t'step is to admit to what you've done to a few responsible people. That won't save your skin, but at least it'll prevent damage to your company's property and keep men working."

Shock drained Reuben Nattrass's cheeks of colour; his mouth was slack, and his eyes were those of a man fumbling to comprehend the full measure of the disaster which had befallen him.

"What tram-rails?" he said thickly.

"Is that your last word?" Adam demanded.

Reuben Nattrass took a deep breath. "I don't know what the flaming hell you're jawing about, Brunskill," he said, licking his lips. "But if that bloody cousin Arthur o' mine has been telling fancy yarns——"

"It's your last word then?" Adam intervened grimly. "Well, it's mine and all."

With a cat-like spring, Reuben Nattrass leapt forward, the violence of his onrush hurling Adam through the double doorway. "That bloody arm o' yours right?" he snarled. "It'd better be, because even if it's noan I'se going to belt you every inch of t'way back to that office of yours."

"My arm's as sound as a bell," Adam told him coolly. "But there's going to be no fight until everything to do with th'hush is over. Then, if you still want one, you can have it. Meanwhile I've summat to see to —the blasting o' that step."

Veins stood out on Reuben Nattrass's forehead. "If you do, Brunskill," he said, "I'll bloody well——"

Adam did not wait for the threat to materialise, but nodded towards a friend, throwing his hands up in illustration of the disruptive forces of high explosives. Daniel waved understanding and then, spinning round, sprinted up the gritstone road to Notion Bridge.

After reaching the top of the steep rise beyond Worm Gutter, Adam and Cherry saw the crowd, more than a thousand strong, arranged in a tight horseshoe around the dam, the lower ends coming close at each side to the channel down which the water would run. Old Hannah's was not the only donkey, either; and about a hundred people were mounted, notable amongst them Sir Charles Grafton and the much more squirely figure of Mr. Miles Buckle, Steward of the Manor.

Greeted the whole way up, Cherry and her young man gradually skirted to the rear of the temporary reservoir, where they climbed the retaining bank, walking upon this, a wide wall of turfs, as far as the crude sluice-gate in the middle of the outer side, a drop of eight or nine feet before them and water lapping at their heels behind.

"Well, here she is, you two," Adam smiled. "Everything ready for her?"

Cherry blushed as she tried to control her skirts. The wind was playful, and many people were strung out below on the line down to Doomsday High Shaft.

"Will it be long?" she inquired.

"Nay, you want to make t'most of it," Sam Kirkbride said.

"One of the penalties incurred by famous adventurers, lass," Hugh Bearpark laughed.

The assembly, which seemed to include every scholar of the Wesleyan Day School, were gossiping avidly about the latest sensation of all, Adam's plain intimation to Reuben Nattrass that his arm was perfectly sound. For weeks the East Side's agent had been making his intentions publicly known, and speculation was rife as to when, in view of his opponent's wedding, the fight would be.

Despite this, hardly anyone amongst the concourse failed to glance every few seconds across the moor, towards a small building at the foot of the pipe-line from Deer Pot. When the quickest eyed of them shouted excitedly on perceiving the first figure to appear at Maybe Shaft, the throng was absolutely silent as one by one men clasped the spindle at the distant eye, to scramble out of the shaft.

"I've to turn this wheel," Cherry gulped, "when Daniel waves?"

Faces were all one way until a white cloth on a pole was jubilantly flaunted, when a mass of heads swung round, in the direction of three men and the young woman they were bending to assist. As frothy trickles began to slip past the opening sluice, a piping cheer went up from the youngsters.

Turf banks have their weaknesses. "Come on, lass," Adam said.

The water was running downhill fast, a creamy surge which quickly became darkly coloured with soil. Then, in succession, clods of earth were thrown up, small stones and larger pieces of rock. The rushing stream scoured deeper, tearing out boulders which, grinding along, added a more ominous note to the prevailing sound. For eleven minutes the torrent raged, when the deafening noise died and peace returned to the far-spreading moor. There was a moment's inaction, and then young and old swarmed into a sharply-scored defile which, in years to come, when clothed with fine turf upon which a few rocks might be strewn, would strike an observer as some queer, dried-up water-course.

"I'm that worked up, Adam love," Cherry confessed. "I hope I haven't nipped you black and blue."

Long before reaching the lode they knew it was not barren, too many faces were delighted for that. Sir Charles Grafton, riding away, offered a word of congratulation, and Mr. Buckle reined in to do the same, adding that the Manor had no complaints. Adam, of course, made an inspection, but ever mindful that water at high pressure might be viciously surging forward far beneath their feet, did not linger.

Acutely aware of this also, Cherry did her utmost to hide her fears about the possibility that shortly Reuben Nattrass would have immeasurably more reason for hating Adam. "Oh, it's wonderful," she said brightly. "I know there isn't a terrible lot, but every bit helps, doesn't it?"

They had joined the stream of spectators winding along the trod, and although he was wearing a grimy working suit and she was attired suitably for an official office recently performed, they were proceeding arm-in-arm.

"I thought t'mineral looked fairly promising, lass," Adam replied.

Nearby, Edmund Kearton was walking alongside Mr. Wade's horse. The West Side Company's chairman, noticing them, smiled down at Cherry as he told her that in due course she could hope to receive a souvenir of her discovery, a garden ornament cast in lead from the first bings of ore taken from the hush.

"Oh, I'd love summat like that, as a reminder," Cherry glowed. "And it is kind of you, Mr. Wade. Isn't it, Adam?"

"It is that, sir," said Adam. "It'll right set off the front garden."

"Aye, so long as it's proper," Mr. Kearton complained. "I'm being no party to one o' them naked figures of a Greek woman as has been mentioned. The garden o' Modesty is seen from the Chapel, but what might please th'eye of a dissolute nobleman in his park——"

Handkerchief out, the spinner's trumpeting drowned the undertaker's words. But, though scarlet-faced afterwards, Mr. Wade managed wheezily to convey to Cherry that she would be consulted before anything was decided.

Just then Richard Blenkiron nodded at Adam, his demeanour so unusual that Cherry turned to stare at him. Since childhood she had known the blacksmith's jollity and deep-chested laughter, and the fiery temper, too, but never before had he appeared as he was now: a man of iron-hard mouth and vengeful eyes.

"Adam," she whispered, "whatever's up wi' Mr. Blenkiron?"

When Adam had steered her on to a narrow track which, within a few hundred yards, gave a view down Winterings Gill, he answered her while peering keenly ahead. "Maybe he knows all about how your uncle were deceived, love," he murmured. "I don't think either Mr. Guy or Mr. Dougill will let the grass grow under their feet."

"I wonder what they'll do about it?" Cherry said.

"We'll see," Adam muttered. "As we'll soon see about summat else, too."

Cherry looked up at him and then, following his glance, gazed down the ravine, at the grey buildings around Bucker Level. "The hush water," she said, her breath catching. "It'll run out of th'East Side workings down yonder, won't it? Where we pass."

Adam nodded. "That's my reckoning, love, but I don't know when exactly, though I shouldn't think it'll be long."

In front, the advance guard of a long line of pedestrians and horsemen dipped over a bluff, to wind downwards to the wharf-like road leading from the North Smelt Mill to Notion Bridge.

The alarm was given by a sightseeing party of East Side groovers who, returning across the moor to their places in the rises of Martha Level, heard water swashing furiously past the sump of a ventilation shaft. Far away the crowd was streaming along Mine Road, but the frantic signals of men who suspected what had happened were understood. In the vicinity of Bucker Level, women and children were rushed to the refuge of higher ground, smelters from the Mill threw down tools and ran for life, and mates from the dressing floors scrambled up the dead heap. Within a minute or so the small heights overlooking the broad cutting in the line of the level's tail were peopled by the throng.

Cherry was pale. "Oh, I'm so glad they're all out of danger afore it comes."

"It wouldn't have hurt anybody in Mine Road anyhow, love," Adam said, patting her hand. "And I think all t'chaps that were working had been keeping a sharp look-out. Freestone John warned everybody, you know. No——"

"It's here," an angular man shouted.

A couple of immense rats, fleeing from the level, heralded a wall of water which extended to within a few inches of the barrel roof, tip of foam poised on ravening prow. Uprooting rails and sleepers, the flood tore along the tramroad, with never a check until it surged through the wide door of Bucker Smelt Mill, where ore hearths exploded thunderously, bringing down the roof in a tangle of ruin, a cascade of shattered timbers and broken stone slates. A mighty backwash came out, and that swung downhill, towards the dressing floors, whose iron shades, launders and machines were swept aside in a trice.

Adam grasped Cherry's arm, to whirl her across a strip of waste ground to Winterings Gill, the same thought in his head as possessed Matt and Len, who had joined them. But though the beck was swollen it was no more so than during a heavy rainstorm. "The smelt mill cushioned it," Adam muttered.

"Aye, an' all the slime pits helped," nodded Len, to which Mary Jane's father added: "Thousands of gallons must have gone into 'em."

"Well, Cherry love," Adam said with relief, "no damage that the Lord or anybody else can complain of. You see, in everything else we're covered—where Daniel blasted this morning right through to where they'd piled them rails is all well within our own sett, and so it's nobody else's business what we've been doing . . . at least not having regard to t'very definite declaration we've had from the other side."

"Oh, I'm so glad, love," Cherry murmured as they returned to augment the crowd gaping at the wreckage. Groove and mine timber, washed out of Bucker Level, littered the ground, and across it Mr. Rutter picked a path to them. For once he was without a smile when mentioning a Corvy banker. "What'll William Storey say to this here, what'll William Storey say to this here?" he gasped.

Adam was more interested in a gentleman on the spot. Mr. Buckle's remarks carried well. "How do you account for this, Nattrass?" he demanded. "In view of the letter Mr. Storey consulted you about before writing."

"This is limestone country, as I'se oft telled you," Reuben Nattrass growled. "And water can travel in it by ways unbeknown to man."

"I am no mining man," the lawyer retorted, "but I am certain that such a large volume of water could not have arrived at once without an unhindered passage, not by filtering through crevices in the rock."

Quivering with rage he singled out Luther Thwaites, whom he warned to be prepared to ride to Corvy within the hour. Mrs. Peacock was also requested to air two beds for the night.

* * * *

As her uncle's future well-being had been taken into most capable hands, all that remained for Cherry to ensure at Yew Tree House before she left for good was its spotlessness from top to bottom. During the afternoon of the hush, when after careful survey she decided all was satisfactory, Dinah called. The two girls sipped cups of tea and, as groups along the whole length of Main Street were doing, chatted about recent events, although, in their case, the certainty of a bloody encounter between Adam and Reuben Nattrass was not mentioned. Then, revived, they set off for Modesty, carrying a dinner service between them in a clothes basket.

When returning, their path beyond Nick Turn was blocked by a crowd clustered round the policeman's notice-board. Upon this, largely effacing an intimation about stolen sheep, a bill had been tacked. It was written in home-done capitals and signed by Richard Blenkiron, chairman of the Parish Council.

"Come on, one o' you," Old Hannah was saying crossly. "Here's me and Kit's twitching while you lot mumble: 'What's it about? . . . Why ever have we . . .'"

As Cuthbert Daykin cleared his throat, the two girls succeeded in edging nearer. The blacksmith's communication was to the point, and read:

A PARISH MEETING WILL BE HELD AT THE WEST END TO-MORROW AT 10 A.M. IF WET IN THE LITERARY INSTITUTE. ALL ATTEND.

When through the press, Cherry and her friend, voices cautiously hushed, attempted to link the announcement with the secret they shared, the malpractices which had nearly broken Mr. Alderson. Near Calvert's Wynd Bart bumped into them, a sheet of stiff paper in his hand.

"Are you putting up notices an' all?" Dinah asked him.

"As a matter o' fact I am," he replied to her astonishment. "You see, Adam's shutting t'mines in the morning so as everybody can go to a Parish Meeting that Mr. Blenkiron's let us know he's calling."

"Where is Adam, Bart?" Cherry inquired, a thought worriedly. "He didn't say what he were doing when he left."

Unconsciously she was given assurance. Adam was occupied with several members of the committee, re-arranging supervisory duties to include the new ground at the hush.

Dinah's next remark was made as they passed the schoolmaster's house. "My, isn't everything a to-do," she marvelled.

She was not the only person who thought that. For the remainder of the day Winterings hummed with talk, and streams of callers retired baffled from Smithy House on learning that the smith was not in the village. In the early evening Mr. Storey's fly drove furiously in from Corvy, and, past midnight, lamps burned in the dining-room of the Plug and Feathers, where the East Side Company's directors and agent were assembled. Much of this news spread through the Dale, reaching the ears of many gentlemen of acumen who believed in keeping themselves acquainted with everything that was going on.

2

The throng outside the Plug and Feathers fell silent when, promptly at ten o'clock, Richard Blenkiron and two elderly gentlemen appeared at the front door. Watched by every soul present, including Mrs. Peacock, her servant girls, and one or two friends, who leaned dangerously out of the bedroom windows, the blacksmith at once ascended the mounting block, from which he did not speak long, merely enough to introduce formally James Guy and John Dougill, whose persons and qualifications anyhow were familiar to all.

"Well, that's all from me," he concluded. "You'll be telled how a highly-respected chap has been shamefully used, and a young lass treated abominably because she donned trousers. And you'll hear why she did—because t'young fellow who unearthed all this wanted an extra pair of hands."

As an opening these remarks were exceedingly effective, and ears were strained not to miss a word when James Guy, replacing him on the mounting-block, quietly began his account. Methodically the old mining-authority outlined a damning case, from proving the ownership of the lightweight tram-rails to exhibiting a portion of a very unique luckstone and a plan with the East Side Company's stamp on it. Gradually more and more heads turned towards a sarcastic-mouthed, raven-haired young man whom Mr. Guy finally addressed.

"Well, have you owt to say, Reuben Nattrass?" he inquired sternly.

However damning the indictment sounded, an outright denial would later have revealed many loopholes in the evidence, as Adam well knew, and it was a relief to him when his cousin took the bit between his teeth. "Nowt," was the savage reply. "'Cepting, of course, to ask what you long-faced lot reckon you can do about it?"

The rising growl of angry men expressed the general feeling, but a pale-eyed individual standing on the parapet of the bridge, tangled of whiskers and beard, made a tangible suggestion. James Pedley had discovered it was not wholly profitable to sully his own brother, and he welcomed a new and popular scapegoat. "Into t'water with him," he thundered. "Aye——"

"Hold on," Mr. Kearton shouted. "He deserves, it but we can't have——"

"Over t'Brig wi' him," the fanatic screamed. "Him as were innocent, Adam Brunskill, who in my human frailty I decried myself, were chucked over, so let Reuben Nattrass pursue t'same thorny path. By all as is holy, brethren . . ."

Fists clenched, eyes vicious, Reuben Nattrass eyed the circle closing in upon him. "Who's going to be the first volunteer?" he jeered. "Now I'se noan particular and if he'd prefer a few mates to——"

Mr. William Storey created a diversion by dismissing the culprit from his company's service. To those who had dealt with him only as a banker it seemed strange that his fury was not about the damage suffered at Bucker Level and Smelt Mill, which the previous night he had been planning to restore. "The most fearful aspect of this shocking business, Nattrass," he stormed, "is your contempt for the well-established ethics of a fine profession. Deliberately to cause a fellow adventurer——"

"You put your bloody head in an ore-hearth," Reuben Nattrass grunted, more interested in the scuffle taking place in the vicinity, where men who would have meted out the most salutary punishment the village knew were being forcibly restrained by others. "Well," he sneered, "I don't think th'avengers are so anxious to put out all they could or they'd have been at me by now, an' so I'll be on my way. But I'll be about if any on you wants me."

He pushed forward, to walk unhurriedly across the cobbles and then along Main Street to his father's house.

Then tongues were loosed, and very soon three separate crowds were formed, by those congratulating Titus Alderson, down whose cheeks tears of gladness streamed, others who expressed regret to Cherry, and by those surrounding Adam, with constant traffic between the three. Altogether quite a few minutes passed before Cherry, joyous but a little dim-eyed, was able to slip her hand into her future husband's arm. She brought an account of how Mrs. Roberty Will, rather shamefacedly, had felicitated her uncle.

"It were a real effort for her, love," she said, beginning to smile, "and I think that were why she gave Mr. Plews such a dressing-down about them shares. Anyroad," her eyes were dancing now, "Screw Tom were so wild he set on to George Nattrass, saying he'd led him into it. And when he made a slighting remark about your Uncle George as a businessman——"

"The fat 'ud be in the fire," Adam grinned.

Mr. Wade was tapping the window of the bar and, when they looked up, he beckoned them inside, where, in the seclusion of the inglenook corner, he said that Mr. Storey had been making tentative approaches about some form of amalgamation. "I gather he now intends to make a clean sweep, and if possible join our board in due course," he chuckled. "What would you say to that, Brunskill?"

"All to the good, sir," Adam replied without hesitation. "Mr. Storey happens to be a gentleman who's genuinely wrapped up in lead-mining and within limits he's noan averse to paying for his hobby. And that means groovers here have all the more chance o' making some sort of livelihood."

The spinner pondered this, nodded eventually in acceptance, and then remarked that he and Mr. Rutter had decided upon extending invitations in this connection to two others, whom he named.

"Adam and . . . and my uncle," Cherry gulped. "As directors!"

"Yes, my dear, and for themselves, not because they have a preponderance of shares," smiled Mr. Wade. "And as your uncle knows nothing of it yet I suggest you send him along to me this evening. He . . . umph! would prefer to hear it officially, I'm sure."

"I'm sure, too," Adam agreed. "And as for myself, I'm very grateful to you, sir. But if you've no objection I'd like to think it over. You see, from now on I shall be farming."

"Quite so," Mr. Wade said. "But I trust you will be able to combine the two, for a time at least. I . . . er . . . imagine," his cheeks ballooned out, "that many others will have the same hope."

On this note they separated, Mr. Wade for Half House, the younger people to the kitchen, to give his message to Mr. Alderson.

"Well now, lass," Adam said, "I'm occupied with another little matter to-morrow, at Greets Church, so I think I'll get up to the hush and do a bit more thinking out on t'spot."

In other circumstances Cherry would have replied suitably. As it was, brightness faded from her face. "All right, love," she said. "Are you . . . are you going alone?"

Adam stared. "Am I . . ." he began, and then realising her fears, squeezed her hand. "Don't worry, lass, I can take care of myself if owt happens."

Before leaving, Adam believed he had dispelled much that frightened her. Whether that were so or not she was smiling gaily when their hands slipped away from each other's, he to edge through the crush towards the door, she to join a lively group of her friends in the bar, amongst them Dinah, who Daniel, there also, believed was "coming round." They had much to enliven them, not least a bitter quarrel between the Nattrass brothers, who, to wind up an unfortunate spell of many weeks, had just spent a few awkward minutes with Mr. Storey. The banker, when requesting their resignations as East Side directors, had left them in no doubt as to whether they would have to pay on their guarantees.

William Nattrass's jowls were quivering. "It's that bloody silly scheme o' yours wi' Brunskill as has caused everything. You reckoned you'd getten a man o' straw for the job——"

The cheese-factor's lips thinned. "Your Reuben's got about as many damned brains as you have. But if either on you had a few more——"

Mrs. Peacock did not even trouble to pat her hair. "Outside, both o' you," she said peremptorily. "Sharp an' all."

Hardly had the discomfited pair left her establishment when Cuthbert Daykin, in thickly addressing Lodge Trotter, raised a laugh as big as that signalling their ignominious departure. The postmaster had been sitting as inconspicuously as possible, lest the differences between George and William Nattrass should bring attention to himself, but the shopkeeper was his undoing.

"Were you addressing me, Daykin?" he snapped, broad black *pince-nez* ribbon a-flutter.

Cuthbert Daykin, virtually a teetotaller, had been drinking steadily since the East Side Company's latest disaster. "I am," he hiccoughed, "because I'se proposing engaging you to put a stop to all this here cracking up o' yon Brunskill. You'll be instructed to take proceedings against him for coaxing me out of highly valuable property, to wit my West Side shares."

When a much amused gathering recovered from this, John Dougill capped the matter by observing that a few shareholders assembled one evening in Greets had not required coaxing to transfer their shares to the young man. "In fact," he went on unsmilingly, "them as lives in t'Market Place vows there were such a hurry to turn the papers over for the next man to sign that Screw Tom's parlour curtains were blowing as if there were a gale."

As so often before in its history, the Plug and Feathers resounded with merriment.

"Well, I'll have to run on home to mend the fire, love," Cherry said indistinctly, laughing despite her foreboding.

"See you to-night, then," Dinah said. "I hear all the chaps are having a do for Adam."

"At Matt's, yes," Cherry said. "Well, good-bye, love."

Her progress towards the door was not swift, through a throng of men the majority of whom had something to say to her, but at last she was outside, where she responded to the smiles of a group of ladies whose conversation ceased abruptly at her approach. Heads were put together again as she got farther away, when a deputation to the mistress of the Plug and Feathers was determined upon. Mrs. Peacock was extremely stiff with the delegates at first, pointing out that the wedding was to be very quiet, attended only by those who had trusted in the couple, and that she herself was providing a repast on the return. Mrs. Harker, however, amongst the elect as it were, enabled her to view the matter in rather a different light.

"I quite agree wi' every word you've said, Lucy," she declared. "But on t'other hand ought we to prevent the village trying to show how sorry it is, that's the question."

Mrs. Peacock began to thaw. "Well, of course, if it's intended as a mark of public approval towards the pair, that's another thing. And maybe it's my duty to withdraw gracefully."

On being assured of this she became easier still, and the conference closed rosily over glasses of port wine, by which time Mrs. Peacock had offered to contribute towards the wedding feast everything she had made for the more modest affair, including the wedding cake. In extremely good humour the ladies concerned left the Plug and Feathers by the back door, and when outside, chatted gaily and trilled frequently, so cosily glowing inwardly that the exact time for the midday meal seemed much less important than usual.

That afternoon decorations were smuggled into the Literary Institute, where the urns were scalded out and polished. Mysterious activities proceeded elsewhere, and from several of the more well-to-do homes the fragrant smells of baking and cooking went on into the evening. The shops of both Emma Ann Metcalfe and Cuthbert Daykin began to do a brisk business, and a discussion of a rather hypocritical nature took place between two inveterate enemies before the Wesleyan Day School scholars were dismissed.

It was true there was the feeling of snow in the air, but hardly strong enough for the schoolmaster to close the school for the following day.

"We don't want t'youngsters to be stranded, do we?" Mr. Kearton remarked.

"That is precisely . . . er . . . the point I desired to raise, Mr. Kearton," Mr. Kidd appeared highly gratified.

So that was settled: the children would be able to take part in the celebrations of the morrow.

Modesty shone throughout and, so that none of its perfection should be undone, Adam called there on his way from work, to collect clothing, toilet articles and nightshirt, taking these along to Old Hannah's, where he was sleeping that night.

A new tie desirable, he next walked to Cuthbert Daykin's, where the proprietor, with much less abandon than usual, was in the midst of singing *Come with me to Fairyland*, the result of which was that Emma Ann Metcalfe slipped in from next door. Incidentally, gossip insisted that she was becoming bolder, point being given to this in the present instance, when she came forward to wish to-morrow's bridegroom all happiness. During the ensuing conversation, Adam learned just why Cuthbert Daykin's manner had been strange recently.

"Well, I realised what t'position were about them shares, Adam," she smiled. "But lately, since you've made 'em of some value, this silly here——"

Mr. Daykin quivered. "Really, Mrs. Metcalfe," he said distantly.

"Now come on, Cuthbert dear," little Emma Ann said lightly. "You know very well it's summat else as is t'matter." An air of gravity not entirely unallied with amusement clothed her while she explained her neighbour's method of recouping himself for the amount he had paid out to Adam. "What you lose on the swings you gain on t'roundabouts, he calls it," she went on, guilty of a slight giggle.

Even Adam was staggered. "He bought a hundred East Side shares?"

Cuthbert Daykin's florid cheeks were fiery. "Without speculation," he asserted loudly, but got no farther on a most unpromising theme. Eyes tightly closed, he groaned dismally. "My head," he murmured, "it's like as if I'd getten t'Saw Mill inside it."

"What you need is a nice strong cup o' tea, lad," Mrs. Metcalfe soothed him fondly, taking his arm.

Ruminating about the follies to which man can sometimes lend himself, Adam walked to Yew Tree House, where Cherry was full of the stream of visitors she had had during the afternoon.

"They all seemed right suited about everything, but the queer thing were as not one of 'em mentioned our wedding, love," she said. "I'm wondering if there's feeling about it not taking place in the Chapel."

"If there was, lass," Adam reassured her, "they wouldn't have bothered to come."

"Anyhow, I'm glad it's a quiet do," she said. "We've had enough excitement for just now."

Adam smiled. "To tell you the truth, I don't care much either way, so long as you an' me are duly wed."

Suddenly Cherry was very solemn. "And neither do I, Adam love."

A few minutes later they were compelled to rise hastily from the big chair when the committee, too much in earnest to be embarrassed, arrived in force to ask Adam if he would re-consider his decision to abandon mining, of which a report was circulating. Freestone John, with other interests himself, was their spokesman, and he began by explaining that out of the better Pays of recent months many had been able to save a little by continuing to live tight, in the hope of renting one or two fields and buying a beast or so.

"The fact is, friend, that though we've long known as lead-mining i' Skewdale were finished, we've all getten it into our heads that if you'll spare a bit o' time from your farming—well, it might make just t'difference for a while."

For a short space the only sound was that of the ticking of the grandfather clock, and then Freestone John, from out of the half-circle of silently waiting men, spoke to Cherry. "You know, lass," he said kindly, "you ought to be consulted about this. If Adam takes on a sort of supervising, there'll oft be occasions when t'milking has to be left to you, and jobs like that."

Cherry's eyes were moist. "Oh, I'll do it gladly," she said.

One by one glances turned in Adam's direction, until all of them were gazing his way. "Aye . . ." he nodded, moved by their trust. "I'll tell Mr. Wade as soon as possible."

There was no hilarity, just hand-shakes and quiet words of thanks. When the door closed behind the callers and Adam returned to the kitchen, he looked steadily at the girl who would be his wife.

"We'll pull together, you an' me, lass," he said tenderly. "I've no fears about that."

"I haven't either," she whispered, overbrimming with love.

Further visitors made it impossible for them to have any more time to themselves, save the brief moment in the passage when Daniel and Wingy were walking down to the gate. Gently Adam kissed her.

"Meet you to-morrow in church, love," he said.

Her eyes were starry. "Yes . . . yes, Adam," she said.

With his friends Adam went along Main Street in the fine snow which had begun to fall. At the end of Calvert's Wynd they called for Blind Kit, with whom was Sam Kirkbride, and Hugh Bearpark and Len Rukin were rooted out of the reading-room of the Literary Institute.

Outside the alehouse beyond the chapel garth Wingy and Len Rukin found diversion in the shape of Cyprian Metcalfe, blind-drunk. Each seized one of his arms, to rush him over the hump of the Brig, taking him so far up the main road that, when bringing him back, they met their oncoming companions not far below the Royal Alfred. Emma Ann's husband, fighting alarmingly for breath, was laid on the grass verge to recover.

The lively party continued, over sprawling Snorr Bridge to Lane End beyond Badger Hall, where they entered a cottage over whose roof a mighty ash, vaguely seen, spread its branches. Bidding Simon Sunter open bottled beer for them, Matt Tiplady brought out shaving brush and a bar of kitchen soap. Vigorously stropping his razor on the back of a calf-bound book, he then began to remove a dark stubble four days old.

"Oh aye," he grinned through the lather, "I'm sprucing myself up for t'wedding. A chap . . . er . . . owes summat to his self-respect."

"H'mm," Adam chuckled, eyeing him. "And who's said that?"

It was a pleasant evening, of talk and laughter, the host whittling walking-sticks meanwhile, a sideline he could safely pursue in the presence of Will Skidmore, who came later with his father.

The gathering broke up before ten o'clock, when Adam was escorted to the door of a bow-windowed shop in the kitchen behind which, with a like concern, he was rationed by Old Hannah to a ten minutes' chat before dismissal to a mattress of pigeon feathers upstairs.

3

The countryside was dusted finely with snow, a delicate mantle of many soft folds rising from the bottoms of the dale to the high lines of the fells, where it met the cold blue of the northern sky. It was chilly when Adam slipped out of bed, but he was soon warm in the kitchen, where a fire banked with cinders had remained alight all night. Until he decided to start out early to walk to Greets by himself, his activities were leisurely, but after that he hastened, and, when Old Hannah came downstairs, he had had breakfast and hers awaited her. She thoroughly approved the project.

"Aye, there couldn't be a more beautiful morning for a chap to be setting out to keep an appointment wi' a real bonny lass," she said, opening the window to throw crumbs to a pet robin. "When he comes wi' the trap, I'll tell Daniel you've gone."

Savouring the lovely scene, Adam covered the miles of highway. Everything he saw enchanted him, such was his mood, whether it were the widely-spaced track of a fleeting hare, the first sight of Greets' grey huddle of houses over a quickly descending moorland brow, or the medieval brasses in the ancient church. Daniel, very resplendent, arrived as he was inspecting a colourful Munich-made stained-glass window, to the memory of a young son of the Graftons who had lost his life when exploring the lead-mines.

"Top o' the morning, lad," his friend grinned. "Well, I'm a bit late, so we'd better sit down i' front yonder, as I'm telled we have to do."

Soon the handful of special friends began to enter, when the best man, elbowing his charge, rose and took up station against the coming of the bride on her Uncle Titus's arm. And, at last, simply but prettily dressed, she was there, alongside Adam, listening to the Vicar's solemn words. Occasionally the couple glanced sideways at one another, glances of love which, however, attained a different significance when each increasingly became aware of many tip-toeing feet, and the creaking of more and more pews. On becoming man and wife, a legitimate curiosity was satisfied. Turning, they saw row after row of smiling faces, familiar faces.

"Well, love," Adam bent nearer to her, "Winterings has stolen a march on us all right. Nearly everybody's here."

"An' I'm glad, after all," Cherry glowed. "They're our folk, aren't they?"

"Aye, lass," he squeezed her arm.

The vestry was crowded to capacity when Blind Kit asked the bridal pair to attend a little spread arranged in their honour. "You'll noan be offending anybody either," he said, smiling all over his scarred face. "And if you don't believe me you can inquire of Mrs. Peacock there, who has very kindly surrendered her undoubted rights in t'matter."

"We'll be very glad, Kit," Adam said. "Eh, love?"

"It'll be lovely," nodded Cherry, radiant.

In due course they ran the gauntlet outside the church door, an assault which delighted a very small gentleman in braided morning coat and pepper-and-salt breeches. That is until Dr. Seaton remembered the bridegroom's insinuation, when, from the broad back of Mighty Joe, he extended an accusing arm.

"A monstrous allegation," he roared. "You, with a silly grin . . . a monstrous allegation I say."

"Yes, sir," Adam replied dutifully.

Appeased, but still on the warpath, the little doctor transferred his attentions elsewhere, singling out several ladies and gentlemen to comment upon their respective disorders.

Anthony Skidmore hastily whispered to Adam: "For t'Lord's sake set off sharp, lad. I've forgotten to leave him a specimen o' my water, and if he spots me he's capable o' demanding a sample on t'spot."

Others besides the master of Badger Hall were alarmed, and a mass of wedding-goers, almost hysterical with suppressed laughter, scattered towards the waiting vehicles—in the van, fear lending speed to their feet, those with most reason to fear becoming the next victim.

Beneath a brilliantly blue sky and a sun which shone dazzlingly upon the snow-clad hills, the procession up Skewdale made a brave show. No one walked back to Winterings, every soul accommodated in one or another of the traps, dog-carts, brakes, wagonettes or coup-carts forming the long line. At the front, Mr. and Mrs. Adam Brunskill rode in style in an open landau hired out in summer to visitors to the Dale, and more than once, before pulling up at the Literary Institute, the newly-weds stood up to look behind, at conveyances gay with nuptial favours, at drivers who flourished whips just for the pleasure of trailing long, white streamers.

"Well, here we've been brought, so this must be the spot," Adam laughed when the carriage clattered to a standstill in Main Street. Greeted by helpers who had stayed behind to put the finishing touches to preparations in the Institute, he helped his wife out.

Directed by a chorus of half a dozen people, they went into the big back room, pausing involuntarily on the threshold to marvel at the festive decorations, rows of tables groaning with good things, and a stupendous array of wedding presents.

"Adam!" Cherry gasped, housewifely instincts stirred by ornaments, pans, tablecloths, blankets and cutlery, preliminary glimpse only. "Look!"

Many were the speakers later on, amongst them Titus Alderson, who, very conscious of his directorship, paid tribute to his niece's husband, an avowal earning tremendous applause. And an uncertain truce ended when Mr. Kearton, with surprising freedom for him, speculated as to who would wear the trousers in the marriage, plumping for the lady because, as is now known, "she's used to 'em."

"A most indelicate remark," Mr. Kidd observed very audibly, waving a pudgy-fingered hand. "To say I am astonished would be——"

The joiner halted. "Are you insinuating as I've said summat coarse?" he demanded. Extremely irate, he continued to castigate, but, lost as he was, there came a moment when he was aware that everyone's attention was elsewhere.

A man of powerful figure, mouth set cruelly, stood within the doorway. For a while he stared unwaveringly at the bride, and then the relentless glance moved to the one to whom she now belonged.

"Three o'clock do you, Brunskill?" he said thinly. "Outside t'Plug."

Adam nodded. "Very nicely, Cousin Reuben."

The resentment of a company outraged by the brutal interruption began to be heard. A few pieces of crockery came to grief as guests jumped up.

"I don't know as Winterings intends you being here much longer," Nathan Wharton shouted, to be supplemented by Mark Iveson's furious question: "Why couldn't you have waited instead o' spoiling their wedding day?"

Reuben Nattrass's eyes glittered. "I haven't even started spoiling t'wedding yet," he glowered. "But I bloody well will all right."

Cherry was deathly pale and, when the door slammed, Adam jerked his head towards his oldest friends, Simon and his wife and Daniel. "Jane," he said urgently, "tell her I've a bit on a reputation in certain ways, will you?"

"I'll do my best, lad," Jane Sunter replied, her lovely eyes furious. "But it's her husband who has to face that big brute an' not mine. Yes, Cherry love, I know how you must be feeling, but don't take on too much."

"Adam'll handle him all right," Daniel said earnestly.

Simon Sunter's stutter was at its worst. "If you'-d s-s-seen some of the t-t-t'things Adam's done, Cherry. When he g-g-gets going . . ."

Closely surrounded by her husband's intimates, Cherry got herself in hand. "I won't be silly any more," she promised, trying to make the best of it even though her lips trembled.

Watched sympathetically, Adam put his arm around her shoulders. "That's the stuff, lass," he said. "And another thing, love, there's quite a while before me and Cousin Reuben tries conclusions, and for my part I'm noan allowing him to ruin everything betwixt now and then. Of course you may have i' mind other wedding days, but for myself——"

"Oh, Adam," Cherry smiled.

Mr. Blenkiron leaned across gravely. "Adam's right," he said. "Make the most o' this great day in your lives, love. Mind you, I'm noan saying it isn't a wicked shame as it's going to end as we know, because it is."

Adam eyed the blacksmith. "Aye," he murmured dryly.

It could not be supposed that guests were other than profoundly shocked by what had occurred, but nevertheless, given the lead by the young couple, the tone soon improved, becoming almost boisterous when a move was made outdoors, where Adam duly threw small pieces of wedding cake on to the flagstones, washed for the purpose, in the alley at the side of the Literary Institute, a ringing cheer arising when the plate splintered into fragments, the best of good luck. Then Daniel Dolphin, as best man, tossed a handful of coppers into Main Street, the excited calls of young searchers changing into piercing yells when a shovelful of hot coins fresh from the fire was indiscriminately strewn as well.

The unmarried men's race, to Town Foot and back, the prize a piece of vari-coloured silk ribbon belonging to the bride, was easily won by Wingy Blenkiron.

"I don't know why ever you go in for it," Dinah said to the victor. "You've always been t'fastest sprinter about here."

The postman laughed. "Well, it's just a bit o' fun, lass."

Dinah shrugged, a gesture unseen in her before. "But what on earth will be the use to you of scores an scores of lasses' ribbons?"

"Scores and——" Richard Blenkiron's fiery-haired son repeated. Then he flushed alarmingly. "Hey you!" he growled. "And now I'm going to tell you summat."

Unaware that matters between two of her friends had approached a disastrous crisis, Cherry joined Adam, to whom Annamaria Rutter, very woebegone, had just cautiously admitted to hearing from Arthur Nattrass.

Adam knew about the message of warning sent to Cherry. "Well, when you write, tell him to come home," he said. "So far as he's concerned nowt's going to happen in the matter o' them rails."

Her mouth opened. "He'll noan get into bother, like?" she faltered, eyes welling when Adam shook his head. "I'll . . . I'll write him to-morrow."

Cherry was willing to forget. "I should, lass," she said. "Of course it'll noan be nice for him at first, but he'll get over it in a while."

Annamaria laughed in the middle of her tears. "Get over it! 'Course he will, love . . . he'll bob up like a cork i' no time. But I'll watch who he mates with in future, I will that."

While certain defects in Arthur Nattrass's character were being discussed, tactfully by Adam and frankly by the culprit's young lady, Cherry noticed Dinah, who seemed immeasurably distressed. She hurried to her, and as quickly hurried back to Adam, to tell him she thought she ought to go along to Yew Tree House to change her clothes. Under her breath she added: "Dinah's right upset about summat, an' I'd like to take her away sharp."

"Right, love," Adam smiled, surreptitiously squeezing her arm. "I'll be here waiting for you."

Not very long afterwards the crowd outside the Literary Institute was startled by a piercing scream from down Main Street. A group of young men at once tore towards Nick Turn, beyond which they found Fronick Blenkiron leaning against the pillar-box in Mrs. Metcalfe's wall, not far from hysterics.

"Whatever's up?" Bart Hugill asked.

"Your . . . your brother," she moaned.

"Has *he* got down?" the clerk muttered. "But——"

The voice of his former young lady rose to an astonishing height. "Is he down?" she screeched. "I were nobbut looking for a brooch I'd lost an' he seized hold o' me and tried to tug me towards Town Foot . . . and if I hadn't managed to loose myself . . ."

Very upset, Bart Hugill ran forward while the others bore the stricken young woman back to the Literary Institute, where a new subject, poor Rive Rags's ominous lapse, took the place of talk about the wedding and the fight which was to succeed it. There were many serious faces amongst those with daughters—a harmless lunatic was one thing, but a crazed creature with ideas about young women quite another.

"I shall see t'doctor about having him put away," Mrs. Blenkiron declared. "But for t'mercy o' Providence our Fronick 'ud have been ravaged by now."

That was the position when footsteps were heard flying along the village. Bart Hugill skidded to a standstill at the kerb.

"Alf were nobbut trying to show Fronick summat," he gulped. "Reuben Nattrass has grabbed Cherry an' taken her up Sorrow Near; and he's knocked out Dinah an' all."

"He's done what?" roared Richard Blenkiron.

Anthony Skidmore began to speak, his blazing temper that of them all. "Minnie, lass, you be off to Dinah," he said to his wife. "Now how many hosses have we getten? We'll divide up, some galloping down to Half and then up Heugh Syke on to t'moor. Others take Sorrow Near . . ."

"And the remainder on foot as fast as you can," Blind Kit shouted.

"By God, I'se missed my eyes, but never as now. If he harms that lass——"

Their tight expressions implicit of a desire for action rather than words, men hastened to play their parts. Within two minutes Main Street echoed with the hectic drumming of hoofs on stone setts and the rapid patter of Sunday boots.

Ahead of them all, on a horse snatched from a hitching bracket at the Plug and Feathers, Adam rode as frantically up Sleety Slape as a willing beast would take him, in pursuit of a man who, deeply involved in another matter, was not of a nature to reflect about the added penalty for an even more fearful crime.

"But I'm certain he'll be back again to keep his appointment wi' me," he told himself, cold sweat on his forehead. "He's bent on it, and for that he's reckless enough an' so sure of himself that he'll never hesitate to face up to everybody at after. But if I'm right he'll noan go far with her, which I reckon means that a chap with his knowledge of the Old Man 'ul make underground. And the gainest place for that will be one o' them disused levels to th'eastward of Bucker Smelt Mill."

At the South Mill, springing off, he sped round the corner, the office door bursting open under the first assault of his shoulder. Provided with candles, he remounted, to race over the two bridges, thence diagonally to climb the far side of the gill, his main hope to gain height. Beyond a covered watercourse he swung his horse, now nearly spent, to the left, for a desperate scramble upwards on the top of a snow-capped flue which rose steadily towards its octagonal-shaped terminal tower.

At a point where turfs covered the stone arching of the chimney he paused, praying for a sight of his quarry as his glance ranged over the wild moor. The scattering of sheep gave him a clue. "Yon ravine," he muttered. "That's it then."

Jumping from his horse he sped down the precipitous slope from the smelt mill flue, a single false step promising disaster. The level of the moor attained, he started out at an equally break-neck pace across the heather, over becks and deep hushes, his line never deviating save once when, deliberately risking the passage of a green-and-white mottled patch, he was almost bogged down. Within less than ten minutes he slid along a rocky spar. Good fortune was with him, for, in a small area where old workings were many, and four closely-adjacent gills cut into the rising moorland like outspread fingers ' he found newly-made clog marks.

After sixty or so fathoms of worming and burrowing, the groovers of another day had driven a straight gallery, and when Adam rounded the last bend, he saw a faint glow. "Cherry," he shouted, "I'm here."

Her sweet-voiced but desperately frightened reply came and a deeper cry of derision. As Adam hastened along, a vague, rumbling noise began, the light died away, but in a while showed again, the period between its further appearances becoming shorter as the growling accompaniment increased.

Athwart his path, in a traverse cross-cut, an old waterwheel barred progress, the way-gates to each side tumbled in and impassable. One section of the wheel, a quarter of the whole, was devoid of struts and bracing, a moving segment through which Adam glimpsed Cherry's ashen cheeks and her companion's grin as he threw aside the long joggle-handle for starting and stopping the waterwheel.

"Well, well, well," Reuben Nattrass raised his candle to allow its rays to reach through to his cousin at every revolution of the wheel. "This must be what they call t'courage o' desperation."

A pulse was beating in Adam's forehead, his deep-set eyes were merciless. "Let her go, you damned fool," he said, his tone deadly. "Don't you realise what you're doing?"

He was dealing with a man who seemed consumed with a ruthless desire for revenge. "Aye, I know all right," Reuben Nattrass retorted. "An' a rare difference it's going to make to your wedding day—and all as goes wi' it after an' all."

Assessing speed and distance, Adam retreated a few small steps from the wheel each time its solid portion cut him off from his adversary's view. "Aye," he scoffed, "it's easy for you to talk that road when there's summat between us."

Reuben Nattrass chuckled. "No, Brunskill, you're a right 'un for setting traps, but you're noan goading me until I'se had a spell wi' this pretty in a real nice little love-nest as I know of. But, mind you, I'll noan forget to be at t'Plug to give you any satis——"

Before the groaning wheel had completed another full circuit the candle was dashed from him. In a brief span Cherry saw the swift passage of her lover through the gap in the waterwheel, flying as if he had been diving into the river after rapidly running along an overhanging bluff. As the arrow-like line of his body curved downwards, his outstretched hands fastened upon her abductor's shoulders. A pinpoint of light flashed in the air, and then darkness descended.

Fingers locked in anguish, lips moving in urgent prayer, Cherry listened, her back pressed tightly against the rough, damp walls of the old level. She heard the flesh and bone thud of a heavy fall, deep-chested breathing, the grunt when a powerful blow found its mark, and the quick shift of feet to obtain a better purchase. Thus she waited, so sick with apprehension as to be dimly aware that her senses might soon be lost. At last, when an overburdened heart held her rigid with its sharp pain, she thought she heard a voice far away.

"Adam," she said faintly, wondering if the buzzing in her ears had deceived her. "Adam . . ."

"Aye, I'm all right, love," Adam Brunskill replied fondly.

"Oh, Adam," she murmured. "I . . . I . . ."

"Come on, lass," he said. "Find your way toward me and then feel in my pockets for matches and a candle."

The indignity of being seen when helpless may have been too much for Reuben Nattrass. Before Cherry could delve as she had been asked, another fierce struggle began in the darkness; it ended with a cry of pain.

"That's a foretaste o' what you'll get if you use your feet on me again, Cousin Reuben," she heard Adam say. "I'll break it next go."

This time Cherry was able to find box of matches and candle, and soon, strangely bright by contrast, the candlelight shone upon two men, one with deep furrows of iron purpose extending from nose to corners of mouth, the other's expression that of insensate fury.

"Let go on me an' fight like a man," Reuben Nattrass choked. "You've getten me wi' a fancy lock——"

"Aye, a Cornish friend as you once heard of taught me it," Adam nodded grimly, his grasp firm on an out-turned captive wrist. "And it's staying for t'moment . . . as surety for your appearance at the Brig, where you're in for that fight you're seeking."

"The fight's going to be here," Reuben Nattrass's breath hissed. "You seem to forget as we've to pass t'waterwheel, and you can't stop that single-handed."

A few baulks of slimy timber leaned upright against the side of the gallery. Eyeing one carefully, Adam motioned Cherry to retreat. Judging the instant, his leg lashed out and the beam tippled, falling into the open segment of the wheel. Instantaneously the old working was filled agonisingly with the rending squeals of tortured wood and metal, the violent reports of a piece of machinery coming asunder and the clatter of falling fragments.

It was strangely silent afterwards, when a clear path to the day lay before them.

"Go in front an' light us, love," Adam smiled. "And don't have a spill through hurrying overmuch."

The little procession, headed by a white-faced girl carrying a candle, advanced through the Old Man—along drifts whose crumbling timbers alone held up the sides, past rotting trap-doors covering ancient sumps, upon a sole deep in slippery sludge chill with spring water—until at last a tiny glimmer of grey began to show ahead.

At the edge of the scar overlooking Malaga, closely surrounded by enraged horsemen and pedestrians, there was scant doubt that Reuben Nattrass would have been lynched had not Cherry testified to being unharmed. Adam's announcement, too, that the fight would take place as arranged, was also of value in turning the scales.

Deliberately avoiding the company of others, Adam and Cherry walked down to Yew Tree House, his arm around her. In the kitchen, before leaving for the West End, he tried to bring comfort. "Don't fret, lass," he said, gently raising her chin. "And don't forget, either, that I've never lost a fight in my life."

Cherry's eyes were too bright. "Oh, I know now that you're a lot stronger than most," she retorted. "But . . . but the real truth is that you've never gone in much for fighting. Leastways, that's what you've always made out."

Adam kissed her lightly. "No, I haven't, love, but I shall be all right. In fact I'm wanting nowt else just now except to go on yonder an' get it finished with."

She swallowed painfully. "You are brave, love."

Perhaps it was quite the wrong thing to do, but Adam laughed, for she looked so pathetic in her endeavour to be courageous. An intolerable surge of love for her swelled in him, and he took her closely in his arms again.

"Well . . . lass," he murmured, releasing her suddenly, "I'd better be off."

It was very quiet at Town Foot, since the last eager sightseer had raced towards the Plug and Feathers.

Cherry smiled mistily. "Good-bye, love," she said.

Determined to end her misery as quickly as possible, Adam left the house. Between the green-painted gate and Nick Turn he seemed to be striding through a village whose inhabitants had deserted it, abandoning everything.

As was traditional when really serious fights took place in Winterings, the space between Lucy Peacock's establishment and the front of the untenanted Bridge Inn opposite was always kept clear, spectators lining two sides of the arena only, the approach to the Brig and the entrance into Main Street.

The antagonists had stripped to the waist, each revealing a satiny skin rippling with muscles which in Reuben Nattrass were slightly bunched, whereas Adam's arms tapered more or less regularly from the shoulder to the wrist.

"Well, are you damned well ready?" Reuben Nattrass bawled.

"Aye," Adam nodded.

The other, as if savagely eager not to lose time in meting out the most cruel punishment within his formidable power, closed the distance with a rush, but, receiving a poking left with a sting in it and, when he ran in again, a flashing right hook which sank deeply into his ribs, was compelled to change his tactics, keeping left foot and left hand to the fore. For the next minutes the patter of clogs and boots, the thud of blows and quick breathing, were the major sounds against the lullaby of the falls.

"S-s-seems as Adam's b-b-bent on beating him at his own game," Simon Sunter stuttered. "I m-mean he's noan just picking him up and ch-ch-chucking him about."

"Going to t'body mostly an' all," Daniel whispered. "Look at t'reddish marks as is already showing. If them wallops, hit at Adam's strength, doesn't affect yon fellow's bellows afore long . . ."

On the surface neither fighter appeared to have sustained any real damage, and now, the first fury of assault and countermeasure over, they were sparring. Then, as if realising that the struggle was taking place before a throng who had never known him as other than a swift and overwhelming champion, Reuben Nattrass increased the pace. Adam ducked a whistling right-hand to the jaw, but was jarred by a vicious crack on the ear; meantime his own fists played an endless tattoo on the enemy's body, which in patches was gradually dulling from bright red towards purple. Neither slackened for an instant.

"They can't keep on at this lick much longer," Richard Blenkiron muttered.

Possibly Reuben Nattrass had the greater reason to appreciate this. Bleeding knuckles to the fore, cut on his opponent's teeth, his right hand whizzed forward, but merely grazed a shoulder. Then he brought up another right to the mouth, a left under the eye, and a straight drive to the temple. Under the insane fury of the attack, Adam began to give ground, a fact which did not escape the wiseacres.

Against the mounting-block Adam's retreat across the cobblestones ended. Toe to toe, blows were rained, during which it came noticeable that Reuben Nattrass was a little slower and more prone to be erratic. Missing completely with a terrific left-hander, he was nailed on the mouth and suffered a smashing counter on the nose from a man whose target, it was also noticed, had shifted upwards. Cushioning the force of a desperate pile-driver on his forearm, Adam proved this again with a right-swing whose hard impact on the jaw rang out quite clearly.

As Reuben Nattrass staggered, a distraught figure darted out of the crowd. Caught off-balance by Isa Skidmore's frenzied thrust from behind, Adam tripped, stumbling to one knee, a roar of anger rising from the spectators when her brother, teeth bared and bloodshot eyes those of a madman, got his head in chancery.

"He'll noan ever get away," Edmund Kearton groaned.

"You wait," Richard Blenkiron yelped. "If Adam gets really wild . . . An' he's up again."

Linked together, spinning like a top, the fighters whirled crazily towards the Brig, and then back again. During this mad progress the former East Side agent was able to strike thrice, but before more blood streamed down his elbow from his victim's nose, he was pinned against the wall of the inn, the choice his, to yield his hold or accept grave internal injury by crushing.

"What did I tell you?" the blacksmith gasped. "If that lad had wanted to cut loose by his own methods he could have ended t'fight within a minute o' starting it. I happen to know . . ."

To all intents and purposes that was the finish for Reuben Nattrass. Every semblance of cool craftsmanship deserting him, he butted at the stomach with his head, but, side-stepped, received a blow which sent him rocking. Relentlessly Adam pursued him, hitting from the shoulder; blood poured from the bruiser's eyes and deeply-slit cheeks, from a mouth warmly-filled. His sorry guard penetrated again and again, Reuben Nattrass's features became more shapeless, his head that of a Fair doll waggling from side to side. Unsure on his legs, he was knocked finally to the floor with a straight left.

"That'll do, you've had enough," Adam said, his quiet words distinct to a couple of hundred folk who hardly breathed or moved. "Be off home an' clean yourself up . . . because you're leaving here for good, by six o'clock to-night. If not, you'll face t'consequences in a penal court for what you've done to-day and for what you did to Mr. Alderson aforehand. Six o'clock, mind you, and not a minute afterwards."

He turned away, looking about for Bob and Ward, who had been entrusted with his clothing. Almost immediately the lines of spectators shouted a warning, and, luckily jumping the right way, the heavy piece of rock hurtled harmlessly past him, thrown by a man who had summoned up his forces for the effort.

"And for that, Nattrass," Adam growled, smashing down the other's defences before grabbing him around the middle, when he hoisted him high above his head, "you're going over t'Brig."

A mass of sightseers barred his progress, in their forefront Edmund Kearton, with arms extended. "No, lad," the undertaker shouted. "You've been terribly ill-used I know, but I tried to prevent 'em putting you over and I'm stopping this now . . ."

Adam did not argue. His trunk twisted as his right shoulder dipped, and then, above the close-packed ranks of those before him, and carrying over the parapet beyond, a burly body sailed through the air, to vanish as it fell almost twenty-five feet into the pool at the foot of the waterfall. A gasp of amazement went up and then the sound of scampering feet. Every soul present watched Reuben Nattrass claw himself out of the water and painfully climb the side of the gill, his route homeward taking him along the pastures at the back, out of sight of those who had seen him toppled from a mighty pinnacle.

Pausing only for a blunt word with William Nattrass, repetition of the intimation addressed to his son, Adam hurried into the Plug and

Feathers, where he washed himself, doing what he could to improve his appearance.

Titus Alderson critically eyed a swollen ear, a puffy cheek, and a nose larger than its normal state. "Well, you can't hide that lot, Adam lad," was his verdict. "But you'll noan frighten the life out on her now."

"That'll do then," Adam smiled.

Outdoors, every man of sporting inclinations would have enjoyed a talk with him, but he was weaving his way amongst them too swiftly for that, to race along Main Street to Town Foot. Dinah, anxious not to intrude, bobbed out of the doorway of Yew Tree House as soon as he touched the gate. She was bruised on the forehead but made light of the accident caused by Reuben Nattrass when he pushed her, fiercely explaining that she would have been able to resist much more successfully if she had not caught her heel in her skirt, to crash against the wall.

"Nay, lass, I know very well you'd have stuck by Cherry if you hadn't fainted," Adam assured her. "Anyway I hope it's no worse than you're telling me."

"I feel that ashamed o' myself," she confessed.

She left at once, and then Adam went into the kitchen, where Cherry's glance moved searchingly over him. Then quietly, after looking at the scars of battle, she began to cry, her head cradled against his breast. "You're awful knocked about," she said almost inaudibly. "But at least they've not had to carry you back. I've had . . . the most terrible visions of——"

"Well, you can forget 'em, love," he consoled her. "And you can forget about Reuben Nattrass, too."

"It's all over?" she murmured.

"Aye, lass," Adam said, nuzzling aside soft hair to kiss her ear. "All, all over, and we're taking up the day as if nothing like this business had ever happened."

"Oh, love, let's," she sniffed blissfully.

"From this moment, lass," Adam announced. "Everything bright an' shining, and the clouds all gone."

After brushing off the worst of their mud, it was decided to walk to Modesty, leaving behind the carpet bag containing the remainder of her clothes, which Adam would return for later. And this they did, arm-in-arm, Cherry faithfully adhering to the letter of their compact.

In the vicinity of the Literary Institute a host of delighted people greeted them, but Adam did not think it advisable for her to stay long. At Old Hannah's, however, they paused to inspect a card on the door, not anticipating what might be its precise significance. The picture on it was of two heads pillowed closely, the main caption reading: BY GOD'S BLESSING, TWO SHALL BE ONE. A secondary line was on a less lofty plane, the script writer almost certainly having followed his client's exact order. It said: BACK AGAIN AFTER I'VE DRUNK THEIR HEALTHS, WHENEVER THAT MIGHT BE.

"H'mm," Adam grinned. "I reckon I've missed summat by not going through all them cards. I will one day."

The wedding card, or its illustration at least, offered a splendid opportunity for one particular species of wit, and Cherry with some nervousness noticed the approach of several people. "Let's be off, love," she suggested. "I want to arrange where all the wedding presents are put when they carry 'em along."

They were further detained, between the Plug and Feathers and the Brig, when Richard Blenkiron's mighty bellow arrested their progress. The blacksmith, wreathed in smiles, hastened towards them. "If I never live to see another, I'm satisfied, lad," he said impressively.

Adam stared. "See another what?"

Mr. Blenkiron stared, too. "Why, a fight!" he ejaculated. "By! but didn't I enjoy it."

For quite a time he enthused, until Cherry saw present-bringing traffic start at the Institute. "Could you come in one evening to go into all th'upper cuts properly, Mr. Blenkiron?" she proposed demurely, mentioning also that she would remove any ornaments within arm's length. "To Modesty, where we're going to live, I mean. We've been wed to-day, you know."

For a few seconds the blacksmith's face was a study, then he burst into homeric laughter. "And here I've been keeping you while you've a sight more important things on," he chuckled deeply. "Well, Cherry love, I don't recollect whether I kissed you in t'vestry . . ."

Cherry dimpled. "You did."

". . . but I'se going to do now," he said, dispatching the bridegroom a broad wink. "Aye, I am that."

Inside the front gate of Modesty Bob and Ward sprang upon them, and from there to the one step an unbelievable quantity of rice was thrown. The boys desisted, however, when Adam carried his bride over the threshold.

"Is that what you do wi' 'em, Adam lad?" Ward remarked.

"That's it, Ward lad," Adam grinned.

Within the hall, shouldering the door until it shut, Adam cradled his wife with her face near his own. "Happy, love?" he asked, to which, too full for words, she nodded, eyes dim with emotion. "Aye, me an' all, lass," he said before their lips met in a long kiss.

The tramp of feet compelled them to return to a very practical matter, the reception of wedding gifts, porterage being effected mainly by close friends, amongst whom Fronick Blenkiron obviously considered herself. Bart Hugill was on the job, too, and once, when arriving laden, was stopped by his former young lady, out-going.

"I'm right sorry for that mistake," she apologised. "I really ought to have guessed as Alf were trying to tell me summat very special, because he's always been so good and biddable, like."

"Aye, well, you'd be startled, lass," Bart mumbled, reddening.

"I should have had more sense," Fronick persisted. "Anyroad," she smiled, sweetly earnest, "I'm right sorry."

Sardonically Wingy Blenkiron watched his sister as she tripped away. Subsequently he was not entirely silent, charging his friend with 'weakening,' and adding certain observations far more caustic than that.

"Hold on!" Bart ejaculated. "You're running down your own sister, lad."

Wingy groaned. "God in heaven!" he muttered.

Dinah did not arrive until the last item had been delivered from the Literary Institute. Noticeably pale, she attributed this to a bad headache, as was quite feasible. "I think I'll get along home, Cherry," she said. "I'll look in when next I come shopping, so good-bye, love. An' good-bye, Adam."

When she left the room the third person present, one pointedly excluded by her, started to voice his complaints. Angered by her friend's misery, Cherry did not allow him to proceed far. "Yes, she's had a horrible bump, but that's not why she's so out o' sorts," she declared. "It's because you've been nasty with her."

"She were nasty wi' me," Wingy growled.

Adam's bride took a deep breath. "Sometimes, Wingy, you say you're nobbut half a man. Well, you're wrong. You're not even a quarter o' one, not an eighth o' one, not a——"

"It'll get difficult, love," Adam remarked, "when t'fractions become real small 'uns. So if I were you, I'd leave it as he's noan a man at all."

Wingy Blenkiron visibly struggled with himself. "Well," he said at last, "I've never smacked a lass, but I'm sorely tempted just now, and so I'll be off. And . . ." he glared at his traducer's husband, "it's noan because I'm scared on owt you could do."

When the door closed, Cherry expressed her vexation. "He's just daft," she said. "Dinah an' him were always mad on each other, but when he lost his arm . . . well, he just slid out of it. I could box his ears, I could really."

Neither darkness nor an early tea-time was far ahead, and so Adam lighted the lamp, its soft illumination revealing a kitchen already possessing that inviting brightness which had from the first attracted him at Yew Tree House. Then Cherry put the kettle on the fire and shortly they ate their first meal alone together in their own home.

Afterwards, refusing assistance, Cherry cleared away, while Adam, smoking his pipe, kept his eye on the clock. At a few minutes before six he remarked casually that he might as well saunter to her uncle's for the bag, an excuse which ensured his presence just beyond Nick Turn on the hour. Others, out of curiosity, were also there to see if Reuben Nattrass left Winterings, but Anthony Skidmore's errand was in keeping with the stern look on his face. Shot-gun under his arm, the owner of Badger Hall stood in the carrier's yard, near to a vehicle into which a small amount of luggage had been loaded.

Satisfied, Adam continued to Town Foot, where he collected his wife's belongings. The hoof-beats of a spirited mare were audible as he started back, and near the Wood Yard gates he met the dog-cart, father and son in it.

At the sight of the man who had humiliated him, Reuben Nattrass's arm went up, and the whip in it. Quickly Adam dropped his slight burden and, stooping, grasped the varnished spokes of a wheel, lifting until William Nattrass's wheezy cry of fear rang out.

"Any more o' that, Cousin Reuben," he promised, "an' I'll tipple the lot over, you and your passenger and t'horse and all."

In the light of the well-polished carriage lamps cousin surveyed cousin. "You'd have enjoyed nowt better, would you, than to have left me wi' a real weal across my face?" Adam smiled faintly. "But I'll bet you'd have preferred it to have been a different sort o' blow, eh?"

Dark eyes gleamed, but a small grin appeared on a much battered face. "Maybe I would, Cousin Adam," Reuben Nattrass grunted, busy managing a curveting animal. "Aye, I reckon you're noan without a drop o' Nattrass blood in you."

"A rare compliment fro' you, Cousin Reuben," Adam nodded appreciatively.

The restive horse had its way, but, as it leapt forward, a lash whistled viciously, not for its punishment but for the marking of the young man who had last spoken.

Adam, wary, ducked just in time.

"By . . ." he chuckled, as lights rapidly receded down the high road, "but he meant business then."

No sooner had he reached home than there was a discreet tap on the kitchen door. Quietly, Floss padding at his heels, Matt Tiplady limped in, to deliver a bass from which fur and feathers protruded. "Only an extra little present from us at Lane End," he winked, "so shove it in t'larder."

"I thought you'd given up your wicked games, Matt," Cherry laughed.

The visitor pointed a stern finger. "Now look here, Cherry lass," he began strongly, "on the question o' game every law in this land is founded on shifting sand. If right were right——"

"I know what this means, so make yourself comfortable, lad," said Adam gravely. "Aye, it can easily be two or three o'clock in the morning when I let you out."

Matt Tiplady gaped, and then grinned from ear to ear. "I can take a hint, Adam lad," he guffawed. "Aye, at after that, I'll make myself scarce. Well, good night to both on you."

That kept Adam and his wife amused for some time. Then, while Cherry set the table in readiness for supper later, Adam went outdoors to the wood place. They had made up their minds to spend the evening in the parlour, where a big coal fire had burned all day, but both had a preference for their own logs.

On his return Cherry was standing quite motionless in the kitchen. She looked exactly as if she believed that Reuben Nattrass, with the means for vengeance, awaited the master of the house beyond the passage door. "There's summat moving, love," she gulped. "I heard as plain as anything."

"Maybe a window with t'catch off, lass," Adam laughed.

Striking a match, he lighted a candle and, picking up the candlestick, went with soft tread into the hall, Cherry never far behind. A sound catching his ear, Adam's fingers closed upon the knob of the best room. The door's hinges creaked as he opened it, but that slight noise was as nothing to the noise of upheaval within, and most certainly Cherry's heart was in her mouth until the combination of flickering firelight and the candle her suddenly uproarious husband bore illuminated the figures in the scene, Dinah tightly embraced by Wingy's left arm.

"Well, I'm damned!" Adam said delightedly. "There'll be a charge for this, Wingy lad."

"And I'll pay," the postman grinned.

Cherry and Dinah were kissing each other, an example which spread, both gentlemen, after wringing hands interminably, kissing the ladies. Muddled explanations followed while a bottle of port was opened to mark the occasion, but, as was natural, each couple wanted to be alone and so it was not very long before Dinah, holding her young man's arm, started out for Badger Hall, to tell her parents the news.

At the gate, however, Wingy with laughter in his voice shouted to the effect that Mr. and Mrs. Brunskill could expect further company very shortly.

As Adam and Cherry certainly expected one very privileged caller, this was not surprising. But, alongside the white-haired lady they had in mind, a much smaller lady trotted, a grey-eyed little girl.

"Now we're noan stopping, loves," Old Hannah smiled as she was ushered in. "I daresay Mary Jane here 'ul try to persuade me to linger, but as soon as she's carried out t'special errand she's on——"

Mary Jane nearly exploded with indignation. "I know very well as newly-weds wants to be left to theirsen," she declared.

"Oh you do, love?" Old Hannah observed penitently. "In that case, I'm sorry, lass. Anyroad . . ." she seemed to be making an effort to contain herself, "hadn't you better have that word wi' Cherry as you mentioned?"

Matt's small daughter looked hopefully at the tall young man. "It's private-like, Adam," she pointed out.

"You could whisper, couldn't you, love?" Old Hannah suggested.

The proposal had hardly been acted upon when Mrs. Batty laughed until her eyes streamed. By then, however, Cherry had sufficient inkling of Mary Jane's desires to cause her cheeks to redden.

"Adam, love," she said, trying to appear calm, "I think it'd be better if you popped into t'parlour for a minute or two. If this goes on much longer my ear 'ul be wet through."

When, with becoming courtesy, he had withdrawn, Mary Jane glanced with satisfaction at the closed door. "Makes it awkward when chaps hang about sometimes, doesn't it?" she piped. "You'd think they'd have enough sense to shift off when women wants to speak specially to one another."

"You would, love," Cherry agreed.

Mary Jane, without masculine handicap, proceeded to make her ambitions crystal clear. "Can I help right fro' the very beginning when you have your first, Cherry lass?" she inquired. "That's summat I'se never been in at afore, and it's all experience."

"Well . . . well, love," Cherry hedged. "I might not have any."

"Won't you just, lass," Old Hannah chimed in confidently, but amplified this bald statement with an observation which heightened rather than lessened the blush of a newly-married young woman. "The good Lord lending a hand, that is."

Ignoring the cackling of an old lady who had discerned ribaldry in her own remark, Mary Jane pressed for an answer.

"We'll have to . . . to see, love," Cherry told her. "Maybe we could talk it over later, if ever the time arrives.

Mary Jane seemed very pleased. "I could come to tea."

Suddenly Cherry was overcome by an irresistible impulse to laugh, too, so that Adam on his return found the two older ladies a trifle exhausted, though Mary Jane, perplexed a little by her elders' strange behaviour, was as composed as ever.

"Well, loves," Old Hannah smiled, rising, "me an' this young lady is off now." Fondly she looked at them and then, placing her hands on their shoulders in turn, kissed them both.

Cherry and her husband watched the old lady and the little girl as far as the gate, where final greetings were exchanged, when Adam, his arm around a slim waist, closed the door. The hallway was brilliantly illuminated by the tall staircase window, a rectangle of pearly-white light. "Cherry lass," he said, "what do you say if we walk up the pastures for a stretch?"

"I'd like, love," Cherry exclaimed. "It's a perfect night."

A bustle started in the Brunskill household. Adam mended the fires and, as Cherry hastened for warm wrappings, found their clogs. "Ready, love?" he shouted. "We'll go out by t'back door."

Good friends were spending the evening celebrating the occasion, and the full blast of a hunting song, with Hugh Bearpark's accompaniment on the bassoon, reached out from the Plug and Feathers. Lusty voices were joined in an old favourite.

"*There's no joy can compare,*
To the hunting the hare,
In the morning,
In the morning . . ."

Gradually, as they climbed towards the Common Pasture, through their own meadows and grazings, past haybarns and cow-places, the snow crisp beneath their feet, the 'tantarras' and 'hurras' died away, until everything was still save for the faint music of water trickling downhill. At the lower verge of the fell they faced about to stare at the Dale, so clear in the moonlight that the haze of peat smoke drifting from the chimneys of the little grey village below could be plainly seen.

"Isn't it lovely, Adam?" Cherry whispered.

"Aye, love," her husband replied.

Within the shelter of his arm Cherry tried to resolve a matter which sometimes worried her, beginning rather indirectly by saying how glad she was he would continue to take some part in mining. "But there's summat else as troubles me a bit, love," she confessed. "You see . . . well, you were doing so champion lead-mining in Spain and your manager thought so much of you that . . . Adam," she turned swiftly to him, "I know you could have gone on to be real successful and I'm hoping you'll never regret settling down here."

"What if I did, love?" Adam asked. "Would you leave here and go willingly with me anywhere?"

"*Anywhere*, Adam," she told him.

His grip hardened. "And now let me tell you summat . . . that I might have done better in Spain, but it'd have been in a foreign land, noan in a spot I love as dearly as you do. And above all, lass, let me tell you that money and success isn't the most important things in t'world. What is, is to be wi' them you love, and if it's in the place you love, all the better."

Cherry was trembling. "I'm that, Adam . . . I mean I'm wi' the one I love and always will love."

Adam Brunskill's glance roamed over the prospect before them—

Lovely Lady and Silver Seat wearing white mantles, the shimmering course of the Skew, and steely pin-points where light was reflected in a nearby waterfall.

"This is what I've wanted, love," he said so very surely. "Just this . . . and you."

"I'm . . . I'm so happy . . . I ache with happiness," Cherry said, her voice low.

"Aye, love," he murmured, taking her into his arms. "That's it . . . with both of us."

Sheep were moving below and far away a sheep-dog barked, the sound carrying thinly but clearly in the silence. A young man with resolute deep-set eyes and a sweet young woman looked at each other and then, closely together, began to descend the fellside, towards a screen of trees, lofty spruce and umbrella-headed Scots pines. Beyond these nestled a creeper-covered little farmhouse, Modesty.

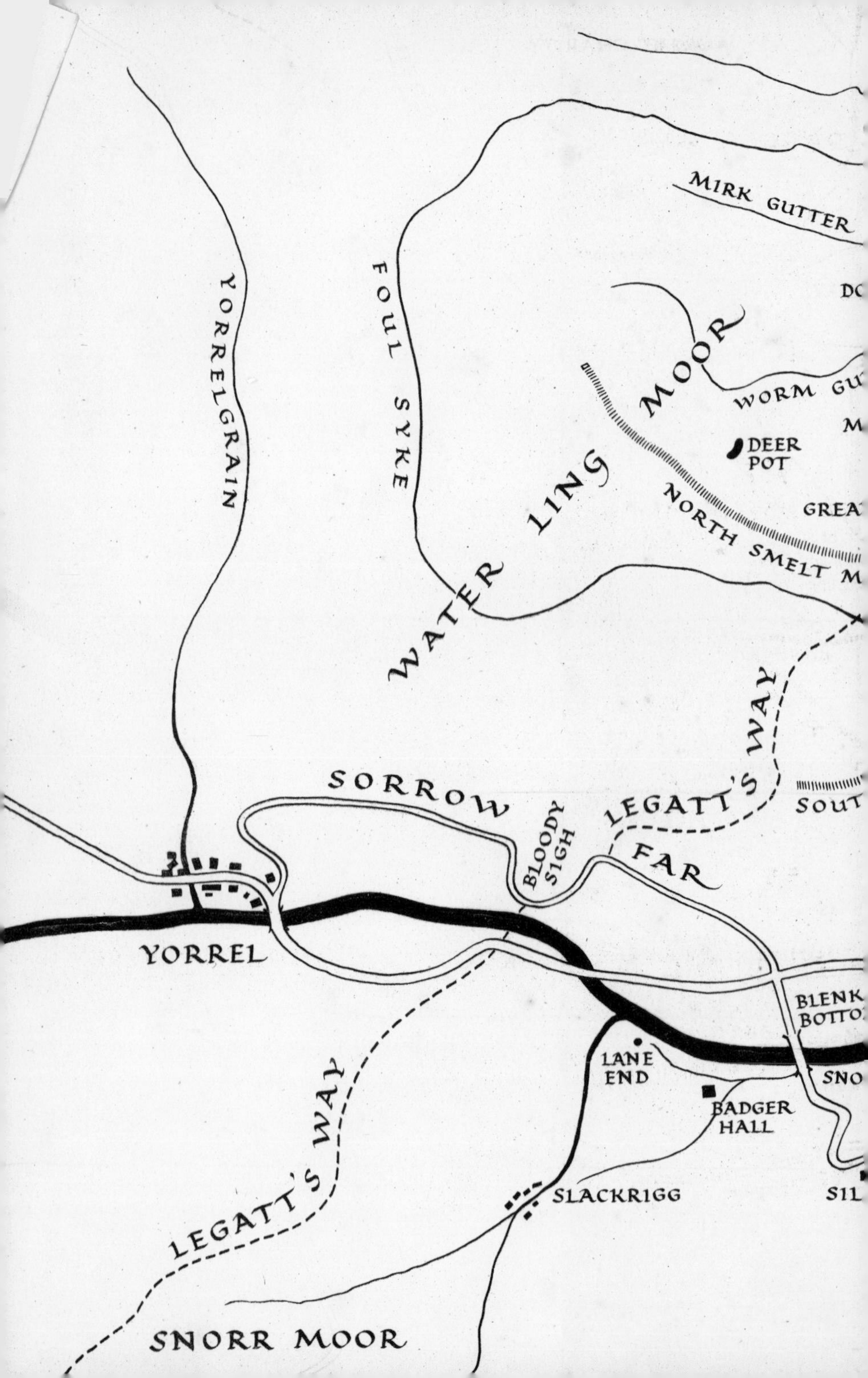

MIRK GUTTER

YORRELGRAIN

FOUL SYKE

WATER LING MOOR

DO

WORM GU

M

DEER
POT

NORTH SMELT M

GREAT

LEGATT'S WAY

SORROW

BLOODY
SIGH

FAR

SOUT

YORREL

BLENK
BOTTO

LANE
END

SNO

BADGER
HALL

LEGATT'S WAY

SLACKRIGG

SIL

SNORR MOOR